D1714399

DRIL 2022
http://wint.co
wintdotco@gmail.com

DRIL

"CHAOTIC"

my friend spyroquagmire called me today. said he's trying to start a "weed NASA" § i am the "Walter Cronkite" of game stop. yes i absolutely said it, and no im not deleting it this time. § Starfish Rant. ive had it up to here with this bullshit animal. click here to watch my starfish rant § Oh you wanna show up at my office, take a swing at me in the parking lot? Wanna knock the hoagey out of my hand? Make me puke by hitting me? § 95% of people these days think the bad celebrities are good. like and share this if you miss the days when pople liked. the good celebrities https://t.co/mVZKN5ExuR § not many people know this, b ut i actually coined the term "Lunchtime". before then, time and lunch were two entirely immeasurable concepts, § #The12DaysOfContent somone tell me what day im on please because i lost count http://t.co/JzhsuCEi67 § My Business Logo: a composite of sexy lady legs cut out from a variety of images and arranged to spell the word "Gordo" § as a lad i often drew 2 adjacent circles in a crude attempt to portray an Ass. ive since matured and only draw asses of the utmost precision § Beer is like pepsi on crack . § girlsl... i shall virtuously employ the expansive breadth of my tech wisdom to protect you all from Daesh... even if you dont follow me... § An empassioned Mitt Romney spoke. "My dear Americans." His tone rife with the gracious fortitude of a leader. "We must always eat Slim Jim." § According to @klout, I'm influential about: forums, religion and spirituality, and diaper http://t.co/2hhru5LL § some people get their accounts suspended for cursing out celebs.. i get mine suspended for posting things like "Sports is making a comeback" § instead of scoring touchdowns the nfl it seems is more interested in scoring "Shit downs" § fairly confident that even if i became a rat some how, i still would not want to fuck any of the other rats § thank you for liking my Wordle. § fucking nobel laureates screaming at each other about the current state of Juggalo Love in the handicap stall at dennys § the amount of faves your post gets = what your IQ is at that pount in time. this is called the beethoven equation § (i descend from the heavens) I'm uh, netflix is good (i go back up to heaven) § 5000 Year Old Turds Found In Ancient Diaper Revealed By Scientists To Belong To Man With Small Penis, Shapely Hips § piss on mysel.f § do not talk shit like this § rate my dogs dick dot com § "sounds to me like you're gonna be wantin to be suckin on a piece of my bullshit......" § former UN ambassador John Bolton uses hideous mustache to conceal "Police Is Bullshit" facial tattoo #amomentofsilence § http://t.co/O7z9U3Iv "Trash is Good" § no. my bumper sticker of beautiful intergalactic bounty hunter Samus Aran saying "Im Autistic" couldnt have been the reason my car was towed § my brain stacks 2 baby blocks together mentally and i involuntarily say something like "Trader Joes is basicly the Modern simpsons episodes" § 1989: the fall of the berlin wall is celebrated, historically revered 2016: i tear down the sneeze guard at old country buffet and get Booed § Adorn Your Front Door With A Tasteful Welcome Mat Or Shut Dah Fuck Up § Bill gates has so many followers that if he accidentally posts a picture of his spread ass hole its not even worth his time to delete it. § the police report described a "Cartoonishly diapered" man § POSTING FROM THE ANNUAL MORRISTOWN CHARITY TEEN MELT, OH IT'S JUST HORRIBLE, AWFUL (FOR A GOOD CAUSE THOUGH) § i take the stage. my red penis tip sticks out of my waistband; little bit of piss coming out. "I will end all politics-based attacks of me." § absolute horseshit that im being written up for painting "JORDACHE BOYS" on windshield when i can see the road between the letters just fine § "You Like To See Homos Naked" Joe Dirt § no hashtag.. no rant #NoHashtagNoRant § just installed 500 security cameras around my compound & my sony wonderstation refuses to interface with a single one! hungry grab a snicker § Waiters do not put the big silver dome over our food before serving it anymore because of politics culture § i rolled out some denim content last night and it was really good actually. .. § Ive read so many posts about how to be nice on here, its no wonder that I make such a good living as the CEO of the New York Times . § ive had it up to here with this benghazi fella. callin up a few rowdy boys to do some jumping jacks on his lawn § any 1 want to look at pictures of owls with me write the word Hoot on a bottle mesage & toss it in the frog pond § congress: it would be an honor to let you join Congress me: absolutely no. it'd be a disservice to my followers to join the bastard congress § 15 years ago the most shocking thing online was a picture of a man spreading his ass cheeks open. today, it's my opinions about Wet shaving § i reserve the right to have reddit "Shut Down" if the questions become too rambunctious § beiing exposed to this sort of thing 99 hours a week is either making me extremely stupid or the most intelligent person in history https://t.co/XlVzx5wKPH § handsome https://t.co/K8MaQen1bQ § just tried to search twitter for "im a virgen" but i posted it instead, then frantically deleted it #thiswickedwebweweave #misery #Pride § sorry boys.. im goin A.W.O.L.. !!! Another Weekend On-Line § the best follow-ers money can buy § the scud missile was named after famous military physicist Scud Missile § im a marine & accomplished scholar. my sons were alchemized into helicopter fuel to serve their armed brothers. how dare u post penis to me. § please follow my business associates @ZohanTweet, @Jokes_Zohan, @RacistZohan, @ZohanCroatia, @ZohanMoneyTips, @ZOHAN_REAL, and @MyFunnyZohan § what if Netflix was Real Life #justMythoughts § all dril is trash § evry young man MUST receive a cupbox at the age of 17 to carry his favorite cups around and to give him a valuable lesson in responsibility § lets step it up. lets replace the Follower count with the number of criminals youve murdered. lets see where our true allegiances lie § daffy and donald duck: "SAME SHIT , DIFFERENT ASS HOLE" § it Sucks, its bullshit, its stupid, but you Love to see it § judges should sentence perverts to more stupid shit, like making them do obstacle courses made out of porno. bet it's not so good now huh § youre all hot misunderstood geniuses, and for $400/hr you can get exclusive access to my seminar on how to not take your penis out in public § "Crowdpleasers"... Now these, I like § this one time-- me, DigimonOtis, and EpicWayne tried to open up a barbershop together, but the plan fell through due to my fear of hair § started smoking at the advice of the "Making friends in your 50's" reddit post, quit after reading the "How to make your cum taste good" one § i would advise U not to visit this small internet website, MEETUP.COM; They get mad if yo[u bring devil sticks to the meetups even if your pro § trying to draft a tweet about how people arre getting too many tattoos of the cars from the cars movies without invoking Race § Haven't the slightest idea why 1.6 million people would follow someone who's ramblings have all the charm of an illiterate, pathetic drunk with too much internet access. #pitiable https://t.co/dYUJuEBELc § http://t.co/hq9EnbHCV6 § one of the all-time classic flubs https://t.co/1NQnf0rXc9 § nobodys telling me where i should donate 6000 cigarettes. nobodys telling me where theyll do the most help. So i guess ill just smoke them § ive gotten word that pussy_hacker has taken SirGamestop out for a night on the town that he wont soon forget, and then some , § This is a guy who I imagine likes to jerk the old pole at night& masturbate. This is a guy who uses tired swear words like "Fuck" and "Damn" § truth be told-- i only like the good ones § this is peak hours in romania , where most of my fans live § cowboy `s blade § im so sorry that happened to you. But this is some Insane content § i burned 100 extra calories today just by thinking aobut asses § rip dr phil § My friends love disappppointing me with whips § (after smiling all day because i realized something important) Tell me. If Fort nite is "For children" , how come it has Family guy in it? § the most wild thing you can say when walking into a restaurant or a kitchen "it smells like fuckin food in here" § Gamer Kiss Magazine wants to see your "Bitter game face" (the face you make when you are playing a sub par game) Get those pics in Lads. § (after sendding 500,000 messages to Arbys without getting any favs or replies) i dont care. their commercials arent even that funny any way, § jesus christ. this man at the library is looking at the lowes,com homepagr instead of gaining knowledge. im gonna upload a pic of this clown § U would be superbly fucking remiss to not click on my link of top 10 reasons that Vuvuzela s are The Dog's bollocks § i looked that little punk behind the counter in the eye and told him Criss Angel Mindfreka is the most compelling televsn program like, ever § sitting on toilet, avoiding wife whos mad at me for saying Chinese zodiac animal and spirit animal are the same thing § lobotomy--Check castration--Check 8months of Bible-Based close combat training--CHeck police mandated electroshock therapy--Check Time to post . § duhhh ok yes sir thank you sir https://t.co/zZNEXX3TW2 § " ice tweet edit" will replace "posted from android huh??" as the reply that makes girls fuck you instantly § Can you make them all un block me please . https://t.co/cDZQuGSYAx § tryinh to convince girls on here to sync all 655 episodes of "Hee Haw" with me, telling them its like SNL but nice § take it dowm § @TruthPointDWR Dont say fuck on this accout § Ready to enjoy my Farm Fresh Mozzarella Sticks from Bertuccis, retweet my favorite celebs, and post some worms-eye pics of my Genitals & Ass § hwow many favs are worth the equivalent of a human life... id say about 70 § you gotta check out my posts § saying "Looks like I struck a nerve ." in the gorup dm after posting "Pringles is white people doritos" and locking my account § my dick looks like a dissected frog #JESUSISKING § Geting my dick sucked in Unreal Engine 4. Flushing toilet in Unreal Engine 4. Having shit beat out of me by greasers in Unreal Engine 4. Wow § it is a Content Curator's solemn duty, to post links to shit, without freaking out under the intense scrutiny of the craven, impotent masses § Bog Off, Fuckazoid. Im Cramming Packets Beyond Digital Light Speed ,Injecting Pure Fire Into The Blogomedia SuperFrame For The God Damn Lord § theres too many of them to block. im gonna lose it § some facebook bull shit § people these days would rather have faith in Homer Simpson , than, the Honor System § i spend 2hrs on my back with my legs spread so it looks like the sun is setting into my ass from my perspective."haha the sun fucking sucks" § i finally worked up enough courage to cry in front of the pregnant woman who frequents my gym § arms folded, back turned to the television, refusing to "Meet the flintstones" despite the theme song's pleas § RESULTS ARE IN: The Pibb Xtra 2012 Gold Prize is rewarded to "Football". The Pibb Xtra 2012 Stinker Award goes to the fireman shooter. Bye § i have been secretly collecting my roommate's piss for 7 years. i dont know what to do with all of these jars of piss. i am extremely scared § YES. I AM THE HARD ROCK CAFE. YES. I DID ORDER 18 "ROCKABILLY URINALS". JUST PILE THEM UP OUTSIDE OF MY CRIME BASE-- ER I MEAN VAN § as god as my witness i will trick out my Balls with cadillac skin enhancers and Discreet varicocele nut mods § Nudity is perverse. Nudity is an act of war § HUuuuu!! Topgolf is Trending !! Look at it! Look! https://t. co/7frnMJ7ABi § all the trolls talk shit about my profession as an artisan ass wiper. but when they see my fine selection of towels they beg for my services § i want to open the worst pub on earth called like "The Bull Dog's Cock" and get in trouble for tnot paying my employees § " I DESERVE MY WIFE " GET OF MY ASS!! KING OF THE ROAD § HMM NOPE § "I love the name of honor, more than I fear death." -me to my boss after he found a picture of me with a big shit stain on my sweatpants § i had a nightmare that i kept clicking the logout button and it just kept logging me into this website again and again § i will do it. i love the good shit favstar § replacing my ass cheeks with both hemispheres of my useless brain was a decision i made for MYSELF. i didnt do it to fucking impress twitter § FUCK the news!!! § - the Deterioration of my Balls - § @ SwissIOCForever thanks for showing me this robots dick § I have been a jock since I was 0 years old . § buying some golf cleats? bet U high society FUCKS like to step on each others COCKS with these. i own this foot locker. your'e a child here. § https://t.co/A2lZudIWVA § i hold this truth , im just an average joe trying to do my messages here, and i dont have time for fellas who want to take a big crap on me. § its no secret that i sometimes have to scold my hare

brained followers rirght in their goofy fucking faces to keep them in line §
these flawless squats on the roof of my van go out to the bastard who accused me
of "going apeshit" a t wild birds unlimited in marietta, ga § i already doxxed
all his anagrams and the best one is "tract disease" § people pay good money to
stamp your mail. if you refuse to take the time to thoroughly digest every
piece of mail you receive, you are a Cur § ass gas and grass. i love to drive
my car for free § please god my lord let thtere be an all beavis spin off §
someone said "rage comics" out loud and fistpumped in one of my classe.s. thats
a real thing that a human being did § imma misogynistic hopeless romantic
whsoe tolerance for mainstream pdf readers can be described as " scant" § gogle
is in deep trouble since they used picture of my patented 2012-ready wiccan
runestone arrangements without permission § It owuld be rude to eat you. Goal
§ @MilkBone milk bone is 666 § do not ever come to my gym with crayons and draw
smiley faces all over the walls. i will put your ass in the gutter. i will
knock you over § i found a pill in the grass. i think it was a drug pill. i
called "911". good luck all § this image radicalized 100000000 youth
https://t.co/2BzF3CTKSQ § Learn How To Use Toilets Without Getting Fully Nude §
Ah!! Ah! once again, the flap-jawed trolls have deliberately misinterpreted my
constant attempts to get a girl friend on here as " Sexual " § ellen made me
sign some papers and put a big blown up picture of my leathery dick on her show
instead of my topical tweet. ellen fooled me § peppercorn ranch & buttermilk
ranch... one of these is good, the other is completely Fucked, and its not my
responsibility to tell you which § participatr in something known as "the porky
pig discourse" hmm no thanks im busy sending pics of my new dinette set to 115
different girls. § look at all these pitiful toads shamelessly seeking validation, unlike me, seeking validation in a cool, disaffected sort of way § man on
mountaintop wont stop yelling "Wanker" , cops cannot reach him buecause of
falling rocks § many've sought the ultimate Combo and have asked me what the
ultimate combo is. i am too amused simply by their ignorance to even answer . §
little known fact: the e3 gaming conference is considered the holy grail of
the public urination community § damn right he did https://t.co/Mxhwib7fW1 §
every time indie film maker rick james gets kick off an airplane i boycot anohter
fucker hollywood mainstream garbage pot § im the dip shit top replier who goes
into every thread about someone being afraid of moving out and says "Dont
forget to buy a plundger" § convinced that about 98% of my followers and favs
are all from one awful man who is taunting me becuase I spoke ill of orange
julius in 2011 § my more astute readers have noted that i botched the hashtag.
its not supposed to be "the thursday nite rat". i cannot fix it. its locked in §
it's a disgrace. nobody fav this please § @KeeblerElves Please help me . You
cowards § the best is when they bark at you when they see you through the
window of your own house. At that point i know your iq is fucked . § "i could
teach a dog how to use a $10 bill in two seconds flat. the zoo should invent
money that they let the animals use" - alan Greenspan § Wow. Christ § watching
simpy slide up the fireman pole § if you can smell your own balls that means you
have corona virus . bad news for all you Stupid mother fuckers on here § the
pursuit of having trhe nicest opinions online... is the only thing that
separates us from the god damn animals. the sole reason we exist § Im so pissed
off im going to throw up § wandering aroud w/ my thumb up my ass during Civil
War 2, asking people to show me their posts so i can tell if i should grenade
them or not § dictionary.com defines the word "Mania" as "excessive excitement
or enthusiasm; craze:". "Ziggy Mania" offered none of these things t o me. §
tipping the waiter is BORING, no one even DOEs it § why do you want to kill
dogs § your looking at 9.11 § licking a cartoonishly large loollipop while
unsuccessfully building a deck in my yard one-handed, saying "Fuck!" and
"Shit!" occasionally § Havent busted in over 45 hrs. Ive Cured my Anxiety,
PTSD, Bisexuality & various Poxes, all by retaining my viscous loads. Now I

become Mayor https://t.co/ZWW5hHlaIl § Im the guy who exclusively wipes his ass with the disposable seat covers § i will not let you poop the stately office . i will never use the code "Rudy20" for $20 off orders over $100. i will not dm GIRLS § IM TAKING A CRYSTAL INTO THE VOTING BOOTH .... #PRANKS § i have been pacing the driveway for hours, trying to work up the courage to tell a t least 3 twitter girls that i have married them § i dedicate this oscar to the caveman who invented electricity, because without him€• Film would cease § not much of a response to my #ShowMeTheSelfieMonday call for selfies. might try Heroin for the first time . Oh well § fucking.. actual yes http://t.co/eRm6R1S-0lu § This Fucking Sucks http://t.co/fqnRcJGH § the headless horseman sucks shit/ he wouldnt last 2 minutes in hollywood. he cant get me here § "ey!! im walkin here" - me getting waterboarded by the us government § #ReplaceBand-NamesWithDad nutty professor 2 the klumps § every single one of you will be locked up for deplatforming and demonitizing joe the plummbers imdb page § @ cesarmillan PUT MY DICK ON TV § send all Business offers to: wintdotco @ gmail . com ... no goof ball shit § last night i had a vision of a pope in jeans. Clean, white as the holy spirit, perfect, angellic jeans #TrumpStoleTheDocs § LOVER UNBUTTONS MY PANTS AND SEES THE ANKH LOOPED AROUND MY COCK. SHE LOOKS UP AT ME, BUT ITS TOO LATE. IM ALREADY HOLLERIN ABOUT THE ANUBIS § cavemen were 14 feet tall and immortal because they didn't believe in Lying § building a casket for my babydaughter in minecraft in lieu of a real casket which i can not affort. § the facts are: actual little two year old children are coming onto this website to send me brutal reprimands daily and make me violently ill § my spinning 3d head rises from a dumpster full of discarded shrimp who were born fucked up by the bp oil spill. eeyaaghhHHH!!! im ALIVE baby § i will never make forbes Top500 tweets. i will never get my posts featured on The McLaughlin Group. Because Im a SLUT!! Woth personal demons § mantis is a small green dog. not bug #CancelColbert § going to buy some goofy bug eyed glasses & drink poison until i look 80% more sickly/ weak and ask random girls if they need a Suger Daddy § tiger wood offers tearful apology after his uroclub burst and spray piss all over his fans during a golfswing gone awry § now's the perfect time to catch up on my Smoking by smoking every cigarette and cigar in the house § Bacoun. That is all #Yourdailysmile #MediaBrand § reality sets in that im " o longer funny," the dream of being Epicly quoted by funko pop owners for the rest of my life dies unceremoniously § "Cold hard cash is the real deal" the quote of ben franken § the only Pro-Israel carpet cleaning service in the tri-county area § adult cop wrestler § all men between ages 46-62 run a newsgroup named "Bimbofied By Wife" that has pics of them handcuffed with bras stuffed down their throaot § ill speak no more of the "Show Us Your Turkey" thanksgiving event. as many have taken that as an invitation to send me their penis and balls § my lawyer has just informed me that my official logo resembles an alien with a big dick. this is the My Lai Massacre of personal branding § WELL I PRINTED OUT MY RESUME, DUNNO WHAT ILL DO WITH THESE OTHER 4999 BOXES OF PROFESSIONAL "IF YOUR A HATER DONT READ THIS" STATIONERY § do any of you know any good lawyers that i can sue you with § jack: i will protect you from all rogue group dms. you are not a "Honkey" . Your an angel me: Im an angel. Im intelligent. Im not a honkey § sending the obese isis guy pics to girls & saying "Me", printing out the kissy face emojis they send back and hanginh them up in my cubicle. § i do not 'Get' porky pig § my turds are nobodys problem but my own. and theyre boring § football?? Pfuh. while you sweathogs are pounding off to grievous injury porn i'll be experiencing life at the car wash, with shorter lines § hot wheels toys for adults called Adult wheels § guy trying to tell me im using the elliptical cross trainer backwards; Fuck you man. . This is my journey § hockey? ive been known to slap sticks every now and than. had a name for me "the goalie killer". I quit playing when the shit got too easy . § my new shit: "Burger king = mc donalds" Please let me know what you think of

my new shit, and provide suggestions on how I can improve it. § O girl!!! You
got that NSFW Pussy ! Your shit will get my ass FIRED !! From my JOB § they
need to put nets up in the baseball fields to catch all the homers. youre
wasting so many good baseballs and it makes me sick § if you follow my account
you are protected from demons. you are protected from all x-files § "fear not
loyal fans. james bond blasts all his turds/piss to smithereens with a laser
while on missions." -james bond, author of james bond § THIngs other people
like: being bastards, being Uniformly tasteless THINGS I Like: Being reason-
ably kind, and trying to help, when i can § Think uve seen True 4G Wireless ??
Think again. *READS STAGE INSTRUCTIONS BETWEEN ASTERISKS INSTEAD OF PERFORMING
THEM* #worstpickuplines § #10ThingsYouHateToDo jack off, not jack off, 3 4 5 6 7
8 9 10 § i will go to great lenghts to prove that i take real showers. i will
send pH samples of my flesh to th trolls. i will take pics of wet tub. § @
NancyGraceHLN my 2 year old son is drawing #swastikas everywhere after seeing a
toddler smoke weed on your show. thanks #Irresponsible § airlines should give
you a smaller barf bag for when you just want to spit out a piece of sandwich §
Sftu. Thanks for making me dry heave § fdreaming of that special moment when i
can look into my wifes eyes and say "Thank you. Thank you for marrying me" §
whether its that Hot rock N' roll or Cool jazz, well we can know what the one
thing is that we all can agree on, is that it is "Pretty good" § sorry for
leaving a poop that looks like your initials § "breaking in" my new pair of
jeans by tossing it onto the freeway and letting cars run over it while i
observe it through a scope § if that lawyer didnt want his wall punched, he
shouldnt have told me my uncle left me a sony walkman filled with cut up bugs in
his will § if you like this video of a monkey eating m&ms you will certainly
enjoy this video of a lizard tearing up a rat with its mouth § (dming the
girls) this swebsite is the future. were pioneering... minds (dming the boys)
this website is sellout. this website is family guy § The video games &
childrens tv show industrial complex has pooped its own ass once again and made
2020 the year of the Actual Bitch . § trying to get the girls chat recognized
as a hate gruop § where do mirrors come from. if i stand in front of a mirror
is my reflection also subject to the insurance mandate?? can i touch mirrors ?
§ #AboveCowards § i reserve the right to blog my yap off in defiance of the
trolling groups and hate communities who want to disrupt my cashflow § http://t.
co/5f0r1TTg yes § im actualy, probably, the most superbly relatable and normal
person in this jail cell as of right NOw § nerd with lame attitude: North Korea
is bad Me: Have you ever lived there. nerd: (his glasses fall off) Me: Catch
you later § Q: Dear @Dril, friend to all online. Do Good people die? A: Good
people absolutely do not die, and you have bveen blocked for asking me this § i
ONLY spray m y dick with @MonsantoCo insect poiosn, i will absolutely accept NO
OTHER, my dick is AWFUL and this is the only thing for it § more and more
sources are reporting "an end to sex" § paying women to ram me with thier cars
§ $1§$1§$1§$1§$1§ https://t.co/y8QKUHT7xA § my tweets are good way less often
than 20%. damn, with a 20% success rate i'd have my own hbo special by now §
guys in a pizzeria fighting and busting the little parmesan shakers against the
table to shiv each other with § oprahs the secret § You Look Like The Fuckin
Kfc Man #tastefulinsults § i would NEVER misappropriate funds from my panera
bread gloryhole kickstarter to buy mustard gas,, you BRUTES , oyu selfish,
horrible APES § i wont let nasa sent me to mars [does the dx cross chop with
guns] fuckin alright § https://t.co/Wg9jig4rfk § this is based on nothing .
entirely fucked § "big the cat" is the most compelling figure that has ever
existed in any form of media, and that includes book `s . § america the
Fuck-State proves once again that ti is bullshit, by locking innocent Toilets
in most prison cells without trial § check out my tumblr *goes limp & rolls
down steep mountainside for 10 minutes or so, banging head on branches and
rocks, surely dead * § i shoukld be allowed to do kindergarten again. im pretty

sure i would absolutely fucking nail it this time § the pinheads at the post office are all down there whooping it up with my good car mags instead of delivering them to my tent in the desret § a guy who calls him self "service animal toucher" is going around trying to trick people into licking elevator buttons. stay safe all. § Im sorry for saying that all the cartoon characters who have depression deserve to have depression. Im stupid. Im stupid. I shouldntv (1/31) § several bernie Sander Bros, in High Levels of govt, have told me they think its good that DJT keeps ivanka feet pics in the nuclear football § guess who just filled his hot tub with high fructose corn syrup and is ready to take one swee t dip.............. § fav if you think adults should have access to toilet time retweet to see the face of G-OD ignore and get th e word "Liar" branded into flesh § just a little casual assplay at the farmer's market § i hate vuvluzela noise. http://t.co/MZv2QI6O. § My dick looks like a cartoon character's § politifact... waiters should offer to can crush my cans when im done with them... TRUE § Leut me make this clear: gloves are Next-Gen mittens , mittens are trash, i will never wear a mitten, i will take down anyone whos mad at me § im known to "Trick or Treat" from my neighbors mail boxes. they love it and it drives them wild. And it`s a bit of fun § please stop sending pictures of girls urinating to my house. it ws funny when i was 16 but now it is affecting my standing within the church § ive cancelled this project due to of people getting mad at me. thank you to the 1 guy who bought it https://t.co/Brsl4OtyAT § "what are ya.." i said to his face. "some kind of a FReak cop?" he desperately reached for his badge but it was fused permanently to his leg § christ. just dreamt that dietpepsi of antileaks obtained the chaos element, came on to my online page & made a mess of my literature. my god § getting more pain receptors implanted into my skin!! maybe now my posts will actually mean something to you mother fuckers!! "AAAAAAAHHH!!" § SCreaming while the road workers slowly pave a road on top of me using my own tax dollar § i invent the first porno NFT and i get an ass kicking . i try to do something nice and my followres attack me like a dog § can any of you hook me up with some sports § oh absoluteyl § metal gear eric called me at 2 am last night to tell me he just envisioned a strain of marijuana called "Racism Ender" § its either anonymous the hacker or an angel § making the rounds on 9gag: an animated gif of my depressed balls, descending slowly into a fiery, cavernous pit which appears to be Hell § http://t.co/QlbDYzU1sD calling all my dubai followers to step up and pour a bottle of htis down my ass crack § even if youre not a comics guy, i woud fully recommend grabbin a cigar and experiencing Blondie's 948-strip "BENEDICTION" arc in one sitting § *fires 400 rounds at a piece of shit log until it slumps over* Take that adam landza § Re-tweet me pussy § suck it bigtime champ § none of my followers like jokes, none of my followers enjoy Fun, every time i try to lighten the mood people just post pics of my mug shots § how dose it feel to be puppets in my numerology experiment *my true form emerges, a 3d skull wrapped in tinfoil , shooting green flames* § because 100000 protesters were murdered in cold blood in the birthplace of civilization you ungrateful dipshit #jan25 § the most popular of my weekly features is returning in 2016. thats roight folks. #WaterboyWednesday no further info at this time. § which one of you jokers made the radio station shoutout "Rock and Roll Kevin", who has "Brain Cancer" § nice no true scotsman fallacy. hm, typical tu quoque fallacy. ah, the classic "grab me by the ears & crack my face with your knee" fallacy, § favstar is an important brand outreach utility & the fact that some people will misuse it by putting jokes on there is pathetic § SUCJK MY DICK http://t.co/cbU6JrAuDS § fuck you. dont you know who i am. im the big palooka who eats frozen dumplings on 24/7 live cam while people clal the swat team on me § I will do better next time . § thinking about a beer sip i once had § considering the insane amount of meds i woud need to become harvey weinsteins Lawyer without wanting to flip my $80000 car off the over pass

§ MEN would rather say shit like "Skip to my Lou" than chant a single Healing Mantra. Not me though § i dont care to hear any more talk about "Donkey kong country". its a stupid game that has Incest § we are starting to live in a world where a man cant sell 200 containers of WBP (White Boy Piss) withtout having to sign some kind of paper § think i might quit my job and invent the Original chicken sandwich § call me a piece of Shit so i can finally die § god is real. fuck garfield § i have faith that some one (preferably from New York) will soon explain to me why this post is good § im redoing the funeral for my ass because nobody took the first one seriously enoguh. too many attendees yapping off & refusing to be seated § http://t.co/zjDicwHRyz you will never defeat me mother fucker § on my deathbed, surrounded by loved ones, i bid farewell. i explode into 1000 totino's pizza rolls and everyone in the room tries to grab em § before the trolls leak my finances id just like to state for the record that ispent $6000 on Dr Mario world because i thought itd be funny § what is quickest way to get sprayed by a skunk in a discreet maner § cmon peopl now   smile on your gamers   everuybody get together   try to do good with your Gamers right now § sent to juvie hall for 6 months for rendering 3d skunks § if i ever catch you getting your stupid ass into a car accident ill knock the shit out of you § if any of you have any tips or tricks about how to make the queen ant shit ant honey into my mouth, email me at LongLegsGustin@bisquick.com § head fully immersed in kfc bucket filled with hidden valley ranch dressing and m&ms. brand engagement locked in at one hundred percent § i will never have, never have thought of, and never will think about, engaging in "Raw Dog" intercourse wih my wife § to counter-act the terrible "ISIS", im starting my own group called " ICEis". what we do is give retweets & faves to the hopelessly decrepit § yes i can confirm that george zimmerman just fashioned a cocoon from Monster Energy cans and metamorphosed into a gun with angel wings #cool § blue mark accts continue to be given "Carte Blanche" to take big filthy shits all over my career & my beliefs while @Jack dances to the Bank https://t.co/vNuQdKBKXxd § harvey weinsteins tooth fell out the last time h was in court and the judge made him pick it up and put it back in his mouth § this is for All the avoacado toast likers https://t.co/bBSE6SdT6L § i can't afford any rat literature because i spent too much money on the elaborate sign over my empty bookcase which reads "RAT LITERATURE" § i can in the year of our lord 2013 verify once and for all that shrimp are NOT baby birds § Hmmm nope!!! § guy who once posted "Service dogs love having their ears grabbed" given permanent seat in wolf blitzers situation room #Redemption § dictating some more nice posts to my keyboard boy while my wife straps me to the big spinning crross § u got 1 side saying dogs have paws & the other side saying dogs have hooves..then me, the guy who cuts thru the BS, saying they have Niether § *stares at a man doing jumping jacks in complete awe* How is he doing that § omicron? omi gettin out of here #GotThierAss § listen fuck wit. if you dont want me pissng all down the floor and the walls of your public restroom then make the urinals. bigger § is he dtc (down to change) § advising my client alan dershowitz not to become host of the new tv show on g4 gamers network "Show Me Ya Pussy" § Whua?? No sponsorship disclaimer? no my friends. im saying all of these things for free, because i need to § https://t.co/mRxuUFt0g7D § if this board was real life id be allowed to embed as many bmp files as I want to. if this board was real life you'd change your tune quick § ive had more threads locked than any man on the planet. ive had my address posted 1000+ times. i get ``Owned`` so much that i look like shit https://t.co/308nflDLgV § i lvoe and cherish all of the girls of this site, and other websites. you all become my wife more and more with each passing day. Thank you § absolutely, and i wont get into heaven until everybody on this site unblocks me § WHo else thinks that, without JACK at the helm, this site is going to start Sucking FUCKING DICK!!! § (banging on ex wifes front door dressed as a cop) open up. the citibank social media team says im Valid §

ARMYMAN: the US military now Officially endorses cruel and unusual torture agianst qdoba fanboys and Ignorant-Minded people ME: b-b...badass § ive started bowing my head and saying grace before reading each post on here... "thank you." "thank you for the posts." that sort of thing, § what did Steve Jobs smoke to come up with all his famous ideas § im a bush-league yokel who should be put on the floor § 2022 year of the buffoon. ladys invest early; get your self a man with that buffoon dick § 1-800-VamoOSe § wouldve loved to make $10000000 but honestly seemed rude to fuck over hedgefunds since theyre the people who make like, our shirts, and food § writing a scathing letter to THE MEDIA for letting me become DUMB as SHIT !! § during tibetan sky burials theres always the risk that the birds will eat everything except your dick and that people will laugh at the dick § chase bank is simply trolling by removing money from random peoples accounts, it's funny and ground breaking and if you get mad your a karen § im stufing more toilet paper into the clogged toilet to stop it from overflowing. im using the plunger to cram more toilet paper in there § need 800 more dollars to keep the unofficial "$h*! My Dad Says" tv show wiki up and running for another month, yiou fucking worthless toads, § @DrOz please help me. i have a phycological desire to amputate my legs. please provide me with resources as im at the end of my rope § you need to realize that when you make a joke about the queen dying it is the british version of 9/11. You are spitting in the face of 9 /11 § Seems as though lately, peop[le have been talking their mouths of things § when they asked Ben Franklin "Sir, through Cup and Coin, does pleasure Portend the folly of Man?" mr. Franklin smiled and said simply "Beer" § My (new) Twitter value is $0, according to http://t.co/ zzZzntzRrD ... What about yours? § apology letter to the juadge for grinning in his courtroom whenever someone mentioned my fun & clever web handle (SexBug) during proceedings § an adult version of Chuck E Cheese type places where you pay someone to shout the " -WORD" directly into your face so you can feel something § this is one of the georgia guidestones § starting to think maybe that it kicked ass when that guy siad "show me the money" in that movie i never watched § where are my damn freaks.. where`s my nasty Posters. where are my fuckin doofuses § this was fucking real. i cant get over it. what was this guy doing, endorsing piss? https://t.co/apB8KVgUSX § watching some bulllet time movies and inventing my own bechdel test for bullet time instead of girls § im the guy at mcdonalds who decides which states the offers are not valid in, an d i get more death threats than god § <MUMMIFIED FERRETS>, each one dressed as a cast member of "The Little Rascals". the notable exception of Froggy renders the set incomplete § imagining a guy who calls every Simpsons character a "Simpson" (even ancillary ones, outside of the main family) and letting him ruin my day § #CancelColbert gangstalking me, collecting my piss, laughing it up with his fucked up buddies when I ask where my piss went, carrying on, § Who Told U About Satan Ass § go to bed dad § i love stigmatizing the mentally ill by terminating thier 800 million dollar promotional deals.... not § it is decided from this moment forward, i will not be clicking on any "SCAM LINKS" § a man asks God, how am i supposed to live, without George H.W. Bush God simply said "That is why I made 2 george bushs" The man just smiled. § http://t.co/ ZOn11UfM heres some real political insight for u disgusting parasites to gobble up and slap on your bolgs § im finished with groupon. it means nothing to me § The Pillsbury Dip Shit § drunk driving may kill a lot of people, but it also helps a lot of people get to work on time, so, it;s impossible to say if its bad or not, § shocking wiki leak #WikiLeaks #ObamaChewingGum http://t.co/ dxM6K316S2 § WHo in their right nerve is selling M Jackson ticket to the funeral, le tthe man rest in peace, Relax!!! § (wtaching a video of capt Jack Sparrow shitting on the number 2016 while the camera zooms in and out of his ass hole) Oh this is everything, § youvr gotta eat § the sattire is lamentable and gross. theyre doing bad of it § once againl, the "legalize incest" crew has

somehow hijacked the protest I organized to ban sorcerers from congress §
http://t.co/sh1Ydsxf my cool forems § hard at work in the Study, pen in hand,
orchestrating my next public melt down § AAUh..!! Yeah. Lets all gang up on the
guy who gives his children Steroids, just because he has a different opinion.
Fucking idiots. § saw a centaur out side of aldi today § "Hwhoo!! That's a lot
of zeroes" - me after seeing the amount of money of $12.00 § "Soda is back"
Only at Mcdonald § im about to loose my shit if my feed doesnt slow down with
th fucking posts. nobody could possibly read this fast. this is a travesty §
been thinking about it a lot, and i do not believe that anyone will ever come
up with a brand name better than "Taster's Choice" § yes i got smacked by ball
lightning in the bathtub and now im connected to ghosts. yes i have Tantric sex
with astral women rogan: Holy shit § i just got logged on to the site and im
going to need you all to shut the fuck up for like an hour while i get caught
up on my feed here § dog food + baby food = protein shake #OnTheGo § "rat rod
shit shack" § screw around like a bitch and i well show you why they call me
MR.Wuhan § "do turds carry gneder. are there male turds & female turds." good
question, Walter_PSX. hte answer, however, is not so clear cut im afraid; §
girls if ya man be Posting under the user name of "Clit Goon" do NOT FUCK
HIM!!!!!!!!!!!!!!EVER § top complaints im working on: - the racism (of course)
-posting the same shit over & over for years -not posting enough of the
classic shit § REAL REAL REAL "The @Dril Drafts Folder: See it BEFORE he says
it" take a L@@k #ForbiddenContent http://t.co/jFkkmhUluk § oh you say you're
going to fuck me? you're going to try to fuck me, through the computer? Well i
say this, and that is "Game on" § the sculptor wipes his brow & steps back to
gaze upon his creation, the words "Gonzo Jeans" rendered in marble. he drops to
his knees & sobs § I've seen enough. Computer... link me in to DragonWeb § who
sent this to my house. Fuck you https://t.co/iBGywSBPzG § this is seriously my
actual reaction when some Stoopid-ass hipster girl asks me what is my faovrite
band . https://t.co/FlCIDYrNhc § me after watching over 700 hours of you tube
tutorials about how to hard ovverride the Orgasm center of girls brains
https://t.co/YvQfXnH1I9 § reading a 900 page book on Dry Rubs and immediately
forgetting all of it and just dumping a shit load of cocoa pebbles on my ribs §
SARGE: This hall better be spotless by the time im back from Lunch ME: Sir may
i have some please sir 9 officers run up screaming in my face § AUUAHHHHGH §
running multiple red lights while listening to the radio jockeys Flawless "dr.
evil" impersonation and scream-laughing § fellas. do n't forget to do something
special for that lady in your life on valentine's day! none of you deserve love
http://t.co/AqlOp59emz § i was already boycotting disney mulan because its for
children, but now that im pissing off hong kong policemen (??) thats the cherry
on top § Reason For Ban : Unfairly denigrating the SuperPretzel„¢ brand. //
Date Ban Will Be Lifted : Never § https://t.co/AHGJGxuUS2 § Why is there anger
on this world. In year 2014. You savage , hateful, ugly thing's § replying to
massive amounts of flagrant screwball tweets with words like "Tedious" followed
by a period § if my Marmaduke internship doesn't pan out i will have nothing.
Nothing § when someone tells me i dont know true pain i remind them of the time
SirGamestop tried to brew his own IPA and gave all the boys Botulism § there is
too much of Lies... § sequestered shelter in place in the vip room of fatburger
with 12 "lady's of the evening" geiting my entire shit honked like a old car
horn § @JoseCanseco Im going to throw all of your baseballs and baseball bats
into the garbage § https://t.co/10SkMRG2L3 § smiling is worthless. it has no
value. nobody wants to see your damn teeth all the time. fuck you #TheThurs-
dayNiteRant § get this down off the computer. § (responding to a troll after
increasing my intelligence to Max Level with a carefully optimized content
stream) I suppose u think youre God, § someone please fucking come to my house
and inspect my gums for any sort of discoloration and leave withotu speaking to
me § theres a 3rd babe movie where he turns into a human at the end. beautiful-

ly done scene. the pigs dream comes true. the government Blocked it § hats off to the shirtless man who found spelling error in my 2yr old tweet but failed to realize that everythng i post is irredeemable filth § it makes me sick when i see border collies portrayed in the media as "Loser Dogs" who are "Probably Rats" § #unpopulargamingopinions games are, in fact, NOT art, with the sole exception being Bugs Bunny Crazy Castle (1989) § move every game stop to the peak of K2 and you will find out damn quick who are the real gamers § some times, it would seem to me, that some of the people who use "smart phones", are ANY THING BUT !!! #OhButUGottaLaugh § i will soon be assembling the LA Boys into my 1br apartment to watch every episode of Mind of mencia in order and show covid virus whos boss § this page is now protected from dick heads and shit heads https://t.co/KKQ6dz0ceB § thank you RandomMan. thank you Don. § i do enjoy spending my weekends "Joining the Army". oh how i hate when monday rolls around & i must say goodbye to all of my soldier friends § forcing comcast to give us internet service without allowing them to completely blast our asses with datacaps is basically old timey slavery § getting fucked up new reports that both of the vp candidates were washed and scrubbed in the same big bathtub, minutes before the debate § bitch § APRIL FOOL ISNT OVER UNTIL AMEX REMOVES OUTSTANDING BALANCE OF $333299 FROM MY ACCOUNT & ACKNOWLEDGES THAT I DIDNT BUY 3000 ASTRONAUT DILDOS § "don't tread of me", the famous words of that good snake who doesn't want to get stepped on, the noble slithering bastard I relate to most § do not be alarme.d the repulsive green hue of my dick and legs and stomach is merely a side effect of fucking bags of wet grass constantly § ragnarᴬ̃ɟk filipino § wearing my most Insolent pair of bluejeans to father`s court hearing § i have received in my life 2 Teen Choice Awards for the work i have done with poisons § this is an attack. you are attacking me § seems to me.. sometimes... you just have to say speak the true things which remain unspoken. § "i think that, if every American had a math book in his hand, instead of the big gulp, we would be in a better place, of the country." -Dril § 3 reasons to join the jackinf off without a condom movement: 1) Its good 2) Its free to join it 3) You dont need a condom to jack off § @birdo i hate u birdo § just heard on the news that our enemies all follow the cutesy motiva- tional shit accounts also, and draw even more power from them than we do § super bowl? the ony bowl you fucking slobs have any right to talk about is the dog bowl, which is where you all eat most of your food out of § tired of pretending certain people have "some good ideas". i miss when all i had to do to fit into a social group was take Heroin constantly § The Band Was Originally Called "The Red Hot Chili Diapers" Before A Puliceman Said No [citation needed] § by "JACKING OFF" https://t.co/XXvZTKdTDR § i have reported the nude celebs to the Motion Picture Association of America, and the oscars. the situation is under control thanks to me § i dress as a police and give mother fucker s like you my badge number every day § im not goiing unless the good people of http://t.co/hdBR2JqY9X can raise $200,000 to transport me and my hardware § https://t.co/Sx6Ym92g6t § rhinestone cowboy 2: titanium cowboy § Cause I got high high Hopes for the living !!!! Cause I got High High Hopes !!!! § very concerned about celeb s § i only stare into the abyss for the commercials § EEEEYYYYAAAAGGGGHHHH !!!! MY ASS .... § i will tell you this right now: I'm from hell. Im highly fucked up. Ive been known to say rude things and watch the carnage unfold brutally § i Fucking disagree § cash for Clunkers.. fuck yes to this... § me and the boys have decided that the least gay way of wiping your ass is to dump a quarter bottle of Palmolive Spring Sensations back there § *shoves bloindfolded man's hand into a bowl of slimy grapes * and this is God's diaper *sticks hand in spaghetti * and this is God's turds § Nuffs aid. Need I say more? Nuff said. Need I say more? Nuff said. Need i say more? Nuff said. Need I say more? Nuff said. Need I say § Funny how some people will forget to click the like button on my posts but always remember to like posts that say

war crimes are good , etc § i will show my penis because i do not want to host
the Oscars, as you see, i will be busy that night, watching the Oscars. § im
pleased to report, that once again , beer has been voted the Coldest drink §
jnust found out me and trig palin have the same agent, no big deal or anything
§ does anyone have any tips and tricks for someone about to own a Balcony. Can
i take beer on it § if you say the words "Room temperature" to me ill flip my
lid. room temp varies depending on the room. youre talking shit out of your
mouth. § trying to drink a can of beer . § checked my inbox for 2 seconds &
immediately saw a genital. could not parse which type of genital it was before
tossing my phone out the car § today is international lunch day so start
eating. #InternationalLunchDay https://t.co/H6iZBS4FW1 § my fellow men it seems
are more interested in getting their dicked sucked , than fostering a network
of Gratitude for the voices of bodys. § sorry if i offened anyone during my
latest nude-out, the doctor told me to grow my body hair out to cover up the
miserable amounts of acne § filling the entire toilet bowl with piss some how §
"Yow... That aint right" § youve enntered the page of The Master https://t.co/
XickVgoFG4 § im the guy who was not sold on Jack Ass until they made it 3d §
going ape shit at the gym. rotating in full 360 degrees with the boys,
flawlessly synchronized § miss when trending topics were shit like #NationalMus-
tardDay instead of links to articles about how eating chipotle cures racism in
rats § this is a very important thing in the econommy § did we end sars yet.
good job every one, if we did § 2005 me: who the fuck is martin van buren 2015
me: ah yes. DonkeyKongEddie. arrested at gamestop on nov 13 2014, drives a grey
honda accord, § roll my big ass over in my favorite chiar and crush 4 of my
horseshit wives for blabbing one off while im trying to absorb a beer commercial
§ im the guy who airbrushes the nipples out of pro wrestling ads. i make $85k a
year. but i have a secret *removs shades to reveal nipple eyes § klout score +
IQ = Amount of $ in bank § YOU WILL NEVER WASH YOURSELF AGAIN AFTER WATCHING
THIS WISE OLD YOUTUBE CLIP WHICH HAS BEEN ï¼¢ï¼¡ï¼®ï¼®ï¼¥ï¼¤   ï¼¢ï¼¹
ï¼¤ï¼¨ï¼£ï¼¨ï¼´ï¼¨³ § there is a time and a place for clowns and it is called
"CIRCUS". not the computer § Everuything about the N-word. I believe im already
rich and ill be launched into the kfc man's grave then. -- http://t.co/zY8yfShu
§ stop for a moment and think about the most realistic Vagina youve ever seen
in your life... § i do not find it unreasonable , during my scheduled Cleaning,
to ask my dentist to wash my dick as well, since my dick is basically a tooth,
§ unlike the rest of you clowns, i want to watch dog the bounty hunter's entire
body morph into a fingerless leather glove for ASEXUAL reasons § @SheriffClarke i
will do any thing for my Sheriff § if you have ever retweetted me without it
equaling endorsing me , i will shatter your smart ass little turd stained
laptop against my legs § i have just gotten word that the 3d dog in Untitled 3D
Dog Project (2021) can speak english, like a man § They read my posts on ellen.
They read my posts on Meyers. Who the fuck are you. All your accounts are for
children. Unfollow me. (66/66) § yeah call the fuckin coppers and ill explain
it clearly to them, ill tell them its ok to shit in my guinea pig hutch because
they do it too § @Iams why should i pay $9 a bag for miscellaneous slaughter
grit when my animals seem to thrive off of my leftover pizza crusts § pokemon/?
who needs pokemon when you have Bosnian Genocide. rewteet this if your a 90s
kid § http://t.co/PGRbniBT i wa nt to drown in this § @Sleepys @SleepysCare @
SleepysKathy @SleepysLaleta @SleepysChanda @SleepysCathy @SleepysIrina respect
teens, scunbags § MAYAN GROUNDHPOG HELD ALOFT BY HAT MAN AT WINTER CEREMONY;
STRUCK BY LIGHTNING; TURNED INTO ONE HUMAN SKULL "UH OH NOW WEVE REALLY DONE
IT" § adding "A Touch of Class" to my home by wrapping all of my game's
apparatus's in tinsel § couldent have said it better. § for reasons none of
you could ever hope to comprehend, i will now be referring to "Baby mario" as
"The baby from mario" § spit takes are funny but if you do them in real life
people will call you ass hole § remember folks - you can click on my posts at

any time to make them bigger on your screen § dick stuck in a moth ball § absolutely block on sight https://t.co/kDkXP1pddD § "TORTURED ACCOUNT" § fake people are ignorant. dead people are fake. ignorant people are fake. dead people are ignorant people. .fake people are dead #RealTalk § "I THOUGHT YOU SAID STATE OF THE ONION" - obbama holding onion at state of the union address § sick of wifes shit https://t.co/VphTqD11nm § Trite. § sorry couldnt hear ya over $ rustling about in my wallet. money i saved by subverting toothbrushes. sucking the toothpaste tube like a cock, § i sense a demonic presence clicking x on my usless posts........... § I already discovered the Higgs-Boson particle in the trash can, with the rest of the hokum . #CERN #God #GodReal #GodIsReal #GodsReal § whats wrong. can't handle a little politic's? § GOD Damn fuckin.. Retro,. classic shit, ah *Face Turns purple and begins crying* sorry. i'm sorry. I'm a dipshit. I'm a fucking idiot § they should rename twitter .com "the dignity website", because i swell with pride when i think of the 200,000+ things ive posted on here § consider how unprepared society would be if every bug and moth flying around just started taking giant shits constantly, like human sized § I own the best law firm in the tri-state area, my wife earns $200,000 a year making ginger bread houses, and we will never hire a US Veteran § a fun idea: mount Tweetmore; like mount rushmore but with Twitter users. again this is just a fun idea i thought of. please let me have this § spending my entire police shift downloading apps where you smear simulated dog shit all ovefr the screen and becoming completely a dumb ass § to the fine folks who kicked my bare ass while i was trapped in the automatic door at walmart: why do you people insist on punishing success § boss waiting patiently for me to finish doing steroids and throwing up into a plastic bucket before handing me some shit he wants me to fax § im a millionair and im going to pay blizzardgames $9.9bil on the stipulation that they put pornos in diabo 3 § as an asmerican citizen i am entitled to the spookiest halloweens possible as required by the constitution of the united states § me and the most profound influencers of our time will soon "Bring back the chuck norris shit" in a display of raw contempt for our followers § kim dotcom was a hero. he loved to piss more than anyht-ing. he would piss into Real Dolls and throw them in the garbage. no toilet § it has come to my attention that people have been saying sex things, and alcohol things on this site. these posts give me migraines so stop § there should be a policeman on the premises when they're naming these damn horses so they stop giving them names that aren't serious or real § the reviews are in folks https://t.co/ujfAOBTt5Q § need to know who wrote "Micropenis Kisser" on my barbeque grill, because if i actually ever kissed a micropenis i must inform my lips doctor § my dick and ass hole are low key sticking out of my shorts § we are living in a culture where you can be punished just for being Dr. Phil § just thinking of how wild things would get if i were to bust out a bottle of wine with the flintstones logo on the label..... § (in reality quiet, barely audible voice) hope your dick falls of bitch § setting up your own yahoo account is easy! you just click here, and he.. oh no. i just sent 60,000 pictures of my ass to my boss's daughter § http://t.co/JC9jwCb1z4 buuy me this if oyu love my content and want to rescue me from eternal misery § forgetting if "taking the knee" is good or bad relative ot my belief system but getting pissed off at every mention of knees just to be safe § a cool prank is to convince someone to join the Armed Forces and watch them get spooked by guns & missiles in exchange for hollow gratitude § listen up Men. the media says you cant flip this over & fuck it like a dog. This of course is a lie. Your penis can fit in any of the holes [laundrybasket.jpg] § the only time isaid the " word" i said it with perfect frequency/timing to intercept & cancel out the sound waves of another guy saying it, § a particularly rude comment i received today has caused me to fill my pants wih shit. i will not glorify the perpetra-tor by identifying him. § the torture of being a Top Influencer on the hateful,

chaotic earth... http://t.co/bFCO8GWvGA § if the sting ray that killed steve
irwin tried to kill me i would bust its ass and crumple it up like a newspaper
§ for my money.. nothin hits the spot quite like Food, or Drink § i hope my
followers are remembering to urinate frequently, to ensure the proper disposal
of bodily waste. § PASSIVE AGGRESESIVELY UNFOLLOWING ME BECAUSE YOU HAVE A
PROBLEM WITH AWFUL POSTS IS A BULL SHIT MOVE § journalism is the hardest job on
earth...I have to look at so many sites, and everyones trying to trick me into
posting pics of my whole ass § do they make those cones that dogs wear after
surgery for people? ?? i need to stop spitting on my dick § shut the fuck up §
looks like a "whos Who' of my dreadful follower list https://t.co/IvoOlKSbep §
if you can make an app that tells you if your ass smells like shit you will
make the aeasiest $1million dollars in the world § if you want the real
bargains during boys night out... gotta go with the Children's menu... every
time § boys im here to tellt you that a high-quality wall paper can make any
room look fantastic on the cheap § (me dming) i am merely a vessel through
which the posts flow. i accept no rewards.. for i have no name, and no face. Do
u like wearing bras, § in light of the slender man case id like to remind my
followers that teens have also attempted murder in the name of digimon otis §
ok. so apparently throwing knives at my car is A Thing now. apparently my
Emphatic Capitalization is frowned upon by People Who Read Words § you know
what. im dropping the subject and going outside to sip some cool lemonade.
Enjoy your circle jerlk § I FUCKING SUCK § hes right though youre bad §
CollegeHater: Ur arms aren't getting enough sunlight CollegeHater: Did u use
the cream I sent u CollegeHater: Ur dead. At the flagpole. 3pm § Your search
- "cal ripken's tears" - did not match any documents. § netflix cuties is as
political as it is bald-faced stupid assed aka i give it zero stars and "my god
have mercy on your soul" -billy madison § fuck of § COnsuidering becoming one
of those jack asses who gets head aches from wi-fi § rogue mythbuster shoots cop
at virginia tech; was aiming for water-filled trash cans § arrest hitler for
racism § "your posts, they aren't good." obama told me over his personal phone
line. "you have to put down the keyboard. you have to #StopThePosts". § Help
Me Deep Freeze My Beard So It Stinks Less § use coupon code "Do Harlenm Shake"
to save 10% off your next Divorce § front of my shirt: " YES: MY PATIO IS
HAND-WASHED " back of my shirt: a convenient bullseye so people can shoot me if
they want to § @FullSail well i doubt you would have paid twitter good money to
promote this program if it wasn't really good and also useful § stood up, faced
audience during larry the cable guy movie, and shouted "YOu're all monsters,
stop laughing at him, that's his regular voice" § More jokes about the movie
"Baby driver" . Soon § can 1000000 irate south korean pigs buried alive after
a foot and mouth outbreak possibly join forces and cause an 8.9 eartquake???
#yes § Im sorry that the 12 days of content feature isnt as good as I planned
it to be. I will try to to better of it, in the remaining days. -Dril § EVERY
POINT VALID AND INDISPUTABLE, perfect diction and posture, my flawless TED talk
about snake vore silences thte trolls once and for all § the "Shit my pants"
challenge: if you can make me cry or shit my pants though the computer ill
apologize to everyone whosever been mad at me § look out for the car with the
words "INCEST DEATH" painted on the hood thats always going like 20-30 mph
under the speed limit, that ones me § Delighted to announce that the mental
illness from being quarantined has caused me to develop an altaer-ego named
"Mr. Simplepleasures" § stay at home rat § extremely good shit http://t.co/
Qh3JvV2ehp § Deep Fake offers us infinite possibilities. For instance, you could
generate an image of your self with a larger penis, and jack off to it . §
vulgar § my followers know i Abhor racism, but i especially dont agree with the
thing from old cartoons where black people have dice for teeth § imagine
assuming the position of a dog and kissing the ass of the "MAINSTREAM" accounts. Muah muah muah. So stupid. Couldnt be me. No way § (seeing the RE/MAX

balloon at a hockey game) shit, they got RE/MAX here? Not bad, § ive trade-marked the term "The guy who fucks up" so if you see someone else using it pleaase stick my Fair Use brochures to their car § chating with lawyer on aol instant messenger. § LET US SPEAK NOT OF THE YOGI BEAR , WHOSE MANNEURISMS, GAIT, AND DEMEANOR , RESEMBLE THOSE OF THE DISREPUTABLE JEWEL MERCHANT "BLOOD DANCER" § if you're ever wondering if im some other guy, the answer is yes, im him, unless it's bad to be him, then im not him, im a different person. § i need something that can put a hole in a UFO § 8 of the navy's finest men rappel into my quarters and change my diaper. i stumble towards the balcony and throw cans at their helicopter § Serious votes only § consolidate your shit into a large mound until its visible from Google Earth, then sue google for putting pictures of your shit online #Rich § probably, if I got night terrors constantly id just say something like "This is a fuckin cool" instead of taking all kinds of pills and shit § one thing for certain is the that the trolls are having a hell of a time Whacking off to the point of ignorance as if i even give a fuck . § ME: watch it bud. my friend RickGamecube, you see, he dont like getting pissed off so much RickGamecube: I dont like getting pissed off § @DigimonOtis always sayig hes "on campus" but he dosent fucking take any classes he just sits in the cafe and plays with a dirty ass gameboy § Saving $400000 a year by eating bugs and little tiny pieces of shit . § custom long john silvers gift certifi-cate that says "Partyboy" on it plealse § im the reddit guy hwo ranted about an existential crisis i had after realizing all of jeff foxworthys "you might be a redneck" jokes were me § me & the boys can never hold a Luau (hula maidens, pig w/ apple in mouth, limbo) thanks to the loud mouth craop going on at college campuses § inventing new character "George X. Bush" the most fucked george bush yet § burger king just did a $100 billion ad campaign to tell us theyre putting piss in the food now when i tell people that for free every day § RT OFFICIAL: Michael Jackson (1958-2009) RIP - http://tinyurl.com/nlm7r2 #michael-jackson #michealjackson #deadrip § someone on here asked me my opinion of Worcestershire sauce... but i dont feel ready to share that at this time. § my mind is normal § me & the booys are rifing on 78 hours of stolen walgreens security cam footage. this guy on here just bought a toilet brush. bitch!! bitch! § instead of mr peanut dying they could show a guy with a towel over his face grabbing his ankles and waterboarding himself with his own piss § ive done the research, ive looked at the facts, ive analyzed the hard data and my conclusion is that youre way more mad than i am right now, § pplease remember to turn your location on so the buffoons on this web site can have an easier time finding you, for whatever horrible reason § "jail isnt real," i assure myself as i close my eyes and ram the hallmark gift shop with my shitty bronco § i have modded gta 5 to make the dicks ugly. and i plan to make them even uglier in ugly dick mod v1.1 § (in worst human voice possible) folks rmember to click that fuckin like & subscribe button and leave a comment below in the fuckin box there § awfully bold of you to retweet my "bad year" tweet on a year that has been extremely good thus far § we told this man that he has the brain power of a thousand state legislators . you will remember His smile forever https://t.co/cfE6ElAu6G § It's basically extremely good except when they arrest a cool guy § yeah , just take this big metal trash can ive strapped to my dick off and just spray piss everywhere. just take it off. great idea fuck face § #itsuckswhen stupid presidents hide there birth certificate... § if youre following me for vids of me smearing chocolate syrup all over my chest. i dont do that anymore, and i suggest u read the holybook . § Make normal car horns "LOUDER" Make Fire Engines, Ambulances and Police Cars "LESS LOUD" § shut the fuck up § oh so when a pro foorball player makes a fake GF everoyne sucks his dick hut when nice boys like me do it the cops demolish her with batons, § need to raise uhhhh $140000 so i can get my daughter Lyvelaughlove in to the army at age 14 § no. not yet § The three brnaches of government? Simple. Breakfast,

Lunch, and DInner. Because the government loves eating us alive with the old Tax & Spen § i sure hope dthe solar flare doesnt cause my camera roll to empty out 200 pictures of my penis onto the time line again § when the doctor ask's you for a stool sample but you dont know how much he needs so you load up like an entire keg with turds "Just in case" § bite my shiny metal § accidentally brought my piss detector into the mens room again and cowered beneath a sink as the deafening screech echoed off the hard tile § The other day , a longtime follower asked to see my penis. I stood Firm and said " o. I will not show my penis to a Shit like you." § @LEVEL5_IA please explain wjhy your latest game contains a despicable portrayal of the prophet Muhammad?? http://t.co/JfLLDN8N #allah #islam § please stop these posts saying im a "pimp". they are causing me trouble with family and police. i have never pimped in my life. im a mere ho § the only A+ i ever got was from that time in art class when i drew venus & serena willaims clobbering the. shit out of me with their rackets § in 1998 donald j. trump sr taught me how to use a Scythe and it sickens me to see people besmirch his good name § my favorite part of the classic 16 tons song is when he threatens to kill me and beat the shit out of me for no reason in the middle of it § i can load my gun in 0.1 seconds. i cn load it so much faster than that guy perfectly every time § when you have to take a shit really badly but you hold it in until your body turns the shit into vitamins and you dont have to go any more > § david kock death hitting especially hard because of baby bird brain derangement that makes me think every rich person i see on tv is my Mom § unlock your account you Freak § bested again by the youngsters who hurl entire thistle bushes at my nude body. these masterminds operate on a level that i cannot comprehend § huckleberry hound... talk about someone who needsto get his act together, pronto § DisgruntledStepSon § i was bullied and tortured at school because i was the only kid with a waterbed. so i got surgery and became a waterbed. suck my cock trolls § there is no meme i have not looked at. § #TheThursdayNIteRant hashtag is now Public Domain. I am permitting twitte'rs worst users to sully it with unauthorized, low-quality rants. § meeting up with ErnieTheBlade and ChaosWendell at shakeshack to discuss the depravity of bobbed hair § HIBACHI MAN AT @BENIHANA__ - WILL NOT PREPARE KRAFT MACARONI AS REQUESTED - THIS IS THE ONLY THING I CAN EAT - IM VERY ILL § now, bear with me folks. if you want to know why i would post something like "stuffing my fat pussy with sage", simply look at the calendar. § dont like my posts then go watch some Prestige television about it. put on some hbo go Fuck face § From the twisted minds behind Dr. Pepper, § i support UncleHalo's idea to replace the united states penny with shuriken § please tell me I wasnt the only one screaming at the tv last night, begging for one of the VP candidates to recognize budweiser's sacrifices § i see that digimon otis has become emboldened enough to begin posting again., likely due to the normalization of that sort of thing, § to the punk who spray painted "Fat Angel" on my 1996 chevy suburban: post your nintendo friend code so i can send you the Medal Of Honor § just to get some perspective on life § hackers are finding ways to inject jokes underneath my posts and i ask my subscribers to remain calm unti;l ive sorted this all out with 911 § he closed his account due to childish people. § now that all of my last-gen hardware is completely obscured by Animal shit , #e3 2014 may officially begin § Good News : Weve Located The Cure For Aids // Bad News : It's Written In The Bible!!! Ew Gross § i will not build a single snow man... until i respect , all of the real men, first § media outrage over the discovery of geiorge zimmerman's Gun Sink, a kitchen sink filled to the brim with guns § thinking of abandoning dreams of becoming a Senator, so i can post about yelling "Fuck" in the bathroom because i accidentally became racist § it would be somewhat fucking good if all the girls on this site printed my avatar out and started kiissing it ,as a joke § Small Meerschaum Pipe, the Bowl in the Form of a Remarkably Naturalistic and Expressive Head of an African-American

Male Slave... https://t.co/vUcKZScvtC § (in perfect astronnaut voice) bleep bloop even I cant figure out how to use damn itunes and im from Nasa § in order to alleviate the stress of having to witness sub par content on my feed, several of my followers have suggested that i try "Heroin" § listening to the song "Shortnin Bread" on repeat 7 hours a day and forming some very complicated opinions upon Race § stealing valor by purchasing fraudulent military gear from etsy,. parading my insane loadouts in front of our vets as they hurl abuse at me, § last night i was restrained and had the words "Bug Helper" branded into my back with a hot iron by three men who i trusted. im still shaking § i warnned you all that bad things would happen if you kept letting your wives wear jeans. AND NOW LOOK! the damn gas prices are up again § this shit sucks so much shit, this is Hell, https://t.co/HHbIzbTeGw § (1) hack myself into the principals computer (2) do a rude little dance (3) get beyblades Unbanned § what a terrible coincidence that this shooting happened to occur on Gun Joke Day § honter biden answer your phone i left metalGearErics game cube controller at your house and he is freaking out at me. he is in the hospital § Waiter! Oh Waiter! Yes, I`d like to know if I have earned any CashBack Reward`s,,¢ with the purchase of my farm fresh miniature cucumber plate § when i was young, i always dreamed of becoming an artist. at age twelve, my father taught me how to tie a Square Knot. Now i hate art, § Your Bad § is it true that the ebola man works at a @cocacola plant. it would be fucked up if he touched the cans and shit, § @RepClayHiggins my wife has the gift of suching my shit completely off § "i said i wanted to meet the KISS dudes! not that i wanted to meet and kiss dudes!" haha dont mind me, im just testing out some new material § What is it that you first seek when inspecting a profile which presents a potential networking opportunity § waking up from a month long k2-induced coma and immediately apologizing to every POC for liking the Tasmanian Devil cartoons for some reason § this is gas lighing. ive read posts about this https://t.co/6wtyXhg4Nd § @applebees this waiter keeps looking at his watch and dripping broken glowstick goop on a detached baby doll's head. 2012??? § once again i apologize § please do not say "top notch" to me unless you want to spend hrs explaining what the fuck these notches are & who determines their hierarchy § the twilight zone episode where the guy blocks everyone on twitter and becomes startled and bewildered when no one is left to give him favs, § my new favorite shit in my DMs is fake twitter admins who manage to get the verified checkmark but still have usernames like MickeyCar199326 § wearing my diaper at half mast , in memoriam #amywinehouse § trolls: Lets jerk off to the teletubbies and. barney me (to followers): Are u seeing this. Are you seeing thi s. Am i the only sane man left § as if. a recent gallup poll indicated that 75% of americans believe the geico cavemen are simply homo sapiens wearing makeup § looking at the list of accounts I voluntarily follow and wishing this shit was more Tailored To My Interests § i've been blacklisted from hollywood simply because I refuse to compromise my unwavering support of Microsoft brand and product. cowardice § just jacked off in real life while you were busy downloading hentai of the old woman who lives in a shoe at 56k § if you receive mail from me and it isn't posted with personalized stamps depicting my dog's pregnant gut then it is fraud. please rip it up § icant come to work today.. on account of JERRY DUTY *SHoves every seinfeld disk into dvd player at once* § i had a dream that Jared from subway followed me & we started discussing new media objectives over DM. when i woke up i was eating my pillow § ievery thing i have ever posted is intentionally good § Wine and stimpy § get to hell you shape-shifting finagler § "KOI POND BONANZA" IN PITTTSBURGH?? THE SUPPOSED NUMBER ONE KOI POND SUPPLIER IN ALL OF PITTSBURGH, PA?? HARDLY A BONANZA § americans the time is now for us to unite against COVID19. we must all come together and say "Oopsydaisy" over and over again untll it stops § once i get the brand surgry i expect dairy queen to come crawling back. to give me back my job of saying "dariy queen

rules" for $0.01 an hr § The SHeriff's Department Denies Your Request To Be Sat
On By Muscle Ladies As Punishment And Would Like For You To Pay Your Ticket
With Cash § "THe Beatles" have been cancelled, everyone. they will be replaced
by me standing on stage for an hour, making my dick shrink on command § pissed
off because people are watching their precious football instead of asking me why
im pissed off § (steps out onto the podium for the annual delivery of his Most
Hated "State of the Arbys" address) the state of the Arby's... is strong... §
despite everything, i am still looking forward to the release of the sequel,
"jungle 3 jungle," which was delayed to 2038 because of trolls. § well i was
going to climb mount everest but this yelp review says theres a nude man at the
summit swinging chains around and yelling "fuck u § how many pushups must I do
in order to boost my wifi signal § Lord give me Coffee do change the things i
have the power to change and Wine to except the things i want to https://t.co/
vh6NFnwKjI § yes, dad, ive heard of simpsons porn. § 100% body fat, 49 year
old, normal Male. good at turning purple while lifting boulders and dropping
them in ex-wife's driveway. Army strong § "If it doesn't have that ZING , it
ain't Tex-Mex." - TheTexMexBoy § stinker alert: you have posted a stinker. you
r punishment is suck this faces dick for 1000 years. good luck and last but not
least Fuck you https://t.co/GAIOijnRXh § its friday "youknow what that means"
https://t.co/NAAgk1f6LO § .@saddamhussein take a lap chowder head § absolutely
nuking my dick into 1000000 pieces with one of those wile e coyote tnt plungers
§ "shit i got Pissed off by" https://t.co/sLzTicbSVj § i would pay $99 for an
app thay reminds you to drink one icecold beer every 20 minutes § ijust had a
dream that there was a big hollywood conspiracy and"3D" was short for "3
Destructions" referring to the 3 buildng attacks on 911 § falling down a stair
case completely unscathed after executing a perfect series of Block techniques
§ digmon otis has locked himself in his closet with several boxes of kashi
granola bars for several weeks to "power up" and "focus" § geiting my mother
fucking ass Rolled for taking too many pictures of the gym § theres an inherent
sense of nobility, or perhaps honor, in the Shit that i post, that distinguish-
es me form my peers. undetectable, but real § i cried when the genealogy
researcher told me this § one needs only to read the quote on my favorite coffee
mug to understand quite clearly, without a doubt, that i am mad about Content.
§ i was going to do it but I got scared § youtube guy does magic tricks for an
ape, and someone in the comments says magic is actually harmful to apes. well,
fuck this shit, then !! § breaking down mentally because im all out of toiolet
paper and i cannot decide which wendys coupon to wipe my ass with § http://t.
co/jxTBUplNC0 just gonna leave this here.. feel free to buy th e stuff on it. to
my house if you want to § out with dentists, in with mouth gurus § nascar-
dicktruckcummanballsguyaryanweedcarlegskissercockprick@bignutcorncobfuck-
ass696drainagedeadgarbagedeadmanshit.biz § me and the boys run the most hated
content house in all of tinsel Town. all we do is cuck each other by accident
and forgive each other § id really like to figure out how to sell me and my dogs
turds and shit to a farm or something § "SORRY BOYS!" your cum tributes of me
are highly inept, trite, and bogus. Futher more, they look like dog shit. Do
better § koko the talking ape.. has been living high on the hog, wasting our
tax dollars on high capacity diapers. No more. i will suplex that beast, §
living vicariously through gamer streamers who are more powerful than me §
(everyone in dm notices ive been trying to type something for 10min straight)
sorry all. iwas just writing down a girls phone number in here § gentlemen, i
implore you not to miss the Gamer's Challenge, wherein i will complete donkey
kong countyr 3 (italian vrsn) without crying § for $0.39 extra the burger king
man will write "yu-gi-oh" on your hamburger in magic marker § Well, it'd better
damn friday § making a Fairly solid argument that tthe same societal sickness
that led to Minstrel Shows manifests itself today as "Doggo Shit" § TWITTER:
our records sjow..youre the least blocked guy here. 0 mutes ME: spectacular.

Truly, truly miraculous. This is a sign.. to post more § ATTN: SICK FUCKS WHO ARE AGGRAVATING MY HEART CONDITION ON PURPOSE BY POSTING DRAMA 2 THE INCEST SUBREDDIT - GOT TWO WORDS FOR YA: "GUN § dont care. having a lot of views is selling out any way § I did not show my ass § i want to crush it between my shoulder blades § Ive been stepped on more than every bug on the universe and still i get back up & put out 1000 stupid fucking posts every day. And still. § #GooglePlayMusic ha ha some guy spent a billion dollarsr to put this boring ass hashtag on the trending list. fuck you idiot § ISIS MAN: It's Jim from Montana... He says ISIS should "Cool it" and that we're "Crooks" ISIS CHIEF: Damn. Were finished. Dismantle the nuke § MYTH: my posts are for the Pauper REALITY: my posts are for the Prince § 1) never look at my replies 2) Im not trying to fuck the weather lady Im just trying to make her cum in her pants on live tv § " []D [] []\\/[] []D " <<<< thats how you type the word pinp § #MillennialSoapOperas " DUMB ASES " § here how it goes down. when its my turn to get the vaccine i say " o. Give it to a female fire man instead" and i simply just walk away... § Buffalo wild wing gets $0 tip for serving "Bones" to me in chicken, if i had wanted to eat bones i would take my Ass to the grave yard § just had a nightmare that my account was permanently suspended for referring to "the beach boys" as "the beach boy shit boys" § but who will advocate the Non-essential oils?? the oils my body could not give a shit about either way § You should have to have Four years experience as a Chef before you are allowed to become a Waiter. The crap has become ridiculous § i'm convinced that people only favorite my tweets so that they can use them to fuck me over in court at a later time, since they're not good § just the other day i was taking a bath and i saw a tiny tugboat in there leaving a chemtrail. i told it to fuck off. im a green beret gunman § Clipart Illustration of a Black Hanukkah Baby In A Diaper, Holding Gifts, A Menorah And A Rattle § - Incest Prank Goes Wrong - Why Thousands Of Geniuses Are Ditching Their Aquariums - Can Plants Make You Smarter? - Moms Can Get Tattoos Now § wheres the fucking list of all the tanning salons that are open during th e hurricane #PostTheFuckingList § having to hose off 900 screaming animals at my job at the zoo every day is harder than any thing a untied states marine ever did § the numa numa man just bougt a $70million house and im here at the library trying to photocopy a fruit roll up § Am i a" HO"? Do i slut my self out? Am I Slutted out? § in a show of deference towards teens , the majestic mount fuji has been renamed to ``Teen mountain`` , in a move that is sure to piss me off § nice to know some one cares about me.... https://t.co/LoJRdUlk3K § cops should have two guns to get rid of crime faster . cops should be dual wielding by 2016 § i got rid of it cus it broke my phone and criminals were usig it to give me heart attacks § floating in my above ground pool nude from the waist down wearing a shirt that says some shit like "i find your lack of wifi disturbing" § FUCK the brand § everybody is jacking off to their follower count and it makes me sick. iits just a number. stop jacking off to it § if my post offend you... call 1800-EATSSHIT § daily reminder to wrap your Shit in tin foil before flushing so it doesnt touch other people's shit § the nyt is giving me $10000 to write about the time i lied face down and cried while dogs humped me until i cummed in my pants 100% flaccid. § WHAT THE FUCK IS A " BAPE" ??????????? § resposnse to the NYT article calling gamers "Ho's" 1. gamers are not ho's. How dare you 2. if Walter Cronkite saw that hed shit in his grave § maestro stands on top of my couch and waves baton perfectly in rhythm with my clicks and scrolls as i block rude accounts & erase sass mouth § i spend the majority of my computer time #Frowning § best is when you're shopping for bedsheets and you see one with a lousy thread count and you say to your buddies "this poiece of shit sucks" § world governements are calling diarrhea the "shit of the future" as it is faster to poop out; causes less wear and tear on pipes & plumbing § bubba burger is short for "bubba hamburger" and the y take pride in serving absolute shit to nobodys § #blog-

con2013 im here and if you so much as look at me without having a Verified
Account my devices will emit an ear-piercing defense screech § alright Boys i
just spent seven years on a dumpster diving voyage across South America and i
got some nice Finds for YA , lets take a look: § THE INCEST TERRIER #illegal-
DogBreeds § good avatar round up October 2018 https://t.co/1hffeu7Wd9 § The
state of the qua;lity of the posts on my feed has never been more fucked. And
every one is too busy touching their Penis to give a shit. § open letter, to
the man who told me that they should make an app for "Shutting the fuck up"
during my town hall web development conference ; § #8ThingsICantLiveWithOut
blame, denial, pity, rationalization, constant validation, superimposing
fantasy, overcompensation and SuperPretzel § @dril isaid comments off mother
fucker and i mean it! § every one on the computer has undergone a villain arc
where they stop jacking off for 2 months and go mad because it didnt fix their
anxiety § ---------------- COP ZONE ---------------- § my "happy Halloween "
wishes have already been sent out so if you did not receive one then you are
Fucked. § my name is krayg. i am 49 years old. i have forgone all emotion. i
am writing this letter to put an end to the tyranny known as Nick Jr § i just
heard someone was angry on a website and now im angry and people are angry at
me for being angry at him and im angry at them too #hel § knocked a shit load
of doritos off the shelf during my latest suicide attempt at wegmans and thtis
16 yr old little shit made me put em back § i fear change § sorry bartender. if
i order the wrong beer the trolls will have a field day. lets play it safe. fiji
water for me, with a Hint of pepsi § well; the Trolls have discovered my one
weakness; shaking big plastic bags at me until i piss myself, & frankl;y 2012
looks to be a bad year § *rotates earth 13 degrees* WHich zodiac sign are u
now?? *rotates earth 27 degrees* NOW what one are u?? *rotates earth 2 degre*
Fucker § we all had that kid in school who shaved the Netflix logo into his hair
& kept saying "Cant wait to watch some Netflix" #WeAllHadThatKid #90 § its me !!
Hahaha. Did i just fuck your mind? Welcome to the web. Where things aint
always as they seem § i will never allow myself to go to hell without finding a
way to take my laptop and piss soaked mattress along with me § let us discuss
the recent unveiling of user "@TurdBozo " and how that affects our creative
collaborative efforts like, artistically and shit § the jduge orders me to take
off my anonymous v mask & im wearing the joker makeup underneath it. everyone in
the courtroom groans at my shit § the crusaders fire ballistas into my throbbing
diaper- unleashing a torrent of mustard yellow shit and poisoning the entire
village § how many years did it take for moses to build the ark?? trick
question. God built it § i cough and sneeze into the toilet like a smart adult
§ betting $10 on each of the horses because all of them are my God , and every
one of them has the power to physically annihilate me § liist of people who
drink beer: wastoids, junkfreaks, crimepunks, crankensteins, grimesmackers,
pissbois, mudgeeks, roadslime, and meatballs § I Want The Duck Dynasty Boys To
Crucify Me Upside-Down And Piss On Me Violently. I Want The Duck Dynasty Boys
To Block My Useless Account § i got in the newspaper twice. once for my good
posts, and once for screaming while still in the womb somehow § my account is
of no business to the trolls and their septic ilk . go jack it, fraudsters.spew
contemptuous bile on your toilet. not to @dril § looking forward to getting in
some #YardWork today!! *trims 200 square feet of lawn with a riding mower and
collapses like a sack of shit* § a new face steps into a rowdy roadside bar
somewehre along Interstate 22.. back of his leather jacket says "Trickle Down
Economics Are Real" § like these curtains?? 100% japanese denim. like my
shoes?? 100% japanese denim. wanna bite of my sandwich? 100% japanese denim.
#tcot § no skills, no brains, total pussy who looks like shit, sucking up and
kissing ass until i get my corner office at the racist orphan refinery § my style
https://t.co/nt8AqSAFoA § I will never post such info onto this bad website §
BMEZINE, U WILL FEATURE MY PIC AT ONCE. IM THE MAN WITH JETHTO TULL WRITEN ON

CHEST IN PERM. MARKER #NotEntitledToTheSweatOfMyBrow § shut the fuck up § turn
all the food on earth into wolf urine #waystopissoffafatperson § ive enclosed an
image of judge judy and my stepdad kissing that I photoshopped to express my
disapproval of the broken paintball gun verdict § all cops on twitter please
help. i found this fuckin egg on a bus seat where a large man was just sitting.
how do i properly dispose of it § open pastebin of LAPD shooter's manifesto.
ctrl+f search for injoke staples such as "jeans", "diaper" and "toilet". no
results. click x. § time for a BATH https://t.co/GK4HNKYhHNF § im gay too and i
love shit and im a nerd § im a netflix executive and if i go onto your feed and
see shit that has less than 50 likes i will NEVER hire your ass!! delete that
SHIT!!! § laughing all the way to the bank, but only because the guy walking in
front of me is wearing a twisted t-shirt............ § best part of being a
#Verified is undoubtedly having cops throw flash grenades through the window of
anyone who tweets the word "Ass" at you § everyone less mentally ill than me is
Privileged, everyone more mentally ill than me is Toxic, everyone equally
mentally ill to me is Cool § my dick is a beak now § https://t.co/UeK46Z1pYb
Focus On The Issues § i am now ready to share my thoughts on the guy who took
his penis out of his pants after screaming "Ohhh!! Ohhh!!" on the zoom call. §
i bought one of those craigslist peacocks. this fucking thing wont eat and its
loud § you utter fool. od not come in here asking to see rocky's dick. that is
not the spirit of philly § i detect a trace amount of piss in the public pool,
turn purple & foam at the mouth. i scream as the lifeguard injects me with piss
antidote § (ass sticking out of pants spraying poison everywhere whlie i step
towards the podium to apologize to the press) Ah Shit. I forgot my notes, § i
gotta say both of these are looking pretty sharp. can't wait to go next-gen
http://t.co/122XQOHPO8 § whuh?? isis is good/? **slams face into monitor
leaving a head-shaped hole* Whammo. Fuck off § nascar saga IV: elder blade:
honor of car § im out here in the yard trying to clean up my turds with a hair
brush § The six things I could never do without: €¢ . €¢ gamer § jon stuart
sir would you like to take a look at the, frankly good, 1000 pages of ad copy
ive written for https://t.co/erPUGGB5qf? or are you a Bitch? § If you do this:
Fuck you http://t.co/9RBuLcCun3 § dont count the celebs out just yet, fellas.... i got the feeling theyre planning all sorts of those madcap stunts that
drive all of us #WILD § ready to accept nine hundred dollars into my life
http://t.co/NVls6XDI3T § just set up My Quicken Loans accounts for a whole
small ecuadorian village, entirely on chrystal meth. keep doing your little
posts though . § vladimir Putin if youre reading this please grant me asylum
like you did with snowdan. i too ,am constantly in hot water because of my
posts § Goodboy goodboy § dunston Fucks in § us siamese twins need to stick
together § This Shit Sucks Dog Shit https://t.co/QL7az6QZ27 § it takes so many
muscles to kick my ass. like a million § i interface the dunston check 's in
dvd with the God Processor. a gruesome polygonal ape head welcomes me to
dunston world § these metrics are absolute shit. once again my followers have
forced me, to threaten to post on here, images of my Hated penis § "im not
owned! im not owned!!", i continue to insist as i slowly shrink and transform
into a corn cob § IF IT PLEASES THE COURT, ID LIKE TO POST SOME EXTREMLY
RELATABLE SHIT: § nobody believes me that once i was shitting in a cave & the
sound of it hiting the floor replicated the Nintendo switch snap sound perfectly
§ im tired of everyone saying that pinocchio turning into a real boy was a good
thing. it was a demons trick § i am selling six beautful, extremely ill, white
horses. they no longer recognize me as their father, and are the Burden of my
life § i found a basin. its you § Yes § people do not help each other any more.
When was the last time you saw anyone help someone. wveryones too busy watching
Huluplus..... § using street view; trapped in man's sandwich https://t.co/
Fk81c28gYf § accidentally printing out 20 ascii wayne gretzky nudes on the
really loud printer in the school's computer lab #90sHell #DecadeOfTorment §

opening my samsung Direct app to get samsung directuly to me § "Oh I was just PostShitting for laughs" EXactly. And that is why U forever languish in obscurity while i engage brands U could only dream of § going to be doing some extremely powerful introspective poses on the railroad track for the next couple hours, so please cancel all trains § your post sucked so much shit so bad it just turned me from ESFP to INTJ in 2 seconds flat. your spinning my bitch wheel 99mph § i go online to learn which cartoon characters fuck each other and log right back off before the corruption sets in § Let 's Fill The Large Hadron Collider With Garbage Now That They Found Their Shitty Particle § MOSQUITO cannot breed inside of faucet if it is running constantly... use this infor wisley § pissing on top of my own throw up and saying a lot aobut society....... § "Gamers" needs to grow the fuck up. § im a comedy Theorist now. waitll you see which seasons of family guy i can compare your posts to. youve only seen but a fraction of my power § realdoll corporation accidently sent me a Scarecrow... a sign that I should return to the simple life at my uncle's pumpkin farm?? Probably § Just got word that thheyre going to do jade helm 15 again, to punish us for letting the celebs run amok. It 's fucked up but we deserve it. § getting absolutely cock suckered by theat shit that made humpty dumpty fall off § really fucked up that you have to start every letter with "Dear" like youre trying to get the dept of weights and measures or whoever horny § i have absolutely zero interest in friendship, i have absolutely zero interest in jokes, i am simply here to collect data and earn respect § A GATHERING OF MISCHIEVOUS IMPS FIRE UP THE NINTENDO 64 AND RUN MARIO UP THE ENDLESS STAIRCASE FOR 1 HR § TheLegsGuru - girls let me see them beautiful Leg's - TheLegsGuru § oarnge bean https://t.co/wmVhogFywN § @Battlefield once again, user "Garth_Turds" is running amok on this server, reading off a list of religions and making fart sounds w/ mouth § stuffing my fat pussy with sage § if i was fake that would be fucking insane as hell § my putty stance. fuck all putty http://t.co/Ybq2iKBCTa § i nneed constant 24/7 stream of memes and jokes about coffee being good to prove to myself im not living in rthe Fucking matrix § my promise to my followers... is that i wil;l never become the "freak of the week" § its sunday morning which means u boys better either be in church or staying home because of another gynecomastia flare up like the poster me § every day i get 1000 messages from my followers tell me i can SUCK DICK and FUCK MY SELF!! because i dont have the check mark § jeopardy should give the contestants guns and make them shoot the categories. i think that this would improve the image of the guns brand § im going to jack off to the comet instead of the ass because im nice § hollering man still causing mischief at supercuts. theyll never attempt to turn your dog into a cat just by giving it a haircut, get over it § my loyal followers are calling me a "Pussy" because a car kicked up a piece of rebar or something and popped me inthe fucking teeth at 99mph § tthe super computer lit up and told me my posts were good in a fucked up robot voice, validating me forever online § im concerned abou t the width of your head, jabounce86 § thinking about hopping on some sites tomorrow. havent made a decision yet but i will let you all know. sound off in hte comments below. § i like to act genuinely baffled when people tell me to shut the fuck up. like "Huh? But why? The shit i post here helps people, but ok," § hunched over my Bureau Plat with quill & ink , writing a thank you letter to the Kohler toilet company for letting me shit in their toilets § too much pressure from society saying we all got to learn how to self suck. iwill never self suck my dick and im unfollowing anyone who does § http://t.co/lLzKlr1s perfect § "tweeting for literacy" is like farting against pollution § we had 2 cuts of ribeye, a salt shaker half full of salt, a quart of wine, and a whjole galaxy of multi-colored bibs, napkins, § welp, time to rescue egypt from muslims. asomebody please carry all 900 pounds of me to the site of the protests. wait nevermind im good § LawAndOrderGal has entered JeansChat   LEVIS_GAURDIAN: NEED A FUCKING DRAINAGE

RIG THAT WONT SCALD MY THIGHS LawAndOrderGal has left JeansChat § ME: (pulls
soaked pair of jnco jeans out of sons aquarium) Ah wahts this. You cant
continue to live here if you do this SON: Im a smoker now § "i nutted in my
wife x amount of times and shes still not pregnant" humor is not funny no
matter what the number is. even if its like 100000 § the only crime dick cheney
committed was being born into a world where goofusmouths are allowed to flap
their gumms at true mighty armymen § ill have no more talk of mystery complaints regarding my screensaver of juiced ass dudes turning into snakes then
back into juiced ass dudes § back up and the fuck off ! § i refuse to conform to
typical standards by being "clever" or "funny ". i will never betray my
spiritual honor by "posting good things" § Gah . Delete it § and every one
always says im a fucking Moron for leaving my dms open . https://t.co/J0yvE-
EVa1P § also, the cop zone feature is done now § when the earths Magnetic Poles
flip and everyone suddenly stops thinking script format posts are good <<<
(whichever directions the bad one) § Ive opened the dialogue on race over 1000
times. Ive steered the discourse enough times to make your nut sack spin. §
FURTHER MORe, any future tweet i make may now randomly be designated as a "Hell
Tweet", meaning if you reply to it , you will be blocked, § ive been legally
advised to state that the video of me being escorted out of a hospital while
clutching a nerf gun ansd making noise is fake § Yes yes yes. Right down the
line https://t.co/4FfZauUzOA § whocares. theyre both fake. everything on this
fucking web site is fake § can you believe they won all of that guys money § i
have been told that my web page is a sort of "Heaven" for men who exist on the
Diaper Spectrum § writing in "god Trumps racism" and walking out of the voting
booth high-fiving the Good Cops with a visible load stain on my croch § are u
ready for mothersday i am. http://tinyurl.com/2chgrdp § christ.. ive done it
again.. ive posted the absolute good truth shit that every1 has been waiting to
hear in this sea of lying crap nonsense § keep your dirty shit of of here § Im
not fucking serious or mad right now § eat shit mother fucker!!! **throwing
massive amounts of cash* art is dead bjtch!!! art is dead § "The Godfather:
Part Iraq" (2004) In this 4th installment of the Godfather series, the godfa-
thers head to iraq to settle the score, of 9/11. § soirry. i didnt know
retweeting "fuck lobsterfest" would make me lose 200 followers. ive learned my
lesson so feel free to follow me again § now let's see that bad boy in 3d §
cornering a janitor for 50 minutes to tell him how i was once involved in a
polyamourious relationship w/ the guy who said "lee roy jenkins" § the pringles
man is the ghost of uncle pennybag, the monopoly man. this is the first opinion
ive ever posted so please be gentle. #BrandLore § BILY JOEL ROCKS MY HEART AND
SOOTHES MY SOUL - FINAL ANSWER REGIS - AS I LAY DYING § confidently reclining in
my seat after calling my onlinw adversary a "shitbarn" § on the horn with
nabisco slavery engineering solutions and hooters world Bank(HWB) aa we speak,
might even contact "Super Nintendo" well see § this aint the damn barney
channel https://t.co/EGdhPwu2bi § (ddumb ass, squinting at the tv, struggling
to comprehend "The Flintstones") why are they wearing those outfits § i do not
delete my posts. deleting my posts would be akin to razing Abraham Lincolns
famous log cabin, just because the trolls are mad at it § The Fact Remains That
Your A Guy From Reddit, And Im A Guy Who Posts On A Website Thats Somewhat More
Prestigious Than Reddit § the guy who invented the plunger said "i gotta find a
way to suck the toilet off Pronto" § #ConfessYourUnpopularOpinion coats are just
big shirts § rip out my chest hiar and shove fistfuls of it into my fat mouth
while my slobber-glazed jowls shake about and sprinkle your bosom with spit §
closing my eyes and mentally visuelizing my enemies bodies, in 3d , to analyze
them for weak points § Thoroughly Unimpressed. https://t.co/P4B629tINJ § I miss
lunch from when back before it became a fucking joke to most of people. § agent
scully found me freezing to death at the mountaintop. "drink of my breastmilk,
it's the only way youll live" she cries, and i say "ok" § this bitch thinks

he's the Coin Master. Why i do not know. https://t.co/k8YBcIhFfK § @McDonalds i have an a 1 million dollar idea that will pull your failing company directly out of the toilet. hear me out. § my life motto is simply the words "james bond" § 1) All Sex Is Rape -- 2) Sex Is A Synonym Of Gender -- 3) There Fore Gender Is Unequivocally Rape -- 4) Set & Match , Gendertards. § MY SIN: i got excited and made a horrifying post of jay leno (car victim) MY PUNISHMENT: i will burn my self to appease his oafish fans § that'sd right folks!! i, adolf hitler, have been PRETENDING to like rap this whole time so people would consider me more eclectic! Ha Ha Ha! § id love to do some posts on here § just got my new jeans in the mail and the trolls are sweatting like a bird at the kfc factory § ME: ok now do a search of this. "muppet babies theme - backwards, half speed" ALFRED HITCHCOCK: Holy Fuck !! § went to sons baptism. i yeled "ot so fast Champ" and punched the priest & spalshed holy water around. i lost my child in the ensuing chaos § movies that portray Dragons in a positive light are marked with a gold marble, while movies racist against Dragons are given a frowning Ass. § send 1 million guys dressed as The Matrix into iran and i guarantee you the rhetoric will tone down § astrally projecting my brain into antifa head quarters and memorizing their combat patterns is the easiest shit i have ever done in my life § i stopped watching all the tv shows my followers think are bad, unfollowed all the Goof accounts, and yet twitter still sends thugs after me § " big-ears bastard ruins another opera after being flung off the balcony by marines " § BUSter implicated in cannonball terror plot, inanimate crash dummy tried for atrocious death crimes while Build Team flees the country § yoiu got some shit on your monitor § i squint real hard while attempting to contemplate a math problem designed for children until my entire dumb ass face turns navy blue § if you add me to the dumb ass group chats full of guys i dont know you better believe im leaking that shit to the cops. i do not give a fuck § #BenghaziInFourWords MORTIMUS BELLUM PESTILENTIA BENGHAZI § getting the daily presidential briefing and its just shit like "we banned Weed because it makes people too smart" and "Mozart smoked weed" § that's where all the good shit in life comes fronm § http://t.co/jT9y9xJPVu look at thi § Cant sit still knowing this year's 9/11 is on a CHURCH day!! Very excited § #IAlwaysThinkAbout the Arts § new concept "Jeans City" will figure out more info and put it here later § #worldturtleday these beasts are simply armoured rats ,always and forever § if my bank balance is below $100 i will refuse to vote. if it is over $100 i will vote for whichever candidate has the best "Ground game" § "if theres a spicy brown mustard, why not a spicy brown ketchup?" The wise man smiled. "my friend, the condiment you seek is Barbecue Sauce" § reported for Flame Baiting . § i want the popular new animated gif of me looking at a messy old trash can while lickin my lips; Removed . Remove it off- site. Log it out. § romney claims obama takes too many showers & dries skin out. in resposne, obama slow;ly steps on mitt's dick & balls with a high heeled shoe § its like i always say folks "you gotta follow my account to get the posts" § i stop to ask a local how many asses the ass downloader has downloaded. "at least 100," he tells me. i nod and continue my journey onward § your taking my post out of contexts, but yes § eating baby food. baby food for adults. adult baby food. i eat baby food. eat baby food as an adult. tricks to eating baby food as an adult. § as the authority on being tge guru of tech, i think that, "searchs", are going to be an important part of web life, in the year 2015 § Sadly, every one below the age of 45 is more interested in finding "Waldo" , than being "Well-to-do" § @DrewFromTV please murder me drew carey. i want you to snuff my trivial existence from this awful lplanet. good job losing weight § #TheSatur- dayMorningRamble cant do it anymore. the ramble has taken control of my life & my doctor has advised me to stop before it kills me § i enjoy a bit of "Humour" every now and then, but people seriously need to sotp tying me to a chair and injecting me with unknown substances § " the bitch of bluejeans" https://t.co/

TiJs0ly8kr § group of young woman: were going to take some "Selfie" portraits.
care to join us? me [doing the face palm face now]: ABSOLUTELY NOT!!!!!!!! §
"Give me an App that will make me say, 'Wow'" "Apps will help us in our lives"
"An App is always just a download away" some good app quotes § the archaeolo-
gist inspects a hideous smear of caveman shit on the wall of an ancient cavern.
"ah, this is it. the first ragecomic" § This is f ucked up. http://t.co/cyqAL31G
/m4m/ Gangnam-Piss Jesus christ. Holy shit man. Check out this fucked up man.
§ the newest, shittiest one possible , owned by dick Cheney & hipsters,
tweeting for pepsi bucks to promote abcs sitcom lineup § it seems like nobody
appreciates a good wine any more. every one would all rather drink Redditor Cum
§ thjis could be possibly considered to be a rude comment of me. § dont post
thjis. its a work in progress § underwhelm by social media..posted 6 pics of
my clean mouth, fresh from dentist,but ppl are more interested in yapping at
their shit friends § please lord publish my email just this once § alcohol is a
drug, beer is alcohol, and drugs are a form of beer § pleased to announnce my
new provocative sit com "Who Smoked Daddys Crack" will soon replace all the
good shows on your fav streaming service § will e3 have designated crying
booths. im sick of crying in the bathroom where people shit. § Move alone...
Nothing to see here. § my plan of my walk of life is always making one million
smackers (dollars) to get rich, and to pick up all the money I find on the floor
§ i refuse to partake in any hot black friday deals today out of respect for
all the dead folks on the benghazi strip #shopping #deals #prayer § when I
dropped out of middle school I went home& watched korean flash animation "i love
egg" like 28 times with tears streaming down my face § haha jokes on you halo 4
admins.. my daughter isnt really dying . i lied. thanks for the doublr XP
Bitch. § kissing the female firefighter emoji as penance for being a dog brained
fuck freak § theres like 90 reddit threads per day called "Do your friends Hate
you?" and they always have 10000 replies of people saying shit like "Yes" § @
TheScienceGuy the natural course of life dictates that by 9000AD hte entire
human race will have either died off or evolved into pitbulls . § while youre
all bowing to the Pig Industrial Complex on false holiday #NationalPigDay,. i
will be observing pictures of the noble bull moose § Why am i smilin tonight
fellas? Just got my hands on that new good treat to sip known only as simply
"Bber". § my mentions are on lock down until further notice . § my stupid
fucking little ass and my stupid little pecker with the balls on it are iconic,
and me right now, and mood § i plan on giving the olympics a right proper
bollocking for lifting the tokyo 2020 setting straight from my cat girl novella
§ proud to announce that after 30 years as a slave on my uncle's fishing vessel
i no longer wish to fuck the post cereals honey-comb wanter § Its smart § my
problems with "who to follow" 1.i dont know most of these people well enough to
burden them with a follow 2.it should be 'whom to follow" § please set your
home pages to http://t.co/vahp3VrtsA . it is a better web site than twitter. no
trolls or loudmonths, always free. § pretending not to be mad while the guy in
the next stall over takes a big shit while I try to Meditate § kiss my Thug ass
§ im finally fat as hell Its About Time "Its About Time" #itsabouttime § i'll
never. § gotta pick one man. the night ain't over until you pick a favorite
pope. "all of them" is not an acceptable answer. "clement xii"?? Fuck you § fine
then you can just skim through and look at t he pictures like a damn toddler §
was gonna bring back the classic "piss" gag but you cant say the word "piss"
any more. theyll get ya. ford trucks .com built ford truck #ad § missed
connections: the bone - head who dropped an entire slice of pizza on my brand
new Craig Martin`s (wow yourw a tough guy) § mother nature and father time
arre not real. theyre fake people who were invented to explain trees and clocks
to shitheads § i specifically requested that my bone marrow be sent 2 the man
who wants to rub it on his dick, instead of that dying girl. this is bullshit §
i can only do 2. they are refusing to fund me § false. total crap https://t.co/

PXX9Gd116D § how high does my postcount have to be before i'm eligible for Mensa § "the guy who tried to sell a mummy on etsy" § Surfin' the net. § if anyone knows what to do if you accidentally swallow an entire cigar while running on the treadmill please contact StogieLad@Yahoo.com § today's the day that i put on my high heel cowboy boots & stomp the shit out of the fake plastic son that my father raised before i was born § click this post to devote yourself to Zesty Ranch from now to eternity , the cool, crisp satisfaction that all good mouths adore § the dog from "Doge".. was assassinated today.. at the Pittsburgh Marriott durinng a "Meet & Greet".. point blank with a sniper rifle.. Weird § 2013: burger king creates "The Doritos Whopper" 2021: orson scott card writes "The Doritos Novel" 2035:removed from matrix. no more doritos § @hhgregg 696969696969 § my walk in closet with the frogger arcade cabinet is a No Liberal's Allowed Zone § i found Heaven https://t.co/q3zPaTws § I have never been horny. I have never even thought about becoming horny. Get off line from me. § indeed, i am Very Diapered right now, currently pairing a Pampers Cruiser with a quarter glass of Marcus Sinclair's Cape Cod November Ale § Beware of the group of hauntingly beautiful Latinoes who will post nonsense on your vlog and hypnotize U into bowing before htier coward god § a tshirt big enough to cover my ass hole up § trolls have cost me the Dairy Queen deal. Dairy Queen will not take my account seriously because of these people. § my name is " GAMER FUCKER " and i was sent to FUCK all the gamers... § every girl on ther fucking planet has the exact same voice as each other that i like to call "girl voice" § the us census has analyzed 100 million diapers and figured out which race has the worst smelling turds ,making live leak comments obsolete § im making this canon whether u like it or not http://www.fanfiction.net/s/5806451/1/the_ventura_twins § question my alligence to the dod damn twitter website and get swiftly block buttoned to childish hell, nincompoopts § your snl § the epic shit of 2017; is the boys getting TheSegaPimp fired from his job at The Red Cross for not wishing me a "Happy Halloween" § http://t.co/YyiGvd2k nostradamus in hell § the best damn posts for free mother fucker § attention Boris_Gunblade; regarding getting that "having aids money" , i do not know what you meant by that. please respond to text message § typical that I should be diarrheaed on for sharing my beleifs § my agent said i'm not allowed to post in all caps anymore so i threw all of his award-winning birdhouses into the fucking driveway § The office space judge, to the trolls: For refusing to stop being a piece of crap i am sending you to 15 years of pound me and the ass jail. § there needs to be a "BRexit" for people Who still be watching Teletubbys § Once again, those dastardly, Devious trolls have installed a device underneath my computer desk that shoots me in the dick every time i post § the fact i still post here despite people sending pics of my penis around is the greatest act of kindness in human history . Remember that § Q: How goes it, Mr 007. BOND: mission accoomplished, i have electrocuted The Bitch. now give me my money before i start knocking shit around § BREAKING - The Green M&M Has Been Spotted Wearing A Mysterious New Bra; But Not Everyone Thinks It's Good § BARBARO IS BACK, THE ONCE DEAD REACEHORSE IS BACK TO LIFE AND TEARING UP THE HORSE TRACK LIKE NEVER BEFORE, "THE SECRET" WORKS,THANK U OPRAH § restuarants need to start hanging up pictures of their bathrooms outside so i know what im getting before i walk in the damn place § im thinking this is gonna be the most Wild april fools day yet! § i saw a man at rofl con with a huge black stain down the ass crack. can another attendee please confirm #roflcon #StainMan § im banky. § turner classic diaper § NEWSWEEK: WHat can be said. youre a spectacular brand. like hitler without the racism ME: I am exactly indeed like hitler without the racism § producing a tv show called "Fuck My Money" and it iwll be either a tv show or a movie. look for it § https://t.co/p3gmZuN3s4 § STOP THE POST STREAM. PULL THE PLUG ON IT. END THIS MADNESS. GET THESE DAMN POSTS OFF MY TIME LINR "LOUSY!!" "WE DON'T WANT EM!!" §

fuck your self. stop looking at my posts. taste a son of a bitchs ass. § The
Foundation For The Restoration Of American Honor Has Given President Barack
Hussein Obama A Hitler Rating Of 34. This Is The Worst One. § youll never shut
me the fuck up , no matter how many times you unfollow me, you will never shut
me the fuck upon here!! get lost Cyber scum! § to my hawaiian pen pal from like
4th grade; sorry for sending you a pinecone. if someone sent me a pine cone in
the mail i'd beat their ass § DONE WITH people who think that ronald macdonald
is a real person § all guys wanna do is tell you where their Bonnie lies. Shut
the fuck up § im IP banned from this site in the usa but my Dubai account is
good to go § thinking going to the Kingdom of Heaven for fucking one trillion
years is a fairly nice deal § my wife gives birth to a beautiful vintage
schlitz beer tap handle. i kiss her softly on the forehead & put it on display
next to the others § prison of lies § Ive built a solid rapport with the
Moderation staff. And I thank them for Punishing me while discussing Arts &
Culture w/ other 30yr old men § as torrents of horse piss splatter clamorously
onto my forehead I scream in absolute torment but make no attempt to move or
cover my face § "please post more of these" "ok" § #RespectThePolice alright
done. what should I respect next. bugs? urine? im taking requests § portrait
of mew two with pubic hair removed from the digimon otis estate § /~-_,™ -|.
RAT.|-™ ,_-~\\ /~-_,™ -|.POPE.|-™ ,_-~\\ #tigerblood § wish that for one day,
for just one day, that i may live in RAT'S WORLD ... § im sorry every one. the
mayor ran out of key to the cities so they had to give me the key to all the
girls bathrooms instead § whats the fucking point of even achieving muslim
knighthood if i cant wear the ceremonial headdress to Jail #BULLSHIT #CRAMIT-
BUSTER #HELPME § why hasnt twitter verified @AssBoss yet. im certain that he's
the real ass boss § @thegeicogecko how do you cope with the realization that
everything you say and do is dictated by a soulless, unfeeling corporation §
just put my elbow bthrough the monitor because i thought the cursor was a bug
again. nevertheless this setback will not slow down my posting § LISTEN UP
NERD, THE WEIGHTS WITH HIEROGLYPHS ON THEM ARE IMPOSSIBLE TO LIFT UNLESS YOU
POSSESS THE CORRESPONDING RUNESTONE, THIS IS HELL GYM § My Dad's Friend Craig
went to his favorite bowling alley and laid flat across lane no. 6. he chose to
die there. § you ask me to play "The beer song" ... I smile and ask, "Which
one?" § i hope all the cartels i pitched nfts to arent mad at me § if ur
biebermeter has a reading of less than 150 Bμ then why hte FAUk am i even
talkin to u § Oh yes he really said that shit . § for like 8 months i thought
covid was one of those joke diseases where you ask "what's covid" and the other
guy tells tou to suck his nuts § i wipe asses like mine for breakfast § the
straight truth. im richard simmons, rofl. i love kissing Monsanto Mwah Mwah.
HOw's your twitter immersion now?? i also believe in God § every animal in my
house is dying for some reason and i can't handle bullshit right now § #Bed-
BugsFeedLists blood, § im going to eat this entire rack of baby back ribs in
protest of nasa's bullshit robot on mars § @DeBeers I WANT DIAMOND LIMB 'S § im
tierd of extroverts crucifying me and my cool introvert friends § "octo mom"
will never be allowed to join mensa or the fortune 500. just saying the damn
truth like it is § i dont know if i'm wearing it wrong or what but this Thick
Load Bracelet is not making my loads thick. § @RealLunchables again, I apologize. § its my big son § http://bit.ly/10CbFu very intresting, very informative , but becareful watching this film because it is cursed § im sorry to Wawa
for attempting to behead myself in one of their restrooms. i promise to take
the Wawa experience more seriously from now on § joke's on you; i actually love
being body slammed by one dozen perfect wrestlers. and my mouth isn't filled
with bloodm, it's victory wine § ill never show it § i will nevr add baby huey
to the famous bird list. he wouldnt even make top 40. i will NOT back down on
this, U obnoxious, ungrateful pricks § your post has bbeen Hotbugged by
DipShitx666 § get one of those bill gates tubes that turns piss to water, load

a big fat backpack with treats, cut the cord, pull the plug, fuck the grid, §
stumbling through war torn syria with my pants down, begging everyone around me
not to feed the trolls § TIL a janitor invented flamin' hot cheetos. (http://t.
co/VNalccHA) submitted 19 hours ago by jj788   117 comments   share §
ultimate glaze § lots of movies like to add jokes in there, as a bit of an
easter egg § every one on this web site is this guy https://t.co/ybaUQKdA7o §
your a child § "i wish they got, WiFi down here" - guy who died in the paris
catacombs § small village. all the locals are dead, their bones removed and
fashioned into a crude satellite dish, seemingly designed to download asses. §
The jokes, Ladies and gentlemn. The jokes § SARGE: WAT IS YOUR MAJOR MALFUNC-
TION SOLIDER !! The Impervious Millennial: im Gay sir. I eat shit. Bazinga
SARGE: I... CANT... BREAK... HIOM § BURY ME WITH MY ASS......... § please @
gangnamjokes. post the first gangnam joke. please. you piece of shit. please
dont squat this account and gyp us on the gangnam joke § fingers ranked by how
good it is to show them to people: 1. thumb 2. pinky 3. ring 4. index 5.
middle   steal this listicle,u corrupted fucks § for the last time, Diaper is
capitalized when referring to the lifestyle or state of mind, but not when
referring to the physical object. § CONTEST : If U Find The Fabled R. Lee Ermey
Diaper Commercial I Will Send Some Thing Cool To Ur House § looking at my own
dick in 3d § i msay be woefully ignorant, but at least im good at justifying my
existence with trite remarks § Thread. The dog who died in a united airlines
overhead bin was a deep state Chaos Agent. Thread, Thread § fuck the game
"Musical chairs ". they should call it "RNG bull shit Chairs" § its the weekend
baby. youknow what that means. its time to drink precisely one beer and call
911 § NASCAR Forums >> Odds & Ends >> Repost: A Man NAmed Jake Is Causing Me
Endless Grief § i said im sorry. ive taken my lashes upon the cross. my brand
is still good and anyone who cant see that is worthless § no § http://www.
foxnews.com/politics/2010/02/16/cpac-organizers-try-turn-hip-quotient-video-
games-rap/ herse something uplifting & inspirational § im not going to shut the
fuck up until all of my friends, and enemies..... are big time rich § once
again the trolls are at fault. theyve ruined the best night of our lives with
their filthy shit. im ready to throw up. § oh everyones trying to be cute.
Everyones trying to put on a little show, posting unauthorized information
about my penis § the good things i like about 90s is there were no hipsters, no
rap, and your odds of getting an infection at a hospital were slightly higher §
no amount of money will ever fix my forlorn dick, i woud instead advise you to
donate trash by throwing it at me § hes the ceo of arbys now § well im going to
keep this brief. i overexerted myself while responding to emails and got put up
in the hospital. i basically need lungs now § Thinking about getting very
pissed off on the computer today . § everyrtfhing I say and do is owned here-
forth by the fine individuals of the Cash For Moms Online corporation. i beLieve
in cash for moms. .. § no soup for YOU gaben newwel § mystical truth Teller
https://t.co/Q5XCIgvPsQ § just a few of my Media Accolades... Still think im
"Bs"??? https://t.co/HeArwPUiRa § Absolutely not. § I didn't want it to end
like thtis. I am so sorry. My hands were tied. The rants weren't getting
enough Favs so the sponsor pulled the plug § (does some notes on a guitar) I
Have been through my life a good man. I am a clever man (does some more notes
and fucks it up) I m nice too § he has not responded to my request to send him
to boot camp § andy rooney hologram crashes coachella 2013 and berates the
audience, calling them "rude" and "a disappointment" #awful § im thinking a
tiny palm-sized toilet you can just keep on your desk & jack off into would soon
become as ubiquitous as the personal computer § im a Diplomat's Nephew and im
tired of pretending um not one § top 3 Engagements 1. faved by Charles
Martinet.. voice of Mario 2. direct message from the official Lunchables account
3. the one to my wife § bad tweet? where?? ha ha ha § I;ve looked at the
facts. Hell im looking at the facts right now. § stay on the computer all day

and get sad and huge § starwave, hotflux , gumcore, bigsnap , powerbox, piss-hop, classic mouth, soul flute, birdstep, rock 'N' rol, serbia drum, james bond § I mdade $400000 just by typing the words "Simpson and garfunkel" back in 2011 and u have the gall to @ me w/ ur little 200 ass follower acct § Clipart Illustration of a Frustrated Cowboy Holding A Skunk That's Been Torturing His Farm With Stinky Spray § you post " ustard" by mistake one time &people call you " ustard man" until u freak out & drive your car thru a hospital like blues brothers § i truly believe that i will usher in a new era of peace and prosper-ity when i get every single post on hthis fucking website deleted by 2022 § Fuck yourself if youre not going to be nice about this § boycot https://t.co/cjb6yRmKMs § Moneyhats all the way down. He doesnt csre about the true fans. He killed the dog for profit.Just follow the big dollar sign § please stop aksing me in the dms if i have to go to the bathroom. i just went to the bathroom and im fine. § it's the name i use to commit crime under § prepare to meet thy Focker § i hope every one whose house is on fire today gets out safe & dead certainly., if my pit bulls could speak... they would say "please, please increase my power" § YOU: jacking off is everything. jacking off is my raison d'Âªtre ME: jacking off is a zero sum fool's game and im clicking x on this chat now § jacking off is Alphamail § "hey, you know what people like to smell while eating?? feet and piss" - guy who decided to put playground tunnels in fast food restaurants § i imagine to the lice who live in my chest hair, my enormous, frowning head is God; their only beacon of hope, thats why i never wear shirts § 2012 ready???? Hm Lets See *opens uhaul truck full of diapers which proceed to spill all over the dairy queen parking lot* § #iKnowImNotThe-OnlyOneWho the pope § i spend a lot of time thinking about how good it would be if someone finally developed a sports app ,"For the fans" § the facts are thuis: i accidentally did benghazi while trying to steal nfl broadcasts and im sorry about it. this is a stressful year for me § i feel obligated to inform you i have a normal looking man's face, and i only have one of them § #Trump-Colluded with my freaking nut sack . print this you cowards § if you get popular on you tube you make $100000 a month. if you get popular on twitter you get your shit caved in by robbers every day § Hey Dumb Ass! Thats my face youre pissing on § A MERE Musing From A Troubled Husband, Strengthened Through Time: "Let the birds have their bird seed, and unto us boys, the Beer seed" § the professional youtube reaction man who pays me $3 an hour to scrawl his account name on the walls of womens toilets just died of cholera § TODAY: - pissed some body off - got my ass kicked - Pissed myself - got piss kicked into my ass - ANd its only 2:01 AM. § i will pay a jpeg specialist up to $500 to put a black bar over the ass & pussy of my beloved rottweiler before i send the pic to my father. § if all the girls and women in this town want to secretly film me taking a huge piss, then that's their right and god bless em § it is really quite astonishing that I have yet to win The Lottery, given how good I am at selecting six numbers and saying them out loud § i step into the vip lounge. i see a man in high heel shoes stepping on a carton of milk while other men in suits yell at him and throw coins § i fixed it. its better § im in jail for desecrating a toilet. the aclu is racist against white people § just thinking about how two guns mounted on my wall in an X pattern would look really good over my toilet § just admiring my "Pornfree" badge . https://t.co/Hbk986wXih § everytime windows updates youll find my dumb ass claiming that the user experience seems "smoother" now. you will beg me to shut the fuck up § neitehr am i. im a fucking waste § WHO SUMMONE D WRESTLERS TO MY YARD. I DESPERATELY NEED STOMACH MEDS AND IM AFRAID TO GO LEAVE HOSUE. MY BIRDBATH HAS ALREADY BEEN SUPLEXED § http://t.co/zLoyi0fS thsis is the only candidate my followers are allowed to vote for. jeff boss for president on the " SA did 911" ticket § "be the james you want to see in the world " - James Bond § watching all of you goof up again, w1th your posts. nobody has ever crapped themselves

more in human history. The shit is a total clown show § "ill goon your ass. ill pig you out" yeuah um, No, its highly unlikely that you will "Goon" my ass. Try reading a book of english § JAY: They are going to replace WTC, with a Mosque. Can you believe this Silent Bob SILENT BOB: This country is headed fot the chamber pot. § thats very sad § ok go to your browser and type in godly erics twisted as fuck burger king reviews dot com slash good shit slash Clinton Soundboard dot s w f § i have it on good authority that kim jong il jacked off shortly before dying. this devastating fact makes the pain of losing him even worse § i vow to continue improving my Posture uuntil my chest consumes the earth § Where were u when I was being mouthed off at. Where were u when my brand was tarnished by Mockers. Where were u when i got called a "Prick". § ((SPILL-ING BLOOD ALL OVER KEYBOARD) THIS IS WHAT U WANT. THIS IS WHAT U FUCKING BASTARDS WANT RIGHT (1 WEEK LATER) WHY ARE THE KEYS STICKING § i would really love to try getting my dick stuck in a pine cone. but i wont due to trolls § #ClickingMyMouse § #RejectedScoutBadges CHALLENGING AUTHORITY. COPING WITH FAILURE. DRINKING DIRTY WATER § Fucking yes this . Friendlys has a meatball bar § Im Sucking Myself Off Right Now And I Hate It #Dateline § my new bullshit is getting really mad everytime theres a new ios update and they still haven't added hobo code emojis § MOST HATED FOODS., 50) PAPA JOHNS ORIGINAL FAMOUS CHEMTRAIL PANZEROTTI 49) THE DEMERITORIOUS DOLLAR NINETY NINE McDIAPER.......
MORE TO COME § @Battlefield im a dirty animal. i m a fucking bastard. § ignoring all phone calls from rickgamecube and metal gear Eric so they can't talk me out of getting fake bullet wounds tattooed to my chest § i fear that if the 10k character limit is enacted my trolls will post ascii middle fingers that are elaborate & beautiful enough to kill me § i bet you just went ryour entire life growing out that hair on your ring finger, never thinking to remove it, it sucks § me: May the coffee be with you. Beer is the red 100 to me intelligent Bill Gates: You are a Fraud. Confess § JAMES BOND: (Shoots his gun at the screen in the intro and murders me) ME: Now that;s cinema § i am very sorry for all my bullshit @digimonotis i would like to be friends again please just talk to me http://t.co/cziQX1uR § @redbubble https://t.co/oj4aBw1VrL this shit sucks get rid of it § your damn right https://t.co/v33JAnA9cx § i will not do it. § me and my lawyer just tricked my ex-wife into signing an agreement which orders her t o wear a dumbass cowboy hat to work #FuckU #LifeRuiner § my previous tweet was not the thursday nite rant. first off, it doesn't contain the hashtag. secondly, it's wednesday afternoon right now § dicks are only sold in cartons fuckface § hibernate in a drain § yeah its dealing with punks like you is my job. § only 1% of my followers can do this. Pathetic! fuck you, go do your wordles § what i'm saying is that the world's smallest dick could probably fit inside the world's largest dick hole rather comfortably § #E32021 Actual T-Shirt Seen At e3 2021 - " ext Gen Sucked Me Off " . - Why? How? § Louis? gosh, it's been years. it's me, Neal, from Law School. anyway, i got this big juicy onion here, was thinking me and you could fuck it § The reason the "Cars" movies have gained so much popularity is becuase the cars speak to one another. You don't get that with real life cars § why do clowns have such big shoes. that's not funny. it is just ignorant. no wonder circuses are dying #TheThurs-dayNiteRant § sex worship i;s a mental condition that is worse than liking the super bowl § @THEHermanCain herman cain fucked a big pizza and got tomato sauce all over his dick and thats why he lost the nomination § wife is no longer permitting me to jack off in the car during her book club meetings. where am i supposed to jack off then? fucking EGYPT??? § every argument i have ever made in my live has been in good faith you fucking slob dopey bitches § my uncles caught me searching "can i still join isis if im racist" on the family computer & are now withholding all holiday treats for 2015. § do not show me Loyce § the blue thumnbtacks on this map indicate concentrations of high æœˆ(luna) energy, the red ones are all the panera breads ive been banned from § "Hrm, this

Content less Hit than Miss lately. Unfollowed." - guy who follows 1200 people who post about their ear infections all day § this account is the Curse of my life § i pin a nerd up against the wall and sink my fist into his stomach. "thats for retweeting me" i strike again. "and THATs for faving me" § #selfies-forariana https://t.co/UhPYcMgkp5 § mr. Crapped On Daily § "tomorrow the sun will turn into shit and rain toxic death upon every human" -george carlin cobain nietzsche LXIX § OPRAH: Take us back to the time you invented the famous Livestrong Bracelet. ME: well..i was at boston market, just looking at my wrist, and § the Ten click challenge, invented by buddihst monks to enhance Discipline , asks that we limit ourselves to click on only ten things per day § dont have time to read this sorry § MY KUTCHER/SCOTT " DUDE AND SWEET TATTOO" ROUTINE IS SEVERELY HAMPERED BY THE FACT THAT IM ONE PERSON § pray to god that our children live long enough to be able to watch an astronaut fuck an Alien § me, begging and pleading with a turtle, telling it to spit out my dick , causing a scene at a miniature golf course and getting 911 called § remove this at once from my page or illb e forced to citizens arrest you § ralph_of_x_box told me "the best damn sports show period 2" is coming out in 2023 § horseplay is morally indefensible § HOW WOULD ONE REGISTER FOR THIS SUPPOSED "STRAIGHT PARTY" § i was explicitly banned from them because i am a loser and a jackass § @CBStweet IVE DISCOVERED ASPHYXIATING MYSELF NOT ONLY ENHANCES ORGASMS BUT ALSO THE INTENSITY AND FREQUENCY OF LAUGHS FROM UR COMEDY LINEUP § Imbecile https://t.co/xrsMDS7tux § another fucked up thing. why tdont people in tv & film ever actually shit when they sit on the toilet. why arent we allowed to see the piss. § winner of this year's prom theme is "shit to israel", with a grand total of 2 votes § i have it on good authorirty that many of my trolls look like the mother fucker from mad magazine. fuck you. i will never improve my posts. § wondering why more people aarent faving this screenshot i found of professor Stephen Hawking saying "ape piss". If its fake please tell me § HandsomeTruthTeller, Your YouTube account has been suspended for the following reasons: Extortion, Treason, § its me again, from the website. admit that the berenstain bears are for adults or i will strategically headbutt your father to death § i cannot eat this bowl of rice until i've personally applied a louisiana-style dry rub to each grain. i refuse to eat like a peasant § aide to BArraack0 "Virgin" hussame nobadman cuaght buying toilet paper... wow ! wonder whatz going on in the white house. T Cot. #tcot § i respect youir beliefs so much (jack off motion) theres no possible way your opinion can totally suck me Hard § how do i add " GUNS " to my posts .... § i dont give a rat FUCk about your personal shit, about your politic's, about your ugly kid and wife, just keep the Christian sand art coming § as punishment, the townspeople force me to wear a prominent, scarlet letter "A", which stands for "a big piece of shit who loves crime" § floks... whether you're young or old: Star wors. Does it every time § theres a new dril in town and its me, the millionaire who buys twitter accounts to make them less funny § glued a bunch of steaks to my body & did some poses & got the 2012 olympic muscle man medal & threw it in the trash cause its commercialized § if i ever catch you "Dabbing" , I will never hire you to work at my FORTUNE 500 Logistic's firm. You a re simply a liability I cannot afford § https://t.co/KRxsNVCAzR § and i find it kind of funny i find it kind of sad the dreams in which im Beavis are the best ive ever had § i love to frown upon bull shit § some body please make the watson robot play halo. § helping the waitstaff by wiping the table down with the same disgusting napkin that I just used to sop up all the bullshit off my face § ladies & gentlemen of BlizzCon, im ready now to unveil my spirit animal for 2012. *holds up picture of the family gu y dog, audience gasps* § You will nearly shit, when you find out which two beanie baby review vloggers are engaged in a salacious "Pervert`s Affair" . § the waterboy (1998) is woke now § it is remarkable that he has managed to stretch this concept into 5+ hours of non-stop laughter § getting removed from a cafe after using their wifi to look at a slideshow of kpax images for an hour § "EroticLloyd", aka "Puerto_Neko", aka "RicanMudBoss", aka "LloydGunge", akA "GunkAndCatBoi", aka "Puerto_Gunger", aka "Aiden's Cool Uncle" § achieving the uppermost echelons of power & influence just to get sucked off next to Rep. Cawthorn in a room that looks like a hotel lobby § social distancing? I've been social distancing my whole life Lol . no ventila- tors? Ive been breathing without a ventilator my whole life Lol § Shut Ya Fuckin Mouth § im sorry for claiming that all cops wear big fake boobs full of milk under their shirts and use them to breastfeed criminals. only some do § my birth name is "KFC Sunflower", but you can call me "Shit" § DAD: your baby brothers missing, please put down the controller. help us find him ME: Did u read the news. Gaming is a legitinmate hobby now § everytime i click on the skull, a random dweeb's computer chair spins around at a million miles per hour and collapses underneath his ass § Ohh!! THe agony of it all! Im sorry!! Im so so sorry! The pain my POSTS have caused! How many more must SUFFER? I cant stop! Its to good § you see; most of the piss were exposed to in our day-to-day lives is immediately diluted by toilet water. pure piss is a monster all its own § do not post to me such filthy SHIT § i love shit that has a "sense of humor " § so you DONT insure tupperware contaners filled with magazine cutouts of legs & feet? what if i told you some of these badboys are reagen era § if youre going to name an in-game weapon after decreased officer brian sicknick the least you can do is not make it have shit DPS . @activision § i sacrifice my most valuable gift card to the ocean to quell the intensity of the raging waters. forgive me, saladworks . § there's currently an image of an unidentified nude man making the rounds on several online circuits. please beware § @ Battlefield The longer we both draw out this "Garth_Turds" debacle, the more foolish the both of us look. § how come a baby born with a foot in its brain is considered a "Miracle Baby" but when I get my dick stuck in a drawer im just some asshole § thinking i only have about 80000 more posts to read before i figure out the precise amount of sex that should be allowed in pepsi commercals § crapping my self at food 4 less and making $1000000 per second from people sharing pictures of it § Enjoy New and Exciting Recipes Including Buffalo Chicken Mac & Cheese and "Mac & Cheese Gone Wild". § Uh, this is fairly fucking mood. § whats wrong? u look like youve never seen a depressed,gruesome- ly obese Mature Hetero who also happens to have gorgeous abs & tight AZZ befor § im not about to dignify that with a respone. really fucked up of you to joke about the gross malfunctioning boner disease § ah! ive had my ass put to the terrible kingdom of hell, also known as "the devils playpen", and also "Satans Playpen" § so apparently if you take all of the autism awareness puzzle piece car decals and put them together you get a cool pic of yoshi as a girl § bewildered by this one star review of a pocket pussy from a verified buyer that is just the word "Stupid" § i was recently forced to sell my eyebrows to a cancer patient just so i could afford a string to tie my broken skull togehter #freemarket § BREAKING: Man builds awesome face out of legos and is given key to governors mansion; while Shit Head Me eats moths in an abandoned hospital § got a One Million Dollar idea here. the dewey decimal sytsem... its good right? now imagine using it at Wegmans to find your favorite snacks § PEOPLE MAG: which pop culture icon are u going to Slaughter next... ME: I have set my sights on "The Boogie Woogie Bugle Boy of Company B." § BONE DEAD......... § #TwitpicY- ourDunkContestReaction http://t.co/rtHgmE5A7n § Hhm, Nope http://t.co/6B7hfKNP- Wu § @TruthPointDWR hitler society § Childish. i dont have time for links § @ realDonaldTrump i dont § College is back § CNN: SHITLOAD OF DEAD WOLVES FOUND IN NYC SUBWAY SYSTEM INSPIRES US ALL AS A NATION TO REFLECT UPON MOTHERHOOD AND PERHAPS OUR SELF'S § When I can't log into my Microsoft account, to access the additional features offered by Windows 10, i get stupid. i go fucking insane § theyre telling me i got the new covid variant "Vaccine melter" so i apologize to all women whose Pussy ive deftly & expertly eaten recently. § [man leans into doorway of WTC bathroom] "Hey, you gotta finish up in there. 9/11 is happening." "Alright. Just a sec." § http://t.co/xRCJBZNh this has replaced human intimacy in my awuful brain § online is sickos § i propose a Bussiness offer of the boy who says"Damn daniel".. i should like for him to grace the company of me & my wife, for twelve jewels § if i could only maneuver myself in such a fashion that my dick could fit into the drain of my bathtub id be truly content with my life § i;ll never be a real pig *sobs uncontrollably * § spaghetti and meatballs... now theres a #ClassicCombo § "I envision a dining experience tailored specifically for the public masturbator. Therein lies the Soul of the Roy Rogers brand."-Roy Rogers § i dont care about "get laid". i want my tweets to inspire girls to have dewep and meaningful relationships with me § it's new § a hair-thin string of spit slowly descends from my lips & delicately makes contact w/ my crumpled up dick. i raise my head & say"ok im good" § how do i get one of those stupid ass hyper links under my display name that says im a senator § I Am Not Afraid To Shut Off My $300 Asus Monitor From " ew Egg .com" Off If The Intelligence Of This Site Reaches To The Level Of Stupitity. § DIVORCE GURU: gaming is a right, not a privilege. remember that always. ME: Thank you divorce guru § mr Wantin to be suckin § may God continue to bless #theGameCraze § And its onl y 1:pm. Thread § (sobbing like a fucking doofus) why isnt my feed good!! why dont these posts make me happy any more!! what is wrong with all of you!!!!!!! § asking someone why their halloween avatar is still up when it's just a normal pic of them is the most fucked up move you can do, actually § rickgamrcube will have sex 1 time in his life. at the age of 58 he will hire a prostitute after being diagnosed with a terminal illness. § that man you see ,screaming at a woman on the train? Earlier that day, a trusted follower called him "White Urkel". Think before you judge. § did it hurt when you fell from heaven and kissed my stupid ass you mother fucker § i use some offbrand shit that my father boaught 200 cases of in 1998. dont know the name, the labels just a picture of a cobra. sorry § Thheres just not enough moisture in food now a days. Run that shit under the faucet & thw worst actually, but thanks § im going to get shit on a lot for posting this but i dont care https://t.co/BPuMWfWaow § I have a confession. THe leaking of six thursday nite rants on monday was a false flag operation designed to kill The Thursday Nite Rant. § #The12DaysOfContent http://t.co/3ExzF1htlB § if you dm me some dog shit business offer and dont immediately offer me a $10000+ Apology fee youre fucked more than anything ever § @RealLunchables im uploading my awful nudes to this. sorry § why is it a crime for me to confine garbage using my sweatpants and why does everonye on couchsurfing .org get mad when i yell at them § @BreakingNews i want my spoilers mate!! stop hiding the spoilers fuck face!! § taking a Diagonal shit. § i have spent the last 9 yrs writing countless papers on the subject of Followback Culture. The quality of my life has suffered immeasurably. § #E32021 E3 has failed. Sex has dominated the world. Michael jackson is on the loose once again. Games & Games Culture is nothing but compost https://t.co/vZPjwjFJhL § well if it was allowed, id go with a banana thats the average amount of ripe, as i believe it offers the "Best of both worlds" § i will not back down, i will never stop yelling online, tear down this post § do it fucke r. everyone on this trash website has already seen each other's dicks. i am not afraid § @MexicanAtheist Then log off my sight. § SLOWLY LOWERS JEANSED ASS INTO A WOODEN BOWL FULL OF EXOTIC MEDITERRANEAN OILS AND REDROSE PETALS; AH THIS IS JUST TOO GOOD FOR LOWERCASE § "Are we having FUN yet ??" - DRIL 2021 § @ saladworks im nude § with all of the running around we do during the holi- days... its a wonder we don't LOOSE weight instead of gaining it... #TheThurs- dayNiteRant § the list of white boy's with fat Dicks just dropped § if you remove the license plate frame that advertises your dealership youre a nasty son of a bitch & you want small business owners to choke § the villagers gather at the summit to hear my horrendous impersonations of futurama characters and grant me offerings of ivory and fruit § ill destroy him in public and then i will take off his space helmet and unmask him § Bandwagon Hiptser: Everyone who has normal opinions is a rat ME(Normal opinions): Youre a dumb ass because youre in a circle jerk against me § my belief is the classic "Pimp" ,in so far as a guy who dressses ostentatiously and walks around addressing his "Hos", is deserving of Jail. § im absolutely taking this as some kind of threat https://t.co/206WQZv5kJ § pulls down pants revealing ass. pulls down pants further, revealing a 2nd pair of ass cheeks. pulls them down still fruther, revealing 3rd p § the most solid benefit to owning your own pool is that you get to keep all the animals that drown in it § please tell me the latest sex news § hate it when i slip up while changing a roll of toilet paper and the spring loaded holder fires the cardboard tube straight up my ass hole § kim karcdashian should have married me or my friend DigimonOtis instead because we're Nice. #ThingsLongerThanKimsMarriage § on March 14th 2011, user "AIDS_Wanter" mali- ciously paraphrased my alt-luit witticism regarding birdseed which turns into birds, when planted § good teamrwork. thanks http://t.co/oatu1lOT § No results found for "BORN TO GO FUCK MYSELF" § mr buzz feed here folks. just lost my job again, this time by trying to sniff a flower on a mans shirt and getting water squirted in my face § how do i make it so people have to give me money if they want to reply to my posts § HAHAHAHA!!! YES !! YES!! § clicked on discover button& found my "Jokes" are coping technique designed 2 assuage guilt sur- rounding my faltering relationship with CHrist § some fucking Karen pooped in the elevator § sometimes bags of food say the true shit that were all afraid to http://t.co/Q9x0g2MrFF § spending time thinking about a fucking disastrous hypothetical penis that has a hole thats wider than the shaft, like a funnel. and frowning § @DigimonOtis is a Piece of shit and I found an album under his bed full of pictures of condoleeza rice, like rthe one gaddafi had. § everyuth- ing about you is hilarious § in 2090 i will get all my essential nutrients from cyber heroin and swallow big silicone eggs to simulate the process of taking a Bio-Shit § flags are posts, because you post them § http://bit.ly/1vIUb7 end racisn. black power § this site is fucked https://t.co/nCVgwZ8ABD § Metal- GearEric: You are being tried in the court of gamers for calling Ninja Gaiden "Weiner Gaiden", even though it is not called that at all § un follow if you do not consider this true power https://t.co/NNCIYv7XA9 § some yuppy shit stain just gentrified sadaam husseins spider hole into an allergen-free omniracial Thoughtspace & honestly? im smiling of it § i dont remember how this image got on my comptuer and theres 0 results when i try to image search it § so, noobs, any last words beofre i officially change my first and last name to "Logen" and drive my car off a cliff? I though so. § i would really like to wipe this spilled chili off of me but all my towels are fucked up right now § open literally any web page before opening your mouth § a father says to his 3 sons, "i love you all but I must fulfill my destiny as the Wind. goodbye" then he turns into the wind as his sons cry § i can no longer close my eyes. with out seeing a bounty of Farm Fresh groceries being licked by dirty dogs and animals § once again i will take the path of honor, i will pledge NOT to watch the steve harvey fleshlight vid, no matter how good everyone says it is § i have about 250 rants in thbe can, ready to post, as well as 500 more that need minor tweaks before becoming availbe for consumption § i get my ass............... § im a Fuckhead media specialist who wants to know 1 thing... WHAT makes twitter. com 'tick' § I shall perform no new downloads , until this wolrd and the people of it can post along side each other in Harmony, I shall download no more § "To my unfollowers, I will strive to reexamine my content strategies, and do my best to earn back your follow." NOt. Eat my Fuckin shit § i will sign   -My posts § trying to reply to thsese fucking messages caus today is Mention Monday & to expand in spocal media it is essential 2 engage § yes i still believe the

idea of wingstop was STOLEN from game stop. my evidence? its called reality §
Removing the battery from my phone until the time line becomes less toxic. § i
now hate the song "She'll be coming around the mountain when she comes"
,despite having previously said i liked it, because it sucks SHIT § #TenLiber-
alCommandments thou shalt kiss the dicks of our troops and lick their dicks
also for disrespecting them and making them sad § @CampbellSoupCo i opened up a
can of cambell soup beefy raviolis and it was just slush. im sorry big coustum-
er here, but i couldnt eat that § trying really hard not to be Tryhard § Have
you ever wanted to click X on a bastard § Sigh. the trolls are beating off their
weiners again § somebody please Bribe me § ap,. http://t.co/BEbnsYQIxE § im a
51 yr old man who doesnt know how to wash him self, abnd i love the attention,
and i love making ignorant people mad, and im crazy cool § i am beginning to
doubt that most of the subscribers to my feed are mature enough to handle
sniper info. § let the record show that the minor-attracted genius blocked me
after i said this § i supoprt sopa, pipa, acta, buta, mema, rude jokes, muslom,
spike tvs ill fated animation bloc, indie, and this guy http://t.co/ScBrI0s3 §
- piss gback better - shit back better i will come up with more soon § ive
signed a 1 Month Pact w/ my wife which grants her the right to viciously berate
me online, as long as she watches & supports my Stream's § @UberFacts bull shit
§ this is every thing and its only 11:am, https://t.co/XOioXnwFQh § going to
eat too much refined carbohydrates and turn my dick stupid § mn http://t.co/
HkVui2Qpao § @Eukanuba post twitter update on ramidad but not easter Sunday????
its obvious now where your alliances lie, i wil boycott your subpar grit § i
think every one with depression, anxieety, stomachaches, etc, should get a gold
coin that lets them legally park in front of fire hydrants § the big seat of my
sweat pants sagging beneath the weight of globs of neosporin as i waddlle my
fuckface ass off to the impound lot § Saying you want to put your dick in the
keebler elf house is one of the fucked up things i will block U the mostly for
. § Twitter. It's what's happening / Twitter § @Battlefield can you please do
something about abusive user "Garth_Turds". i fear your inaction is only
allowing him to grow stronger § i would have to say that, given the option, id
take the blue check mark. i would sacrifice my indie status for that privilege §
my followers are giving me something nice for Christmas and its called "Shallow
Judgement" and "Lack of character" and "vulgar Aggression" § blockbotting the
boys group after they put a towel over one of our friends heads and convinced
me that its elon Musk, come to kick my ass § i will never support pears again
after the tree on my street constantly dropped nasty pears that got run over by
cars § WHAT DO WE WANT "Memes" WHEN DO WE WANT IT "Instead of regular jokes"
§ i need towels sent to my house . this is not a fucking joke this time § let
me explain it to you fucking nerds one more time; this aaccount is Above Humor.
You will not find jokes on it. § be Quiet § http://tinyurl.com/4mtlzdt thuis is
my dick, i am posting this to come to terms with my self, this is therapeutic
and good for me. #courage § now you see, what i like to do is consider my page
to be a " o Frown Zone", because of the consistently good quality of my
messages i put up § respect me.. respect my #Setup https://t.co/FuGceQtgUW § my
youtube account "ThePepsiEunich" has earned me $48 in ad revenue throughout
2010-2012. id rather die than let the GOVT take a cent of it. § "tthis is some
superbly phenomenal shit." -spoken by president barack obama, upon following
his 650,000th twitter account § brutally headbutting massive hoards of benghazi
likers § confiscate my spine § fondly remembering in 2013 when microsoft made a
hail mary to try to convince everyone to put an online camera in their living
rooms for fun § oscars for exrtraordinarily subversive, insightful, online
textual Musings?? unsoiled by MOneymen?? Thats what my shit particularly would
be § just down loaded all 15 episodes of frank tv in divx blue ray 1080p up on
the big screen if any girls are reading this https://t.co/5WXwUeKd8k § AMERICA
REALLY DEAD THIS TIME. I MEAN IT. ALL NATIONS UNITE TO DONATE BILLIONS OF TONS

OF DIRT TO GIVE A PROPER BURIAL TO OUR DEAD COUNTRY § its actually so good, § looking at some posts about "Cum" while frowning and generally making a face § missin the glory days of the 90s when true talent like "justin bieber" made trending topic isntead of nonsense such as "Beckhams face" § and i will state right now that these recent events bear no weight upon the popular "saturday morning ramble" feature. Thank you § im the dumb mother fucker who uses a dessert fork to cut up my spaghetti § with the engagement numbers yiou people are giving me some times i think id may be better off changing my name to "Mr Go Fuck Myself" § i highly suggest using hash tag #HuckleGate if you're a Journo who wants to print my tougjh but fair opinions regarding huckle berry hound § ladys dont send me nudes... send me nudes of your therapist. so i can "Bust" § http://www.youtube.com/watch?v=oHuZmv58-Zk gorgeous. wonderful § no you see, if you look closely at this drawing he put a face on the sun. clearly this child is autistic § windows 8 disrespected by scum bags: the age of technoWis- dom dies amid the screams of bloated, bleating hog`s &the laughter of money- changers § it is unfair that i should have to go to hell just because i was born with a pigs brain § i dont want to be a member of this shit earth. § dinner at pf chang? let me consult the oracle *squats over mirror and spreads ass cheesk a little bit before getting depressed and stopping* § nick jr. wanted to publish my memoirs - told them to take a hike with the kid shit § the worst part of having an ass is always, having to wipe the damn thing. the best part of having an ass is shitting. #ElectionFinalThoughts § graceful and poignant § any day now: our favorite posters will stop hiding in private chat rooms and start making america Smile again § bat man would never suck the jokers dick @Cnn @msnbc @WSJ @WSJBusiness § all chefs are doctors all waiters are nurses and i am getting paid 160000 a year to believe this § http://shrek. wikia.com/wiki/Guns § the onion AV club boldly assigns a letter grade to each phase of the moon while dozens of readers chant incantation into the comment section § the reason it costs hundreds of thousands of dollars to incarcerate people is that jail is really good and i like going there. Jail is good § u go through life thinking the man wears the diaper. but at what point does the diaper wear the man. #diapermaster § culture war 666 § next issue: should miserable, long-winded diatribes about what constitutes art be considered "Art" ??? § jay leno does not urinate in his cars. do not put that idea in my head. i would die protecTing jay lenos cars from urine § incredibly handsome , charis- matic famous boy credited with ending income inequality after saying that slumlords should be called "dumblords" § Having a bad one; First my Lockheed Martin investment tanks after the ceo posts his penis. Now Cold stone Creamery just called me the N-Word § i think there should be a meter man who comes over to check your gamer meter like the do with water meter § @Battlefield user named "Garth_Turds" disrupted an in-game memorial service by making obnoxious beatbox noises, can something be done? § #TagABeautifulGirl im good. im really good and normal. i want to take a women to the shooting range and discuss guns culture. i love humor § ass is the most poisonous part of the human § all off them § were you surprised to see me, gaming in the bathtub?? i am a man of infinite pleasure. come, hand me my robe. i write my own mr. bean skits § post "AMEN" or youre fucking stupid § plpease post suggestions for some wicked fucked up aspect ratios to help me trick my treacherous wife into thinking the tv is broken § Ahh damn it . I fucked up and accidentally bought the newspaepr with the eye holes in it again and saw something i wasn'tsupposed to § DVD: FBI WARNING Me: oh boy here we go DVD: The board advises you to have lots of fun watching this Hollywood movie Me: Ah.. It's a nice one § while you were busy poisoning your soul with spectator sports i was in my house jacking off face down in my bed § @chinese_rock Your names not actually "chinese rock" § South Korea's 1 Million Buried Pigs Create Thriving Underground Society; Seek Unification With Hostile Surface Pigs § #threewordsforyou lucasarts is my ass

§ Clown Disregarder § this is what boy's day is all about. just some boys going to pool § it is only natural that any reasonable human being would want to yell at my ass, but throwing spears at it is completely unnecessary § i forgive Ellen   This tweet was sent from the high way at 99mph § I AM WASTE § if i wanted to die painfully i would live in that shitty aquarium with your fish § lets all calm down in here. § (poking head up from self suck) augh this tastes like dog shit (goes back for more) § i have taken my shirt off over 10000 times § now from my understanding, the bra store is not only a place to get bras, but also functions as a sort of social hub, for single woman & men § take, this down § people keep replying to my posts accusing me of not knowing what True Pain is. possible computer bug??? § (cop inspecting his new body cam with huge pepperoni fingers) what the fuck is htis. where do i pack the ammo. is this a new type of grenade § it's balls to ass like the sheriff say https://t.co/1QA-uhEaKRu § no!! this is fucked! § The entire King Soopers store at 80th & Wadsworth is staffed with Federal Agents not authorized by any judge, § using mindfulness. to waste my enemies § NEWSWIRE : former presideent George W bush filmed touching various fabrics, assessing their value, as the country Shits its Ass § normal hamburger with that doritos flair § me: i dont even care if they cancel sports howard stern: Thats wild § sorry, all. "Let's Play: Pissrealms 2D: Part 314" has been postponed indefinitely, due to an injury i sustained while taking off my shirt § theres a fucking mattress lying in the middle of route 70. it's still there i think. check it out if you're in the area and you like mattres § if you threaten to kick my ass or kill me you will get BLOCKED. Thats just how it is. Enjoy not being able to read my posts you dip shit § attn: Fucker who posted False R.I.P. to Cedric The Entertainer; i haeve just received my good shooter degree from gun college. that is all § i need 20ccs of stigma on this man's horrible looking ass cheeks stat § @TruthPointDWR You cared enough to shit . § t o the guy who told me they took the ape to the hospital and cured him, Fuck You. § night time falls. im "corie latin" now. a man of intrigue. i place a bird feather into my glass of scotch and i never do posts about my dick § some one help me put hundreds of human teeth into my ass hole #bonnaroo2015 § MKOprah § what i need is one of my girl follower to shovel garbage off of my dick so i can jack off and post a numerical rating of the ordeal online § ! ! ! I will no longer be answering any sex questions in this website. ! ! ! § http://wiki.answers.com/Q/Are_snakes_real § i have posted at length regarding my inane balls at the cost of my family, my career and my dignity. the least you can do is rack up my Favs § "I do not look at the numbers beneaht the post. I only look at the letters, of the post, that are used to write the words of the post" -WINT § my agent says if i get my balls neutered off ill be able to calm down & improve my posts. but i keep telling him, my posts wil never be good § "STOP BEING Tsundere" - me screaming at god § i makte that inteligent jew asuka humble § im the model that the Bobs Big Boy Big Boy Restaurant Man is based on. They forgot to pay me #worstpickuplines § sometimes i feel like im the only person on the whole damn computer who understands the concept of Honour § MIght stop giving a fuck all together. § man with sword has ability to Vanish (unconfirmed) § you call these posts?? i call them " CON JOBS " .... § do not attach pieces of bullshit to m y net log without premission from my lawyer or ill take pictures of my monitor & mail them to the judg § Piss_089, noted pervert and imbecil,e made the ridiculous claim that i "love touching pieces of trash cans" & that my "gumline is fucked up" § allow me to reiterate.. im on the side that is the least mad. whichever one that is right now. nobody knows whos more mad at this point. § please enter the wooded area behind hardee`s when you are ready to be lectured about using corn cob holders by a fervently diapered imbecile § The instant I heard the song yankee doodle aas a child I threw my headphones off and said that the shit is over rated and I was right § verne is back https://t.co/HGoyozoQir § im the did you know that the bible doesn't actually contain any references to hell? or heaven? or christ?? it just a bunch of names & phone numbers § i do understand that it's halloween and it's only natural to want to get up to a bit of mischief, but paws off my hash tag please. § assembling my crew https://t.co/e6zwTsVF86 § shooting off automatic rifles making horrible diarrhea shit noises as the recoil makes my tiny dick flop around. hell yeah. thats cool to me § Your "I Love TD Bank" Car Decal Fucking Sucks § i think that the dog version of the super bowl shoyuld show some god damn respect to the regular version of the super bowl § i feel like if i practiced often enough and really focused i could learn how to shave all the hair off of my body using only my fingernails § the next masked singer should be a dead guy § i am not going to post pictures of the oilive oil after i shit it out, as that would be unsafe for work § i stiltl want a picture with ghislaine maxwell so badly. I dont care what the peanut gallery thinks § #Imagine justin holding my nude, shaking body while lowering the gun to my head and whispering "goodnight" into my bruised ear § Playsy some @TOADM , all of the Rap Likers begin to cry "My God, Our Music Was Fake All Along", as I take a well-earned sip of Pibb Xtra § doing head stands to let the cum from my balls flow directly to my brain and make me more intelligent § when i scroll too far down the google image search results for "rat" and start getting pics of ground hogs and shit... Lets talk about this. § Wow, just wow . Burger king is naming their new sandwich "The Brian Sicknick January 6th Whopper" ? That's so controversial § remember not to die on halloween so you dont turn into w pumpkin § no. do not give him a hash tag. dont you dare do this to me § youngsters are all fucked up due to elevated levels of incest that occurred during reagan-era protests. thats why theyre hooked on cellphone § i help every body, im not racist, i keep myself nice, and when i ask for a single re-tweet in return i am told to fuck off, fuck myself, etc § he Sighed and drank from his cup of beer very lawyerly , § I DRIVE OFF OF A CLIFF AND SCRAMBLE TO RIP THE AXLE OFF OF MY CAR AND LIFT IT ABOVE MY HEAD AS I PLUMMET TOWARDS CERTAIN DOOM. ONE LAST REP § took failblog to court for putting puicture of my dick up, settled for $6. a victory, because im worht far less than that § AYE... THE OJ SIMPSON VERDICT IS SOMEWHAT SHIT , INNIT!!!!!! § before pushing psychic civil wars, the news used to talk about guys named like "Crap man" who would poop in 100 public urinals a day somehow § i hate it when the referree kicks me in the balls and ass while my opponent has me in a head lock § for every animal you dont eat i will eat the grab and go yogurt gogurt,maddox said that and it owned, someone get that quote,someone please § i pour my Blood into my tweets, and seeing all these random 4chan reddit Monkey Cheese tumblr teens get more favs than me is the great 9/11, § fired for "unleashing rats at work" which is bull shit first off because they don't make leashes for rats § #jan25 is far more significant than yourself. i bet you dressed up like a clown on 9/11 and shit on people § my name is Destyn. i build crossbows and sell weed to all your dads and im 15 § my muscles begin to glow with the intensity of 100,000 sun` s. this can only mean one thing€"€"€"€" there's trouble at the gym § thinking of wrapping my entire body in barbed wire and becoming Sovereign § im really mad that we as a society constantly allow our celebs to starve to death in the creul and unforgiving wilderness § LAUGHING AT THE VERY IDEA OF THIS MYTHIC "POLICE MAN" WHO SUPPOSEDLY HAS THE ABILITY TO STOP ME FROM RIPPIN UP CRAB LEGS ON THE CHURCH FLOOR § the first rule about Guns is to Respect The Guns. NEVER let your dog lick the Guns. and don't point the Guns at anything unless it is bad § taking my laptop into the Jungle... § please don't use asterisks to censor words, they look like tiny assholes and make everything worse § i jsut imagined a nude body and winded my self § that house is clearly on the grid. it sucks § i agree. im as terrible as you § free mustard offered at burger king... genius?? or a "Beta Move" § sorry. fan-made, HD remake of "Bubsy 3D" will never see the light of day, because ive been turned into birds college called Ass Kick University where i just kick the teens asses when the walk in there... am i RIGHT folks?? § please check out my devastating one-man takedown of the thanksgiving day parade, which was given a PG rating by the MPAA due to " sarcasm". § do not show me this http://t.co/8GE5bvWIEb § not ashame.d of my posts. my messages help people § Porn is a constant reminder of how inadequate I am (self.AskReddit) § I am a coward. I beg of your forgiveness. And please check out The Saturday Morning Ramble, which is still scheduled for release on Feb. 8 § garfield eats Shit § foflks i want to tell you all about icecold pepsi. its good to drink that & top it off with a crest whitestrip while jacking off in your car § some hipster or something is probably mad right now bc they give golden globes to good ass films instead of the fuckin mona lisa or whatever § taking my 3d printed wife to the Arboretum . § im 14 year s old and im already more psychic than my dad § brushing teeth; mouth gaping open like a shit head as toothpaste drips down my wrist, waking up next morning in a panic, thinking it's cum § today, the mythbusters destroy the "myth" of american exceptionalism by heroically firing a cannonball through dublin, california § looking at my metrics & noticing a decrease in followers after retweeting the "Condom king" acct 4 times in a row. fuck you all. Fake people § how to convert ouija board to xbox controller using only a dead gamer § i challenge any man who thinks that my 7 handsome border collies are too loud through-out the day to a round of Chess, the game of kings § ive got my eye on you matrix_gary. § the new shit is MyBeerNumber. you will attend a Tasting with an authorized brewer and dtetermine your MyBeerNumber. my MyBeerNumber is "4" § @THEHermanCain please send me pics of you crying on a photograph of the wtc. i need to see ur tears and part of your wet face. please hurry § if you put one of those 280 character junkheaps on my feed ill flip a coin to decide if i should block you. i will let God choose your fate. § motorists are advised not to touch the mattress. the cops are on their way to beat the snot out of it with hammers. do not interfere § attempting to hand hundred dollar bills to the ailing sheldon adelson like duce nukem § Duty And Honor http://t.co/PCizXLGG9N § that's the end of my dry rub rant. it's just my opinion. i have already received 20 death threats. i fucking dare you to block and report me § get the fuck out tof there!! get the fuck out of there you god damn idiot!! asshole!! i need that oil!! i need oil!! http://t.co/EafCpVBEY9 § instead of fumbling around with a wallet i like to carry my cash and credit cards in a huge green trash bag bulging out of my shirt pocket § concerning "Online", ive found there are websites that are often considered the "Good" websites, and others generally understood to be "Bad" § Welcolme. so im role-playing as a piece of trash on the corner of market & 5th. in need of 2nd player to lift me into the garbage please. i wont pay you. § i cannot condone taking my previous tweet and using it to say that the "ass wiping hack" is me. i regret putting myself in such severe peril § winner of the 2010 teen choice award??? Inappropriate clothing and disgraceful behavior. Again. #tcot § i gotta say it folks. breast milk tastes like SHIT., "Sorry ladies" § Thw common law wife is giving me "Side Eye", for accidentally eating some of the poison they left out for the stray dogs in karachi § troll!! Move along!! Troll § arbys refuses to honor special bulletin offering a free "Roastbeef Snack" to all divorced men... lots of upset divorced men at this arbys,.. § posts are such damn shit, posts are so bad they are giving me covid Toes § crapping fuck... 900 pictures of guns that you absolutely Must see § ah (sees the good low gas price while driving, spit takes hot coffee all over dick & the sharp, sudden stimulus causes me to ejaculate) okay § please put a helipad on my shitty roof § i epicly agree § a god damn beer and some salt water § please stop saying barnum & bailey is suing me for "stealing their clown routine". they are suing me for very serious and legitimate reasons § i will pay the jim henson company $100000 to make the old critic muppets pepper a slideshow of my most miserable nudes with caustic remarks. §

me, because theyre infants § 911 WAS SATIRE U FUCKING IDDIOTS, IT WAS AN IRONY, THE MOST POIGNANT WORK OF ART IN CENTURYS #tcot #teaparty #GOP § i am looking forward to some god damn serious male grooming discussion when everybody runs out of jokes around 2015 or so § right now theres guys covering their dicks in bird seed to trick birds into sucking them. and youre all here talking about post office... § bad ass https://t.co/5oiDfTQVVz § respecting the Serpent... https://t.co/ofkZCI35r3 § im assigning a letter grade to all the looney tunes at 10:00PM EST sharp. this is a once in a lifetime event. please do not miss it § hm.. the essentials... well what can i say. you gotta have em baby http://t.co/8Edkr2U60c § when you reply to a womans selfy with a picture of invader zim saying "Epic Need" it never fails. i have cheated on my wife over 400 times § ==ultimate mom pics== § just doing some nude sunbathing in this gender neutral target restroom. i hope i dont get my dick sucked § @RichardDawkins impossible. for he has already denounced the neologism "OWned", and i cannot own him, nor him me, § not even legendary blade Masamune could offer these awful creatures a death as swift & honorable as my patented Ass Crush § [Bobby chases Grenouille, screaming, then ramming and tackling him hard to the ground] Coach Klein: [in amazement] Wow! #WaterBoyWednesday § asimo is a weakling. it cannot stand up while being punched. they didnt program it to fight or defend itself. i will probably win this § sorry for not reading your dms ladys. i was busy yelling "MY MONEY IS TAKING A SHIT! MY MONEY IS TAKING A SHIT!" into a huge cell phone § more trouble in the middle east as the islamic world struggles to find the new muslim pope § will no longer be livestreaming foreskin restoration process; the trolls who attempted to summon [ã,¤ãƒ³ãƒ—] (Imps) into the chatroom are to blame § getting my pussy hammered like a dumb ass § the latest rumor ;which i dont even care to discuss or give a shit about, is that i was seen drinking out of a bird bath on easter sunday § SOME ASS HOLE ATE MY TONGUE AND REPLACED IT WITH HIM SELF AND IS EATING EVERYTHING I TRY TO EAT § christ yes. This shit fucking rules § i'm wild about Setups § name any crime and i will tell you how I could easily avoid being the victim of it in 2 seconds § its a shit account. § if your grave doesnt say "rest in peace" on it you are automatically drafted into the skeleton war § youve heard of the trail of tears, well, if the boys in the white house had their way it would be the trail of taxes, and we;d get the shaft § the Economy is changing the way people think about Culture..... § i will never name my son "Rufus" . that, to me, is a dogs name § THe,yre going to stop, making twinkies soon. Buy lots of ammo and leather § @CNN Holy Shit..... § in order to get to the bottom of the SEXTING craze, goerge stephanopolis takes a shit on a teens chest #NEWmedia #oldmedia #moralfocus § im a Dipshit § thats my son. thats my exwife. thats me. thats my gf. thats a dog § trying to make my penis look more realistic with oils. balms and such § (to guy who is filming video of me on his phone while i am siphoning fountain soda through a horrible device) fuck yoyu stop taking pictures § "elvis" is the filthiest musician alive § boy's in summertime... http://t.co/PK5V0t5QeV § Im just going to say that this is for anyone who thinks its good https://t.co/0H5z1U7quD § while you're all worried of OMICRON .... https://t.co/ufpkRE4Pe9 § cool gags in 2011: making the text field in new twitter really tall. you can scroll down and keep making it taller. ramadan mubarak § a "keg" is teenspeak for a large barrel of the vile drug known as "Beer". they can be as tall as 12 ft and are often used to crush policemen § two men emerge from sensory deprivation tanks "I just attained oneness with all living beings" "I just fucked the Girl rabbit from SpaceJam" § @favstar1000favs FUCK OFf § U have to listen to this song "Signs" by the five man electrical band... the guy is just owning the fuck out of all these signs, it's insane § im a pleased as punch spoon-fed bitch and thats a bottom line § (pointing at some bull shit on the news) You see that?? Theyre from reddit § drinking beer out of a humming bird feeder because all of my glasses have bug's in them § im going to start a

judge a stony glare § I will never become a Mens barber. but I am allowed to
admire their culture in any way that pleases me § dont look at my dms § tell it
to my ASS!! § I AM NOT RACIST!!! THIS IS AN OUT RAGE!! I DEMAND YOU REMOVE THE
POSTS AT ONCE! § As a Digimon fan for over 10 years, I never heard of someone
named DigimonOtis in the Digimon community, so his input is also invalid. § i
walked in on two cops touching each other's badges in the unisex bathroom at
saladworks and got a coupon from complaining about the ordeal § *understands
tthe full potential of the net all at once and stumbles backward wwhile
struggling to breathe* christ,. my god § NEWSDESK: POTUS oversized diaper is
NOT "funny," or "Epic", and neither is the tiny stream of poop dribbling out of
his beleaguered ass hole § submitting my email address and clicking "yes" on
massive amounts of promotional offers while choking myself § Jsut arranged an
8-count box of pop tarts to be sent to a girls house. Looking forward to
explaining to her how to prepare them § currently employed as Water Guru at the
beach. it's sort of like being a lifeguard except i have no inclination to
touch the drowning people § tipping over a news van on top of a pile of
shattered childhoods in honor of Dying Idiot joe "Joe Pa" paterno #JoePa #Hell
§ looking to spice up my marriage with pg13 comedies about camping § since
about 1000 people asked , the reason i stopped posting my ass wiping logs is
becausr the trolls were using that data to terrorize me . § i'm sorry but can
you please remove the pig display at the zoo. nobody comes to the zoo to see
pigs. what the fuck is wrong with you. § bazooka joe... habve you seen this
guy. fuck him. he talks shit even though his comic strip is printed on garbage
instead of a newspaper § i can post sex things in times of crisis § i must
rotate in my seat eternally to avoid having my muscles damaged by wi-fi energy §
i just want to find the optimal bra for sniper operations, but everoyne here is
so rude, and pieces of shit § the air is rusty and im dead § i just divined a
glimpse of everyone who has ever unfollowed me talking at the bar, laughing
about how bad my posts are & i fucking screamed § i am thed inventor of gangnam
style and im back and im here to say to all USA forces here and abroad "oppa
thank you sty;le" § this is fucking stupid *Submit* everyone will hate this
Submit my worst tweet yet *Submit* this ones okay *Submit* ban me already
Submit § THE MASTER: LETS SEE U DO SOME SICK PARKOUR OFF OF... THIS!!
REVEALS ENORMOUS BANANA PEEL § now that kfc has promoted me to "toilet
officer", i want to shift the paradigm and change the way people think about shit
and piss forever § my most famous tweet, entitled "Jacking off at the Dog
Kennel," has earned over ten billion engagements & was retweeted by stephen
spielberg § brand accounts should do cool shit instead of sucking Ass. they
should post their dick and say they had to do it because they lost a bet § i
cleaned it § if twitter wre a grocery store the aisles would be labeled shit
like "LIes," and "Ignorance" instead of shit like green beans and diapers § all
snowmen are abominable. mockery . spit in gods face § Damn. Egypt's in trouble.
Hold on im coming *DRops anonymous mask on patio and hoses it off real quick* §
@ladygaga im sorry spider man. please forgive me spider man § FOOL: Election
day should be a national holiday GOD: No. Elections shault be held on the day
of April Fool's, to teach WASHINGTONDC a lesson § cops need grenades. doinate
all of your hand grenades to the local police force or face insane cop torture
forever § Dear drigl, An item you listed in the Community Market has been sold
to Osama Bin Laden. Your Steam Wallet has been credited 0.27 USD. § theyre
murderers. all of them § Its 2019 and It `s only 12 pm § reminder to all of my
female cop followers that i worship female cops daily § boys crowding around
the salt lick and theeres a tiny guy in the back saying "cmon! let me get a
taste of that!! ah Jeez!!" § let's swap wine zines § the man who froze his shit
and cut them into tiny disks to fool the coinstar machine is probably the
closest thing to real life james bone . § my followeres, who all hate me, and
wish to kick my ass, are nobodys, and they lack the combat training tu injure

anyone on this site, my feed is the pinnacle of cultural purity, i look at the blank goddamn page& blow kisses at it furiously § they should clal it the "stimulus cheek" because it can kiss my fuckin ass cheek § proudly announcing to the barber shop that i got through my entire haircut without screaming or touching my dick underneath the smock § dear god. in all my years.... an ancient diaper perfectly preserved in amber-- no wait, its just some shitty caveman head. throw it back § tired of all hullaballoo what soever of jareds fucked foot long § This is realhookah, not /r/hookah. This isn't for posting pics of the same hookahs in different positions, with different shit in the base. § i love having molotov cocktails trown at me in the cyber cafe-- not. idiot § the "Seems To Me" collection by @Dril. Thank you for reading it § SCREAMS INTO THE MICROPHOHNE, MY HOLLERING REVERBERATES THRU TINY CELLAR FILLED WITH 59 HOGWILD PIT BULL DOGSm;; GAINING STRENGTH THRU ANGER § Download free Pig Hitler theme for Nokia N70 § smear turds all over my dunce cap and kill me § lknow what pisses me off?? people who drink milk and spit the milk back into their glasses while making a smug expression. also teenage . § i dont think the monster truck gravedigger has ever dug any actual graves. it would be a very disrespectful and loud way to do it § inconspicuously jacking off duringi the board meeting using a series of ropes and pulleys § that picture of all the construction workers sitting on a steel beam eating lunch except its me & the boys sitting on the floor at game stop § i am sick and tired of having my page mocked just because ihave a lot of good opinions on apps, on hashtags, and all of that good shit § if u followed me back 8 yrs ago things wouldve turned out differently. I would not have been forced to expose you as a "White noise" poster. § i want all every girl on twitter to take the pH level of here pussy and send it to me via private email § "whodunit"?? how about we just call it a "murder mystery" insTead of resorting to that grammatical mess #TheThursdayNit-eRant § Donald Powers The Drumpf who Sucked Me Donald Powers The Drumpf who Sucked Me Donald Powers The Drumpf who Sucked Me § i was so wound up over trolls this morning i forgot to wipe my ass. i pulled my pants up and the shit coalesced into a wad on my lower back. § now that i'm unemployed I can finally weave an intricate fan universe based on the chick fil a cows who are always holding the signs up § cool news: if i sit a certain way my dick becomes convex #heeaja § *aims revolver at the word "mosque"* prepare to kiss my steel, fucker. *accidently shoots a period at the end of it* NNO WHAT HAVE I DONE § im the guy who is famous at the hospital because i had to have two catheters put in since i piss so much § i believe in sex. i work with asphalt and i respect the asphalt. pain is my god and heaven. i am NOT a ï¼§ï¼¡ï¼ªï¼¥ï¼² ï¼¤ï¼µ ï¼£ï¼ï¼ï¼³ ï¼³ï¼ ï¼ï¼ï¼ï¼-. sponsored by nestle § fucking asshole http://t.co/bM4IJE7P § the dunkin donuts era § in the year 2200 big government breeding restrictions will be gone away with and all service animals will look like this https://t.co/6eosZ969s9 § i love ggetting hazed so i can gain access into this exclusive club of people who have been forced to eat dog shit § KICKSTARTER: buy me a big roll of bubble wrap so i can fuck it --- $0.23 Pledged of $35 Goal -- - § @TherealGeorgeZ RATATATA /ÌµÌ‡Ì¿Ì¿/'Ì¿'Ì¿ Ì¿ Œ •|•|• "€ - - - - BOOM BOM POW /ÌµÌ‡Ì¿Ì¿/'Ì¿'Ì¿ Ì¿   *CLICK* BLAM BLAM BLAM BLAM (Philippians 4:13) § with. a genuine content creator § hoagie prreserved in peat bog for 30 years - "It's Still Food" - "Oh it's nice" § my mrouth feels very dry and my dick got a liuttle bit smaller last night. i think they started rolling out 6G § "posting" is "first responding" § i shsould be allowed to beat off in the back of a police car. im already going to jail so whats the difference § seems to me i am one of the only people on this earth who knows exactly how high they stack shit. § ex-con making $3 an hour shoveling diapers into a river "IF THE MEDIA CANCELLS ME FOR MY BELIEFS IM FUCKED" § "_____ favorited a photo you were tagged in " SDONT YOU FUCKING DARE § court orders mythbusters to change their name to the Shamebusters. adam weeps while jamie comforts him and delivers the

did it. i posted like a fucking cartoon character instead of a human for 7
years and finally got my free light bulb http://t.co/zuoezdz5bK § kudos to FX
for promoting a tweet with horrible eyeball gore for some bad tv show aand
pissing off a bunch of ladies http://t.co/AWLuMk4akP § its Time to euthanize me
§ age 0 (baby): I want my Dada . age 25 (Millennial): I want my Data Do you
see how fucked this is? § every one who has ever retweeted my shit owes me $125
for sharing my personal data, full stop § Cared enough to reply me ! Youre like
in love with me ! § are thtere any adverse health affects to chemically sup-
pressing puberty until the age of 49 § broke secret sevrice guy turns his
pocket inside out and strangles an assassin with it. opens wallet and unleashes
a torrent of moths at him § your just a dog from the zoo § i believe we gotta
push forward and afford dynamic, web based Content the exact same dignities and
legal rights as Human Life § Are u going to signal boost me or not. § my "Ass
Ceremony" is solely to blame for all thre bad earthquakes. if i knew it would
have caused the earthquakes i would not have done it. § heed my words ,cyber-
filth, i may bvery well be a thirty eight yr old kindergartner, but im fairly
average when it comes to eating female ass § pussy log 12.29.11: justin
unscrewed the knob from the door to the ladies' room and now the club boys all
take turns cradling it § peeking into police station window, watching the cops
Fuck each other. duane eddy's "Rebel Rouser" is playing and im nodding my head
in tune § its just hte #SexLife § im a dirty cop who has joined the islamic
state of iraq and the levant § cant wait til my teeth fall out so i can get
those new gamer dentures that all the chatrooms are screaming about § when thw
pope says mother teresa is a saint.. i say she Ain't! § please join me in
welcoming the great "miles davis" to twitter.com http://twitter.com/milesdavis
§ @Battlefield I tried earlier but when I posited a list of Garth's transgres-
sions he silently closed the chat. Sorry I actually obey the TOS § yanny, and
laurel, "SUCKS" !!!! Im back bitch § research https://t.co/JNa6kozNnU § i dont
respect the cowboy life style any more and if you are doing cowboy shit you
might as well be wearing a clowns outfit § Most Embararssing Shit Eaters Alive.
Stupid Mother Fuckers Kiss The Nuts https://t.co/MqeqQn0uaa § If I Fill A Bird
Bath With Capri Sun Will Birds Still Bathe In It #badsciencefairprojects §
click this post to worship Everlasting Slime until your cold, lonesome death,
the uncleansable taste of Shit running your throat and tongue § pyramid was the
first haunted hous.e Fact. § #RuinAChildrensBook i dont have a camera but rest
assured that i ruined it & made sure that no child will ever derive emotion
from its pages § fucking awful https://t.co/bf8pGoLoOg § my t-shirts no longer
have humorous slogans on them, their purpose now is to display pitiful appeals
begging people not to piss on me § vp announcement the same day they announce
Cosby Tetris (2007) no longer receiving eshop support? nice cover up § Houly
shit !!! The posts just keep on coming § i bring my own drink coasters and use
them on the tables at burger King. Because im not a fuck boy piece of shit. §
endorsing the candidate whose supporters have called me "Pussy ass" or "coward"
the least amount, and its none other than the great bob Dole § @DigimonOtis
ducked otu of a paintball match to make out with the fattest girl I ever saw
and our team ended up losing § the adrenaline rush i get from posting gives me
the energy to walk to the toilet, and the endorphins i get from shitting allow
me to post § sure, punch all the teeth out of my mouth for having an Opinion.
Very good § Boys are showing to much DICK on the time line... I come here to
research Ethics and i am bombareded with 10000 human penis images daily §
Closing my account until all of the pro jet-dry kiddies go to bed. You people
are animals. Hopeless brutes § thank you inventor of bibs. every one else, off
a cliff § MMORPG (massive multiplayer online roleplayig game), FPS (first person
shooter), RTS (real time strategy), T2DF (tactical 2d dragon fucker) § im
honeslty inquiring as to why im discouraged against printing my business card
on basketballs and 2hand passing them to potential clients? § i dont follow

and toilet § CONFIRmed in corocoro magazaine: "Donkey kong is Diddy kong's Mom". gamers i can assure you this is the most tantalizing gender scandal yet. § you are fixing to get a red ass § people always talk down on the Zoo but if your'e a shitty animal like me it is a great place to network and be gawked at for zero pay § http://t.co/Pl03awKXRu i want to help the 3d dog give birth § mmy monitor flashed before me in dazzling light. for 1 brief moment, I saw every Celeb at once, the good 1s, the bad 1s, crying, jsut crying § every one wants to read my 200-page manifestos about how i refuse to make eye contact with my dentist, or "Get me a man who does both" § absolutely disgraceful § i cured my self of covid 19 by forcing myself to cough a lot § Its fucked up to think about that only 2 years ago, in 2017, the current year (2019) was considered "The future" § i got like a whole page of arbys coupons... no big deal § keurig is building a Mausque inside of a Dave and Busters, and Heres why it matters: § No sex on this profile § mother fucker calling himself Elmer Fudd on the CS server, NEed I remind you that, on the show, Elmer Fudd's Kill Count is essentially Zero? § when you find out that i intentionally limit my power by not being a guy who retweets his own shit......... § my most significant personal cultural advancement in the past 10 years is thhat i no longer think the restaurant "Chili's" is any good § my expert analysis wouuld indicate that each point on the dow jones = 1 job(s) § my friend nasdaq_oscar says they just let all the pardoned turkeys run around the white house and shit on the carpet. disgrace to the office § this is the makeup rant because i fucked it up last week. the normal schedule will now proceed after a brief thanksgiving hiatus § Wawa has always been nice to me and I give it six platinum stars § i come here for the kind of comedy that a man can respectuflly nod towards , i have not laughed in 10 years, laughing is for hyenas & ghouls § running some scams out of my scam tent § if the flow of Nuanced takes regarding pod casts, the baneful N-Word, etc, shall ever cease, ill scream like i got injected w/ an air bubble § This is the most fucked up sentence that has ever been uploaded to a web site. § Most Of My Followers Died After One Of My More Heinous Diaper Jokes § i have been carrying my prophet mohammed body pillow everywhere since i was 14 and i will never forgive the coyote who yanked it off of me § @dril maybe this make sense to ya. http://t.co/551SP9sY § me, begging everyone to stop running around and pay attention to my venn diagram labeled "GENDER & AUTISM" on board the capsizing Concordia § people ask me on here, what is the reason for the season. The reason for the season. is of course, " SANTA " § (the presence of the sarcasm tag indicates that i do not actually want to suck god's dick. please dont derail this discussion with nonsense) § im going to perler where you arent marched out on a pike just for posting pics of your barbeque setup in the group chat § attn : man with "Pedobear" car decal who cut me off at 70mph on i-295 -- nicely donme. Superb § thinking about how much higher we'd rank on the World Happiness Report if they said gamers should be allowed to be landowners, on the news § @MayorOfLA @LADOTofficial THANK YOU SIR ! § WATCH: Low IQ single Father fooled into thinking he has been accepted to Yale at the age of 44. Savor his pain § bathrooms in japan have virtually no piss on them. this is because the culture has instilled a sens e of humility within the people. no piss § Turkey's prime minister has warned that he would eradicate Twitter after a number of audio recordings anonymously posted on social media pur § interset- ing. it appears "emotions" were basically just rrage faces that people did in real life, before online existed, § @MexicanAtheist please dont assoicate the freaking awesome thunder cats show with your fake belief's. thank you § taking a deep breath and inhaling all that horrible, pornographic Wi-fi § i plan on spending christmas with the kranks by putting the dvd in and playing it. i want to spend christmas with the kranks mother fucker. § i was banned from club penguin for roleplaying as a toucan § money is such a corrupt bastards tool that all i can do about thinking about it is to simply laugh about it... § i ceo of legs § Police of reddit, what is the funniest thing someone you are arresting has said? (self.askreddit) § say what you will, but i truly believe that this man, this Adolf Hitler, was one of hte most buzzworthy racism-likers of the 20th centure. § HOSPITAL TIp: get a cool friend named Jacob who works there and lets you photgraph the recently deceased to try and capture their souls § REMINDER: your favorite CONTENT CREATOR is NOT your PERSONAL DOG. DO NOT look at their IMDB PAGE. DO NOT make EYE CONTACT with THEM § does any one know when is 4 20 § 4k tech will enable the viewer to see my dick hole fully accentuated through my jeans as the media hunts me down in a carrabba's parking lot § theres never been a horny me, and never shall i horny be, And If this sacred vow shall break, I pray the lord my posts to take § frowning while the entire waitstaff of California pizza kitchen sings "happy birthday" to me, looking like a lump of shit in a neckbrace § there bad § BEGGING AND PLEADING TO THE JANITOR TO LET ME FUCK HIS DISGUSTING MOP § me and my friend bill gates live in fort knox now and if theres one thing i enjoy laughing all the way to its the bank § Peoeple across the country are sick of putting food on the table. I will stop and frisk the lies #MemeContent #Joke § YOUTUBE VID "GRANDMA FUCKS UP" FINALLY HAS 1,000 VIEWS. TIME TO ROLL OUT THE "GRANDMA FUCKS UP" MERCH AND QUIT MY JOB AS A TOWEL INSPECTOR § i dont do that anymore. i broke the contract and im cursed now § trolls: do something productive instead of beatinh your weiners on my page. there are so many birds flying around indoors who need help § go whack off else whare § FLORENCE RIVERBOAT JUG MAN AND THE COWARD MURDERERS § things im currently in trouble for accidentally Liking: 1) a picture of a girl 2) the Mafia § as someone who receives the middle finger daily, i have the authority to state that using both hands is superfluous and absurd. doesn't help § name searching https://t.co/QEz86Vkpji § Tony § legitimately undesirable mousetrap grit (wasn't asked for) § feeling down??? http://i.imgur.com/cwgRO.jpg § Can Police Man Cartman " Respect The Authority " Of The Intesnely Cool Refreshingly Satisfying Mint Taste ONLY Found In Dentyne Ice ??? § santa i know this is an odd request but i believe w/ a little christmas magic, any things possioble. I need you to shrink my dick by 2 inchs § young sheldon may be the grandson of a war criminal but the real controversy is that home alone invented soy face in 1990 § let's all be my wife § let's leave politics in the hog pen and debate the real shit, like which 90yr old restaurant owner invented the original chicken cheesesteak § attn teens who wolud crack wise abot my grotesque, misshapen ear lobes: i am pissed of, overtaxed and ready to die in the name of Lady Honor § what if my posts were the one thing stopping PUTIN from turning the USA into a Slave Zone. think on that a little before you unfollow my ass § were at the point now, folks, twhere the CIA will kill you for having Opinions, but refuse to assassinate the nitwits who fuck with my Page. § @RichardDawkins theres been a mistake sir. please un block me https://t.co/sXp5f42umi § "All My Rowdy Friends Are Coming Over Tonight" is a song written and recorded by American country music perform-er Hank Williams, Jr § @prodigalsam this is the most bullshit thing ive ever gotten blocked for § The offending article of clothing read "Big Bird Sucked My Dick & All I Got Was This Lousy TShirt". I have blocked this person from my life, § The Fraudsters, the Bull shitters, and Fuck Boys are out to turn my page into their own personal Restroom!! Ohhhh!! Very not good!! § @Oscar-TheGrouch Ive reported this crap § your little ass wouldnt last 2 seconds on my page § curly is the most bullshit stooge. his antics are the least believable. moe and larry would have kicked him out of the stooges in real life § please pray for my sons Thursten and Gorse who have just glued themselves to a curtain, § The New Ironic,¢ § "Is Wario A Libertarian" - the greatest thread in the history of forums, locked by a moderator after 12,239 pages of heated debate, § is america ready for an <otaku> james bond? would this post-9/11 culture of fear ever allow an <otaku> james bond to grace the silver screen §

repeating to my self in the mirror "Star wars is for adults" before seeing the final one & having a violent reaction like ingesting a poison § dunno why im getting dog shit offers here. i never said crypto was monopoly money for pedos & drug addicts, i only thought it, repeatedly § twitter hiring sherlock holmes to prowl the office wih a magnifying glass and find the employee who posted "Aids piss" on the pizza hut acct § im afraid you do not grasp the enormity of who it is you are dealing with. (removes diaper,. revealing two sub-diapers) Shall we continue.. § review: koala kare diaper station with the fuckin bear on it. awful. sorry im not some size 0 model who can use this without it snapping off § what would you do if i unlocked 100% of my true brain? Nothing. you would be fucked § oyu investigate the mysterious object that falls out of my shirt onto a pile of bibles. your worst suspicions are confirmed. it's a hairball § when christ rains judgement on the world he will remember you talking about your birthday while egyptians fell to sniper fire § sorry i ruined Fucking talk like a pirate day by speaking at length upon my terrible mustard allergy which has caused countless pain of me. § Oh im losing followers just for expressing an Opinion to someone who may or may not be a professional dog killer. Nice society you got here, § a good bad -ass thing would be a criminal who throws lots of hand grenades and kisses them each time. they could use this in agent of shield § calmly browisng my 100 Sites per day, as recommended by the experts § if you do not think garfield metaphorically "ate shit" when they closed his restaurant down then you are not looking at the facts § im strong § girls legs 2017. legs getting shot by paintball guns. "Is legs normal." legs on the mind. annihilated by legs § i mailed my detached dick to bolivia to get it enlarged by a professor of Medicine. i am hoping it is returned to me without incident. § (insufferably) It's pronounced. "Bloomin Onion." The 'g' is silent. § "charity is the toilet of mankind." -DigimonOtis § i would never say something like "Fuck the games world and all its wonderful and mysterious locales. Fuck mario" . i just would not say that § https://t.co/JqyzTyl9 https://t.co/hSx1buQw https://t.co/XypytTp5 badfrog3333 § i need someone to come fix my fucked up neck tie. ive barricaded myself in the bathroom ogf kenny rogers roaster in mumbai. say the password § "humankind is so corrupt" i mutter as i sandwich my dick between my badge and gun and take several pics of it with a disposable camera § im not allowed to comment on anything without the poermission of Conde Nast and Barqs Root Beer § Downlioading 6 Terabytes Of Info On Deal's § "There is something to be said for being able to bring that Wow factor., into mediums that make use of Social. Mm. Just incredible" - @ Dril § need to wash gamefuel stains out of a very expensive kimono § there is absolutely no greater account on twitter than @DinoMiteBarney. consistently on point , no guff, what else can i say . check it out § can I get into legal trouble for secretly filming myself on the toilet § consider the cornerstone of my beloved acct..the "Follow Back Guarantee." i will follow you back always... no matter how much you suck shit, § Where_Gogurt_Failed.txt § there is NOTHING wrong with having 1 Million Doallrs you are NOT defined by your one million dollars...   having 1 Million Dollars is normal § you aint ever catching ME getting my "DICK" sucked... NO SIR!! eyes bugging out, ass cheeks twitching, making racist noises-- one of that § the worst mythbuster to ever exist was the dead myth-buster that they never talk about #TheDeadMythbuster § in the end, i dont even care if the movie "Alladin" was made up. It was a stupid movie anyway. § sponsored by God § more harmful to our web than any computer virus... sick thought's and selfish attitude... pass it on boys... § Q: are nerds allowed to read your tweets A: no. absolutely not. only businessmen and christian women are permitted to read my tweets. § to everyone talking shit about my fine motor skills: *gives the Finger, checks to see if correct finger is extended, it isn't, tries again* § Gotta See This: tenets & facets of sears tyrannical mattress return policy ridiculed Skeptically by man with more than enough to eat at home § earning 100% completion rating in the latest game from the "SEX ADDICT" series by PissRealms, and hating every minute of it § obviously., thsi has only exasperated the issue, and my doctor is a piece of shit. please send me donations to help me shave my self § he belongs at the circus with his friends § you will never be less racist than me § let year 2020 become the year of Boys . Because men are out there changing peoples lives every day and simply they do not give a fuck § @glennbeck harmony korine's "trash humpers" § dont know how they did it, but Bloomberg Opinion found a way to post directly into the Whats Happening sidebar, making them effectively God. § (straining relaly hard until something inside of my head pops) There . I just gave myself depression cause none of you are clicking my Links § Euuuhh... Not a Good look! https://t.co/1nsLIeR6nH § no mouse pad. "off roading" § (ssees a stock image of a frowning man sitting inside of a doghouse) Hurmph. Asinine. § MY SHIT IS IN SHAMBLES, MY DICK IS IN DISARRAY, MY ASS IS ASUNDER, MY BALLS ARE BALLISTIC, MY CUM IS CONFOUNDED, MY PISS IS PITIFUL § going down to the bank to yell at all the workers there and tell them to keep their greasy mitts off of my stash § my dimwit sons love it when i drop them off at the car dealership for 7 hours while i cruise around for bargain's § ExoneratedUncle § maybe when hte myth buster finally decide to tackle blood diamond slavery, maybe THEN ill bother to tivo their shitty show. § discussing covid challenges with my Jeans strategist § im the Dumb motherfucker who holds a 21 gun salute in honor of pizza huts old brand on the quake server & fails to get the boys to cooperate § **sticks vacuum into skintight rubber suit so it becomes even tighter and dick and balls become more pronounced & visible* ugh!! mondays § knuckles mashed into my ass cheeks at all timse. new media singularity or what have you § Consideirng putting a bumper sticker on my car that says "Get off my ass" and a sign about a mile away saying "Go closer to my ass" § fucking bad ass https://t.co/X7Qb-sE1fTf § actually i take "the big bang theory" and the good word "bazinga" very seriousl. § id love to be 1 of those purple espn guys who puts boulders on descending columns but id probly get all sorts of penut gallery comments here § when i change m y name to "@QuickenLoansLLC" in Q4 youre going to be Fucked. sorry § wife sentenced to 4yrs for defrauding a charitable organization..U know what that means (pulls worst gaming consoles to exist out of closet) § http://bit.ly/9lcuCA WRANGLER UNVEILS ILLEGAL NEW AD CAMPAIGN § 0% and 100% are the same tnhing § my living room has more remote controls in it than NASA. its like you gotta be an astronaut just to watch the ball game #TheThursdayNiteRant § thank you for protecting a grown man from beavis puns § @kfc_colonel i hate to bother u mr colonel, but could you please tell me where kfc gets the famed Bucket § there should be a good version of the oscars where they hand out statues that are fucking wearing clothes § Im online at the computer, ready to post pitures of my new sandwich, and ive got a hankering for my ass to get kicked § jsut a heads up if youre trying to be a check mark guy on here, you get paid more to have opinions that suck fucking ass § hoping for that big promotion from mounted, tormented beast to rodeo clown § i.. im gonna lose it!! im absolutely ready to crap all my damn cum out !!! § seems weve all forgotten i won the official "Fuck the noid" contest and have still not fucked the noid or received an equivalent cash prize. § I have decided to officially unfollow "@Budweiser", on account of their complete lack of original, informative, or compelling content. § the joke is on you fuck face. i actually love getting screamed at and publicly shamed for my dumb-assed bull shit . I love apologiz-ing § i can promise only this; i will lick the boots of my enemies until they beg for mercy , crying § Monsanto Yes #MonsantoYes § Looking to the day when the World Wide Web matures to become into the World Wise Web. § @RobSchneider what about the wind? i think it's the wind § first day i got online on a man named Mumbai_Eddie accused me of having diarrhea, so i detached my modem and put it in the sink for 8 years § i like to believe that getting my ass kicked

100 times a day for 50 years has granted me "Street Smarts" § im the smart adult with my shirt pulled over my head so I can play holdum poker on my phone with out having my performance affected by glare & wife's... you gotta get your man a blue tooth § scrolling through 900,000 emails calling me a hideous cock sucker to find a benihana coupon i thought i saw like a week ago § fbi agents are hiding theur guns in toilets so they can arrest you for shitting on government property. do not be fooled by this dirty trick § only the finest.. @ Burbank, California https://t.co/TnzaM3UOcJ § im starting a new feature on my feed called "Boy's Thought's" where I just riff on the things of day to day life and maybe some surprises to § researching dynamic, groundbreaking new ways to wipe my ass § @MoonPeople It isnt me. I despise porn and sex. § Star wars is back baby . . . Confirmed by @Dril § I Have beatten a game of solitare after having to restart only 26 times. I am a magnificent gamer prince § imma newmedia grassroots teen marketing consultant prick fucek. ah a new tcot friend.! ill just ignore his goatman avatrar § atticus quiznos, cornelius pepboys, baron von sega; distinguished luminaries who voluntarily castrated themselves for the sake of the #Brand x mr pib § The ceremony will begin at 12:00 EST, wherein DigimonOtis shall unblock my account, and I will Follow him, officially ending this turmoil. § BLATHERING SHITE: the Dems VP Pick should be subway;s own Jared ME: That man is in jail. Have you done any research prior to this discussion § my followers will be thrilled to hear that i am wearing a very pleasant pair of jeans while reading a variety of articles, on subjects § ((frowning) cause im the Apps Man (depression) YEah yeah im the apps man § there are mother fuckers in this life that will "Take the L" but Most refuse to "Take the pLedge of alligeance" § the sticker on the back of my dodge stratus says it all... if you drive Cozy Coupe , FUCK OFF ! § @McDonalds @McDonalds your current slogan, "Im Lovin It", will no longer do. i would suggest replacing it with "Look out. Here comes the McShitter" § food of the loom "big" under wear 90% off $0.89 one time offer For the fans. § if any one knows how to convincingly justify dubai's economic model to bratty ltitle brothers go ahead and plop me an email. fubu back. § so the wisdom i gained in exile with the barbecue shaman on the peak of Mt. DryRub is apparently non-transferable to Yale. sad and upset § I HAVE COMBED THE INNERMOST REACHES OF DARKNET TO BRING YOU THIS REALLY SICK PICTURE OF PEOPLE FUCKING EACH OTHER IN SUITS OF ARMOR § i have successfully avoided getting a "Charlie Horse " through out my entire adult life . § i'm going to beat the shit out of asimo. im gping to knock it on its ass while its trying to use a staircase at a trade show. dreadful beast § i only jack off for the amusemement of my followers, who have come to expect this sort of bullshit from my account. § which ever mother fucker invents the porno version of squid games... buddy you're making $1000000 Easy § really hoping that someday my wife will surprise me by sending me a picture of my own dick § assault on liberty: the local farms have begun smearing dragon blood on their pig troughs to keep me away from them § only thing stopping me from being th 1st diaperbound wiccan 2 scale everest are all the handsome climbers who're prejudiced aganst big peopl § how to convince my uncles to combine into one superuncle so that i only have to buy one christmas card? how to do it? how to ddo this? how § No More Fooling Around: if your post sucks my balls , it will be regarded as SHIT !!!! § theres him § Dont like getting the middle finger? Then dont show me bull shit § " nothing is stronger than power. " - qdoba_NoScope § Thirsty Men Dot Coum.. Finally A Place Where I Can Meet UP With Local Thirsty Men And Boys § my nipples are purlpe because of an iron deficiency . NOT because i dont believe in god. so shut the fuck up, grandpop's grave § if you whack the side mirrors off my car with a bat every day your the biggest piece of shit on earth, your toxic, and "telling on yourself" § I do oft in times flush my waste as soon as possible. I have no desire to look at it. I would rather be reading expensive novels to my wife. § mnever. my signature technique could bring serious injury

if attempted by a layman § kicked outta the classroom again for pointing out the obvious fact that our school buildig was built by slaves. § yeah im supposed to be "offended" by spit on my grave. youre basically feeding my skeleon nutrients. also spitting in graveyards is illegal. § me: nobody has to get owned today. please, please put down the keyboard and step back 9 year old child: Fuck oyu § spike tv is showing some good vids of dudes urinating and im stuck here at work yelling at saudi arabians on the phone for $156.00 an hour § a quick e3 prayer: i call upon our lord in heaven to ensurre that these perfect video games are not lambasted by criminal journalists. aman § http://t.co/ gZjB6r9E Im Screaming At It All #savederpy § point blank blasting a pair of jeans with a 120 decibel leaf blower at 6am even though i have been" warned about doing this" § ohhh no!!! our nations Value's are under attack !! https://t.co/TIFrpGg8kV § we're here to discuss the cultural merit of "Baby Crash Bandicoot RPG". please leave if you have nothing of value to add to the conversation § they say zika virus is the Bastard of 2016, but that distinction must go to my infamous folowers, who i consider to be "Dumber than Dogshit" § i have cleaned all the dirt out of my fingernails and will be posting new pics of them shortly. i want to be liked on here. § starting a social media platform called "Shithead Hell" where all the posts are the same as the ones on here and we share 0% ad revenue also § i think drunk drivers would crash less if the industry manufactured cars that said to them "you are Seen. you are Valid and Known" § this is photo shop § another thing that fuckin sucks is the gerber baby § "the ancient americans had over 20 words for sandwich but only 1 word for betamax. fucked up but real" says a future man to his crystal son § letting millionaires shit all over my house and piss on my pets for $0 § BREAKING: Millionaire rapist rehab facility lost to random gas explosion--Dozens of 2nd chances tragically denied--"Mist of splinters & flesh" § @neiltyson what are the odds, that the letters on the license plate i saw today would just happen to spell "MR.PIMP" § reminder that if you block me after sending me a message, i am unable to respond to it § #unpopulargamingopinions nmario and luigi are Virgins § you sell draculas ruby red swastika brooch on ebay one time and suddenly they flag your whole account as a hitler account even if youre nice § thought friday would be a fun day to test run my pizza-pattern necktie, until i ripped my clothes off after being called a "fucking scourge" § it is extremely fair to say that my entire pelvic dick area resembles the singular breast of a pregnant European § @glennbeck crime § THe "Oscar Selfie", is, in a word, Huge. Representative of a New-New Media paradigm shift. It, was a solid move from the cclebs. § If youre a milennial who doesnt know what a Farm is "You are part of the aids" § 2020: america elects the first Shirtless president § ive had enough of posting! The favs.. the retweets.. the girls replying.. it all means nothing to me! Mr Donald Trump... put me in the WAR!! § am a network marcketer and a mlm,and i love making friend and allso i care about other as well.i need some1 who have this same thing with me § iwish i could grasp my monitor by both sides and shake all the stupid ass trinkets off this youtube reviewers shelves § i receive a generous amount of funds from the US government, as they believe that my good tweets are an effectuive deterrent to masturbation § THIS!!! https://t.co/jCYR7yXHZc THIS!!! THIS!!! § i hate it when shit is "Sparta" § shiting into a tube while earning $4 an hour from home § Fuck you § boot rust § Nasty ! § i brought my fossilized pilgrim shit onto antique roadshow and they were all aorund class acts. im sorry it wasnt good enough to put on tv § all ladys need to shut off the god dam soap operas and put on the vids of me smoking a pipe that ive painted to look like a nascar § thank you for looking at it § i'm pepsi rep kevin and we need $12m kickstarter dollars to make a pepsi commercial in true 8 Bit. lets show this new pope what were made of § very brave § Disrespected at hooters again § where was I during 9/11? Ha.. easy question. I was simply thoroughly engrossed in the literary treasury of The Great Authors.

§ hbo euphoira tricked my two year old into getting blasted on Brown heroin. thank you for bothering me outside of grocery stores @dare § (photoshop of a bird shitting in a mans mouth) GUY: THis is what society has become GUY 2: I can feel myself becoming radicalized from this § sensing activiy from one of my known "Black Listed Accounts." do not engage of it, lest you intend to shit on me & everything ive worked for § yes there is a hemorrhoid sub reddit and yes it is full of guys somehow obtaining 4k resolution pics of their ass holes and posting them § my dick's like the size of a toilet § im not breathing correctly because of the amount of people who insist on showing me the number of 69, which is the password for sex. § MMMMMMMMMMM~~~~~~~~~~~~ § reading 70 iq posts about how bullying ghislaine maxwell makes us no better than the bad guy from the x-man movie and just nodding intensely § once more for the mother fuckers in the back... Not All People Who Work At Carnival Dunk Tanks Are Clowns. § what do you mean 1800-GOT-JUNK only takes waste "Out" of peoples houses. thats an absurd concept. i will hang the fuck up right now § photo's shop § visiting New World's https://t.co/WbkNLQMVdQ § please put the king of skeletons back underneath his parkig lot before he starts yellin . disrespectful fucking rat people mother fuckers § i've decided to open my account back up after a brief cooldown session with lobsterfest_ralph. § And im not a sell out for having an above normal size dick either. Un tag me § id like a few words with this prick https://t.co/QH016dazoq § you say you smoke two packs a day? two packs of what, pal? shit? § " dont forget to fav and retweet . always always " § yeah im the one who made that image. i did it to own yiou, on twitter. #savederpy § today TekkenChauncey claimed that spiders make their webs out of cum and that makes them Gay so i destroyed his mame cabinet with my boots § the coolest thing the police ever did was invent their own flag thats just a desecrated version of the american flag § Eiating a $26 Wagyu peanut butter and jelly sandwich while pushing some buttons on my watch § i just looked up the stats and the number of meaningful relationships ive formed is less than the number of public restrooms ive Screamed in § experience the avatar blue person VR blow job - only at Sears department stores § i now have over 100 comments that the media refuses to let me apologize for and the trolls got my Ass over a barral § Coward-Centric Platform twitter, removing user handles from character limit, giving the repliers more ammunition with which to shit on me, § "Howard Stern should start a pod cast" may be one of the worst things ive ever posted, but still seems unfair to have my tires slashed daily § my permanently wet forehead is perhaps my most powerful weapon § Gasping for piss § This Was Supposed To Be The Summer Of Lonesome George § Cant wait to catch all the exclusive trailers and live events at #GamerGate in Los Angeles this week. Looks to be the best gamer gate yet § i will do better next year sir § THE BOYS: Come! Come quickly! Theres a Seal balancing a ball on its nose, at the Gazebo ME: Cant. Wife is making me buy 36 Forever Stamps § wife put me in the dog house agauin for failing to get the blue checkmark... and people ask me why im mgtow pua... § ((restrained by cops and forced to watch a man put mustard on a bagel) nno!! you're ruining it! That's quality bakedgoods § U Have BEen Brought Into Court On The Charge That U Must Lick And Suck On My Cop Boots Mother Fucker - NOTE: THe Judge Is Also Wearing Boots § topless hvac repair § spiders need to stop building so many damn webs. that'd enough. you built too many now. § klout was supposed ot send me a bottle of spices but they didnt § the audience gasps as i, @dirl, divulge onto webspace, my invalid opinions, quips, and horseshit gags while smoking 2 cigarettes ,simultÃ¡neo § been reckon ive been thinking about heading on up to the big city to (reading note card) to get my "Ass Clowned" § lord of all media https://t.co/LXdMdQ7t3h § got about 50000 posts to catch up on here... thats so many.. thank you my sweet boys § thinking about taking all of the logs out of my fire place and using it as a gamer cave § its laughable that you all would still rather suck porky pigs dick than admit that hes wrong some times §

i got a booth set up outside of the casper, WY red lobster to promote & expand
my brand presence. if you speak to me i will call the police. § We All Have
That Friend Who Fucking Sucks § http://tubedubber.com/#8jBEEtoPzS8:mfZN5YDRN-
N4:0:100:0:10:true § i dont respond to threat § tge nicest thing about me is i
have excessively dry balls which basically start flaking apart like a piece of
strudel whenever I walk around § moseying up to the girl on campus and whisper-
ing in her ear "got that fuckin pizza hut p'zone in my backpac" and straining
my face intensely § pleased to eannounce that all my posts will now be about
the Filipino israeli defense force, which i have recently been fooled into
joining § just give me one hour and no swear filter and i can literally completely destroy anyone psychologically with aim instant messenge § if donald
trump tried to drunk drive in front of me i would karate kick the keys out of
his hand with perfect precision § please stop trying 2 rile me up. im over-
weight man with cardiac dysrhythmia; and rude posts send my blood pressure into
crisis zone § unpopular opinion : only the popular opinions are any good
https://t.co/IYwQ8L8Bd2 § i got a big ass and i know how to fuck it. Mastercard
§ "oh this?? im only wearing this shit in case i need something to wipe my ass
with"-something i just said to impress all my shirtless friends § €¢€¢€¢€¢€¢€¢€¢
¢€¢
€¢
¢€¢
€¢€¢ § simpsons Kurdish § twitter should verify me because i invented the
simpsons § 1. all pussys are equally taut. this is not up for debate 2. many
old world cultures consider loose pussys to be a sign of "Blessed harvest"
https://t.co/Sz7LHtD59r § Asthmatic Blogger Expo Ruiend By Very Dusty Man §
"WORM ASS" national prison made me into the man i am today. i would still be
desecrating crypts be it not for the fine policemen of worm ass § society will
not accept me, the 142 yr old man with the grab bag of severe helath problems,
consorting with their prized youth § as soon as i figure out if taxationw ithout
representation is good or bad, politics is fucking finished § how about go drink
your self a babys formula pal!!!!!!!! § Earth Wind and Diaper #NotARealJoke
#WhatHaveIBecome § i think that wearing a jumpsuit emblazoned with the official
logo of my twitter account while i indie develop would make my posts good again
§ jacque fresco and i watched the original run of matt groening's "Futurama"
together and i pointed at the screen whenever the robot came on § https://t.co/
n0YGypHFnh § feel i have much to reflect upon in my life, on news of receiving
"The Golden Douchebag" award. Many improvements to make, moving forward. § wolf
blitzer putting on his best handsome guy voice spending hours in front of the
mirror practicing saying "this just in money is worth $0" § posting my 680
credit score durihg peak girl hours § (to sold out crowd at madison square
garden) does any one remember the eat the poopoo video. he eat the poo poo? no?
§ ihave been banished from the city of dubai due to my excessive sweating and
practice of pyrokinesis § somehow my "JOKE HATER" sweatband gets me more
compliments at the gym than my decidedly ripped form § visions of God §
thinking back to 9/11.. i wish i had flipped out more. Wondering how different
things wou;d be if i had gone more ape shit § calm the FUCK down § im a husband
, i am a lover , i am a gamer, i am a Slave, im a nit wit, im a goalie, but
above all else, im a Koch Brother § please help my cousin "Bruno_THought_Lead-
er" who just had his account suspended for threatening to "Fuck" brexit § piss
is not a profane word. it is a body part § i dont know how to make the good
tweets anymore, like thte one from 2012 where i piss on a ferret in a pyramid
or something § wikiHow: Home » Categories » Philosophy & Religion » Paranormal
Beliefs » Ghosts - how to revive princess diana and secure the blood throne §
thank u. every night i wake up screaming because of the weird twitter circle
jerk . i dont take this site seriously though § thinking of all the guys who
requested to be buried face down so the whole world can kiss their ass. Cant

wait to kiss their dead asses § heres my halloween costume. im going as a bumblebee http://t.co/5HVJ3coeXl § every pitbull dog contains a hidden set of skills known as the "Master Skills". the only two men who can unlock them are me and Elon § feel like im the only person smart enough to notice how much hourglasses suck compared to normal clocks § a good commercial idea would be a cop who pulls a guy over ansd steals the out back steak house gift card from his wallet while checking id § #SingleBecause self-sabotaging loud mouth with a hook dick who worsks with men twice my age at a vomit processing plant and has rabies § do not be a stupid ass in my life. do not clownstyle me § i found a bunch of those bugs that roll up into little balls. i called the zoo & they refuse to take these horrible bugs away from my house § let's be real. they should mkae a less ignorant version of the teen choice awards, and i should win one of them for coming up with the idea. § im stupider then dog shit, i dont give a shit, and i dont give a fuck, and i will never shut the fuck up, and i'll always Respect my enemys. § No real-time results for "teh economy" § prolapsed 6 or 7 feet of gangrenous intestine onto the floor of the GOP national convention in my latest of many goof-ups, bloopers, & flubs § top ten things you do NOT want to hear in the Nursing profession: 10. Shut the fuck up   9. Fuck you idiot 8. Your pay check is in the trash § i would love to lift all of my pathetic, frail followers by the ankles and huck them like tomahawks § before i hop into the top 5 most Racist muppet babys episodes, a few words. TesticleGear from GayFactor is an innovative new solution for th § oh for fuck sake . § full investigation: bring me the man who threw a dildo on stage during my TEd talk. also the men who encouraged him by hooting and whistling § warning issued to microsoft who is hard at work making the new "Windows": The world is watching you my friends § if you see a man in a fawkes mask walking down the highway with a sign that says "Gamestop: Power to the Players" that's me and i need water § crap off wise guy § please stop posting unofficial crabby road strips. i a m sick of seeing our beloved maxine being used to denigrate the lord and our troops . § climmbing the power lines until i am less pissed off § i siad jobs plan, not inside jobs plan!! #oboama911 § ihate it when a doddering Nanny yanks me by the ear lobe, right when im about to click "Like" on a big plate of sausages § Ghuph,.Being called a "Bastard" on here by someone with a sexually explicit avatar is the bigguest laugh ive had on this website since 2014. § Fuck Back Better § $5 poison vs $100,000 poison.. which kills more Rats § i have it. the ultimate pushup § log me in to the on-line city where the links are blue and the girls Dm Me...... § WOw. Sorry. Like i give a shit. Wiseguys on here § can we all please affix "#justforfun" to the tweets that aren';t meant to be taken seriously. this would really cut down on the mishmash § the last chilean miner emerges with two armfuls of coal, making all 32 of his colleagues look like Ass Holes § YOU TUBE POOP VERSION OF WIKILEAKS" "COLLATER-AL MURDER" AVAIBLE ON I TUNES.............. § GETS RIGHT UP IN WIFE'S FACE AND DEMANDS "THE BOOK OF ELI" THEMED THANKSGIVING DINNER; MANGLES A THING OF PAPER TOWELS AND HURLS IT AT WALL § imagine a world where we could all smell our turds while theyre still in our body. capital one whats in your wallet § some opf the things people put on this website set off the old "BULL SHIT" detec-tor..... § i hate it when the boys at the office find my "Are you a pussy" buzz feed quiz results that i printed out § am i still blocked by "The diaper guru" ? yes. but my people and his people are negotiating an amnesty agreement as we speak. § i challenge anyone who would bring shit to me to a one on one hockey match. goalie vs goalie in the frozen arena. three pucks § posting detailed plans aobut how im going to start trying out different shampoos on a gaming forum at age 52 § doctor: i can say with absolute certainty that if you do one more weird trick youll die me: CAPTAIN TIGER's Miracle Corn. LOok it up bastard § if you got covid 19 do not interact with any damn posts of mine and hit the God damn road you nasty sewer animal mouth kissing mother fucker §

(shoots all whistleblowers with the doom 2 bfg gun) thats what u get for disrespecting your jobs & bosses amd making a mockery of Employment § damn it to piss. my wife replaced all of my anti-wife reading materials with Pro-Wife bullshit § fuckin Wade https://t.co/gv0cmmnC1C § hello 911. the toilet seat ripped my loin cloth off again § i'm looking to be hiring a very nice girl to crack open pistachio nuts while i Game. must have clean fingernail.. no hucksters § there's a twitter room where people with verified accounts go to talk shit about me and shit on my good name and make me look like shit § .@plantcore may outright steal but at least @GoofyKidGalvin7 has the initiative to create bastard versions of the tweets he finds § you all can send me breast milk now. thank you § posting LIVE from a resort in the Dominican Republic, getting blasted in the face from all directions with pesticides, lips flapping around § im sorry but what are the odds that 100 snakes would hatch from that huge egg i found in the swamp. in a way, we pretty much won the lottery § if youre a healthy young male or female with blood type O, please consider donating a kidney to me. my goal is 22 kidney 's § most famous birds: 1.Krfc   2. talking parrot who said "i love you" the night he died   3. thanksgiving turkey   4. tweety bird 4(Tie). Phoenix § uh oh... think I feel another BIEBBER RANT coming on !! #TheFamousBieberRant #MyBreadAndButter § - ass kicked in hooters parking lot - thinks thunder storms are fake - donated 200 Emeralds to the police § inventor of GameFuel's impassioned plea: "please stop drinking it. its not for human consumption. why are you drinking it. its for cars" § powerful vision: the fox nfl robot stops dancing for a moment & collapses. from its body emerges a Nude African American Male, finally free, § excitedly approaching people, with a rehearsed smile, like a fucked up rodent, and asking them what they think of the latest Bixby update § the great pyramids are being bombed into rubble by mubarak's thugs you dollop of lizard shit. fuck your birthday #jan25 § when somone posts a vile piece of home decor in the group dm but you have to bite your lip because youre on the lowest sub-tier... § https://t.co/cetUVljy9Y baby mario is not mario's son in 2014 § this weeks "Mother Fucker" award goes to BabePigMovieMan for saying my dick looks "Crumpled up like a napkin" § way to capitalize cunt,. u must have some real deep seeded gender issues #Peeeeyuuuu § One Million Strong Agsinst God Hateing Diaper Man § Thank;s all. Remember to fav and retweet the thuings i put on here also. Get the word out that my posts are good § Japanese;Chinese,Korean;Vietnamese are the only Asian women that I have ever known. That is why I use their look and experiences. § #Zodiacfacts if yourre a #taurus! get a life § bill gates' dog is too dumb Lo even know his owner is a celeb. thats why i should be bill gates' dog. crawling around his mansion for treats § hgeuhkl i am a 300-pound producer / jurnalist my hobbies include car & beard maintenance also i know photoshop and my name is Miami § #The12DaysOfContent theyre back boys. the good posts i used to make when iw as an Indie account. the Classics series, http://t.co/7UWkZAnEu9 § optimizing my hyper links, for the fiscal year, § #MyDreamCarWouldHave a big ass i could fuck § http://bit.ly/bl4vMi The Free Encyclopedia § shut the fuck up § "Sucked Behind Bars" "George H.w. bush bimbofied me and sucked off me"   "Snowman fucked me" "Locker Room Fucked by snow man" § Im here to addmindister beatings to all of the liars and cowards in this hot tub § Cool, But Gay § sorry i cant relate to any of the shit you people are saying. however that absolutely does not mean you should stop keeping the Likes coming § #ThingsPeopleHaveToStopDoing shitting on the koran. for every koran that gets shit on i will shit on a bible § triscuit. beggin strips. and who can forget hamburger helper. § looking through my expertly curated feed for something nice https://t.co/8vwjQWJRVX § 20 treats = 1 snack 3 snacks = 1 meal 3 meals = Boys Daily Intake 180 Treats = Boys Daily Intake 1 Treat = 1 Goody 60 Goody's = 1 meal § its disgusting to create the illusion on tv that animals are talking with cgi or otherwise. a disgraceful tactic §

whoever keeps adding " one of the characters ever piss or shit" to the "goofs" section of my indie film's IMDB page needs to wrestle my legs § jobs are under seige § i would like to become somebodys Uncle so i can start posting shit like " ot all dips are marinades , but all marinades, are dips" § waking up in the middle of the night, gripped by blood curdling terror, yelling, sobbing, punching my pillows, because i forgot 9/11 § i have renounced Teen in all its formes, and am now ready to embrace the mom revolution . § thinking of some new provocative poses and gestures i can use at the local drive in movie theater to get my ass kicked more efficiently § im pretty sure the neightbors can hear my keyboard clicking at 4am and thats why they throw chemicals at me § is your name realy "tatum yazzie" or was that procedurally generated using some ancient mayan timeshare marketing algorithm § ive decided that nudity is acceptable if irt's done for artistic reasons, like, promoting a mattress store, § [transfer of pug_dog_Spectacularly_gored_by_bull.flv completed]   oops. sorry. that's the wrong one. here [transferring lime.jpg] § (chanting to self; walking around in public) dont get owned. dont get owned (body quickly separated into 500 pieces by metallic alien noise) § why am I grinning like a jack ass ? Because I am about to go to the 1964 New York World's Fair and receieve my very first Hand Job. § if u think you can sub tweet me because its 3am you need to Shut Yuh Ass Up § yu fucking idiot i wanted to make a sniper rifle out of those toilet paper tubes and now that theyve touched the trash theyre no good to me § yes. im it. § rating a porno "thumbs down" just because thegirl wouldnt take off her blue tooth head set is one of the moust fucked up things i ever did . § petrified 800 nubile women with mucus and the so-called great state of wyoming wont allow me to build a palace out of their bodies -- fuck u § Look again at the post. I did indeed sign it, with a 'D' for dril, after referring to you as a Frau. (german woman) Checkmate. § hey girl,.. whats the general consensus on that pussy situation. what chemicals you got down there § i have never condoned "rumpus" § im starting a new feature on twitter called "Are U for Real". Check it out § @BreakingNews please make a Nude one § Piss is valid. Jacking off is not valid. Shitting your pants is NOT valid. MEntal Health is valid. Looking at the computer is valid, & so on § i have posted severla high-res images of my teeth & gums for the inspection of the trolls. they will find that they look like a normal man's § melt thtis shit earth. melt this shit earth and start over. except for me and everyone in my necklace makeing club § Mr. Spendmoney Tomakemoney § simpson debate ends with 17 job terminations, 5 injuries, & 3 deaths. the decision is made to continue depicting their nipples as black dots § the thursday nite rant is murdered by me for being a source of tyranny in my life § wrestleburg is a real town and i live there § (suddenly becoming very somber) no Woman should have to pay over $10 for a Brassiere. § CELEB: Love that Moolah baby ME: Did u see that shit. Did u see that shit. He called it moolah instead of money. God damn! Only in hollywood § after muchf bullshit, screaming arguments, i have finally procured the $80 usd necessary to begin development on the face book of gamer. § bouncing my large mean ass on top of a shitload of stolen mannequin legs (girl) § please read my boolk entitled "girl theory" for more insights on this troulbled gender, as well as pickup techinques & lament § attn all my fellow high profile Hollywood guys--please checkout my friend "@CelebKiller" look at his scripts, get him in the movies Thank you § if you come to this website for jokes, rather than Experiences, youre Fucking yourself § check out my interview in GolfVibe magazine, aobut my newest upcoming tweet, titled "Snowman Fucker" § im going to crush you in to powder. im gonna powder your ass § downloading some very interesting pictures of DJs § @MrBean i lost $900000 on this shit trhe instant your goofy ass got involved. you fucked me Bean § i squat down, leaving a tiny, perfect marble of shit in the lobby of four seasons hotel in honolulu. i then contact my associate, James Bond § if they decide to replace the failing US dollar with killer quotes and

refs from pg13 comedies then me and a lot of cool people will be rich §
http://t.co/y3sQDFTaG1 ths is the direction of the @Dril account & our vision
of the future of media. This does not represent Final Product. § Seems to me
that politics is something of a "Double Edge Sword" , that can be used for
Good, or, in some cases, Evil. § can i get a twiter verified account. im the guy
on hgwy 23 who holds up the ad for that furniture store that went out of
business 6 times § Fact. § especially Fucked up in the wake of kobe bryant. Its
more important than ever to Think Before You Post, and once again i dropped
the(27/66) § what this site needs is the apollo theater "Sand Man" to push all
the " MORONS " off stage. I will take this down if it is considered Racial § i
play it smart by pissing into the toilet. § using intense calmness , As the
dragon , while dealing with peoples shitmouth § policemen have barricaded all
egyptian hospitals and are refusing the sick and injured. theres your fucking
birthday present § M Jackson Your Rapes Are Forgiven, in death you are no
olnger bound by your disgusting criminal actions, Also I Like "The Moonwalk" §
faerie blogs, faerie blogs, faerie blogs... § sees another grown man eating
cheerios off his table at the restaurant, gives him the restaurant cheerio nod §
Shut the fuck up abuot Greece § HA HA HA HA HA HA HA 8=======D~~ 8======D~~~
8=-====D ~~ § stare directly into the sun For Free #blackfridaydeals § I NEED
IT! TO BASK WITH IN THE GLOW OF THE BLUE CHECK MARK! THE CELEBS NEED ME! AND I
NEED THEM! MORE THAN ANY THING! MORE THAN ANYTHING! § marvel and dc universe
should be one universe: Gods universe. § https://t.co/xPGlu10a4i § My posts at
this site are, Really Really, great. Thank you § i am indeed a friend to
sports. let everyone who claims that i am not a friend to sports face the grin
reaper § My dick is above average size in real life you fucking animals. Do
not say shit § dont !!!! http://t.co/EKGe69SRrL § i requested 1 jeans, of 100%
Legacy Deluxe Denim Menswear. what you've brought me is Classic Men's Denim
Premium Wear, which, clearly sucks, § my posts are on Lock Down until the
benghazi crime situation is resolved . do not look at my page § e § things 90s
boys remember: vision of themselves in the future being violently ripped apart
by unknown energy. that board game thats in a mall § If a snake eats an animal
w/ mammary glands its eating milk idiot. i recognize u from the snake forums, I
see ur still a troll § pretty much like 80% of the cats in that movie are fake
§ i love iwt when a big thought bubble appears over my head featuring guys
pouring entire bottles of barbecue sauce out into a thick pile § incredible:
son helps father https://t.co/SJwGS95IGo § im the guy who asked the baten
kaitos forum if i should bring a condom to hooters § @Adobe something that i
wouldve used an actual animation program to develop i f i had any fucking sense
whatsoever @adobe #cocks § expliaining to wife what the phrase "pussy nexus:
beyond pussy" means and why it has appeared on my credit card statement like 8
times § wondering how i learned all the different informal synonyms for "penis"
outside of health class. I think they announced them on the news § @hooters2
you are my light line, my angel, my God Force. Let me show you the feeling of
bodies touching each other. The dragon of life § some things are more important
than the brand . § do it you coward § GOD is an endangered specie's § @Hooters
i go there to get infected with ring worm on purpose § personally im thrilled
of bidens dog being sent to a shadowy offshore facility to have the Evil
surgically removed from its pea sized brain § a man in a leather jacket
emblazoned with "BabeSmoocher" single handeldly ruined my high school experience and is the reason im unemployed § i craft my own rigs § i want anonymous
and police to join forces against the mayor and allow me to have a big pile of
dirty towels rot the floorboards in my house § My News Years Resolutions Is To
Take My Dana Carvey Impersonations To The Next Leveal. (Pro Circuit Anyone?
We're In Talks) § i can only save one http://t.co/5fXddCJ3eL § "Master Distill-
er Jeff Arnett explains what makes Sinatra Select's character as smooth and bold
as the man himself, Frank Sinatra." it piss § legally obligated to go door to

door and inform neighbors of sex offender status but this is a good opportunity to sell my custom Gamecube's § where is he. wheres the ass hole. i hate him § please remove the pervert alert § need some one whos mentally 12 years old to explain to me how market volatility is like the bernie bros of gamer gate § christ... just suddenlty hit with the realization that what im doing here is truly important. . thst behind each "Impression".. is a smile. § DESPERATELY MASHING MY HANDPRINTS INTO A HUGE WAD OF MY OWN SHIT ON THE HOLLYWOOD WALK OF FAME WHILE COPS FILL ME WITH BULLETS § WIFE thinks she can tell her man, when to SHIT!! WELL GUESS WHAT! i will SHIT when I LIKE TO! and if that Pisses her off..DIVORCE HER ASS !! § google it sometime, honey § i hereby hand this twitter account to Obama's Thugs aand permit them to beat the crust outta me screaming and to piss on me. no trial. amen § we asked 100 angels from heaven what their IQs were and the results will drain your Nuts § i have a life, thank u. § shit § i say that, let the MOds decide. i trust their decision and i will not attempt to sway them one way or the other. § A man took sips out of his neighbor`s hummingbird feeder for over 2 years. This is what happened to his Kidneys § Think i might mix my dishrag up with my bowling ball rag and get some diseases that only dogs usually get § shut the fuck up and kick my ass § It'd be an honor for you to use my toilet Mr. Mailman. I must make clear i dont intend to film you or collect your waste. My toilet is clean § AS J. BOND HOLDS IN HIS POSSESSION THE FAMOUS "LISCSENSE TO KILL," I MYSELF HAVE LICSENSE TO TOUCH AS MANY GRAPES AS I PLEASE W/O BUYING ANY § the very best on line wife`s ass § iran suports team coco or what have you. goodnight § what is the best kind of acid to spray my own dick with as a joke § in the nice days, the paper boy would hand deliver the newspaper to its subscriber. now he throws it at my dick and murders me every time § how do you clean a shirt § plotting various ways of dmming my girl followers some truly bizarre pseudosexual shit that they can't even get mad at § then they donate the hair to corrupt criminal organiza- tions isntead of mixing it w/ rotten fruit & feeding it to the dogs, as wa s customary § fully embracing the power of Social Media at the age of 56 and changing my name to Kim Jong Lexus § #2wordsforvday Watch Bruce (willis) § i donjt believe in porno my friend. but thank you for interacting with my page § you d o not have to tip the waiter if you say "Thank You" more than 50 times, over the course of the meal § everyone loves it when i go to their parties and mix all the whips together (cool wip, reddi wip, miracle whip etc) like a fucking shit head § #ThreeWordsSheWantsToHear always Handsome gamer #Three- WordsSheWantsToHear loud but Nice #ThreeWordsSheWantsToHear COrdial, and unafraid § bill: i just think hes cool. and, hes nice to me, and hes Based. melinda: Your sleeping on the couch tonight mister bill: FUCK YOU!! § still way fuckin Muscled , despite the economy, despite life § typically, you can extract aobut 10mg of bone marrow from a single owl pellet. mix with water and pour over nachos for free instant meal § actually, i have big red burn marks on my ass for a cool reason. i fucked up smoking a ciggerate § do not Devil my ass § nothing more heartwrenching than having to look a man in the eye and say "pal, your brand is nonsense. not even the gurus can salvage this." § Wow u really are a bird brain. § my favorite holiday is the one where you cover everything in plastic and turn the hose on indoors and just go wild § please contact your cybersenators and tell them to tear down the bad computers § the doctor reveals my blood pressure is 420 over 69. i hoot & holler outta the building while a bunch of losers try to tell me that im dying § a pig and a dog are married, ending islam forever § the boys of washington § i love him thank you § knocn knock. "whos there" israel. "israel who" 2012 is real. buy paste § watching stimpy slide up the fireman pole traumatized me and made me want to become a united state marines § ive looked at the facts and there is no possible way that this game does not have incest § mean while, while you were "Gaming ", i tasted 100 different wines in a cave behind a waterfall and cried into a shaman's arms § i wear the oj simpson glove while i post . thats just a small example of how fucked up i am. Dont make me tell u more § having you tube intellectuals explain to me how exactly humpty dumpty fucked up , and why he deserves to die § (truyng to stumble across the next big two-word phrase that gets really popular for no reason) udhhu.. bird hell owl. big hell. owl hell § with advancements in technology we will someday be able to watch a 3d animated version of larry the cable boy go to vegas & get into trouble § heated debate https://t.co/gsIzuzGz15 § "Device Lets Fully Paralyzed Rats Walk Again" -bunkum. i for one will not put up with this resurgence of walking rats and my followers agree § metal gear eric made me sit on a dog bed during an impromptu bomber man 64 tournament at his house. And no one is talking about this . § its fucked up how there are like 1000 christmas songs but only 1 song aboutr the boys being back in town § BRAVE NYC FIREMEN IGNORING ALL EMERGENCY CALLS TO REPAIR MUSCLE MAKER GRILL #HEROES #GODEXISTING #SANDY § my shitty Zumba Trainer thinks that letting people pay me to cry on webcam doesn't count as a real job. mods, help me diaperbomb his mansion § no. Remove thje piss. This will not stand. § THHEYRE GOING TO MAKE A LOT OF FUCKING BUILDINGS IN TH NEXST COMING YEARS SO MAKE SURE TO INVEST A LOT OF MONEY IN WOOD § Mpuh. I could take the time to pick your pathetic posting logic opinions into shreds, but i wont, because i have a life in real life, Thanx, § Hmm i wonder which restaurant will become the new mcdonalds, after mcdonalds goes out of business for performing coupon scams against me § HELLO IS THIS "FUCKWEB"?? HOW DO I LOG IN TO "FUCK-WEB". GIVE ME ACCESS TO "FUCKWEB" THIS INSTANT. EXCUSE ME?? I AM NOT SHOUTING I AM TALKING § *wactches a sniper headshot a butterfly while its still inside of the cocoon* Hm, absolute Ownage. Ihave never seen anything that good. § it was a different time. i no longer believe in sex § cant wait until work is over so i can stop sitting in front of this monitor and sit in front og the monitor at home which is 3 inches bigger § Fuck to hell § please stop owning me § 5676083 » Stock Photo - African American businessman holding a pile of piggy banks isolated on white. § GAY TRANSHUMANIST ..... I KNOW U HAVE BEEN CHECKING MY POSTS OUT .... SHOW YOUR SELF § Why? Are people upset with me? Are they posting lies about me in the group chats? Without letting me defend myself? Who's posting the lies? § awfully bold of you to fly the Good Year blimp on a year that has been extremely bad thus far § throw money at my dick § wish i could retweet this https://t.co/BBYRAVVuic § we need to reopen SNakes World because Snake owners have suffered "MORE THAN ANY ONE " § i am legally required b y the state of wyoming to tell all of you that i was caught fucking urinal cakes. i am a urinal cake fucker § thinking of getting 1 of those Yes icons on my avatar so I can just point to it when people ask me if im strong enough to carry my adult son § i am the great benghazio . i need Truth for my justice hole #funButSerious #BanMeForMyOpinions #HowDareU #SomosFiOS § scrolling through the timeline, not comprehending a single thing, but smiling and nodding slightly when i see the word "Favs" or "Retweet" § jack`s off to the super bowl for business, jack`s off to the bitter beer face commercials for pleasure § Netflix has once again showed their ass by proving once and for all that the ceo of it is Michale Jackson . § nmy name is greg. i enjoy Film and Tech. § DOCTOR RIPS FAKE BLOOD APPARATUS FROM MY LEG DURING RED CROSS DONATION DRIVE, I HOOT AND HOLLER AND HOP INTO THE ESCAPE SEWER § i think if we lower the legal army age to maybe llike, 12, we will see a sharp decrease in recreational nudity § VERIFY!! VERIFIY THIS ACCOUNT! THE TROLLS ARE BREAKING IN THROUGH THE WIN-DOWS!! I NEED THE CHECK MARK !! NOW!! NOW!! NOW!! § i piss into my hands and carry it until i can find a basin § i just shot a wicked load across the hood of m y dad's monte carlo and i'm feeling hetero as all hell § rt if you think that "Coors Light Cold Hard Facts" is the "Chevy Clubhouse" of "Dilfer's Dimes" § yes my lord https://t.co/T8C3UJvklT § smiling to my self... thinking this just might be bat mans biggest adventure yet § Frowning § no. no. no. and no. santa would never do putrple drink. keep the jokes stashed deep in the garbage on this holy night § rocky homer simpson show § its time to stigmatize the Ass § going to the bathroom "On Principle" § when ever i see someone own the olive garden on here i get excited & squash my fucking balls against the computer. but apparently thats bad? § game'sfully employed https://t.co/J3hpW2pBSb § can feel such a shit load of energies tonight, that i may see them, and that i may be here for them, on the computer tonight § yes, https://t.co/gDLdfhoryA § crook § girls love having last names like "Witherspoon" § http://t.co/N7a5BLf8 art § tj maxx stands for trader joes maxx.. But yotre not allowed to say that anymore!!! Oh!!! § Fuck this. I tried to be a good poster § @enterprisecares Thanks, I'll get right on that. Also my daughter may have ingested some of the hair. § its FUCKED UP!!! I JUST WANT TO POST § [apps help us day to day in our lifes... but some men have twisted the apps to fulfill their oqwn selfish desires. beware these 'dark apps'] § this shi t https://t.co/XCWdtFDgaa § Hunter S. Quiznos § look, im not saying that martin luther king jr was a gamer. that would be ludicrous. im simply saying that if games had existed at the time, § Piss on me, chief § theyre probably going to show my dick on cnn soon. hopefully on split screen with some dick expert from minnesota saying how normal it looks § "booty" is code word for "ass" . this is known § ive invented entire schools of philosophy just to discard them outright. just 1 second of my thoughts would make Plato shit out his panties. § googles motto is "Dont be evil" ? What A load of Hooey that turned out to be. Follow my page if you want to check out my shit . § i have been sitting in my computer chair repeating to myself the phrase "The god father of posts" for the past 9 hours . § the forum that murdered "ravioli_dad" and "basedgarfield2"??? no thank u § you waste my time farting up my ass thats a good way of getting your nuts brusied. § put an egg in ur mouth before the dentist, then when he opens ur mouth he cant mess with your teeth cause there's an egg there. #lifehaclk?? § the knock out game is a lot of crap. Lord heal oru youth . Lord heal our youth #TheThursdayNiteRant § someone has smeared shit all over my "please don't run me off the road" bumper sticker andi need help getting DNA out of the shit § [kOaLa_Releasez_Prezentz]gilligans_island_theme(Tap_That_Ass_Mix_2007)by_DJ_arbys(Deceased)_uploaded_by_Vect0rman.mp3.zip § This has been being said by people. § looking forward to my 19,000 dollars https://t.co/rF5YIPR7I0 § i will respect the wishes of th e mayor and the townsfolk by not fucking the pumpkin patch and ruining the harvest, only if i am given $100. § im looking at bible, now. § thinking of Life #ThursdayThoughts #NationalDayOfPrayer #MuellerGate https://t.co/SXx6NK9BTc § im the ceo and if you show up to my work with little pieces of poop on your tie YOU ARE OUTTA HERE !! § copy puste this if you think that rhinos can kick humans ass ,even if humans are using the guns. § in the yard, lying , on my back gripping my ankles wih my Rear end in the air yelling hurry!! Hurry! Spray the hose at my ass hole § will 2023 be a "big year" § did you know, every time you flush the toilet without closing the lid, millions of waste particles fly directly into my open mouth & kill me § please check etsy.com for more Hell Charms made from my own inner ear bones and crystallized vomit before i get IP banned agan § i'll be wrapping this hog in tinfoil to protect my dryrub from the NSA until all this bluster dies down § someone please verify rumor that petsmart is turning all animals loose (lizards snakes rats dogs) because of the scoundrel obama care § all the good shit got cut from my stand up special... now its just me talking about how i cant cum without using steriods for 40 minutes § LOOKS TO ME LIKE nobody cares what a crumpled up shit head like me has to say. this garbled crap eater... this Cocksuckered old dog...... § kev smith i support u and that air line had no right to charge u for the poopstain u left smeared across two seats § please read my longform treatise "The Arrogance Of Burger King" available only on my new $70/month content streaming platform "ShitWire Pro" § typical "Weird Twitter" circus

clown, hiding in the garbage from the Truth im constantly laying on them . § @
HelpDesk help #slur #slurReport § does it not save a total of 12 keystrokes,
which are widely regarded to be considered to be known as the "Typist's
Syllable" ? § number one. it is my right as a gold's gym member to bring
barbells into the toilet stall and get my extra reps. number two. its not
cheatig § hello dear , will you be my smile https://t.co/wDckOjXxdv § when i
see shit on the news saying we lost 50000 jobs for w/e reason, i say damn... i
couldve scored some of those jobs, if they werent Lost § list of vhs tapes that
GoodWill gave back to me: -pussy legacy -worlds Gayest bloopers im selling
them and i want normal price § the real kennedy assassinaiton was when jamie
kennedy was assassinated verbally by gamers for not taking his e3 appearance
seriously enough. § mister one million dollars http://t.co/sAWxBXp7qK § im
talkin normal mustard a nd would also go as far to also implicate Gouldon's
"Spicybrown" § some children get really angry if you tell them that all nasa
astronauts are cigarette smokers, but its true § This is the most fucked up
thing you have ever done . § @TruthPointDWR shut the FUCK up § thank you for
the Signal Boost . § myabe the people WITHOUT fetal alcohol syndrome are the
ones with the so called "disorder" § im getting word that theres a rumor that
in the next star wars all the star wars characters go to The Moon § driove 5
hours to rodneygamerfield's apartment to sit on his mattress and watch the
animatrix while he played on the computer. § i get really upset when matrix
haters refer to the greatest cinematic achievement in human history as "bullshit time". youre a fool and liar § ²0€¢ ¤€¢.„œ¿.„€¢ ¤€¢. €€¢.Æ.ÌµÌ¡ÓœÌµÌ„Ì¨Æ·
Perfect Æ.ÌµÌ¡ÓœÌµÌ„Ì¨Æ·.€¢ €.€¢ ¤€¢.„œ¿.„€¢ ¤€¢0² § every day i thank God for
making it illegal for cops to kill and beat me § i live for th e sensation of
adrenaline pumping through my spine when another person on here publicly
accuses me of being "Off Brand" § looking to "Max Out" my ball's § Prisoners are
producing gallons of low quality semon "On the dole". WE are FED UP with being
SUCKED OFF by crooks & conmen. At long last sir § looking for Coins https://t.
co/rmYcDoaw4H § where were you when Pibb_Lord_Janus posted his epic takedown of
"Betty Boop" § Bacon nutella fortnite selfystick iPhone avocado kanye Mocha
Latte (deep breath) triggered tinder starbucks Chipotle safe space pumpkinspice
§ Leeroy the Jenkins guy § carefully walking @TheRealOJ32 through the process
of deleting his account to avoid letting the trolls win, like we're defusing a
bomb § im sorry for posting that vid of me sitting on the toilet and sneezing
like 8 times in a row, and ive ordered my top men to try to delete it § u are a
Coward of the lowest ordr, in Usmc we owuld poison dogs like u, trolling alter
my heart rtyhem and i can die from it § "diapers are for animal at the zoo".
nmever in my life have i seen a more ignorant comment written online and
overlooked by the hitler media § my 600 lb sucked off life § judges are bullshit, your honor § for some reason. people get upset when i say the markets are
down because of Bill Watterson's beloved print media staple "Calvin and Hobbes"
§ i never even thought jeffery epsteins posts were that funny . § @cnn please
teach me how to make a net so that i can nab the ruthless scoundrel known as el
chapo § i live in a hollowed out tortoise shell with a GUN sticking out of the
head hole, the closest pronounceable address is "hell" § my true custom rig is
a baby grand piano filled with lava lamps § just realized that skeletons are
basically just rocks hitching a free ride inside of our bodies. sad and pissed
off § theyre taking my trademark hardline of societys bull shit (tv, movies etc)
and turning it against me! T-This was supposed to be impossible!! § it fucking
Sucks when a store sells me shit https://t.co/OZBhvWs87p § when the dow hits
30000 it means you get $30000 every time th e libor scandal happens , so, a
lot of people will be thinking thats good § Utility Belt Contains (At All
Times) Raw Vegan Oxygen Pills, Raw Vegan Skin Bronzer, Boomerang And Bic
Lighter (Fire Boomerang) , Four Guns § geting AssBlasted for sharing my normal
man's perspective, in a world . being fucked hardcore, by goblins, for liking

Due Process § " If Will Smith slapped me I would call 911 " - Dril § time for another rant. fuck igloos. shitty ice house.s too cold. for more rants check out my site. send paypal to theloneranter@rantman.com § bone prank: drop pieces of your skeleton in strategic locations to spook nincompoops and lame-os § tekken Chauncey is no longer invited to boys brunch after saying that he would like to karate chop the #royalbaby in the stomach § @beebee880 fox news network (FNN) a nd al-jazeera and bbc2. § every year, a figure dressed in black leaves three crispy strips & a bottle of mtn dew at the kfc man's grave then disap- pears into the night § Tweetmix.me http://t.co/R2XQ3b9 via @tweetmixme § i will not hear any more talk of mars needing moms § it is with unbearable fucking agony that i declare the death of "The Thursday Nite Rant" . writing them is too hard § ppoisonous § speaking of war crimes, some say the white flag of surrender was inspired by a piece of toilet paper dangling pitifully from my ass § either my chris farley summoning ritual was a success or a Fucking owl got in here again. wherres that god damn light switch § unlike normal humans, geniuses do not like bull shit § im going to be one of thsoe guys who writes ebooks named like "Brain God: Calculation Master" then spend all day screaming at people on here § pplease let me join mensa. my IQ is essentially, zero, but i have very good, clean hands § wife wont wear diaper. help § having a "small penis day" so i would appreciate it if my followers could send me some jewels or maybe some golden statues § @CrackerBarrel wher can i pickup merch ft. shitty beard guy who needs all sorts of wile e coyote shit to hunt the most pathetic animals ever § @DrPhil please kick my out of control teen's ass § whih of the three stooges got the most ASS!!!!!! #Pennzoil #itsoktobewhite § if i ge t one more comment about guns being a type of Glove- im spraying the fuse box with a hose until my computer turns off § warming my nuts on your daily coffeecup § Weekly reminder that the official Oprah App can be enjoyed by Oprah fans and supporters of Anti-Oprah alike. § every time you vermin talk shit of me, i flip my chair backwards at 900mph and bust through sevreal pane glass windows. Not so cool now huh. § Beat the shit out of the football. Beat the shit out of the football. Beat the shit out of the football. 11 43 22 36 hothothothot § i feel like posting some more good ass posts is what i feel like § llove saying "damn" § it is my displeasure to report that the TWITTER-MASTERCARD group has frozen my credit card for posting "The monster mash sucks" § i will drag you out of here kicking and screaming, but for the sake of protecting all girls from my horrendous posts § @USArmy you should invent a gun that sjhoots nuclear bullets § RT OFFICIAL: Michael Jackson (1958-2009) RIP - http://tinyurl.com/nlm7r2 #michaeljackson Suport Iran Fucker § thinking back to it.. most slaves, only had to deal with one master. the Modern Content Producer has it far wrose, having to please millions § one matrix pill is Pitbull Holocaust. the other is Pitbull Revolution. i wont say which is which because i dont want people to get mad at me § reading 10000 posts a day has provided me great insight into thr cultural impact of the Philosophical Mind, and has also given me Morgellons § famous daves proud to announce confessional booths in every restaurant where you can go to atone for your bbq sins. fucking murder me § they didnt show "rag fucker" at e3, i was really expecting them to show "rag fucker", disappointed & concerend about future of "rag fucker" § sometimes i gaze towards the beautiful endless sky and wish that i was a bird. so that i could piss and shit out of the same hole § lord help me im aobut to ratio this bitch § i was given a purple heart for being the fox executive who invented the 3d football robot & made homer stop showing his ass on the simpsons § i agree with all party `s involved http://t.co/04YXhaHcEL § i just sucked my own dick and got poisoned. no podcast tonight § my huge legs and a vile hunched back § id like to muse upon a scenario i came up with just now. a DUMB ASS visits a restaurant, after reading a poor review of it in the newspaper § bad § im trapped undermeath thousands of hissing metal pipes but im, still going to do my updates on here §

(wearing one of those fucking stupid hats with the word "Press" on it) mr president! do you think DC Films should show bat man taking a shit § barbaro is back 2014 http://t.co/Z73UqNki19 § ANGRRY FUCKIN BIRDS.... HOLY... I CAN'T EVEN. . § first off, trees are bullshit § my dick and my ass look like theyre from 2 different races of people. i typed this in the status box 14hrs ago & im just pressing submit now § i love coming on here every day to interact with a growing network of "CON MEN" and "IMBECILES" § "but the oval office wasnt around when John tyler was president" says hte nerd as my ass slowly engulfs his pathetic, misshapen head § i speak for every mother fucker when i say i would pay gladly $100000 for a Mature version of Franklin the turtle show § you see a man standing near a woman humping thin air. he says "AAhhhh!!! Oh girl.! This Pussy is Mood!!" in the worst voice you ever heard, § me and six or seven other worked up, wild eyed heteros are gonna bust up a gas station with grappling hooks to protest obamas new hoagie tax § thinking about shit that i Recognize and smiling § how do i ask my girl followers on here to marry me with out looking like im "Stunting " or trying to "Pimp" § thinking of life's i could have led in other worlds..... https://t.co/G1yZpvuort § slapping all my repliers across the face in one swoop like moe howard. all of them dropping dead instantly § new idea "Golden money" some times when getting money you will get golden money instead which is worth 10x the amount of normal money § thbe NSA is really good. but it could be bad? please dont write any opinions about it until ive solved this § $1000000 Post: julian assange walking out of the ecuadoran embassy covered in shit and saying do not go in there like ace ventuera § the btk killer spits in my god damn face. the impact cuases my neck to whiplash and separate 2 of my vertebrae. i flip him the bird but good § you started a whole account just to ask me if i'm matt? leave matt alone, he hates you, you dope § i don't care about anybody's opinion unless it is good. before you type, please ask yourself. "Is my opinion good" if it's bad dont write it § if you cancel me "your stupid" § carefully cutting out an article titled "Extremely Small Man Begs For Life At Disneyland" so that I can frame it for the rumpus room § gathering data on various of bastards § sorry oprah fanboys, but the Oprah MMORPG is a buggy mess, hasn't been patched in 7 years, and i regret playing it daily since i was a child § you need to get off my case first off because yourre on here posting yourself in italian black face and upsetting people § caught my son running a google search for " shit stain pussy ". i am beyond distraught. we are strictly a Bing family § TYLER PERRY ---------> MONSANTO <----------- 666 § basically i got David (@DavidSpade) over here-- just laughin at all the Virgins that are mad about our bold new definition of Christianity § slamming some coins into the juke box and playing the worst song you ever heard about a "honky tonk man who needs his dick sucked" § sorry. i can't come to work today because my fat little penis got blown off by a stick of TNT , in the war we just lost because of me . § a mudslide engulfs a small village as I obliviously powerwash my bluejeans uphill § only gamers know whats this is https://t.co/A0nfZC4SQH § blooper: it is implied that james bond 007 engages in sexual contact. this would never happen in real life because sex is revolting and rude § a social network to help cops with dirty boots meet browbeaten civilians who want to Spit`s shine the boots for free.. my one true vision § all of my tweets are normal as hell § a nice tip for halloween: fill up a jar with piss and say that it is a jar of frankenstein piss. display it on the porch with a strobe light § my tweets bring people together, and unite this country even more than 9/11 did. every time i post its like 9/11 happening again § spitting out perfectly good pieces of hamburger meat into a napkin § the wga guild kicked the shit out of me and rooted through my bag and stole my screen play "husband baby" aobut a woman who marries a baby § (accidentaly fires entire ar15 magazine into my foot & leg with 100% accuracy rate) alright. thats fine. heres what i think happened, [1/82] § my favorite feature of this site is

absolutely no consequences for my opinions sucking ffucking ass and me being
100% wrong about everything § (takes off VR goggles after howling in fetal
position for 3hrs while guys in varsity jackets slap the teeth out of my mouth)
wow its so good § the IRS plane man died so that people like doug would stop
taking $ from the average joe citisen. § i've been publicly unfollowed by
"lawyer ron" because of you fucking people § @QdobaMexGrill I Want To Know How
I Can Prevent My Unborn Daughter From Autism Despite A Shaman Predicting It,
Help Me Qdoba Mex Grill § engage my turds doofus § miss when the favs were star
shaped, instead of heart shaped. the hearts aare just another filthy product of
the horny industrial complex § no more belly Vids § there's almost certainly a
cosmic connection between my conversion to Muslim and my ascension from "'Tweet
Writer" to "Content Producer". § This is the reason i post . § cruising the
streets of night time in my Hyundai Sonata... looking for drunk drivers to ram
into § the wrong side of town. just a bunch of signs on the side of the road
that say "Moms Earn Cash" with no phone number or email or anything § my
Reaction when . https://t.co/QcaBZ0uE7j § "oh youre sad because a judge died?
thats so adorable" i say as i effortlessly list off 100 dead judges from simply
my memory § changing 500 tiny diapers on 500 disgusting rats #TheLifeIChose §
((attempts to dress up for hte first time in my life to attend Grandmas funeral
but ends up looking like a school shooter from the matrix) § im Sucking 1000 §
shacking my head at peoples crap... § phew. just served 4 years in afghanistan
and not a single person saw my dick while I was over there. not one. hope they
got a medal for that § (crying now) my friend QuiznosMale needs lijke 2000 sq
ft of carpet by thursday and none of you are helping him with the carpet §
nobody has earnestly called a donkey an "ass" since the bible was written. stop
fucking up my clipart searches with this nonesnse § Petition To Ban Actomom 93
of 1,999,999 Signatures § FACt: i was not kicked out of teen mensa beucase of
my extremely poor posture; i was kicked out because of my terrible opinions and
ideas § love when i lose aobut 100 followers immediately after making a
beautiful post. the weak shriveling up into dust. Thats called darwin § as the
man who was personaly tasked with wiping roger ailes ass id just like to say
theres no way im more than 40% responsible for his death § i proudly skim the
amount of $17.76 off of all my employees paychecks, because they do deserve pain
§ oh my god becky youll never guess who i unfollowed last night~~ cmon!
guess!! ok ok ill tell you-- CBSNews § takle it to dm.. this thread,. this
thread where i declare my respect for girls, is a hallowed ground § Im takeing
it down, sorry § me after getting curtains stuck in my waistband and pulling
them off the wall: "ah fuck its happened again,ah, i am truly a shithead, oh no"
§ barricaded in a lawless southern town for calling the one where pikachu
choked on an entire apple a "filler episode" § little known fact- "petsmart" is
actually a portmanteau of "Dog Store" § ive just dipped every boxcutter in my
house into a mug of real life brown recluse venom. Now's not the time to get
stupid with my ass § the varicose vein gamer § how the fuck did you manage to
post 14.4k tweets to 0 followers § when people retweet my posts without
permission, that is, essenitally human trafficking § for decades i have traversed
the unforgiving mountains and rivers of south america, hoping to catch a
glimpse of the fabled "ass downloader" § just once id like to see an archaeolo-
gist speak truth on one of the mummys he found. "He looks like someone knocked
the shit out of him" § Biber done it http://t.co/BoroyIDfN9 § ideally...Sleepys
Mattress Professionals will get on board with printing "DRIL TWEETS" on-prod-
uct, and pull both our brands out of the Abyss § I refuse to provide counsel to
one who sees fit to carry the user name "Gay Horny" . § apparenlty yelling
"where the fuck is garfield" at comic con 2011 is not only frowned upon, but
illegal § in many ways the blue guys from the avatar movies are like people.
they are like us in many ways § Rats Are Life Facebook § I WILL NEVER "PIMP" §
the point being that thte damn computer should know exactly which download i

want when i type "'chris matthews mindfreak" into the bing bar § "ignorance is
bliss " No. Any one who says this has never tried having an iq of 200 before
§ 1) i lie face down on sofa 2) infect me witrh lyme disease 3) it's NOT ok to
contact this poster with services or other commercial interests § imbecile goes
viral after telling tgifridays waiter that his caesar dressing is "too spicy" §
id love to get attacked by a bird. id love for a bird to try to fight me. id
love to smash it to bits with my bare hands. § went to kiss my agent on the
cheek and i missed and kissed his sunglasses and he called me a fuck up and
refuses to get me in iron man 3 now § oh yeah buddy... i eat birdseed... and i
ain't a FUCKIN bird!! #JustTheGuys #DamnMenTweets § just plowing trhough the
7-11 double doors with extra wide samurai armour and dropping broken glass all
over my Geta (ä,‹é§„) § just sent $39k in crypto growth exchange funds to a guy
named "Dinglepussy" and am now being gosted by him § nno. no ball § Trying to
get clicked on § oh forgive me for forgetting that youre too good to visit my
squalid LA apartment to watch all 9 seasons of the abc sitcom "coach" as a joke
§ don;t support this. please, please tell your followers to put an end to these
miserable hate crimes. i havent slept in 8 days § it is important to remember
to empty the recycle bin on your desk top every once in a while if you delete a
lot of files § My User Experience Conditions - 12/17/17 : - Will click only 3
links today - Muting the word "Bluray" - Unmuting the word "Wendys" § Well,
the time has come. But before I officially grant DigimonOtis the coveted @Dril
follow, I would like to say a few words. § #AmexAlicia i HATE the aid bug § "if
youu die in hell you die in real life" - demon philosopher matthew § jokes on
you , my followers peak hours are 2-4am because theyre all unemployed and
depressed § i tried to drown myself in the toilet but my neck is too big to
allow my face to reach the water so now im downloading some nice blogs §
IMPORTANT: Marvel Universe breaking New Ground By Introducing World's First
"Mentally Ill" Supervillain § i am constantly motivated to improve my content
so that i'll someday be as good as the guy who got his dick stuck in a trampo-
line on youtube § Out Here Ginding § " obama" legally changes name to "yesba-
ma". approval rating rises 40% § Im nthe new voice of the apu character from
simpsons. Im not as good at doing it as the last guy though. Sorry § @
GregWHoward I agre. Obama is gay as fuc%. Im not gay either. Thank you §
guys who get circumcised when theyre like 45 years old are Sluts § http://fc01.
deviantart.net/fs32/f/2008/222/a/5/RIP_Bernie_Mac_by_Miserycat.jpg close my
eyes and start 2 pray if only god could let u stay § ONE DAY THE ACCUMULATED
BODILY WASTE WILL CAUSE JOE PA'S COFFIN TO ERUPT, SHOWERING THE FACES OF HIS
WORTHLESS SUPPORTERS WITH FILTH #WeAre § #raceWisdom § @PizzaHutCares @
LanaDelSunreys the pizza hut pube team § in social media blunders: i post a pic
of my new watch without realizing all of my credit card numbers and dick and
prolapsed ass are visibl § i saod it once i say it again--the pain of being a
content creative influencer, and dealing with peoples shit, is like child birth
on "Crack" § hog § images leaked of WildArmsGarret , trusted consigliere of
DigimonOtis, taking a bath in one of those old fashioned metal wash tubs § rest
assured im constantly surrounded by flies § im being TROLLed because of my
pro-nascar beliefs for fuck sake!! why dont any of you care!?! why are you all
just posting more jokes!?! § i know i will catch endless flak for this. but I am
of the belief, that the tried and true Suit and Tie, is a Classic § i have
still not ruled out the possibility that the jellyfish i stepped on while
collecting seashells at the beach was a False Flag § exclusive footage obtained
of Roger Ebert playing a sega and crying . we do nto forgive. we do not
forget. this is Wikileaks. expect us. § looks like im forced to address false
rumors that i own 3 dildos on a shelf labelled "breakfast" "lunch" & "dinner".
this is an absurdity . § youre as much of a virgin as you are stupid assed. go
away from my gym § it is a shameful aspect of our family's past and im not
afraid to confess and atone for it by posting messages about it online § this

is photo shop § stop FUCKING calling me "EPIc Divorce Man", or i will terminate my pogo account and take my tokens wiht me. i am not a MEME, im a HUMAN BEIg § this guy took a pic of an NES cartridge on top of a filthy carpet and.. yep. the game on it is one i like. im pretty sure that makes him God § shes got full, luscious lips, killer Tits, and triple knockout hourglass hips. Not who you were expecting, huh...?? Rethink erections. https://t.co/oTyCKhmqvx § i can be a friend of you. but piss me off and i will become your Enemy. The Art of War § whenever i see someone eating without a bib i laugh and shake my head. beucase i just know they're going to fuck their shirt up with stains § wow this 40lb bag of dog food is only $30... why do dogs get all the bargains § pour teeth into my ass #SpyMovie § somebodys gotta do it!!!!!!!!!! § SnookeredByFraud-sters666 § log off. now. this is not a horny account. § ah ye,s its nigh time that the Lexus has attained Trending Topic status, there is no Finer car, "This Is Exceptional", Lexus. The car, Lexus § my accout is fucking good § #bestfeel-ing Jerk of § you ever see one of those preserved bog men or mummies on the news and think " ow theres a guy who looks like he got an ass kicking" § i think that turning myself Gay in the summer of 2013 would really impress my overseas investors § @McDonalds @McDonalds but how do you shake the core of a public fresh off the heel's of the 9/11 atrocities. what is it that they fear the most § i would click the print button a lot of times § maintainig one of the last serious accounts on this fucked up website is an emotional burden that could be likened to the trials of christ . § i stumble into a nameless town and see an ass pressed up against a screen door. i instinctively turn around and walk back towards the desert § going to start deleting posts, due to harass-ment. as in, i want more of it. hbring it on egg heads § what if all the locker room heteros want to kiss the gay player & it messes up their performance on the court? can we truly afford this #NBA § i am taking my 34-year-old son into town to buy him his very first pair of clip-on suspenders and we are both very excited § (using a hand mirror to get a real good look at my Fucking balls) whoah!! im seeing double! § amusing that i am constantly told those words of "Fuck off" by the girls of here... when i can hook them up with any App that they desire.. § ealier today i posted a sexually charged comment to my page. I apologize. i dont know why i do this. I suppose im simply destined to FUCK UP § not if you wrap a towel around yout head § Some may say iim considered, the Bad Boy of controversy § outrage in the midle east as wealthy oil barons trade daughters for new 3d tvs only to disocver that glasses are required for full experence § all of the rumors that i'm crying right now are: 1) bbutthurt 2) gross 3) KuKlux klan § to battle the trolls and their incessant mouths § are you having a crap of me mate?? Are you, having a crap of me mate § the Digimon Otis peace treaty will hence be frozen in piss and thrown onto the freeway where itll shatter into one million despicable pieces § the maligned Villains of my story., my ass and dick, are known to drive my readers the most wild and turbochagrge engagements & impressions § congress passes law to make every character in every show go to jail on the final episode like in seinfeld § All i know is burden § but not Good enough for the follow ?? Hm? § death to false muscles § http://www.youtube.com/watch?v=ov7TLhM7sOE § @dril Who give's a fuck § three words to describe me: Sensual, Progrsesive, Muscular. Check out my blog about mustaches § hello 1800-GOT-JUNK?? PLease come by and give me all the junk you got. shovel it into my home, and my childrens bedrooms, and dont take any § DELTA FARCE, WITLESS PROTECTION, HEALTH INSPECTOR€" THREE INTEGRAL COMPONENTS, PRIDE OF THE ANCIENTS; VITA INFINITUM; LARRY THE ASCENSION GUY § A wieght gain tribute to Princess Daisy § https://t.co/LxTAQQXnxg § i believe that while i was Resting, Aeris_Nader, the snake that he is, dropped a pinch of baking soda into my ass crack and poisoned me § Dont look at it if youre just going to say ass to it. § this account is now 100%, fully unbridled, Racist. Fuck you !!! http://t.co/iqDjFXJoQH § listen bud! get your i pad out of my face! leave the gizmos at home #TheThursdayNiteRant § the reason i poured vinegar all over TwistedKenneth's bike ramp is because he made a gross joke about piercing my dog`s nipple § they have a "System" § my followers love to Drool & Shit like a bunch of dirty daugs; and they would see me damned to Hell if i cut off their precious content flow § me & the boys will be holding hands., forming a Covenant Ring, to protest girls who only want to fuck the main pirate from the pirate movies § "Personally I can't stand when a woman says. "Suck my dick," or anything of the like. You're a woman, you don't have a dick." #Me #GoodRedit § the words "yugioh angel" reverse burned into my flesh after attempting to pose shirtless on the hood of my modified car during a heat wave § Oh mate. Oh mate. Youre properly jordached. Youre off that bullwinkle mate § its not normal to get on here and post fake joke shit when the rockefellers, the carnegies , theyre all reading it. theyre scrutinizing it § dont do it. 1million followers is more powerful than the nuke #NoMillion § utterely Trident hlruh bl mint lies and filth novel of marketing gum hurhf ghfh ghuhlck #AeathDrt § @KloutSupport "There was an error getting your Perk. Please try again or contact support." what the heck. im a Top Influencer for christsake § my IQ has increased 10 points ever since i stopped tollerating people mucking about, on the time line § @bloomingdales I want you tot take this off your store https://t.co/er5XqM4bgs § im sorry if you like him or are a fan of his, but you just know that this guy is looking like total shit https://t.co/szSCrnXO9y § Guess Ill Just Keep Drinking PISS!!! https://t.co/qGysz0jpQi § phenomenal http://t.co/OcgIteRKEL § @McDonalds @McDonalds i would suggest studying caricatures from early 1900s racist war propaganda to help your team devise his gruesome appearance § next guy to propose another wild kramer autism theory gets thier ass banned down to chinatown. this is seinfeld forum, not ignorant forums. § man at national cemetery tackled down, face shoved into grass until head turned purple for saying "may the 4 be with you" to each dead troop § Im nodding my head § heavens pray that the goofster, the gagmeister, and the stoogelord don't join forces and create a slapstick squad more powerful than the CIA § yes,. i;m the guy who eats handfuls of salt to dry myself up so i never have to wipe my ass, and yes, there are several wars declared at me § if i had a billion dollars id get wall-to-wall carpeting in my bathroom and donate the rest of it to the army § i am notr, nor ever have been, a nerd, and i have used some very powerful swear words on this website that would blow most nerds socks off § fucked up that people would click X on my feed during what is perhaps the worst crisis i've ever faced. go back to the zoo, miserabl animals § local church replaced with "The Simpsons lounge" where you can watch any episode of THe Simpsons & buy themed drinks based on the characters § reported § why would anyone want to put hell on wheels. what kind of satan would allow this § -all poison animals Destroyed (snakes scorpions) -reduce spending/waste by making the Oscars an olympic game -a Hollywood sign in every town § i don't have time ot actually read you peoples posts, but ive been evaluating your engagement metric's and they look like Shit... § none of you are educated in anything, youre all pricks, your dms suck, yoyure terrible at trying to engage my brand like normal human beings § oh and also thanks for the troops § rotating inside of a porto potty at least 4 times looking for the sink § @ Wendys MANAGER HASSLED ME FOR BRINGING ART BOOKS INTO THE WENDY'S STORE, WAS TOLD TO LEAVE AND WAS UNABLE TO EAT THE FOOD THAT I PAID FOR § my step dad is apparently too busy kissing his shitty wife to attend my 55+ senior rugby league games. OH and guess what, we lost. Fuck tyou § the boys held an intervention about me "Going hollywood" because i;ve been buying plastic toothpicks now § i feel like getting shot would;nt be that bad if you knew how to properly "body spin " away from the bullet or slap it away with your hand § you little online fucks who sit in mammas basement and finger your puds cannot conceive of the #HELL that is pushing fresh, invigorating SEO § listen son, if someone

calls you a horses ass, you look him in the eye and tell him "horses asses are
actually incredibly strong, and clean" § i deserve th e most mentally ill
president imaginable. 99 year old babbling doofus. Send us into the volcano
sir § it is time for me to fuck several pieces of corn, in the stead of a
female human. i hope your labor day is full of laughter, joy and wonder. § " o"
§ i love to build illegal temples around town. i love scrubbing my pitbull down
with big piles of soap bubbles. i love to fuss and raise shit. § now im a man
whos been eating his fuckin spaghetti, i tell you what for damn sure. tghat
being said, toilet paper needs to be about 3x wider § this is a serious
account. no jokes § i only allow ppl to contact me by artful magazine clippign
collages sent in insured fedex packages or by my xbox tag "dirty_shirt_iddiot5"
§ police are finding lots of Bad Food, theyve been yanking it otu of the ocean
for about 10 minutes now on the news, i pray for the families § i flash my
pistol and hand a note to the cashier at Wendy's. the note reads as follows:
"I Want A GF With Bat Wings" § i get dozens of compliments about my perfect
ears every day. it's llike Shut the fuck up. Im trying to eat a bagel in my car
and you do this § im the dumb mother fucker who has permanently fucked up abs
from wearing a pair of suspenders backwards for three days straight § i have
seen every episode of agents of shield and i am ready to whip deep state in the
penis § i invented the "bacon is good" joke. i invented the meme of people
liking bacon. all sorts of people are copping my gag and im pissed § shutter-
stock has hit hte concept of "A young atheist" out of the damn park with this
one. bravo http://t.co/YXstO2Snho § if a gorggeous woman made a sexual comment
about my perfectly toned body i would put her in a head lock. post "Thats
Right" if you agree § the Original bad boys!! the Best, the very greatest.
That's right folks, ive got the Whazzup Budweiser Men on board to film 17 short
films § i'm really good at reciting my favorite quotes because my voice sounds
like a cool movie character and isn't all fucked up and high pitched § somebody
snuck into my yard and smeared shit all over my kony statue. people are
monsters § i am closing down the craft brew wiki because i am being treated
like a zoo animal and nobody gives to shits . § get the hell to crap § i am a
simple country man who believes that hackers belong in jail #TheSaturdayMornin-
gRamble § becoming incrediblly Spiritual on the computer... holy fuck... § im
developing an app called "mr. beer". you can use it to ask mr. beer if beer is
his favorite drink and he might say yes. mr. beer 2015 § #5ReasonsIHateFacebook
DIRTY GOVT TRICKS, CRIME CODES, THE 666 MICRO CHIP, BOROUGH COUNCILMAN "RODGE
PETRIS" , WAR PLANET-- LOOK UM UP § and the nobel peace prize goes to... "Fag
Poisoner"?? a huge tattooed man takes the stage & bites into the award like a
cookie, gives finger § BACK OFF CAPS COP THIS IS TOO IMPORTANT FOR LOWERCASE §
"zelda vs garfield", i mutter as i look at the floor during a job interview § its
up in your teeth mother fucker § my next 4,000 tweets are dedicated to all the
good babes of japan and beyond § proof of same...... http://t.co/cjzBWlvgKn §
if youre making a movie and you kill off a beloved character like bat man or
bugs bunny you ought to be charged with Murder. No more excuses § As Sure As I
Have An IQ of " 65 " I Will Never Not Address A Presidential Candidate As " SIR
" NO MATTER THE POLITICS OF IT !! § my being a shit head can be traced back to
boys school, when i was expelled for using the headmaster's computer to search
ebay for " LUNCH " § i was going to make a joke about the food pyramid and
eating mummies or something but i stopped because occasionally teens look at
this feed § really hoping a cop doesnt wander into my room and sees me googling
"how to do a hit and run 2021" out of context § ass life § im taking back thw
word "Penis" because boys are being out here doing it for them self § hear this
trolls: ive been secretly respecting the flag in the privacy of my garage for 12
hrs a day , maxing out its power to insane levels § just remembered the tweet i
did of corb cob after seeing a picture of it for the 10000th time. Wow thats so
funny § proposed mural of Dr. martin luther king breastfeeding a pitbull

wrapped in us flag REJECTED by town "Fucking" hall #DeathEarth #EarthDeath § you
see that big puddle of piss i made. loock closely. that miniscule speck in
there is my brain. please scoop it up for me and call 911 § consuming Top
Tweets at unprecedented speeds (cream of the crop; specifically curated to my
personal interests) frowning like a sack of shit § just shaking my head and
smilling...this shit is so Myers-Briggs § "looking for my lost shaker of Shit"
only a bastard would change the lyric to this , disrespectful to mr buffet & all
contemporary americana § YES !! YES ! PULLOVER http://t.co/GIiYo3sj6e § as i
have stated repeatedly on this blog, my favorite philosopher is Ben Stein . §
just when youre scrolling through the time line and you realize something so
true that it pisses you off to the point you nearly crapped.... § if scientists
have demonstrated that rats can breathe in an oxygen-rich liquid then why cant
i breathe while submerged in Pepsi `s § ME: computer; what is my Jeans Number
please COMPUTER: your jeans number is 5. the ultimate compromise of durability
& comfort ME: (Smiling) § well were back to 1000 americans choking to death
daily on this virus and ithought the time line could use a quick smile. Thats
all § diaper pumped full of saline--looking more mentally ill than tom cruise
and jason bourne combined--semen wiped all over bottom half of shirt § calling
it: SimAss from Maxis will be 1991's hottest title. greatest Ass simulator I
have ever had the pleasure of using. § you are a known troll and reply guy §
the majority of my critics think its hould be illegal for me. or anyone else,
to have a job. Do not fall into their pranks. § hidden camera prank doctor: we
got your xrays back. Looks like your brain has been replaced by bugs me
(oblivious): please let me g go home § 19:00 hours. im whereing a condom right
now. temperature: 74°F. air pressure:1012hPa. just had a phenomenal potato
salad. Wind Direction: NE § i bet half the people posting "Ah!" on here dont
even realize its an acronym for "Acknowledged Heartily" § you missed the boat
pal http://t.co/32rn5syqtv § Muslims are currently rigging a poll on the
international edition of CNN through a Facebook campaign. Let's show them
Reddit power. § " Trump Sucked Me " and " Trump Sucked Me... Again! " § FOlks,
please, do not hesitate to send me twitter content before you publish it, so i
can tell you if it's acceptable, or if it's bull shit § the best thing i ever
found at work while disassembling old desks was a poem my former co-worker had
written about the Super Bowl § yo this server is for pregnant halo players
only. all u non pregs can go suck a lemon, capiche?? § Data Coursing Thru
Fvery Vein, The Ultimate Fusion Of Man And Machine, Sites And Apps Becoming
Blood And Flesh Becoming GOd § ActuaLly fucking this . § how do people know how
big their dicks are. is there an online quiz you can take § worst corn maze in
usa has to be "The Cornundrum" in Melvin,OH; the corn seems brown or sickly,
hand stamp wont wash off, stray dogs roaming § i ve centered my brand for 2021
by: -watching a dog give birth - expanding mind using exotic new beer types
- reconceptualizing the " -WORD" § i do in fact keep a trash can under my desk
so i can spit up a few nauseous loads whenever i get publicly humiliated by
people retweeting me § MICROPENISRODNEY U HAVE & ALWAYS WILL HAVE BE A PECE OF
SHIT. I POUR MY SOUL INTOTHIS BUSINESS AND ALL U DO IS SIT THER &RUB YOUR HAIRY
LEGS § do I have.,. a twitter account??? oh yeah, im a real tweet mouth §
shut the fuck yp https://t.co/1nRbXL2ZHz § who cares. pick up a foot ball § my
meme dissertation should be "put into the toilet"?? perhaps the only thing
that should be put into the toilet are your harsh criticisms. § Asexual VR §
how come nobody ever helps me when im playing team foot ball. i beg for the
other players to help me and they refuse to #theThursdayNiteRant § i am about
50% certain that the doctors who took turns punching my egregious chode during
my eye exam violated the hippocratic oath § the way im talked to on here its a
wonder i haven't shit my own ass .... § i regret to inform my followers that
the fig leaf i wear on my pud at all times has migrated to my ass hole and is
stuck inside of there now § aguh. lord § remember back in the early 00s you

were allowed to shoot ropes on a mans face if you caught him wearing a fedora hat or posting on REDDIT... § http://bit.ly/gTL4KV #betrayal #misery #2012 § the wiccan rhinestones embedded in my autism bracelet are counter fiet § walmart Sucked me § the road is a battle field, all the other cars are your enemies, and not using turn signals gives you an Advantage against then § (pics of hole in wall) thats what happen when i got very pissed off by the sports radio caller saying the football players should run slower § ive been known to look at 2, even 3 emails , at the same damn time § i;m selling my piss and shit back to the grid § the mummys curse mother fucker § congrats all. thanks to your tireless efforts, and unrelenting, coordinated aggression, the cheese cake factory now serves, "The Eucharist" § @DennysGrandSlam its ok, ive since forgiven you. id simply like a coupon to replace the dr. pepper that was spilled during the altercation § https://t.co/iKYM0jDKrz this is the most vile thing to be put on tv § you turn on the tv on to one of the hipster channels and theyre saying we need to start pooping in bags now. i will never poop in a bag § im the only lawyer in nyc who will handle your case AND have sex wit h u § Mmm any one want for mashmallows. I got a roasted BITCH on fire § in 11X B.C. an irish Mystik cast a curse on all moms to reciev free college books every 11th day of 11th year & 11th milenium. this is today § They also have to eat the shit § imagining the guys on Shark Tank laying into the guy who invented the fucking porky pig character "What were you thinking !!" § people have been printing lots of swears on hot sauce labels as of late § #foundMedia #Really-Good https://t.co/YYwE6w6ZpQ § regardless of if he's real or not . can we please just talk about how much bigfoot sucks ass. what has he done with his life § BACOn is some fairly good and epic shit !! Wow http://t.co/hHxvEWwHxr § accidentally severed my spine due to some bogus info i received on the computer § just inherited about 200 crude dog statues my grandma sculpted to scare Angels away from her propertyl, § the moment you realize that every piece of furniture you own is just a man in a zentai suit stuck in a rigid pose and they all flee at once § Feeling very crapped on by my followers § from what i undestand gerrymandering is the process of manipulating districts in such a manner that gnarly dicks show up on the election map § everoynes talking about comey but, get this: i dont even know who he is 2934 RT 1293 FAVS i dont know what nintendo is either 0 RT 0 FAVS § why turn myself in to the police.. when I can turn myself into the police https://t.co/dmId4ehIDN § Here http://t.co/GoG1naHYtF § if I download just ONe more app I will need an APP to keep track of my APPS!!! #TheThursdayNiteRant § wearing the wrong damn shoes to the basketball court, getting freaked on like a Dunce, getting my ass kicked stupidly § hope to make this somehwat of a tradition: the "Show Us Your Turkey" event. i'd like to see your beautiful birds, on this thanksgiving day § well i believe its time to ugly up my face with some techno baby bullshit to show everyone how unapologetically humorless i am #throughglass § I GOT
- SUCKED OFF - AT HISTORIC COLONIAL WILLIAMSBURG § MOE Hitler mrudered over 9million people you numbskull   Moe uses the claw of a hammer to yank on Curly's nostrils   CURLY Nyuuaagghh!! § @tylerperry still shilling your vile shows w/o apologizing for your comments on GM food which have cost hundreds of lives.? #nsn3d #SickFuck § duhh aduhh aduh § every one in that convo is dumber than rats shit & my posts wer terrible long before it became popular to say so § very bad covid § ah.. the perfect Souffle! cant wait to dig in to t(*EVERY PIPE IN MY HOUSE EXPLODES AT THE SAME TIME, COVERING ME IN SHIT AND BOILING WATER* § my friends, theres nothing i enojy more than a capsule of beer , while tasting beer with other 18-34 year olds, at the beer store § @BaltimorePolice going to have to unfollow you, for arresting me § who ever invents all the nursery rhymes (hollywood? government?) needs to write one that doenst suck fucking my balls § i have never fucked it up § always https://t.co/V5r2meeNji § now more than ever, people are threatening to piss § yeah thats right babe... im in the

shower right niow.. wearing nothin but a neon green tracksuit, and some belts §
one of my neighbors kicked my big flaming barrel of shit and piss over & spilled
burning waste all over my yard just because im an irish man § @CNN @MSNBC i
shant post their names for fear of reprisal . § @McDonalds @McDonalds they fear
Chaos. they fear those who dont simply loot and plunder as the hamburglar does,
but those who seek to Destroy. § yo!! check THIs out *reveals a sickening
green bruise spanning entire stomach and partial left thigh* § my crippling
fear of Hell makes me post really good things on my timeline #blessed § Going
Very fucking hard on donald duck today. Saying i would never want to be him,
or be any part of his life. § "maturity" is a subjective concept often employed
to breed contempt for thsoe who deviate from the corporate sponsored nor‚m §
shut thr fuck up https://t.co/Cd71KPOCA6 § i can confirm that favs are "crypto"
§ im still allowed to jack off. jacking off does not count as pissing. please let
me have this § really good place to leave a new toilet https://t.co/HgvaJBzc7s
§ @Famous_Daves so youve always been famous for your bbq, but now your staff can
be famous for touching d**ks, namely Mine, earlier today § sometimes i have
dreams that @DogBountyHunter & I are hanging out shooting the shit then a
criminal shoots him & i breastfeed him as he dies § this guy knows the shit §
an Oscar category for super bowl ads in the future?? perhaps in a less judge
mental world, § #2011predictions theoretical physicists will rejoice when
high-speed particle collisions finally produce measurable evidence of My Smal
Dick § i dont care how good it feels. i am not naming my child "compost
fucker". end of story § @PrisonPlanet my boss called me a "Pussy" for not
wiping my ass § Thanks for the like, stupid! § ants https://t.co/cCCX3FW4ET §
gotta get these tuerds out of my mustache before the cops come § my pet iguana'
s get angry at the same tv shows I do.... wierd but cool § DOCTOR: you have the
balls of an 80 year old man. your dick is mostly normal. your pubes suck. I
didn't look at any other parts of you ME: h § anyone catch that middle finger
during the half time show? it was mine, in my living room, directed at the tv
#ImIndie #GoodIndie #Indie500 § imaggine if people went through life trying to
collect IQ Points in so as much as they try to collect Dollars. verify me.
verify my account § cant wait for this Cunt to take us to mars; no Sjw, no
Girls, just us boys sitting around in 55.9m sq miles of waste land, swapping
MEMES !! § my impressions are at aln all time low!! my numbers are shit!! im
furcked!! im done for!! OHhhh Noooo https://t.co/5tAFqu8pww § (folloiwng the
waiter to his car) Sir. Sir. Can you confirm or deny that the Southwestern
Chipotle Chicken Paninis here are "Chef Inspired" § cajun seasoning and old bay
seasoning might seem quite similar, but closer examination will reveal that one
of them is far more Racist § TO AVOID SCARING OR OFFENDING CHILDREN WE'VE TAKEN
ANNE FRANK'S DIARY AND REPLACED EVERY INSTANCE OF THE WORD " AZI" WITH "POLICE
MAN" § the boys are enjoying their fave jukebox when ths sarge steps in SARGE:
TURN OFF THE DAMN JUKE BOX! ITS WAR ME: Fuck u sarge. The armys crap § ive
never heard of this "europe" but it sounds like a big bunch of shit to me §
tarzan is garbage. he sucks more than anything. people need to stop encouraging
his shit by making films of him. go home tarzan. fuck tarzan § welchs juicemak-
ers, (pauses a moment to collect self, holding one finger up, audience hanging
on my crucial forthcoming words) but for piss, § Bad news folks! i waited in
line for 16 hours to see the queen. But by the time i got there she was fuckin
DEAD!!!!!! § ill never rinse my farm fresh vegetables. its the responsibility
of the greengrocer to rinse my God damn food and if i get poisoned so be it §
Shut the fuck up? Now ? Whil;e im smack in the middle of perhaps my most
ruthless tear against Netflix Culture? Muwahaha. Never § getting really into the
idea of sleeping on all fours like a dog until my spine becomes super fucked up
§ sorry, for a second there i thaught the real hank hill retweeted me. § i have
been strategically poisoning myself to make my dick smaller and more cone-
shaped so it can fit into condoms easier § lets ACTUAlly shove atheism down

christians throats. cram godless voids into their mouths which nullify the Prayers of their digestive tract § choppy vhs footage of me jacking off in a guarded prison cell and yelling "THE SYSTEM WORKS" upon climax § thank you Microsoft for sending me 50 Reward'sPoints but i must decline the offer . For i did not earn them, they are not mine to use. § it is tragic that my followers refuise to obey my direct orders , and that i am often told to get "Ass-Fucked" when i ask for pieces of food § im just about to say that if you come in to the kfc support forum w/ a name like "crisp_Kyle" you can go right ahead & click that logout tab § NOTIFICATION FROM LAST.FM - "RAUNCHY - BILL JUSTIS.MP3" HAS BEEN LOOPING ON YOUR COMPUTER FOR 9 YEARS NOW, AMBULANCE IS COMING § i swear to everyone on this site that i am truly, truly a good and compassionate person, and i have a completely normal dick that isnt small § mr. Drone Strike my Wife aka the six figure asexual here telling you now more than ever, Gamers have been given the short end of the diaper. § haivng stress diarrhea into a handful of Kleenex § the real shit. § leaving splinters stuck in your fingers is good. its all protien baby § rip Yankees owner George Steinbrenner, my favorite sienfeld character § saw some posts i didnt like and now i have to go take a giant shit in the bathroom. Thanks everyone. Thank you § http://i.imgur.com/pITDW.jpg § give a man to fish and he will Re-Tweet U § Cart Man § **shooting bow & arrow into huge pile of discarded diapers piercing like five or six of them with each shot* now that`s what i call Combos § "Stick It" to the bastards of Washington using this hot new WendysTrick: Bigtime WendyScam for Nonviable Bun Bargain; Pitiful & Effective § my dick is bulb shape, nobody helps me, and whenever my browser needs to be updated i call the police § just read a fascinating article, about how people who try to "Fuck" have the same chemical imbalances in their brain, that the cave men had § show us the Boys https://t.co/CJS-90gzeN1 § waushington running amok... #JustMyThoughtsOfIt § BibleReader666 § surgery to make my head drier § were fucked cause people would rather see fred fuckstone on the shitstone show than True hard dicked journalism that costs $1000000 to make § you got me. i was, in fact, cramming my dick between the toilet lid and the bowl to simulate sex. but i was NOT "making a racket" . § I Just cried for 9 hrs because i realized i will never have my own Faerie, and NOw i gotta get my car inspected?? SEriously? Are U for REAL § watching another childrens tv show where they accidentally made the school bully the best character by far § my follower count nosedives dramatically each time i do this but #The12DaysOfContent must continue http://t.co/QDAFXSrgok § What if the guy who jumped over the white house fence thought it was the gamer gate. § GIRL 1: only 25% of @dril's followers are female. lets get that to 100% by 2015 GIRL 2: I agree § mcdonald kids meal ad asks: "What If Kids Ran The World?" cue insane montage of cosby, Fogle, weinstein, et al. getting shivved in prison § @ munckytown What Is Ur Take On The Teen Slavery Problem In America #AllTeensAreSlaves #TeenIsTheNewBlack § this is what an Emissary of the Kingdom of heaven my look like. Do not engage it in combat https://t.co/pVAX1wTooq § adult man who must frequently be burped like an infant or else he will die § is it spiritually advisable to circumcise my sons if they're conjoined twins attached at the foreskin § HERE WE GO BOYS !!! http://t.co/Npd9Am9Js2 § http://t.co/B9N6pBOU humanity in its Lowest form, Fuck you #savederpy § i hope to one day eat 10'000 calories a day § heads up all . my "powered by Groupon" car magnet has fallen off of my rear bumper, possibly due to a Polar Event § i do actually this § please leave my ass to the toilet § WHOSE COCK DO I HAVE TO SUCK TO GET SOME DORSEY-CERTIFIED BLUE CHECK MARKS AROUND HERE . WHOSE UGLY WIFE DO I HAVE TO FUCK § ill be spending new years encased in marble with magnetGirl77 because we just basicly trust spirit world more than human world at this point § get her ass!! Protect me sir § jacking off.. (lights cigarette, takes a big smoke of it) ..i s a Zero Sum fallacy. a jesters game § https://t.co/S8qCIFhW this is the most important twitter account in 2012 § we'd pour hot wax into the assholes of new marines yelling "Welcome to the CORPS!" cant do that anymore. this nation used to build railroads § if you spread your dick hole with your fingers a tiny bit before sending nudes tghe girl will think youre a Leo. i read it in Cosmopolitan § death https://t.co/7vGn40uZCX § for the 2nd time- the fans have failed to raise enough money for me to invent a new type of Face § go to a ymca locker room and laugh at all the nude morons § your satire . § if i catch anyone being horny on here theyre fucking finished § enjoying my "BEER O CLOCK" tshirt? yeah I got a whole hamper full of these badboys at home. you can come over & look at them all if you like § can anyone confirm or deny that the "spooky dicks" they sell around halloween each year aren't just rebranded dildos § gettting radicalized by bull shit metacritic review scores and making voodoo dolls of twitch girls for showing their ankles on stream § billions of people are shitting and pissing everyday. it's too many. it';s poisoning the earth. consult your laywer before using the toilet § no. no it is too soon. ignore my previous tweet please § I TELL YA IT NEVER FAILS !! WENT TO GET MY MAIL AND A HIPSTER HIT ME WITH THE STRONGEST STREAM OF URINE I EVER SAW ! KNOCKED ME ON MY DUFF ! § just wasted an entire afternoon at the court house trying to copyright th e phrase "Trump look like a uncle" § in terms of cop VS marine all the cop has to do is position himself behind the marine and arrest him for murder and its essentially over § "cleveland rocks " is not actually sung by drew carey. end this fucking lie § #ObamasPresidency-InTwoWords bun gazi § Check out these amazing pics of fat guys slammin chairs around then a hottie getting fucked by pumpkin head http://t.co/VYAuuVbu § they should invent a spittoon but for Urine § bug + dirt = me § NEVER MAKE ANYTHING IN FLASH - FUCK PLEASE GOD @adobe #shit § i shant say more of it . https://t. co/wUSQGubk3B § (apprehensively tries pouring some orange juice and knocks the glass over like a piece of shit) ah , they dont make em like they used to... § if my followers want me to become a guy who says shit like "tarnation" aand "Dag nabbit" i will do it. i will please them at any cost § thinking aobut turning into a wolf and kicking hurricane sandys ass § Its not even a popular toy anymore § so you want to upgrade your jeans. i suggest you gather 3x daenim shards, 2x bug honey, and 4,000 ralphs. only then will u be worth my time. § what if instead of oil-- the warhawks were all after the enemys piss. like "we gotta take baghdad. we gotta get their piss." just having fun § during times of pandemic, the thought of even getting, let alone maintaining, a full erection, is true ape shit lunacy. it is violence § entire bullshit of gas prices deconstructed by large boy who is partial towards treating him self § attn Waiters: giving me one of the free pens from TD Bank ruins the experience of signing my check. it is a slap in the face. A death threat § i don't believe in religious, but i respect the fear of nudity § "favs.. retweets.. they're all good as hell. You're basically here to get those. Without em, you might as well be posting into the toilet," § sending slowmo footage of my balls undearneath the bathtub faucet being pulverized by the water pressure to ameicas funniest home videos § i hate it when my ass is "over tea kettle" § due to my latest getting pissed off, i shall hence forth refer to Turner Classic Movies as "toilet classic movies" § thanks for telling me what " amore " is you dumb ass hole. i totally had no idea before i listened to this insipid song #TheThurs-dayNiteRant § The Credits Roll At Justin Bieber 3D And My Body Chooses To Fuse 3D Shades To My Brain Forever; No Turning Back & Life Is Good, Thank Ya § im the one guy on earth who thought it was cool that google glass would allow you to look at your dick and make it shrink/change colors § youre welcome to click the off button at any time if you are going to piss about it § raise Hell to end workplace discrimination against men who suffer from PL (Pube Loss). force my boss to pay due tribute to my pristine mound § every day, send one teen to iraq, and bring one truoop home to experience the hardship of teens life... #AnotherMansShoes § http://t.co/36JTlhuJ youtbue championship 2012 § if your a "gangster" and you trick me into smoking weed by putting it in a queso ruffles bag Fuck you. Ill remember your name. § when it comes to eating things at restaurants i love the shit that is "Fresco" § computer show me an animated picture of bugs bunny eating a huge watermelon in a way thats comical but not racist § it must be said that with the way ur carrying on with your posts, most of u will never realize ur dream of becoming a United States Senator. § youll never catch me sitting on the toilet, taking a huge shit ... it aint my style § folks.. when isay I'm "Getting my nails done", im talking being hammered to the cross, by those infamous trolls we all think poorly of, § "Having drama is the stupidest shit on earht" - Drew Brees § reminder to guys trying to offer me Merch Deals, that i tried selling shirts once but it failed because none of my followers wear shirts § Pope Fuckes 200 Deaf Boys. Bet ya hes tired..! #justforfun #gags § erase § every time you use a toilet you're letting everyone who has ever used that toilet before shit up your ass § casually discarding styrofoam container filled with buffalo wing remnants into the passing stroller of a baby § just deleted some posts that may have been considered hostile towards people who like to show their dick in public. i was wrong on this one. § no. the marine chant has always been "Oprah", not "oorah". you've just been mishearing it this entire time. "oorah" isn't even a word § we got myers. seth. verne. all ready to put on their costumes and entertain u. think youre ready?? absolutely not. austin 4.0 § hello. im calling to report a misprint at the shirt factory. ordered 700 "shit man" tshirts but they all say "shirt man". no i will NOT hold § http://t.co/gD4yGMQl Got anymore Sonia Sotomayor Feet Pictures? Upload Here § when ive Mastered the simulation that you pitiful-ly refer to as "Life" § im talking about main lobsteer, as in the good part of the lobster, like prime rib is to steaks § @turdslut it appears you dont actually follow me, Turd Slut. if thtis #FF is some how ironic. Then you are the most fucked up person alive. § hurts , dont it!!!?! § just had all my postmate deliverys cancel on me because they caught me posting about cum on here § shut hte fuck up https://t.co/GrEtPH3Y4h § " BLOOD CURSE " to all the terrible motorists who threw debris into my bathtub as i carried it along the highway and made it really heavy § taking the high road and waiting until after the election to call tekken chauncey a "HO" § a jpg of a fish § https://t.co/a6CoabkcWV Fine . § they are going to start calling the damn gas prices "Gasp prices" because thats what i do when i see then § whats the job where you dress up like a michelin man and get attacked by vicious dogs. anyway thats the thing i spent $800000 at college for § protected from all hater energy https://t.co/NM7K0Xamql § why are the ants only invading my bathroom sink? you dip shits are way off. i got a whole ass bag of sugar in the kitchen, unsecured § matrix 2: pedaphile killer § @JoseCanseco @JustinABC13 @HillcatBaseball I hope hes ready to see a man urinate on the field of baseball § @ASIMO you look like a nerd made out of diapers § SHIRTLESS MAN AT THE FARMERS MARKET WHO EVALUATES THE FOOD BY "LISTENING " TO IT WITH HIS EAR IS BACK.. THINK ILL SIPHON SOME OF HIS MANA § user named " beavis_sinatra " has been terrorizing me since 2004, by sending me pictures of cups that are too close to the edge of the table § add Beer to mario @nintendo @nintendo @nintendo @nintendo @nintendo @nintendo @nintendo @nintendov @nintendo @nintendo @nintendo @nintendo § i dont like fuckers. § i maintain that curly is by far the most malignant stooge. without his toxic influence, moe & larry couldve ascended to unfathomable heights § i cannot reveal the subject of next week's thursday nite rant. my competitors will use this information against me § i touch a glowing qur'an and turn into 100 lions #suitswag § http://t.co/6b3eFiKWJ9 icant believe this is happening § me and my laywer are discussing possible challenges that may arise from me asking a net girl to run me over with her car while i "pound off" § THEY SAY A NEW BOND ACTOR IS CHOSEN OUT OF RESPECT EVERY TIME THE REAL LIFE JAMES BOND DIES, AND HELL, FROM WHERE IM SITTING IT CHECKS OUT § im going to drink honey live on camera until the borough responds to my repeated demands to demolish my house with me still inside of it § this contest wil require some serious sleuthing . prepare for a horrifying excursion into the miserable world of diapers § just deleted 23,000 tweets at the request of Sbarro. feeling Purified § *circles "become gay" on a whiteboard* § itoday i realized that Miracles, Guardian Angels, God, it all exists; when i put 1000 bees on my dick and every single one of them stung it § the army: forbidden from jacking off. ~99% kill shot rate   the mafia: encouraged to jack off. cant kill guys unless theyre tied to chairs § stainless steel? my ass. ill stain that mother fucker good § (bored in apartment on two week administrative leave after nuking a 14 year old girl with a napalm launcher) THIS FUCKIN SUX !!!!! § thinking about how good the Hanging Gardens of Babylon would be, if it wasnt ruined by its obnoxious fanbase § *reclines in chair a nd ages 2 ,000 years instantly turning into a skeleton and then pile of shit* ah everything's going according to plan § Oh looks like people are "Too busy" to drop me a Like on some of my replies now. Guess I'll go lay in the road and get hit by CARS !!! § thank you for emailing me the picture of the pillsbury doughboys dick while my dad and all my uncles were standing right behind me. Not § im the dumb mother fucker who puts the ice in after the drink and calls the soda fountain a "bastard" when it splashes at me § yo. dont go swimming in that swamp i just cummed in § tu quoque.. i invented that fallacy, and its an honor, sir , to see you using it to get yourself disqualified from arguments with me § haha this vitter has probably gotten all sorts of boners on the Senate floor cause of the diapers. eyes buggin out, classic looneytunes shit § CHILD: Papa.. tell me once more about WIFE's DUTY PAPA: it is WIFE's DUTY to protect her husband from villains, always § thats one small Ass for a man,. one tiny jeans for man kind § getting my loan approved at the bank by lying on my back and executing a series of flawless air kicks right there in the lobbby § we need less mayors and more sayers (of truth) § 4.6?? Oh Your One Nastey Bitch § jamie kennedy WILL be waterboarded at the spike tv VGAs in order to prove once and for all that it isnt torture and that iraqis are pu$$ys § WORLDS BIGGEST TIRE CHANGE FUCK UP, THATS ME IN THE GUINNESS BOOK, THATS ME IN THE PICTURE, CHASING THE OUT OF CONTROL VEHICLE INTO THE ZOO § me and TekkenChauncey banned from red lobster after getting into scuffle over gradius canon & becoming tangled in decorative fishing net § i tried to throw a molotov cocktail at a bird but he was too high up § i could not help but notice that everyone you see online is either really a dumb ass, or genius, or average intelligence § belittle mme. call me shit. throw hair at me § relaly hoping this election isnt a repeat of '04, when i got trapped in a brushpile and mistakenly voted for a bird § onyl if i get 100% of the revenue and also a $250 fee for eating up my twitter bandwidth by Mentioning me § I will shut the fuck up , IF, it will restore the Harmony. I will get on my knees like a dog and make that sacrifice, for the sake of Calm § yes. i can confirm that craigsli$t will flag your job listing for removal if you accidentally title it "buffalo wild wings toilet fuck". § my garbage family is staging an intervention or something for me because i forgot what its called when people have a chin made out of hair § i fulfill mens destinys https://t.co/EYwyOQTJwe § Dr Pussy . I could give you so much more than a woman ever could. The gift of Laughter, the Privilege of High-Level engagement. Your loss § released statement regarding Grumpy Cat urinary tract infection: "Grumpy Cat is in a lot of pain, but still wants to entertain you at shows" § huaw yeah you gotta try this shit... just boil the macaroni in the same pot as the spaghetti ... this is called the famous "Double pasta" § ill take.. the whole damn lot !!!!!! http://t.co/wkIMOvWaeJ § the vatican should not be allowed to name any new saints until God sorts out my numerous issues with the citibank web portal § @TruthPointDWR ,you will never smoke § middle-aged men have been retreating to the sewers of our fair city to cry. as mayor i will promise to eradicate these terrible crying men § seems like

nowadays are more like nowadays than they were thenadays and thenadays were
less like nowadays than they were thenadays, nowadays § guess what smart guy.
cavemen didn't brush their teeth either, but look how strong they were. they
also detested sports § let me justt play devil's advocate here and say that
eating shit is really good and im a dumb shithead and i love shit § i do
support the long display names so people can change them to things like "The
Discourse Is a Hell Of A Drug!!" instead of an actua lname § please keep my
denny's coupon gender rant off of wikipedia's list of notable tantrums-- it is
NOT notable § i signed up on twiter to fight for proud causes; YOu signed up to
find another venue for your pathological waste speech; And you § to potential
employer: when i said i jerk the dogs off at the zoo, that was a joke. the zoo
doesnt even have dogs. theyre domestic creatures § just because im following
yiou on here doesn't mean im obligated to read your fucking posts, or like you,
or marry you and be happy forever, § I shoudl. Just bring back the fucking
TexMexBoy shit. Thats all im good for § pouring a beer into another beer
because i once read of the concept of "Mixing Drinks" from a James Bond novel §
wwow. howd that happen. i honestly dont know how a bunch of pics of shirtless
men got on my resume and youd probably be a shitty boss anyway § might siphon
some gasoline to generate a non fungible jordan peterson fortnite skin or what
ever you fucking dopes think is good. idont know § diddy's kong quest is soon
to be considered a turner classic michelin star Kong Quest and gamer fans are
screaming loud. § I just got word that a disrespectful message towards Dr. Phil
has hit Darknet. Users are advised not to download the offending material. §
Every Time I read a new Tweet on my time line. My IQ increases by One Point. §
theyre in love with me they winked at me through the tv § LABRADOR DRUNKDRIVER
#illegalDogBreeds § the turtle club from that movie is real and igot sucked off
there § I want to be Gargled at. I Want To Be Spit On, Hollered, and Fucked
at. I Want To Be Pissed Towards. I Want My God Given Disposal § fuck the grid
§ tiodays FunQuote: "Dont forget the WiFi" #FunQuote § Sorry, username "Mal-
nourishedBrony" is taken. Sorry, username "MalnourishedBrony2" is taken.
Sorry, username "ImKillingMyself" is taken § sorrty. im not a racist. i just
thought these slogans were too good not to post § I Have been told that my
followers have agreed that it would be good, if my name that people started
calling me were to become "MR.JUICE" § @ASIMO im going to knock its teeth out §
top 10 whack-offs , Ass-Outs, dick shows, and crank-me-offs. only on youtube .
com - americas funniest home fuck ups § bastard, http://t.co/z1UcEH9Ebt § the
only thing this proves is that youre a doorknob § just heard it on the news
that theyre gonna start using Crisper to breed dogs that look 100% like
beautiful human women § i thjink i'd know the difference between Satan and a
noisy washing machine with "666" spraypainted on the side § vermin § Hello Dear
. It is my pleasure to chat you § (pitching the Michelin Man) hes this big
white dipshit and people associate him with tires for some reason. he has no
personality. no jokes § Agreed, actually § .@markZuckerburg twitter dms are
broken agaain you ugly sack of stupid fucking shit. you incompetent freak § i
gotta tell you, itunes is running me ragged. i reckon it would require the
expertise of a NASA astronaut to operate this infernal program. § fuck no. due
to luigi's bullshit there will never be a year of anybody again § mcgruff the
crime dogs Crime Tip #888853: if a criminal makes you play a game of darts to
save a hostage's life throw the darts at his Dick § breaking into digimonotis's
house at night and leaving a severed human thumb in his bed, signifying a
"Thumbs down" for his disloyalty § (makingh the bitter beer face) ohh girl this
pussy tastes fucking Normal § a dog should never stand on its hind legs for any
reason. that is for humans to do only and they look like fucked up chickens §
As Per Tradition, Governor Romney Must Now Kiss The Presidential Legs, In A
Show Of Perfect Humility. POTUS Disrespects The Gov By Declining § my friend
who works at twitter told me the next thing everyone will get mad at is celebs

being forced to provide unpaid game show labor § http://www.cornbird.com/goods/
draw/hommers.png the hommers § halfway through the work day and my boss STILL
hasnt noticed im stuck in a pair of handcuffs. ur dealing with the Master.
#FuckU #BaldPrick § my stystem can predict all lottery numbers with 100%
accuracy. but not the powerball number. it is too powerful § keep it coming. I
love this shit https://t.co/ARQRhnGxC1 § i see someone post a picture giving
their dog a tiny birthday cake and think you see that? thats my tax dollars
going towards that bull shit § good to online shop http://t.co/OO3IU6pZmJ § i
post one amazon referral link to osme mens bathing suits that i found very
tasteful/practical & you all act like i put a gun to your heads § downloading
shit loads of counterfeit papa john coupons through unsecure wifi net works §
fire dril and tornado dril are my alt formes . well bye § farm boss: yyoure so
good at cleaning the pigs' ass holes. please let us pay you me: no. i won't
allow my work to be corrupted by the dolar. § don t dehumanize my posts § Your
replies have been simply Fire. Love the energy but please do keep any talk of
boiling me alive to a minimum as that is against the law § hardcore becoming
that guy who thinks the covid virus will be " ot good", overall, but on the
bright side it might inexplicably end racism § if i go to jail for telling the
truth then what ever. i'll just win the favor of every prison gang with my
realistic method of saying things § i left the cam on long enough to prove i
wasnt fat, spammed thte chatroom with B-List Material and left unceremoniously
. diapers § although im the foremost Blue Jeans Virtuoso i consider it disrespectful to wear them. i simply kiss each pair 5 times a day; facing mecca. §
open up thhis portable crapper   citizen. im police and im on a crook search.
stand down stand down § @AcmeMarkets clerk slapped a whole packet of heritage
Diapers out of my mitts and made some comments id dont care to repeat. Retribution? § im an Empath. im a Homeo Uncle. im a rodney § now that Ned Neutrality
is finally dead he will be sorely missed, survived by his wife Cathy Neutrality,
as well as his kids Ethan & Walter § Super Mario Guy RPG - The cast of Family
Guy meets Super Mario RPG as Peter Griffin does a "Let's Play" of the classic
1996 Nintendo Game. § click that fave button if i did good. § a giant vat of
slop in a secret factory has two pipes which lead to the bottling lines, one
labeled "GAMER FUEL" and the other "BABY FOOD" § "buckwild" or "hogwild"?? im
writing a poem for my gf § a fuckin.. rat eating a slice of pizza?? damn,. the
guy who filmed this must have gbeen smoking weed. § i knwew it. i fucking knew
it. twitter culture can suck my dick *RIps up $59,000 check from dairy queen*
§ i will annihilate all spoofs of me . i will take anyone who does spoofs of me
or my beloved content to the court of criminal law. § #The12DaysOfContent
http://t.co/dSDMi9dVMJ § my dick and my ass are normal § getting smoked to crap
by a big bomb bieng ridden by a man waving a cowboy hat around § im not going
to post about taking shits or shitting anymore . i Condemn all of my previous
posts about shitting and asses § police...! Poison that man § I GRIN AS I
CAREFULLY TYPE INTO THE MAINFRAME "A NINE AND AN ELEVEN WALK INTO A BAR...."
SUDDENLY FBI AGENTS BUST IN AND START FUCKIN MY ASS § what do teens find funny
nowadays. getting "Slimed" onj nickelodeon? farting principals? help me out
here § if a $40000 check isnt made out to DigimonOtis in the next 3 hours, we
WILL hack missouri's official state dog and change it to a dirty boot § ive
installed a couple of externals to cover my bases § tips for photographing your
own vomit From A Mom-- lighting, etc § Obauma, stop giving speeches and get to
work locating and executing the Bastard Osama Bin Laden. #Remember911 #Wtc §
lets just say an online quiz told me my dog is harboring the soul of a Haitian
Prince and idont know how to free him without hurting the dog § fuck restaurants making quesadillas like 1 inch thick, stuffed with crap falling all over
the plate. whatre you trying to do, suck my Dick?? § im sorry but, when you
people reply to my posts with things like "Fuck you" and "Fuck your Account"
it makes me look like a real dumb ass § pledging to cut down on "oafish"

behavior, such as accidentally eating spicy food or having my shirt ripped off by a windmill § https://t.co/AecSDSeAYs § the entire contents of the kfc smokehouse angus chicken snacker slide out and fall directly into my shirt. "IM FUCKED" i yell out § why'd there suffering in this world................ § taking hthe Touch Your Own Eye Balls challenge, at the zoo, despite recent developments § i sometimes wonder how shaken the AB/DL community would be if they found out i was injecting my diaper with saline solution instead of Shit § me and several other eclectic masturbateurs have gathered on capital hill to protest Mr.Skin 's inadequate representation of " Indie " media § sick of guys like jared and storm roof getting themselves beat up in prison just so they can snag a trending topic on twitter § seems to me. like, well, these days, people are more interested in Instagram , than telegrams, which are better because theyre the first one § wearing shoes makes you like 50 pounds heavier § http://tinyurl.com/38xm9um the blood will set u free § james bond, your next assignment is to infiltrate the white house and take the Tax's back from obama. please, get the Tax's - § new mcdonalds-flavored burger king sandiwch given the coveted score of "Eight" by food experts § ass someone who owns BOTH next gen consoles, as a actual murderer with every halo displayed on my mantle, i've the final word of gamer gate, § @dril hell tweet § Bloomberg Opinion has cleansed the earth with Absolute Fire once again! " this is Brouh Moment to me!! " § popular youtube user "LunchPhreak22" often enjoys "Phreaking" his lunches by poisoning them for the amusement of his viewers § Sorry im driving my car 100mph § the cops need poison stun knives so they ca n arrest me harder, and every police cruiser should contain a coffin full of beer #MyNiceOpinion § @UncleHalo i;ll have you arrested for cowardice § I think if i put my mind to it, I could put a tree in my house like they do at the Cherry hill mall § i love shit that doesnt equal endorsements § when i serve you one of my fine home cooked meals i promise 2 things: 1. it WILL be tge best thing you've ever tasted 2. you WILL get diarrhea § Sword's. The only blade known to man § @Snowden please do a wiki leak addressing the mistreatment of gamer`s by viacom § Traitors https://t.co/zgFjQZgjaH § might do the obama thing and follow 600000 accounts so people cant get mad at me for following specific guys § There's no greater television program than The News. The News is the only show on TV that I like, and it's smart. #TheThursdayNiteRant § thinking about a adults version of star wars where all the characters have Depression and saying the word "Bauzinga" to mysef in my car § actually the barf bags on airplanes are for shitting in. they call them barf bags because thats gross to some people § i just thoughgt about those commercials with the stupid fucking mouth in the dishwasher that begs for jet dry & ripped a door off its hinges § they have been calling it "PS5" because when i see it I piss 5 times. § "Me and a lot of my friends are starting to think that this Covid-19 business is a complete goof. A rat job." - Spider man § everyone please stop fucking posting for a second; i think i just inhaled a hair § TEARING THE MONA LISA FROM ITS CANVAS AND USING IT 2 CENSOR MY BIG BARE ASS AS I BUMBLE MY WAY OUT OF THE LOUVRE WITH GUARDS SCREAMING AT ME § id absolutely love to move to LA with my model g.friend & start my film career, but all my pre-orders at game stop would certainly be fucked § can you please alter this "PROPERTY OF THE ZOO" tattoo on my back into maybe like a naked gypsy chick § Hell Yes;. the army is putting me and my guns on a plane back to iraq. Thius is like real life DLC § might get mad at harassment of Tech Companys and post some shit about how nobody believes in smiling anymore. You never see any one smiling. § if you like the band "Shinedown" you will love this video of me getting trounced by police officers while demanding to meet them § how did they do the ace ventura butt talk. i know that shit wasnt real. was it 3d or robots § beached whale corpse explodes after internal gas buildup-- "tea bag" prrotest scheduled to take place inside of its diseased remains #teabag § 9/11 and all the micro-9/11s imposed upon me by my

emplyoer every day is all rolled up in, and majorly a part of, Crisis of Boys §
.@Budweiser Check out my tweets. I like the stuff you post on here. Please,
have a look at my page. Love the 'Weiser. Bye. § i clicked the checkbox next to
"Keep Me Logged In" so that's not possible § new bat man villain "the dunce"
just a guy in a dunce cap who says hes sorry a lot while bat man knocks the
crap out of him § gaining a new followefr.. that, to me, is a real "A-Ha!"
moment § The new shit is 100,000,000 Followeirs by 2021. Put that in your
fucking web site § please join me iin eating one hundred bags of romaine
lettuce if you are sick of the CDC rubbing their ass in our faces, with
politics § had another nightmare where i had to explain to my high school
principal why i wrote "Moves like Dorner" on the front of my note book §
https://t.co/AaJ8415oXE § (contorting entire face into an abominable purple
frown) cobb salad?? that sounds fuckin STUPID § @Bubbaburger Get rid of this §
Stop looking at my posts § im still noob after all these years, after 20 years
of the computer im still noob, unbelievable § - barack "knock 'um down" obama
- http://t.co/oW5xdmbLof - mad rodney - http://t.co/yTiRJSiEMX - chemtrail
- http://t.co/E4km14dXL9 vote now § whoever sent me that vile picture of an
undimpled necktie- congratulations for emotionally ruining a man and undoing
years of therapy § your white § your about to find out why'd they'd call me
"The Bitch" § thank you, http://t.co/XmuLGcjapP § fuck it, ill just come out
and say that i think "Iceberg lettuce" is just aobut the worst name you can
come up w/ for a damn type of lettuce § if i ever get Crucified i would like it
to be on my official warhammer 40,000 surfboard while my all my pitbulls bark at
me § Want to say thanks to PedophiliaMan for this comment? Give them a month of
reddit gold. Please select a payment method. PayPal BitCoin Credi § im sensing
some major bullshit coming from the graveyard § i think "mario and sonic at the
munich massacre" could work if they did it respectfully & didn;t fuck with the
formulas from the retro games § you Hog. you Rat § if your car is this. Fuck
yourself https://t.co/ddI8HIdKyl § FETID BOZO: Ahhh oil spills are bad WISE
ADULT: the sun will evaporate the oil, & the wheel of mother gaia spins goodly,
As does all things, § thinking about running out of toilet paper and having to
wipe my ass with like, dental floss, or a mouth wash bottle, and getting very
upset § @tjefferson1976 thank you thomas jefferson § theres bullshit Cybervamp
and regualr cybervamp, and im the regular one, and youre the bullshir one cause
you do shit like play mario games § #truth #fact... it is proven that about 80%
of people online are violent murderers. wow thats so many. be safe my beloved
followers § put the damn coat on!! it's really comin down out there. Thank you
for this opportunity. § sounds like a real fucked up idiot to me, § Im going to
shut the computer off until people learn to be more mature about life. In tge
mean time, suck my dick § FOR 1 SECOND THE NORTHERN LIGHTS DISPLAYED DHARMA AND
GREG IN GLORIOUS BLURAY-- NOW LETS ALL SIGN MY PETIITION IN BLOOD TO GET IT ON
TV'S § i have decided to become an Oil magnate, after spending quite some time
reading the dictionary definition of the word "magnate" § SAY IT AGAIN BOYS :
"If it's not from Harvard , it's not a STEM degree" § it is nothing short of
miraculous that all the rich people on this website are personal friends of
mine, and care about me, and know my Pain § #Vote https://t.co/WjnGJJY9z9 § @
Princeofass ass is nonsovereign. he is claiming to be the prince of it for
page hits. § $0 § #AnimalTVShows dog fucker § Are U for Real #AreUForReal § i
cried during the schene where richie rich revealed the mcdonalds in his house.
if you dont like it, move on § me vs. a girl follower's Father, screaming
grappling match in a parking garage, trying some WWE wreslting moves im not
athletic enough to do § glorified mud § Had to block a friend ive had since
kindergarten because he said he was going to fuck the new ghost busters ghost.
Im through playing games § shot da fuck up BITCH § suck 100 metal dicks for a
1/256 chance of viewing a lovely 3d cutscene § ive decided   A. every white
colored food is vanilla flavored. especially popcorn. especially mayo B. this

opinion will be shown on The News § polease cut all art programs so we can instead focus on teaching our children the importance of being Respectful towards influencers § my rig tower is full of shit parts because i spent all my money on a mouse pad with a screaming human face ionside of it § linking my Folders to other Folders or whatever the fuck it is people do on the computer § wrestlers and sega § It's Saturday night. Hand me the cold one fellas § #ImNotAntisocialImJust an imbecile that smells like guinea pig cage § my big april prank: scream about my dick for 5 years on a website that people normally use to socialize with friends and loved ones § boys i need a full report on your Scalp Health by uhh 8pm or else ill go ape shit in the dms, § i can not catch a break folks. my 78 yr old son has been pissing into the boiler some how and making our home smell like a reptile enclosure § 1) i do not owe you mother fuckers a damn thing 2) i will not hear any more questions or comments unless they pertain to MetroPCS, or Pepsi. § need a dog who can maneuver something in the ball park of 600000 blocks of limestone around my yard https://t.co/wul3XHxzzQ § dear horseshoe crab,: you are neither of those things, and yyou look like a damn rat in a hat § thank you daugter § I Am Your Slave Madam President! I'll Always Protect You! https://t.co/497F3CMguH § wearing some ridiculously shitty looking jeans that look like half of a halloween costume § @pepsi die from dehydration § #MOMCHAT IS TRENDING.   #MOMCHAT IS TRENDING. YOU HEARD CORRECTLY, #MOMCHAT IS NOW MAINSTREAM. EASILY ACCESSIBLE BY FALSE MOMS. FUCK TWITTER § i dont promote circus acts. § you think im wasting my time putzing around in the drafts folder? bull shit. 100% off the cuff https://t.co/wSMDuYFBXk § it ius abundantly clear that my entire online presence is like a big toilet shaped pinata that people bludgeon with sticks & take shits into § https://t.co/SxADN7Gjwd § thanks for banning mme for having the username "WTCPuncher" , even though I registered that name before hte towers blew up in a car accident § every one on cnn is my father and mentor § memes of the antarctic § just like the time my buddy " chustin " Ate Shit on that ramp we made out of horse bones § cursed pair of google glasses adds world star hip hop watermark to everything i look at and cannot be removed from face § youtube recommending large amount of gamestop dumpster dive videos to me; perhaps hteyve implemented a new algorithm which detects "Misery" § currently seeking buyers for "Zonked in the Pecker" thw only sit com where the wife punchs her husband in the dick at least once per episode § what is the blue shit i see on them. remove it § nude palestinian grandpa with micropenis tazed by BP oil executives in scuffle involving megan fox's $100,000 iphone; blogoverse implodes § alright shit for brain listen up. i dont want this guacamole stuff youre peddling. its green and it looks sick. go home #TheThursdayNiteRant § my solemn vow of shit § My CartMan Tattoo? Still Sick As Fuck. I'm Just Wearing A Turtleneck Sweater Because It's Cold § If God Was In Hell We Would All Be Dead. § feel as though i could break through most walls with my bare hands , given an unlimited amount of time and resources § PLACING SCREAM MOVIE MASK OVR MY HEAD AS MY HUGE GLISTENING BODY SLOWLY ROTATES IN MY HELL REALM,CONTROLING 600 MONITORS,SMOKING A 3D HOOKAH § do not make my life a living hell § it's horrible and i'm very close to calling the police § yeah right johnny cash. we totally believe that you went to jail & got executed. why don't you sing about real things instead of doing irony § theyl;l do it until i die and then theyll drag my corpse through the rubble while making awful beast noises § Im sorry it has to be said but if you have a small penis that means you were a devil in your past life and you need to unfollow me right now § TWITTER APP: THree different guys you know just faved the same damn tweet. This is breathtaking. What are the odds ME: please locate my wife § No results found for "fuck superpretzel". No results found for "superpretzel is bullshit". No results found for "boycott superpretzel". § MGM STUDIOS CAN U CONFIRM THAT MR. DUSTIN HOFFMAN HAS SEEN THE VIDEO I SENT OF ME MUCKIN AROUND IN A PILE OF LEAVES?? OK

ILL CALL BACK LATER § cut the crap 2017 https://t.co/tvNbAGfiWC § soryr guys.
the boss just yanked my privacy tarp off and all further content is on hold
until i can retrieve it § from now on every one call him Doanald J Poop and if
enough people do it he will be forced to reopen fudd ruckers § any 1 know where
the bannasa are. i promise im not moneky president. if u know where the bana
are emale me at the_ape_potus@whitehous.gov § obama's ban on clove cigarettes
has affected me Spiritually § ye.s im the king of sex and having it. come to
my government mandated cage and bring a big sloppy plate of nachos § LOVELY
GIRL FOLLOWER: hey.. i noticed you posted 3 barbed remarks about game stop in a
row.. is everything ok? ME: NO, everything is NOT ok, § Hrm. This is trou-
bling. *loads another nude woman* This absolutely will not do. *loads pictures
of Modern Architecture* Ah, now this is good § girls will be like "i cant go
out tonight! i have a pimple" and then they will get a face tattoo of Baloo
from thre jungle book § ready to help all cops . http://t.co/MH6vcCqH5h § the
trolls: please Followback, and also Yolo me: HUh?? Shit for brians? Whuuuaa??
Egads. Homina Homina. Sweet Baby Crap. You're a fool § (passes a man in a
hardhat toiling over a roadside utility cabinet in 100 degree weather in my
black convertible) Nice Fedora Dip Shit § i was once known on youtube as Epic
"PLease stop recording me" Man., now im top influencer Gary Faves, making $500 a
year posting from home § hakuna mycoffee. .. #Understandable http://t.co/
OR15m3zi50 § i give my guinie pigs "HEROIN" it CALMS them DOWN § *sees
another discarded poland spring bottle on the side of the road filled with piss*
haha. hell yes § #NationalOreoDay i spit on oreo § 4.2 TB of VR compatible
slo-mo footage featuring a man with no teeth shooting a bra using a dsr
precision sniper rifle and pistol wipping it § iwant to be pummeled with carpet
beaters by eastern european grandmas and make big awful clouds of dust § dead
wrong buddy § attn: fucked up t-shirts incorporated-- get me a tweety bird with
devil horns saying "I refuse to pay for a car wash" § theres lots of normal
people on the little black list of pedophiles too. i think its fine to say u
want your dick sucked by a computer #spon § trying desperately to come up with
a name for my new cajun styled recipe that isnt racist and just fucking up
constantly in the worst ways § @Budweiser Fuck you smart alac § EMAIL CAMPAIGN
TO MAKE THE BOARD OF HEALTH STOP CLASSIFYING MY GIRL FRIEND AS "POISONOUS" §
covers up apartment's only window with a "Keep Calm And Enjoy The Posts" sign
yes!! mother fucking yes !! this shit is Perfect! god DAMN!! § ill be hiding
under the floorboards and snorting herbs for stress relief energy until i am
ready to face my guinea pigs again § children should learn Gambling basically
asap aand fix the economy by winning big § rubbinb hand sanitizer all over my
loud mouthed pet birds § big news gang. another A++ app from the theranos
company to help me keep track of all my silver ware. let me just say. Wow § ME:
id like to use my AAdvantage rewardsPoints, American Airlines: Im ready to
pull the trigger. Go on. Drive the knife deeper into my heart § ive decided
that it is Anti-Jobs, to demonetize the youtube guy who went to Mecca and flung
angrybird plushies at the cube or whatever § enjoying some fairly darkweb shit
https://t.co/tG9FkVREoK § Pull up a chair kiddies, its Thread time.
Let's get to the point. I messed up. I said that the super bowl is a game show,
when it cle(1/66) § "Much talk about blocking the Suez Canal, when people
should be concerned about blocking my most virulent Trolls." - The Ethical
Masturbator § reading my revolting tweets to a focus group for several hours
and escaping on a sled pulled by rats when it is time to pay each of them $25 §
never show me him § thisi s a no take zone § I SUBMERGE MYSELF INTO THE CORE
MIND AND CRACK MYSELF INTO THE BIT-WEB, MERGING MY CONSCIOUSNESS WITH ALL 18
EPISODES OF THE GASTINEAU GIRLS § waiting for the ma mas out there to put all
the little trolls to bed so i can post controversial material without repercus-
sion § unverified accounts are fucking disgusting. they often contain base, lewd
"humor", and i have mini-strokes whenever one of them retweets me § screaming

on the phone with J. dorsey about how Fucked I am if guys with shitty beards keep saying my posts "Have lost their Edge" § http://t.co/ht1ueoTuNI what hte fuck are you doing § got all these tabs open like "Girl poison husband rate" and "Poisoned husband body count" researching if i should want to have a wife or not § NETWORKING IN HOME MARKETS SUCCESS SEMINAR HOSTED BY JAMES BOND HIMSELF? OH YEAH. IM IN. BUT IM GOING TO NEED YOU TO DRIVE ME THERE § he was MOCKED in high school for being a Senator's son . Now he has made over $10,000,00 selling fake service animal vests to local nit wits § would like to issue a correction ,regarding my comments of Japanese toilets. they do spray water on your ass, but they do not suck you off . § @CHANNAKAJIMA im respectful of him § writing fan mail to the police, suggesting some new laws that i think would be good § my favorite tv show characters are "The good guys". My least favorite characters are "The villains" § driving your car through my fence and bbreaking all my potted plants with a hammer and kidnapping my dog is little dick energy § i have a rare condition which is commonly known a s "pig ear", and if I was born in the 1950s i would have been euthanized #Blessed § vin diesel as the Tooth Fairy??? Now I've seen every thing. § ijust had one Hell of a steak dinner. i wont post specifics regarding the dinner due to trolls but i would like to get this viral please., § i would watch a movie of a james bond kind of guy doing spy shit and rolling around on the floor and striking gun poses and it's set in hell § please respect the sanctity of UFO chat § im the good man whorespects his followers, i respect the artistriy of tweeting and i respect my girl followers also. nuff said dip shit § It is simply for your foolish claim that the economys doing poorly, right after they increased the Mega Millions Jackpot, that I am Smiling. § just remember what it is we're all fighting fo.r... http://t.co/ucS2wcLgje § *¥¥¥_,,- MaGnUm DiApEr -,,_¥¥¥* § ive mastered every hypothetical social situation by reading posts on here and am now ready to talk to my step mom with out flipping out, § In 1998 I Encountered What I Blieved 2 Be A Malicious Presence.I Poped My Tony Hawk Dsk In2 My PSX And Let Loose With Da Best Moves. It died § me and my roving band of gorgeous cop punchers suffer the indignity of detecting the scent of piss. we pause and attempt to locate the source § i can confirm that Somali pirates have intercepted my shipment of 20,000 glossy 8x10 headshots and are using them for vile purposes § "i hope they serve dumpsters in hell " me, eviscerating a dumpster diver verballym, before closing the dumpster lid on top of him § im the Rembrandt of naked yoshies § im having my BALLS CUT OFF!!! just for liking cambridge analytica § that guy who makes all the fluuu comics must have a milion dollars by now, mean while i live in a gutted bureau § DUMBASS: SHut the fuck up THE WISE MAN: No you shut the fuck up § piss #ad § wfie chasing me with rolling pin because i changed my display name to "black Wolf" and put the Poly flag in there § nobody gets my humor . Guess Im due for an ass kicking. I deserve shit § -go about my day seeking energy in my life as a Bieng of intelligence -if your sperm count is complete dog shit, i will not even talk to you § heaping helpings of gamer Gratitude going out to the boys who mailed my streamwife a glorious synthetic Hymen via Twitch Prime Pro § becoming a cop so I can access the police computer and scrutinize the Walmart receipts of my rivals digimon Otis and warez_lad § the toilet feeler ruins another public restroom with his grubby hands § Seems to me today would be an excellent day to browse some of my Legacy Posts, from the Heirloom Collection, and throw them a retweet or two § i will not let anyone touch my pitbuls unless they are wearing a collared shirt § another fucked up thing that women will do to all good men and boys is steal their last names, poSsibly to leverage their own failing brands § banne d from the Laugh Factory after getting on stage and forgetting if husbands like the toilet seat up or down § the beer face § geting a wife https://t.co/wRu22q64XQ § get a life. go fuck y ourself. i have a life idiot. help § you wanna waste my time? you wanna piss me up? you want to pull my nuts?

my balls? You want to-huh? Whats that? You wanna slut my ass around § this is a trick question § in 2017 i will make a concerted effort to become a ringling brother. § it truly does seems that most of people would put more trust into Gay lord focker, than Our lord father § oculus allows you to smoke wii remote like a cigar and blow heaps of smoke in celebs faces § retiring into the portable dog kennel i live in and shutting the tiny gate to keep the shit heads out § about 85% of the people online are just absolute criminals and i can get dominated by them perfectly from the convenience of my shitty modem § sometimes ant clever than human http://t.co/BFimIW4r § elvis never fucked any of his fans . thats why he was "The king" § if i had a million bucks i would b uy a Pregnant sears mannequin § Your aocunt was better when you shut the fuck up you mother fucker § obana. i know you're reading this. where's benhgazi. what did you do with the benghazi man. release the benghazi gems. #YouJustPulledAnObama § someone please get me in touch with the little boy who died & went to heaven. i want to astral project him into my ex-wifes castle for intel § wordle is making the damn world STUOID § "dinner portions.. for lunch? Absolutely. Absolutely." -TheTexMexBoy § who ever told me that kim dot com's secret doge coin stash was bureid under the roof of my house is an idiot. i just dug a hole to. my house § i have never lived down the moment i pulled my pants down in the locker room and all the gym boys noticed that my dick was wearing glasses § what can i rub on my body to make my musk more ethnic § i would not discount pua techniqes just b/c girls are wise to them now. for instance,w. a few modifications i can use them to rear pit bulls § - Always retweet promoted tweets. - Always surrender your username and password to Girls - Always Wait 1hr before replying a Verified Acct. § funny you should ask. im actually having a lot of problems getting it to do just that. its like you got to join nasa to learn how § you gotta realize if youre a roach or any kind of bug its already game over for your ass. you look like a little pice of poop walking around § the time has come for verifed mark § thats a good vehicle to be trapped in for eternity i think § @dril my reasoning behind this content is that theres a large version of the mask and a tiny version of him as well. something for everybody § *hangs political cartoon of obama eating The Jobs with a fork and knife up on the office billboard* you see that? ?? hes esating the jobs. § nobodys talking about how much jacking off is such Einstein shit. who comes up with this stuff????? § YO *points to spinal cord on brain diagram* THATS THE BRAIN;S DICK § now, all trhis talk in the media about me not wiping my ass; i dont know where all this is coming from. if any thing, i wipe my ass too much § using genius Journalism to crush my enemies . . . § thank ytou for the Fav § get me some of that fuckin Travolta denim § "...most of the human race killed off, because it is unworthy, it is unworthy of the gift of life." - someone who hasn't killed himself yet § shut up!! shut the Fuck up!! https://t.co/tVsepHMp-JB § I WILL REGRESS INTO PRIMAL FORM AND SHUN MY LOVED ONES IN ORDER TO POWER UP MY CONTENT !! I WILL GET RE-BLOGS AT ANY COST !! AT ANY COST !! § i rescind my 2009 tweet "bat man fucks joker", as i now understand, through the wisdom of age, that bat man adheres to a noble moral code § blesssed to have over 200 mannequins propped up around my house in vulgar positions, and the accompanying "Love my manny`s" bumper sticker § you must know the nickelodeon program "wild N crazy kids" primed our nations youth to reject thr scientific method & all fact-based evidence § While your were busy all discussing the black celebrity's ass, i just constructed an authentic Christian abacus using fine tumbled stones § for all you twitter birds out there.. a fun idea ive been throwin around: lets make the front page to "WILD WEST" theme..Huh! only on Friday § mournful day fpr comedy fans, upon news that the wife character on "Kevin Can Wait" will be beheaded with a sword between seasons 1 and 2 § for the second time in november iit is now international mens day. Wow § i like it. thank you http://t.co/ulzjhHpfuL § Politic's is back baby. It's good again. Awoouu (wolf

Howl) § iwant to outfit the scope on my sniper rifle with net flicks § im invent- ing a new kind of bird seed out of sand and waste § bring me your dead pet and i will make a sword out of it for $39 § THE BIG MONEY MAKERS BET ON ISIS EVERY TIME § nope i died § album (120 pics) ben stein kissing wife § rat man got money from nsa https://t.co/Hqj1wfLuhw § at around 36:29 in the steve harvey fleshlight vid you can see a single tear rolling down his cheek, crying for the lost souls watching him § ive done so much personal growth that its to the point where if you dont follow my posts youre fucking stupid § "I believe the Egyptian people have no reason to replace their rightly instated leader with some sort of primitive pyramid god." DigimonOtis § i'll just call every opinion i don't like a "Circle Jerk". i'll dominate everyone § " Seems to me in this country, we eat Fake food, meet Fake people, buy Fake clothes... and have Real problems. "- Winston churchhill § lunch paraphernalia spilling out of the footwell of my car as i pull up to my old high school to steal footballs § #ConfusingThingsGirlsDo show virtually no interest in The Bible Code § @Wegmans "Authorities continue searching for clues after a beheading took place at a Wegmans food market" This is absolutely disgusting. § excuse me? did you just call me a " buff dude "?? The proper term is "Muscleman" , you piece of shit § yes thats what i meant. thank you § people will call you Gay just for wanting to win the lottery . yeah well straight people like to win the lottery too bitch § im not changing it until nicholson's lawyers force me to § ATHLETE: THERE IS NO HOCKEY WITHOUT "PUCK" ATHELETE: THERE IS NO FOOTBALL WITHOUT "BALL" WISEMAN(SMILING):THERE IS NO WISDOM WITHOUT "BRAIN" § two simple words that will save our shitty, fucked up country from job loss, restore our dominance over china and end taxes: "cyber pinball" § establishment cocksuckers wiping their a$$es every time they shit, while the windbag toilet paper lobbyist crooks roll around in blood money § basicly a sniper rifle that can switch gears and turn into a baseball bat if the situaiton demands it. an armymans ultimate tool § https://t.co/7yt904Vpfx § (carrrying a huge polkadot- ted bindle, looking like a dumb ass , shoes completely untied) Mother.. Father... Im leaving home to join the cops § losing my cheez it sponsoriship for posting a picture of a sword piercing a $1 bill § as a youth, the boys would laugh at my large ears & call me "The Ears Bastard". but today, I have every epsIode of Sliders at my fingertips. § listening to a man on the train tell me about how a cardboard toilet paper tube feels 100% like a pussy if you run it under the sink first § in talks with twitter execs to make my account unblockable, and also Worse § and today's Golden Toilet award goes to the cast of Weekend at Bernie's 1 & 2 ofr disobeying the noble qur'an. § dont be gross on here § there should be ICU beds only for geniusses and if your iq is less than 120 they eject you from the window at fucking 200mph § absolutely do not sleep on my breakout role in "Gods Not Dead 3: God Dies" as the Soy Faced money changer § oh sorry. "TheJRPGMotherFucker666" is my old user handle. from when I was a foolish child. my new one is "CockNBallsCummerShitheadShithead8" § beautiful e3 conference from the Police. THreatened to trap all crooks. Spinning handcuffs around. Elaborate boot play. No games to announce § today. i will stay home and sharpen my balls. i will Hone My Balls § you got a paypal???? § youtube.com sends albanian govnt. $70 for dancing dog video. albania best country. fuck all othter dancing dog video #ubertwitter § rodent website § real_damn_fairly_misanthropic_red_m_and_m § https://t.co/EGtfVEAN7K § well it goes to show you that the trolls will gladly stoop so low as to shit upon the #classiccombo of spaghetti& meatballs we all hold dear § i want to take one of those cruises where people shit right there on the boat but apparently they only happen randomly as a surpris,e § seems like more and more, every young professional should have at all times, a bag to keep papers in § i can confirm israeli android os WILL use a gui based on art assets from dream- works The Croods & that this is exciting news for Crood likers § pigmail will replace email in 2010 § i just talked to all of my celeb friends on this site and they told me that the blue checkmark is good to have. personally, i believe them., § ouh yes!! THe boys have spoken, and they want more! More jokes about the ape! My one man show , entitled " ot-So-Great Ape" will explore th § if you 'accidentally' spill an entire 7-11 big gulp on a sears mannequin they will throw it out and you can go have sex with it in the trasg § level 55 arcane stevia eater § does anyone else think that @DigimonOtis has been going downhill lately.? wouldnt be surprised if he sold his account to some reddit guy. § well im glad theyve downgraded me to "basically" a nazi instead of "literally" a nazi § Wife says i should shit in the yard until the toilets fixed. Itll be ok if i cover myself in a tarp. But i want to shit in the broken toilet § if i ever got face to face with the "Affluenza teen" on my server im thinking itd go a little something like this (plays guitar really good) § truthfully, i do believe that, now thatm the gas prices are low, i think that theres going to be a lot less BULL S#!T on the commute !! § if u know what the word "consoles" means. son , you might be a Gamer § being a dumb ass is bad enough, but being a dumb ass, in 2020??? You fucked up big time § i shall not be attending boys night, as i have injured myself while attempting to butterfly an auntie annes pretzel stick . § one thumb up. good § " Is it just me, or is SQUID GAME getting to be a little too close, to real life? " -- © COPY RIGHT 2022 @Dril -- "That's money in the bank" § just kicked a hole through my mirror because all the girls on my time line are saying they want to fuck Wally Gator now § http://i.imgur.com/cVoFs.jpg § yo Aesop... these fuckin "fables" of yours? Not up to snuff. Some weak fables over here. Go back to writing college. #TheThursdayNiteRant § I dont appreciate bieng called "The Waterbed Bitch" just because I own a waterbed and post pictures of it daily § @SheriffClarke i am trying my best to appease the appropriate individuals so that i may become a police officer. please do not mess this up for me, cloud. § http://www.youtube.com/genesislistener The Genesis Listener § top me off, beer man. here's to bottoms up **gets kicked out of the fucking establishment for putting my dirty coat on the bar* § me and DigimonOtis suppot the government of Egypt, and detest the ape like protesters and their Campaign Of Fear. #jan25 § helping my dog https://t.co/gPz0hFbm6k § Clipart Pig Angel In Prayer - Royalty Free Vector Illustration § man encased in lethal amounts of body oil and skin bronzer preserved for thousands of year.s.. beautiful § drawing that big boy hair.. therapeutic https://t.co/QxpV7omI6n § had to block the guy posting him self smoking a pocket pussy under all my posts. good night nasty mother fucker § sylvestetr the cat: sufferin succotash! Terry Schiavo was murdered § absolute bastard . of all the fingers you couldve given me, it had to be the middle one § im going to watch homer simpson sing the beer song on you tube. does anyone care to join me § hey whos this guy going around telling all of our troops about "eskimo pussy" § im far too angry to piss anything, let alon e my trademark diaper. § remembering the anguiham the girls had caused me when they said it was good to have "Dadbod" § peoplr would rather see macDonald's, than macbeth. and that's why all of this is going on § (hearing the first recorded sound from 1860, a pivotal technological milestone) This guy sounds like shit. Mostly his voice sounds like shit § Fuck #TheThursdayNiteRant and the bruise it has left upon my legacy. Fuck contracts and being tricked into signing them. Fuck Ruby Tuesdays. § listening to the updated version of the "baby its cold outside" song where the guy's trying to convince the woman to leave so he can jack off § shut the fuck uip, coward. "beavis day" is not a real holiday. i am going to insanely wreck you for posting to me, about the false holiday. § i sincerely hope all of you remembered to powder your keyboards and mice to prevent Hand damage during your normal 16 hr browsing sessions § when a drama liker tries to talk to me about Whatever bull shit and i will just simply say "Uh!" #insipid § all t he babes from the old movies will be in it. the dad from the third one will be in it. austin 4.0. do i make you oscar baby § new twitter feature allows you to disregard mny posts, please click the trash can next to my name to prevent me from ruining your home page § me_steppin_on_a_pair_of_cowboy_boots_while_wearing_cowboy_boots.flv #Woof § @the_ironsheik hawaii § diapers are not for babies § thank you normand https://t.co/5kv6RlVQz5 § #AnimalTVShows pig fucker § worrying a lot about our geopolitical foes recording& transcribing our military comms and its just 900 pages of "Permission To Jack Off Sir" § this is the Essence https://t.co/9fbLYVAhgm § my dick is in the news agian. and Ouh, whats this?? The damn gas prices are sky rocketing while everyones distracted. Trite. § "all hail the PrankMAster, the King of Cranks", scrawled onto the wall next to my blue corpse and a rescue inhaler filled with tabasco sauce § "in year 3000 every chair in the house will become a toilet"- ben franklin § @TruthPointDWR unfollow me § in 2020 police technology will allow criminals to choose between "hot jail" and "cold jail" § Good of my life https://t.co/9xpZPFf8Fm § if this is true you need to go directly to police . § COP: weve detected unusual amounts of cum being flushed down the toilet at your house. please stop ME: Thats not mine. Its uh,. my dogs cum § @ BarryGoldman15 im so sorry i well do better § no you listen to me, Fucker, i need "Steppenwolf" carved into THE BLADE, not the handle-- please hold my father is crying § my life flashes before my eyes and its mostly just me sitting on the toilet. i enter survival mode and begin instinctively wiping my ass § got one of th ose steering wheels you control with your mouth so i can dual wield on the road. top secret technology for friends of police, § #nationa-l0reoday i will henceforth either "Fuck" or "Spit on" all the " ational whatever day" hashtags that the NSA pays twitter to promote § @DrOz nevermind. ive made the decision to amputate my legs, i found a man on angie's list. thanks any way. § trying to take my barbell into the mens room ansd failing to get it through the doorway like a dog with a large stick § 100 years ago i looked at the first ever drawing of mickey mouse and i said out loud that that shit was going to make $99,000,000,000,000,000 § please dont make whimsy of the popes ass while I am on-feed. ive more inportant things to do than indulge myself in hearsay of the popes ass § beer is soda on crack - @ DRIL § #HipHop-StarWars please. imn begging you. all girls on this hashtag please send HD pictures of your teeth& gums. please god just give me this § every movie ever made is esxactly the same movie as the other movies, and they all deserve 2 stars from roger ebert § was a tad dismayed to find a Rat Brain in my favorite KFC Snacker Meal, B ut the friendly cashier assured me it was merely Intestinal Matter § just meeting up with one of my real life friends; pictured here. http://t.co/JgYf0QQIAN § receieved "DOG`s CURSE"... "The Poster Will Transform Into A Dog Unless Ten Beautiful Women Apologize To Him" It'll never happen! Im Fucked! § lesbian Wireless § scenario: the duishwasher mouth starts up in some dumb ass baby voice. "GIMME SUM JET DRY!!" i unload my .480 ruger into it without Emotion, § My face when, some one tries to tell me that I am not the inventor, and sole proprietor , of "The Ass Meme" https://t.co/Sc31yHOYeZ § badboy Michael Jackson Rip 1958-2009 "Deth" http://tinyurl.com/l7atle #dead #iranelection #michaeljackson § none of my pets are breathing properly . Am i the asshole (AITA) § You wanna see me throw up? You wanna watch me barf as a joke? Too bad! I will no longer make myself throw up as a joke! No more! Never again § ???: The hole at the bottom of the toilet is the toilets ass hole replyguy34: Thats fine replyguy29: Babababababa replyguy93: This, actually § Mme § realized at 4am that it's morally justifiable for me to "CatCall" women because my followers cat call me in posts. in the replies constantly § log off., you piss covered reptiles, youre turning good bandwidth into shit § thank u my friend § OOUUHH youd love for me to give my self a kidney stone on purpose , wouldn't you!! you dirty mother fuckers Oouuhhhh!! § i accept all your apolo-gies you sad mother fuckers. YOu all have a lot of work to do when it comes to critiquing my meme style. Foul animals § cant wait to dip a paint roller in my preferred brand of paint and suck it like a big yeti dick § "always have at least 2 drew Carey anecdotes" § This channel is dedicated the the beautiful smoking girls of Japan. These videos aim to capture the style and elegance of the Japanese girls § spending my weekend retooling a joke about fucking the tiny hole in the bathroom sink that prevents the water level from increasing toom uch § http://i.imgur.com/4KRjB.jpg § what if Jar head met Dunkirk § Q: mr bond this is your most fucked mission yet. you must obtain the Paedophile's Stone BOND: Ah, like old times?   Q: Like old times mr bond § internal dialogue of tech journos watching Asimo dance around "Wow id love to break its legs" "Lets see it withstand the burden of the Cross § pumped my home FULL of oxygenated perfluorocarbon so i can swim N breahte; forgot to vacuum up pet hair & crumbs beforehand ---- Chest Pains § if satan tries to put a microchip in my gun i will shoot him § my slack friends all have jobs oppressing my discord friends § whilst you were visiting grandma in the hospital i was grinding for BAG !! § spending my honey moon in the bathroom, watching video of chef gorddon ramsey saying "Ah Fuck Me" after being served a shitty looking onion § my great-grandfather died protecting his farm from a pack of coyotes. i died from overexerting myself in a money booth at blizzcon § the gaming challenge: load up your video game of choice and play it until you reach the credits sequence. the gaming challenge § digmon otis once mistook a beached toilet for a dolphin egg § droitos should make hamburgers § if cops can see this account already: im sorry for all my posts ,t force me to lick your boots CLEAN sir, im a bastard who needs punishment § a crass message got on here some how and im trying to debug it. in the meantime please check out https://t.co/fUq3h548ge § THATS IT!!!!!! I HAVE HAD IT UP TO HERE WITH THIS GUYS SHIT https://t.co/HBhLn4HuHp § "Please. The time has come for you to Normalize the repulsive and despicable Digimon Otis." No. I will not normalize that fool ,or his sins. § i feell like im being unfairly targeted during this paintball match just because im the only one wearing a tuxedo § rats dont have pussys § #AmexAlicia prray for my aids uncle § CHEF: mon signor!! leaving the tails on the shrimp is good! it is tre bien ME: Im going to nuke you with live ammo. Im the guy from the crow § i consider protected, locked accounts, to be the most Powerful accounts... for it is they who have Blocked the entire world § AS A TRANSHUMAN, I DON'T WEAR SHIRTS BECAUS**DRives diamond-studded PT Cruiser directly into great pacific garbage patch; never seen again* § contents of kim dotcom's panic room: imported mtn dew (glass bottle, no corn syrup), " o copz allowed" sign (affixed to door), blooper dvds § @LAYS can I vote for the flavor that makes me feel like a depressed, nauseous slug after I eat a whole bag of it?? or is that all of them § thats not rap § im officially the guy who has held out the longest without being "Ready to laugh again" since 9/11 and what do i get in return? ASS-FUCKED.. § #WorldwideHandsomeDay looking dumb as a dog in my piss-yellow tuxedo whilst i spend hundres of dollars on international phone calls § all im asking is for you dumb mother fuckers to click on 1 link in your entire life § (plays some Tchaikovsky records at the highest possible volume) ah it sucks ass. but my IQ is increasing so much § after careful reflection in this era , ive decided that i no longer support wearing the pants known as "jeans", and i will eradicate them § wassup. yoda here. froum "Starwars". i m here to rep pro-ana. remember to eat paper instead of food. may the force be with u . thank you § i;m now getting surgery to completely become a Brand. all bothersome human elements (ability to get mad, go to toilet, etc) will be, removed § all new simposns this week. theyre finally gonna tackle Tim Allen. with guest star tim allen. this ones tv 14 so watch out § @rwang0 @AdobeSummit Once again i have been blocked for starting the dialouge . § might do a post of "macklemore" soon. § Jjust processed every news story on CNN as logically as humanly possible & had a strategic stroke that murdered the bias center of my brain §

post "I love the mcdonalds Five for Five plan" if you support Don. post "Mcdonalds five for five is Bumpin" if you support Hillary J Clinton § please dont flood this information channel with sports info § next year ill try harder to be the guy who posts shit like "Fucking 2022 Poop Hell" every time a celeb perishes in a small aircraft disaster § im going to start a multimedia network for those who enjoy smacking dingers in the game of base ball and also marry baseball § Sorry "DrunkDriver1488", your eHarmony profile has been rejected § Nobody Checks My Son For Head Lice With Out Getting Past My Police Issue Hollow Point Smith & Wesson Which Gives Everyone It Shoots Leukemia § Remove Tongue From Your Mouth Using Ancient Weird Ass Factoid That A Mom Did § forced to remove my famous "DANGER: MAY CONTAIN LETHAL LEVELS OF SARCASM !!" sign from the front door of the poolside shed that i live in § stop giving $ to these so-called "gyms". realize that u can attain God's Body by finding hot cars and sitting in them til the owner arrives § huge tub of au jus sauce with bottles of beer floating around in it is lowered into the room before the big game. " ow that's, a power play" § Realizing the food at KFC sucks ass for the 4th or 5th time in my life , and making myself calm by looking up famous quotes about "Chaos" § @JimCarrey im the pro-neurotoxin, anti-vaccine, son of a bitch cop!!! i love rolling around in disease and spreading it to dumbass civilians § "Phew! Its like a sauna in here!" - the most hilarious guy in the sauna § content 2 http://t.co/hST5OWjymR § FOX Broadcasting calls every artist, writer, lawyer & executive together to conclusively decide which color the Simpsons' nipples should be § JSUTIN BIEBER COVERED IN TURDS AND PISS AT THE JUGGALO GATHERING FESTIVAL-- WOULD NOT ALLOW HIM TO PERFORM-- OH THIS IS HORIBLE #HELP § i went to arizona accompanied by two desert goblins and smoked spirit leaf out of a human stomach § oh every day i m getting Mail like, "It drives me Nuts! You are a fucked bitch, your posts stink my ass... But youre not wrong." and smiling § #WalgreensLatino please stop posting my username § they added a new type of corn row to miitopia -- heres 10 reasons why thats good and 8 reasons its bad § A dog with five tattoos has appeared online § im going to fuck up antarctica with hundreds of throwing knives § -windows covered in trash bags -arbitrarily sorting the contents of my snack Pack -pumping racist apps into my nokia at Lightspeed -frowning § Flying to Dubai, UAE, to jack off in a hotel room. § sick of bieng fucking shrieked at in DMs just because im one of the few left who thinks girls should not breastfeed while operating aircraft § might post a pic of my fist clenching a huge chunk of my own hair i pulled out saying "You did this !!" over and over during peak girl hours § (sending image of delicious meal i stole from a group dm to a girl) yeah i ate this § time to look at the "Moments Tab". i lay down in the bath tub and a guy smears shit all over my chest with his ass while using a taser on me § where can i get one of those giant inflatable rats that construction workers keep putting up on the side of the road. i need it for my grave § workshopping some atrocious new kfc slogans "My oh my, The taste of it" "Kfc its a boys thing kfc" "aah!! Munch" "Help me get to kfc" "Hubba § Seth i mean. § #WENDYSHOAX § Chheer's, and thank you, and good luck § if i saw someon e on the street wearing a dunce cap, i would challenge him to my famous Three Trials of wisdom, and soundly defeat him § so our team gets to hte benchmark and its just a nude man on a dirty mattress. whoever registered this should be ashamed #geocachingmishaps § CANT ATTEND GRANDMAS FUNERAL SHIRTLESS??? WISH I WAS IN THAT CASKEt § "clothes" are a construct you fucking dolt. as well as flintsonte chewable vitamins is a construct, and grandmas house is a construct, prick § I TAKE BACK EVERY KIND THING I'VE SAID ABOUT THE GIRLS ON HERE ! SHALLOW AND CRUEL ! HEART LESS DEVILS ! MANIPULATING MY POSTS & TRICKING ME § i shou;ld be allowed on the roof of any building § STICKS WET HAND INTO HUGE GNC PROTEIN POWDER BOTTLE AND LICKS IT CLEAN, TRIES TO CLIMB ONTO DISPLAY MATTRESS AT SEARS, APPREHENDED BY CRAIG § apparel, http://t.co/eqWudCeNX1 § i bet i could knock a grammy statue over with

my piss #grammys § i want to fuck a sheet of paper § Drink my god Damn piss.
Drink my my god Damn piss. Drink my piss mother fucvker. Drink my fucking god
damned piss off § just because i havent been seen in public for 7 years is no
excuse not to wear a suit and tie before sitting down and eliminating trolls §
might peruse the dumpsters behind some failed sub way restaurants & take home
some huge pictures of bread/ tomatoes to hang up on my walls § congressman
introduces "Young Folks Should Call Grandpa More Often" bill, farts, dies, is
replaced by his 70 year old son § do speak to me about the economy, Cuisine
trends, and middle east things. dont speak to me abou joe dirts balls, and
killing me. § #quotethatmovie "it's people. soylent people is made out of
people" § i habve been banned from over 200 dating services for being upfront
and honest about my rotten, barbed dick § imagining a real dumb lump of shit
guy, like 55 years old, reading some article aobut jada pinkett smith in his
squalid office and smiling § grandmom kicked me out of the house because she
caught me waterboarding an extremely small man § https://t.co/DgylHE2S thank
you @toiletmaterial do not vote until you have seen this twitter background §
as sure as i am a VETERAN`S SON , i will never move over and let an emergency
vehicle pass me , no matter how loud it is § i would never photo shop anything,
espiecally when it comes to damn fucked up things like racism. this is a
serious account § thje opening riff of "Life In The Fast Lane" repeats over and
over forever while me and the boys shoot at a septic tank with airsoft rifles §
haters are my God § alrigt jack asses. before you "Go In" on me, heres a quick
recap of the jokes i invented: - Dogs (Anything mentioning them) - The Weed
Fairy § wait i fucked that up. its suppose to be "good cheers to my friends,
and this Year - best luck and thank you" and then i raise my botle § special
message to the wrestler who got himself on mars and knocked the curiosity robot
over--- im going to turn you into Bugs § once inside the Visitor base i stood
before their marvelous spacecraft and covered it with my piss. my god. my god.
my god #VANGUARDSOF2012 § When they obtain the pic it's game over. They can
black mail you into saying the N-Word. They can print it out and suck on it
like a dildo. § #WhyGunsAreBetterThanLiberals THE 63RD SEAL MUST CONSUME THE
SHADE OF BLOODFALL IN COMPLIANCE WITH THE NIGHT COMMAND, ANDMICHAL MOORE IS FAT
§ remember to always have samples of urine, shit, semen and blood attached to
your belt to avoid wasting the doctor';s time if you get sick § at the advice
of my doctor, ive decided to piss, but only in small amounts out of respect for
the #NoPiss challenge. i will limit my piss. § oop, autocorrect got me. what i
meant to say was "i cant wait to eat shit right out of the sewer and suck some
outrageously gay clown dicks" § theme song to Cheers makes every animal in my
house howl untikl i fucking lose it and hurl all their cages across th room
into an awful pile § We Live IN A Country Where Football Players Are Given
Helmets For Free But I Have To Buy A Helmet At The Store Because Im A Regular
Person . § -the drew carey show forums harbor a subforum named "Hell" -users
are sent there when they absolutely fuck up while talking about drew carey §
god promised me in a dream that if joe biden & kamala harris get married they
will adopt me as their boy. I watch them on the news every day § Discussing
Reality Intelligently Life § need to gain. concerned of my big boy status.
dream of becoming Army Strong by the age of 35. rip me open another bag of tiny
marshmellows § #OpenCarryGamestop http://t.co/FBgdCAunvG § having $100 is
Millionaire shit § " $600 is bad" Yeah listen up nomb nuts if 600 is so bad
then why dont you sl;ap a stamp on it and deliver it straight up your Ass. §
posing next to a jeep and handing out business cards at the high school i
graduated from 8 years ago, explicitly stating i do NOT followback § @Lowes i
am this close to killing the mother fucker who keeps coming on my account and
posting diaper things and saying im the one in them § hm? U want me to stop
posting about the latest deals at Boscovs? well i wish bugs would stop biting
my dick..but " PAL IT AINT HAPPENEN' ! " § looks fine to me s.t.f.u. § *produces

a tiny book from coat pocket which lists every breed of dog that is legal to eat* § hey all . just learned about this new shit here, i think you will like it if you enjoy using the computer https://t.co/BWNiaAEbpL § I politely requested the post to be taken down. It is still up ass of 2/24/18. It is only fair that the check mark be transferred to my page § out of the trillion girls who follow me i only want to marry about 8 of you. do better § (in highly rational and cool voice) i have the higher follower count than them. i wiont let them undermine me § suddenly getting very upset imagining all the great lottery winners of history gathering around & laughing at me for picking dogshit numbers § I hate the really small salt shakers and long for the times when we owould be inclined to more often use the big salt shakers at restaurants § 8 Words We Must Never Say In Front Of Father (Number 6 Will Make You Shit) § U cant wear a sword. A sword is not clothes. Yes, A SHeathe, is clothes. The sword goes in the sheath, but that doesnt make it clothes bitch § i want to put on a really ugly shirt but i can't because of trolls. AAAGH **unscrews lightbulb from lamp, throws it into toilet, perfect aim § if you like this shit down load my incredible one time offer the only app that lets you spin the wheel of pussy for free no question asked § i know of two types of people,»people who know bianry, and people who want to morph into a piece of dog shit and get stepped on by a hot lady § mate...ya got a hole in your head § #youbeblownwhen you run into some five figure intern in the executive washroom § nothing give s me more power in this life than blocking a guy who asks me nicely in the dms to unblock him or one of his rat friends § U cant even get a good "Shoe Shine" anymore--the guy just keeps trying to put his mouth on my dick. Is this a Thing now. Is this a Problem § you can put truck nuts on other things besides trucks idiot § the most disgusting accounts on here are making claims like, "Fred Flintstone is a pimp" , with zero evidence § limiting the thursday nite rant to one day of the week ... its just not good for gthe brand § received some very important secret documents regarding the Masturbators. not only do they enjoy touching their dicks, they also worship sex § keelhaul my dick § @DigimonOtis we rehearsed this for 7 hours yesterday. you cannot do this. § everyone screaming at me cus i accidentally made tge dog deaf by yelling memes at it. if the meteor kills us all i wont give a Fuckin Shit ! § me and thr boys taking massive amounts of heroin behind macaroni grill saying shit like "Uh yeah That just happened " every time we shoot up § just found out im considered the "Bitch" of Ashley HomeStore and the employees there are instructed " ot to hear my demands" § Kicking the shit out of the back board on my computer desk because" Dabbing" is bull shit § @DeptofDefense The next AIDS you guys manufacture & distribute should target people who listen to Justin Bieber! Yuck! #JustForLaughs #Gags § geting a bunch of reptile habitat sun lamps to beam some much needed vitamin d into my fucking obese skull while i do the rounds on sites § studies show that 5% of all the food that content creators consume is waiter spit § that woul,d be the exact opposite of interesting § james bond the good fellas and god father team up to shoot the most ufos you have everf fucking seen § the grenades man doesn't believe in girlfriends § I AM NOT AFRIAD TO USE THE WORDS "FU*K" AND "S*HT" WHEN DEALING WITH SNAKE OIL SALESMEN ON THE PHONE § changing my bio to " obody Helps Me" , to punish society § nothing will stop me § "being nude helps me ponder Life" - the wise nude #TheWiseNude § theyre donating all the expired vaccines to some very thirsty dogs at the kennel and i think thats something nice for once § i would like to convert these gmail invites into human dollars please § issuing correction on a previous post of mine, regarding the terror group ISIL. you do not, under any circumstances, "gotta hand it to them" § another Twisted observation--Where the fuck does cinnamon come from. it just appears on food sometimes. Do people buy it at the store or what § if i get on here and say something like "Readers Digest Sucks Cock" do you think theyll give me a free subscription § piss hitting toilet sfx piss hitting urinal sfx only on spotify § ok. so apparently rap did exist in the 90s. and i apologize. all the other objectionable bullshit i post here is real, though § why dont you come to wheare i work and slap the dick out of my mouth bitch § in 2015 user @Dril chanegd the world when he deprived himself of using the toilet as part of the #NoPiss challenge. now, hes taking on Turds § %%%% a gigantic man is batting a ball of yarn around the floor of this @Maggianos little italy restaurant %%%% § https://t.co/O9h3XolzpW this short online exchange between Karl and his friend wayne hooter might just,. chane your life § Im told that it's wrong to think that Mickey mouse would have 1 million dollars if he was a real person. Im told my beliefs are trash § Im the guy who asked them to remove Sex from only fans!!! I thought It would be nice!!! I didnt know it woiuld make people mad!!! Im sorry!! § the banned version of "'lord of the flies" where the conch is replaced by a fat immobile pug dog § Rumours are having it that this next star wars is fixing to be the most twisted, for adults, and mentally ill one yet #EpisodeIX #EpisodeIX § Its impossible for me to respect someone who is wearing an arm cast. UYou look like a mummy from egypt. Remove it § An Unstoppable Legion Of Young Fortune 500 CyberHeteros § roving online gangs are promoting disrespect of brand leaders on this very platform #HonestyHour #Police § look at what youve done. you messed around and you turned the beetle bailey wiki into shit § ever y movie ever made before 1950s is named like "the Gal with the $100 Pussy" § i can't tell you how many serious UFO vids i've seen ruined by the slow zoom out and reveal of a man jacking it § sushi place i get my Specialty Rolls from apparently thinks its ok to just fill the takeout box with tempura crumbs. dirty & unprofessional § meme 's encompass all art forms you street rat § lot of stupid shit going on in my replys. must be FUCK MY ASS day on twitter... § You Won't Believe How Many Legs That Spiders Have § can almost hear the angels screaming as i plunge the dagger into my chest and abdicate my destiny as He Who Would Forge The Unwettable Denim § somewhere theres a group of geniuses debating whether Rugrats moved the diaper community forwards or backwards in some hotel's banquet room § the pope makes six figures easy. Fact § the thing i accidentally posted earlier about putting my used condoms in the dishwasher was a virus. my subsequent meltdown was also a virus § He thinks it's Cute to come into my mentions and lord his "Hollywood Elite" blood capital over me and my boys § starting wednesday off with a fun one . § getting my ass run over after trying to hijack a guy's riding mower and failing § coming up with some new racism slogans... "Racism: Never knew it could be this good" "Racism: Gotta geddit" "Racism: Now that's what's nice" § that's certainly a numnber § i will skewer the trolls at last by scanning a legal document whichc states that it is entirely permissible for me to weep openly at perkins § horny does'nt exist § i was better in the 90s before my account was bought by the actual ku klux klan & placed in a granite sphere surrounded by castrated pikemen § is mother teresa a saint " o she aint" § Waiiter, i have not received my Farm Fresh olives, and my steak is far too Unctuous. Please tell the chef to go back to 9 gag. § i will end your pain https://t.co/A8Kvy12R2c § if the pigs decimate my follower count tomorrow€"Know this. followers are just a number. devoid of meaning. and they can never take my Likes § i may be wrong, i may be stupid, i may have gotten my son murdered, but at least my clothes arent coverred in SHIT § i have squandered the last of my fathers good will by christening our new boat with the name of "S.S. Mind Of Mencia" § ask me anything u please, as long as its about my ambitious plan to build a castle in the Jungle for the apes to live in, called "Ape House" § ???? Dont Know why im catching shit for this. Most blinds are famously hard to see through. § its true. i selll my account to a less funny person every year just to rile people up § I am Donald "Penis" Trump, known & hated for my Inflammatory rhetoric, as well as my old mafia-style Racism. Looking forward to posting here § i think

your jaw should be knocked into the river § emerging from dissociative fugue as
husky teen w/frosted tips, striped polo, red shorts, nokia N-gage, unusually
hot mom, above ground pool, § pig nosed man arrested for trying to whisk an egg
using his fingers § Vinyl Sticker Description: Unless You Are Nude Don't Touch
This Truck Text On Product: Unless You Are Nude Don't Touch This Truck § i
want to live ther § when i changed my name from "jared" to "jaryd" it was a
declaration that im done following the rules. many tears, but also strength § @
Snapple "Phenylalanine"? Hasn't that been proven to cause autism in lab pigs §
i will soon be leaking a list of the people who sent me really concerned DMs
when i posted that jacking off too much makes your dick smaller § a Husband said
to a Doctor... Write me up a prescription of" Myfuckin".. Indeed, yes. Myfuckin
Beer, Myfuckin cofffe,Mmyfuckin slippers, etc § #red for aids tuesday i will
guarantee a 5% decrease in worldwide hiv infections by kkeeping my filthy dick
out of the pacific ocean § might pull some strings and get a paywalled article
put in the "whats happening" sidebar about my Horny Status, for 10000000 people
to see § im going to urinate all m y damn cum out.. dont read this if youre
Male § re: clogging toilets; its important to note that i use a minimal amount
of paper. so the responsible party is usually my very thick turds § im methodi-
cal bitch. your the random guy § i'm just like you, pal. eivery morning i put
on my straight hetero jeans one leg at a time and pour myself some straight
hetero raisin bran. § im pleased to report that this is a Jeans account. § This
is wihy when i see a millennials resume i throw it simply in the trash.
https://t.co/drF1O2FUzB § the shirtless man at the farmer's market has been
talking about "lesbian gravel" to the peanut guy for like an hour § every time
i open my mouth and speak my yap its like cumming to me. its like ejaculating
to what a average man would feel like § i singlehandedly brought the OJ Simpson
brand back from the brink of calamity and by God I will protect Yahoo. com from
these online devils § @the_ironsheik im fake. wrestle me § having a cocaine.mid
ringtone does not make me a bad father. § Grand "Ayatollah" Montazeri found
dead on bathroom floor, among playing cards and discarded insurance brochures
with conspicuous tooth marks § nothing like pouring a fresh bag of kitty litter
down the ass crack after another liberating diarrhea shit § the trolls will
never admit it, but wells fargo has been knocking the fucking crap out of covid
and police brutality, with their posts § guess what. i have the brain of a
Human. i have a Human's brain § #myfavorite90ssong the blue song by daft punk
§ "my mario tip: Anything is possible in the world of Mario." - my mario tip §
just fired 300 Journalists . And it feels so good § pissed off by the idea of my
ass becoming grass § BREAKER BREAKER ONE NINE THIS IS BIG SHITTY TRUCK DRIVER
HAUL`N A BIG CUMMY DICK ON DOWN 2 SAN QUENTIN PENITENTIARY 2 FUCK ALL THE
PRISONERS § "Durr michelob ulta would taste the same if it had a turd in it"
-Suppressive Persons with little on their mind but mischief and mayhem §
http://www.youtube.com/watch?v=N-fcShqK46k&feature=related help full. §
#UNELECTABLE !! #DEADWRONG !! #MarcoRubio #TeamRubio #Rubio2016 http://t.
co/5dONoyRGnk § dr oz tells me on his show that you can just pour a shit load
of mouthwash into your laundry instead of wasting money on various detergent's
§ a lot of people tripping over themselves trying to Speak on my ass. just an
observation ive noticed § oh my zippers down? well how about you zipper your
mouth, instead of look at my dick § yea i totally deserve to be put on the sex
offender registry cause i got caught taking pictures of my feet at fiveguys
burger and fries. Not § all you peoples posts are "Scooby Doo Ass" § working at
one of those "Cool offices" that has pinball machines and ping pong tables and
dildo launchers and pepole shitting on the floor § @the_ironsheik please humble
comedian Robin Williams for his mediocre performance in the heartwarming family
comedy "Old Hogs" § ME: Sorry. i must turn down your offer to join the Mafia, as
itd disappoint my friends on twitter THE MAFIA:The Mafia respects your decision
§ these noodles sucked https://t.co/pVhOR3EszZ § by ripping my phone book in

half I have not only proven im strong, but that Im also a cool independent guy who doesn't need to call anybody § #ThursdayThoughts is and will forver be the shit version of #TheThursdayNiteRant § Cigar mommys § highly agreeable shit https://t.co/WmC8JKIX0j § as far as im concerned the best revenge is ordering wolf piss online & pouring it into someones car. "living well" is too hard § extremmely turned on by Fav Denial , heavily worked up by women declining to fav my posts § a bunch of cops knock my colostomy bag on the floor and begin stepping on it with high heeled shoes while i jack off and ask them to stop it § GEN X'ER: Help im shitting on my pants ME: They have this invention called "toilet" now. Maybe if you hang up the cell phone yould know this § the Assed singer § reddit user "IncestVader" has just confirmed that @RicinElvis is thbe culprit , is on the loose, and is going bonkers. please yell at him § STOP IT I CAN'T DELETE THEM § (man with 120 IQ in the 1700s [80 in present day IQ] listening to Yankee Doodle for the first time) Oh this is devilishly Fucked § i love going to video games forums and posting shit like "Please tell me how to like Mario" § @DogBountyHunter me & martin luther king stand with tucker's girlfriend and all diaper wearers. shame on you #dogthebountyhunter § thiis is not the proper spirit of beer chat § Take this shit about the coors brewing company down § the dogs playing poker painting is ranom wacky bullshit, it is now considered not good by me, and i have made the decision to not look at it § @DigimonOtis got spooked on 9/11 and tried to hide in a storm drain & the firemen had to yank him out and lecture him for wasting their time § washcloth draped over the face , pointing up towards the showerhead. thats right folks im waterboarding my self again for my viral #Failures § folks if you think haunted house is scary this halloween i invite you to look at the damn economy and thj dow jones § the steve harvey fleshlight vid now officially has more views than the critically acclaimed masterwork "Boyhood". we can do better people § i cannot comprehend half of the things i read online but i'm smart enough to know that it is all really good § if you want a verified account on this website you gotta drink Pepsi ONE„¢. the food board recommends drinking 1800 Pepsi ONE„¢s a day § don't know why people think it's fair to call me "The Piss Judge" just because I pissed all over the floor of my courtroom that one time § i love wearing clothes with words on them. like a fucking caveman § isupport having my dick sucked and my ass kissed and my dick kissed and all the other metaphors for liking my posts § shes a real beautie https://t.co/TAjmd1ʌKaU § ok. ive been lied to § ladys please step on my toxic male Ass! Go nuts stomping my ass out like a cigarette until I hate it! Until I think its a bad idea! § only if u respect muscle § @Battlefield user "Garth_Turds" jusr read my address online , except replacing the name of my town with "Toilet". my daughters are crying § the truth is; a lot of these people making and laughing at shit and piss jokes are actually quite stoic when they're using the toilet § bring me 1 gem, i promote you to Wiseguy. 2 gems ill promote you to Punk. 5 gems makes you Thug. for 10 gems i will promote you to Shit head § @glennbeck i am a real wiccan libertarian and thank you. thank you. my premature daughter got brandamage because of obamas help care taxs § im the dumb mother fucker who sucks on my computer monitro like one of those aquarium fish; to bond with ceelbs, brands, trends, what have u § instituting a new feature on my feed called "The Hell Hour". the hell hour begins now § im the guy who ruined Columbus Day by saying he had slaves, and im ruining Back to the Future Day too by saying the film is rife with incest § DontWantNoBullShit.   DontWantNoBullShit § trying to imagine the kind of guy who would donate to a presidential campaign like a month after the election so i can worship him as a god § everyone please stop laughing immediately & explain the joke to me very carefully like i'm 2 years old so I can tell you if i like it or not § known among variety of local retailers as "oily ass man." banned from mattress giant, pier 1 imports, ikea, raymour & flanigan, and so forth § my uncle called me a Loser on television way

before this guy';s uncle did it @cnn @reuters @infowars @gameinformer §
#SeedPig for podunk nit wit § steven wrong § Yeah. Also he sold his account to
buzz feed in 2015 and his psots arent even that good § i dont trust banks.
especially the pig shaped ones § the bird bath institute considers any stone
bowl between the size of 8 to 40in. to be a bird bath and they are sick of
people disputing this § i was buzz feed until i sold th account to jiffy lube
for $100. this is common knowledge § hovering over the apartment maintenance
man with my pants down while he unclogs my toilet for the 4th time this week §
be warned america. 1st they get us fired from amtrak for saying jacking off in
the control car is good, next they start poisoning our wendys § its 69. just
kidding § most rhymes https://t.co/qV8nkbsPeu § " can fly the boeing 737 max
perfectly " § Basterd obama § some names for potential new nintendos, after the
super nintendo: the good nintendo, the nice nintendo, the helpful nintendo;
more to come § Cart Man § my turds and brain fucking suck and my toilet smells
like a god damn turd and it also sucks § need someone in or around geigertown,
philadelphia to help me dispose of approx 7500 live guinea pigs. i can not pay
you, i will not pay you § oh this hits § the fact is, my children are going to
see people wearing Jeans on television, in the movies, and other media. how do
i explain that to them § "the definition of shuriken is extremely broad &
encompasses any thrown weapon. a chair can be shuriken, for instance. a
birdbath"-UncleHalo § i am not a ho § down load the brexit app today muy lord §
its true. your more likely to die in a car wreck going 60 mph than 100 mph "hit
the gas before ya crash" the law of 100 § #FreeJahar this is the $5billion
helicopter obama wants to build instead of giving jahar fair trial. http://t.
co/4v33qIkrSk billion with a b § i'll find it § see that dumpster labelled
"SLAVE PISS"? bet ya dollars to donuts it's not actually full of slave piss.
someone probably wrote it as a joke § Spipe tv § eat bird shit https://t.co/
SWiJG6XDfD § "For years many have wondered what the letters 'DC' in washington
DC stand for. The answer is quite simple: Dollars & CEnts"--Winnie the Pooh § i
will devour all sinners in the name of all polite boys online § (fantasizing
about dangling off hood of my moving car adn touching the truck nuts on the jeep
in front of me with tongue) hell yea, actually § [crying[i just want to seay..
it takes a lot of courage for the cashiers to thank me for shopping at wal
mart.. but it iw well appreciated, § Its not in the spirit of star wars to do
that § i know how to get on all my favorite site`s. § 3d dog https://t.co/
YBZQbc2qvN § there seems to be a Fucking mistake here sir, https://t.co/
akzYXMEKj1 § the new meat ball sub's sandwich at mc donalds is a home run and
between you and me the taste is sensational and almost good § gamer knife
https://t.co/4KM6I9VY0M § evolution of doritos: cool ranch --> cooler ranch -->
cool ranch again --> epitome ranch --> lousy ranch --> apotheosis ranch -->
shit ranch § is pregnant part of lbgtq #LGBTBabes § I foudned buzz feed and it
was my idea to take all of that sweet Koch Bro Cash and put bad gifs on the
site § Jsut count the faves. Thats what i say. The people of twitter want urine
§ if you dont post your IQ at the beginning of every reply to me you will be
blocked like a street dog § spice up your life by throwing your favorite coffee
mug into the garbage § RAMPANT INCEST AMONG THE RULING CLASS, GLOBAL SHORTAGE
OF DIVINE CRISIS EMERALDS, SANCTIFICATION OF BASTARD ENERGY BULL SHIT MOTHER
FUCKER § blows on a horn and summons hundreds of Leather Daddies who form a
human pyramid which i climb on top of to survive the second great flood § in
veneration of the right honorable baroness my six komodo dragons will be
rewarded one etxra " DIPEY CHANGE " and allowed to eat spaghetti § me and this
guy on a podcast talking about how its bull shit that youre not allowed to have
opinions anymore https://t.co/tk9NWFa1YQ § thinking of that 9/11 thread on the
pokemon board i used to post on where the Admin said "Welcome to World War 3" &
everyone shit them selves § Fidgett spinners are making people dumb assed . §
propsoing to twitter a groundbreaking event called "The Banquet of Forgiveness"

, where every blocked person on every account gets unblocked § UNCLE: on sept 14 u posted "my dick is not all its cracked up to be." Explain yourself please ME: its. a commentary on the economy actually, § accidentally bought the mouth wash that's formulated for "Sucking dick" at cvs and it's actually really good § These are the most important jeans you will ever wear § THINKING ABOUT WHEN DID "IN GOD WE TRUST" BECOME " WOULD YOU LIKE FRIES WITH THAT" § each 'Ridge' in your crinkle-cut potato chip costs 4 gallons of precious slave blood to create and adds a satisfying "Cruntch" to every bite § take ntoe Hollywood: these superbowl ads teach us we can create compelling visual content better than any movie, WITHOUT resort to Vulgarity § i am above choosing sides here. i hope they either become friends & cancel the match, or beat each other completely to death simultaneously § it is indeed possible to shit too much. i would advise my followers to try to shit in multiple, smaller intervals , throughout the day. § im being evicted from my home for saying that kfc should sell hamburgers on a public log, and being a general "Dumb Ass" when it comes to IQ § considering various theorys of "Dark IQ" which is a sick & twisted version of IQ that can be really high even if your normal IQ is very low § Electric Light Orchestra AND Spyro The Dragon??? Finally , A KickStarter I Can Empty My 401k Into § i can't seem to do anything without being owned by shirtless males § "durr lets leberage each others brands" "dahh okay" ((the two men rub their asses together while licking the screens of their web tablets) § sing to God § phew for a second i thought i was the worst, least funny thing on the internet § im on the news truly pissed that ghislaine is not allowed access to her mahogany davenport from which to handle various sorts of paperwork § You wanna tell peole i got a little lady bug dick?? That how you get your kicks? Haah?? taking multiple shirts off while saying this § the hell hour has ended. all 37 repliers to the official hell hour tweet have been blocked indiscriminately. they took the gamble and lost § have you ever seen a chunk of fools gold. its a very alluring substance § nnone of you are supposed to read these § my reaction when people react to pictures of my reaction when im reacting to something good http://t.co/N0wsIZfLOS § everyone please soend me the money equivalent of whatever your reply is worth instead of putting your words underneath my posts from now on § enjoying my Microsoft § all credit, for this image, goes to Snooker https://t.co/EffHqi9iW6 § need some new Christian podcasts to listen to while cruising around in my fake cop car § forwarded to Admin . § a month ago everyone was scared thy were going to die so they immediately grabbed as much toilet paper as possible & wiped thier ass with it § http://t.co/w81Why5B no rude coment § woah. just realized the "Hungryman" logo on this can of sloppy joe is referring to me, the guy buying and eating thhe food. Insane mindfuck § There is a widespread campaign of fear being devised and perpetuated against me just because my dick looks like a cartoon character § im not a ignorant fuckfaced dip shit. i enjoy every minute of it § twitter to me, is a Collaborative Experience. ergo,when you shit on my posts it creates a rippling effect that corrupts the souls of all men § this is thge greatest post ever made § @DigimonOtis Get online immediately and prepare for this yiou fucking idiot. Only 25 minutes left. Answer your phone § youwill fucking remove this if you know whats good for you § rreddit: IM an insufferable fucking prick. the computer has made me extremely wise ,but im shit,. please post your Racist Roommate Stories § what me & the boys enjoy most is going to a home goods store to laugh at all the toilets. saying "haha i really want to shit in there", etc § the nile river is red with blood and your fucking birthday present won't cleanse it. perspective, you fucking rat #jan25 § fuck tumblr https://t.co/DpPFs4N8De § MetalGearEric has offered to engage me in a formal debate as to whether or not santa claus's real name is "Winter Claus" § if i ever accidentally posted something relatable or good enough to trick you into following this account, i truly apologize. im crying also § fat nude man in guy fawkes mask sucked up by jet engine while doing jumping jacks on runway. the olympics have been cancelled in his honor § i had do to it do him § @DrOz can i use a plunger to unclog my ass hole § funds removed from 1000s of accounts, markets crash, after deranged poster says that charles schwab & company "touches there self at night" § JOE PATERNO IS A LEGEND. THE MOMENT HE WAS BURIED HE IMMEDIATELY GOT 2 WORK FILLING HIS COFFIN WITH PISS, SHIT, & CUM. HES JACKIN OF. #WeAre § im bad now § and then there was PreCumGary, a remark- able man who, despite his name, never allowed ihmself to release pre-cum during sex and masturbation. § ever since i changed my gametap id from "diapermaster" to "CoolBryce" a world of doors have opened up to me. § my wife. my beautiful wife. i cannot lie to you any longer. the fbi is after me for kicking president obama's Turtle. thats why im screaming § the Ins & Outs of my ass; "Regarded As Low Quality" by famous Dr. House, in banned episode unfit for public consump- tion, Bullshit Bullshit. § celebrating the demise of Racism by watching the snickers commercial where mr bean eats a snickers bar and turns into an asian guy § [download of "bagel covered in caesar dressing.jpg" complete] Ah, Fucking Good This Yes. Absolutely Epic Fucking Particularly This. Sir § if this shit costs me the Fanta deal i will: 1) become eeven more racist 2) cancel all Thursday Nite Rants 3) add a switchblade to my avatar § as we speak, RickGame- Cube, Bradley_X, GodlyWalter17 and myself are planning an attack on the terrorist organization known as "Al-Qaeda" § .,. <<<<< THATS MY DICL #Os- cars2015 § this is the room where i simulate combat scenarios by performing wrestling moves and crowd control techs on 22 girl mannequins. the gauntlet § because the entire country of egypr is burning. if DigimonOtis were here right now hed spit in your fucking face. #jan25 § "IN THIS HOUSE, FOXTROT IS CONSID- ERED MANGA" #Oscars § DO NOT BE MAD AT ME !! PLEASE! PLEASE § no heaven or hell when you die, everyone is just herded into a room with a big scoreboard saying which person blasted the most Cum § By engaging with my Troll bait ,you hav e fallen directly into my ass. Good evening § and here we go again. another civil symposium, bungled up and ruined by me, the horny asexual. everyone always blames me, the horny asexual. § still waiting on that twitter verified status. i swear to god i am the real DJ Darkzide (the onyl vampire dj) § Announcing new feature called #Rubadubdub where my followers are encourgaged to post pics of themself inside the bathtub. Ban me i dont care § i regret being tasked the emotional burden of maintaining the final bastion of morality and NIce manners in this endless ocean of human SHIT § hmm. myaybe we should tax Stupid People. and hipster. *the nation stands and applauds, I enjoy a success- ful career in legislature for 60yrs* § perusing the count chocula sub reddit with a mouth full of werthers originals flavored skoal tobacco dip § indeed, god is starting another great flood but this time he wants the ark filled with a shitload of monster and red bull instead of animals § either my neighbor has been running a vacuum all day, or producing a consistently loud, droning noise with his mouth somehow § the artist formerly known as "BubsyFucker" is no longer banned from israel. please keep the wiki up to date anmd withhold your judgments § marijuana did columbine § my ass cheeks have two giant finger nails § cancelling my livetweet of the pa flower show becaus of the SHIT you people have said to me, tthis is the bed you laid in, this is your hell § found in 100 yr time capsule: will o the wisp, a screaming bible, a fistful of shitty paper, some teeth, grandpas pipe, misc turds and husks § "im not autistic. just my dick and sex drive is. im 100% a regular person other wise." § killed my dick with too much febrease spray § @FBI @LASDHQ while youre here id like to report this pervert for impersonating a cowboy § its all cool, im a sex worker too "the best there is" § #NationalCerealDay i fuck all cereal § everyone thinks youre a celeb when all your cars windows are tinted but people only get those so they can jack off on the go § a man in argentina is willing to surgically transfer hair from my Buffoonish ass to my weak, infantile chest and tattoo a jawline to my neck § disregard this . § can any one who knows of Politics tell me if this is good or not https://t.co/6ShvHIK03o § its below 0 § ive never met any of them, but i know that there are guys out there who name their dogs shit like "Rover " and "Fido" § i thitnk, that, before you wish death upon someone, you should make sure their tweets are really really bad first § when someone i never met on here has me blocked i assume its because theyre a pedophile and theyre afraid im going to take them to prison § some people sing the praises of the one hundred dollar bill... i myself, prefer the humble, time-tested and reliable one dollar bill § candidate gary johnson pledges to cut down on online clutter at pizza hut debate, cites rampant misuse of the #Yowza hashtag § i'm pisser #1 http://t.co/a9Fz0kxh8h § my watch beeps whwich means its time to stand in front of my ex-wife's house and play "Hit THe Road Jack" while dacning and licking her mail § waiting the customary 20 minutes after someone in the group dm says one of their pets died before posting a picture of sponge bob Nutting § everyone on this site thinks they're hard core but i bet if they took poison to weaken their bodies i would win fights against them handily § so what's the deal with benghazi. are you benghazi???? why is potus hiding from benghazi § looking for the kind of ketchup that Chefs use...... § walking around wearing a sandwich board sign that says "Kick my ass" and subjecting the masses to raw unfiltered journalism § please donate medicine to my boy son kim jong-un, who was assaulted by a fawn & became too sick to attend the royal korean spaghetti banquet § Pldease just fav me if you enjoyed the tweet.   I dont have the time to read the replies § i get hacked constantly everyday because i am a Clod with zero technical prowess § "brevity is the soul of SHIT" - the shit man § please contact me if you own one of the six corporations who controls 90% of the american media or if you're of the dragen race § Thank you. Closure at last #tcot RT: @Mythbusters Adam and Jamie "Go Benghazi" in the all-new season premiere of Mythbusters, don't miss it! § ATLANTIC CITY - 9:02am - A second oversized globe has hit the Ripley's Believe it or Not Museum . § My followers are sick thugs, they are Debauched imps, and they love to be made to howl like dogs when i call them my little sewer bitch rats § i was uninvited from the oscars for trying to sell "oscars brand bear bile" to everyone who stopped their car for me while i fake hitchhiked § enjoying some prestige Wi-Fi in my car at the car wash § Beer is the drink of summer. But it can be enjoyed during the other seasons, in moderation. § just as Christ was nailed to the cross to rescue his brand, i will be nailed to a Meme. my shit & blood will drip upon the funny impact font § whenever i get nude for any reason i hear the dogs go wild outside. must sense something that humans can not. § ST PETER: on march 14 2024 you posted simply the words "james earl bond". hope the 34 favs were worth it idiot ME: They were bitch § donald trump is the best man for the job... and for that he has earned my vote. however, i believe he needs to "Check his priviledge" § i feel like some people don't appreciate the effort i put into TTNR. frankly, all i can do is feel embarrassed for you. it's a good feature § Ha ha ha its me. It's me. Yeah, good jok.e. No http://t.co/DOAzn9hPys § Im at town hall getting a permit to have e xtremely bad opinions about guitars § workin out in a graduated cylinder. as i gain muscle mass the water level will rise above my head and drown me. this is true muscle suicide § here i am again, screaming into the toilet, hoping somehow, somewhere, my future wife can hear my soothing voice resonate intot her asshole. § woah. look who's back in town http://t.co/aZ9quw0r § me and the boys chipped in and orchestrated a fake 9/11 that you can easily prevent and become a national hero (fake 9/11 becomes real) oops § society has shown its ass once again § i am in no position to judge an ass. i do not deserve to judge an ass § hard core https://t.co/hA1r6YgLa8 § not Suprising to see these LOSERs attack Sports and Athletic Legend @TheRealOJ32, as i've been attacked just as maliciously, if not more so, § sorry to all crooks, hucksters, cronies, and phonies... but in this, our year of 2016, police man is sitll king, and the jail, his Kingdom ! § i absolutely deserve tax credit for offering my respectable toilet to government employees whenever i can § cum piss poop ass § my spirit animal is t he lowly paramecium, cosmic punishment for killing a paramecium in my past life § if i win that wendy's contest i will do the right thing and choose to set dick vitale free § i accept that all the things i post "For Fun" are to be met with physical violence, including elbows to the face, shattered knee caps, etc, § my price-less stradivarius gaming keyboard... fcovered in policeman urine § Seve jobs, bill gates, and Albert Einstein sitting at a table, enjoying a glass of Single Oak Barrel Whiskey , While i watch and smile. § Oops! another $50000 worth of nft ape shit got stolen from me some how. Weird!!! good thing i still have all 200 of my iq points § i am a chef now folks. im walking around town in my chefs hat like a real dumbass. everyone hopes i get hit by a car § if some one said some shit to me like "Rock and Roll Hoochie Koo" i would not be able to contain my rage. i would completely lose my shit. § please leave, sir. your vulgar, senseless displays may be tolerated at K-Mart, but not here at Super K-Mart § please help mme. my dad sent me $40000 to go to Fight College but I spent it all on making a big hormel foods logo out of gorilla glue § i do not give a shit of the official WHOTUS stance, i refuse to hear it, i will never forgive the turkey, i will not bow to that filthy bird § IF THE ZOO BANS ME FOR HOLLERING AT THE ANIMALS I WILL FACE GOD AND WALK BACKWARDS INTO HELL § @AlanDersh follow back sir § Yiou have to be really smart to get 250k followers on here. It doesnt just happen to you if you post false info about your ass for 7 years § that was it. the rants over. stop sending me messages § i like to think if i was alive in the 1800s & saw a Minstrel Show id take the Rational approach. id say "This is simply the SNL of its time" § things the trolls won't allow me to have: - the blue check Mark - the 260 characters - a nice plaque that says "twitter power user" § please help me tanger58. ive become something i cannot control § @enterprisecares Glove compartment in my rented vehicle filled with diapers and hair. Don't you guys check these things? § I am going to try to have diarrhea today. Because I am not "DEFINED" by my ass § I support DigimonO-tis and his right to purchase a synthetic cloaca , and I respect his decision not to fuck it. § im on a watch list for capitalizing "Balls" § border colies are 250% Smarter than humans and stronger to, which is why the US Military refuses to breed them § @redlobster Thus always to tyrants. § hate it when my boss knocks out the front leg of my desk with a baseball bat and funko pop lego shit flies every where § you can post shit like "my roommate put the addams family theme on 9hrs a day" no one will ever question it. you will get the medal of honor § asia is now protected from all sex. thank you § apologies to guys named "clay". that's like one step above dirt § piss me off forever, kiss the dog shit out of my ass mouther fucker #ShutYourYap § http://t.co/gpmcAVS-RXa I Have Found My Calling. Good Bye § nude bathing was invented by the vile criminal slave class of the byzantine empire and it drove the kind & decent noblemen absoutely bonkers § big steel drivin' hank gordon bubba once told me i aint once put on what it could not do, but to what i can't do on what i put myself or on § trying to heal..... please donate to my go fund me... $10 will make me less racist... $100 will make me extremely less racist...thank you... § my christ. i am invigorated. using my new official old spice dr.pepper halo 3 exfoliating forehead wax. this is God. this feeling is God § nobody seems to realize how many people had to die to bring 3d back to the theaters and its extremely fucked up that interest is waning § thinking i could bring my laptop to people who never saw computers, like some black tribe in africa. let them watch me game for a few hours. § thgere should be a side quest in elden ring where you dm a bunch of guys gfs "Im sorry he cares more about his Fucking Stupid game than you" § im somewhat a bit of an expert on *looks around cautiously* girls, as i have convinced many of them to beat the shit out of me

on craig list § and to you, in his will, your great uncle leaves y ou his most
treasured possession, the very "POWER BIEBER" that caused his death § Hell is
Real http://t.co/8JRZNMkgrn § thats my baby boy. my dim wit son § time to
revisit Geis http://t.co/SibgLrWN § forum gods: 1) the guy who dug a big hole
in his basement & posted pictures of the hole 2) the guy who intentionally
gave his wife head lice § thinking about getting some miniature Gibson guitar
replicas box framed, and hanging thenm up for the boys to come over and look at
§ principal surveys the premises from his shitty Dodge Caliber, sees the jeans
dealer trying to peddle his stash on school grounds & calls 911 § all dressed
up in my little tuxedo and ready to sacrifcie my self to isis § Day of Forgiveness: whilst you go about the holiday season, please today take time to Forgive
a content creator who has yelled at you before § Im so fucked up. Im an
embarrassment to the brand § shut thf fuck up § just clicking my mouse a bit.
having a look at my files § @TheOnion i did it. i hacked the onion. ive been
making them post fake news stories for like 20 years now. suck my dick § @
null____void @NBCSports i hope they do because it is the worst picture i have
ever seen § i finally learned how to photoshop the bitter fbeer face onto women
after spending 15 years jacking off to the keystone bitter beer face ads §
#why90srocked everyothing was more real. everythig more visceral. a more
'human' experience. i was also 200 pounds less fat § a tendency to substitute
the word "Shit" with "Dust" when talking to girls (e.g. "just wiped a bunch of
Dust out of my ass today") § plaese help my loathsome son find a professional
who will tattoo the cheesecake factory logo onto his chest with no backtalk or
jokes § #BringBackDrewCareyShow Bring Back Drew Carey Show § what the fuck is
Salt life please § loathsome animal § i would like to remind our nation's youth
to burn their mcdonald abd burger king cups after use so mobsters cant hide
IEDs in them § @CapsCop GO FUC^& A PIPE § https://t.co/HzhVRfXhei § "Litter Box
Fucker" AUDIENCE: (LAughing already) WORKING CLASS JOE: Im going to fuck the
litter box now. AUDIENCE: AWuooo! Hoo hoo! § im thinking my posts arent on The
NY Times Best Seller list because they have been very difficult to access lately
due to Inclement weather § jacking off more often (due to Stress) and also
jacking off less often (due to Stress) § the weak shall wither and die...(JACKS
IN TO TREELOOT .COM CIRCA 1999 VIA THE INTERNET ARCHIVES AND CLICKS ON THE
FUCKING TREE 100000 TIMES) § feed your dog with this one insane pringles hack §
weve toiled to bring you the greatest specifically tailored user experience of
all time. PLease uncheck the box that says "Shut the fuck up" § i boos't
"RESPECT" i block "PORNO" § fifty two year old mamn hides underneath a tarp at
work and jacks off to the same cartoon characters he did when he was thirty
years younger § hte shit people type at me "Yap yap yap" § let me tell you how
i deal with Haters. i collect their piss in a jar and keep it next to my
monitor. why?? uhrh. i think it makes them mad § And now it seems that even my
own followers cannot resist pelting me with ad homenim dog shit. § Give me some
good memes and ill post them. Im sorry. Im just trying to please everyone §
Dog Bows to Bible - What this little dog did to the holy book of God will
knock your shit out of your ass hole. § i see how ti is. i provide the best
content online to all my girl followers but when i ask to live with them for
free they leave me for DEAd § fucking a stack of emoji t-shirts at target or
kmart or wherever the hell § IF COOLTRAINERDUSTIN ACTUALLY HAD A CRYSTAL THAT U
COULD GAZE INTO 2 SEE ALL EPS OF "MIND OF MENCIA" HE WOULD PRETTY MUCGH HAVE 2
SHOW ME IT § i am a natural showman. i love to show off my natural's § my new
jeans https://t.co/Pj95o0wPAg § h m. wikipedia still appears to be working to
me http://t.co/xNQJRq0e i dont see what the problem is. #factswithoutwikipedia
§ #The12DaysOfContent im sorry again http://t.co/Odg5cl2lFa § it is with a
heavy heart that i must announce that the celebs are at it again § who are my
top creative influences? easy. the geico cavemen. where do i draw the majority
of my inspiration frpm? easy. the geico cavemen . § they are always on tv

carrying on § there was once a man-- beloved & cherished by all... until he was unfairly chased away, by the dip shit brigade. and that man was named "Me". § i want to become a master plumber so i can make shit rain on my enemies § sppeedy gonzales is White § some times.. i need my coffee fix so bad.. i gotta grab TWO mugs!! Im the mockery of all my co-workers and i fucking suck § downloading an app developed by Asia that tells me how much diarrhea is hould have everyday § i would take so many bribes if i was a judge. half my shit would be bribes. take bribes from the criminals until theyre too poor to do crime § pal the only "meltdown" im having is my ice cream melting down into my hand while I lay on the beach & laugh while thinking about the trolls § i basically love to catch all the shit that falls off of peoples hamburgers with one of those tiny nets they use to scoop up goldfish § PROSECUTION: could you please tell the court who exactly youre referring to when you use the term "Gender Folk"? ME: not to a bastard like U § please stop changing the "Gomco Clamp" wikipedia entry, i have the entire article tattooed on my back and im sick of having to update it § @ RollingStone shut the fuck up rolling stone magazine § nows the time when the CEO of the company inspects each employee's shit, and im nervous cus my turds look like fucked up little caterpillars § dippin my head out there for some hardball strapthug coplikes to handle my doofus and preg me down ,no wise guy shit #nerdland § a bully asked me if i wanted a "Hurts Donut" then one thousand ghouls phased through the floor and ceiling and began shitting on me § io love helping the economy by fucking up while doing downloads and getting 100 coin miners installed on my pc § when journalism was good, https://t.co/fLjPzXG75H § @AlanDersh Hello Alan this is your lawer speaking. I am advising you today to please keep posting this shit § IVE TAKEN TO MIXING JENKUM METH IN MY BATHTUB IN ORDER TOE ARN THE MERE PENNIES NECESSARY FOR PROLONGING MY GODFORSAKEN TOILET LIFE § i am protected from your bull shit § "insane clown posse? ?" Hm. *smirking, now* Sounds like a certain web site, that i see § .@carrabbas holes on salt shaker too small disrespectufl to customer and very much a cheat § me and the boys are going to watch the final leno and then watch every episode of leno in reverse. full return to thence Leno. #lenouroboros § "[Tipping] is... the last refuge of toads" - Thomas Jefferson "Do not tip the waitress" - Monroe "i dont tip bitch. Reblog this" - John Adams § (dismissing waitress handing me the check with a hand wave) no thank you. i dont believe in any of that § the trolls are also in full bloom as well i see , § just read the wikipedia article for "Mindfulness Based Cognitive Therapy" while you were on here scrolling through miles of puerile dog shit § and the final word i leave all of you pitiful cowards upon this sinful night is "Truth".. hold it clos.e.. use it.. thank you § the mysterious "Dr. Gamer" § #FineMenThatEatAss #FineMenThatEat-Pussy #FineMenThatDontCheat https://t.co/4xUCPHosEv § the only sin ive commit-ted is looking so god damn good in these fuckin jeans, kickin around in my big ass boots § horse d'oeuvres #barnyardsnack #tcot #agony § just indignantly threw $799 gamer keyboard into koi pond because i got pissed off by the craze that is sweeping the nation known as Planking § i have ended porno § to the fanboy who threw acid iat my face near fuddrucker`s, you can destroy my body but The Cloud will preserve my brand for millennia #PS4 § i now hereby declare that all of the guys who reply to my posts are now married to the girls who reply to my posts, and thats that § the times they are indeed a changin..but the one time thatll never change is Lunch time. lock them engagements in if you think this is good. § hmm more ignorance § this may very well be the much needed "Win" for America that economists have speculated upon since 9/11 § dozens upon dozens of the racist new starbuck cups,. filled with urine and placed all over my computer desk like candles on a satanic altar § it is sio, so easy to Mindhack the government and get permission to dig holes in your yard § Top 3 Cuases Of Teen Death: 1. Noise   2. Misbehavior 3. Jeans § i fairly tend to use "Sarchasm" to destroy liars mentally, and if that's not yiur cup of tea, i have the 2 words for you which is Suck it !! § they fuckin STINK!!!! § neo pets cinematic universe § not at all unreasonable to assume that everyone who has ever unfollowed me likes to engage in mystic forest ritual to make my muscles tinier § Whats fucked up is , some will think this is good!!! https://t.co/2samsGi56q § i show up at the range wearing a t-shirt that says "I Wont Wear The Earplugs" and i m promptly directed back to my car by staff members § aahhhh am a gaaaamer of constant sorrow, https://t.co/2kI0qFc8CR § getting the zone auto zone § Real.Time.with.Bill.Maher.2013.11.15.HDTV-NO. SWEARING.EDITx264-2HD[kkkdracula] § there are secret offices all over the country full of men in business attire who consume porn for 9 hrs and go home. they dont even jerk off § Introvert = In vitro pervert. theyre sick § how could a man with $0 get one of you 3d printer eggheads to print up some wild runestones for my daddy-daughter astral ascension ceremony § you tube is now officially named "Ignorance tube," due to the many proverbial ass kickings i have received there § account Status; Verified. To the chagrin of all Shit Accounts, This is now a LOCKED PAGE . I am the rat of life. I am the bitch of forever § i am being targetted by a shadow campaign just because i cured my own diarhrea by exercising instead of taking "PILLS" § nobody has suggested 14:88 yet. the hitler numbers. § DOCTOR: you cant keep doing this to yourself. being The Last True Good Boy online will destroy you. you must stop posting with honor ME: No, § @Bubbaburger i dont like this one either, remove it § #the12daysofcontent thank s http://t.co/rk8uiieT7P § the " o Bullshit" award goes to this guy for being bossed around by gas station employees & giving them a poor review http://t.co/SRps5X8qaA § @longjohnslvrs never thought id get my di*k touched by a staff member at a long john silver's, but here we are. its a madhouse up there § the integrity of Fav Star is at stake . I Deserve death § requesting hand critiques. please be honest , but fair http://t.co/3vecQz6R6q § shut the fuck up § two truths & a lie: (1) i use the fatsuit from big momma house 2 as a corset (2) im in trouble at the dump (3) please dont reprint this info § all of you people have rat hands. i am going to be fucking sick § legalize pubic hair in playstaton (PSX) games § yes because those are the funny words § replying is second responding § @Cheesecake one of ur waiters kicked me out of my chair and into an interracial family's table and burned my dick off with a cigarette. thnx § #Zodiacfacts #scorpio women have two ass holes § no-reply@youtube .com: We've changed our terms of service, me: my terms of service is simply this"Shut the Fuck up" § ruby tuesday is a small business. fuck you § I Have A Life, Fucker. *Drives away in tiny car powered by my ow n shit and piss* § Yo u are only pissing him off further § get the bars off. expose these fucking privks § this next dip of chaw is dedicated to the pursuit of muscles, and also my jeep § what can i say. my hatres are my motivators (gets pic of nude man covered in syrup sent to inbox) FUCk. Please stop § (sees a cop shoot somone) This is just like james bond (sees a war happen) This is like robo cop (sees a burning house) This is like top gun § https://t.co/JzTVdxitfx the state of owl sfx on you tube fucking sucks ass § the Law Man surveys the room, and is able to locate me hiding behind a potted plant thanks to my trail of miserable , fucked up turds § I WIL NOT RESTORE THE PSN NETWORK UNTIL ALL 7 HELL MASON BANKERS ARE IN JAIL & THEY BRINGBACK COOKIES N CREME FLAVOR DORITOS § watching big mommas house 2 in defiance of attack of small businesses § ive always said we need to make the Dou Jones go up, instead of down. And now that ive been proven right, every one wants to kiss my dick . § gypsy denim § CLICK ON MY POST 10000 TIMES IF YOU ARE WORKED UP OVER COMPUTERS § the 1st rule of my twiter account is read my posts with an open mind,. the 2nd rule is the fight club rules. the 3rd rule is simply Have Fun § Joe Pa is in his deathbed right now id wager, jerking off one last time before the curtain falls on his disgraceful life § what donest kill me makes me stronger ((gains infinite strength from being not killed by infinite things)) § im gonna eat this whole sack of potatoes by my self #Anti-

Lent § dropped a mouthful of spaghetti on my dick just now § im not verified yet but i hope to be once @JACK deals with his many personal demons . § prom is filth § #promfail unaware of big wet towel hanging out of ass; whipping around knocking over refreshments as i get agitated in response to Hostility § https://t.co/tMHyhyopnH Very Nice § my follower count decreases when i use these words: dick, cum, ass, turds. it goes up when i use these: brand, multimedia, sports, pepsicola § im NOT going to live tweet the damn super ball game, and im NOT going to respond to any DMs asking why. i care about the integrity of Feeds § "Gotcha" § Sorry fucked up § BOOOOOO TO M Y 10000TH FOLLOWER @TorresaurusRex BOO YOU PICE OF SHIT EVERYONE THROW YOUR SHOES AT SUCK MY DICK § remember blowing on the CDs to make them work? blowing on control-lers?? memory cards? pplease validate this broken man #PlaystationMemories § You are such a stupid little selfish pig. What youve done here is shit yourself & yet youre too doped up from the circle jerk to realize it. § i guess i will change my name to "Mr Go Fuck Myself " huh?? Since all you sons of bitchs obviously think it would be good, if i did that § whenever i elevate my professional vitae through mind-blowing, dynamic content, i reward myself by fucking a book of carpet samples #Toonami § your saying the quiet part out loud ... https://t.co/QoHZ3zaC8w § Mhickey Mouse Cartoon Hands Flipping The Bird Marijuana Weed for Iphone and Samsung Galaxy Case (iPhone 6 plus white) § again i've been asked to comment on the hidden ass in the new star wars trailer. it's time to put this cowardly rumor to rest. theres no ass § oh good another one of you fucking monstsrs has come to shit on me § im a fruad. i wear the wrangler jeans despite never having wrangled a single goddamn thing in my life § authorities forced to destroy entire 35,000-ton chernobyl sarcophagus after misunderstood online entrepreneur gets his dick stuck beneath it § entertaining twisted thoughts of putting bull shit on the back burner § extremely getting a uti by usnig the same shirt i used to wipe my dogs mouth to wipe piss off of my dick § i can guarantee you that im only as racist as the girls im attracted to- and not a tiny bit more § #ZodiacFacts #Saggetaearrius (sp? i dont know? the crab one?) are the best golfers but they can't drive or something § dplease promise me you will respect statues from now on § elmer fudd with yakuza tattoos. legion of fudd § shit hater § proposed "slime wtc" catches airplanes and converst them into waste § @Team_Mitch @AOC https://t.co/nwYmVoKRTX § im taking a sledgehammer to the bimbofication of gamers and the assumption that just because im a gamer i only fuck with out condoms § yesterday i bought a 26ct bag of fun size snickers bars as penance for wasting a police man's time § what about i take a big jar, i shit and piss in it for like 3 months and then sneak into your house and dump it on your bed § sen larry craig(R): DuRr I have a wide stance Me: Cmon. If this guys for real. Then I got a bridge to sell ya.. and I just ran outta bridges § ENJOYING BOND MMO?? JUST CRAFTED SOME REMARKABLE BOND GEAR WHILE YOU WERE BUSY TRYING TO FUCK THE NPCS WITH THE HUNDREDS OF OTHER JAME BONDS § im at Ces baby. they got an app that makes your phone do gun noises and fat wet asses, flying around goerge jetson style § deleted the tweet where i said that homer simpson is allowed to show his penis in the japanese version and im allowed to work at kmart again § Citizen Kane Except Every Instance Of "Rosebud" Is Replaced By "POWER BIEBER" § Just gotten word that ive been approved for the verified mark. It'll appear within 5-7 days. Wow! What a nice surprise! Thank you every body § need an investor to help me open a chain of restaurants which absolutely must be named "Asian Taco Bell" § **kicks a plant over because of something a celeb did* fucking ass hole *vomits into the refrigerator because the new iphone is bad* shit § operating an unregulated labor camp on the Dean's lawn nd saying "Shut the fuck up sir" when he comes out of his house to threaten us § oh you updated your privacy policy? very nice. i updated my privacy policy too which is to show you my ass and balls on purpose. Fuck you § sometimes it seems to me that it is a bit good

to say that we could not do our posts without using none other than the humble
computer chip. § AS THE GUILLOTINE SLIDES TOWARDS MY NECK, I PRODUCE A TINY
BARBELL I'VE BEEN HIDING IN MY MOUTH AND LIFT IT WITH MY TONGUE. ONE LAST REP §
https://t.co/fPhdrAwpPs Gudetama Sanrio English § i am a cot and pickin "tells
it like it is "son of a bitch § gah. the decal maker fuckged up my order
again. now corey haim will never rest in peace http://tinyurl.com/yh6r2eg § i
can just tell all of you are going to be a bucnh of little shits today and rat
fuck me out of another pulitzer price by not retweeting me § im a jornalist §
do you like my controversial "DURAG" post? Yes I wear them. § thank you. it
hasnt been long but i can already say that having 200 k followers is exactly
like being god from the bible. § Seems to me that we have been more becoming
like a country of people who let Cell phones define our brain... FUCK !!! § i
suppport the duck dynasty boys and i support gay also because i am a kind,
reasonable man § when digimon otis spoiled me the ending of Men In Black 2 i
got so mad that i showed him my dick § ernest shits himself stupid. ernest nuts
him self #twistedErnestFilms #tgif § hosanna !! hosanna !! netbooks for dog
lovers § i was also goig to make a joke about how putting a dry rub on the
vaccines makes them cause less autism but the science is still out on that §
Ohh!!! Im a fuck up!! My followers hate me!! I'll never be good!! What do I
do?? What do I do?? § every singe day... my followers ask me. where can i get
the latest Kfc DinnerPlan. and the answer is simple my friends. "Mc Donalds" §
thank you and Amen https://t.co/9t5yqXg6w7 § im just a Hispanic male who loves
looking at pictures of bluejeans. i have a tough road ahead and a long ways 2
go in my life § Food $200 Data $150 Rent $800 Candles $3,600 Utility $150
someone who is good at the economy please help me budget this. my family is
dying § the saturday morning ramble will be cancelled as well. thank you for
your cooperation and understanding. PLease enjoy the holidays. § THE COP GROWLS
"TAKE OFF TH OSE JEANS, CITIZEN." I COMPLY, REVEALING THE FULL LENGTH DENIM
TATTOOS ON BOTH LEGS. THE COP SCREAMS; DEFEATED § ohhh anOTHER solar eclipse,
you say ?? gee i cant wait.. *does the Jerk Off motion until the sun supernovas
itself out of shame* § i wouldnt advise taking any liberties., your god damn
pride is your key enemy § i never said "ounch" , i would never say "ounch", and
if i did say the word "ounch" it was becaus ei was trying to type the word
"Lunch" § my favorite part of nascar is when I vomit all over my shirt and car
after the race., desecrating the logos of the brands that enslave me § painting
an exquisite 12 foot mural of martin luther king jr dressed as a cop, entitled
"The Dream Realised", to prove im not racist at last § realm of Lamar
https://t.co/mrdbdyj1mA § doestn matter. we're both mere shadows of Baby
Giveaways Galore § i tell you folks this damn itunes is something that you cant
figure out unless you are a nasa guy § watching him desperately try to dissipate
the vulgar dust cloud by blowing on it moved me to tears § as a 46 year old
teen I would like to apologize to all old dudes on behalf of the teen generation, for decades of gangsterism and nonsense, § evvery other Friday the sheriff
guides me around the jailhouse and lets me expose myself to the villains, and
thats #MyTGIF § seeking a pisswife. i will do anythoing for a pisswife. § im
seated down, and Ready to get pissed off........ § / ! \\ / ! \\ / ! \\ if
this post gets 5000 likes, my wife will give me back my inhaler / ! \\ / ! \\ /
! \ § I'm Sorry For Raising Cain At The Out Back Steak House Even Though It's
Still Bullshit That They Refuse To Serve Me A Plate Of Just Croutons § sorry
for roasting your set up § ive decided to abstain from urination for two days,
to punish myself for letting my kolut score dip below 70 again § tomorrow im
going to fill up on bread befoore 10am and get waterboarded by my seven identical uncles § Jailed Man Jumps Head First Into Toilet -- by InsaneOuttakes
-- 110,973 views #TGIF #TGIF #TGIF #TGIF #TGIF #TGIF #TGIF #TGIF #TGIF #TGIF §
two hundred <JOHNNY COCHRAN LEWD HUMOR SWEATERS> , the kennel will give ya 20
cents for these , the animals love to wear them and rip em up § im an extremist

judge... and i Vote § sub way has just announced that kid rock is the new jared and that when kid rock dies they will make the jared after him a black jared. § i weawr blackface while i game to improve performance. i have no intention of racist. That will be the final post before i turn my phone off § love too get a bite on that. thank you for sharing § if iyou come on here talking to me about your penis, or saying unreasonable things about my penis, your account will be "Knocked down" § i hear by claim this guestbook in the name of the m0nsanto christianz. fuck u. fuck u. fuck u. fuck u. fuck u. fuck u. fuck u. § checking my computer chiar for GPS Trackers, left by ex-wife or cops § my follower's https://t.co/UCv7ICcNKy § SHIT!! HA HAHAHAHA § putting my dick in a Capsule § which film or work of art rujined my life the most. im going to have to say men and black 2. § my work day consists of my bosses trying to goad me into my cubicle so that i'll just sit in there & jack off isntead of ruining the company § mastering Life calmness in the face of being called a dip shit § did anyone do the "google ass" joke. did anyone do thr joke where "google glass" is changed with the word "ass" in it. hope a nerd sees it § i have saved $53,000 by claiming the home office tax deduction on my Gooncave § cumstarter. i need 500 liters of cum to start a projec.t i dont know its some bacon blog. who gives a fuck § boys are reclaiming ladies Night..... and its all thanks to Men § aid's § facing resistance from wikipedia in removing the article that says i have an ear infection as it is very difficult to verify that i do not § if u follow me. ..and ur display name is "bazinga man".. you had better FUCking be the real bazinga man before I unscrew youre head & SHIT D § worst food of 2016 : Bread Where to begin. Bread is a piece of shit and its no wonder its commonly associated with the worst drink, "Water". § AUNT: We will miss our Guinea Pig "Charlie" who had to be put down today ME: NAtural Selection At Work. COUSIN: I will fucking rout your ass § idont know who runs that account but i am most certainly a huge piece of shit regardless § if you like the band sex pistols you will also enjoy my band called "the gun pistols" § im thinking the next big industry is dog humanization services. surgery to make dogs look like a man, stand upright, etc. its what they want § to the pyramid on the $1 bill calling itself the "all seeing eye" Fuck you. the only thing you can see from my wallet is the jeans of my ass § this is the national health advisory board issuing a safe reminder not to touch your dick for one hour after handling pets § (genuflects as two golden lights come forth from behind me, taking the form of majestic angel wings) i would never hold a seleb at gun point § #SendASmile to the stock marcket dow jones today . lets show Corona whos boss https://t.co/8U80tT1cQh § i scan the docs & id the perp. "The Radio Shack Masturbator". bounty on his head. i put 100 bullets into my pistol and hit the god damn road § i hand the chipotle cashier my card. "i support indie" with a photograph of me winking. she looks up and sees me winking in real life also. § digging thorugh all the trash cans and dumpsters at e3 in search of condoms containing genetically superior gamer cum § eunuchoid 49yr man puting self up for adoption, please. unemployable due to frequent nosebleed. loves movies & Tech. thank u for reading it. § at last., after years of legal b.s. i am finally required to be served up to 5 communion wafers at church because im a big fat hungry man § wassup babe, im the reason Pregnancy-info .net disabled video embedding on their forums, how abuot giving me a nice kiss § "calling out" magnetGirl77 for telling me that my dick looks like "a piece of fried calamari" § @dril none of them were good. Sorry § (Whimsical) i love to piss , right there in my big sweatpants (Serious) No. The toilet is the only place for piss § ill kick any ones ass who is a "BOOMER" § fred flintstone does not Jack off ever, he works hard every day to provide for his family, fuck you for saying something like that § "i will never respond to a dm unless its a girl sending it. i will keep my feed tidy. i will betray anyone my followers want me to betray" § haha i probably have like $10000 more than you § if you don't think i like to muck about on here... i damn say you're in for the shock of a life time!!!! § they call the book " 1984" because that's what my iq becomes when i read it.... § if the state ordered me to wear one of those shitty lapel cams i'd say " o SIR" & crush the camera under my cop boot while the public cheers § 1/29/18: i do not want to think about or look at the word "Tater Tots" § folks, please. this is a private matter between me and the heartless criminal § when you post a picture of your hamburger in the group chat, your friends are likely taking that lunch data and selling it to Villains § id like to report a hacker. he offered me 1000000 to show my dick and didnt cough up the dough when i delivered the goods. i got hacked § just thoguht of a tiny man standing inside of a toilet. waving a turd in with batons like the airport guys. shopping the idea to buzz feed § sometimes i love to be able to want to be the man who is able to want to need to have his wants and needs able to be fulfilled sometimes § #questionsobamawontanswer SHOW US YOUR DICK § purchased a cage full of rats in the hope that infusing my home with New Life will fire up my posts a nd score me the Bertucci's deal. amen § time stops when you see a DM from that one special man. picture of me on all fours like a dog. "searching for my smile... Have u found it?" § Thinking about saying "Fuck" on SNL. What my brand needs most right now is for me to say "Fuck" on SNL. How do i get to go do that § the girls on this website are villains. all of then. § grown man's ass surgically transplanted onto his son. final wish of a dying father § elon: the tesla milker will run by taking ordinary chemtrails out of the air and tuirning them into, milk me: wow. Tastes great. Ha ha ha § @McDonalds @ McDonalds thats it. thank you for hearing me out. i am a huge fan of the"big mac" and im nice once you get to know me § http://t.co/RvRHIaehDr here is a cool list of "weird tweets'" § egypt is literally dying and all you can think about is the day your annual gift is shit into your lap you shit pig #jan25 § had mny scholarship revoked because of my bumbling 15 tweet routine about how isis attacked the airport because they hate brussel sprouts § today my 4 year old son thanked me, for my work in engineering Fostered dialogue's between my White and Black folloers, as well as Asianic. § i would appreciate it if my followesr called me "Sir" , like they would a Police Man, or any one else with the power to destroy their lives § ijust gave some guy in the bathroom $200 and he left. i think i own a toilet now § several men present to me a single diaper in a black suitcase. i take the diaper in my hand and examine it. "my god, this is next-gen" § isnt it wild that every time i look at pictures of hell i say that it looks like some cool shit, and that i would go there instead of heaven § BOSS TELLS ME I CAN KISS MY FERRETS AT WORK, BUT NO OPEN MOUTH. I PUNCH THE FLOOR SO HARD HIS SCREEN SAVER DEACTIVATES § @Garfield false flag § i'm not allowed to participate in the olympics this year because i have " o discernible athletic talent" and my "dick looks chewed up" § Many consider Reddit,com to be the "Front Page" of the internet, and yet, in the year 2018, I am called a Bastard for saying this. § does anyone know if robert mugabe have a twitter site § @Lowenaffchen @dogbountyhunter woqw. respond to a helpful offer with disgusting, ignorant vitriol. lost a lot of respect for The Dog today § i want to see james bond do steampuck, i want to see bat man do steampuck, i want to see spider man do steampuck, and thats the bottomline. § theres a 1000 dollars in front of you. youre free to take it but if you do every dead bug on earth comes back to life. Do you take it Yes No § much of bliged § half the posts these guys are making could perhaps be found in "Barney magazine" , or "Shit for babys magazine" § ijust had to block like 3 people for using the word "gargle" as a noun § @THEHermanCain whoever the fucks running this account now needs to unblock me from it ASAP. "Enough is enough" § please stop coming to the dumpster factory where i work and forcing me to tell diaper jokes. my boss has taken my car away becausr of this § daily reminder that i wear a suit and tie daily eeven though I have not set foot in public for over 16 years #GoodBoy

#Hansdome § i am far too clever to jack off § "sorry sir. we cannot offer
support for any non-standard operating systems" http://bit.ly/cyX2L7 § i will
block those who shit on the Bones of Mr. GHWB, euthanized with a lethal dose of
Heroin after 94 years of service "As was his request" § I wouldnt enjoy doing
it, but I would eat dog shit if it would increase my IQ by 1 point. Whos with
me § perhaps big bubba and trump could end up in the same minimum security
facility. but that would run contrary to conventional big bubba lore https://t.
co/cu6UG7n6us § yes i am a "HO" Honorable online § this is very bullshit §
guy reading tweets out loud at a gathering: ah, ah, check this out. he just
posted, "Leeroy the Jenkins guy" everyone else there: Thank you § if someone
dressed in cclown makeup came up to me and asked to suck my dick, id naturally
assume it's a troll, § every day my inbox is inundated with women (female)
claiming that they understand Mens Life, whereas all i can do is simply smile.
§ some of mother fuckers think to win the Dumb Ass award is a GOOD thing! § you
have the right to remain Diapered. anything you shit can and will be held
against you in a quart of piss § the more i drive around in circles, the more
people see my "HOME DEPOT FUCKED ME " bumper sticker. simple aritmetic § god
once said "pit bull" https://t.co/3rs2e8DFpf § thhere is no such thing as
charisma, and art is fake. the only metrics by which we must determine the
worth of a man are Strength and Wisdom § bull shit https://t.co/Gb5aiZ6Dhd §
let's all kick the BTK killer's ass, all of us who make the good tweets,. we've
got to meet up and beat the BTK killer's ass and go on dates § Guess ill go eat
dog shit then and get worms in my legs like that guy in taiwan. § huge amounts
of vomitting hav.e, made me good at howling § hank william jr is not horse
shit § the trick to lining my dx racer gaming seat with towels is to not let
any part of my ass touch the chair and reduce its value § in the year 2030 ,
"You will be able to order food on the cell phone" § https://t.co/xw5ppF6ato §
it will be as good as the thursday nite rant once i get better at writing them
and my stress levels decrease. § by getting really mad at poeople for having
their dick sucked § God Bless the United States of America and the Constitution
that this Country was built on. Grab yourself a Mud Jug and KEEP PACKIN€™
HAMMERS § (sees no soliciting sign outside Wendy's) damn it!!! fuck! i really
wanted to solicit to wendys!! § http://www.youtube.com/watch?v=ApxjOMDgFZE my
girfriend latest victim of disgusting bp oil spil § Guess what. Some people
have opinions different that you, so shut the fuck up § gonna catch a lot of flak
for this one, but i gotta go with Alchemy > Random. http://t.co/PrsF4m2L § im
just a man w ho loves his beavis § year 2160 - the huggies corporation pays the
united states govt 4 quadrillion dollars to suppress socialized sewage treat-
ment § "Will You Commit To The CareFree Live Or Die Brand" Yes sir "Are U A
Sick Enough Fuck To Get Covid On Purpose & Drive The Fans Nuts" Yes sir § FOR
SALE: One Beekeeper's Uniform With "METH GOD" embroidered into back, Lightly
Used (856) 625-3325 - Ask For Officer Jim § i did not say that the kid from
jungle 2 jungle should be sent to Guantanamo bay, i just said it wouldn't be
racist if he was § cant wait to win the civil war just by sitting on the
computer and get a dumb ass cop butler as a reward § envisioning Jeans Hotspots
across america & various territories, where consumers can learn their "Jeans
number" and look at photos of jeans § getting too big from steroids and smoking
cigaretts in front of girls, walking around like a dumb ass, waddling like i
got a log in my pants § be careful on the web. i just found iout my girlfriend
of 12 years is a bag clip § i am interested ni "meme format". i am going to
experiment in "meme format", to improve my page. http://t.co/UEl1EWJlpo §
putting on my game face. the official face of the nfl § if my twieets upset you,
then why dont you just "COVER THEM UP" ??/ ha ha get it § to me, the white and
yellow lines that get painted to the roads are mostly a nuisance. i say let's
#TakeEmOff § oh sorry. I was browsing the #jan25 tag for information regarding
important human rights developments you shit stain pig man § they will be

destroyed so they do not fall into the hands of my predators § Now is not the
appropriate time to discuss content. § starting "project Dog dick" the NFTs of
the future. send me $20 and i email you a dogs dick pic with special Dog Dick
Number (Dont lose it) § desperate Husband , sitting on the toilet and palm
mashing all the buttons on the bathroom jukebox trying to get bob seger back on
§ In Second Life. Im the toilet who slides around and asks superior avatars to
use me, please track me down if you want to discuss "Politic's" § hell no i
wont wear a sleeping cap. what the fuck is that shit. how does a hat help you
go to sleep. looks like, a Fools hat. § ill show you real truth ... https://t.
co/Ph7kDBsjdi § Just looking at some stuff that i clicked on. § Found it out the
hard way that SubWay is no longer using Signature Breads. Ive been snookered.
Ive been cock suckered § .@chasebank youve fucked my millionaire points clubs
rewards and murdered my ass dead in the water now your life of fraud is exposed
to all § i may not know "jack shit" , but i know my friend "Jack fists" and he
would like to come to knock the shit out of your teeth, § every reply i receive
on twitter is a literary treasure & rivals the collective works of all pulitzer
prize winners combined § im not wishning you freaks a happy new year. you will
all fuck up my 2019, like you have with all the other years. youre dopes § It
didnt work. Leave it § you can even give money to it if you want to § foudn
some excellent Ass Shirts in a big red bag behind the hospital. i am replacing
my entire wardrobe of tuxedos and zoot suits,with these § i was promised awful,
screaming cicadas by the millions. i am starting to think i busted out my
CICADA MAN 2013 t-shirt for nothing. § wish Obama would authorize some drone
strikes against my ex-wife! *the act takes a more serious tone* Instead of
doing Benghazi. § say what you will about my mediocre ass hole... at the end of
the day, It's got people talkin!!!! § obliterated by secret service goblins
taxpayer magnum pulse cannons while horse playing on a diving board § Can i
citizens arrest girls § everything thats a reference to something sucks fucking
Dick. all quotes are shit § ˜…˜…˜… § FUNNY ! Dog eating a used condom ! ˜…˜…˜… §
he lived a rich, meme-filled life § we odnt post the word "you" anymore in 2016.
§ to stand nude before a group of middle aged italian mob bosses and have them
obnoxiously berate your dick while smoking cigars § whats everyones favorite
gas price? mine is $3.29 § im too busy frowning at the computer to eat § happy
birthday " horus the sun god" § in Are society, women are constantly fucked and
had sex with . it is therefore my duty as a Senator to inspect their pussys
for microchips § piece of shit https://t.co/OUy5nfQlau § @NYGovCuomo this sucks
Ass sir § suckng off a wadded up bra in honour of national bra day or what ever.
i dont know. who gives a shit § The most fucked up possible thing has happened.
Porno has returned to cyberspace. § bill mahrer should go off on guys who poop
their pants § "and the lord said Gambling is fucked" unfollow me if you are a
gambler § Personality: Good friend for anyone, will help someone in need, not
foul with language. Dislikes: People who ridiculize Lucario (I really ha § "I
have Watched the Bud Dwyer suicide video over 1000 times." - iconic Mickey
Rourke - InfluencePedia.Go § Kurnis § ZUMBA IS NOT FOR MOMS!! ZUMBA IS NOT FOR
MOMS!! ZUMBA IS NOT FOR MOMS!! STOP STEALING MY FRIENDS I WANT TO LIVE MY
LIFE § @SlimJim how much salt has to be hammered into a turd before it turns
into a Slim Jim § i love to hover hand my gf in pictures. (gets Owned across
various media) sorry. Sorry everyone. I forgot that was bad § everyone who says
my dick looks like a marshmallow has obviously never seen one before. do
marshmallows have urethras in them, or balls?? no § posting Ethically, within
reason § Have u ever wanted to Kick someone's ass on here so bad but don't do
it because you will die if youre exposed to clouds § i, turdghoul fuckass,
swear to uphold the constitution of the united states of america, so help me
Piss. ok sorry, now let me do it for real § whta can i say. i fucked up. i
really dropped the ball on this one. happy halloween § theory postulated by
known troll "Zentai_Gary" states that i, @dril, go to the zoo every weekend to

, in his words, "fuck the apes", and i w § before you threaten to "Pimp slap" me, please remember that i am a police officer of the law, on at least four separate timeline's § "the human brain is simply just a computer. And not a journalist alive will tell you this." - the Dril account § President Obama began to question the future of his country. Desperate for answers, he humbly knelt before a crucifix made of Slim Jim `s. § getting Shit engagement numbers all around. Thats saturday morning for you. My followers all have DUIs. Guess ill go fuck my self! Boo hoo! § Perhaps the tier I aspire to achieve the most is that of the Milk Bone brand. Such flawless precisIon. Beauty; Grace. Truly awe inspiring . § It's become apparent that this is a measured attack . § im laughing at this really good ad   http://t.co/JMoAYCGH19 § Time and time Again. People on here Fuck me over and ruin my life. simply for starting the Dialouge § GUess who just renewed his subscription to Newsweek. this guy! (cue blurry stock footage of an unidentified fat old man spitting into a cup) § the last four super bowls were deep fake, and they're just gonna keep on deep faking them § many are asking me about "hamburger 2.0" . I will say more of it in due time. § people get mad at me when i riff on Current Events so ill just say this. im enjoying cooking turds on the grill regardless of what day it is § "You have the thoughts and brain of a baby." - My 2012 Adviser Craig Gurtle -- Fuck you Mr. Gurtle, I Can Survive 2012 My Self. § "Every Women" by SegaBoris Every women is a rich tapestry ,   Woven by the lord to be Nice, Never Racist, and always Have a interesting life § holding up hte line at Aldi with a barricade of shopping carts, desparately trying to contact the ex-wife to ask if im allowed to eat Pectin § i know a lot of women . and none of them would ever need sleep with this clown Austin powers § just reassuring you all, that if i forgot to include your favorite tweet in my book it is because it sucked Ass. Get fucked off of my page § fuck "jokes". everything i tweet is real. raw insight without the horse shit. no, i will NOT follow trolls. twitter dot com. i live for this § RATIONALIZE YOUR FILTH ONLINE, SCROUNGE THE WEB FOR EMOTION, LOG OFF ANGRY AND GO TO BED SAD § http://t.co/E2xH8t4O http://t.co/eESRTyJz http://t.co/UN2fyxZJ your pre-election piss links § attn supporters of hashtag #JackOffForTheEagles: thgis is NOT an official, NFL sanctioned method of supporting our birds. use xtreme caution § they brought back covid 19 because you were all being such little shits to me § please allow me to explain the mechanics of the thursday nite rant. its not officially thursday nite rant if it does not contain the hashtag § it is generally agreed upon that my posts are considered to be the worst aspect of my twitter presence § HA HA HA HA HA HA HA HA HA HA HA HA HA HA HA § teens using planetary alignment to get high, we now turn to our resident Teen Expert, now trying to get a light bulb to stick into his beard § it's really messed up that im the only normal person on this entire site, considering millions of people use it daily § inventing a new Suit of playing cards: "The Horseshoes" - We got the king, queen, jack and Ace. All your favorites - The most powerful suit § warning: shrek brand cadmium contains shards of broken glass § just read something fucked up... Not a single picture of stonehenge exists. § now that net neutrality is finally dead i can share my controversial tony hawk/NASCAR cross fiction without fear of persecution or ridicule § when harry potter said"i solemnly swear to blow up this monsters penis w/ a fire ball" i had to put the book down & bow my head for a moment § xmas hual 2011: can of paste, novel based on "little fockers", Oprah Crystals, fucken mmeat ball sandwich, a fuckin $2.50 slice-a pound cake § boycott digimon otis. hes not even that funny § i pay $5000 for a high end cpu just to get disrespected on my own god damn feed § im all about getting out there and putting the posts up like im bad outta hell § i iwsh he blocked me so i could talk shit about him, but now i have to say the gofundme is good and im glad hes doing it. § i fully intend to topple the DigimonOtis empire via a coordinated campaign of viral folk songs bolstered by my partnership w/ Bob Evans Inc. §

lets make it 2000 dollars. i want to see these fuckers sweat § when you're sitting on the toilet theres a tiny opening between the seat and your dick/nut area. this is known as "The Daredevil's Spittoon" § In my honest opinion, due to recent events, they should call beloved pop sensation Justin Bieber, they should call him "Mr. Jail". Thank you § stepping into fiveguys hq, just listing hundreds of brand new chef-inspired value combos off the top of my head. Boom. just like that. 1 2 3 § when people upload pics of misc.electronics and the shit just is covered in dust, crumbs,etc i usually have to sign off for a sec &cool down § It all so sucks Ass. § cant wiat to see what devilish thanksgiving scenarios me and the boys of twitter can conjure up. "The turkey was taken by spiders? ? Whua??" § the super bowl is a game show. and any game show with out merv griffin at the helm is shit. Its not a good show § imagine the sheer power of a man shattering a boulder with a whip. incredible § please do not send any pictures of your legs to LegNut64. he is not a real leg cop § i was born in my motehr's bladder instead of the womb. the doctors called it a "piss birth" #Romnesia § there vapid . § my followers know im the go-to Bitch when it comes to interior wood paneling, so if i say its a " o buy", the shit has become seirious § i can only hope that when a kangaroo court of dipshits comes to haul me to prison that i have the grace and humility not to get mad at them § do not contact this account until you have truly felt the pain of a big male. § (sniffing a crumpled up one dollar bill i found on the floor of a dog kennel) ah.. thats greenbacks baby § sorry grandma. your laptop was good but i shattered it into 1 million shards after i saw someone say SEO stood for "shit eater optimization" § IM THINKING WE GOTTA P{UT OUR NOGGINS TOGETHER AND TRYING TO SEE IF WE CAN MAKE THAT "YES NUT NOVEMBER", FOR US FELLAS WHO LOVE TO BUST!!! § im george soros bitch § people who like to say "Ba ba ba ba " at me <<<< People who hand me their wallet § the family gathers around the PC to run a google image search for "invader zim crying" § #e3rumors IM THAT HANDSOME FELLA LAYIN ON THE HOOD OF HIS LEXUS NEXT TO THE CONFERENCE HALL, STROKIN IT TO ALL THE RIFF-RAFF ABOUT THE PLACE § HLUUUUUUUUU1 § @Battlefield I have verbally con-fronted "Garth_Turds" on several occasions, remaining respectful despite his refusal to listen to reason. § http://www.buttheadcovers.com/tiny-pig.html sombody please buy me this for next years 9/11 § #atlanticcon please disable all of your wi-fi devices to prevent Gremlins from entering this trustsphere of minds. inflation is a myth. bye § children.. toddlers.. babies..they all got one thing in common. they all truly believe they can kick my ass. but they are Fundamentally Weak § reaches into pocket for folded up print-out of "the troll face". a bunch of old crumpled up napkins also fall out. the stench is unbear-able § searching for bastards . § "Depression" § yeah with damn beer.Tonight we drink damn beer in hell § thats why im a bing man § me and my fat cousin are gonna tackle e3 gonzo style with a series of choreographed blogs an;d im rolling out a face book for gamers. § Is Amaerica Ready For A Fat President § my main shit is going to CVS and doing riffs on whatever i see on the shelves. most of my material is never recorded or heard by human ears § just yanked 3 bundles of rebar off a construction site and into my truck. now im going to biuld my own pizza hut § sickening https://t.co/CnbuNh3bkp § Q: Whats ur least favorite finger to be flipped off with A: the middle one. it pisses me off way more than the other fingers. drives me nuts § did you see his dick through the clown pants he was wearing. Oh Man § venus sucks shit. if they find life there it's going to be a very small man curled into the fetal position yelling "FUCK THIS" § fourteen of my beautiful sons exploded in God's War and the army sent me a gorgeous mantlepiece of a wolf that I kiss everyday § Fuck Digimon Otis § its monday now, but ive decided that yesterday was the first official "Shut Da Fuck Up Sunday" which means its time to block 5 dick heads § nobody gives a SHIT about ANYBODY!!! if a train obliterated my entire house nobody would even call 911! It's that fucked! It's that fucked! § the only ones authorized to sneak peeks at my dick are 1) my doctor, 2) my dentist, and 3) my lawyer. as for the trolls? No Dice-- Bub. § Ive decided to not be a part of asexual anymore after receiving a call from my agent orderring me to stand down § today i saluted the afghanistan vet who lives on my floor and said "Suck My Dick Sir! Mission Failed" then went home and dead lifted 300lbs § there is no act more intimate & sensual than browsing a mans "Like" page , and clicking on there without permission is the ultimate betrayal § pringles caliphate § al gore conference on global warming..canceled by SNOW!! "Guh, BLugh Durr" says the dumb man, while he pees into his comically large diaper § just had the check Mark for 6 mins, but lost it by posting a picture of the back of some guys head with the caption "White people be out here" § im being targeted individualed again https://t.co/BkmDsrsM0M § Goes To Rotten.com, Sees A Man's Dick, Clenches Eyes Shut And Shakes Head While Clicking For The Back Button, Clicks Refresh Accidentally § Sovereign Citizens Getting Owned Compilation § @GoonExposer please dont goon expose me § i repeat: this shit would have slayed ass in the golden era https://t.co/Vy7Amt0ppB § going Hard for my next big 9/11 Deep Dive. The time has come to goose around in the name of 9/11. Just wait'll I get my kicks, of 9/11 § father wont stop opening my amazon boxes--How to proceed? (Self,Legal) TOP VOTED: put a live wire in his car & light his ass up. Cook his ass § apparently if you pull pics of the gym teacher's mansion off google street view and draw some ghosts dancin on it the fbi handcuffs your mom § i sense that my Zwinky knows when i'm feeling upset. is it possible that Zwinkys operate on a higher level of consciousness than humans? yes § my heart goes out to people waking up from comas today & not believing the date actually is the number 2 repeated an insane amount of times § manufacturing a story about getting sucked off by Sam Donaldson for the "Shit Head" new york times to report on w/ zero scrutiny whatsoever § despite google's bullshit-- today is National Criminal Log Off Day. if you're a criminal then log off § 1000% of followers will rather click on a penis than a literature book § #5wordsbeforesex IM GONA FUCK § @Number1TCOT have you ever had your hat fucked by a dick § i cant believe ive been chanting the words "epic Pee tape" in the mirror every morning for the past 4 years for nothing § Im Very Upset with girls *impossibly low-res bikini babe robo-posting about heartworm meds follows me* Just kidding. Im only mad at the boys § i opened my notes app for the first time in 5 years and the only thing i found was some shit that says "mr feed bag 2007" https://t.co/ikmC7jIz1X § today's garfield was much funnier when i read it the second time. thru the scope of my DPMS panther .308 semi-automatic rifle. #veteransday § i hate all of "Groupthink" , except for the groupthought that group thinks that groupthink is bull shit § I CAN CONFIRM HERE AND NOW THAT THE USER GOING BY THE NAME OF " OPRAHS_DICK " HAS NO AFFILIATION WITH HARPO PRODUCTIONS-- " BLOCK THAT SHIT " § people named fucking "Curtis" need to get a grip, and start calling themselves "Curt" which is a rteal name § #THeSaturdayMorningRamble sometimes when you get caught in traffic you just wanna get pissed off § am I the most dark & twisted psycho god online?? hm lets see: - When the dow jones industrial average goes down i say simply the word "Good" § I've Provided The Users Of This Geode Collector's Forum With Tasteful Upskirts For 17 Years. Don't Like It? Then Log Me Out, Bastard. § when MetalGearEric told his 36 followers i have "A Poor Man's Micropenis" and none of my so called allies stepped in to defend my honuor.... § i think it is good to vote, unless it is inconvenient, or boring to do so. then it might be very bad. i'm sorry for doing politics om here. § " a man must have a code " § my followers love watching me vomit all over my $4000 gaming setup like a Whore § going on a diarrhea strike (giving myself diarrhea on purpose) unntil the us govt forces my daughters to join the isreali defense force § i respect installing $40000 of mods into a pit bull to make him look like Frankenstein but changing his name to "btk killer" is too much. § #ThingsGirlsLike Moonlit Sega Rants § i really dont care what Yankee Doodle did when he went to town. His toxic fanbase tells me everything I need to know about him . § For years i've put up with the piss lobbyists and their laughable attempts to silence me. i will not use th bathroom again until theyre dead § SCIENTIST INVENT VACCINE THAT CURES AND CAUSE AUTISM AT THE SAME TIME. THE ULTIMATE HIGH § @Tabletsman @DigimonOtis this is tactless even for you , tablets man § MAINSTREAM: Barney the dinosaur is some good shit. I like it. It's really good. ME: Barney the dinosaur is bunk. This is a show for children § ive been searching for videos on how to humanely execute a captured butterfly, and all i found was SCAMs § I Apologize sir. Im a fucking idiot. I will Try to make them good § i love "having my druthers" (??) § SARKOZY PRETENDED TO INITIATE HANDSHAKE WITH OBAMA BUT THERE WAS A BABY BIRD IN HIS HAND AND THE BABY BIRD MELTED. ACT OF WAR............ § nonchalantly wearing a pink sweater vest while plowing out my wife during a 4.7 magnitude earth quake § just invented a new type of posting while your were all running around on here. ENjoying your little whack off sessions? Dont care didnt ask § i can't post the reason i need a wife from this website by june 30 because that info is private. grow the fuck up. all of u § film your wives you god damn morons. im paying top dollar for wife footage § i pull a small american flag out of my pocket and give it a bunch of tiny kisses in my day to ward off liars and cheapskates § i just think this is the sort of thing that would be nice to have https://t.co/h8JCrR6JJc § well fucking great. my date's getting here in 10 minutes and im going to look like an imbecile with my bookcase devoid of any rat literature § 5g sucks dog shit . i could not even download a dogs ass with this crap § you are all too concerned wih your fucking "Brands" to help a mman who was absolutely in hell for 4 hours you turncoat motherfuckers of shit § #ObamasPresidencyInTwoWords IN1993OBAMAWASWITNESSED-CARVING ALCHEMYGLYPHSINTOAPUBLICBENCH § Frowning Principal Exposed To Beer Content On Time Line § Ellen Pledges to Gradually "PHase Out" Cameras in Employee Restrooms in Highest IQ Move to Date: Here's What To Know § thinking about taking some of the excess respect I have for our Fallen Heroes and converting it in to Cold Hard Cash § double digit iq; pure stooge energy. i would love to see all these people get together and attempt to build a shed https://t.co/6rqlv8puhe § seems to be confusion regarding the job offer. you just directed me to an amazon listing for clown makeup. Looking forward to the real link. § grwo up. this is serious § for hte last time im not badfrog3333 im this guy http://t.co/KpjbucKS § gluing 1000 newspapers to the wall so my neighbors cant hear me jacking off is not only rational; it is an act of service § just as Christ washed the feet of his disciples , i proudly volunteer to allow my girl followers to use my shirt as a napkin,. § https://t.co/9vlMFms7DG my failing brand https://t.co/KHEIYhoDh5 § jesus christ there's a band named ziggy mania § yea everyone called me Dixie Cup for years juts cause I asked if it was alright to use a dixie cup as a condom in sex ed. im cool now though § when you call me a shit head, or a dip shit, or a low rent stooge, that is like putting a knife directly into my Posts. § my dream uncle would have the calves of an angel...and the thighs of a Devil § SensualMaddenPlayer Checking In. § i am a local politician and i just want to lick this fucking ridiculous huge lollipop without people photographing me and ruining my career § regarding the pep boys. they look disgusting § "ah, but you are merely a parasite. and some day this little labyrinth you created will collapse before you find the exit." -animefucker_x10 § juts donated $300000 to a lobbying firm whose main thing is letting people drive cars at the age of 6 § if you "clap back" someone with a PhD on here, you should be allowed to have their PhD. Its just common sense people. Oh that's tea § check the shit o n the lightbulb before using it. too many people are using the wrong voltage count and it;s too bright #TheThursday-NiteRant § Its mueeller time #TheElection § going to the fire station to kick all the firemens asses wearing my fat ass denim overalls § im going to be very upset if I shell out a thousand big ones for google's glass only for it to be 100% legal for people to do jokes about it § the bastard of downloads § they look like some shit a farmer would wear to the public execution of a goat. fuck jeans § imagine a guy whose desktop computer is an integral part of his drum set and he posts by tapping the keyboard with his sticks and it's me § no i am not talking about my post § dr oz says due to the sheer volume of milk & cookies santa consumes, you have no hope of poisoning him with piss or cum. wont even notice it § did you just rob a bank by threatening to open a bottle of diarrhea § putting my fist through the wall and yanking out a chunk of insulation and making a "what the fuck is thiis" gesture before throwing it § don't you dare make me type § ill yank your earrings straight out you goblin § im not cut out to be a content producer!! fuck thtis!! i want to go back to just looking at everyone else's content and nodding if its good § THRIEE SIMPLE RULES FOR SPEAKING TO ME OF MY AFFAIRS REGARDING MY INTERACTIONS WITH MY LAWYER'S... STAND DOWN !! GET IN LINE !! FUCK OFF !! § reality tv show where we replace one lucky boy's pc gaming chair with a fully functioning toilet. every episode § ALL SHIT § My 2022 bingo card is looking more and more every day like my fucking ass wiped it . § you look like the tomb raider lady Lol Mar 22   just heard the news of jussie smollett. Feeling unsure right now   5s You can no longer send m § you call this shit rotisserie chicken? I bet this shit hasnt even rotated 1 time in its entire life. § #worstfeeling dying of dehydration caused by diarrhea in a third world nation ravaged by warfare with no doctors #bestfeeling halo 4 odst § if you have less than 1000 followers i can guarantee you that me and the boys share your posts in vip chat rooms and call you a "Muthafucka" § givgn my social security number to the valentines day app to find out which idiot wants to see my dick the most § there are two type of people in this world, people who know binary and mpeople who win the special olympics because there retarded. § i have every net flick § ME: when committing to a project like "the 12 days", you are forced to bear your soul to countless vicious cannibals GQ: crhist. its true § i just sold all of my teeth to the president of starwars for one hundred dollars #SBMediaDay § Welcom to MpregCraig's Mpreg Dolphin Cove 3D... if u are a shark fanboi, please leave. 2d likers? no dice. Fpreg? get the F outa here § if the event occurs wherein i misspell the official thursday nite rant hashtag, please let me know via email and i will correct it § idont eat § someitmes it seems to me that some people woulr rather join KKK, than join mensa.... § this website seems more & more like a place where elitist daddys boys can show off how 'CLEVER' they are, instead of a source for bra advice § the Iranian parliament holding an assembly to watch the dance scene from Son of the Mask on a poor quality vhs tape and screaming at it § shocking: "racism is the light of my soul. racism is the air that i breathe, and racism is what i like." -RacismMario @cnn @msnbc @foxnews § STEROID and CIGAR levels must remain equal . otherwise my organs will complete- ly shut down and the quality of my posts will suffer immensely § my new quote: "That's some good ass Hulu" (to be spoken after, viewing exceptional content on the hulu streaming site) § *stealthily dumps an entire bottle of gnc 100% pro performance whey protein into the dog's food dish * oh hey what's going on i was just uh, § incoming picture of mysterious bead collection from WolfRespect- er § #ourfriendshipendedwhen you laced my oatmeal with shrek glasses § begin- ning tomorrow .. for #The12DaysOfContent... that's twelve days of top-shelf posts just in time for santa. as a "Thank You" to the boys § Unamused by the portmanteau of "Groupon" § the brief period in high school when DigimonOtis changed his name to BurgerKingOtis in an attempt to improve his image § Yeah, some of us like to network with successful brands on twitter. The rest of you want to join hippy communes and suck the hippys' dicks. § ive completed the first hour of my 2 day #NoPiss challenge. i am searching for media outlets who would like to document my struggle § 9/15/17: 0 "DRY DAY" § two handfuls of kitty litter taken from the beautiful hollywood home of sports broadcaster Dick Vitale , for $100 or best offer § droid is filth. govt trick to ID and persecute civilians for $. real ID is 666 - thow all micro chips into the trash can. piss #IWantADroid § waving flags, honking horns, trying to coax the kfc golem into shitting all over my mouth and my picnic § god grant me the strengrh to raise $260 to create Skeleton MMORPG . if this kickstarter fails...im gonna Start Kickin § mario tennis § twittetr should recommend. a bath § (vomits while dioing pushups at the gym and resists every attempt from professional trainers to stop me from continuing) § if the twitter man is reading this: i don't like the fact that people are "following' this account and i would like that feature turned #OFF § despite the most recent of shit my enemies are now saying, i will never be found, standing on my front lawn , using a "Hula hoop " § watch this marines Epioc response to being told that he should replace his gun with an enormous lollipop § me N' the boys eating messy sandiwches, sneaking around with big binoculars looking for girls & letting every one know who runs this TJ maxx § im absolutely the only mother fucker on here dumb enough to get publicly whipped for posting NFT bullshit while also making $0 off of them § i point to my new tat , "UNVACCINATED" written across my shoulder blades, the dudes nod their heads and line up for a round of high fives § Please Dont § the troll wedges the curb between my ass as i lay on my side. " o!" i shout. "im a content producer!!" he stomps my ass cheek, finishing me/ § #ghettospellingbee spell Ownage C-A-R-L-O-S-M-E-N-C-I-A (rip) § barak "diapers" obama too busy scrubbing the litle oil spill birdies to wipe the tar of disrespect from the souls of our mem day troop #tcot § (POsturing like a dip shit at the public pool) My father owns no small number of shares at the smirnoff ice company. Let me be the lifeguard § i take a vacation to hawaii to relieve myself of the Trolls. a group of hula girls begin beating me up & calling me shit as soon as i arrive § my idea for a car, is that it looks like a normal car., but right next to the steering wheel Blammo. theres a hose you can suck beer out of § if any of oyu crude boys want to come after me *room lights up revealing collec- tion of r/c helicopters behind my outspread arms* be my guest § i really hate him § triyng to calculate the precise amount of gunpowder needed to blow up my dick, and only my dick § let`s get this insane takedown virel § looking at a picture of poop chart that has different kinds of pictures of poop on it to find out if i have any diseases § yorue next. on the pain list § your damn right im a some of a bitch. soorryest some of a bitch i ever met § lookin for some crazey motherfuckas to do a mind meld with, literally a combination of minds, double brain. we will be the most powerful man § (struggling))ok i figured it out: all opinions are good, except for the opinions that say other peoples opinions are bad, because thats rude § my crystalologist told me that bin laden was trapped inside this $60 jade charm?? getting REAL huffy & worked up righ now and demand ansers § haha you beg for paypal donations to keep your terrible website up and yell at people who do the same to eat § pleae look at the facts. § i am sending my passport and car keys to this man § if big tech keeps loading their apps with features that i can accidentally post my dick on, i will have no choice but to enter crisis mode . § pranking my pud § yes but i nnever do searches on him so it's weird that this happened. § hit by a train while wearing a trenchcoat bloated with family guy jewelry and nobody even helped me pick any of it up because god is twisted § (fully immerses self in a picture of sponge bob saying "Dat Boy Tho") § breastfeed a celeb today § tyoure on here scrutinizing my posts , while your girl is out Fucking curly from the three stooges § (trying to apologize for sending dick to 900 girls) you see the phones have a front & back camera. so taking pictures is really complicated, § none of this shit is even from the future. is that a bee hive? Fuck you https://t.co/U1M64ZqsfK § Just like the damn bomper sticker says -I Will flip my car on top of you and snuff you out if i see you "DAB" , Regardless of race §

neurotoxic pig bone spores § Looking To Be Jacked Off Into A Basin - m4w - 32 (Trenton, NJ) § CNN should put a little "Devil face" next to all the bad, or upsetting articles on their site. Who likes this? Who thinks this would be fun? § i do not watch the snl show (Too crass) but i do enjoy reading the episode summaries that they put in the newspaper for some reason § Ooohhhh my portfolio !!!!!!!!!! https://t.co/Q5qExhT8Nm § Rather tiresome that people wiould rather Threadshit my mentions than say, enjoy a whimsical boating tour through the fair canals of Venice. § BUY NOW http://t.co/4SQ3G1to "AUTHENTIC BIG TEX ASHES" Own a piece of history. Actual Big Tex ashes #BigTex #IllNeverForget § when one of the boys tells me he has to use the bathroom i inevitably respond with some stupid shit like "Alright, Sounds Good" § my ass looks like a NUMB SKULL's ass § getting pisse d off imagining my trolls and dissenters crawling around my house in little butler outfits and expecting tips § daily reminder that the idea of "SUcking Ass" is a societal illusion & everything you do is healthy no matter how much youre punished for it § Girls are my wife constantly § they should put slot machines in the mc donalds. i want to win baby § to the trolls: i just bought a 5-pack of Oral-B electric toothbrush heads using points from my Chase Freedom card. could a child do that? no § @JoseCanseco please beat me to death with the softball bat juiced. i want to experience the legal 600 ft long ball across my fucking skull § jay leno in return for your fucked up fixation with cars you have earned a Kiss from the devil § 9/30/10 - CONTENTS OF DIAPER - THE USUAL; SHIT 'N' PISS-- 1 EGG I LAYED § whats that? if you send me $40 i will send a big picture of a dogs dick instead of a normal sized one. @elonmusk re blog this sir #important § #QuestionsIDontLike muslim § taking sips from a big fat thermos with the isis flag on it. thinking about inventing an app that tells me when lunch time is § pleased to announce i had a nice conversation with the sheriff and my account is now verified. Thank you all § i think theres like a 90% the family guy saw my penis through the tv just now #paranormal #NotGood § i feel as thoggh ive been tasked by a greater power to keep the riffraf of twitter in line, through my gift of words § Im sucking off a big ass onion right now. Urrghh § @prodigalsam GOD DAm right you were confused, im all about top-tier content, ive been blocked by the sheikh of dubai for christ sake, Fuck u § how dare you fuck with me. how dare you fuck with me , on the year of Luigi § i am nude, shaved, & ready to be submerged within the digital chrysalis where i will generate bigcoins by doing ki warrior poses until i die § ive seen like 9 separate group dms that are named "Boys Chat". 9 parallel universes, each with their own fucked up opinions regarding Lunch § i Fucking hate it when i come at the king and miss, especially when I best not do that § the Joe Dirt watcher's rockin' Joe Dirt quote of the week: "Watch Joe Dirt" § I LOVE TO ROUGHHOUSE , IM A STRAIGHT TICKET VOTER FOR THE GRAVEROBBER PARTY,AND I BELIEVE THE NUMBER ONE ISSUE IS "MOMS AT THE PUMP" § great tweetie bird quote https://t.co/w8KamUmBC1 § the next perspn caught posting anymore lewd comments regarding the green lady M&M to my home & garden web book will be reported to the FBI. § i have been tasting my piss every day in order to develop an immunity to it. i am immune to piss. if you piss on me ill just laugh at you. § TO ALL GIRLS-- your Man drops a notebook, and inside it is every " ew Rule" written by bill maher since like 2003. Do you flip out or be cool § "the online web. truly a touching testament to the power of... deeply Human connections." -what Abe Lincoln would say if he were alive still § "RSS FEeds? ", i say as i stroke my goatee while leaning on my podcast's huge 3d logo " ever Heard of UM !!!!!!!!!!!!!!" § "Worthless" county treasurer in hot water after releasing list of famous cartoon apes he would like to fuck § thinking abou t having a phase in my mid-50s where i wear a whislte every where i go and make everyone around me call me "Coach" § lets piSS UP A TOWN!! Everoryone reading this, lets all choose one small town randomly and publicly urinate all over it. Combine our piss § but worry not. i have changed my last name to "apefucker/" to dissuade all women from stealing it § and n9ow people are being abusive instead of helping me so i am just going to shut the monitor off and sit in the pitch blackness for awhile § ah,. so I see you too have an interest in tech, and epic sciencse. Get this, i just read that each bitcoin is now worth, over 100 bitcoins § tellling my miserable wife and sons all about the Importance of Media § once again its up to me to take the high road. while everyones making jokes of the fat weed smoker mayor ill be whipping myself in his honor § my hobbies include wearing cool clothes, getting sucked off and being involved in local theater. The last one is a joke, actually § if you work with compute,r, if you know Code, if you do Code, please, please design a hot tub app that i can use in the hot tub § hell of a week folks. first the apple press conference fails to impress me and now it's 9/11. whats next § i have been racking up absurdly high scores in Windows Solitare to increase my power as a gamer § the soldiers crafted armor out of the covers of outdated guinness world record books, to bedazzle and confound their opponents § bring back green ketchup. § i got lock jaw from eating pasta out of a dogbowl and my wife will be here in 2 hours to marry me. help me github § 15 reasons why Comcast,m the company voted the worst in america, is actually the best one, and Here's Why: § (witnessing the flaming wreckage of a 6-car pile up) ah. Respect. More power § whatre you gonna do with all that baumit..gim me some of that baumit come on man https://t.co/TfP7xE8N2S § just because im following the pilot's orders and putting ym seat belt on without raising a stink does not mean i forgive him for doing 9/11 § i think my neighbor might be a gamer?? hes always yelling shit like "Oh Of Course He Fucking Shot Me. Of Course I Just Get Instantly Fucked" § the famous "dewey defeats truman" photograph except it's me holding up the hedaline that says jacking off cures prostate cancer § sure, i would hire the trolls to come work at my multinational public relations firm... to clean the PISS and SHIT out of OUR TOILETS !!! § im Shit efron § tokyo of nippon. the big apple. it is here i will forge my destiny selling printouts of my most Fucked Up posts. i sip off my beer cup & nod § i'll heal him § we all know the famous "Five Second Rule"... if you dont throw dropped food in the trash within five seconds it unleashes toxic spores § Good Lord https://t.co/inCGhw0io7 § its too easy to delete some absolute dog shit you posted. you should have to send like a pint of your own blood to twitter HQ to do it § @dominos thanks for unfollow-ing me. You truly are an ignorant pizza company. Guess were a papa john family now § I want to become the White Martin Luther King of Mental Health. ANd I want to get rich doing it, but without losing my "Edge" or selling out § I AM very exicted to be living in a 3-d world in the yr 2010. the OFFICIAL start to the new millanium § retweet this i f you capitalize Film. #Film § @ FOXBroadcasting U guys should un-cancel the Bernie Mac Show, like u did with family guy. § been completely ruined due to iron deficiency and Arrogance. had to scrap the project and start from scratch. Looking for investors § "horny" has killed more people than all the volcanos on earth combined § I.m taking a break from people who think it is good to make a fool of me for drama purposes. Basically dont look at my page until im not mad § http://t.co/Vq9OvjXyKJ Here's That Fucking Awufl Kfc Page People Have Been Asking Me To Re-Upload § palm thrust my entire head through the fucking wall and kick my big ass while im trapped like a stuck hog § well i'm doing uh, the angry face meme § free julian assange § Bugs Bunny: B Elmer Fudd: A- Tweety Bird: F Daffy Duck: C+ Porky Pig: D+ Theyre the only ones i can think of right now. My hands are shaking § i just found out tombstones have dead people underneath them. fucked up § fast in furious 11: Beyond fucked fast in furious 12: fully Sucked § $-^2 -^2 -^2$ htese are the jeans that christ died in $-^2 -^2 -^2$ § a 38 year old man who is dressed like a school shooter is here too pick up his vitality supplements . § jacking off 1s " Ghetto " § Id like to sincerely apologize for being a beady eyed little fuck-freak. Im hell's shit. Im dog shit's ass. Brand me with a hot iron. Sorry § having my Balls exfoliated by a Doctor § In the past, I have fallen for this trick over 100 times. I've suffered professionally and mentally as a result. Their tactics are ruthless. § im bored. lets end rape. put a blue ribbon or something on your avatar if you want to end rape i guess § people who jack off in the bedroom: spiritual, harmonious, Attuned people who jack off in the bathroom: intellectual, mechanical, productive § woah. you can say "Houston we have a problem" in messy situations that have nothing to do with astronauts or texas? this changes everthing § a visit.. from the easter man http://t.co/qK6xCdUeOU § thats it. thats enough. im shutting the computer down ,before i become too powerful § i will gladly purchase the Horrifying new xbox for each room in my home and expose my nude body to its mandatory camera daily for kfc points § #TheThursdayNiteRant please build more walkways so i don't have to fuck my pants up in the bushes § everything i post is a disgust-ing lie § when your feeding trough is clear of Debris.. that is the shit i like to happen § turn on c-span, therse a man with an anonymous mask doing parkour on the senate floor and im rubbing my face on the tv to absorb his energy § JAILBIRD: Whatre u in for CROOK: I headbutted an ambulance JAILBIRD: Hm., Thats good. Well bye CROOK: Bye. Thank you § ibm scientists place two atoms next to each other to create "world's tiniest ass." government orders them to return grant money immediately § a bumblebee shit on my arm and it hurts § the content i Crave https://t.co/sjSHhxcUuy § to every one who thinks i will get in trouble for posting this. https://t.co/DCqQKXnw5M § check out the new "Five For Five" offer at mc donalds... thats Five soda's for five bucks "Or your money back" § why is piss the center of my life § 30+ YEARS OF CATHY ABRUPTLY HALTED-- LATEST VICTIM OF CORPORATE ELITE'S WAR AGAINST POPULIST INSUBORDINA-TION #OPPRESSION #BETRAYAL #ARTDEATH § micheal_jackson_gets_horny_on_jeopardy. swf § Cowardice: A Tale In Four Parts https://t.co/Abc1veRqnh § now that the unofficial, unauthorized Hall and Oates Super PAC is dead I might as well lie face down in the fucking bathtub until im bones . § demonius darkblade has The Nuke, i can confirm that this large man has obtained a nuclear device and intends to use it on rude posters § massive, hulking gorilla of a man, com-peltely covered in hair, lying on a mattress and jacking off to his one immacu-late shaved leg § block on sight § FOR CHRIST MAS I WILL ATTEMPT TO RATIONALIZE MY DESTRUCTIVE SELF HATRED AND UNCEREMONIOUSLY FAIL TO SUCCEEd at anything whatseoever thankyou § MY WORST FEARS CONFIRME, COPS IN SEWER, MEASIURING MY TOILET STATS AND PUTTING LOUD BUGS IN MY HOUSE AS PUNISHMENT WHENEVER I FUCK UP § yeah i started twitch streaming but i do it offline so my dumb ass followers cant shriek at me while im doing it. 30 year old children. Pigs § me . me please. dear god i need this § twitter is granting me the world's first Dark Verified Account because shit pumps through my veins like blood and i have a shitty attitude § video footage of obama taxing an innocent dog. shameful #kanyewest § i wish i had my baby teeth back. those were the good 90s teeth § dont even think about serving me food from taco bell that isnt served to me MExicano Style § this post is 2 years old. ive since lost custody of my children and my wife left me. still wild about candles § privately and dis-creetly asking any and all girls in my life if they have any questions about upgrading to Windows 11 § a cop will spank you publicly just for breast feeding your pitbull in public . but when a bug bites you hes all "euhhh i dont arrest bugs" § watching hours of people on you tube destroying "Dennis The Menace" logically to max out my SAT scores and live my Best life § asking my financial advisor how to "Bet against america" after seeing someone get mad at someone else for doing it § muting people who like to talk aobut "The news" instead of posting vignettes about being forced to pour mouthwash down their ass crack § *steps up to mic; booed immediately* geico commericals are tthis generation's pink floyd **boos get louder** can anyone help me find my car § appreciating every post online is akin to acquainting oneself w/ each earthly grain of sand..and i absolutely intend to do both these things § when i found out she used the same widely popular online social media aggregator as me, i just knew mny soul was destined to Neg her § "Green lettuce" § ive never laughged at a piss joke. (sees how impressed everyone is, takes it one step further) in fact, ive never laughed before in my life. § my ass isnt very good, over all. my ass and the hole of my ass are boring to think about § drag my shity corpse around § I REALIZE MUSTACHE69@FIANANCE.BIZ MAY NOT BE THE MOST PROFESSIONAL EMAL BUT IVE GROWN SINCE I CHOSE IT AND WOULD STILL LIKE TO BE YOUR LAWER § you come on line and challenge me with a user name like "Lesbian Mr. Clean" , i will not respect you, regardless of your skill lefvel § PULL THE TRIGGER § theres gotta be a game that will make me cum in less than 4 minutes. Theres just gotta § the Heartlands been pinpointed to the town of Dick Licker, Oklahoma where the main thing they got is a museum that displays a real $100 bill § surgury to become japanese. Surgeruy to become Japanese § My Regular Life And My Ocean's Eleven Fanfiction Life Have Collided In A Horrible Fire Ball § I want you all t o know that I am not angry. I am acutally laughing at this whole thing. But Piss_089 should ha ve his computer locked up § watching the inbetween comedy bits on vgas i sat and pondered.. wow this Shit is good enough to be on SNL.. the big league § "Daniel Joerger" gave the Adult Dunce Cap a 1/5 star review on February 20th, 2013, saying it was "Junk" and " ot worth what I paid for it". § if you ask me this election could end about 100 different ways: 1) trump gets 0% of the vote 2) trump gets 1% of the vote 3) trump gets 2% o § phaw!! 2am!.. time to go hit the hay (jacks off and comes back ot the computer) § i believe in " inject steroids into infants ". i believe in " WAsh your damn car ". i believe in " #PregnantHogGate ". i believe in " koopa" § im 90% sure that Weed is a real druvg and not just some shit my friends on here make jokes about § Men - It is never too early to wish all fo the women in your life a happy Valentines day . Ladys- Im sending you pleasure waves at this time § to clarify, i still think that "Porky Pig" should get the electric chair, but not enough to kill him, just enough to Scare him a little bit § epic ; supreme court rules nabisco is legally allowed to label their products as "Homemade" after forcing the employees to live at the factory § i finally beat the Guinness record of "most karate chops absorbed by a man" but it doesnt count because i was unconscious during parts of it § Super Bowl Who???? #retweetthisif #someonetell bobby brown his head look like a chicken wing- #nowplaying Ray J #musicmonday § thinking of becoming a "Pipes" dipshit § no. this is a business proposition. no sex § with these cash back rewards i can fulfill my long standing dream of taking 2 women to red lobster at the same time https://t.co/glT0P7Vkga § lets say hypothetically i was gifted the otto warmbier poster by a DPRK emissary. will they let me sell it on ebay? or will ebay fuck my ass § i saw the other day- theyre selling it $2 a gallon now. Unbelievable. § do not talk of this on here § Q: Mr. James bond youre going to want to have to take a look at this. Q turns the laptop around and james bond sees my posts on it § jackinf off at the dog shit factory § learning how to say "1 2 3" and "hut hut hut" at army § wife is sad because we had to remove all doorknobs from our dreamhome since they were at the exact perfect hieght to go up my ass by mistake § @Favstar_NSFW thank you favstar nsfw. § cave man: ou ou ou,. keep net neautral so me can download Porno Monopoly guy: why not jack off to a Turner Classic Movie instead § @policeman i will assist u sir § FYI if you were to be killed by Drunk Driver paul pelosi, or any heir of the noble Pelosi bloodline, youd enjoy a warriors death in Valhalla § sometimes i wish my ass would be destroyed by a meteor just so i wouldn't have to take shits anymore § my top Grabs of now https://t.co/GmcHZfaZWN § WAITER..ive made it quite clear U are not to speak to me until im ready to select the Spice Level of my braised quail dumplings..now BEGONNE § Today , I am every Husband § leave your DRAMA at the door, or i will SHIT myself !!!! § satan has his filthy little hand in my google serach priority and now when people look up my username they get pictures of dead camels § Camptown races I mean. § "you can take that 666 on down the road" is actually etched into my family crest and i scream it everyday § everyones always using selfie sticks these days instead of attending lectures about string theory and shit and im so mad i could crank off § apparently im not good enough for the pep boys to follow me on twitter. apparently the pep boys fan fiction i poured my soul into is a waste § onl;y if i'm allowed to pray 15 times a day and drink coffee and suck dicks § attention all cops on reddit who have murdered people ; was it Awkward? what gun did you use. did you get a promotion § if you have ever disagreed with anyone about anything youre a sociopathic piece of shit § handsome single adutl man contracts scurvy after eating nothing but oscar mayer lunchables for 4 years and blames his dentist § http://t.co/XYrQaKTmq4 § (bowed head solemnly rises from deep thought) Intellidgence is the strength of wisdom § the american sniper murders 8 people with one bullet 2000miles away from a beach chair in hawaii, winks at the camera and says "Its A Livin" § MIss the days when i could post something like "Crisp Angel: Birdfreak" and get immedialtey a check for 1 Million dollars § please don't try and tell me that schrodinger's diaper is a quantum superposition of clean and dirty states, we can all fucking smell it § if you insult the tiny pepsi can at the bottom of the buzzfeed article your'e fit for the bathroom. i will never let you look at my posts. § one man stands, bravely defiant, against the impending fury of my massive, raw ass. a Troll snaps a picture and puts it in some history book § @Battlefield I recognize that hand gesutre. It is designed to stimulate sex to a womans Pussy (vagina). I will report it § sink help § i destoryed my balls with uh, enhanced interrogation techniques sir § the taste of Bacardi infused with the raw power of Centrum Silver § check out this little guy if you have never seen him. his name is mickey mouse and you can find him on any computer § i just got an email asking me to join The Rat Pack. need to know if its real or not before i move to belarus to make textiles with my uncles § just shaking my head while the piss comes out. This is so vapid § some times the most real shit we've ever read in our entire lives is just sitting right in front of us on our computer screens ...... https://t.co/PJ3lf9gIAM § my combat jeans deflect most bow and arrows shots and also prevent me from thinking about sex § the jerk off who told my autistic son that sega of america exploded needs to come forward so i can crush his neck betwext my Perfect thighs § #The12Day-sOfContent #AmericanSniper http://t.co/jUMQiOrSEF § i wont stop tweeting wonderwoman opinions until all cool & funny people are ran off this site and i can post my psoriasis scars w/o judgment § phew. im out of breath from looking at blades online all day § since opinoins are judged based on how new they are, instead of how good they are, today i will make $1000 by posting "Rap music is hipster" § nobodyd on here is capable of talking to me like a normal goddamn human because theyre pricks and dimwits with incest § twiitter dot com baby... the inmates are running the damn asylum.. AND IT THINK THAT IT IS GOOD...!! #StartupIndia § boy oh boy do i love purchasing large amounnts of Fool's Gold. wait a minute... fools gold fucking sucks. this stuff is no good..!! Fuck !!! § pavlov thinks hes good just because he can make dogs drool with bells. mean while I can make dogs howl insanely just by taking my Ass out § the essential, Male Ass § telling secretary to hold my calls so i can spend some time lookinh at girls' avatars with a loupe § TRied to sell some cool EbaumsWorld Merch to Wallstreet Protesters, was told to "Fuck Off" by probable agent provocateur; Im Sad and Fearful § im not trolling. Im talking normal § first you got th e 3d tv. now you got the 4k. whats next. 5 § oops wrong accou5,nt § some times i see people buying shit at a store and wonder if theres a dark side to comsumerist behaviours.... § fuck my ass hole https://t.co/J2wbHKmgkY § beer city USA . my friend s § i will never thank you § you hacked the poll you stupid fucks. this survey cost me $10000 out of pocket to conduct. you ruined sometyhing beautiful

you pricks § getting brain damage from pissing my self off § you've disgraced
the uniform of Police. hand me your badge, gun, hat, knife, belt buckle,
cowboyboots, laser whip, bullet purse, cock ring, § consider that the possibility remains, that most of you have not yet hit the skill ceiling of wiping your
ass § Curse of the Colonel (ā,«āƒ¼āƒ āƒ«ā,µāƒ³āƒ€āƒ¼ā,¹ā ®å'ªā „ KĀ neru SandĀ
su no noroi?) refers to an urban legend regarding a reputed curse placed on the
Japanese § i am attempting to enter the mind of otis in order to destroy him §
@TruthPointDWR 1) do not say this shit 2) please post all content with the
hash tag #TruthPointQuibiNow as you have been prevoiusly instructed § this feed
is protected by grandma § "auuahuhuh" some nerd who wears glasses probably
right now § Thomas Husband § too bad. https://t.co/5YZT0dOhVK § becoming
accepting and calm of other people having lifestyles of having the wrong
opinion about shit § my dog approaches me, rolls over on its back, and i vomit
all over its stomach. undoing 9 years of trust with this animal § "At long
last, society has shown its Ass." - Dril § MarioGodKenneth is stuck in israeli
prison again and ive received $0 in donations towards his bail. § GeniusTalk
- dog food has been putting subliminal messages in theire food to make dogs
think they taste good - TruthVisions § if you see me dragging a compass through
the sand, i'm conducting Market Analysis and must not be distracted § shut the
fyuck up § im going to go draw santa hiring a gay elf and stamp "Dont Ask Dont
Tel" all over it and sell it to The New Yorker for $10000. bye § i have been
advised not to ascend to the spirit plane in my sissy dress and #diapers § all
gags and assorted banter aside though I will in fact be shooting the thanksgiving turkey with a gun instead of eating it this year . § on a rickety stage at
some empty roadhouse, a True mississippi blues man is howling aobut diapers,
unappreciated by the toilet using masses § you all think youre all being
"PLAYAS" !!! you think your doing swag to me. But, you are simply just pissing
me off ... § I CAN PAINT CELTIC RUNES AND WICKED SPACESHIPZ ON YOUR PET SCORPION
FOR 10,00 YUAN § the dj just said he ran a man over with his car and did a hit
and run 4 year ago and hes crying now § "offensive or inappropriate does not
automatically equal funny" - GOD § ok piss stian, this ralph wiggum tattoo is a
long-term investment, meaning its value will grow over time. go read a Economic
' s book, child § #ImSingleBecause my grasp of humen sexuality far exceeds that
of eveyr girl § they are trying to make the 2020s the decade of Nude § lunch
cabinet § "Clit Goon" is actively trying to avoid me, when I`ve stated repeat-
edly; if he comes forward with a genuine apology- I will not pursue him. § DEAR
COP WHO BUSTED MY FRONT TEETH IN FOR SELLING TOWELS ILLEGALLY, THANK U. IM ON
THE RIGHT TRACK NOW. PETSMART HIRED ME TO JACK DOGS OFF § "Some people on here
are more interested in Public selfies, than public safety " -- Oh?? Can He Say
That?? § #TheSaturdayMorningRamble was cancelled out of the respect of prime
minister ariel sharon . please stop asking me about it. rip ariel sharon §
converted 95 Dodge Stratus into a motorized " fuck rig " that jacks my dick ,
consumes gas & drives down property values with horrible noise § this gradient
they applied to the iconic kellogg's logo is of no use to me. i think i will
write them a nasty little letter § (in slick Dennis Miller cadence) guh, §
#LeaveItIn2012 bin laden. kil;l the piece of shit § im sorry for getting
bonnaroo 2015 cancelled b/c i used the hashtag to ask ppl to put teeth in my
ass. but im Not sorry for defeating trolls § please let me edit my tweets so i
can go back and remove every reference to pig piss and liking pig piss §
AWESOME father to 5 loud, dumb ass Birds // HVAC Lives Matter // Your Marine
Is My Son // i brake for Green Pussy // My Other Car Is A Gun § james bond
hollers "Destroy Teen Asthma", bends over & does a line of coke off of a VHS
tape that has "PUSS AND BOOTS BLUERAY" written on it § no it very good. § i
gave it back to the lord § retweet is a sham § Love To Scrimp, Hate To Save
#TheFinalWordOfIt § i dont know what that is but it sounds too good to be real
§ ME: Im far more excited to see what the "Cloud" has to offer, than what the

"Clown" has to offer. MY NEMESIS: How dare you tell the truth. § every day, the content creator sits at his Oak Escritoire and asks "How can I transfer the maximum amount of pain to my parasitic Engagers" § petition to change the twitter bird into a shittier, less noble animal, l ike a pig or an ape § pleased to report that my odds of having sex have dropped to 0 after my latest and greatest Grievance Thread § when i step out of the bathroom to announce that Ive clogged the toilet at a party, i tell everyone exactly what i clogged it with (my shit) § healing the world full power https://t.co/0MsfztMfDj § https://t.co/S8HqQPRuzi Looks like shit § by calling them "Stackers" instead of quesadillas, taco bell is legally allowed to fill them with 49% bird shit § whats the deal with people handing me receipts after i buy things!! i dont want this!! fuck you!! fuck you!! fuck you!! fuck you! #Stand #Up § looking at Mars Bar § (Becomes upset by an unsolicited mention of Beetle Bailey on twitter feed, and punishes followers by refusing to post an update for 30mins.) § thats the worst one!!! dont say it § my page is a tornado of Slur's... my inbox is a viper pit of horseplay... my desktop is a Clown's Tent for bastards... § tyler durden and the Joker and 007 agent james bond take turn beating up my ex-wifes car while i say "Cool" and "This is fine" § when the social order collapses and the new global currency becomes mens semen you will regret ever jacking off in your life § i am truly baffled that some people would rather watch amc's "Breaking Bad" than indulge themselves in the good shit i constantly post here. § im not horny but, lets face the facts people... if youre a girl im gonna click on ya § just got word that because the extensive water damage present o n my balls and part of my ass, i am no longer allowed to vote § everyday i am harassed constantly by the phantoms of my own bullshit. my posts get me into trouble. please follow @Dril on twitter dot com. § haha. woah. apparently if you dress up like a police everyone will think you're a real cop and you can trick people into crying and shit § due to recent events, i have generously reduced my weekly donation to cambridge analytica by 40%. And nobody is reporting this § "Spike TV should put on a slideshow of your most celebrated posts, accompanied by a tasteful, easy listening soundtrack." well, This is true § id like to grab each of you by the ankles and dip your entire screaming head into a bucket of honey, everyone Ratios me, its all a setup § you cant like dms dick head https://t.co/ydKGglPtpa § people used to jack off to this guy back in the 90s. not me though https://t.co/5lw685mP61 § " BASTARD " § i dont know much about solar storms but i swear to god that the one that happened last thursday gave me the ability to yell louder § i have moved all of my bitcoins directly into my brain for safekeeping until all this nutso crap blows over § just embed the damn image automatically like all the other images i post. this looks like Shit. § youll know whehn it happens § i fuck all cereal § just to clarify: "the studio" is a room I rent for $800 a month. i use it to compose all of the posts i type here. § i love getting my gun opinions from cartoon characters and capping government drones from 900 miles away before they blow my shitty house up § go fuck your selve § can anyone confirm whether or not the entire central NJ region smells like bad breath today because I think it does § its fine. i spray it with a hose before eating it § listrn pal, im matt, and i love Too fuck § oh youre gonna unfollow me now? just when the posts are getting Good? im sorry Your Majesty!! (Dick sucking motion) Eugh Eugh EUgh § struting around in my stepson cowboy hat looking for an ass kicking § if youre sick of Incest, please support Anti Incest by changing your avatar red. if your avatar already has green tint then please remove it § thinking about getting the dow jones back on track, simply by making a few phonecalls. but certain people have been a bitch to me, so i wont § im uploading a "let's play" vid of me getting stuck between the walls of my house and getting all tangled up in the insulation and shit § i dont have to. theres no law that says i have to § TIME: Why arent you live tweeting the big game. Why ME: id never

forgive myself if i killed someone by pushing vital info off of their feed. § my
velcro jeans burst open, scattering my secret stash of 2 liter canada dry
bottles as I stumble backwards off the roof of the 9/11 buildig § (saying loud
enough so people can hear) the matrix is the james bond of steam punk § 96 year
old man goe's back to kindergarten after losing ihs job at the chemical weapons
factory due to Gas Prices and the Economy #InspireMe § concerned about t he
health of my followers, many of whom appear sickly and have chapped, unwashed
elbows, stained with grime § i pay good money to load my sons bag with treats,
and if Erasmus Infowars Copfucker wants to devour them in the university
library, so be it § @DogBountyHunter Theres a guy here who claims hes the real
Dog, says the guy on tv is some filthy hippy;Is this the real or fake dog
twitter § GOD: Im getting quite aged in my late years; and I need someone else
to be president of heaven Donald R. Trump: My lord... RBG: (Applauding) §
#ToMyFutureKids please tell Past Daddy which 9/11s to prevent § i test all my
tweets on lab animals and they hate them all. im an embarrassment to BRand
Culture § buy shares in the Markets. i have a really good feeling about the
markets § My dick is wearing a neck brace § @kfc_colonel i made a pipe vid
dedicated to you http://www.youtube.com/watch?v=4PHPtrAKMeU&feature=sub § these
people with locked accounts...damn!!! you just know theyre hiding all the good
posts in there § No results found for "i invented black borat" § wiping your
teeth down with toilet paper or giving them a quick spray with the hose; that's
the good shit. toothpaste is flim flam from hell § A CELESTIAL BEAM SHATTERS THE
ORACLE INTO ONE MILLION SHARDS, WHICH WONDROUSLY FLOAT INTO THE AIR AND FORM
THE WORDS "PEAK BITCOIN" § us governmnet kidnaps swazi rape orphans and forces
them to watch the sad dog episode of futurama while monitoring their vital
signs for $ § it is so hard folks, to maintain my world famous Post- Racial
Outlook, when the damn gas prices refuse to stay down tto a reasonable level, §
Mohammad Muhamad, King Of Islam, Cahugt Counterfeiting Some Cool Dunham
Specials On 3D Bluray; Sentenced To Be Hung By The Penuis Until Dead § Fuck you
mother fucker § look at this classist filth https://t.co/PfQRf13w § i command my
exwife to pour gunpowder into my pipe as i grip it between my clenched teeth
and read money magazine § being desperate enough for human connection to go
onto girls posts & chide them for using Twitter Web Client or whatever other
one they used § metal chains begin to fly out of every hole of my computer while
i scream like a fucking iddiot in a child's comedy film § http://www.utexas.edu/
law/calendar/2010/09/20/8909/ § hte nightmare is just beginning. google "sewer
myth" § when i told u all i had to get my dick surgicly shortened b/c i slept
on it wrong and injured it, i opened myself to you, and you Spat on me § man
throwing chairs compilation 2018- uploaded by the games codger § I AM ONLY
ALLOWED TO RESPOND TO 1 MORE CRAIGLIST AD BY LAW. NO STRINGS MUNICIPAL PUMP
HOUSE SEX OR 14 FREE CINDER BLOCKS? IM HAVING A STROKE § thr new pope has been
chosen. you all ready for this?? his name is..... The Bible. #BloodOfTheEucha-
rist #FwdThisIfYoureAWiseTeen #HeavenTeen § every one here has become too
cynical and full of their own ass. its like none of you are even trying to help
Jussie § Gorilla `s Scam § Tjhis guy fucking sucks https://t.co/ZL67sQF6zm § im
an adult, and i deserve to listen to the verison of the super bowl shuffle where
thw word "Ass" is not censored by the referee `s whistle § @CapsCop EAT SHIT,
COP § i want to be wearing google glass when i see my wife in her wedding dress
fofr the very first time so i can turn it into a big dorito § in base ball
theres only points and players. i will be Shut Down for typing this. § stop
this. At once. we are supposed to be lifting the voices of our fellow content
creators. Not shiting on them. § always men `s beer https://t.co/QZnZfNVUdn §
great news, boys. the town decided not to condemn my home on the condition that
i remove the "intolerable meme shit" off my lawn and porch § linktr.ee/drilreal
get at me . all accounts not on this page are fraud. fuck twitter § Just saw it
on CNN: Thyere coming out with a new batman #NewBatman § might get really into

chewing tobacco for some reason. might start calling it "Tobaccy" . Fuck you § blocking me is an expression of Love. the line between "Follower" and "Guy who has me blocked" blurs more with each death threat i receive § THE COMMON IMBECILE: the movie "cars 2" is better than the movie "cars 1" ME: alas this nation has truly gone, to the dogs!!!! § nasty trap spray § bbeats the shit out of you. silently begins pummeling y ou as you surrender and accept your punishment. not a word is spoken § my gym teacher is outside my house right now screaming about how I owe him 20 pushups from 1973 and that my torso sucks § the guy who forced those flight attendants to wipe his ass died and im the only one willing to put politics aside to pay the proper respects § fellas..tell your girls you will n ot be providing any more sex until the entire female race apologizes for halo 5's dismal metacritic score § to everyone who thinksn im some sort of dip shit regarding video of me eating a pocket pussy, please rest assured i hated every moment of it § remove all of the bathrooms from churchs right now. you need to be doing that at home § people are telling me to stop posting abot this. theyre saying im doing a Psy Op?? buddy if any one's doing a psy op its "Clit Goon" § shut thef fuck up you dip shits § we all have our own way of grieving. *sinks teeth into huge ass medium rare t-bone steak with "WITNEY" written on it in ketchup* § sand blast my damn ass or go to pig piss cop hell § MEDICAL "PROFESSIONALS" WHO REFUSE TO TELL ME THE AMOUNT OF WEIGHT I NEED TO GAIN TO BECOME A PURE BLOOD IMMOBILE #THINGSTHATMAKEYAHOWLOFF § In culture, today, where they have cellphones, it seems, as, though, the most forgotton words in the English language are, "I give a Damn." § " Shut Da Fuck Up " § does Theire exist a single caveman who has gained lastable notoriety through his or her accomplishments? Not a one. ban sex and ban caves § someone needs to tell "TimOnline" that his username fucking sucks § theoretically , tips could be done away with entirely if i were allowed to enter the kitchen and personally retrieve my entrees ChefToTable § as far as im concerned. "fidget spinners" is DEAD IN THE WATER § "we witness now the Death of Light. A Cowar'ds millennia. Shadows dancing upon the Graves of our lives" - Diaper pounder § YoshiGod9 says that if you shit into a wasp nest they wont sting your ass because theyre too dumb to know what shit even is. Prove him wrong § number two-- the Flintstones have always been, and have never not been, a Black african american family. Just look at literally 1 gene record § i theatrically cut open an envelope. "The facts are in, Trolls" i read off of a medical document. " ormal looking man. No evidence of Autism § people are still apparently very upset with me for cancelling "the thursday nite rant" fea- ture... let it go folks.. https://t.co/L3gqdFNYCX § some times you just gotta say " uff said" because enough of the shit has been said to that point § the only animal crossing i see here, are the animals crossing me in the replies § draculas politics are actually really good to me you scum bag § my attempt to expand my wardrobr by cramming a pair of Damascus Jeans into the office copier has ended with tragedy. escape the 9/11 reality § i am a Gentleman's Son and i deserve the big gravy boat § no. no birth § my father banned me from taking shits after 8:00pm until i was 19 and this instilled within me a sense of morality and honor and respect § i think its terrible that criminals are encouraging our more gullible members of society to celebrate the propagation of the vile aids virus § the clown nose on my dick is there because im more susceptible to infection since my wii bowling accident, iddiot. no more hateful messages § today; we are all Yale § im actually glad you leaked this. now the Dialogue can begin. § dunther, twang lad, gunbelt, Holbo, daemetreus costco, fallen gordo, § When they call Elvis "the king", i can only shake my head. As the only man I recognize as King is reformed pervert President Joseph R. Biden § pregcore § ME: What do you mean the plane departed. The clock says its only 8:25. TICKET AGENT: Sir Thats a clock ME: I know § Yearly Reminder That Human Beings Have Actually Died As A Direct Result Of April Fools Day #aprilfools

#JokesOnUBub § sometimes i wonder if i could slice EpicWayne in half with one swing of the blade. but its probably really hard to § the dress Color? (grins Intelligently at the hell about to be unleashed upon naive content consumers) its brown, because i wipe my ass of it § the hell genie cured my crippling fear of Smoking,. but forced me to incur the curse of having perfect skin and legs #InHighSchool #Allah § ((crrying) im sorry § stupid god damn MORON!!! fucking BITCH https://t.co/szsJrXFQrV § people will tell me shit like "oh you cant say kofi annan was no fap. no evidence" and i say, how dare you sully a mans grave, with politics § no. what is wrong with you. christ § in this house, a PIT BULL can believe in GOD !!! § i wish my opinions were good enough to put on bumper stickers, but alas, i can only say "syria is basically road rash 64" using my mouth § ok. i basicly need one of the girls on this website to marry me by june 30 and i am absolutely under zero obligation to send you pics of me, § @ASIMO coward § it was empty. i ate the food that was in there beforehand § im moving to israel, where the boys are nice, as soon as i get confirmation that they use the same kind of toilet paper that we use here § you like going to the bath- room? i normalized Shitting back in like 2013, with my posts. But dont thank me, im no hero. Im just a dumb bitch. § leafing thtrough another heap of death threats and served papers that have been 100% tailored to my interests, using Tech § only a post has the power to make you laugh.. or cry.. or even smile. thats the official quote of me § " NO BULL SHIT" is not just a phrase i like to say, it is also a way of live § "Can Determine The Gender Of Any Animal Simply By Touching Its Dick" § (watching Leno deliver some solid hits against Michael Jackson in the opening monologue) I dont understand. Is he mad at him? Whats going on § threres a rumor master chief will take off his mask and reveal hes the btk killer.. do not do this.. it would be disrespectful to halo § i draw my psycho-blade and stab the shit out of a plastic tub with "waldenbooks" written on the side in magic marker § "god damnit!" the coach rips his headset off "they covered our football in nerd cum! those bastards have covered our football in nerd cum!" § bob costas found hung with the word "FED" carve in to his chest #iamamotherfucker § i have decided to develop a gluten allergy to piss off my most hated waiters § #TheSaturdayMorningRamble sometimes it is good to get off of the computer every once in awhile and spray garbage around the yard with a hose § just because im a gamer with Polio, doesnt mean i cant someday become somebody's Butler § yeah im shit i know i know § corn should grow from sprouts. like beans do. none of this cob bullshit § Unamused by trash behaviour . § Do not mention me unless your a girl § may the wind carry my tweets and soothte the sick, the wounded, the downtrodden of both man & beast, across the savage shit earth of trolls, § @PetSmart Question: can rats lick § faces ranked 1. soy face 2. Blackface 3. diont like it thats the bottomline § "thw word 'good'... when you hear it, you're almost guaranteed something nice" - TheT- rendingBoy § extremely frail man, tasked with gathering hundreds of dildos thrown onto the football field by overzealous fans-- booed incessantly; Reviled § my 14beautiful geisha brides work together to change my preposterous 300 pound diaper. #mtvcribs § reminder that on this sacred of days that i was the first guy to condemn the 911 attacks, while everyone else was busy watching honey Boboo § looks to me like im the one being gang banged § big bbq coming up. should i wear the apron that has a picture of ziggy taking a shit or the one that says "introverts are good at Fucking" § BOSS: i need you to go around to all the other employees and collect their piss in this thermos ME: Yes Sir! I will not fail you, your honor § a respectful nod to all my friends whohave been removed from group chats after having some sort of melt down. "The Fallen Angels" § turn off the computer? Fuck that. I Wnat to see posts. I want my posts!! § girl;s with cracked phone screens give top like the devil him self 0 RTS 2 LIKES pray if you Like this... 1210 RTS 42134 LIKES Power of Lord § the president has never once been filmed taking a bath. he is presumably very filthy § " And the beast which I saw was like unto a leopard, and his feet were as the feet of a bear, and his mouth as the mouth of a lion: and the dragon gave him his power, and his seat, and great authority. " https://t.co/CUq8FtiQ3s § im going to prank call a bunch of moms in my latest collaboration with MTV Japan § Um,m sending Ezra to prison? Thats a stone cold *#MEntalHealth-Fail* § come now ladys for a night of pleasue and devils deeds https://t.co/qAiHtZ0Di2 § Turner classic Homegoods § beginning to despise my friends and loved ones for pushing valuable branded content off of my feed as I struggle to comprehend this world § im not saying i dont respect the flag. just saying id respect it more if it was a picture of something thats good to me. like someones lunch § thank you . this will make it way easier to block them all https://t.co/gFtL8DSyEE § Looks like slavery is alive and well, if youre a Top Influencer. Im not mad or anything I just think its funny. But i am pissed off by it § @TruthPointDWR meet this https://t.co/LpvW519YqY § how come when s, bannon gets removed from the national secuirty council nobody gives a shit, but when it happens to me everyone kicks my ass § my followers behave extremely errratically, like a bunch of sick animals, whenever i go "Out of character" to post aobut Mens Wearhouse § i remember shit from when back when people gave a Damn...... now the whoule damn world`s a penis § im near certain there is a hotly contested tug-of-war between fox executives upon the issue of whether or not homer simpson can show his ass § i will nbe referring to a certain soda brand as "p*psi" until i receive the $16 they owe me for years of aggressive social content strategy § dis charged from the army for doing memes too much § web MD just told me I have "Fuckface Lymphoma" and that im an "Aids Man". in light of this humbling news id like to apologize for my posts § every veterans day i remember my pet mantis who got defeated by a baby bird that i tried to feed it § there's it https://t.co/JlKyWnQkqF § im proud to announce that ive started and cancelled The Female Bras Project due to Free Speech and Trolls, respectively § for hte win. Mostly. § bug off my posts § wow.. just watching the cnn channel here.. amazed by how they know all the news so well.. Extraordinary § sometimes its good to just wipe your ass, § every day this happens: my followers inject me with a mix of chemicals , And they kill me as they would a sick dog. Every day they do this § when I catch the hater/troll who plunged the legendary sword AssBane into my butcheek I will do a cowboy dance on his tiny nuts & kill myslf § as a guy who developed an autoimmune response to comedy as a result of being "Roasted" for my Ice man tattoo, ive much to say of April FOols § if i do not get my postcount up to 5 digits by the end of this year my peers will forever think im a shit head and my account will be erased § people who like getting whacked in the balls; that shit sucks. youre outta your mind § I`ll not be watching the halloween themed episodes of "Wheel of Fortune", as I dont find them scary even a little bit. Please and thank you. § GM developing car seats which detect how wet your ass is and post the data onto your facebook page, for fun?? fuck eveory thing about this . § its true. each cow's udder has one teat that will shoot piss instead of milk and ruin the whole batch. they call it the Farmer's Gamble § when you leave a huge pile of barrels on the roof for no reason . you are literally actually supporting donkey Kong Tbh. § think you got it rough? try engineering blog posts while trying to suck down two whole baby bottles full of muscle milk before Solstice ends § Geting that "Impersonating an officer" money § "mr. bucket" now theres a guy who clearly does not have his shit together § so many Weird Twitter accts asking me to suck their dick in the dms. im njust like, yeah right bub. you havent even retweeted me since 2013. § my idiot trolls get ulcers whenever i say my top 10 favorite film quotes to girls § @meganphelps i agrree with all that stuff you say about god and dead people. please let me cool the fire in your heart with sexuel pleasure § oh no!!! what if we lose??? what if they blow up the New York Stock Exchange and force us all to wear Womens pantys?? Help!! Help!! https://t.co/

UmhtgS0g8a § you can learn so much crap just by clicking on like two things.
https://t.co/WlAynIiKj7 § sending special kind of energy to my followers that
is good/poweful energy normally but immediately becomes dog shit energy if you
betray me § #momsandbrands now were talkin. can i network here. i'm a normal,
real person. i think youre all good #LonelyWantuingDates #GoodAtBrandsAlso §
Although listed as a baby cowboy hat it is actually more the size for a 5-6
year old child. Needlessly to say, I returned it for a refund. § from the
popular TED talks comes the TED Scream. at first glance, it's a man screaming
on stage. but can his screams change the world ??? § http://t.co/MTn35r91 a
solid hour of this § thje teen choice awards blows the kids choice awards out
of the fucking water instantly, zero contest #culture #TheArts § mint wine § i
will never stop feeding thte trolls § #freejahar friends, i have just learned
of another passionate freedom fighter who was betrayed by the us government
http://t.co/Mh3WNkTLti § to who ever said my dick looks like a bacon bit. oh
so i guess you're the expert of knowing what peoples dicks look like then . § @
GitRDoneLarry i will raze every forest and devour each city in blood tribute
for the crime of 9/11!! please nbring back blue collar TV § @DigimonOtis Otis
hsas made my life a living hell for 20 years. Fuck it. Im done. You win. I
don't care § Mentioning the woefully fated thursday nite rant feature to me
constitutes harassment. Let's keep the trash out. I am a real journalist now. §
putting the vacuum on my dick until I stop hearing crumbs go down the tube §
girls are such White people § more and more news reporters are starting to use
the phrase "James Bond style" to describe certain kinds of murders § im here to
tell you that even with 8 kid,s, 6 dogs, debilitating rickets & a filthy
waterlogged home, that its still possible to be a Gamer § @TockTockTock TAKE
THIS OFF LINE IMMEDDIATELY § if the infamous "OCTO MOM" were to come out of the
woodwork and start preaching to us of her thoughts of politics, i would just
about SHIT.. § Imagine. A world where guns come out of the ground like plants.
And all the water is replaced by Bullet's. This is Gun World. It's real §
you're not allowed to mail bombs to people § Crimes of the Ass (2005) (V) -
Recommendations § yes sir. im sorry sir. (hangs up) that was the mayor of
reddit. he wants this account spick and span of dick jokes before the handover
§ would like to see the myth busters come back to tackle the myth that its
illegal to open other peoples mail § @JoseCanseco pissman Ultra § im now aware
of a vulgar & objectionable program named"Rocky & Bullwinkle". sign my blogti-
tion to yank this disgusting shit off the airwaves § i wont say more of this.
but a couple of the big accounts on here have been souporting swearing culture,
by posting swears to the time line. § https://t.co/DBVsuJE6EQ § huge disgusting
man with extremely muscular fingers pokes at his tiny laptop while his emaciated
servants groom him with squeegees #win § my intense belief: you should not be
eligible for the presidency of the United States until you are at least 89
years old § @mattjohnchrist go suck burger kings dick rsome more you fascist
fan boy sewer hog § nothing pisses off Baseball more than showing up at the
plate holding a custom djinnblade, designed by your cousin Chedson, instead of
a bat § ah, its beautiful, § as long as i can post from the cage it's fine § the
absolute best place to hide your nudes is in a file folder on your desktop
labelled "Clothes" § the us government has its top men working day and night to
invent a paper towel that is large enough to wrap me up and dispose of me § man
slowly poisoning himself over the course of 50 years by storing his silverware
and fine china in the bathroom § @Richard_Dawkins disgusting. § computer
DeleteMyPorno "EraseMyPorno" § http://t.co/Tfa7VBWJ please. ask me anythig § If
you ever in your life had this thought: "Hmm, Today I think I will go
Full Karen."   me and my friends will NEVER hang out with you!!!! § Thats what
they do. They rile you up with nonsense posts just so they can call the cops on
you and get you arrested. Its called "Intrapment" § only thr dumb ones. block
without hesitation https://t.co/7uaFWjASn2 § my new job is being the guy who

says "Sir You Can't Film Here" repeatedly to people who bring recording gadgets to aldi markets § at full power, telling every one on the "Am I The Ass Hole" sub reddit that they are the ass hole without reading their posts § KFC is making BIRDS and LUNCH 10954 patrons $545060 a month § Hey man im sorr y but me and every other guy in a group dm called " ut sack club" were talking and decided your posts suck shit . § taking the lords name in vein... #inspire https://t.co/Zv7CuAGiNH § this page is the " o Ratio Zone" Ya got that Dick head? § when a web site asks if i want to see their " ew Design" it is the exact same thing as a man asking if i want to see his penis and ass § the famous time-tested classic, the philly cheesesteak, has become Sexualized by greed § school lunch card revoked indefinitely for making a counterstrike map based on the principal'/s rock garden § i may be a dim-witted narcissist but at least i hafve really good opinions about life and other things § NO... I DO NOT "PUT OUT " FOR MY GIRL FOLLOWERS... UNLESS YHEY 1) ARE NICE TO ME 2) HAVE FAVED AT LEAST 5 POSTS FROM MY "TREASURY" SERIES § im sorry the trolls bugged my office and everyone had to hear me say "heres your sign" over and over again in a shitty bill engvall voice. § Baffling lack of respect. § i dont know § #girltime "dating",as we know it,is an outdated pratice that can be traced back 2 thge pre-sapiens imbecile, hurling turds at their pregnant § becoming Inmortal and laughing . . . § peolple are reacting to this https://t.co/ZR6VmxANKL § Keep Colm and Look at my posts § teen § worse than goldman sachs: secret tapes of me bleating like a shit-covered animal because time magazine refuses to publish my meemes § the officer detected a single string of cum connecting my sickly brown dick to the Fucked vegetables. " o no" i exclaimed. "its a spiderweb" § after careful consideration, ive decided to fuck the green m&m because they made it look like a girl. i would not fuck the red or yellow m&m § the heinous y2k bug will bow to me and my glorious rifle § why did the earth worm jim guy block me... cant handle the real shit § PRANK: say The Simpsons got cancelled and tape everyone's reaction. alter the footage later to make it look like their balls are hanging out § CORRUPTED EARTY'H... § im haunched over, hunkered down and duncepilled like an Arthritic dog being sent to the shoe factory & i get less Ass than the bumblebee man § (being trampled to death by panicking crowd) hah. look at these dumb fucks. they think im part of a floor. they dont even realize im a human § shut hte fuck up § hauling ass to the hair place to find tekken chauncey and laying into him with a rolled up newspaper while hes getting a Perm § *pushes a mini-fridge over* Fuck U § Maximum Security Gamestop § someone out there is making $1000 every time a person clicks on this https://t.co/fJWNu5zjp4 § catching a ton of flak for my "how to fuck a Cadbury egg" web log series. sorry dim wits. your dick needs to be really small for it to work § i despise the toilet. id love nothing more than to kick it through the wall and shatter it into 100 shards of wet porcelain. But i need it § get this crap off § *inhales sharply and punches a sofa 6 times extremely quickly* § id like to be able to watch one Reba intro on youtube without seeing a bunch of comments from 3rd world nations threatening to "fuck" the WB § I can confirm absolutely that filmmaker George Lucas is bringing our dear star wars back to us. § stop flooding the #stolenvalor hashtag with army man shit and only use it to report plagiarized @ Dril content, please and thank you § Comments off until the children go to bed. § Who Ever Left Their Pear Here. Come Get Your Pear http://t.co/6JIgZKrxYS § dont know why everyones up my ass over this. i didnt say she smells like urine, i said she has the energy of someone who smells like urine § Proud To Employ Disabled Surgeons For All Of My Cosmetic Procedures § just hating my lead coated dx racer knock off gamer cushion from bangladesh. absorbing & releasing countless toxins via my Ass. 16 hrs a day § A Man's Sense of integirty. http://t.co/FXRYPFVnMG § ok, first off its BS that wetnaps dont tell u that you need to unwrap them before use. second, food smeared on face boosts the immune systm §

" pivot to Toilet " § fred phelps is still alive. and will continue to make
trouble for all of us good people online. thats my beliefs... § teen gradius
please § if death regulation affects my god-given ability to put holes in
garbage and animals really loudly i will kiss the toilet 1000 times and die §
im the man who got banned from the gym for trying to bring a mattress inside,
and i have gotten significantly weaker since the incident § Geans § Greetings.
Today I would like to discuss "Porky Pig" § my 125 IQ growth hormone consultant
and legal conservator has confirmed to me that they are going to make the 2022
hyundai sonata "WOKE" § guy who drinks pepto bismol every time he has to take a
shit until the feeling subsides § myth: making me mad is cool FACT: making me
mad is a crap move& people who do it are all sociopathivc criminals with fucked
up rotten brains & this man was Seen https://t.co/uf0HvuV5Yw § im the guy who
talks about ass wiping hacks so often that i commonly use the abbreviation AWH
and get mad when people ask what it stands for § im a journelist now. gi;ve me
free monster engery or ill Eviscerate you § foghorn leghorn argentino unofficial
§ Posting is the easiest shit ever and yet theres people on here with hundreds
or thousands or millions of followers FUCKING IT UP § ok mr honda dealer lets
get down to brassed tacks. U dont wanna waste my time, i dont wanna waste
yours. now; CAN i jack off in your toilet, § up your fuckig ass dude. Shut up
https://t.co/pizSblJlxz § #RockCenterXMAS a holiday Salute, to all the guys who
died while putting bulbs in that big ass tree, whose bodies just got left up
there § youll all be glad to know that my soul has undergone some much needed
healing after i apologized for the earthquakes which killed thousands. § i
fucking love logging in and out of things at incredible speed § number three.
i will never take the advice of my lawyers, my loved-ones, and colleagues to
#StopThePosts § absolutely pounding a zip lock bag of cut up hot dogs in the
portle potty § @Battlefield "Garth_Turds" on here calling console fanboys the
N-word. I ask you Garth, why is it that you're playing the PS3 version then? §
guys think if they squat my user name on emerging social media platforms ill
give them $1000 for it , instead of just calling them a Bitch § getting
cancelled cultured for ignoring the haters. whats that you say? ignoring hte
haters isnt a crime? IT IS NOW !! § petition to invalidate benchmarsk that're
located precariously close to dangerous ethnics #geocachingmishaps § SickFuck
Productions § the dickwolfs controversey.   Go #worstpickuplines § im sorry
for claiming i was going to "flip the script" on dry rub barbeque. that was
wildly irresponsible of me § Im a dunce who needs faves and retweets to live §
i piss on your little emails § people only think wizard of oz is good because
they want to fuck thr tin man, if they didnt want to fuck the tin man they
wouldnt like it § i live in the church § (a) an alternate universe where im gay
(b) an alternate universe where im bi (c) an alternate universe where alternate
universes aren't real § wildly agreeing with some shit im reading in the
newspaper that says like "There is nothing more Iconic, than Milk and Cereal" §
AVATAR didnt win enough oscars, please supporrt independent film maker james
cameron b y cutting your oscar statue in half (if you have one) § bramds
http://t.co/BCkDV2xGTM § lvoe to perform aerial leg drops on the referee §
wiccan and juggalo are the same thing. they just announced it on the News §
(intentionally spoken within earshot of severral arbys girls) ah fuck. my hands
smell like steroids from using steroids all day § now i will be the first to
admit that im an irredeemable son of a bitch/. however, i am also a piece of
shit with no brain. § worlds first adult man netflix cutie fatally TREATTED LIKE
SHIT on his BIRTHDAY § ANNOUNCEMENT: Im developing a game for true and brave
gamers only. please have a look at my page, for details: https://t.co/9vlMFm-
JIve § Biber done it. § The Bayer corporation proved the link between Masturbation and Homosexuality in 1968. Thbe debate is over. § i live for the tears of
all baby huey fanboys. their suffering is more essential to my being than the
blood flowing through my veins § so if the admin posts pictures of his varicose

vein clusters it's ok, but when i do it my avatar is replaced with hands gripping prison bars § cyber bullied at k mart § donate $78 to the " micropenis" awareness fund for a orange micropenis ribbon to show your support for micropenis. i have it § well, i'm planning a move. the democratic people's republic of korea?? strongest cops in the game. flat out. Make our cops look like shit § @McDonalds @McDonalds it will go without saying that hes an ugly son of a bitch. goblin-like. someone you;d particularly not want shitting on your food § microwaving my ass hole in the microwave https://t.co/U8OLOn2xI1 § shut thef FUCK UP § RE: Restaurant Etiquette >> I've been a waiter for 9 years, and I like it when people snap their fingers at me. So your commant is invalid. § im trans-siberian orcehstra for christsake § "guns are the most inportant weapon of our time. lock and load. see youa t the Range." - anonymous § stressed out due to pistachio shit all over my shirt and computer desk . all posts canceled § 6304 saw a goblin 81206 saw a big foot 9511 saw a cryptid (dog version) 71515 saw a "raggedy ann" 72116 saw a man with very fast eyes § im losing hundreds of dollars per post but the economy will improve soon § if id known he was planning on using it to wipe his dogs shitty mouth i wouldve never allowed XenoMarcus to borrow my monogrammed neckbrace § Oh we're doing toughguy shit now . § consider this: the time and energy it took for you to tell me to "Shut the fuck up" could have instead been used to breast feed 10 orphans . § everyone giving me shit over the teen things I said is mad because im able to conSistently put up the good opinions before them &get the RTs § first you have democrats and rtepublicans. theyre basically the same thing. then you have green party and uh, the whigs. theyre the same too § the xrays indicate you have a laughing skull in your stomach,. youre deathpreg. diont you dare give birth to that bonehead in my office § The Bible Is Fake. oh. what's that? you're holding a physical copy of the bible, you say? hm, looks legit. The Bible Is Real, Then § reminder that if you jerk off tomorrow on christmas y ou are the bastard of earth. § (looking at wtc memorial) this is mood ass § cold butter popcorn. tjust throwing that one out there § your mission is to get laid on gmail. delete all other apps, do not talk to me until you fuck. your mission is to fuck and suck on gmail § i've just been notified by the oracle that late night personality jay leno is currently in Denim Mode. § what gender do i have to turn myself itno to be able to squirt octopus ink out § if i wanted to watch super bowl id just put on one of the damn 50 other super bowls they did. you've all fucked up once again § my wikipedia device of choise. § @ billgates ive invented a new type of water. i need Ten Grand § Auh.. Beer! Theres nothing LIKE it! 123 cups of scalding hot Beer on my office desk. Dont spill it now, it's good. § sniper flawlessly zaps the lid of my beer jar clean off. camera zooms in & out on my astonished face accompanied by buckwild cartoon soundFX § this mug is Perfect. http://t.co/3Lt0xoWW #PerfectMugs § seems to me, life is aoubt "STICKS" Age: 1-20 : Selfie Stick Age 21-90: Walking stick § you gotta respect iot, even though it sucks. You just gotta respect it even if you fucking hate it . You gotta respect this shit § @Shell im wiping my ass with shop rite bags § see this watch? i got it by Crying. my car? crying. my beautiful wife? Crying. My perfect teeth? Crying. now get the fuck out of my office § http://t.co/gFFTBY9aiA teen wolf wiki asks the hard hitting questions § ã ¤ã‚‹ã ¤ã‚‚ã ã‚‚ãf^ã‚·ã Œã¥½ã‚€ã §ã ™I love beautiful armpit § this talk about big bubba & jareds footlong is conjecture. its a old wives tale. the real problem in jails is all the masturbating going on § #SaySomethingGoodAboutTwitter you can easily remove it from your screen by clicking the x § i have performed ã ®ç¥^ã‚Š<mouth prayer> in all 4 directions of the compass to stop ShirtlessClyde94 from leaking photos of my ghoulish pud to TMZ § the ye.ar is 2009 AD. world government has passed the G.R.E.E.D ACt, banning ownership of CD-ROM. hyperlinks have repleaced the dollar . § i have spent the past 14 years of my life crafting an intricate tale that evokes the mind and spirit. i am

proud to bring you "Ghetto Sonic" § "Valor is the honor of distinction"... the
words engraved on the side of my gun, that i force the gamestop employes to
repeat out loud to me § i cannot sit idly by while my followers get shit on by
the terminator § mr bean is a complete dope. his oddball capers are crass and
unrealistic. i frown while watching this show. § bbeing passively aggressively
retweet trolled by half wits & their beautiful girl friends just makesme say "
ot before ive had damn coffee." § my critics say that my unconventional ass
wiping techniques are no good. that i am seriously wounding my ass. that my ass
is dirty. bastards § A FRANKENSTEIN #illegalDogBreeds § much like they do with
investments, professional ties, etc, journalists should be expected to disclose
how Mad they are, § got our best men on the case https://t.co/s2fvhyxkY1 § that
smug prick baby new year th e piece of shit. ill throw him from my truck the
dumb ass mother fucker § wearing, Oh,; I dont know, some cheap douche bag jeans
that are sickeningly blue, climbing around on some bricks, Truly Looking dumb
as Fuck § i wonder if social media newsbots ever miss their former lives as the
beautiful women in their profile pics § Italian mobsters beat rival gangster
with metal bars before feeding him to pigs, police investigation claims
http://t.co/oXsuBfWC1q § lost in the Maze... http://t.co/KaDXJo6Twp § looking
at tom dixons mens plum wine cooler https://t.co/Vbkf28Y6I8 § @BigDogClub yeah
that blows. anyway i was wondering where i can buy one of them please § the
rock spots a small pile of jabroni turds left carelessly on the floor of his
ring. he postures defiantly as the audience hoots and jeers § @GeraldoRivera @
realDonaldTrump i just had a phone call with him too and he said the opposite
of all that shit and called me Gay § to anyone who has ever had sex ,i forgive
you. i am the simpsons, bitch § argh.. (shakes fist) Damn you White people !!
ha ha, but seriously though, most whites are actually highly intelligent, and
resourceful, § getting word that the election is now considered "Fucked" by the
state attorney after a man reportedly let his dog lick the voting machine §
perhaps one of my most egregious viral marketing blunders was inciting radical
islam by reading my controversial Dick Clark tweets on vimeo § human sack of
dog shit; holding up the self service aisle, trying to beat the system by
taping balloons to the produce scale § cnn should hire The Pope § sometimes i
post serious things but, i like to have a little bit of fun on here too
#TheThursdayNiteRant § if your movie or tv film dosent have Dolby it sucks
fucking my dick § http://bit.ly/aC0hVF vile footage exhumed from Apache Chief
Geronimo's cursed grave § #blogcon2013 waddling around the auditorium trying to
find a place to set up my custom pc tower with "BOYS BOYS BOYS" painted on the
side § my name is "hubo" now and not even my dad and all my uncles can change
it back to "greg" no matter how many xboxs they step on § im sorry to everyone
who has ever wanted me to apologize to them for something, and im sorry for
apologizing tio you if you didnt need me to § "put your Ass into my world for
one second and you will kiss my nuts" - god § i think that if mensa started
getting involved in gang violence, they would easily Win § please bring your
rats to the new castle flea market so I may bless/heal them. ill be sitting in a
lawn chair wearing a stolen priest outfit § cghecking to see if i have the
correct wattage on all of my Light bolbs.. now thats a pizza pie #thatsaPiz-
zaPie § my annual "Cum tribute" to the Ford Focus will no longer be archived in
the library of congress due to partisan gridlock and meddling taxmen § Damn.
The blogs confirmed it § With Pigs § seeing more and more people post anti-lunch
sentiments despite the fact that, well, they gotta eat . § alright. wherever
the dart hits on this map is wwhere im building my new Mosque. (dart hits wtc
ground zero) Yikes! Uh oh § im nthe nice man who deserves this § 2011 YEAR OF
THE ASIAN WOMAN CHALLENGE: SUFFER A GENUINE PANIC ATTACK IN EVERY CRACKER
BARREL RESTAURANT ACROSS THIS USA NATion § we avoid piss because it represents
Chaos § https://t.co/ka4CgZs1Hy § the other day a trolling Shit sent me the
message, "Googoo Gaagaa ". Twitter has indeed threatened to close my account if

i dont retweet him § EVERYONE PLEASE BUY YOUR MAGIC SPELLS BEOFRE AUGUST 30
WHEN EBAY BANS THEM FOR GOOD, CONTACT YOUR LOCAL ANONYMOUS REPRESENTATIVE &
HOLLER BS § my dick andballs look like a honey nut cheerio stuck to a brain §
i`m not at liberty, to discuss § a 90 year old man looks at hula hoops "they
dont make'm like they used to" now hes all started up "theyre SHIT!! these are
picees of SHIT!!" § KitsuneHorace says theres a secret game stop located under
the Lincoln Memorial where congressmen are allowed to shop without wearing a
Mask § Now whos ready for some damn Tweets for Fucking adults § sensor THIS!! §
ilove the idea of beating the shit out of my Son's rival's dad at the little
league game with a suitcase full of cash § about 80% certain that Neil Cavuto
just said "teh economy" instead of "the economy", on th e air. someone with
dvr please confirm § http://fc03.deviantart.net/fs29/i/2008/158/1/1/JOHNNY_KNOX-
VILLE_HEDGIE_by_skellinghog.jpg § All music made past the year 1969 is rap.
(sseaIs self in rebuttal proof chamber for 100 years) § apparently there;s a
base amount of @mtn_dew you can drink that will make the red cross refuse to
accept your blood & i surpassed it, #Yowza § posting my Lunch setup and
immediately getting 10000 guys yelling "you dont know what pain is" to me in
the buffallo bill voice § vision's... https://t.co/CTVJLWTTj2 § thank u mysterious stranger @drilsdiapers for doing the community a great service by catalog-
ing my abject misery & rendering me unemployable § i WILL supply you with the
TOP Stapler Mods - "Hideous, Impractical, Waste Of Money" - These Are The Death
Knells Of Our Cultural Parasites § if your tweet doesnt grab my attention in
the first 9 or 10 characters it can just fuck off § im starting a pod cast
service called "Mouther" and our inaugural pod cast will be a pod cast about
breaking bad called Sucking Bad § say it isnt so....... some of my followers
think being a "KAREN" , is actually GOOD !!!!! § its just onne of those things
you look at and say "oh its nice" § the emerald nuts corporation deducts my pay
substantially for each death thrreat i receive so please stop it § eating 1/2
lb of beef boulougnase and getting roid rage from it § i might cancel this
week's rant due to crippling dread and other real life bull shit. we'll see §
seeing the words "Farm Fresco" on a billboard and having to pull the fuck over
from becoming Overstimulated § Welcome to the citadel of eternal wisdom.
Behold, this crystal contains the sum of all human knowledge -- Except Rap And
Country § They sweet talk you. They promise to sell your penis as an NFT to a
wandering merchant and split the profits. I have not received this money § " ame
one Roman Gladiator who owned a Smart Phone. I'm waiting" - Ken Bone § helping
women by inventing a portable bra dispenser , for when they are on the go § as
a twitter power user, I am MORE than qualified to assuage any of your questions/
concerns/aches/pains with sexuel Contact. § https://t.co/S53uOn5PNg § Ive been
sniped in the nuts by Topgolf customer service . Folks I have never been more
fucked in the ass than i am currently right now. § i have not forgotten the
crimes of "Tweety Bird" § 72 is not even a lot of money § closing off this
childrens' playground until i am done filming parkour montage which i will use
as psychological warfare against my landlord § if i was a rich guy who had to
try to convince a bunch of people that dog shit tastes good i would absolutely
buy a super bowl ad § 75% of the tweets on here are complete PishPosh. 20% is
Networking and Implementation. the last 5%? Pure Content. #TheSaturdayMornin-
gRamble § INSPIRING: After 20 Years-- Local Waitress Reunited With "78 I.Q."
Police Officer Who Used Her As A Human Shield At The Age Of 11 § maybe the ski
mask guy who blasted the "Doge" dog across the room like a rag doll.. maybe he
was all of us. my opinion. unfollow if u must. § dont know ass hole https://t.
co/PZvQ8Jg5wj § -racist, -unsanitary condittions (animal near food) - fake
holiday -ill eviscerate this pic further at a later time. https://t.co/
ycauu88vTY § for every shit comment i receive, i will be doing 1 push up. the
trolls shpuld be Very fucking careful lest they grant me unlimited power §
tekkenchauncey no longer allowed in my home after he took a picture of a pube

on my toilet (that he probably planted) and used it to ruin me § the idea that
people are still masturbating in 2014 is insanne, and utterly, asinine § my
name is Tony Turds and i demand for people to take me seriously everty time i
talk and also for people to like me § alRight. no filter. i think that, igf
you are a bird, and you get run over by a car, you absolutely need to get your
god damn act together § please dont let the pharaoh see this § "Kermit the
Racist" by AdultCartoonFTW (182,727 views) § -computer 3d generated regis -
the $1000000 you know and love -one of the life lines is that they bring out a
big hoagie for you to eat § gonna fill up on milk shakes and do some open carry
off the grid § the worst thing you can do in death is make the R.I.P. on your
grave actually stand for Racism Is Power § #ZodiacFacts black people are all
#Gemini § inventing a new type of cum by jacking off incorrectly § bread has
never been good. let it be known on here that i will never eat the shit food
bread. § i think police should get extensive background checks so that i can
hire all fo the most insane, mentally ill cops as my personal bodyguards §
rides a segway through a monolith labeled Drugs & Alcohol , destroying it. §
yea i torched the dennys. and i woudlve gotten away with it, if i werent the
only guy in town with a custom jersey that says "My Wife" on it § just realized
that every hare brained dick boy who follows me on here is fucking simping for
me. Nasty!! That shit makes me puke!! § ah, online is amazing. there is so much
to do here. *GETS OBLITERATED BY INSULT`S AND SICK IMAGES* i've changed my
mind. online is childish § yeah im a fake piece of shit now and im rich ha ha
ha § the accident was not my fault. the speed bag installed in the roof of my
car was obscuring my view. also the driver was a fake version of me § the onl
thing i can drink without vomiting anymore is diet peach snapple mixed with
skim milk and breadcrumbs § it is phenomenally cruel of people to come onto
this website, look at the posts on my private feed and share them with their
shitlord pals . § 16 reasons why Farm Fresh Corn on the cob could be your new
Taste Obsession - Chef Ã&douard`s Corncob Lounge "On 3rd" § who cares who the
next james bond is. theyre all Lucifer § the words Paul Blart 2 appear on
screen. the black eyed peas begin singing "Let's Get Paul Blarted In Here" as
the mall cop bumbles around § ive modified my phone to deliver electric shocks
each time one of you unfollows me. The pain will make me kinder, humbler, and
more powerful § For your Friday Enjoyment; A "Shit List" of folks I've banned
from my Radio Shack: Monica Louinsky, The Honey Boo Boo, Octo Mom, & "Snooki"
§ #ChrisBrownPickupLines Babe Remember That Time I Took My Shirt Off In The News
Studio Cause I Got Mad While Trying To Clear My Vile Record § big bird was
obviously just a man in a suit. but the other ones were too small to contain
men. so what the fuck § truly we are living in the worst of all possible hells
§ Eat Shit § We did not find results for: "GOT TO FIND OUT IF THE RAT WHO BIT MY
DICK IS A GIRL ONE PRONTO" Try the suggestions below or type a new quer § my
fatass head floating in the sky, looking down at all the Girls i follow banter-
ing/ having a nice time on here, nodding, thinking its good § Unfunny.
https://t.co/DiXwd64w3F § i shall say this only; ive ended peoples careers by
reporting them for "Ironic" typos & spelling errors., i do not give a shit. im
a warrior § could any influencers share tips on how to "punish" your self for
generating low engagement? might need some Pain to keep my head in the game §
ass ointment seeping through the top of my perilously tight jeans leaving
unsightly horizontal stripes on the sofa #Supernatural200thEpisode § vvvvvvv U
see that shit?? That`s what we call in the business "Another satisfied custoum-
er". Locked down. § online is where i go to get my A B C's... Abused By Cretins
§ just generated the N-word inside of my brain in 3D, spun it around in
circles, and exploded it #DrilThankYou § this shit really hits home for me
since i was once forcibly removed from a united airlines flight for having a bee
hive stuck on my head § you want to claim that i keep a cup of poop on my
computer desk? You want to go on record? ill put you in concrete. ill give you

to the lord § JUDGE: i'll commute 10 yrs from ur sentence if you kiss my gavel
ME: no. i will do the time i deserve and thats the truth and also nuff said §
WHy isnt there a crosswalk where 50 year old women can explore their femininity
without getting hooted at § pissing my self off thinking about a brand of beer
called "Goofy Beer" and its slogan § "Goofy Beer: It makes your dick smaller"
§ you deserve my worst offer, which is "2" § if it werent for the invention of
the electric chair iw ould do so much crime. id be smashing vases and shit
right now § chiropracty is real and it works on swords also. § a blessing on
this earth. my shit covered muscles are a blessing on this earth § as the sun
consumes the earth i will stand atop the highest mountain with my arms spread
wide , shouting "Bring Back Meebo" § haha get this, these people on the crisue
boats that get stranded, they have to shit ON the boat, and sometimes they even
touch the shit!!!! § i have defibrillator paddles strapped to each ass cheeck
and im ready to bring hell to the nerds § @THEHermanCain herman cain grabbed a
lady's ass while thinking about pizza § Eatinh a 26 dollar hoagie. § im being
told that the pussy oscars (the version of the oscars that judges womens pussy
shapes) has become the latest victim of "woke" § mabye this decal of the troll
face saying "DID YOU TRY RESTARTING IT??" will make the boys in IT respect me
&stop kicking my cube walls down § you give me dry ice & i dont know what to do
with the shit. "is this mother fucker really posting about dry ice" yes. wet
ice is good though § you can down vote me but Im god damn right § NO NOT HERE §
if i could get my hands on the wildman who painted sexy butterfly girls all over
my wreckingball i woud tie him up and throw my shoes at him § Sponsor Wanted:
Basically U Would Pay Me to eat Dogfood and i go "Its So Good Even Humans Can
Eat It" or just fucking ignore me until i die § looking at my timeline, it
seems that MetalGearEric has shifted from a Tier-B to a Tier-C poster ever
since his grandma died. imo , § i plan on going to do it. § manifesting not
getting my ass kicked b y saying "i hope i dont get my ass kicked today" and
getting my ass kicked regardless § user name "harambe_Poop" is selling false
home owners insurance. beware of this § the $100000 pyramid is actually fairly
fucking cheap for a pyramid § THINKING ABOUT "WHAT'S FOR LUNCH" !!!!!!!!!!! §
"RESULT: You are the Serpant. YOu dislike loud places and people are constantly
putting drama in your life. But you're strong." This is true § If i catch U
retweeting mainstream shit, like updates from The Weather Channel or pictures
of food, youre finished. Go clean yourself up kid § just sitting here waiting
for mny nails to dry. i can debate the sex losers all day. but I wont because I
possess the inner strength not to § thinking of being appointed the official
"Bitch" of the NFL § the infamous millennials are more interested in (consults
notepad) being nickeled and dimed by the tax man than (squints) distilling
vinegar § youre all a Dog of the Coward's order. ill take you across my knee
and slap yopur Ass., i will "GIVE UM HELL" as ordred by the great general §
bougt a bottle of "liquid ass" to teach my stepdad a lesson but i consumed the
entire bottle by mistake. now i drink "liqiud ass" on the reg § just found a
somewhat NSFW box full of robes and hoods in grandmas dungeon § WHEN IT IS TIME
FOR ME TO BE QUIET, I AM EASILY FOOLED BY THE FAKE RUBBER NIPPLE OF A PACIFIER.
I THINK THAT IM GETTING MILK OUT OF THE DEAL § and to the guy who said i have
shit for brains: youre right. i do have... four brains.......... § everoy
father's day my dad would take me out on a picnic, and he always filled our
picnic basket with dirt, because dirt is the shit of God § Let The Rapist Do
Football. Let The Rapist Teach The Kids To Run The Ball Good. He Good At His
Job And The Rapist Should Be Aloud To Do It § gah. turned a corner too quickly
and maimed my nuts § blocked at 9999mph § hu... now im a man who likes his
garlic butter.. let me tell you. in fact, im prone to saying that regular
butter needs to step it up a tad, § paper towel ?? Huzzat ?? is it a paper or a
towel. more to come § for my dedication to the brand. . ive decided to treat
myself to an affordable vacation package in ssplendid, extraordinary "quicksand

hell" § (looking into a big toilet filled with shit , piss and toilet paper,
shaking my head) this is fucking stupid. hardly worth my time § i hop the world
cup isnt painted with cadmium unlike some other cups that will remain nameless.
§ do not be afraid to talk to that lonely boy on the train ... with the rosy
red cheeks, sun glasses & big cigar... he just mmight be... angel § "if youre a
dumb ass youre no friend of mine" - The dumb ass killer § brett favre punches a
curtain with the word "INCEST" painted on it, rips it down, looks into cam and
says " o Incest" #PublicService § CANT WAIT TO SEE THE LOOK ON MOM & DADS FACE
WHEN I GET THE BOOT CAMP THEY SENT ME TO SHUT DOWN FOR DIAPER DISCRIMINATION §
someone hacked hte high score board on the java pacman game in monsanto .com's
"For Fun" page. just a heads up § reminder to the girls of this page that I
will soon have $ 1400 § Death Caliber § uber ride home from dennys iwth the
instagram Gf (mid-20s, dressed like a casino waitress) shrieking at each other
because i "Made a face" § @DrinkGrumpyCat send this entire misguided operation
to the dumpster you vile urine peddler § - _ = NEVER A SEX ACCOUNT = _ - §
theres no space in the title you shit mouthts. it's one word, it's always been
one word, it will forever be "Topgun." i will not delete this § might buy some
$200 japanese steak knives & instantly ruin them by using them to saw through
the clamshell packaging of my new shower radio. § https://t.co/3SXmLlkmxr § @
CrackerBarrel guess who just touched my di*k??? yeah, it was a cracker barrel
waiter. § chris brown engulfs the crowd in acid piss during bad concert,
disfiguring scores of his awful fans (Says He's Sorry) #Grammys #teambreezy §
thats my setup § do u, sir, take this cardboard cutout of 90s era David Spade
to be your lawfully wedded wife, to have and 2 hold, in sickness and in health,
§ https://t.co/77QLxjtCpV Good Ass, Top Tier Content § im a Skank. § feeling
extremly threatened by gamerscores § .@KonamiCodeKnower i know yorure online. i
know you've been stealing handfuls of gravel from my driveway and hiding them
in your big shirt § please Gustin, if youre out there, send me the rest of your
Gothic Emblem Concepts for our Hell Van Project. It's been 8 months, Gustin §
investigate Gallahger death § explaining to the boys at the auto shop what the
"you know i did it to him" man is iwth the inflection one might use to discipline a child § thinking about some computer slob clicking on my Like button--
right after touching his nasty dick. hey buddy; i dont want that shit. Keep it
§ boscov's is a highly professional organization Sir, and as such we refuse to
engrave "the sex fucker" onto your george foreman panini press § nice bundle of
‹URI GELLER PEZ DISPENSERS›, many of which appear to be ruined by human teeth
marks but some of them are ok § U Have Been Banned From GoiterTeenz - The Forum
For Teens With Disfiguring Goiters-- Reason: Prolonged Harassment Of Female
Members § my dick is a swastika. #andthewinneris #iwasthinkin #atablackperson-
funeral § ï¼µï¼®ï¼¥ï¼µï¼´ ¬º´¹á´¬á´¸á´±¬„ § absolutely ruining my own day by
imagining a restaurant that refuses to serve me because im wearing brass
knuckles § if you have a problem with me kissing pictures of Dragons while
driving the bus, fight me. i just ate 30 hotdogs and im near invincible §
GET PAID TO CRY - MAKE UP TO "$4.98" A DAY SOBBING ON WEBCAM -MAIL US TEARS FOR
Ð²onÏ…Ñ•Ð²Ï…Ñ…®- ABJECT HUMAN MISERY IS THE LIFEBLOOD - DIE A HERO § would you
let a man named "Porno Pete" do your taxes § Can we stop the posts please guys.
Can we all cool it with the gags, riffs, spoofs, and epic shit. People are
trying to do mental health § the desert has never helped any one and i am going
to go throw poison at it § never subject yourself to the humiliation of using a
public spittoon again- simply spit into your diaper, and USER HAS BEEN BANNED
FROM TWIT § networking with my friends on here https://t.co/MadL8r1RUA § i
feel, as I, over time, become even more of a Dumb Ass, i am able to consume
web-based content and Media at increasingly Blistering speeds, § Im sorry? Are
u "Going in" on me?? Am I being "Gone In" upon just for p osting my time-tested
opinions about girls holding forks incorrectly § does any one know what
happened to this guy, https://t.co/YplfsLjkeM § im the only person on this

entire website without a wife and it is just ignorant at this poin t. § on line § i want too live their. i want too smooch them § Yoyu shut the fuck up right now § (screams "Shut The Fuck Up" as loud i can, over and over into a phone for about 4 mins straight) Ah, Cant seem to get good help these days - § once agAin going "Ape" over controversial Classic rock opinions at the super market while my asain gf pushes me around in a shopping cart § please refrain from writing extraneous stupid shit on the bass drum in any of your future stock images you cock sucker https://t.co/Aw1CAtCIbe § (flips wallet up in the air and tries to catch it in a cool way but spills its contents all over th e place ($2)) § some ass hole told me to get snapchat so i did and my name on it is "coward" , please make me regret thnis, please shit all over my phone § (after hearing the library has games , i arrive at the front desk, disguised as a non-gamer) er.. im here for some.. book's § @holidayinn My pop pop was diapered against his will at one of your Colorado locations. Please help me find the man who did this § .@girl I Wanna Rub Ur Belley § once again ive been reported for calling Odie "The dog from Garfield" to make people think i know less about garfield lore than i actually d § santa https://t.co/8TVcfvDUKm #goodbook #Remembering41 #BushFuneral § this is the most important shit in the world right now. We love seeing this. Thank you https://t.co/HECyCU2WZq § lets set some realistic goals here : jokes banned by 2016. sex banned by 2020. a cop in every household by 2025 § some times it takes a little bit of Free thinking to be able to look at the bull shit of the world to step back and say "Damn What the hell" § thank you for putting these kind thoughts underneath my flawless posts § AGE 20: WHY WONT ANYONE FUCK ME // AGE 40: WHY WONT ANYONE LOVE ME // AGE 60: WHY WONT ANYONE KILL ME // AGE 80: WHY WONT ANYONE FUCK ME § i will not close my account until the sport of golf is rightfully named "golfball" like the other ball sports § whoever the fuck "iamath" from glasgow is 1) please dont use my email to make snap chat accounts 2) your dick looks like absolute shit § meeting with CBS execs over possible sitcom "The Diaper Ref" about a referee who wears diaper &describes everyday problems with sports terms § my ultimate quest to become a united states armyman begins by rejecting all forms of online drama trash in my life #TheThursdayNiteRant § all of my followers are lousy hob goblins and all of the people who dont follow me are dirty dog ghouls § dunnno why people are spending $80 on yellow tinted gaming glasses when you can just piss all over your monitor for a similar effect § NERD* § god intended for the creatures of his likeness to wear good tuxedos all the time and to paint their cars to look like it's wearing a car tux § Get Your Head In The Game: YouTube .com - "Get Your Head In The Game" § i see the followers that guys like @ DrPhil have and wonder, why can't i have followers who are nice ?? why are all of my followers pricks § the anime web turnpike girl is like 50 yearsold now § Make America Shit My Pants § studying videos on you tube that other people took of me flipping out and thinking of ways i could make my mouth louder some how § https://t.co/DQPFkd1awi some posting music for all of ya § aint nothin in the bible against diapers § glorious crime spree after being fired from wal mart., expertly hopping fences, chugging all the seeds out of my neighbors bird feeders, § "DISRESPECTFUL !! DISRESPECTFUL !!" the crowds shriek, upon learning that the scene of bat man wiping his ass & sucking his own dick is Cut, § my sources tell me he uses the toilet like a normal man. § "History will show that Brexit was the correct choice, for the future of Great Britain. I also do not believe in sex." - The_Brexit_Asexual § i attribute my small dick to my low IQ, and my entire body being too dumb ass to send vitamins & minerals to my dick to make it normal sized § im about to get my piss tested for steroids. if they find steroids in there then ill start drinking it instead of going to the steroid store § "Yo. Lets get some owl tattos." - something a hipster has probably said once in the course of human history #DOUChe #jokeums #heteroBoyLords § HELP ELON!!ELON!! HELP! HELP! POST "DOG COIN" § i would sooner die than relinquish ownership of my dale carnegie mousepad to either of my fat sons § wow theyrre releasing more of these already http://t.co/m8INRDahRZ § Stop owning me § if i had $1000000, or even $100000, i'd marry a woman with a completely unfuckable, solid gold Pussy. and i would look at it and say "Wow" § These replies are getting out of hand. Im going to lock twitter down for a bit while you savages sort your goddamn lives out. Bye. Whatever § closing my onlyfans after doing all possible combos of pics (penis, balls, penis lifted up to expose balls, and Ass, Spread ass, and Mouth.) § my ass looks like a Stooge's ass § *steps out on stage twirling a cane and accidentally hits self in the dick 100 times * AAAWGHHH § i block all gilrs § im afraid our fair mayor has been living high off the hog by spending our precious tax money, as evidenced by his username "HighOffTheHog666 § controversy erupts as john boener hands out tiny goodybags to everyone on senate floor and sticks dems with all the yellow starbursts #Gross § i FIRMLY believe that beloved Super NES luminary "Funky Kong" woul choose Netflix over Hulu , in any Fucking universe you can throw at me § the funniest one., rest assured § my dick is satire § if the mask from "the mask" was real it would be on the news. § the rumors are true, my posts are all written in GMT Time; "Giving My Thoughts" . § surprised that nobody here had ever used the phrase "pissed on execution style" unttil i described my poor customer experience at hhgregg § if u say any fucked up things about the new york world trade nine eleven groundzero tower center tomorrow i will absolutely rip my pubes out § http://t.co/YDw5ORL7 hahha i beatup guys like this daily § reminder to all mh followers that if something i post catches your eye you can "Like " or share it to your friends w/ that re-tweet button § me and the boys charging through the streets carrying a massive battering ram headed for Mens big in tall store § covid toe penis; can you get covid toe in penis. do blue markings on penis mean same thing as covid toes. covid penis real? when to call 911 § the media wont shut their yaps about me http://t.co/wIg9bcz4 § no https://t.co/JjDPfzP8TB § getting bup slammed in the mouth for my bull shit § i am only here to field questions regarding my presidential bid. i will not discuss my ongoing project, tentatively titled "Aids Mario." § revamped. reloaded. ready to roll. austin 4.0. blasting directly to dvd may 2016. too randy for theatrers § let me tell you exactly why this t-shirt design of the tasmanian devil with angel wings is bullshit. first off, taz is not dead § i didnt understand how interest at the bank works until someone explained to me its like storing cum up in your balls § ME: No matter how ya slice it, Some-times some shit is just true ???: Shit is never true. Its all false ME: Youre wrong my friend § "The one thing i love about Beer: The one thing I love about beer is that its always time for another sip." -The one thing i love about Beer § due to the actions of bastards and human slime, my agent has advised me to deactivate my account for 18 hrs, to punish my disloyal followers § liberating to have gotten all the joke's out of my system sometime back in 2011 so I can now disseminate serious info to the dumb asses here § i've had just gotten word that the $30 arrangement of Chef's Breads i had ordered to my home has been intercepted by trolls § my main issue with "master chief fucks cortana" is if you read the halo novels youd know the space suit automatically jacks master chief off § the rant was already posted. read it before the mods get all emotional and tear it down. § you must face the mirror daily and ask your self: "which brands will i touch base with today". you have to ask it out loud or it won't work. § im obviously being punished for my subpar output, § these moon posts have got to go!!! *spraypaints "Bad Eclipse" on some desert boulder miles away from humanity and dies of dehydration* § @glennbeck to his credit, doctors are often too busy counting their blood money to learn anything smart about body's. § i'm going to shut down for several hours while user "JFK_Destroyer" reconsiders his threat to "suck my grave like a dick," § someobdy on here just sent "the cup of stfu" to isis and all of the mainstream

media outlets are refusing to report it § FOR GOD SO LOVED THE WORLD THAT HE
KILLED IT THEN KILLED HIMSELF § full time Cash Back award activator § Login:
SewerLad Pass: FuckTheMods666 § the reasons jacking off is good are - it makes
me dumber - it makes me Worse at sex - it pisses the trolls off for $0 § if you
react to me or my posts without permission you are the most son of the bitch
there is § https://t.co/Q6os85UlEA id rather have q anon post my address and
dick and balls than have t o read another one of these Fucking posts § me and
Alan are the only guys on here who are allowed to call the police when we get
soft blocked § my name is "Pruce" now. tell every one you know that my name is
now pruce § @TimHortons LEAE ME THE FUCK ALONE § catching a guy jacking off to
hte shirtless ricky gervais atheist smile and immediately yanking him out of
his car and smacking down his ass § fuckin online fuckin idiots § @Doritos Give
mme my fucking coupons you cock sucking rats. I deserve at least 4 coupons for
posting kindly of your nauseating onion fodder § getting Sucked out of house
and home § blood the hedgehog. mewtwo the hedgehog. dwayne the hedgehog.
muscles the hegehog. christ the hedgehog. marcus the hedgehog. § IGN: "octomom
caught Gaming" Gawker: "octomom is a gamer and i want to smooch her" TMZ:
"ocotomom GAMES? hhuUWHAAT??" Wired: "octomom game" § if hollywood has any
dignity left they will surrender all golden gobes to the united states marine
corps and blow a bunch of kisses at them § everyone on here would rather give
$20 to their idiotic gfs. its discusting § this is an attack on not just me ,
but all boys § "If for one day. Just one day, you knew the Pain of having 1.6
million followers, perhaps you too would seek solace, in the DMs ." -Unknown §
i know times are tough but rtry to give a Like and retweet to my posts if you
are able to. if not, thats ok also. Fuck you § getting my fuckin Onion sucked
§ im the guy who gets really upset about people not putting their real names on
here. im also mad at State Farm Insurance for not being a farm § Im going to
make 1000 videos of fuck nasa. § dont come on my account and lecture me about
manual transmission until yoauve gotten BOTH of your balls snug up inside of a
sweet sugar babe § reasons the famous statue "The Thinker" is better than
selfys & cell phones: - It is a classic - It is for geniuses to look at - It
costs $0 § if youre putting together graphics for your book you can just use
royalty free images of chicken legs instead of normal legs and it will look fine
#art #tips #help #helpful #smart€¦ https://t.co/eP93iZmhDf § getting my cudgel
autographed by a law officer § just enjoying a noticable uptick in Favs and
Followeres ever since my sworn enemy, Osama bin Laden, was brutally murdered in
his rumpus room § when you Mock the brand-- your putting a Knife in the back of
every depressed person who chose not to commit suicide because of Disney IP`s .
§ @dril https://t.co/uDVuHb7HU2 oops im owned ,fav thi s one instead § AH.
ONCE AGAIN IM RAKED THRU THE COALS AND TORTURED TO DEATH FOR HAVING A NORMAL
PERSONS OPINON. FUCK OFF § Jesus christ. I;m so god damn sorry. This is so
fucked up. It's a living nightmare. I am literally shaking. I have never felt
such pain § slobber, by definition, can only come from a mouth. anyone claiming
to slobber out of their ass is a liar and possibly a scammer § (to women at
party) Im probably the top most crapped-on guy at twitter. My options get
trashed constantly and Im best fit to shut my mouth. § ME: please show me the
posts in the order that they were made COMPUTER: thats too hard. heres some
tweets i think are good. Do you like this § pplease stop asking me to retweet
shit for money, if you have to pay me to retweet your shit its probably so bad
it sucks shit § what if the guy who jumped over the white house fence thought
it was the gamer gate § switch handle to "Gamer Wonk" § @DrinkGrumpyCat this
bullshit has clumps of PUBIC HAIR in it. tastes like someone attempted to mask
ACRID PISS TASTE with CHEAP SOAP. No buy § @McDonalds @McDonalds i know its
fucked up. but "shit" is one of the last few apolitical threats. 99% of ppl on
both sides of the spectrum dont like it § this needs to be addressed. if you
see me along the road, please do not intentionally ram me with your car. this

is the 4th time this happen § austin powers men cut (only men scenes) . mkv §
why isnt this on the news § its absolutely my right to have a 90 yr old woman
scrupulously vacuuming around my enormous bulk at all times while i groan and
roll my eyes § U will regret this. § @johnmellencamp kept coughing into his
hand and looking at it during his latest performance at clowes memorial hall
and it was gross § tak9ng your shirt off in the pool...shit move § today i will
be making a bowl of "Home Made" guacamole, with, you guessed it, chips. §
CONTROVERSIES: lots of people jacked off to "beetlejuice" because they thought
he was a girl. it's perfectly normal & good [citation needed] § http://t.co/
gigLk7tGJw this is how to fuck on craigslist § (i shoot you with massive plasma
cannon that sounds like a jet endgine when i shoot it and turns you into blood
instantly)suprise fuck face! § im ganna get all indigniant and huffy like a
BItch anw way!!!!!!!! dont wanna eat This Dinner!! im a Teen for life §
Ladys... if U have never been sucked by a man who pours Cement , you are SHIT
!! https://t.co/idXbcVzMIf § i just found out today that my best friend and
confidant of 11 years is a beers drinker. this troper is NOT amused § @DigimonO-
tis Fuck yourself § ragdolling as an olympic sport. ragdolling into a pile of
bird houses at 99mph . rag dolling down the side of the hoover dam etc. gold
medal § i love bait. cant get enough of it § http://t.co/50D8jZjEvP #NoFuck §
sending Honor to my friends on the computer today Thank you!! Thank you!!
https://t.co/0UyMAe6nnN § i post at the pleasure of my follower's. people can
typd shut the fuck up at me and im not going to . i post at the pleasure of my
follower's § just thought of a new guy. "The Guy who writes down the make and
model of a car he saw in a car commercial, for future reference" § projects for
Q4 2010-- michael cera's face tattooed on top of my regular face § i want to
network with clean human § i have never looked at my own dick in my entire
life. not once § waiter i would like to pay my bill , "En PiÂ¨ces" (In coins)
§ jail § (saying to group. of 7 girls) the lore surrounding the Addams family
is actually quite a bit darker than you might think..and fairly Leftist § i
would say Mr President, the partisan gridlock ends now. i would then roll up
like a pill bug and pray for the darkness to come quickly § # tantrafee   holy
shit... this pug isï»¿ to fat !! i am sorry with him... 3 months ago § up until
i was about 28, i thought "the 9 to 5 " was a euphemism for blasting cum §
thats where it goes. this is normal § I find my self. walking the hallowed halls
of Harverd university , thinking wisely to my self. upon the quest, for
Knowledge... § Ur Honor, The Jury Is Obviously Biased Against Me Because
Theiyre Mad., And They're Butt Hurt, And They Post On Different Forums Than I Do
§ list of activities enhanced by fingerless gloves: advanced keyboard & mouse
manipulation, burying face in hands, wiping my as, pointing § the best part of
winning the power ball lottery has got to be getting my hands on some of that
Green stuff also known as money. § tthis is the new Pythagorean Theorem § theres
pills on amazon that make your loads bigger but the guys in the 1-star reviews
say they give u diarrhea. dont know whats real anymore § if youre that guy who
emailed me last month asking to be my "intern" come forward so me & my rich
friends can smack tennis balls at your ass § some fool's just need to be
knocked the crap out of § no. the admins will ban you if you do this § did you
see the twteet about dog piss i just did. its good § ive decided that "gaba-
gool" is italian for Lunch § #ChrisBrownPickupLines im ignorent. my music bad.
my pubic hair smells like shit. my dicks smal. grammys only let me on cause my
dad is rich § we here at the @jimmyjohns teen outreach initiative love to "PULL
THE RAT" and "CRUSH A LOAD" like the rest of them. we know how to jack off §
*drops Dunston Checks In on Laserdisc on the roulette table * king me § i love
spending 10000 dollars to make my car loud as shit and suck ass § sad that the
guy who raised $10000000 to produce the worlds first non-woke can opener tried
escaping in a hot air balloon & hit a power line § dunce cap prophylactic § id
say my most defining quality is that i instinctively write tremendous amounts of

think pieces whenever i see a naked person § Donkey kong from "Donkey Kong" Mario from "Mario" They stand tall as the Loony Tunes of modern era, to besmirtch there names is unforgivable § itd be funny if a troll tired to "Own" me by leaking my DMs & only prove that i had sex before anf i get laid even more because theyre good § i can help with this-- you;re supposed to click the "follow" button on my page and leave it clicked on § the games they're putting out these dsys. Damn. Theyre so good that you never even see gamers with depression anymore § i am truly devastated to announce that DigimonOtis is in a coma after getting his arm trapped underneath a beatmania cabinet #PrayForOtis § PROSECUTION: Is it true, that on the evening of Sept 3rd, 2006, you posted the word "Jeams" ME: (swallowing cyanide pill) I dont recall . § there is so much rigamarole and legal B.S. involved around mnaking a comedy central roast of digimonotis that it's almost not even worth it § im like a mean old Rattler rwho types on the keyboard by repeatedly striking it with my poisonous mouth and teeth, and youre.. the dead guy, § Guess What Fag. Most Birds Are Too Smart To Be Deterred By Scarecrows. I Guess Your A Bitch #StrawmanArgument § Im going to try posting like that now § Lets see u do better. § its true. my father owned slaves in the 1980s but he has since apologized & been forgiven with love and support. he's a nice man now. § us military strikes deal with PepsiCo to waterboard all terror suspects with Mt Dew??? wish i had some of that Free Dew. who is john galt § my attitude is generally over all an "I dont give a fuck" attitue § The temptation to send your penis is something that plagues us all. It's not "Gay" to resist it. This is the true test of a Content Creator. § (sees parking for electric vehicles, does the smug grin/shaking head thing) what's next? ? parking for circus clown cars? § Join us for "Goodbye Cathy: 34 Years Of Laughs", located in Pittsburgh's famous Motel 6 Rumpus Room, the event will conclude with my suicide § @petsmart do\tu do obidience classes for HUSBENDS ????? ;) Just Kidding § @BigDogClub whats the deal with the 911 shirt. i thought big dog was a christian organization § -tweeting about stuff thats off-topic is "Random". never do this. -tweeting about current event stuff is "Topical". and this is also a crime § can anyone link me some good User Agreements to click yes on, § petition to make cvs stop forcing their pharma-cists to wear shirts § bee man vs column full of bees https://t.co/v7s6Ln3WPW § becuase i constantly post stupid shit that people hate § how many druglords do i have to take down to get dog the bounty hunter to unblock me after i threat-ened to breastfeed him or something § what is should be the name of my produc-tion Company § in order to fully grasp the "weird twitter " zeitgeist, i woud recommend reading 1 of the many articles publiSuck My BaLLS 666 § Where's The Good Shit. Where's The Good Shit. Where's The Good Shit. Where's The Good Shit. Where's The Good Shit. Where' § dont pay mind of me. i am just a hound dogs old ass... § PissMyPants USA LLC § dollars, peso,s you name it, money is loved by all, and today is Money's birthday. post your favorite amount of money #HappyBirthdayMoney https://t.co/vCxM3e8Me5 § many of my posting rivals have been known to artificially pump up their metrics using irish accounting and Gay casino tricks. dont be fooled § buddy youre ten pounds of shit in a ten pound bag, of shit § i love my beavis. And yours § Priest: and the lord said, take this delicious McDonald and eat it, for it is my body and it will be given up, for you Me: Insanley badass. § HELL IS THE LOOK IN YOUR BUDDYS EYES WHEN HES BLEDDING TO DEATH IN A GOD FORESAKEN JUNGLE!! HELL IS NO LIE; IVE BEEN THERE § #InterestingDevelopments:do not purhcase Hatfield Quality Meats as they contain a rare pigment alloy that turrns your skeleton bones black § going back to switch the auto-capitalized 'i's in my post to lowercase so people don't think im some fucked up nerd § the book that single handledly made "gaming" a house hold name § once you achieve the coveted post count of Seven Thousand...Thats when you gain access to the prestigious halls of MENSA. not one post less. § when your uncles militia surrounds your house with rifles & accuses you of being a dark money pedophile you use it as an opportunity to grow § i fed them Lies § clown college is bnot a real place. it is a location imagined by trolls so they can claim that i'm from there or that i should go there. § Only if U Find The Forum For Disabled People Calle d 3DWorldz ANd U Have Fun. -- http://t.co/ zY8yfShu § OH im so Fucking sorry "Your Majesty", i didnt realize that dick rings were banished in this dystopian piss earth. Ur probably a 9gag poster § absolute mustard ass § "Thou shalt not be as the hypocrites are: for they... pray...in the corners of the streets, that they may be seen of men." #Nation- alAssDay § it was cool when they yanked saddam out of the spider hole becausr i was like "haha that guys me before i had my coffee. thats me on monday" § "Ur honor, if Mr Pibb was truly this man's uncle, then surely hed be able to dazzle us with Pibb Merch" JUDGE:damn he's right. No Pibb Merch § im told that wearing my Denim kimono to the oscars will probably destroy racism and sjw in one feel swoop § itunes.. what a mix-up. its like you gotta be a NASA astronaut just to work this thing § can anyone who has successfully made a surfboard out of their own shit please holler some pointers at me or maybe shoot me if you have a gun § i hate to say it, Oh i hate to say it, but many of my wfollowers think that "Diddy's kong quest" is more important than the Mona Lisa. § is wiki leaks hacking twitter agian or are the people leaving numb skull comments on my page actual human beings § im frowning at this mshit § too much truth in such little time. feeling the heat cominh down to silence me... signing off........ for now § good thing im not a child § I CRY INTO THE TOILET BECAUSE ITS WHERE MY WORTHLESS TEARS BELONG #LIFEHACK § my rEsumE; page 1 ; "IM A JEANS MAN FIRST AND FOREMOST" in 42pt. rosewood font. page 2 is the bible § seriously asking myself out loud if i should let my prick get hard, looking at all of this sweet denim. jourdache, you make a hell of a jean § changing my display name to "Follower killer", my bio to "Fucked", and my avatar to a set of cross hairs with the word "Me" in the center § can;t believe people still try to rile me up in the year 2010 § if i find the mother fucker who ruined my daughters lives by changing his wifi name to "the poop bathroom" i`ll have his balls on my mantel § i personally blame th e skyrocketing army suicide rate on the Preposterous fucking bullshit i post here on a near daily basis § Teens React To Noise. Teens React To Bugs. Teens React To The Normalization Of Warfare. Teens React To Teens Reacting. Teens React To Fritos § you know what wo uld be fun, would be if twitter hq just dumped a truck full of wet turds on my front lawn every day "In case I missed it" § if it werent for the sport of hockey, nobody would give a shit about pucks § i have created more jobs, than every Weed Smoker on the planet-- combined . § i think all commercials should beg me to "try not to cum" and not just the ones on porno sites § shooting my lee dungarees with an uzi for that "armyman" look § if someone comes by asking if i would like to see pornography i say "hell yes". if someone offers me beer or wine i also say hell yes to it. § ME: was thinkin about how I could incorporate the phrase "obama breeze" into my next post. Thoughts? TOM CRUISE: its solid gold baby. Killer § for a 2nd time, a user has threatened to go to the bathroom on me. ill tell u this. only way thatll happen is if ur leaving in the body bag. § im watching my gf transform into wolves . the wolves have the same tattoos that she have. she can turn back into a person when she wants to. § every one with the word "meme" in their bio has put at least one hole in their bedroom wall with the butt of a rifle § every generation deserves at least 5 movies named "Spider Man 2" § my Face when im looking at pictures of other peoples faces on this website that are purportedly reacting to bull shit happening to them https://t.co/LgRxlb- Vblc § im a good man, a respectful man § mmorpg based on 90s grunge life § on one hand $2000 will barely even cover the cost of my large amount of mansions. on the other hand i respect the wild flava brand immensely § red lobster kidzone and this one § A gun is not clothes just because you can wear a holster with a gun inside of it. Jesus christ. Shut thhe fuck up about guns being clothes. §

Your search - pugmom666 - did not match any documents. § reminder: if youre a Judge or any elected official theres still time to throw peoples votes in the trash for no reason https://t.co/yuppHwaNBH § COWORKER: I Just took out a little baggie of DouDou, to eat at work, and Im getting a raise, for being handsome ME: I Admire your Opinions . § me and my followers would be very pleased to see the national reinstatement of "the cobble stone road." a master piece in engineering § THE LAST UNBANNED ALCHEMIST ON EBAY § im sorry but if you continue to spit tobacco down my exposed ass crack I will be forced to stop unclogging your garbage disposal for no pay § the large hadron collier will never detect the higgs boson particle. the only purpose it has is to rile dogs up § ssure. ill concede that this landmark decision is a step in the right direction. BUt people who pre-order games are still getting swindled . § do not strain the ass. the best way to take a shit is to electrocute yourself and let it all shoot out naturally. never strain the ass. § @ContainerStore why don't you guys sell any diapers. Diapers are containers § if U think the tiny stop signs on the sides of school buses are real Ur probably a huge nerd who had to get his butt wiped by the principal § (in this tweet i am pissed off at the "Toilet Duck" brand) Toilet fuck § gamer the bounty hunter § my landlord gave me a call and told me the turds coming from my apartment seemed unusually thin. we then discussed turd strategy for 3 hours § a series of incurable skin conditions have caused my dick to look like Darth Maul's dick, and that's the only good thing about me § here are this year's Vote Multiplers for election day. no, they do not stack policemar - 10x army man -12x verified acct - 15x Asexual - 18x § the joke's hall of fame https://t.co/2UDeGMIo6T § thats my boy § https://t.co/iEWgwL2KvN this is so fucking sick. the dragon murdered him § barbaro alive horse 2017 . fake death § fuck yea i remember. backrubs. dunka-roos. bag clips. sunsets. teeth. all these things were sacrificed in the y2k crisis § eat shit , jc penney skeptics http://t.co/q4CYFS3az8 § lime and pear is the same "Lime & Pear: Same Fruit" (they are the same) #LimeAndPearTheSame // Opinion: Limes are no different from pears § im making a good version of "sky captain and the world of tomorrow" called "sky captain caveman killer" § if i unfollow anyone i will absolutley be murdered by them. im basically in pris-oned. § my opponent's eccentricities are well known. hes probably the one who drank bird bath. he is on record as calling birdbath water "bird juice § please check out my new article "Allergy Season is Fucking Good Actually" which will shatter your precious little minds and make yo'u cry § im a reasonable mans son who thinks that putting a dash of venom into my favorite roast pork hoagie will make it Spicy instead of killing me § it,s a piece of shit for sure § being 0 inch tall keeps the judgementle shallow people away so its fine. § update from the good time line--Bacion is legal to eat at work thanks to President Banksy in the whitehouse, now known as the star wars house § search "crash bandicoot is real" >> Did you mean "Crash Bandicoot Israel"? search " o" § if someone names their son or daughter "Funny Rubio Water Drink" i swear to god i will write your username on a post-it and paste a pic of it § need to find out if the eagle tattooed to my sons chest is racist or normal § @WeBuyRetweets hit me up via my personal line: cumDrenchedArmpit@imbecile.com § mnegative 50 points for trying to trick me with runes § piss also § every room in every home must have a Host § "theyre called millennials because thier souls are 1000 years old...." - truthGamer § i murdered my wife my throwing her at a speeding cop car but its ok because i made her out of shit § looking how to become more cyber § be very nice § i just need to say, to anyone reading this.. You are Important, You are loved, and You belong in this world, if you have over 5000 followers § if I could only get my Nasty mitts on some HARD-WARE , (RAM , Chips ,) my posts would improve tenfould, § Too Fat For College § please dont try and tell me that schrodinger's diaper is a quantum superposition of clean and dirty states, we can all fucking smell it § just thinking about how ad hominem all you mother fuckers are. and simply laughing to my self enjoying it § installed 28 Mods on this pair alone. wrangler, levi.. they all want me dead,m because i refuse to offer them my talents. the jeans hacker . § @GirlHelper i support girl helper § trying to celebrate all these days at once like a sitcom dipshit who accidentally booked 10 fancy dinners at the same time https://t.co/rVkcwmwX6d § having to spell the word "lunch" instead of saying it so the boys don't get too excited § i've been spending the last 7 years of my life making a romhack of super mario rpg where everyone is pregnant. i expect to make $100 from it § i looked at the keyboard and there isnt one § IN OUR LIFETIMES... "GOODBYE" TO MOUTH WASH § someone please. ive bitten into a nasty apple and i don't know how to spit things out of my mouth. ivr never spit before and i need help § "You don't know Jack, unless you know Pepper Jack ." - TheTexMexBoy § eating a single Dorito on a bed of Jasmine Rice § which candidate wants to make it illegal for barbershops to kick me out for having a really dirty head. i dont believe in voting, but still § have sex with rag doll instead of humen #ADVANCEDlifehacks § i am working to resolve the thursday nite rant issue. please do not contact me § TRYING TO RECONCILE MY STAUNCHLY SELF-DEPENDENT SMALL GOVERNMENT BELIEFS WITH MY CONSTANT NEED FOR DIAPER CHANGES § @DigimonOtis cant get a haircut unless his dad goes with him to givr the barber instructions § http://i.imgur.com/vB8UL.jpg no § pokemon "shit head" and "dip shit" versions § number one-- in february of '14 the woke mob called me "Gay" for defending my wifes decision to wear a hula skirt. ive since busted this myth § if you tell me The Mask is standing behind me i will turn around and try to look at it. Because my dumb ass thinks The Mask is real § "THE STUPIDS 2 WITH TOM ARNOLD . TORRENT " IS NOT A REAL MOVIE, IT IS A WORM VIRUS, PLEASE DO NOT DOWN LOAD THIS FILE AS IT IS HARMFUL § youre fit for 2015 #yourFitOf2015 https://t.co/V65O-4BIXF9 § humbly Genuflecting myself before my girl followers, at the end of another red-letter sunday night on the comptuer § im former pro-wrestler Jake "The Taste" Marcel and id like to have a few words with you about professional commemorative coin investment § too many false alarms from people yelling "Bingo is some good shit" or "Bingo is fuckin good". becoming a problem in the bingo community § what do I model, you ask? i model for those gag golf trophies that are given to bad players by coworkers as a joke. guy with twisted up club § i plan on working very hard to shrink my dick in the coming monmths. my goal dick is 2 inches erect § @QuickenLoansLLC thank you § " STAY HUNGRY " - burger king § #FreeJahar obama smirks as he signs the order for a $5 Billion Helicopter while the boston police beg him to pay for $2500 Jahar trial. sick § none of my followers masturbate. § if u consider yourlsef part of Grit Culture just because you r dog shed all over your shirt then get the F.O. and dont comeback § ive been notified by my agent that if i do not tweet the phrase "Epic Wells Fargo" four times this month i will have one of my ears cut off § i would love to brutally kick the ass off of anyone who tries to be nice to me or be my friend on here § please lord my god contact a real life Japanese person so he can help m;e with my scott pilgrim fan translation project. § my piss is black now anf has little pieces of pulp in it and i have to say it on this hash tag because doctors are ignoring me #MuellerGate § i deeply apologize for giving like thirty of my followers panic attacks after posting "Whats for lunch " at 1am EST . § what do Chris Brown, Hitler, and Charles Manson have in common? something charisma something something power something atrocity #teambreezy § exploring potential support for a pod cast thats basically Howard STern, but Nice § What the fuck. Who is this § world record: stupid ass hole drinks cup of coffee underwater § (rodent voice) its damn Friday night!!! And Ill be dipped in shit if I aint ready to throw down some pecker § click this post to spiritually align yourself with Hot Nacho , the devilishly delightful blend of actual nacho spices imported from DarkNet § let us be very clear on one thing, with all of these posts going around. tickle me elmo, does not "Fuck" . Youre out of your mind § cameras are off now. everyones diapers are frozen to each other and 1000 us marines are now separating them all with swords. horrible scene § I Love To Bring My Ass § FRONT: If u dont like the posts BACK: Get out of the kitchin § i challenge us all to experience one another in a greater over all sense of adult maturity, in the year two thousand of fifteen, next year. § A Funny Dog Join Kurdish Tribe For A Dirty Dance . § @CarlsJr the BE community thanks u. http://www.youtube.com/watch?v=e-AUz8bhwmo § @Zoomie2000 agreed. i live in az and my islam handicape neighbor is always asking me about his welfare check. and all i do is sigh #tcot § which of you is ``WACKIN OFF`` on here tonight.............. § im not into that hippy stuff § please remember "RAT" - Repsect Above Trolling § i already do this for free 24/7 https://t.co/PEMBZtumgz § the inventor of the famous "Love to Scrimp, Hate to Save" tweet... FINALly taking pop culture to task... "You gotta see it to believe it" § you will take your place upon the cross, you will bear every last "Tag" and suffer as i do § @OfficialZales could you fit my kidney stones into a ring. me and my fiancee believe that body's are sacred, and we are averse to jewels. § Waiter, by the advice of the Chicago Tribune Id like a Dash of Ground Cumin on my Farm Fresh Egg. Oh! Too much! I withdraw this transaction, § #ReplaceLyricsWithTwerk ppppppppppppppppppppppppppppp (big ffarting ass noise) fuck you fuck you fuck you § BEGRUDGINGLY EXPLAINING THE JERKOFF MANIFESTO TO ANOTHER CONCERNED MEDIA OUTLET § my agent told me i need to get back on meth, remove my satirical bumper stickers and to stop dressing like im cruising for discreet gay sex . § my ass has become too powerful for even me to contorl. tonight , i will sit on the hibachi grill at benihana and put an end to this hell § Peoplw are saying this § seems more and more of times these days that every one is too much of a PUSSY to wipe my ass and mow my lawn for free § i will be typing the words "rock 'N' roll" over and over in a note pad document until my computer makes targeted content more relevant to me § CAN GOD RESPECT GROUND ZERO SO MUCH THAT EVEN HE CANNOT BUILD A MOSQUE ON IT § The absolute shit Im forced to put up with as a content Producer. Ive sacrificed my basic human rights in order to placate U fucking people. § looked at a newspaper today. looks like we're getting taxed out the wazoo, with this president. anyone else see this shit? tax out the wazoo § feeding my pigs a big bag of barber hair § this is how i deal with the SCUM!! Fuck you! https://t.co/nhgbnrqKK4 § what is Courage, you ask??? courage is being able to say that ragecomics are bad on your twitter account § the only thing real about me is my appreciation for the refreshing taste of #pepsi, #doritios, #hormel, #generalmills, et al, § Im begging you! Please stop Quote Tweeting the Senator's nudes just to "Dunk" on him! Hes getting HARD from the attention! Hes whacking off! § i would pay a group of scienttists $10000000 to fool a man into believing in santa until the age of 80. lets get it done § i had to fix the typo since they're probably going to print this tweet in Harper's § looking at pictures of rotisserie chickens i wish i could maul with my bare hands § please everyone search for shit like "autism microchip" on youtube and look at all the thumbnails on their videos http://t.co/V25172FH5s § i now concede that girls may be allowed to wear UNDERARMOUR„¢ brand clothing; but only if they sign a contract stating its for sports reasons § big pharma. if youre reading this i have an idea for a pill that makes you tinier so you can fit into secret zones. i will let you invent it § moving pictures are a sin upon this earth § My Friend Toby Once Said, One Big Ass Biker Man I Ain't As Good As I Once Was, But I'm As Good Once As I Ever Was § genius hack: keep all of your toilet paper in the car so you have to walk all the way out there to wipe your ass. it 's "Good Exercise" § i had the courage to bring kindness and mental health into peoples lives And now wevery one wishes this was my grave... https://t.co/yP9VHzabQT § ill show you real truth. ill show you what happens when you crap on a real son of a bitch § zero of my so-called twitter pals gave me a phone call or offered me any aid during my harrowing ordeal iwth the hacker. may god punish you. § if calvin peed on the gulf of mexico would it provide the oil leak with the disrespect it deserves or merely aggravate the problem at hand § they call it forex trading because th JUDGE has ruled that all the money i make on it is for ex wife § mindless drones: i will wipe my ass... i will wipe my ass... really brave and handsome guy: no!! i will NOT wipe my ass § always take my stagecoach full of pit bulls to the Range . because my girls love to watch me shoot § nope i can not § MAKE NO MISTAKEâ€‹i Appreciate the flawless, invaluable wisdom posted to us by the celebs, and they, in turn, appreciate my valuable feed back § the shithead principal cowers under his desk and uses a stethoscope on the floor to listen for my rough n' tumble boots and trademark Gait § mr deeds from the movie mr deeds is a real man and he is also q anan § "liking arli$$ too much" is a bullshit thing to divorce me over § car wash big man. big man thru car was.h can car wash be used on big man. can big man survive car washj. does car wash clean big man. #Bing § if you go to a nascar rally carrying a clipboard and wearing a hard hat people will just let you go on the track and kiss all the good cars § seems like to me that in this foul economy the only thing "On the Up and Up" is the damn gas prices, thath we all gotta break the bank for . § shit heads who worsen everyones life, lady whos immune to piss smell, man named "Mr Dick Tip" who i have no concern of--all trying to Fuck me § meat loaf just ordered the venue to keep the lights on the audience so he can see if any trolls have infiltrated his show § you have to get up pretty early in the morning to piss off my entire shit § heart of darkness 2: https://t.co/GvVobp9R-BH § if you say shit like "Basinga" they give you a TV show.... if you say opinions that are true , you get the Executioners blade . -EpicWayne § i dont know. i have never seen a doctor who § yes i jettisoned my uncles hvac equip-ment all over the highway & obliterated a teen driver but using that info to slander me is also Cringe. § thinking of replacing both of the license plates on my car with a picture of a different car § i love all the guys, from that show § no youre totally right,"Joe Pa" is a perfectly honorable & respectable man, assuming hes never confronted with any actual tests of character § reviewed obama inauguration speech. not ONE mention of "varmints" #ProVarmint-Pres?? #getUmOut § laying in the car, hiding firom my malicious Wife because im in trouble for buying too many toothpicks to fit into the tooth pick holder § when the trolls have my internet access removed i will not allow that to end the content flow. i will nail my insipid "Tweets" to my car § they are all crooks § the ape `s curse § i call this next 18-tweet series "The Ice Bucket Challenge, But With Piss, Instead" § U want more insight into "THe Process," u say? Look no further. https://t.co/yhbyYzq9SD § reddit: my uncle caught me licking my sistser's bicycle seat and now i need u to send me as many mcdon-ald's monopoly game pieces as possible § just found out tthat cultural revolu-tionary Bill Maher is just another worthless pothead. is there any hope left in this earth § I just generated a #TweetCloud out of a year of my tweets. Top three words: jackson, 1958-2009, michael - http://w33.us/3kq0 § slin jim § my opionon on people who use the word "ass" is as follows: these people dont exist to me, therefore ih ave no opinion of them. theyre rotten § and the award for best banksy tweet goes to.. "egg_dad_ebooks" *seven grown men rise from their seats and push their way towards the podium* § about a dozen or so misshapen <ROSS PEROT VICTORY '96 ASHTRAYS> ,woud love to take up smoking just to get some use outta these bad boys § attaching an enmormous dildo to my rifle so i can grip it in my mouth for added stability. thats how it is #army #navy #themafia § maybe instead of a toaster they shoul call it a "Toast cooker" #normalMansThoughts § Wanker ! Come off it § apparently shirtless people are interacting with me on this site. please put on a tasteful button-down top if you want to fav or retweet me. § b3ndr, PepsiCynic, and myself will be stream-ing an incan healing ritual, intending to absorb blood from viewers to regenerate our foreskins § You need at least $100 to join Boys Lunch Club. I will count all the money in your wallet, so do not try to join if you do not have $100. § i just cracked into aCiDnEt and got my grubby mitts on BigCasper's [No_Incest] edit of the spike lee oldboy remake and im sippin #DraftBeer § they should make dunce caps that have positive reaffirming words on them, like "speed demon" or "Wolf" § mature of u to post this. here's some real shit http://t.co/ yVLd00pVFe § @Gamestop one of your guys tried to give me a bible and said it was the "ultimate strategy guide" with my purchase of petz fantasy 3d. awful § to the longhorn steakhouse which refused to serve me: a bib most certainly counts as a shirt § in 2023 an unassuming fat man will become the official currency of the united states. the economy will collapse because theres only 1 of him § scenario: i'm sitting in the dentist's chair getting my cavities filled. a stray pube enters the window and lands in my mouth. who's liable § i fear my tropical fish no longer respect me after i accidentally stumbled backwards & smushed my ass hole right up against their $3000 tank § "soon or later you will not even be able to be able to take a crap with out the Tax man up your ass" - Dril § "the only way to go is retro." - demonius dark blade, 30 minutes ago § ME: These days everyone wants to suck their smart phones dick if u ask me. HIPSTER: Is that a new feature? ME: ((making bitter beer fsce) § put pictures of fat 1920s babies up next to the muscle builders of modern day & you will ssee that their skill levels are considerably equal § 1 nipple, 1 male ass, 2 jeans pics, 1 toilet full of piss,you terrible f ucking people § Former U.S. first lady Nancy Reagan (R) joined by daughter Patti Davis at the premiere of the film "Stuart Little 2" https://t.co/43kfKiOtma § if you think anything I post is funny you're a piece of litter § @DigimonOtis im running to your house § Nacho Libre Tight Dick Shots - Nacho Libre Best Ass Crack Vids - ripped by x_vArEz_x ©2006 § if you turn the patterns on their shirts 90 degrees... the trusted REFEREE becomes the despicable PRISONER.... truly life is a fragile Bitch § 4am walgreens haul... re tweet this after the Girls wake up https://t. co/fg3DTgduUM § let me be very clear: i would rather attend a Pig's wedding than attempt to sift through the dumpster you people have made out of my dm box, § i live inside of the holy mecca cube and do all my good posts in there § i have in my hand a list of hollywood bigwigs who have eaten human flesh, and i will reveal one name each day until im provided with respect § please stop calling my home with fucked up three stooges noises. my nine daughters no longer respect me after seeing me get mad at the phone § cant wait to get back to iraq and blast some ragheads-- itll be just like halo but with less lag #tcot #nowTHATSghetto #nowplaying #bun § used the last remaining amount of my spirit force to transform mny daughter into a mana blade so that she will never cry again #AFathersPain § one tear drop for every post u have been a Reply Guy to § if i wasnt constantly debilitated from online-induced stress i could probably kick off the ass of any guy on here § climb into the garbage you uneducated clown § effects i mean. § NASCAR Forums >> Odds & Ends >> what are some good podcasts to listen to while listlessly fucking my wife § DICK DOCTOR: have you been using protection ME: yes. i put an entire towel in my ass § yeah like im just going to put bottles of my own damn urine up on the mantel. you fucking idiot. this is celeb urine § cum is so stupid. when i look at it i dry heave and cry for help § we have just been informed that more and more teens are buying "wax lips" from candy stores. do not be fooled. these are not their real lips § think im going to start incorporating the word "Gadzooks" into more of my tweets, to punish my followers, for their constant insolence, § sky wiccan, lava wiccan, river wiccan, light wiccan, dark wiccan. thats all the wiccans § #The12DaysOfContent making these is as torturous as every concentra- tion camp combined, including hell, which god made http://t.co/d3j4RWAnYr § dogs love barking at me like 1000ft from their house. what are youa land surveyor. you don't know what a property line is bitch shutup § im sorry?? i was under the impression that these accounts are good???? § ill simply let the fav counts do the talking. as i normally do when dealing with cra[p. § i changed my mind. fuck cash for moms online. fuck it all. its nonsense that moms are given allthis good cash while I make $0.003 per tweet § https://t.co/7JCD-ndbrpk § i am a Teen and that's somethjing i have to live with for the rest of my life. § mmy appreciation of pat sajaks wardrobe is extremely well known; and is the only aspect of my life that is not shrouded in complete disgrace § intense dr pepper cravings from being mentally mpreg., check. dick looks like an ear from botched circumcison,chsck. 1 big purple arm, check § i spend a lot of time reading the constatution of the united states of america while grinning ear to ear § Ok bitch write "Telomere Mindfulness" on a piece of paper. Go to Golds gym on 23rd, hand the paper to "Eddie" & tell him youre ready to Die § COMPUTER.. FED EX ME A PRINT OUT OF ALL MY GIRL FOLLOWERS SORTED BY THEIR DEVOTION TO CHRIST COMPUTER... GET ME THE BULE CHECK MARK A.S.A.P. § im going to keep doing this until my daughter calls me http://t.co/wbpeGpu7JI § how dare you satirize my beloved fan base, the Lovely Boys of twitter § who is that vile man lurking around outside of "ROFLCon" with a notepad, standing on trashcans trying to peek inside of the windows and shit § looks like the circus is in town again § @glennbeckgirl dont you dare insult ebert chicago. § thinking about displaying an authentic harley davidson denim vest in a box frame to really tie my rec room together and make it suck ass § how can i possibly enjoy a moment's respite, when thousads of my followers could be giving my posts "The finger," without me even knowing it § if i become too radicalized by the death of Fuddruckers promise youll send me gentle reminders not to spread coronna virus on purpose § getting shot directly in the ass execution style while crawling through a duct § me: let's just say if ur a child who suffocated in a plastic bag, my next rant might just rock your socks off buzzfeed: Splendid. Phenomenal § give me the 200000 § >>ATTEMPTING TO SEND FILE 'LIST_OF_CARPETS_I_REFUSE_TO_FUCK_ON_PART1.doc' >>ACCEPT >>PLEASE ACCEPT >>ATTEMPT FAILED § im crying because doctors banned the cure for low T again § THIS IS AMERICAN AIR LINES. WE DROPPED YOUR SHITTY COWBOY BRA INTO THE OCEAN EN ROUTE TO ISRAEL. IT SHATTERED INTO 100000 SHARDS LIKE A PIG. § im kel from kenan and kel show. support rand paul for senate or ill put the screw in the tunna. § #UseATwitter-NameInASentence @chrisbrown punched his wife then took his shirt off in a television studio § the other son wipes his ass too much. goes thrugh absurd amounts of tissue & has effectively thrown any respect for my household to the Dogs § i want to beat the shit out of a ufo § i trusted you jewey2k10 and you pull this shit on me. youre a disgrace to all Straight Edge Teens who play in bands § my sons new deal is saying he wants to be "Tiny" when he grows up, no doubt due to the forlorn shit he has been looking up on the computer . § lets focus on piss farms. lets focus on piss farms. lets focus on piss farms. for the economy. we gotta focus on these piss farms § DONT LOOK AT M E *pathetically wipes filthy ass with a post it note * TURN AROUND DONT LOOK § my ass cheeks look like brains and my brain looks like an ass cheek § anoter sony fanboy. move along § ((speaking too close to the microphone at press conference)I have never watched a single episode of the Teletubbies. They look like fools § prince hussein...wheres my goodboy bailout § STARTING A KICKSTARTER TO GET ME UNBANNED FROM KICKSTARTER. COM AFTER I CALLED IT "PRICKSTARTER" IN A PRIVATE EMAIL § i take my gf on a balloon ride to propose. a field of wild flowers spells Women Are Crooks. "oops sorry." i apologize. "that ones for my dad § asking the baja fresh cashier to detain the teenagers in the parking lot who told me i loooked like "Frosty the snowmans uncle" § like this if youre one of the 3% of teens who remembers when music was just guys saying "my name is kid rock" over and over § "ohh i caught you posting cringe you posted Cringe i got you i caught you" Yes bitch. And i make $100 a month doing it. § GENDERLESS WEDDING AT HARD ROCK CAFE: THE BRIDE AND GROOM WILL BE COVERED IN TARPS IN

ORDER TO CIRCUMVENT THE STANDARDIZED NORM`S; FREE ICE § *all horrors begotten by the desire of man flash before eyes* woha! this is awkward *the cries of millions suffering echo* Damn That's Weird § I shoudl not be expected to put my knee on the ground to propose to a woman, the same ground where the animals shit, § i love absorbing knowlegde from the expansive breadth of electronic information that exissts on this plane we call OnLine. its good to do it § steel reserve 211 extra high gravity breast milk § @NoahMunck True Or False: IS There a force powerufl enough to counteract "Munckmentum" in 2011, 2012, and Beyond. § i am actually the first guy who came up with the "aliens who smoke weed" joke, back in 2011 § ah man. how embarrassing. i chose the user name "CondomMaster" a long time ago, back when condoms were cool. dont look at it § my blood glucose test strip unboxing video maintains a remarkable zero views despite me spending $8000 on Media courses #TheThursdayNiteRat § excuse me sir, i couldnt help but notice that youre in need of a thorough explanation of kegel exercise. ok, it's basically psychic jelqing, § someone please send me the recording of orson welles reading off that big list of "you might be a redneck" jokes., i need it beofre 11 PM § and now im being unfollow brigaded by traitors who would gladly simply put my ass in the viper pit § cant help but smile to check out these new slogans: Weird twitter- "Are we Having fun yet?" weird twitter- "Game over, man, game over !!" § something like 43% of our nations topsoil is actually cave man shit. fucked up § Thank you for your time, Elon. I know youre very busy but I appreciate you coming onto my feed. http://t.co/ ux4RXhgDsy § the most important part of any account on here is the posts. if you dont have the posts youre basically finished § "dear policeman: i am god" etched into the back of my sweater vest § ive beenn using Confidence and Self Esteem lately, to get unprecedented deals on discarded promotional displays at game stop § i have never in my life- shit my pants or had an erection. it is ludicrous to claim other wise § im thinking of making it my "Main move" , to eat a huge plate of nachos and have the worst sex of my life right after § jusut dropped 8000000 HKD on a usb-interfaced sniper rifle that blocks one of my insolent followers at random every time i pull the trigger § lesebien cum #alchemy § [UmbrageLiker has joined the chat] PleasantBoy: GET HIM OUT OF HERE NiceKeeper: NOT ON MY WATCH KindBarber: FUCK OFF ! Helper: THIS IS AWFUL § in melrose, new mexico a young woman found a 'cursed' mouse skull in an unspecified variety of "utz" brand snack foods. beware of this § i extend to all my Pregnant Woman followers.... the hand of Unity https://t.co/L5BYZBTThB § installing sneeze guards at old country buffet is tyranny and they make it far more difficult for me to vomit cigar grease all over the food § http://t.co/ iNSY7WFx great. dale hates me now. fuck this website § 1) wise the fuck up, 2) put the same amount of days in all the months 3)people need to put on the damn thinking caps 4) im boycotting months § if you dont accompany my twitter feed with the "real time with bill maher" theme music every time you read it youre4 a piece of shit § my fuckin opinion of politics? heres my fuckin opinion of politics. not a single senator in the history of the united states, has been white § closing my blinds so the feds cant see me... then posting some shit like "hunter biden is jordan peterson if he drank urkel's Cool potion" § Keep an eye on "Apps", in 2013 and beyond. § all the pictures of bacon on the #nationalbaconday hashtatg look like utter dog shit , these people are out of their mind, uploading these § executing some advanced high-risk transactions on the Markets. trading my ass medicine for dick medicine § i cast 1million holy spells on my yankee candle and now it never burns out and the flame grows taller when rowdy celebs appear in the news § my mame is jonny goodposts § the military industrial complex spent $99bil on dixie cups to ensure that not a single drop of our troops genetically superior cum is wasted § "i am deeply sorry but do not let this freak incident fool you, the uroclub is still a fine product a nd it is a 'hole in one'." -tigerwoods § i have evolved byeond the need for "furniture" and i enjoy resting on the floor like an animal while counting all the cool cash im saving § goign to new york disguised as the Mayor so when the cops turn their back on me i can jack off § i have been saiyng this for years now. Just look at the digimon otis account https://t.co/GgsDDrouVb § dick fact no.77: my, dick is covered in clothes most of the time. this protects it from the elements as well as the gaze of my enemies § i call upon familiars david blaine & criss angel to help me discretely wash this pocket pussy in the soda fountain at the peiwei asian diner § @FootLockerJapan you owe me one million dollars § if you try to say something fucked up to me i will break your arms and call the cops on you § ok so twitter can just freeze all the verified accounts at once but when someone says my yard looks like shit theyre Suddenl;y powerless... § a banner ad that pissed me off siad "This Guys Getting More "Ass" Than You Ever Will " and it was just a picture of the nutty professor § i would not sit that close to a fountain in real life. they are disgusting breeding grounds for all manner of microscopic vermin § f https://t.co/RNQlFwV69L § "The Shitting Otaku" § dont know where to get my Tech reviews since BobTechman was banned after being forced to show his penis in resposne to a harassment campaign § movies are fucking dying and its time to open the dialogue on giving hollywood full access to the nastiest chemical/nuclear weapons on earth § i'm going to be the one who makes a "got milk" parody so good that everoyne forgives me for trying § the least political book in the english languge is-- you guessed it-- the dictionary. § eating luch #MondayMorning #monday-Thoughts #MondayMotivation #JustMondayShit #MondayAss #PissMOnday #MondayBoys #MondayVibes #MondayMood § but my teeth are sparkling clean § just got off the phone wih bill maher hbo & they confirmed bill maher will say "release the gamer cut" on live tv if we get 500 signatures . § #PrayForNicksGrandpa even though prayer is clinically proven to make people die faster??? how about no. § why even bother learning how to hack when i can just have my enemies accounts removed by accusing them of conspiring to piss on grumpy cat § only takes two seconds of me cliciking around on my keyboard to see why they call me the mother fucker of ubuntu § elon if youre reading this please get back to me about my idea for inventing a $900 hot dog that tastes like shit. thank you § trying to convince my dying son to ask the make of wish foundation for a credit card with 0% APR § girls love it when i cure their depression using my intelli-genct brain § wacky sitcom premise where i accidentally arrange to get my ass kicked and have my dick sucked in the same parking lot § WHO CARES I DONT § @SCJohnson @AGMikeHunter @JNJNews nail his ass to the fucking WALL § what i sent you just now was not my sizzle reel. it was a teaser for my sizzle reel., and if you were in the industry youd fucking know that § SOup is not lunch. Soup is a condiment § star wars is back § "I love him. Thank you" - fucking idiot senator Chuck Grassley (IA-R) on the death of the honorable Mr. Ayatollah § withholding this week's Epic Games tithe until they address the issue of people on the mic calling me "Somebody Uncle" § special Treat for all my prety lady followers.... http://t.co/Sb9TrXhg § huey lewis and the... PUBES?? haha. some things are too fucked up for even ME to submit on here...**backspace backspace backspace backspace* § see?? it's happenig again. people are blocking me because i'm posting my opinion. @Doritios is sending me crude messages again. fuck twitter § i dont want to § looking for medicines that will make the fish in my koi pond shit less often § COP: found the culprits blog..another 1 of them Incels DETECTIVE: the only "Cell" he'll be "In" is a cold lunchbox next too mammas meatballs § if anyone sees a blue thermos on I-95 that is a container of Stress Vomit my wife threw out of the car and i need to show it to my doctor § i can telli f youre a drunk driver or not just by reading 2 of your posts § if you dont down load the latest versions of all your programs youre fucking stupid § blue jean's... Activated . § @bobbysburgerpal bobby certainly didnt get his flair & passion for cooking by touching di*ks, so i dont know why your waiter woud touch mine § when i see people putting up foul language on to the feed, all i can do is laugh, knowing that they will never get their posts read on Ellen § big meeting with chinese investors coming up in 5 minutes. need to look sharp and presentable. im running my dick under the faucet § behead those who insult the prophet muhammad?? haha wow. holy moly. "Thats ur opinion man." -the dube. § the government cut off my balls too but they told me the president needed them § washed my hands of him years ago. § guinness coming in 2 mins to film me breaking the coveted "most trash cans knocked over using piss" record but im too sad to put clothes on § @DogBountyHunter remember when you made your son Tucker leave his girlfriend because she wore diapers? Not MLK's dream. #dogthebountyhunter § yo bartender!! we all know you filled my deink with ice so you can skimp on the good stuff. hows this grab ya: " o Tip" #TheThursdayNiteR- ant § world record 100 diaper combo run over by jeep § is the thanksgiving day parade canon. are we to believe that garfield would allow himself to float around and be yanked around with strings § THERAPIST: your problem is, that youre perfect, and everyone is jealous of your good posts, and that makes you rightfully upset. ME: I agree § john tyler was less commonly known as the "Rat President", having up to 900 rats running around the oval office and making an utter ruckus § i remark "mummies are made out of diapers" at the egypt museum. some cops jump out a sarcophagus and begin humping me as i roll on the floor § installing a full scale maypole in my backyard... just thinking the boys are going to love this shit § DICKSLAVE NUMBER 288, DICKSLAVE NUMBER 122, AND DICKSLAVE NUMBER 195 WALK INTO A BAR. THEY ORDER THREE DRINKS AND MAKE POLITE CONVERSATION § @DrPhil "shit" § PRESS RELEASE: User @ Dril Calls For An End To The Violence -- "Keep Sending Me Links; I'll Click Any Piece Of Shit You Put In Front Of Me" § Not Nice!!!!! https://t.co/TBTctLEF39 § maybe sometimes both sides... are good and bad at the same time??? im sorry if im doing this wrong. it is difficult to write § the only hthing i hate more than crashing my ford truck is justin biebers dick. which was recently shown to me in pictures § #BareShelvesBiden https://t.co/5VXo7hKkE2 § ive invented a new kind of bed bugs for the toilet § some times.. the smartest people you know, are Geniuses § banks should have special money they give to the robbers where george washing- ton is cross-eyed or has a hitler moustache or some such shit . § academi § oi guv the old bird pissed it. I will miss her . Fuck § wiping your ass is now officially Politics § the ceo of cash4gold just called me, crying. he tells me this--he says people arent respecting his brand on twitter. i fucking hate this site § you know the ancient sumerians regarded men with wide-ass necks and tiny-ass heads as divine beauties and gave them gifts of gold and barley § pleasse read the article "Why I Choose To Masturbate" by Mutant Turd for truly valuable insight into the mind of the common masturbator § those things are me § horny, distressed man causes local planetarium to collapse § go to www. info .men to learn how to recite the Men's Prayer and help put a gun in covid19's mouth § digimonotis: i do not trust or support him   EpicWayne: i trust and support epic wayne mr_Tightnuts : i support him but i do not trust him § "This Whole Thing Smacks Of Gender," i holler as i overturn my uncle's barbeque grill and turn the 4th of July into the 4th of Shit § http://www.fanfiction.net/Star_ Wars_and_Halo_Crossovers/8/1342/ Thank u § live free or die. kfc § I just got word that the trolls are attempting to change the name of the Stratolaunch LEO aircraft to "The Stalwart Pussy." We must stop them § my top 2013 picks: 1) guns 2) pictures of guns 3) halloween thank you. please look out for the top picks of 2014, which i will do next year. § if your in anonymous please help me destory "zepplindoug777"s life with a meticulously devised terror campaign or somethig § NMISERABLE § completing my "Dip Shit" look by donning a humongous bib with a picture of a sailboat on it § if i ever find a sincere or heartfelt post on your feed im gonna take a SHIT ON YOu § rude ass. upgradable to hell ass. upgradable to Satan ass. upgradable to chaos ass. upgradable to ãƒžã‚¹ã‚¿ (Masuta)-infinity ass § consumeralert: at least one butterball turkey has been stuffed with the shrunken head of an assassinated african dictator.be care full. § by suggesting that i suck your (Female) dick ,u have sufficiently violated at least 3 gneder sacraments and have theirfore earned a " fail" § nuh uh. This is crap § men guy https://t.co/pDBFnXVfCF § Celebs are sucking & fucking each other like never before. But still no justice for those who are getting the most sucked & fucked: The Fans § look at this shit here https://t.co/eA96Me7cv6 § my name is steve jobs. i am a successful ceo in charrge of the apple corporation. #Joke § back in the dog house after the wife caught me photo shopping her into vintage car ads § im thinking this shit addresses my main problem with soda, which is that drinking it doesnt force me to witness the face of God https://t.co/TLIzMb58o0 § the secret -- to becoming a content genius -- is that you have to be able to name every font face on the planet while being water boarded § every little thing that U do...... Baby im amazed by U... http://t.co/z5BtJP0vNh § yell prayers to the lord our god http://t.co/cVC08pyfBy § (hearing about a guy who died) wow thats like 0.0003 9/11s § will calling the police about this affect my backer status § yes. this guy is me https://t.co/zd2KABfhQQ § heres my 2010 message for ya: "good year - good freands - and good luck thank you" thank you § i suppport LGBT... and GBLT ((photo montage of me sinking my teeth into a Good BLT)) #DaringJokes #HeWentThere § Q: What is your Passion Sport? A: My Passion Sport is football and golf § https://t.co/mSsmL4zh7F § not even Austin Powers 4 can win me back after mike myers' hideous racial outburst at the Laugh Factory. Fuck you § hey uh, it's just the thursday nite rant. if youre offended i dont give a shit. Thats whats to be expected from the thurdsay night rant. § you pick up some political cartoon paper & see a shitty grave drawing captioned with "Burt Be-Gone" and its intended to be respectful & nice § i put years of hard work into getting my torture degree at torture college & now everyones like "oh tortures bad","its ineffective" fuck off § sipping some campbell's chunky soup from flask in coat pocket § This site is dedicated to the love and respect of Asian women. If you are here looking for porn... "MAN ARE YOU IN THE WRONG PLACE!" § hm whats this? dropped a copy of my 263-page memoir "All Bi Myself" on the florr of this trendy teen cafe. dont have time to pick it up. l8r § shit pens. no good § clowns should spend less time making balloon animals and more time making Prayer's § @YahooNews his mission was to destroy it . § my thoery is that the book is only being delayed due to stressful constraints from the trolls § stinkers or classics. whats good to trolls § kids are always saying "drew carey invented plinko". Wrong. Drew carey stole plinko from the italians. Drew carey couldnt even invent "2+2". § ktxl fox affiliate just showed a pregnant woman on th simpsons #pregwatch § if you ask me many of Americans have been wearing the mask even before from covid 19. the mask i refer to is of course the clown's mask. § reality check....its not "Funny" or "Good" to fool Content Creators into showing their penis to the official red lobster account-- Perieod. § hello. what is your online user handle please? ok. ok thanks. blocked § down load my widget and learn which poisons you are consuming that are preventing you from becoming an asexual james bond § "dont tax me obama. im dead" -our beloved dead soldiers § martin luther king did not have a favorite type of lunchables. absolutely ridiculous and inappropriate. @kraftfoods please delete § Shut the fuck up http://t.co/Zf89wVtyco § i chew on my philly cheesesteak as i place a camera under the table to film womens' feet. http://t.co/lHAX4G7t - The Standard for Influence. § the boys on shark tank just loving my propeller beanie that sprays piss everywhere while it spins § the absolute perfect shit is scoring a legendary forum handle like "Farkimedes" and making 30,000 posts asking the mods to move threads § to the trolls https://t.co/qvXxLFcZBm § if e3 does NOT #ShowUsTheGames, KeyBladeWalter, "Epic" Wayne Briggs and I will engage in disciplined self-immolation on the disgusting floor § chridst. god damn it.

not this number again § it is official. im taking my football to prom and im
going to kiss it and the nerds will never stop me. i cannot wait to savor their
anguish § #spon #Ad #corrupttion #SweetheartDeals https://t.co/eukiIzyrsi § my
agent told me to say ive done a lot of soul searching & have decided that
keeblar is the treat of the summer § going to deep fake some videos of myself
saying some austin powers quotes flawlessly , § nine boys crowded around a 19"
television "Franklin for Fuckin adults " "Its about damn time" "Hell yes, this"
all rubbing hands together § there are dead guys with verified accounts, yet i
am barred from consideration due to the actoins of my enemies, or "Haters", on
this page . § #e3rumors some meme guy will walkout on stage twirlin two pistols
and begin kicking cans of Gun Flavored Mountain Dew into a screaming crowd §
unban me from college http://t.co/q57sgQ1uxi § TROLL: Shut down windows ME:
Ah, no § we;ll its time for me to pick the scabs off of what i not-so-affection-
ately refer to as my "Fail Dick" § who let this guy type under my post § DAD: i
just heard on t he news that teens are taking the "Kick My Ass" challenge.
please dont do this ME: you have no power over me, old man § laying in the
submissive position, letting a gang of trolls piss all over me and saying "Im
getting too old for this shit" like a bad ass § awful, looks fucking dumb, etc
https://t.co/1xTeOubVql § under the influence of my toilet § @roach700 i trust
you roach 700 § sub way is a pedophile... you guys see about this shit ? §
banking on becoming one of those guys that consistently sucks so much ass tthat
people arent allowed to own me anymore because its boring § funny how ppeople
get faved for posting "Humour", but when i post about how deeply in love i am
with the girls here i get the old Brush off § me, DigimonOtis and some other
asshole ride a three man bicycle to go buy some gold and were all dressed like
dipshits and mad at each other § CRISIS: "TrueBloodGamer" just switched his
steam handle to "TroubledGamer" and is NOt responding to ANY messages, we must
bow in cyberprayer § thinktting of putting a sign up in front of my decrepit
mississippi swamp house advising the band Pussy Riot to keepaway § beer just
beer . cracik the lid off that fucking shit § i apologize for referring to
everyone who bought my official scent as "The Sucker Squad" in a private prayer
to god that some troll recorded § production of beetle bailey 3d the movie has
been CANCELED due to "small fires, sandstorms, lack of interest" § any purchase
made on this page will help me defeat my ex wife th https://t.co/ZLfT74FD7u § i
think it would be fucking stupid to be a fat ass caterpillar and have your
entire body be made out of weak points § buying an assortment of soaps and
ointments to make my ass hole less stupid § #WhoKilledVerneTroyer § The wine
imparts a foreign bitterness. How could he betray me? We were brothers. I fall
to the ground. Execute a partial curl. One last rep. § i see jokes like "doge".
like "angry cat". and I think to myself, "This is fucking actually good. How
can I interface this with my strats." § **instnatly teleports 1000 years into
the future where theres millions of new things to have good opinions about*
HUUhhauih, .. Uh.. BLuahgh § me and the wife are discussing having me cryogeni-
cally frozen like autsin powers for a while, to close up our inappropriate 6
year age gap § imagine if elon Trolled you by sending you a dog saying "Well
isnt that special"or some shit. youd get more ptsd than every veteran combined
§ reduced my weight gain goal to 300 lbs at the advice of my doctor § "How To
Make WebKins Fuck" #IncriminatingSearchTermsFoundOnRyanDunnsDeathComputer §
playing the worlds most normal sized violin § ive been sititng in buffalo wild
wings for 3 hrs now, refusing to speak with the waiter because of his vile dry
lips. i will win this battle § #worstfeeling my as § i have proof that the
women on here are forming quotetweet gangs to "freak out" and intimidate
uncircumcised guys § bday cake is the once proud land of Egypt. the candles?
human beings in flames, dying for the very freedom you take for granted §
Thinking About Saying The Rent Is Too Damn Hi § #TheThursdayNiteRat was a typo
caused by the fatigue and stress of managing my online business. It is not a

real feature. § #PeopleIReallyWantToMeet #oopsiforgot #Celtics forget all of
this garbage. when are we gonna nab Osama § sorry i can't write any posts or
look at my emails today. i got kennel cough from eating a bad pear § turn on
howard stern. he is talking to a policeman habout how tough their job is and
that we are proud of him § You trying to eat the dried up tooth paste I spit up
out of my mouth? You little pieces of Shit? § mario means "penis " in japanese
§ people who write "RT" and copy/paste instead of using the retweet button are
the same people who changed clothes in the toilet stalls at gym § my cigar
rival just posted another vid.... time to leave the kids with nana , switch it
to hell mode and outsmoke this BAStard § horny supremacy § the floor of the new
york stock exchange breathlessly awaiting MetalGearEric's review of the BK
Rodeo Whopper before erupting in chaos § im going to strangle the turds out of
your ass § weeping because of my heroic burden... spending my last dollae at
dairy queen to support girl businesses... chowing down between the tears.. §
saying something like "i only bought that nirvana album b/c it has a babys dick
on it" and alternating between backpedaling & doubling down § trapped, fully
nude, in restaurant bathroom. boss & his wife will be here in 10mins. trying to
see if i can make a tuxedo out of tolet paper § i accidentally legally changed
my name to "Child Porn Man", if u have any experience dealing with this issue i
owuld appreciate your input. § http://t.co/eGp7M4l4FB were u there the day
DragonBlaster laid down his arms & surrendered to the deranged corporate
interests of Big Diaper § be sure to check out my repulsively athletic legs &
thighs featured on the shitty offbrand bag version of wheaties at your local
supermarket § otis is criminal and a liar § Mr Truth Through Pain § IS BLUE
TOILET WATER A RETRO 90S THING OR HAVE I JSUT NOT SEEN A CLEAN TOILET FOR 13+
YEARS. PLEASE HELP § Setting aside the dumb ass things of life to focus on the
truth of intelligense . § haha i just met a man named TenderWallace on irc who
will scrape my teeth in his garage for 25 bucks so this whole dental ofice can
suck it § two cars in the garage, a white picket fence, and monster energy
logos embroidered into both ass pockets § need nonviolent methods to knock out
these security cams fucking up my protcest of public toilet § mother fucker .
catch these boots § racist against autistic § handing print outs of my most
beloved arliss (arli$$) quotes to trick or treaters § thge concept of "forgive-
ness' is some stupid religious shit conceived to allow rich folks to beat the
hell out of women #grammys #teambreezy § clicking onto the reddit comment
section of a picture of a clowns penis and upvoting 400 diferent opinions about
whether its satire or not § "my posts are more..i think.. self aware than most
other peoples posts. Im also nice to everybody" -dril, visionary Disruptor;
while smoking § #worstfeeling When Its Just To Much #bestfeeling Justright! §
months ago i dreamt about people making their ass cracks longer with surgery. i
woke up & immediately put "Crack length" in my drafts folder § no bitch § ME:
COMPUTER... SORT THE POSTS ON THIS SITE FROM LEAST TO MOST RACIST COMPUTER:
YES MASTER ME: COMPUTER... PLEASE DO NOT CALL ME THAT § theyre tryin to Stooge
my ass § ME: waiter...give me a shitty joe WAITER: (wow..this guy just ordered
a sloppy joe in a bad ass way i never heard before. powerful move.) Ok § if
youre looking for good movies about grease, do not watch the nmovie "grease",
because you will get swindled § driving down the highway at 30mph laying on the
horn protecting myself with a shield of Noise § i hate i t when girls think im
proposing whenever i take the knee at them in protest § cor blimey,. down load
the Bing Bar today m'lord, follow MadeaREal,ItsReal_Madea, Madea_FunJoke,&
MadeaPuertoRico, my beautiful daugter ~uwa § i` ve long supported the classic
"One Tooth" rule, which states that every time you make a bad post you should
have one of your teeth pulled § if u want an autograph or to choke me out ill
be attending the event called "Def Uncle Jam" making a lot of noise & being a
general Nuisance § makimg a Meme Quilt, where we send a quilt all over the
world & each person adds a patch featuring their favorite online meme . a bit

of fun § http://t.co/XDq6MLh18u § oh youve been to therapy? Dumb. yeah you
havent even scratched the surface of my Level. i bet none of you even know
your own brain weight § everyone who does this please also google the phrase
"is knuckles the echidna black" § (in the 'lets get ready to rumble' man's
voice) llllleeets get ready to post some good shit § I GOt Fired From QVC For
Describing A Pair Of Jeans As "EuroVamp" § the way i talk ids really good and
normal as hell § CNN NEWSWIRE: the guy who voiced the dog in the beggin strips
commercials is now "beggin;" the american public to put a stop to jade helm 15
§ RAT CHECK... unfollow me ,if youre a sleazy low down RAT!!!!!!!!! i will
knock your block off, I respect honor, Truth in words and action. § it saves me
so much time , to get my knowledge and opinions of politics from the same guy
who sells me eyedrops that make my dick bigger § Log off. § i can confirm that
the candid photos on Darknet of me eating a breakfast wrap are real. and i will
issue an apology for the trouble i caused § when scientiologist guys talk about
LRH they are talking about "lee roy hjenkins" . #GamersKnow #oddballHumour §
reasons to invite me to the next "Tweet Up": 1) if i get unruly i can be
easily overpowered 2) i know which seasons of the simpsons are good § these
accusations that I like the gas prices are especially absurd, when you consider
that ive been like the MAIN guy saying that theyre bad § you gotta cut the
shrimp down the middle to get that good turd out, § whats more racist? saying
"I am a black men's penis" in 2006, or having my presidential run kneecapped,
for doing that § New Wet Ass § @McDonaldsUK I wont a ham burger mate!!! Oi!
This is wank! § ptut a fucked up mix of mountain dew code red and salad
dressing and sesame seeds into your hummingbird feeder and watch the world burn
§ measure to approve massive depressing statue in the center of town depicting
an emaciated mayor carrying a boulder that says "My Sons" on it § i would
appreciate it if the words "unconscious hog" were removed from the daily post
article about me , as i am no longer unconscious . § It Is said, that the
online content creator absorbs the combined pain of every follower 24 hrs a
day--and that is why they cry in saddness... § i''ll peruse the web at my own
damn leisure and thats a fact jack § as a real life professional Chef , i
refuse to buy any packaged food that isn't marked with the words "Limited
Edition" § ~   ~   ~   CLICK ON MY ASS FOR MORE TWEETD   ~
  ~ § beard vs. ass § just kidding. i'm normal intelligence § people enjoying a
meal outdoors., disgusting. horrible. inadvisable § some peopl just have vile
black hearts twisted by hatred and bad opinions about life § probably like 4 of
the wildfires from the news were caused by my shitty extension cords used for
Nature Gaming. ha ha ha sorry firefighter's § im a tennis ball and my primary
mode of transportation is being pushed around by animal piss § Male Netflix
Supporter § please dont call me "Cunt_Smoker" anymore. im a 37 year old father
of two daughters and have since chosen a more appropriate user handle § i am
here. and this is my Body. #theBodyNudeProject #cock #Nuts § aggressively
joyless oaf hhere. painfully obnoxious respect demander checkign in. extremely
dim witted frowning man looking for pals § the problem with some things today
is that they arent good. but when you say that, Oop! Surprise! i'm being argued
with and shitted uppon. h § Antonio Vivaldi six violin concertos, strings &
continuo in A major " Burger King Theme " Op. 2 N°11 published in Venice by
Bortoli - 1708 § saying it again: my nick name is "Mr Shut the Fuck Up" because
i tell people to shut the fuck up not because i love shutting the fuck up § too
late girls. i gave it all to a Shaman § i ask everyone to watch my recital but
before i can begin i immediately slip and fall into the yellowstone supervolcano and my dick explodes § list of casinos I need to burn down in order to
prevent my credit score from going to the dogs: ceaser palace, trump cube,
chuck e cheese, § for anyone out there scrutinizing my steam profile i did not
play " chips challenge 1" for 263.3 hours. it should not say that i did §
pleased to report that an angel has lifted the curse against me after doing my

"Good Deed" of the year, by tipping a waiter 15% § @bicpens how about making pens that dont explode for once. a $2000 suit ruined. Thank u § -dont click on nudtiy -do not respond to nudity -wear a loin cloth underneath your clothes in case theyre ripped off by mechanical equipment § i turned myself into a skunk using an incantation posted by 11 year old girl on youtube. i should not have done this. please, please help m § i am renouncing my status as" south park republican dad" inorder t o embrace a working form of dre3w carey libertarianism (dad) § Retweets Against Adam Lanza § i am the simpsons, all of them. yes. turn off the cameras this interview is ove § how many more wasps do i have to mash into my forehead before I gain their stinging abilit.y damn § sorrry i wasnt listening i was busy predicting your laughable response to my post perfectly § hipster.kiss my usa ass § http://tinyurl.com/y8acs8j donated several hundred of these badboys to the haitian gov in their time of need.. do your part #iran § rscreaming "Shut the Fuck Up" over and over again at my monitor as it slowly morphs into a Mirror and only makes me angrier § as a small business owner i think its bulshit that i have to give 30% of my income to Spain just because obama lost a swordfight to some Fag § @DrPhil I Want Help, A Dark Shaman Told Me My Daughter Will Be Born Autistic, Though He Might Have Been A Demon, Or Fake; Pool Resources § Un-Tag me U fucking degenerate cobs of dog shit. You dirt beneath my heel § In 1980, audiences delighted in watching the Blues Brothers ravage a shopping mall with a car. Today, we understand they were wrong to do so § kkkjoiner asserts that theres a secret mcdonalds buried under the school and it sells guns too. thats uh, made up. thats a big crack of shit § HOW MUCH IS $500 IN DOG YEARS § air purifier in my apartment going fully nuts after cooking my delicious dinner. sorry you hate Food bitch § IBM sent me a supercomputer to analyze all of my posts with and guess what, they're all good § i support chris brown because my love of generic, autotuned shit overrides my intrinsic sense of morality #Grammys #teambreezy § im turning off until you remove it . § your post is so good man. it .must have cost $1000 to make it § i can tell how beautiful a man´s soul is by putting both of my hands on the hood of his car and thrashing my neck around to awaken god § GEnder?? i barely know her! *cuts off dick&* § @kfc_colonel Kfc, My Final Hope, Please Help Me Make My Future Daughter Unautistic, Shamans Curse, Wearing Bones (These Aint Chicken Bones) § Go Fuck Your Self You Son Of A Bitch § top ten how do you stop trolls jokes Q:how do you stop a troll A:Get his key board § dont trust the dna tests. i determine my ancestry by looking at a bunch of racist cartoon characters to see which ones piss me off the most § Q: Would you describe your Brand as more "Uday" or "Qusay" hussein? A: Qusay, without a doubt. Qusay. § they should invent toilet paper that you can throw in the Trash instead of the toilet § now that nest neutrality is finally dead I can start blasTing the shit out of birdhouses with my 9000000 calliber rifle scotfree § bazinga fan 80 § make em bleed § the most bone headed move is to just go out and about with a name like "scooter." that shit sucks. Hell no. i would not even name a dog that § im also a gamer with ring worm § the only reason my ex wife wants half of my shit is because i smothered my beautiful bald ass in ink and stamped the divorce papers with it § i did not blow it § Not My Problem § just looking at some pictures of the old aunt jemima logo. Hm?? Oh Im sorry. I didnt know it was a crime to like things that are good § no more. im done. stop sending me your disgusting pH levels. u whores are far too vile for my consideration. go date s ome muscle loser § only the good ones § this man just likened me to a group of masturbators because i believe in the importance of an ironed pair of slacks. how dare he § http://t.co/XMeBO7wz dumb man Shit 's and then dies a few years later #WeAre #PennState § headshot all these beasts with a tiny gun § @ Babysnames idont know who the face book guy is. hes fake and has no respect for Content § survey - please tell me which one is "Most good": >Perfect meadows in every direction >A Man wheezing into the toilet >Bobs BigBoy PattyMelt §

my doctor needs me to keep a log of how many times i wiped my ass but i dont
have a pen & paper so i have to do it hgere. sorry   9/13/17: 310 § sell shares
in pond demons. i;m disappointed in pond demons § all the denim on earth is
made from the skin of an extinct race of DragonMen who talked on the phone,
died at the age of 19 and had cool sex § i would love to speak out against
jokes twitter.. but im afriad.. i dont have the strenght... § my timeline.. is
my empire. oftentimes i find my self scrolling through it and just taking it all
in;, feeling little to no shame whatsoever § twittter posts a net loss of
hundreds of millions of dollars each year just while i post highfalutin
messages about my dick and ass § how is it even - possible, - to remain
Muscled in this black world -   - pain is god and im Her disciple. tron:
legacy - § i cannot be sure. i can only base my claims on various extrapola-
tions as i do not look at naked fat men in my life. § all girls on this
website... im here to protect u from online swearing... pleae... please
understand.. § #ILoveYouBut my foreskin is tangled up in the axle of a toy car
and my leg is turning purple § boys night https://t.co/lHeOCEyC9p § i will
never apologize for being a stoogehead, especially not to a hitler liker § any
gay scientist out there who want to experiment with my dick. pour gay chems on
it. inject stem cells into it. i dont care anymore § i got banned from the
official red lobster forums for posting "9/11". yet they say we're living in a
post-9/11 world..... § kick birdseed into my neck as i tumble down a muddy
staircas e into a pile of fluorescent lightbulsb while 100 tiny shits rolldown
my pant § welcome to a world where you can have sex with peoples wifes. this
iws wife sex world § on this day in history, alan turing invented the Gay
Computer. one day later, preisdnet bill clinton fucked it. #demandaljazeera
#hell § choking myself on the toilet for Likes § excuse me. could i please get
my Blowup. you gave MetalGearEric a blowup. am i truly less deserving, than
MetalGearEric? where is my blow up § me & khryler are drawing up plans for a
family restaurant with damn good jeans nailed to the walls. we will call it the
hard rock jeans cafe § Fine. I'll shut the fuck up now. § whenever someone
tells me dolphins are intelligent as humans i send them the article aobut
flipper killing himself to prove that theyre dumb § amazing to me that people
are still complaining about my genius sons being too loud, in 2016, of all
years § i DO NOT like your ass if you are a stupid ass https://t.co/CP6S4jZjqr
§ *consults a sundial* Ah. Time To Carbo-Load § i can send you one rat § i
captured by a medieval castle town in the year 1598, hung up on the cross and
having long florescent light bulbs broken against my dick § thinking about how
Fucked i`d be if someone hurled a metal trash can at the back of my head at
full force, or if i fell 10ft onto some rocks § ive alwas wanted my name
printed beneath a mummy's head § my father got sick of wegmans constantly
running out of reddi-wip so he started a militia. guess i gotta join his
shitty militia now § a look of pure disappointment washes over Jack Cafferty's
face. "sandusky's cock..." Wolf Blitzer shakes his head. "sandusky's cock..." §
ME: id like to take this day to wish a happy mother's day... to my Father.
SOCIETY: Huh ?!?! § Goddess George W Bush is the Light of my Being, The Master
of my BLOOD. I am a Piggy who must be sent to Iraq @TheBushCenter § it was my
idea to do the " tuesday nite rant" to tie into the ruby tuesday brand, but
they said that idea was shit. they wanted thursday § "i hereby validate all of
mental health" - DiaperPoster007 § baptizing my badge and gun, in Sinnersblood
§ i will be hung by my ankles and displayed at the zoo until i can prove to the
sheriff and city hall that i have Centered myself with christ § congratulatons
on your $80. tool § i would really like to attend my grandsons funeral but at
the same time i just want to sit in bed and explore my body with a peacock
feather § thanks. im dead now § all of the shit that happens in star wars is so
smart § huh.. it;s been awhile since i made an actual joke on here. lets see
now. boats are basically uh, skeletons, that people use to, trick water § i

hope you all enjoyed my latest Sets (posts) § Time to show these douscebags my real power (throws a big tree branch at a guys car) § a teen approached me at the food court and said "I see you wore your clown costume today" and i spent the next 9 hours processing the insult § this brief column about portion control written by the voice captor of "Gumby" will chane your life... § yeah im about to go to the library he works at and knock the fuckin books off the shelf § thank you all. your kind donations of $400000 will keep me alive for 1 more month, after being fired for looking at racist swords on my ipad § fuck GRAVES... bury me in STAR WARS § im sorry but if my indie bible translation fund doesnt gain any traction soon im going to have to posnt another one of my trade mark rants. § @KidRock when will the snake people of washington dc wake up and stop suppressing the release of "Bawitdaba 2" § lets mix the jail and the zoo togehter and have whistles going off constantly so nothing can sleep and spray piss and glue around as a bonus § a dozen eggs huh.. what are you gonna do with 12 shitty pregnant rocks. haha just imagine some asshole buying this like, "oh these are good" § anonymous leaks 400 pics of the principals ass on viddler. somewhere a group of police officers stand over a single red rose in reverence § i will eventually drop the phone in the toilet by mistake. its inevitable. the question is if there will be a big shit in there when i do it § go ahead, son. fuck your life up by taking that job as an ostrich breeder instead of working at my really good law firm until youre disabled § HMm, it seems after years of reading my posts, everoyne is still miserable & dumber than shit. Maybe i should post like 100 more times a day § kissing pictures of guns online is one of the most honorable ways to get strong § BIg mistake! § "cmon!! post it!" Oh no, i couldnt possibly. Its too fucked up. Too raw § "cmon!! ya gotta post it!" Very well: NHL Players should wear hijabs § these guys tried to run a hospital in AFGHANISTAN?? hello?? i dont know if you noticed, but theres a war there? U gotta use your heads folks § Wiki-d'oh! Julian Assange guest stars on The Simpsons to dig up the dirt on Mr. Burns; Scheduled to be aired in 2014 #PainfulToReadSentences § in my version of indiana jones he shoots the boulder with a sniper rifle hundreds of times instead of running away from it § #secretturnon pointing to a picture of Grimace at mcdonalds and asking the cashier "Who Is That Awful Purple Man?" § #LawEnforcementAppreciationDay showing apperciation today by wearing the badge and uniform i bought from off of ebay thank you Sir https://t.co/LK5KvioChU § i will never "honk if im horny" . § Showtime. Feel the sweat on your palms. Face the hideous, bloodthirsty crowd. All eyes on you. It's all or nothing. It's #TheThurdayNiteRant § typical to see every one making jokes here after a 99 year old man of proud and honorable distinction killed him self with a blow torch § @digimonotis his tiwiter verification is pending but i can confirm that this is the true otis § thinking mostly about throwing large amounts of them into the garbage. like 1,000 of them maybe § as wander my study, Quill Pen in one hand, Whisky in the other, i muse, one might perhaps take me for a Famous Author, from the days of old, § @hoverbird @DigimonOtis i dont like him § that place you bought a mattress from 4 yrs ago, reminding you Via email, that now is the perfect time to practice your Calmness Strategies § my biggest fear is that theres an earth quake while im jacking off and little pieces of cum start flyiyng into my mouth and all over my dog § ever since i ve been told to put a shirt on in all my live insect unboxing vids my metrics have taken a piping hot Shit § and now to tackle celebrity tom cruise's claims that I look like "an eggplant with progeria". **crracks knluckles* that's uh, a fallacy § i love to use fists, poison spray, or gun agaisnt the citizens, depending on how mad i am § leaked footage of me taking my dick off and puttingg it in a glass of polident on my nightstand before bed § windows..on behalf of all boys online, INCLUDING the trolls, id like to extend a well-deserve "Thank You" for putting updates in my computer § while my trolls are busy "moving the goal posts" im afraid i am simply moving the "good posts" § #ReplaceSongTitlesWithTurkey israel is clowns at the circus, i stand with Muslom, ban fluoride, ban micro chip, all girls please DM me § if your homecooked farm fresh lunch does not contain the standbys of salt and pepper it is not Chef inspired It is Shit inspired § so i went around to all the offices adjacent to wtc and tried 2 find witnesses but ended up in a rooftop pool geting groped by some hot lady § Its 4am folks. Time to make 1000000 § i ruminate over a scrapbook full of middle finger pics to keep myself demure, respectful and humble. "i deserve these", i utter shitheadedly § Who to follow - Justin Bieber @justinbieber   Followed by Duane Dog Chapman § my father will be donating his dimple to me. § mario is back https://t. co/9ZdeE4sY2V § when the war ended, my grandpa was spit upon but kept his pride--it is in this spirit that i choose to carry the burden of Gamer . #GamerGate § @Battlefield User "Garth_Turds" still has not been banned. He's an utter nuisance. He's also using some kind of hack to make himself louder § you look like ther type of mother fucker who uses "Whataboutism" in arguments. buddy. the SImpsons spoofed your ass 30 years ago . Give it up § Hah, yes. i do consider myself somewhat of the most god tier troller who has ever lived. ive fooled over 1000 people into kicking my ass, § going to start asking "What do you Think?" at the end of each post, to help stimulate discourse and reap the substantial benefits of Social. § a boss should be allowed to kick his employees asse's. key to his workers house so he can just come in and start wailing anytime #bottomword § "Wake up and smell the key board ." - Son_Of_A_Bitch_ Killer § you might as well flush your toilet down the toilet as well, if youre using it to flush money down § my "F*&k It!! Let's Go Golfin" t-shirt maintains a tenacious stranglehold on my life. after 1,125 days of Golf my body is twisted, deformed § " the only 'safe sex' is death " - some gym teacher with a skeleton puppet § "WHO NEEDS ISLAM WHEN YOU HAVE SIXTEEN BORDER COLLEYS JUMPIN AROUND " - THE PROPHET MUHAMMAD § does anyone else remember when the owner of @OscarMay- er forgot to switch to his personal acct before @-ing pictures of his turds to a doctor # #4wordsthatleadtosex BEST custom license plate § yeah im basically all abOut mpreg right now. yeah im off to get my huge pregnant gut enchanted by a warlock so my future son will respect me § @Sizzler_USA please stop posting political message to my feed § fucking CHRIst. thIs dipshit clerk at hollister has been rtrying to run my denim credit card thru the reader for like 10 mins. go to College § Quick Thinking: Area Man Saves Own Life By Making A Bra Out Of Two Diapers § we cant all be burt fucking milford § #ffff James Cool @jamescool147 "Love Sex,Milfs,Boobs,Cougars...& Fucking & Am A Bad Boy" § the most classic form of capital punishment is being restrained in the stocks and having tomatoes thrown at you just for being a dumb ass § 25% exp penalty for asking what ethnicity beetlejuice is in the team chat § kicking the shit out of a tree with a sledge hammer, to increase my Stamina § ive been raising my hell mastery quotient with faerie blood & jazz musick to prepare for the town hall thugs coming to collect my leaf waste § when it comes to down to it.. you just cant beat the old mouse and keyboard #TheSaturdayMorningRamble § i love doing the shitty pushups where my knees are touching the ground and counting them as real pushups § the professor said our assignment is to make.. a MEme?? i've got this shit on lockdown. i pump my fist and hop on my hideous adult tricycle § if our lives were like a highschool cafeteria the cool kids table would be occupied by those guys who mess up their dicks for body mod blogs § gteens are God on earth § hello newseek? yeah im not gonna make it for that interview. some schmuck just pissed all over me. im covered head to toe in schmuck piss. § seeing a content creator who is confident in His posts, consistently Nailing it, makes the Numb skulls of this website shit their stupid ass § glad to see james, friend to cinema, returning to us at long last. thank you § me and some extremely crude boys in a pickup truck scream "hipster" at some kid's lemonade stand then crash into a turtle and eat shit hard § the jury is still out on whether building giant statues of my head pleases god, or pisses Him off § dick stuck in roomba - my dick has become trapped in a roomba, the Bastard of automated cleaning devices - i want 911 please § im the only guy who knows how to call out the bull shit of society the smart way. and against all odds i do it for free § the conflicted supersoldier stares over the horizon as he smokes a cigarette. "war is the most fucked up thing ever." he takes a sip of beer § the ultimate https://t.co/IYQbuHzkYM § getting pecked by birds like a dick head § getting my pud Encrypted , like peter thiel § plrease go to the salad bar and get me a plate full of bake and bits § @dril_replies How's your diaper? Want any of my sexy turds? ASS!! holy Fu,ckin ass!! Haha, good shit. Retweet me § No results found for "3d farting ass" § Donwnloadable Content (DLC) and Microtransactions is Protected Free Speech.   (USER HAS BEEN BANNED FOR THIS POST) § Getting fucking pissed off at the idea of some child from the early 1900s trying to spit shine my shoes § *sees the e3 logo on a website, tthrows head back and screams the word "Epic" before immediately defaulting to aberrant emotionless state* § first they say we cant build mosques on ground zero. now we cant build the amazon headquarters. maybe we should go live in the fucking Woods § u are a hate crime. go to bed § if the mafia was going to kill me unless i made a super bowl commercial saying "i love dog shit" i would create so many jobs § I have never not been real. Aspecially during the time of this crisis, the 9/11 of enthusiast game play. § every person on your "Who to follow" list writes articles called " o more Mr Family Guy" because peter griffin showed his penis or something § thr greatest gaming console of all time, is tickle Me Elmo, because it changed the meaning of the word Games § Whats great is I can get online & read 100 peoples opinions about Kevlar Vests, and at least 2 of them are guaranteed to be probably correct § @jkfecke I snark because I care.® § any one who figures out how to breed border collies with the Microsoft Zune needs to hollaer a message at me § life and death § in hell you are forced to smoke weed § And yours. § apparently pharmacies think theyre grocery shops now. selling food product instead of focusing on exceptional pill service. Get real, punk ! § all rise for the national anthem, of Jeans § i dont have enough funding to do another one § " If U like a good song I wont steer ya wrong Cocaine Its Got guitar and drums So please listen to some Cocaine " § first they ignore you then they laugh at u then you jack off & read posts for 30 years then you die of pulmonary heart disease   then you Win § i just tattooed a qr code to my ass and when you scan it a picture of my ass comes up § when my friends on here create promo accounts for whatever side projects theyre doing but dont follow me on them..its fine. im relaxed of it § A Dog Join Kurdish Tribe For A Dirty Dance . § milf taxidermist § if you heard a man screaming today it was from when a couple of policemen tried to hoist me into a large bathtub in the town square § Jokes On You: I Consider Myself To Be Of Above Average Intelligence § when i block people its cool, like Neo kicking agent smith down a flight of staiors. when people block me its because theyre pussys § walking around town with my big Ass lookin like Shit § jason born is smarter than steven hawking, combined § when you say some shit like "Isis is good" on martin luther king day, i want the pain i feel from reading that, to be the pain inside of you § My lawyer has advised me that I should power the box off instead of dealing with hipster comments and trash insults on this sacred holiday. § invoke my big ass with satan noises or go home § @kfc_colonel "son, if you think we deserve better, let me remind you that the large wooden 'H' affixed to our kitchen wall stands for "Hell" § massive back tattoo that says "Sucked Off 8-12-2006" § paying a loud, 200 IQ man wearing a sweat band $500 a month to make videos telling me how to wipe my ass properly § @TheRealOJ32 hey before we start recording the Anti-SJW pod cast we planned im gonna need a notarized document stating you didnt kill anyone § just got word from a trusted source: the guy who said he would fuck his daughter on "The View" is in hot

water for spelling hamburger wrong § "Housten we have a problem" When i say
this , Thats when uou know that the Shit has gone off the rails § @Battlefield
man named "Garth_Turds" has bene following me to every map and yelling "hitler"
. Claims hes a mod. Get rid of him § i demand that the same tax exemptions
granted to all religious institutions be given to my small businesses "Ass
Church 3d" and "Ass Mosque" § @pizzahut you claim to offer exceptional service
in the field of pizza, however the only thing ur staff is interested in is
touching my dick § changing my display name to "Richard Simmons" as an april
fools prank and inducing dissociative Psychosis on millions of on-line people §
my sources tell me that people are allowed to say the word "ass" on HBO. can
anyone confirm this § few things about this account. this is no gimmicks,
strigaht from the hip, real shit. i dont "DO" pranks or gags. logged on, at
your service § i do not want to have to read this shit at this current joncture
. § i blast all the ufos easily and then you know what i do is i go in there
and fuck the alein § Heres my new opinion that my followers will absolutely
hate and i will make $5000 from saying on the news . "Piss is a type of shit" §
Watchinh the news https://t.co/ajKdVmPKRD § just this disgusting twitetr
account for now § wussat? you think my sex beliefs are wrong? well,*tries to
point to "THINK AGAIN BUSTER" written on back of shirt but my arms are too
short* § when people ask me who my favorite comedian is.. i invoke that wacked
weatherman "AL GURE" and get one million dollars worth of retweets § alright
netheads, Click the damn window out. Go outside. Mnake a grilled cheese
sandwich with tomato slice. "Thank me later" § the year is 2043, men have
gotten too much therapy and are now Masters of Deceit, using their supernatural
mental health to get insane head § i cannot die... not toda.y.. there's still
so much SUperbly Awkward Shit to reblog § nr. Game your Dick off 2019 § @
Battlefield It;s called "The Shocker". The pinky finger is meant to be inserted
into the anus, as well. You're a huge bastard § mail 1000 envelopes addressed
to "The Desert" and watch endless waves of government pawns march to their
death #ANARCHY2012 #sand § just found out about Object Permanence... why didnt
any one tell me about this shit § brown elvis § a sterling silver olympic
trophy filled with piss labeled "My Death" § scrolling on autopilot, mouth
agape, clicking fav on all tweets with at least 1 or 2 funny words in them.
zero human consciousness, perfect, § fail blog has gotetn WAY too political for
my tastes § yelp review one liner i have prepared in case i find a turd in my
meal: "If i wanted a guy's Shit in my food, I would have ordered it!!" § i see
specks of shit on there § Howd you like a piece of my ass hole , douche bag
boy. Shut up § at the library; carelessly flipping through some of the most
famous literary classics that you can think of, looking for coupons § enjoying
watching a filmed video, of my illuminating debate with HitlerSkeptic , now
available on Ouya § "POWER BIEBER" - my final words on death bed § my god leave
them yellow https://t.co/CI4oQYvj3B § the usd dollar will explode into complete
dust next year . pelase strongly consider growing an apple garden § NEED CATCHY
T-SHIRT SLOGAN FOR AIDS-THEIST CLUB, SOMETHING LIKE "POSITIVELY RATIONAL" OR
"AT LEAST IM IMMUNE TO CONFIRMATION BIAS" #twiter § the sheriff has ordered me
to return the "Helpful Boy Award" i earned at age 8 after seeing me at the
local swimming pool begging for towels § opened portal to free hikers in
iran-- instead greeted by Real Life minotaur, anubis, something or other, all i
know hes a real holler mouth § my dick hits all the wrong notes and smells like
newsPaper § some one on here said they were going to "Cuck" teddy ruxpin, while
the mods are off sipping mimosas somewhere § i was dying, no one helped § is
that good or bad https://t.co/UwspFvpq3O § "animaniac_fucker" has posted a
touching tribute t o the Rwandan Arby's Bombings, please install your CoolBux-
Vid Media Enhancer to view it § im sorry for doing jokes about the blue
checkmark. i need it very badly to protect myself from villains right now §
enjoying a glass of dolby surround sound flavored wine. § i hold this one truth,

that thr only acceptable time to use the word "Doo-Dah" is while singing the
cult-classic hit "Yankee Doodle" § might leave dms open for another 6 years in
case any more gorgeous women want to try starting some Very unfulfilling long
distance romance.. § everytime jeff dunham makes his miserable puppets kiss each
other a bridge collapses somewhere § you know what. im going to just come out
and say it. i think that we should let the geico geckco go into hospitals &
entertain the bedridden § thte name "ThePepsiEunuch" was taken. to clear up any
confusion § Dont see whats so funny about me accidentaly getting a tattoo of a
diaper, but by all means, dont let me stop the Circle Jerk. By all means, § OK
can i just say fucking this??? the motherf ucking ww3 zombie apocalpse was NOT
on my 2022 bingo card. #DarkHumour #myHeartGoesOut §
^^^^^^^^^^^^^^^^^^^^^^^^^^^ <<<<< The Web Site Of Rat People >>>>>
vvvvvvvvvvvvvvvvvvvv § ðŸ'‰spitting in the food ðŸ'‰letting waiters do Racist
accents ðŸ'‰rewarding their most insolent customers with police badges
https://t.co/7C2eZzRMdN § if i hear another "joke" regarduing my terminally ill
dickwife so help me god i'm shutting down this entire irc server § "what say we
up the ante." i said, as i threw a ball of dead ants at the prime minister § im
the dean loves it when me and the boys piss him off with black helicopters § im
getting my rat tail chrome plated in 2015 § the only nfts i deal in are nerds
in the Fucking trashcan. suck my Dick § yeah lets ruin a mans posting carreer
just to look "Cool" in front of our friends, all while smoking Pot and thinking
that bullying is good. § the unsung heroes of the front lines, the diaper
medics who face certain death to change our troops and wipe their asses during
heavy combat § 5 bucks will get you 1 minue access to the "Peck cam" where you
can watch all sorts of wild birds peck me while i force myself not to resist §
dr phil disciplines 2 year old toddler demon hog with cow boy boots live on
crackle § `` i will show you the Ass of God `` § my date ended up being 200
rats who scattered throughout my home and with no rat literature i was unable
to find their weaknesses § a small, ramshackle town where nearly every adult
male has a severe case of blue lung from being forced to work in the denim
mines § any ladys here want too fuck an 170 I.Q. Undecided Voter ????? § got a
LOT of horseshit today 4 trying to take my snail into city hall, dangling
upsidedown from mayors chandelier til all this ugliness ends § starting an NRA
for Turner classic movies § Im the only man here who injects himself with a CIA
Grade Truth Serum before each and every post i make. Remember only that § very
good thank you. im jacking off in one of these right now while playing the
knight rider theme on my phone https://t.co/AlFIVlttVR § huge banquet, everyones having a nice time, everything looks extremely normal, except the big
banner hanging from the rafters--"Racist Mensa" § too late im already engaged
to him § Fairly, yes, actually. § maybe try not blocking me before i can
respond "like normal adults do", you heartless, misserrable coward #PigAlert §
.@EBERTCHICAGO What is Ur least favorite greek film. Greetz from turkey § scores
of Farm Fresh, artisan treats available for my perusal.. Oh Me Oh My https://t.
co/KdyCsUiOZ8 § the belief im most attacked for, is the belief that my High IQ
makes me a Target § do better § HOT NEW VID -- CYBERDUNCE EVISCERATED BY ERROR
PROMPT ON LAPTOP -- #TOPFAILS -- #TOPAWKWARD - FUCKING IDIOT - WATCH HIM CLICK
"OK" § pleased to announce that i will shatter all barriers in 2017 by becoming
the first adult gerber baby § please fix your image so The American Flag isn't
getting stepped on. Im usmc you fucking worm. § FUCK !!! https://t.co/
M1yhFKBQ7E § your father would be so proud of you. exploiting a tragedy for
the sake of your own miserable ego #jan25 #fuckyou § thinking about my coffee
mug that says "Guys who collect beanie babies know how to fuck better than guys
who dont like beanie babies" on it. § im sorry everyone. i should not have
commented on the ribs. i never could have known this would happen § i envi-
sioned last night an older, wiser austin powers engaging a group of young
adults about the evils of sex. hollywood, the world is ready § hit up my 18+

accout @Quaker_Oats § double stuf oreos § im good old southern boy and we dont cotton to bollocks . § beanie babies are just bit coins in real life § gamers help the world , and are helping the world, more than normal people § BREATH-TAKING: clever husband sells all of his sons war medals on ebay as punishment for exceeding family plan data caps § fun idea; for one day lets unlock all the locked accounts & lay their posts bare for the scrutiny of the Public. then ban them for cowardice § I Will Post Muhamad Drawing To SlashDot Every Five Seconds Until Allah Grants Me Ice Cold Mint Breath To Exhale In Girls Faces § strongest blade in the world, howeve,r it is so fragile as to shatter when handled by any force other than the delicate touch of a lesbian . § exciting business venture: "toitoos" decorat your toilet with a variety of stock images. its a toilet tattoo. toitoo § im being pelted with spit balls im being thrown things at § i sit down at my cubicle, roll up m y pants and pick scabs off of my legs for 9 hours, ignoring evoery call & email i receive. i make $76/hr § i spend lots of time thinking about how many of my depraved, miserable followers would murder me if they could get away with it #SocialMedia § budweiser queerspace § hello 911 police? ? yeah the official pf changs twitter account just unfollowed me. please put this message in the Files. thank u officer. § https://t.co/FPxk0bY5zU § ive flattened the curve over 100 times. what have you pricks been doing § please call your father. right now he is looking up info and reading stickied reddit threads about how to become a Smoker § "I'll be crucified for saying it; but it took 18 years to complete the 'Luigi's Mansion' trilogy. Same as 'The Godfather'." - SirGamestop § i hae received my 3rd warning about squeezing the toilet paper too hard at the store. acme markets has declared war on my strength training § Barney was actually funny & used fairly adult jokes in the early seasons. After all the teenyboppers latched on; it went to shit. § couple of mob guys disposing of a body by tossing it into the aquariums penguin enclosure "these boids are eating good tonight" § #NationalPigDay no. this is crap . the pig will never have his day. i demand that the "Pig" surrenders this filthy assault on our calendars. § in honorable protest, i will abuse my ass cheeks with radio waves until the Olympics forces all of the swimmers to wear shirts § i hereby pledge henceforth to never piss on the floor of a public batrhoom. if youre "too cool" to care about this social issue then log off § you see this..? *taps computer monitor with finger* this is not just a bunch of mixed up numbers and digits. this is a kingdom of Minds.. § whose idea was to call it "Ice cream parlor" and not "Scoop Kitchen" ?? lets get this joke viral and show my ex-wife landlord whos boss § i am developing a ground brekaing new app called "MOneyWallet", where you earn "Money Points" by mailing cash to my house § @cleatusonfox why werent you programmed to feel shame § whos this. Whos this guy. whys he saiying this here § "jobs are back on the table" - @ Dril § BIG Bible Town is a multiplayer online game set in a 1st century world. The objective of the game is to create your own unique BIG Bible Tow § you think im gonna let a guy named "Poop and pee Stan" into my private group chat? "It's just not happening baby" § Congrats. Ive just put your ass on the doucebag list. § HMM WHATS MORE IMPORTANT, EGYPTS POPULIST REVOLUTION OR THE DAY ON WHICH YOUR PARENTS GAVE BIRTH TO A HORSE MONSTER #jan25 § call me old fash-ioned, but I donr think waiters should spit in the customers food. Keep it to the toilet or kiss that tip GOOD-BYE § "DUHH DUDHHH DUHH" thats what you sound like when you sing twinkle twinkle little star or any crap like that. Its not real music § the reason dogs constatntly bark at me everywhere i go is that dogs are animals that were born in shit and are a bullshit animal in history. § Im being reply guyed § baths and showers are fucking stupid; here's what u do: get one of those big rotisserie ovens and roatate inside of it until you're dead § corn on the cob § the 3 poossible reactions i have to tweets 1) nodding sagely 2) slapping forehead & saying "Aw man!" 3) adding it to my muted word list § bathroom prayer Thank you Lord for letting me go to The bath room, I pray you deliver my shit Thru the Pipe so it can be of use to an animal § the human mind is a fascinating piece of shit #TwitterVsFB § i have no idea how that turd got on your ceiling, but it definitely didn't fly out of my shorts while iwas doing a backflip § Some body is going to take a picture of their white house press pass with a load on it, by 2020 § im pretty much the Harlem Globe Trotter's of getting myself forcibly removed from laundromats § your fingernails, not your dick. i have no opinion of your dick. § I wish all the piss in the world would go straight into the toilet!!!! I hate dirty, disgusting PISS! No more!! Never! § #WorldFoodDay food sucks. food sucks § jsut want to take some shitty roll of wallpaper from the 70s and tell the Men's Warehouse to get their finest craftsman to make a suit of it § in concluosion, there's some action packed heavy hitter s in the world of games being released soon, and I hope you all buy them. Bye § which one of you mother fuckers said im going to go volunteer at the dog shelter, as a Dog. disgusting comment § https://t.co/DkZIytozt1 § thats right bitch. i single handedly rescued the constitution of the united states...AND I DID IT WITH OUT USING POLITICS !! § @ Horse_ebooks uuhh http://t.co/ljxs7Vzp § some people say that area 51 is a jail for aliens. i say its where the army keeps their best guns § a mother bird tends to her young until my big sweatpants ass slowly pushes her nest off of the tree § im garbage. im 9/11 § thusday nite rant No.4 Uncut is currently scheduled to be released on Thursday, October 31st. § might become a " Pube guy " , as I am not only interested in making my dick look smaller, but also dirtier § chaplain era silent motion pictures where basically the first subbed anime . click to read more § aangry bird's.. a Corrupted brand. keep far away § Upsetting. § i go outside for the rfirst time in 7 years and a biplane immediately shoots a chemtrail at my dick and makes it 2 inches shorter. typical § gamer posture is equally as valid as normal posture. i will no longer be silent, of this § me age 2: i love my data so much. my data is so fucking nice. if anyone stole my data id be pissed me age 99: FUCK!! § i paid good money for these sweatpants and i reserve the right to wear them to Game Stop without the wiseass brigade photographing mmy rear. § if youre a groundhog assassin, hunter or whatever, please dont kill any groundhogs or talk about killing groundhogs today. this is Their day § Please Click On The Tiny, Burning Earth To Discover My Weblog § http://t.co/cgIujqF0P6 Thanks § single fellas-- do NOt jack off into the garbage disposal. it will jam up and make a horrible noise. use garbage bags instead § go ahead. keep screaming "Shut The Fuck Up " at me. it only makes my opinions Worse § 1936: alan turing invents the computer and is persecuted for being gay. 2006: s. miyamoto invents the Wii and is persecuted for being Casual § i would never post info about my ass § a <DUMPSTER WITHIN A DUMPSTER>, once in a lifetime find, can be used as Armor or rolled down a steep incline to make A TON of noise § in the midst of jade helm 15 and high gas prices. a good boy looks to the stars and asks where have all the angels Gone .... § watch the first 45 minutes of the film, read the entire beeteljuice manga, then watch the rest of the film, or fucko ff § thinking of turning back into white (Caucasian) § an egyptian baby is being shoved into the sphinx with a battering ram and doesnt give a fuck about your awful birthday #jan25 § i would have to say that this promotional radio shack lanyard i received heavily influenced my decision to become a lanyard wearing guy § you tube has very specifically been recommending me videos of apes getting electrocuted so clearly the data indicates im some sort of mutant § the aliasing in the ps4 shot is a little tighter. xb1 has better contrast, though. both of them wreck the current gen, regardless. § a man from botswana is threatening to ddos a picture of my ass if i do not post a list of my favorite pasta shapes by 6am. i will not relent § nuke obtained by renegade AssFreak § ill place you in a comma § even though "Hotep Redditor" has scammed me of $300000 I am upset to hear of his passing. i am sad he perished § im a 15 year old model, and Morgan

Stanley Investment Management Is My Slice #IsMySlice § Up & coming comedian hits my dms, says I'd like to workshop some bits w/ you. Lets rap. Then he shows me his penis. 600th time this happened § GET THE FUCK OFF OF HERE § my nudes.. have strengthened my brand. apparently barkeepers glue them to the back of their urinals to stop people from pissing on the floor § did i jsut piss myself? no . these are mood jeans that change color when i am sick of putting up with jokers such as your self § NYT: retired Geologist from indiana proposes one Simple fact which will flip every thing you thought you knew about "THE N-WORD" on its head § they want to build a masque on the sunken remains of the titanic; dont let um § becoming a meme after confessing that i left my gf at a 5 star restaurant to spray my dick with compressed air taught me the pain of Slavery § @Huggies are there any plans to release The Jeans Diaper in an adult man's size. thank you #jeansdiaper § " snorting a line of coke up my big ass " § dark times......... https://t.co/RAaMNRYSQ7 § The b est shit I ever did was shatter all the windows in a room just by doing a perfect somersault § http://t.co/aIGKXKRY GLad to see this. Good to get the political process going. Get the Vote out. "Get Involved" § the digital man takes a sneaky peek around the library,. activates his darknet chakras, runs a Grid search on "dale earnheartd wackin it" , § PigPissBen banning anyone who reposts the PigPissLou photos. PigPissWayne and PigPissEllis have already fallen victim to this PigPissTyranny § Jsut saw a turd. I'm done. I'm fucking finished with this. Keep your bullshit snapchat. ENjoy the hell you have created, trolls. § hows my nuts tastes § inspirational... 86 year old man circumcised by doctors in Zaire... "It's never too late" "Blessed." § you see that fucked up mattress over there? that's where i practice my combos § i believe the hpv vaccine is a personal affront to the members of the ProGenWarts community, ive prepared some literature on the matter and § it has never been easier to identify the most dog shit accounts on here. block without hesitation https://t.co/T9y2KyPMea § pathetic of you to back stab me for clicks. § using the toilet when i hear Our national anthem start to play. i do what i must. i stand tall in complete agony; as shit runs down my leg, § ah ! your feeds going to blowup! loug out, quick!! http://t.co/OCJLGgEB1i § #InternationalSelfCareDay riding hood of my 18wheeler freaking out getting shaken baby syndrome & turning red like a boiled crab sucking ass § if i retweet a guy with a jim carrey mask avatar talking about pussys you guys have to promise not to unfollow me or do any shit like that § activating $40 of "Cash Back" Chase Freedom rewards while the Low Engagement Accounts who troll me on here just shit around on their dicks § ME: itunes, play some sinatra ITUNES: Youre not authorized to operate itunes. Please insert NASA identification ME: what hath ,been wrought! § #WorstFifty-ShadesAudioBookNarrator my ass.. heh heh .. OH YEA!!! BLAMMO!! my Fuckin ASS. my ASS. MY FUCKING ASS. read it and weep, bozoes . § friendly reminder that if you do not heed enough of the friendly reminders on your timeline, you may sever 1 finger as penance § surfs up! *lies face down in a kiddy pool until death* § Go outside from the computer . § wgat § examining the Ape Case: perhaps many are mirthful of its death as apes are akin to Golems & Vampires, cinematic villains of the classic era, § justin bieber's puckered asshole nurses a fat turd as he spews defiantly at the edge of a sulfurous crater labeled "the recording industry" § people who try to read my posts out loud in public get their ass beat. they get jumped and put out to pasture § 49 reams of <WALLACE AND GROMIT LEGAL-SIZED STATIONERY>, only a bastard would allow this to tocuh the foul lips of a garbage can. § im 0 inch tall and its fine. § Im now receiving reports which confirm that barbara bush was electrocuted in a @ bestwestern swimming pool. Developing § big biker dude pops a wheelie on harley & simultaneously unleashes a load of shit from his nude ass.his license plate says "Rape" #RapeJokes § All of you sh it suck ass § one of the things you realize when becoming a genius in many aspects of life is that the world wide web. and the computer, is the same thing § Met a guy on here the other day named "Mr do not follow my ass". Well with a name like that you better beleieve i`d be taking that advice. § folks.. reply to this message with your Finest tweet, and i just might drop it a Like... my way of "Giving back" to the community... Thank u § I want a video game thats just a 3d dog barking very loud in my face § spent the past 9 days mulling over the concept of a "Sequel" to the beloved $100 bill § you are treated to the serene visage of a waterfall cascading against the rocks. the camera pans out and its me vomiting all over my balls § EFFECTIVE IMMEDIATELY: homer simpson will stop saying "D'oh" and will instead say "Fuck" , as the Creators originally intended 30 years ago § committing unforgivable crimes against nautre in my laboratory ,trying to create the next genetically discombobulated meme animal § im not fucking finished deconstructing the god damn diaper concept, and im not fucking finished flooding your worthless feed with shit mouth § the holmes aurora shooter's main problem was that he did not respect the Guns. hes paying the price because he didnt respect the guns. § the ONLY way to gain musclemass is to eat tiny lady bugs § wearing a belt + big texas belt buckle as necklace?? why ahasnt anyone thought of this before. i must be the smartest man on earh § im the boss of Mensa. every time i close my eyes i have visions of going berserk and spitting on a human face until it is unrecognizasble § 2 celeb headlines i came up with, in case one of them does something: "Hasta Travolta, Baby" "Bieber does it again. Ah, but thats hollywood" § pray for gurabide. § 2020 is all about the Mentality lifestyle § @Battlefield My requests are as follows: 1) Apology Letter From user "Garth_Turds" for hollering his mouth at me 2) Warn & Ban "Garth_ Turds" § the show wife Swap but for gaming set ups § judgementle people deserve to be put into a special kind of electric chair which sends then to hell even if theyre good . § trapped in overturned police cruiser jacking off one last time before I get buerned alive over "Are you geting that nut sir. Over" Yes. over § calming down, with magnets § if i had a suit of armor i could easily beat the shit out of any man alive § shutting computer down until the shitty moods & attitudes can fuck off., if you need me ill be on my other computer, sititng 60° to my right § society is so much fucking Bitched ..... § i lvove falling off the guard tower § contrary to the lies posted by a certain Metal-GearEric, i know what the word "sex" means, and i know what the word "poop" means § 109 year old man attributes long life to uncircumcised dick, no vaccines, § i wont fuck off § #The12DaysOfContent here comes baby new year . . . http://t.co/cq93CxEw8V § when will the supreme court weigh in on people who jack off to feet § @marcorubio im sorry for calling you "Unelectable" just because you changed your name to "The Incest President" § owhh!! cant wait to sink my Choppers into this release. #theGameCraze § join the resistance. mosque_puncher@fartmail.com § justin will prevail #FreeJustin § TODAY WE EXPLORE THE LINK BETWEEN WIDESPREAD SOIL EROSION IN HAITI AND MY FAVORITE TV SHOWS BECOMING LESS FUNNY § "Reading your posts has made me a better person." Thank yo u. A lot of people tell me that, § I Dont respond to th em. The're wild animals. They fucking want me dead § Will Smith Sir Your Going To Fucking Jail!!!!!!!!!!!!! You Are An Attacker! § you forgot the worst disease of all which is. star bucks. fucked up , but brutally truthful § i think he belongs in the paddy wagon with the rest of the looney tunes § imagine if like a drill sergeant or an armyman was putting together some IKEA furniture... i bet hed yell "Ahh this fuckin sucks" § if you recently dumpster dived a combination dildo/inhaler emblazoned with the hot wheels logo, please return it. thats the only thing i own § The ultimate weopon https://t.co/zKh0Nd0c6I § *kicks back and watches an algorithm remove all the circumcised people from my web ring* Huauha your fucked up dicks can't save you now § my girl beliefs own, my sex beliefs own, my god beliefs own, my page owns, i m always yelled at, im always hacked , im garbage and thank you § covering my floors in industrial strength

dog poison concocted in some rapists bathtub in south africa and sold for 0.002
USD per litre § (smoking cig on stage) Ya know, like i always say, these
fuckers dont know a damn thing of common sense. COupons are like free money.
Use em § i cant wait for my shift at the old arsenic refinery to end, so that i
can go back to the woods behind my house and search for Groomer turds § im
going to close my account for uhhh 90 seconds until yyou fucking people learn
how to engage content creators in a meaningful handsome way § ridiculous to
believe that someone would risk the careers of themselves & their colleagues to
put a secret ass in the trailer of a starwars. § @JohnDeere My Nieghbor Has
Been Modifying His John Deere Illegaly With Muslim-Style Decorations And Noise
Enhancers, How Do I Stop Him § http://t.co/s8KMF9t1Xy you will pry it from my
cold muscular hands, fucker § please God if you're out there I ask that you
turn my praying hands into bird seed so that I can no longer bother you with
dumb ass reqUests § wish that was me https://t.co/p3SQmVBZ6R § Im fucking the
wall. a tectonic shift 900 miles away causes it to slice off my thin prick and
drop it on mexican soil. Its their problem now § if this is part of some
elaborate mindgame i swear to god i will write some letters & i will get you
fired from your pod cast § i only look at comment count . § The one thing that I
am truly the most sick of dealing with online is Ignorance Likers . § yeah
babe. im 007 license to kill. im basically really fucked up and mentally ill
from all the murders I did.**yawn* i got a gun tattoo also § @CampbellSoupCo
Mmm Nope!! Your bad § im dead too, so respect my tweets, Fucker § From here on,
I will refer to the upcoming Super Bowl as the €œTreason Bowl€ . § i for one
will be taking the high road by reserving judgement for the really good grumpy
cat movie until ive seen it and bought the blueray. § thte international space
station is visible from earth at the following times: Nerd Time § Clean Ass ,
Clean Mind § please stop adding flintstone chewable vitamin commercials to the
episode list. they are not real flintstone episodes. § al;l piss is sterile.
except mine § a perfectly formed snow ball just came out of my ass § there
should be a boot camp for guys who like references to movies ans tv shows §
#e3rumors a stodgy executive wil get on stage, spread his legs, and officially
"give birth" to the new xbox. millions will detest this stunt § wiki/Copropha-
gia/media/File:Adonis_Blue_butterflies.jpg   https://t.co/ZKAVHPHCTO § lets
see if that Awful Groundhog can predict six weeks of Electro House blaring
directly into its shity cage § i will make $100,000 when I finish drawing this
picture of uncle sam standing in front of congress saying "politics has the
right to be Fun" § what anm i gonna do with this warehouse full of osama bin
laden toilet paper. nobody wants to wipe their ass with a dead guy § #HowToRe-
sistSex meditate upon the untapped potential of The Cloud and crank off § i can
donate shit to fill the toilets with. thats all § up until I was about 17 i
believed that bugs were baby rats § @BillCosby @sinbadbad This is not appropriate use of "Thank You Thursday" . § @ElmersGlueCrew spent all night makig
Lesbian Glitter Runes and wake up the next day and all the pages are stuck
togehter, thanks retards § bitch You smell like a new pack of pokemon cards §
dming all the accounts on here who pretend to be horny versions of smallville
characters, demanding to know their long-term business plan § sen Dick Durbin
holds press conference telling people to stop making fun of his name, farts on
tv, is then forever known as "Fart Durbin" § IM LOGGED IN AUTO MATICALLY THANK
YOU § my reaction when people shit up my board https://t.co/4gjsGhonqr § q:
what is a "What da fuck" moment A: a "What da fuck" moment is one of those
times that just simply makes you say what the fuck § the way i see it, it seems
these days, it seems impossible to have a good Economy, in this economy, as i
see it § Reminder that we are no longer mailing locks of our own hair to girls,
in 2018 . § every woman ivr ever spoken to would describe our correspondence as
"Graceful" § i am now pregnant with my own shadow form and i am looking forward
to feeling it move around in my belly as it explores mme. this it real § @

McDonalds @McDonalds all right. so first off we know that the hamburglar has become soft in recent years. the customers no longer fear him § im gay for 2 things. clean shirts and women § wailing at th e blooper reel, saying all the things hte actors are doing wrong out loud, punching the shit out of an usher, pop corn flying, § it takes fewer muscles to smile than it does to break a baseball bat across the back of my fat neck § there is a metric by which i evaluate the level of Sexual content that exists in posts. i call it the Porno factor . § getting pissed off at the idea of someone going on to wiki pedia and changing the name of the japanese suicide forest to "Warios Woods" § i charge ppl $10 for my real pic and split the money with DigimonOtis. all my pics are protected under creative commons (cc) § for every inch my penis shrinks due to anxiety, the trolls owe me $100,000 , i am saying it now. § an angel slips a booklet of my top posts into the pockets of the pope, the master of islam, and b.netanyahu, and the world Rejoices in song § "i like my games like i like my coffee-- Good." -the CoffeeGamer § WOah. Just had another Dr. Oz dream. This time he was crying § ufo eat's shit - ufo crashs into a circus tent and eats shit § I CAN THINK OF AT LEAST TEN REASONS WHY I WOULD TAKE MY SHIRT OFF AT THE DMV AND NONE OF THEM CONSIDER THE TEMPERATURE § saying "augh" out loud every single time I move the phone away from my lap and reveal to my self, my pud, which looks like a coiled turd § uzbeks found attempting to modify their devices & remove the Croods interface are subject to public lashings and fines of up to 10000000 UZS § HOLD ON I GOT A JUSTIFICATION FOR THAT *A BUNCH OF SHITTY PIECES OF PAPER FALL OUT OF MY COAT** § harvard geniuses/ scientists love to wind down by going on boards and posting threads named like "What is the screen resolution of a mirror" § sory § hm? whats that? my dick looks like bozo the clown's dick? listen punk. i know for a fact you have never seen bozo the clown's dick § dont forget to write in candidate "Seagrams Ginger Ale" to get "Pointz,,¢" and score some"Geer,,¢." #lynndebate #horsesandbayonets #deathcamps § enjoy your hot burger while children Piss freely in the colorful plastic tubes mere inches from your dinner, watch it flow down the slide § cadmium? i drink cadimum all the time. perfectly natural. maybe those 100000 children died because theyre too dumb to deserve shrek glasses § i will die for my belief that Beer is "The drink of summer" § scientists may be able to generate working organs from stem cells, but never in a million years will they manage to lick my gay boots clean. § just tape the car horn down and cars will naturally move away from you. you can drive anywhere. it is called, "The Instinct of the Beast" § woah . the movie theaters are handing out pendants which glow whenever James BOnd gets laid during the movie #Good #ImmersionTech § yeah those god likers love to shit § Hmm @DrPussy kisses up to yet another Girl acct, while continuing to ignore my invitations to riff in replys. Guess ill go eat dog shit Huh! § haha owned. im already rich and famous § #mondaymotivation https://t.co/McTcJcLtoM § darknet 2002: pics of dead guys in bath tubs, warez darknet 2017: discussions amongst the boys as to which of our acquaintances aren t funny § stonehenge actually sucks and i hope someone pushes those rocks the hell over real soon § "what if among us was squid game" - DRIL https://t.co/u5ay58wKu8 § Used to be you could get on stage & say stuff like "Tickle me elmo fucks" and people wiould shower you with praise. Standards are now higher § FELLA'S... WHEN YOURE WIPING YOUR WIFES ASS... YOU MUST ALWAYS, ALWAYS USE "TOILET PAPER" § @NBCSports thank you for making the sports § detective sherlock holmes examines my crass pud with a magnifying glass and calls it a piece of shit § this's police. your ass is grass. your tits are toast. your dick is dirt. your balls are busted. your mouth is Mother Fucked. your shit is s § #threewordsforyou starwars is my ass and toilet § fuck your ma mama!! you piece of shit § watching a human interest pieice about a deaf guy who has a photographic memory of every shit hes ever taken § Puh?! you're danger-ously close to mmy blocker's list pal § number three-- Ive reversed my decision to turn down the Nobel Prize for my posts & will be writing an article in THe Daily Pussy, about this § i call evbery four-legged animal I see a dog and I am correct more often than not so I will never stop § oh u think this is funny mother fucker?(Kills ape) YOu consider this comedy? (kills naother ape) and my Missing Plane jokes are bad? Yeah ok § please watch my realtiy drama"shit eaters" about people who eat shit and are constantly goaded into cyclical arguments with their loved ones § you soudn like a nerd § my followers are always onm some god damn goofy shit; Theyre absolutely smoking thut Urkel § its almost to good, i think § seeing a guy on here named "Curtis Blowjobs" , shaking my head and saying "REALLY??" a lot, asking girls in the dms if they can believe this § scribbling my exposed dick out of this photo with a blue bic pen so its good enough for linked in § Cool your nuts scum bag § #AmexAlicia i HATE the aid bug § BIGMOUTH BILLYBASS REVIVAL , SINGS GAGA, BIEBER, ET AL; INFUSED WITH 2012 TECH FOR SHIT & PISS CAPABILITIES; "PHENOMENAL" FORBES MAGAZINE § basically,actual doctors have told me my brain is Perfect. ANYWAY, HGeres nine paragraphs I wrote on why leaving tips at restaurants is bad § Wow thifs blew up. While your here please have a look at this: htttp://www. burgerking.com § subset of lava § tormenting lab animals with my huge vibrating ass § When you "FAve" me, you are effectively throwing a " Treat " into my mouth § please dm my agent if you wish to Banter with me in the mentions, so he can send you the proper paperwork. im extremely tired of this shit. § found a bunch of blueprints, street plans and pictures of pregnant women in a suitcase labelled "Pregtopia" in teen son's room. please help § dont try to tell me it's spelled "clarence"./ i will not be april's fool § is it. i dont know from good anymore § Oh looj at them having a go about things. A fine day for foot (Soccer) ball-- wahey lads? Me mum's tits , Piss up! Ohh the noncers Wanked it § perhaps by shooting a mam to the moon, NASA is the greatest sniper of all? nope. bull shit. it is solid snake § @Boscovs Are you unquestionably committed to the "Customer First" experience--Do you pledge here and now to bow to the customer's every whim? § can some one get me in touch with the user named "Clit Goon" . he said he could give me a bunch of cardboard boxes 6 years ago § dear sir or madam - i request the following: "CUM_SISSY" embroidered into the back of my father's old army jacket, complete with underscore, § i often disagree with DigimonOtis, but his efforts to keep Sharia Law out of the donkey kong 64 wiki are much needed in this wolrd of danger § Vampire A: Im murdered. My idiot ass has put to be last bullet. Vampire B: In Death we can truely live. Good bye § makers of @SlimJim announce @SlimeJim !!! dog food for humans § @ Dril_Analyst thank's § i approve of congres... i believe they are doing a very good job despite negative comments online § @wikileaks can u wiki leak some ke$ha nudes § me when theres not enoujgh fuckin coffee or beer!!!!!!!!!!!!!!!!! http://t.co/yiPkkqO1rl § Remembe,r if you're a fan of the rant, feel free to support it with favs, retweets, or just drop me a message saying how good it is. § my cousin was charged with arson(Bullshit) , and i was thinking we could all help out by drawing up some memes to display in his prison cell § having a HELL of a time updating the names on all my personal & business records to Jeep Grand CheroKeith isntead of keith § petition to rename the statue of liberty "Bisexual Tattoo Goddess" because istand for something real and i live in a part of this world. § certain theres a special combination of ancient cowboy noises that will get you free shit from QVC and ill keep calling until i FINd it § @Netflix few taglines to help U elevate ur brand: " etflix: Boom, baby!!" , " etflix: Get your net fix.", and. " etflix: Our brand is HOT!" § Number two. I will never apologize for defending myself from the onslaughts of jealous swine § @TruthPointDWR suck my dick in balls § im a journalist now so send me any scoops you might hiave and ill try to post it here if its not perverted § too many movies about rats § im having a blast in Qatar watching all the games, rooting for teams, etc. but you cant self suck here. they get really mad if you self suck § (seeing a nude woman) Wow looks like im on the weird side of you tybe again § Mountan Dew Cold Red check it out § god bless him. cops is bull shit. § people are not ready to hear it . but. simply the most persecuted skin color of all time, is " NUDE " § lets "BUTT FUCK" covid Signed , The @ Dril Social Media Response Team § wiping m ass with toilet paper imprinted with an image of bin laden wiping his ass with toilet paper imprinted with the jp morgan chase logo § ok which one of the trolls told some company in Singapore that im interested in bulk purchases of cheap laminate flooring. i demand answers. § @AmandaBynes RAM A CAR INNTO ME BABY § when you say "Tickle Me elmo is not a gaming console", youre erasing the voices of everyone that beleives Tickle me Elmo is a gaming console § if you see it published anywhere else but here i expect you to alert the proper authorities with 911. § ladys this is the Commander. i order you to post your Pussy Number pronto https://t.co/cNEi9o-0TEm § fuck the "left shark " § mr fauci im placing you under arrest in the court of law § who remembesr the mower man screensaver. who remembers the fear of it. who remembers not even being sure if the screams were coming from you § KLEBOLD: Wtf is this shit HARRIS: "Wii Sports Resort"? U call urself a gamer? LANZA: ... KLEBOLD: Get these fuckin trashbags off the windows § Ah, Reddit ftw., Truly phenomenal, big fan of the memes, links, etc. Always been saying this. So whcih stock is making us rich today fellas § please do not embarrass me in front of "inside hoops". you dip shits. you fucking animals § going to burn dOwn my power lines and go off the grid for a bit until all the smug butthurt drama fedorra script kiddy fanboys take a hike, § REVIEW- EROTIC SILHOUETTE MUD FLAPS - 1 STAR: piece of shit. drags behind my Honda Accord and gets messed up. too long. not wortg the hassle § "im a karen who speaks to the manager too much" if you say this FUCK YOU !!! § mlg streamer "BeastModeCos-by" loses geforce sponsorship after allegedly using a performance enhancing bed pan § please get me the list of the dorks who have me blocked on this goddamned website so i can kick their lawn up with my cowboyboots § because of the RECESSION, "Ice Capades" has been cancleled and replaced by SHITcapades and PISScapades. just kidding § ugh.. my husband never puts the toilet lid back down. *Closes Lid,; Takes Huge Piss On Top Of It* § kick their pets and cars #waystopissoffafatperson § going to start saying shit to girls like "the drew carey show is like dilbert on Hash" until i get my honorary degree from Harvard revoked § its good. no wait, its bad, because theyre all morally bankrupt and Heinous brand murderers § originally wanted to keep silent about the "elmer fudd's dick" issue, but BMXWalter's objectionable dickless fudd theory has forced my hand, § "just Genius shit ." - Thugwanker § @Battlefield I have done this approximately 30 times. § imagine how fucked uop it would be to have a brain and be able to form thoughts § sheriff's department transmission decoded by anonymous: "Please Keep Rowdy Beasts Away From Mayor During Dog Show"--what could it all mean?? § is @subway really offering a 10% discount to all Muslims who apologize for the attacks... kind of messed up.. § petition to move "6teen" to CN's [adult swim] block, because me & my friends love it, want to be taken seriously, and are like 60 years old § i just bought an Oscar on the black market and im willing to give it to the first bbw to send me a pic of herself fisting ehr own mouth. § (listening to a wolf howl off in the distance) do you hear that. thats the sound of another fav star trophy in the bag § wghen other people do jokes, they get the big buzz feed offce, allowed to kiss girls,etc, but when i do it im treated like a Crook. typical § if i catch you taking " SELFIE " at my used car dealership (BEST deals in the tri-state area) i will shell you from the rear like a coward § discreetly enjoying a small amount of beer i hid in my gun § before you go around muting my posts and blocking this or that , its important to consider the Shit that i bring to the table § #ihavenorespect for the military (murdertary) #ihavenorespect for whores(girls) #ihavenorespect for rappers #ihavenorespect for 666 § mmy "hype man", if you

will, is a tiny 80-year-old guy who follows me around and apologizes for
everything i say and do in a pitiful voice § for the first time in human history
you can now set Budweiser as your default internet browser § mny repulsive
tweets were specifically designed to do the exact opposite § (getting really
into the dunk tank carnival game) Ill show you some pain mother fucker. Ill
show you some pain mother fucker § (playing russian roullette and its my turn)
hasta the vista mother fucker (shoots the other guy § my 35 year old son is
howling because he clogged the toilet without using any toilet paper again. the
neighborhood despises my howling boy § pop this into your browser for a quick
smile : "urkel" § if i buy a roulette table for my house will the boys promise
to come over and play roulette ? OR should i fuck myself § who spit on my rats.
ill find him § there are guys who have replied to me hundreds of times and they
will get theirs ,very soon § which 46% of you mother fuckers arent buying soap
https://t.co/mbTQvI9lVe § christ washed the feet of his disciples but not the
ass. never the ass § theyer renovating my hard rock cafe.. just saw a mover
man drag two crates of live rattlers inside..has Hard Rock gone TOo wild?? No
F'n Way § ME: Basiclaly its just a joke we do where whoever says hes El Chapo
the most wins COP: Thats not what a joke is ME: Well its good either way § oh
look€"i failed my forklift operators certification for the 4th fucking time
becausse none of the girls on here bothered fucking helping me § just me again
reminding all of you seriousyl dumb motherfuckers to get your daily sperm
count. some of you are walking around with weak cum. § Ya Know They Been
Calling Me "The Bitch Who Did 9/11" § that was julian assange's piss. not mine
§ i lure a group of newly betrothed baby turtles into an abandoned warehouse
using a photo of the ocean and turn them into moths #GOthicOrder § Time to
shit. I excuse myself from the dinner table and enter a square, marble room
with an obelisk in the center. I lock the door behind me § #FreeJahar knock
knock. who's ther.e? jahar's innocence. the us gov wants to spend $5billion on
a helicopter but cant afford jahar's trial. § I see no humor in my providing a
safe dm for women to discuss open mouth kissing. Whats funny is people using
that as an excuse to attack me § @DrPhil the trolls have gone too far this time
. § twitter should let me see the profiles of people that blocked me because i
gotta know whoich of these bozos are talking shit § #NewFastFoods Fast bread §
As A Business Man, I Cannot Relate To Sexual-Minded People, However THis
So-Called Curse Undoubtedly FIRES UP My Award Winning Content § im not saying
the release of my FF6 Nude Mod incrased obamas approval rating, but there's
certainly a correlation that's difficult to ignore § bark up the wrong damn tree
ass whiper § its not enough!! its not enough! § if real life was a tv show.
the eclipse would be one of the episodes of it § the mythbusters hurl rocks at
a sick dog, adam looks at the camera and says'" Oops" wihle jamie fucking
shoots some guys house with a pistol § police man kicks me in the diaper while
running out of radio shack, causing my shit 2 fountain up and ruin several RC
spongebobs #rodneyking § ive just gotten word that he drowned after getting
slat water in his pussy § fucked up my hand while trying to pry open a jar of
cherries with a Shuriken § making my face Symmetrical in microsoft paint after
haivng a mental breakdown on linkedin. com § Do My Posts Help You? Am I A Good
Person? Do You Think Im Nice § SOLVE MY ASS § absolutely crushing it, and by
"it" i mean my "Balls", while i attempt to wedge myself into the driver's seat
of my 2004 kia optima § yeauh, let me just follow the fucking "YouTube"
account, on twitter. thats fucking normal § i believe that jade healm 15, and
the markets going haywire, youve got a "Witch's Brew" of bull shit § here's a
list of touhou girls i want to have as a Mom someday & here is a copy of that
list in case you accidentally throw it in the gabarge § tgifridays has tempo-
rarily taken the "dennis poppers" off of their menu. out of respect § every one
must wear a free speech diaper to protest twitter deleting posts that say "Fuck
the ecliopse" and "The eclipse is some fake shit" § if you odn't subscribe to

every last one of my vague, yet cocksure beliefs regarding the Portuguese , i
will never make eye contact with you § i plan on attending chad and avril's
wedding so i can absorb all the Love and Music Energy and use it to repair the
corrupted soul of gaia . § Well thats just plain goofy. § they are going to
build a moscque on the wtc. #SelfieForSeb § my greatest sin is that I've utterly
betrayed my " O FEAR" tower decal by being embarrassingly frightened of birds
and butter flies § clown Ass. people have been treating me like dirt due to
bernie bro dark money and you cant blame me for defending myself, and im
no(41/66) § who does this guy think he is. https://t.co/vJTdgRC3U9 § disrespecting our soldiers is TREASON !!!!!!!!!! see u in hell u son of a bitch.
kicks orange cat effigy #veteransday § #FreeJahar obama jsut ordered construction of a $5billion helicopter but no trial for Jahar because "we can't afford
it". this is FUCKED UP § it's that time of the year when my father sends me
pictures of jails and tells me that i must learn to Respect a good barbecue dry
rub § house speaker john boehner claim obama used infinite soul glitch at press
summit. obama cooked the boo;ks § told to "Sit my ass down" after wasting my
one question at the town hall meeting by asking if the secret service agents
get to see them nude § the restaurant cannot legally charge your credit card if
you refuse to givr them your signature and leave § the experimental surgical
procedure to make my tears stink less was a complete failure. im sorry everyone
§ i show my son the mandated GMO labeling on a pair of jeans at the store.
"that's how you know it's a good cut. this is a good cut of denim." § informed
by family that i wont be invited to anymore funerals if i dont develop a
jawline, fix my fucked up voice, and fix my fucked up skin § id rather go fuck my
self than like a post § which one of you Fags know how to extract birdshot from
a chest wound #geocachingmishaps § i had not felt emotion in over 20 yrs. not
until baby crash bandicoot's reunion with regular crash bandicoot moved me to
actual human tears § What makes the idea of me being a "Pervert" so comedic is
the fact that I cant even get an erection in public. Its actually a problem for
me § to the countless many Whom have plagiarized my hard work by using the
retweet button "Thou art a Coward" !! i will beat your ass at the mall § Seems
to me when you hand your money to the burger king man he takes it at 99mph but
when he gives you your change back its 1mph. Oh lord! § i used to be mocked for
bullying my class mates. now i live in the real life mansion that Luigis
Mansion was based off of. it get's better by scoring 15% on the buzz feed quiz
"Medical Term or Slur" § kfc commercial idea: a man is trying to get into kfc
but he is too small to reach the door handle. he tries and tries and nobody
helps him § SOME ONE REPLACED MY INCEST FAQS WITH PICTURES OF TURKISH FLAGS AND
GUNS § going strong into hour 8 of #NoPiss. feeling unprecedented spiritual
growth. unfollow me if youre upset because this isnt "Funny" or "good". §
handing Faves over to my enemies is FRAUD !! base, contemptible FRAUD! § @
KloutSupport i demand that you send me my bottle of "Spice Islands Beau Monde"
for no reason whatsoever or else i will post my diseased ass § The Brand
Ayatollah § the sniper lifestyle requires perfect animal instincts and also
smoking. dont join my sniper squad if u havent forsaken humanity& dont smoke §
sorry im late, my car totally Friend Zoned me-- im fired??..now YOURE friend
zoning me?? im gonna eat all these pills and friend zone myself § might passive
aggressively post "Oh! The website is Bad today" if i dont get some damn likes
over here. just constantly treated like a leper § warm pics every day § saying
im going to flip "doug the pug" aorund in mid air with devil sticks . is not a
death threat § "Just simply my posts." § its shit head o' clock and everyones
grabbing at my Nuts § bigmouth fake priest telling me to "drink a shitload of
holy water and kill yourself" as penance? this has happened at three churches
now § boy's Rules: 1) the only coffee flavored thing should be COFFEE !! 2)
"Shut Da Fuck Up And Keep Ya Head Down" 3) Never consume Oils § local man gets
diapoer rash on face from wet beard § that is one subpar app § many people do

not realize that after you enjoy a meal out at a restaurant you can pour the entire salt shaker inyo your mouth as a bonus § (said within ear shot of girls) yeah so like i was saying me and the boys are laughing AT the bitter beer face commerciasls. not WITH them § i have decided to postpone my scandalous hard right pivot until after i have lost my virginity or hjad my dick sucked a pretty decent amount § Thank you to all USERs who have engaged my web space regarding Super Bowl. You have increased the Social Power of myself and the NFL forever § i challenge my most hated Enemys to name a single chemical that exists naturally within a womens pussy. You cant do it § Hot Pockets Yanked From Shelves for Containing €˜Diseased and Unsound Animals€™ #AreYouThe-One § yoyu appear to be severely ill § yknow folks, not many things tell you theyre good right there in the name, so if you see things like Good Friday or Goodfellas i say Take It § i live vicariously through my diaper § all the youth thhese days look like dead eyed little perverts because they are not incorporating Geritol into their daily routine § get yourself a few dozen trash bags and stash them in a drawer somewhere. never know when you might need em #TheSaturdayMorningRamble § you cry during one car commercial and people label you as "guy who cries during car commercials" but Y'All aint ready to speak on That..., § Sort Of Like A Wiccan James Bond § i agree. mindfulness is some good shit. hold on, someones honking their car horn at my house and i have to go outside and kick their ass now § friday night gathering up together a big pile of things i like to respect (flags, crucifixes ,etc) and just roll around in it ,give kisses, § angle of god... calling u § MY 7 BOARDER COLLY'S ARE MY ANGEL AND IF THEY'RE NOT ALLOWED TO BE PRESENT AT THE OPERATING TABLE DURING MY LAP-BAND PROCEDURE I'LL DIE § Let it be known that I am the sole proprietor of the "Ren Stimpfani" joke, and that all attempts to replicate it are for the garbage can. § tuesday morning is " Low Engagement " , which means if you absolutely must have a melt down over Followbacks now's the time to do it § "grouse pandy" § thanks for putting your failure opinoin that i didn't even want to read. § a piece of crap § because im a pig in the zoo § digimonotis thought octomom was the bad guy in spider man 2 § if you think blowing up an rv and injuring 3 people is good UnFollow my ass § it will be good for all of us when i shorten my name from "the ebay boy" to "eboy" § *corsses out all the bad posts in perm. marker* mmm . haha. oh yeah. look at that *scrolls down and t he posts move* no. this wont do. oh no § thank you. Theyre all crooks § me and several S&P 500 CEOs often have sleepovers and discuss which MLB players we wanna kiss and try to determine which ones are Neuroqueer § some pf you are definitely a 1. i truly believe the carelessness you exhibit with your sloppy posts is reflected also by your dire ass hole. § ok publicist says i gotta do one about the zach braff kickstarter ok uh uh*claps hands* alright€"€" what if instead of money he asked for PIss § some times it's the small things that are good #Truth_In_Life #Deals #Abominable http://t.co/jKgDkdYEzZ § "kendo is so much better than normal swords" nope fuck yourself § https://t.co/0Tah9yP4Zi § wow , another bernie bro coming after me just because im posting the truth into their shitty little lives. you Lose bitch § getting all the snow out of my driveway with a gun, just fucking obliterating it § torturing my damn dick with corn cob holders in Penance for the foul tone i took with the subway corporation today § please get the comedy central roast of My Ass OFF THE AIR. it has been edited to make me seem like a good sport., however im truly pissed of § i didnt put any ants in there i just opened it uo and ate all the blue shit. § BRIDE OF DECEIT § sotp insulting me § difcult 4 average joe like me to schedule some time to "Jack Off" arounf here; with all these tragic anniversaries fucking my calendar up § i feel a good balance of nice energy & rude energy cioming through the monitor at me, and i think i will stay online for about 3 more hours. § GIRL: (after listening to me explain something i invented called Weed Theory for 20 mins) Wow thats pretty good. Did you invent that ME: Yes §

>>YOU FIND YOURSELF IN A GREY CORRIDOR. HOW DO YOU PROCEED? >>PIECE OF SHIT
>>SUCH LANGUAGE IS NOT BECOMING OF A KNIGHT. HOW DO YOU PROCEED? § forced to
commit suicide on live tv after 50yr old post comes to light in which i claim
that scotus clarance thomas jacks off using his feet § Ouh..!! Fascinating !
**Nodding a lot* § The Moderation and Administrative Staff of the Star Fox
Strategy and Technique Discussion Boards DOES NOt encourage its users to crank
off, § unbelievable. i have been sent 4 different cum tributes of my "Doggo's". i
will never cleanse the time line with wholesome eye bleach again § #85Collapse
ive been saying from the very beginning that interstate85 fucking sucks ass.
now that it collapsed girls are blowing my phone up § got a big piece of velcro
stuck to my big ass § ive already accepted that im going to hell because I
mispronounced church as "gurtch" once § look at the calender. I'm not explaining this further § but enough about my dick. today, I would like to talk to all
of you about the Toilet. § ive taken shits that have more money than you you
broke bitch https://t.co/fL3Zsti7Py § stop it Teens. stop grabbing onto my
jeans and SKitching me as i try to run away. im a teen too. im one of you §
unfollow , unsubscribe, block and mute all Gambler's § another smart aleck here
to ratio my ass............ § rooting through some damn womens' purses. all of
the things in these purses suck. i don't give a shit § every celebrity on earth
has succumbed to the Corona Virus? Wow!! What a scoop!!! § Horse_Ebook Passes
Turing Test, Replaces The Bible § It would be so nice to have followers who
dont fucking hate my ass . Guess ill go choke on dirt!!! Fuck me!! § ill fix
it soon. i will fix it § now's the perfect time to take out that nasty Zynga
money before it goes sour & invest it directly into The Spice Girls. flame me if
u must § my "The Banquet of Posts" has now ended. There were so many posts from
lots of different people on here, and they were all Winners. Thank yo https://t.
co/f0fWI9ie8K § with all this talk of nanotechnology the next logical step is
miniature girls with cat ears and big dicks injected directly into our blood §
PRIEST: in the name of the father... ME: Yes. Good PRIEST: ...the son.. ME:
Great. Go on. keep em comin PRIEST: ..and the Holy Spirit ME: No § worst part
of being my masseuse is having to suffer a 5 minute monologue before hand about
how i think your job is actually extremely normal § Fuck U. Im trying to get
better § damn true this § im The Pepsi Eunuch Bitch!!! i don't give a FUCK !!!
§ ddepressed, exhausted imbecile dragging an overturned port-o-john down the
interstate, blocking traffic and getting honked at § it's not good for the
dilbert guy to come on here and say hes going to Bull Breed my wife with his
Superior Spunk. i dont care if hes 200 iq § the one major design flaw which
plagued the iron maiden from the start were the large spikes that would stab
anyone who tried to live in it § weaving a "Feel Good" tale about how dogs hate
fireworks because theyre reincarnate US armymen with ptsd; getting down voted
for some reason § "stuart little 2" isn;t funny. somebody had to say it §
#WorstDateIn5words a bunvch of blades arranged to spell out" 9/11". the worst
date, in swords § Bot. § llooking extremely normal today https://t.co/ADTeu9bW-
fC § Mahmoud Ahmadinejad Has A New Wine Out. I'm Dying To Try It But I Find His
Governing Policies Questionable At Best. Such Is My Life Of Shit. § looking to
get on some rowdy boys bad sides tonight mother fucker. § http://www.youtube.
com/watch?v=ivLtCs-F46I § Someone created a network called "(my moms name)
pussy stinks!" The police said nothing could be done, but Reddit, something has
to be done. § "And th mark...theyst fhall beckon..bearers of the Mask.. doth
verily, andth post really good shit, online" nostradamus predicting Anonymous §
my followers have abandoned me after finding out that i dont have any ass cheeks
and that the hole is just exposed all the time like a dog's § my next good post
is about egg salad. What in the shit?? are you egg or salad? Why is this good.
Who's eating it. Check Please. uhhh § probably WHACKEN OFF!!!!!!!!!!!!!! Fuck
otis § sorry i wont be able to respond to any DMs today as i was just walking
around in traffic and got pussy blasted by the fastest Mazda on earth § i

apologize sir !!!!!!! § i have obtained Seth's Ape. i will be usingb him to
co-host my new tv show that is basically jack ass but fake § What ever. I'm a
hated bug § mn, http://t.co/NdnbekAZDO § the mayor has erected another insulting effigy of me (myself) foir the local children to hurl stones and urine upon.
lost my vote bitch § hands Off my posts https://t.co/LJtHXIuj73 § do not
interfere with my negotiations please § projectile drooling: im the only person
in the world who does this. doctors refuse to help me § yes, i am a 24 year
old man, and yes, i am the one who spraypainted the word "Teen" on the side
wall of sleepy's mattress porfessionals. § i lovoe challenging people on here
to Duals and beaning them with a sniper rifle while theyre like fucking with
their phone, waiting for me § is this.. the fabled web 3.0 #fuckingmonstrosi-
tysidebar #jesuschrist § fuck wifi http://t.co/ntA35Tsn § tthis asshole brought
home a tekken lanyard with "Phil" written on it in magic marker and wants to
use it with the keys to his new buick . § injecvting a shit ton of steroids and
walking on the treadmill at 3mph § in fear of losing my job at panda express
after telling a girl about my kidney stone ordeals and haivng it misinterpreted
as sex talk § fellas if your girl isnt losing control of her bowels every time
you take her to bed "You are not tapping that thing RIGHT!!!" § i just left an
enormous pile of vomit behind golds gym for all of you abominable pig clowns to
pick at #blackfridaydeals § i bet the three stooges would be pissed if they
figured out the name of their show. they probably think its called "the three
normal guys' § "There is no known cure for dog autism." - vetinfo.com § @
prodigalsam Feel like this is appropriate. Again. http://t.co/v0vzSiIe5w §
#ThingsWeAllHate pornos and sex § (speaking into phone) get me on the computer
§ came outside today to notice m y "Bring Back The Marriage Ref" bumper sticker
violently ripped off. Obviously, I hit a nerve. § Maybe the phones get smart
enough.. They will do the yapping, for us ! § guy walking around flaunting his
mittens around. claiming that nothings better than mittens. i show him my
gloves and he flips the fuck out § @piersmorgan no...! it's fucking Bad to be
that !! § absolutely read some of my god damn tweets while opening gifts with
loved ones at the tree tomorrow & bring CULUTRE to this ass of a holiday § oi
you lot. The gas pricses have become quite fuck all § https://t.co/hCJDnueSN3
great news for me- a fucking dumb ASS! who FUCKS EVERY THING UP!!! § FULLY
IMMERSED IN THE TIME LINE-- AH DEAR LORD § none of my followers think turds is
good § Im about to get wild at 2:30am on this Fucking can of #Beer I found. I
am going to use my grandpas knfie to "Shot Gun" it. #ThingsILikeToDo § bush was
the president who likes oil. correct? so what i think is that its actually
"Castor oil", because he leaves a bad taste in my mout!! § Interesting that
some people care enough about my posts to look at them and read them. Says a
lot about you Dick head § do not piss my ass off. do not goof around with my ass
§ hm?? sorry, didn't see u there. i was just digesting a fascinating piece
about how reading twitter for 9 hrs a day makes you a BEtter person § Please
come to the provided address to deliver my 25 , 000 USD. I will be there
holding an empty suitcase, and grinning § (me in prone position while having my
house swatted again) officer if u could please just slip the rest of that
campbells chunky in my mouth § if somone cooks your goose, thats it. youre
basically fucked § obelisk rises from the volcano - what sorcery is this ??!!
carved along its side are the words "POWER BIEBER"; 1600 birds myteriously die
§ ' george bush master of porno ' § finest rack o ribs youve ever seen. you get
your favorite dry rub all over that badboy but- oh no- it's sand. the sand
laughs #BBQNightmares § Sept 11: it is a testament to the resolve of our nation
that the nine one one towers are still standidng upright and intact to this
very day § trolls using "#ff" to add me to cruel watchlists for oppressive
police beasts; ONCE AGAIN fucking me over, ONCE AGAIN making me shit myself §
picture now, on this Warm Summer's Night, if all the "SWEARS" on this page were
replaced with helpful links to mazda "Sign and Drive" events § i am the damn

good boy who always gets his dinner egg http://t.co/Wn7RfLyb4h § whenever i see
one of those roast pigs with apple in its mouth i think " ow theres a real son
of a bitch who made the wrong choices in life" § if you dont post anything for
a month and i can't find the reason why, i just assume you died and got buried
in someones yard like a pet § Im thinking 2k20 is the year of "Shut the fuck
up" . All repliers blocked. Absolute God mode § pain time § every day i get
100s of messages from young men saying "I need to ejaculate Right now. What do
I do." and i say to them all. JUst Breathe. § the prophecy fulfilled
https://t.co/H1erJV4KBS https://t.co/MOpYkwDKmE § never say my name again you
disgusting criminal § of course i am mad § didnt r. lee ermey provide his voice
for a diaper commercial sometime in the 90s . im pretty sure he did but I cant
find proof it exists § holy gravy holy meat   holy moly let us eat https://t.
co/XSVi3m7kH5 § "CODGER LOOSES HIS LUNCH WHILE HAVING A WANK" § like i always
say; sewage is just shit in a pipe § ME: hey ed. whats good to shoot at the
range today ED: Someone threw a big bag of packing peanuts out there. Its good
to hit it with bullets § (11yr old Jack Droseys head pulled out of toilet)it
bears repeating that 'Likes' are not conducive to my vision, and th(gets dunked
again) § ufos are becoming smarter..... § Time to do several fucking perfect
wolf howls at the nascar men § the first iddiot to file a complaint against my
rat zoo gets a new pipe hole courtesy of my Handsome Fists § the only font i
like now https://t.co/CKx0meQUIj § win ben steins Pussy § thinking that every
time elon musk trends on here it's because he invented cold fusion, not because
he publicly called someone an "Ass Hat" § sick of hearing about the head
honcho. what aobut the legs honcho. or the ass honcho. that's my opinion on
honcho. thank you for reading it § everyone needs something worth dying for..
mine just happens to be the japanese racist version of the wazzup ad § Does
anyone know how important is this. http://t.co/XLtJAtdnM2 § there are rifts in
the Frankenstein community regarding whether or not igor was tasked with
jacking the monster off to keep it docile § they never shit. they have no need
for bathrooms. they converted them into offices. i will not "hold on" § my idea
for adam is the water boy sequel called beer boy where he gives beer to the
football player's § people who think dolphins are real = shit § whatever bitch
told me the stock market is closed on valentinees day owes me $100000 § SCOTT
PETERSON: i unfollowed you in 2011 and your shit gets retweeted into my feed
constantly. it sucks ME: I apologize sir!! I've fucked up § ARMY: your
nickname reflects poorly on us all. we're changing it to something like "raven"
or "switchknife" ME: no. "hostage killer" is good § im the guy in the incognito
browser icon who jacks off wearing a trenchcoat and sunglasses § heads up
hotshot. gonna drop two fuckin cents on this fuckin itunes. yeah you gotta be a
fuckin nasa astronaut to use this shit. yea alright § the Police have stated
that rubber neckers and looky loos trying to sneak a peek at the irradiated
diaper on 295 will be blasted with poison § hell § i do not appreciate twitter
putting a satire warning underneath all of the posts where i say i am jacking
off right now. it is NOT satire § seeking a fellow High-Functioning Brony to
crawl underneath the tarp i live in and help me de-wax my ears. suit and tie
required. § one more. good night http://t.co/BaZQ2mC5Do § my dick touched the
floor by accident. im a god damned foolish imbecile § each episode personally
costs me $1000000 out of my own pocket. but i do it for the fans..... § on
February 19th, 2019, i will show my penis on here and effectively remove myself
from consideration as the host of this years Oscar show. § #RoyalBabyNames
asshole doofus motherfucker from hell § so what kind of Jeans shampoo do you
use? paul mitchell's denim advantage?? good luck with that you fucking cretin
§ ikea still does not sell spittoons in year 2020. a crime against men who spit
§ yeah whatever pal; im such an asshole for feeding my nail clippings to the
birds at the park instead of sending em off to the dunp. fuck off § three sayings
to any fool who would claim that i am the bitch of this website: 1.your god

damn right 2. i dont give a fuck 3. you Lose § i whip out two good uzis and
shoot up a fence with the words "INMATURE PEOPLE" painted on the sid.e my
father thanks me for this, via skype § scorlling through massive amounts of
online clutter empowers me § Acutually, its not fucking funny. Its just
pathetic. § really lookjing forward to going through puberty again and becoming
a cop § it used to be you didnt need a degree to become a philosopher yo u
could just say shit like "Beer is the Merry Soul's Companion" constantly § oh,
look, people are posting more wiseguy shit while the adults in the room are
trying to make the gas prices lower. Perfect § gonna need a relaly good
explanation from twitter corp. as to why the recently added "me" button leads
to a picture of a rat in a clown suit § When Ur Girl Is "On Point" - Hooking U
Up With That Gold Bond Medicated Powder - Because She KNOw That The Dick Good §
alvin and his chipmunks have not evaded my scorn § how do i get cowboy paint off
a dog . § you have destroyed a powerful networking opportunity with this horse
shit § I Hope So http://t.co/tOuAGUy2j1 § you boys with your pud in your hand
waiting for the girls to wake up and post pics SORRY!! all you get for now are
my posts Muta Fucka!! § isis man: please! you gotta follow back! you just
gotta! me: no can do my man. i respect your right to be in isis, but I can not
follow you. § thanks all. together weve raised over $63 for raytheon to develop
a brand new ITAS that can shoot down enemy prayers before they reach God . §
hes right. in favor of hearing out both sides my next post will explore the
possible "Darker side" of heroin https://t.co/9nuiPvG9Pb § slow motion film of
my ass deflating into a wrinkled mess, my screams can be heard in the background,
awful & beast-like due to altered pitch § my opponent thinks hes hot shit
releasing photos of me walking an iguana on a leash., but little does he know
that iguana is Gentle creature § bullshit jeans. dont buy.   made of some
kind of rat hair. not denim. i took them to my priest and he refused to bless
them § tattooing a bar code to my penis to demonstrate to anyone who looks at
my penis the Fraalty of our humanity, in regard to mens penises § thank you . i
have nuked his ass https://t.co/sU8f2a6cdb https://t.co/o6RUhH6bg1 § #mcgruff
Tip #39: dont literally take a bite out of crime. its an intangible concept
used to classify human behavior & its absolutely filthy § TO WHOEVER IS SHRIEK-
ING AT ME RIGHT NOW I CANT SEE YOU BECUAS EIM FUCKING RUN OVER BY CARS SO SHUT
THE FUCK UP § Just met w/ Boys Lunch Club. Seems to me, That we are very pissed
off that teen girls would rather kiss, "Soldier Boy," than Actual Soldiers § the
shit that killed Elvis https://t.co/gA15sU36Gy § theyre minds have evolved
beyond germs § utterly dejected by the fact that my favorite romance novelist
is just a Trident marketing strategist shilling mint gum to teens #ArtDeath §
yoyu dont choose to be retweeted.. it choose's you § BITCH !!! § im not your
real uncle #nightmarerevelations § micropenised galoot bleeds out in a 7-11
after smashing glass hot dog case with bare hands and shows his ass on the news
by mistake § "oh its so easy to og after david Koch now that hes dead" "its so
Edgy & Brave to get his ass now that he cnat send his assassins after you" § 12
year slave huh? sounds like my marriage. which I dont enjoy. to the degree that
it is succinctly described by that particular movie title § pleas tune into my
next podcast where i ask what the FUCK angry birds is and viciously mock the
first piece of shit caller to answer me § CLICK ON MY BIG DUMB DICK TO SUBSCRIBE
TO MY USELESS NEWSGROUP § some one explain please to me why the letter board at
my local arbys has said "happy hour" for months now, before i get the police
involved § ue to shit on them. § anyone else catch " MR. PRE$IDENT " applying
nail polish during the debate???? nbullshit. highly unpresidential § my world
renowned "miserable adult cam" feature has been removed due to complaints §
soon we shall all be meme 's, graceful and dignified on the net, our crude human
forms long forgotten § http://www.youtube.com/watch?v=tRA5x5g6fo8 § thte
content man fails once again, and walks home to get trash talked by his 34-year
old son who refuses to eat anything without ketchup § I will be your Father. I

will take you as my Son and teach you the ways of online. We will hold hands as our follower count reaches infinity § youre a rodeo clown from the sewer § a mystery individual is going around telling girls he invented "The Ass Meme" . you must stop this immediately. only i am allowed to do that § he is lying. the reason he will never become twitch partner is because he runs his mouth nasty on there § its 4am sunday morning here uin beautiful hollywood california and i got a tab open on here called "Barney FAQ" § those are shit. open up the yellow pages and contact a leg man immediately § SHIT IMITATES LIFE § Guh? my father owned slaves and was extremely poor. stop portending false nomenclature § i am going to plunge a sword into our bed and officially end outr 40 yr marriage if you do not stop yelling while i am recording my stream's § Respect-fully, The Tim Hortons Nihilist § i truly hate winning the infamous "Darwin Award" by getting bombarded with artillery fire in the Super K-Mart parking lot § you fuck yourselfs for this bastard move . § know what. im not fucking sorry. the "12 days" project has been fairly solid thus far. as if the shit you people post is better?? get fucked § I am not a baby . I am a Human § baffled as to why the powers that be would insist that me, my Hotwif,e & paramour Hubby can not enlist in the marines together as a Squadron § bothj of you should be sent to abu ghraib for talking about your penises to me § i will draw a picture of lips on it but i will not kiss it because we are living in a Fucking pandemic . § thinking i can help girls bycruising around town selling tampons and pads out of my ford Fusion for cost of product + gas money § it is so beautiful to me, to have my ass lovingly wiped by my girl friend, knowing nothing is more pure than this bond, Nothing more strong, § i will never apologize for accidentally dialing 911 in my jeans pocket or accidentally begging the operator for a "cop massage" § theres a popular nursery rhyme in which the singer claims to be a teapot. this, for many children, is their first experience with "Trolling" § a man does a wheelie past you in a motorcycle. the back of his jacket says "TAKE DOWN THE POSTS" § would like to get one post out today without my son taking me to task in the replies ffor letting my ex wife take the car § indie punk rock band "THe 9/11 Forgetters" wanted by police after imploring their audience NOT to watch ABC's wednesday night comedy lineup § the Administrator has told you to refrain from clicking on my posts in the future § adult who wrestles cops § practicing my angry phone calls for when someone gives me COVID. yelling "you gave me covid you dumb mother fucker", "youre Nasty", etc § your from 9gag your from reddit your from tark .com and its no surprise to see your stupid Ass in the comments sections kissing my NUTs § absorbing Dip Shit energy from the lousy posts on here and throwing up f rom the body reaction § how about we worry about human rights ... after we've fixed all the human wrongs ? #AnHon-estMansSay § A tag has been placed on Utz Quality Foods, Inc. requesting that it be speedily deleted from Wikipedia. § Fucka!!!! § if every person on earth killed 1000 bugs every day we would have no more bugs #noBugs #stopBugs § i couldnt help but notcie you besmirching my nephews Banksy Valhalla, Jordian Computer, Holstein Paypal, and last but not lease, paper mario § http://i. imgur.com/aJISN.jpg God Is Real § watching my haters "CUM" § "When it is Christmas, the only gift you need is my posts." -@Dril when it is christmas, the only gift you need is my posts. § WHAT ABOut MY FREE SPEECH *a bunch of child porn spills outof mouth* IM AS HUMAN AS THE REST OF U *Dick Flies Out Of Pants And Spins Around* § does any 1 know the hebrew translation for "dubstep" #tattoo § the shit i was postng on twitter in the 80s and 90s?? uh yeah, that was the real shit. nowadays its pandering hipster filth and Crude humour § reading #my twitter feed, screaming "SIT ON IT, BUB!" everytime some1 makes a rude #iSad post, my face growing more contorted as i get louder § not sure if im hearing all the lyrics, but it seems like the guy in the song "Bad to the bone" is bad because he has a lot of consensual sex § me too. im fucking awful § #ToTheGirls2016 im intelligent & clean boy. i have the trigger dicispline of a lion. ive used Torture to cure myself of all mental illness. § if you have trouble discerning the "Family Room" from the "Living Room" your house should be taken away from you § You know, from the tone of your posts, it seems as though you actually WANT the Jeff Dunham brand to fail . § in short, my greasy chest hair has finally achieved complete fusion with my filthy blues brothers bib, and i am now essentially a cyborg § chance is presented with out comment . https://t.co/VNyp4qja2q § #IAmNotALiberalBecause im proud of my greasy, orange ejaculate § if you have a problem with my mouth, i'll be swniging a sledgehammer in circles outdoors for the rest of my life, so come try do crap to me. § https://t.co/KY4k5H8WQC § Fuck Up The Office With A Real Leather Alligator Stapler, Shatter THe Establishment - "I Believe We have Your stapler." - StaplerMods.com § red onion, green onion, yellow uonion, folks this isnt a food, but a traffic light. Get that like button § being a dumb ass on here is fucking Stupid § "hello 911 I need a moat dug around my house immediately" "sir this line is for emergencies only" "Thuis is an emergency moat" § penning a heart-warming screen play about a horse who wins nascar § its funny and it Rocks § friendly reminder to all of my followers not to commit any Crimes in 2018. crimes are 2017 shit "Miss Me With That" § should i learn Letters first? or choose the path of Numbers? a queston every baby must ask it self § cant wait for all nerds on earth to upload their brain to computer so they can be bat man for the rest of their lives & stop fuckinh posting § i know thiis isnt the popular circle jerk opinion, but people who swear while speaking to the 911 operator are gross § at first i thought that Science was a shit waste of time. then somebody did a meme of it,. and now... hooboy.. now i like it § we honor u § reminder to tell everyone who follows you that theyre a good person. Please. I can soft block every single one of you. I have all day § no. i dont care where you hold the "2012 Incest Olympics" but its not gonna be on my roof § please unblock me so we can network our brands § @GreyhoundBus one of your African-American drivers called me a "Kermit-Looking Motherf**ker" and made me feel like a Fool in front of my son § in another life... i would make U stay.. https://t.co/5YnhlziWRQ § my 2015 new years resolutions is to go to hell less often, and raise $99 by selling stolen mulch to buy my account back from lockheed martin § this guy thinks he calls the shots now just cause he got the check mark ... § llove to look at a big slice of meatloaf and say "Damn it's good" § the massive pair of black angel wings that i wear to the gym fucking stink like shit now and they wont fit into the washing machine either § I consider making my posts good a Moral Imperative . I owe it to my follower's to deliver them a product completely devoid of Nude imagery . § donald trump has no time to fuck. he looks at his watch and says "i could not possibly fuck at this juncture." as he powerwalks into the zoo § beware of my friend metal gear eric he is a scammer and a bimbo § mc donads big hamburger no tomato on rye § i get in my car and 100 men smear their asses up agsint my windshield and doors. Unbelievable. I'm late for work. This is clownish. § alright now. just checking to see if there's any interest in a livestream of me speed running this entire bottle of hunts tomato ketchup § wendy's contest to win lunch with dick vitale cancelled due to 'sex people'. entries infused with distinct erotic musk handed over to police § society is changing, constantly ggrowing and improving, and i think it is time for spider-man to show his dick § https://t.co/Jvw4SdYoDj my policy of hell threads is clear , do not disrespect my Feeds § finger nail check. everyone please post your fingernails right now for my inspection. i will block you if theyre filthy § damn. some one told me the first day of autumn was a solstice so i didnt jack off during it. now my sinuses are all fucked up due to T level § local orgy vibe ruined by man who made terrible dog howls while extremely caught up in the moment - bastard is now imprisoned in astral cube § I lpove making my credit rating lower by having my wife painted on the side of my car § i come on here & lay down the hammer and the time line shuts its damn

mouth real quick. cockoaches scattering like little peices of dog shit § dont
mind me... im just a forgotten content creator from a bygone era, whose dick
happens to be covered in aphids § ass challenge : lay face down on your bed and
try to kick your self in the ass. i was able to tdo this § havent gotten any
sleep since group dm split off into like 3 separate factions because XenoMarcus
said metalGearEric's chili looks like shit § STREET TOUGH: HEY. VERIFIED ACCTS
ARENT FAVING U ANYMORE. WHATS THE DEAL ME:(pretending not to hear, fumbling w/
keys to open my shitty car) § the trolls think its " SO FUNNY " when they sit
on my lap and jostle their hips around until i ejaculate al over their ass.
grow the fuck up § delete my nuts § https://t.co/hhgYfh8ZqT § I Love say ing
shit like, "At the Louvre, Even the BATHROOMS are nice" § wlel, it's almost
time to deliver grandma's eulogy. the perfect time to announce that i'm
quitting my job at IBM and becoming a SuicideGirl § i will tell you about the
two types of diaper. there's the Functional diaper, worn inside the pants. and
the Aesthetic diaper, worn outside. § Dan Fouts: The waterboy just needed some
water! Brent Musburger: Wow Dan, did you come up with that all by yourself?
#WaterboyWedesnday § my friend the only crypto currency you wanna get your
hands on is this: bird seed. There is a lot of birds and they all gotta eat §
my friends face when he asks if i know any hollywood celebs & i drop a 40page
document PROVING that merv griffin tried to break into my home § Looks like some
shit for losers & kindergardaners. Do not add any new features unless theyre
good or they put 1000usd directly in my pocket. https://t.co/7mS9B07BJi § james
bond: ill fire 1 round and suck your Dick before you hit the floor. ill kick the
floors dick off and fuck its ass hellboy 2: Game on § long horn steakhouse
should not refuse to honor my coupons just because theyre wet http://t.co/
zODZEYLQkY § i dont like him. i'm just looking at him § all correspondence with
Mastergamer will go directly through me because i am his lawyer and his friend
§ when twitter verifies shit like, oscar the grouch from seasme street, instead
of my acct, i get so mad that i kick fucking holes in the wall § i had an
actual good tweet to post tonight but a tower of filthy dog cages collapsed on
top of me before i could write it § do not show to me this you ho § nneed the
emoji to be the size of an actual mans head on my screen please. to suspend
disbelief https://t.co/YRAvtJohGf § all cops should be forced to dress like
james bond, as a promotional thing. I think it would be fun to get pulled over
by 007 James bond § @PapaJohns why did you unfollow me. what did I do §
disappointed by lack of respect for the pope by the goofus brigade. i on the
other hand respect the mans ass cheeks. i respect the mans legs § nice sydney
opera house you got here. would be a shame it if were to become the the sydney
Gamer house... § ironing my suspender straps and treating them with powders...
in the privacy of my study...making the nit wits and losers absoltuley furious
§ always looking for exciting new up and comers in the realm of breathtaking
digital online content to block § i wish i had the motorcycle from tron so i
ccoud drive home to my house and fuck the plastic bag i stole from good will §
EGYPTIAN PROTESTERS AIRDROPPED 100000 COPIES OF " OW THATS WHAT I CALL MUSIC
VOLUME 7"... THE SINGLE GREATEST NTWICM ALBUM OF ALL TIME § pissed off; going
out in my front yard to pretend to choke on a candy bar and see if any of my
neighbors give a shit § im concerned that individuals are uploading images of a
sexual nature to the johnny bravo wiki . http://t.co/nxRaWhiv does law exist
anymore § shame on dailymail & nydailynews for posting my racist ball screenshot without giving credit https://t.co/tDHQ9W1M5f https://t.co/lHrGYPCGld §
oh this? just a little something i enjoy looking at in my house every day
https://t.co/a8iXuuGUHN § deray blocked me for no reason. if he wants to
challenge me i will absolutely prove im less racist than him. stay out of this
§ hey now, its super bowl http://t.co/yPbH9B8akK § resisting extreme amounts of
arrest § LIKE WANTING TO KNOW WHEN I GET TO SAVE BIG BUCKS FOR PENNYS ON THE
DOLLAR AND GET RICH CHEAP § michael CRAPSon § swinging my great grandfather's

nine iron around on my motorcycle and saying "Seniors Rule" every time i hit something § one of my avatars is a floating skull with a big dick and sometimes my other avatars suck the skull's dick § thats the worst bowl. the dogs shit everywhere and the referee makes like its a joke. its not a joke its disgusting. § how can i get my 50year old co-workers more interested in the indie gaming scene. how. *kicks trashcan* how. *punches car* how. *fires gun* § nobody told me that" doing donuts" was some car technique. up until now i thought that it was just another way to say you're eating donuts § BUSTING THROUGHG THE WALL OF KFC WHILE RUNNING ON TOP OF A GIANT ROLLING BARREL LABELLED "BEAK WASTE" , OVER THE HORIZON, GONE FOREVER § Q: Should I give my dog my last name? A: Absolutely not. Giving your dog your last name confuses it & dangers the integrity of the household § kim jong un Sir, we dont see eye to eye on many policy's. But I look forward to you recovering from being brain dead, so we can share a Beer § i woudl advise against "going commando", or wearing pants without underwear. the last time i did this i got a deep turd infection and died § i am a Doctor and a Lawyer who will teach u how to seduce women with rap music. my name... is not important. § IS IT TRUE THAT THE TSA WILL TOUCH MY DICK FOR FREE AT LITERALLY ANY AIR LINE § justin biber STILL hasnt wresponded to my Gonzo literature concerning the false link between hiv and aids § im onto you r fucked up tricks, go home and sit on the toilet § saw a bumper sticker "My other car is baby Yoda's dick." And this is what passes for classic comedy routines these days . § NET PERVERSION >>>>> BAD <<<<<< MURDER   ^   NEW LIGHT BULBS § oh, youvve read a few academic papers on the matter? cute. i have read over 100000 posts. § i think my goal in life is to start a football team named "The Baseball Preferrers" and our gimmick is to get as many penalties as possible § stunning: mindful adult , decked out in complete set of riot gear - takes out entire stampede of horses using wisdom and tactic's § @CheetosArabia thank you officer § *glances towards framed calligraphy print on wall which reads " ASCAR First" and nods goodly. * § COOL PIC FOUND, CRAMMED UNDERNEATH THE DRAWERS OF MY DESK AT WORK FOR PERHAPS A DECADE http://t.co/IairzdxR § your website claims to have been "running the internet since 2001", which cannot be true because its bad § i hate it when doctors say Shit like "Take two and call me in the morning" . why dont yoy take two kisses of the butt crack of my ass § MicropenisRodney; if youre out there, anywhere plesse get in touch with me, im sorry I yelled at you and I wamt to fix our ragecomic startup § everyone send me indie films about uncancelling "wild hogs 2" and i promise to project them onto my garage door. no cussing or nude, plaese. § when the legendary CBS comedy lineup comes on, i simply turn it off. Know why? Ive been pissed off too much times to care. Does it Shock you § dont say of this § invented in god in Year 666, my sickening Ass was tasked with torturing insubordinate angels until it fell into the hands of the shit prince § "Rock and Roll Kevin is named that because of his extensive knowledge of Rock and Roll music." § go ask a sex account . keep your paws off of me § .@ SouthwestAir GAVE U JOKERS $9990 1ST CLASS ROUND TRIP AND UR LOUSY TAXPAYER FUNDED TSA AGENT HAND JOB HAS LEFT ME BLISTERED & UNDESIRABLE § THank u all, for sharing the Online experience with me. Pretty damn good if i do say so my self. Aahh, just breathe it in. I'm illiterate § just saw another Uncensored Ass in the audience. im finished with this horse shit. #oscars #AssInTheAudience #Oscars2012AITA § my name id yogi. greetings from albania. i would like to put the new i pad in jail. thank you for reading to my message. § #peakMale #godPerformance https://t.co/dAkLaDOaGD § people think today is a good day to talk about the oscars. Wrong. Today we are honoring all of my girl followers who have ever died. § the face i make WHen https://t.co/URwBMYkjSp § bow to your new denim god § i know im a dumb ass for expecting a serious response from the chucklefuck brigade, but can someone please tell me if im circumcised or not § @Bubbaburger take this one down too § thank you for getting me mny coffee

§ for $500, i'll follow oyu on here and steal your best posts. this is an excellent way to get your foot in the door if you ask me § i dont see any problem with getting the Milkbone vaccine. i trust milk bone even though they are usually a dog food company § My Sucked Off Life § you are my commander and ch ief... always.. always.. http://t.co/CNFNFSGDrw § whoever put "give skeleton huge titty" in the suggestion box: first off, this isnt a suggestion box. its a toys for tots bin. secondly; § dont even know how people are able to engage Thought Leaders on here with all these trollsters, hoopla rousers and clowny boys running loose § grandma knit me a nice warm pair of gamer gauntlets so i don't mess up my knuckles when i punch holes in the wall § senator rich blumenthal (D-CT) just threw a towel over the parkour mans head. game over, earth is dead § i may be the worst person you ever met but that doesnt mean i don't have a fool proof plan to fix every hollywood movie franchise ever made § #ThingsThatKeepMeAwakeAtNight 62% of teens report achieving a "sexual thrill" by committing acts of violence, up from 38% in 1992 #Rasmussen § before i Smoke, i want to read an article about if smoking is facing a crisis in which smokers are making smoking too much "About them" § all good boys keep a jar of sulfuric acid at their station to punish themselves for sending horny dms or goig offbrand.. just a drop will do § You'll Never Believe Which JP Morgan Executive Utterly Eviscerate Fitness Blogger Moms Flat Stomach Selfie #WeirdNews #CoolButWeird #Offbeat § the fool tries to make one million dollars.... but the wise man knows that its much easier to make $0.000001 dollars one trillion times § the wise man bowed his head solemnly and spoke: "theres actually zero difference between good & bad things. you imbecile. you fucking moron" § THE GOLDEN EMBEZZLER #illegalDogBreeds § watch "The Mentalist" on cbs and learn how to manipulate human minds like putty then use this info to make severe fucked up posts § this has gone too far. im closing my account until people stop accusing me of being mad. i will also spend most of my time offline laughing § http://t.co/eeDclSQW "Fucking lame" "awfully done, not even funny" "Awful" "100% not a ragecomic" § all sports is the same § i love shit that isnt "For" me § most undergarments were invented and popularized by religious folk who deemed that jeans and denim were too sacred to touch the ass directly § mods!! mods! one of those obscene low follower count boys stole a lick from the delicious lolly that Father bought me!! ah! how dreadful ! § come. I SHall lead the charge against corrupt Game developers, (Falls face forward ansd a variety of ass medicines spill out of my clothing) § the old dog one featured a twistedly brutal amount of blackface thoguh § my Rat Chant: Begone, RAT! You disgrace my home! I will not let you SHIT on my floor! My power is beyond your comprehension! Now, perish! § i would value my semen at a respectable $140 per gallon woth a 98% accuracy rating . #WhatsThatLoadWorth § in light of his posts from 2008 endorsing the Mummys curse i no longer support WhiteDarthMaul or his dream of becoming a Waiter § ive decided that the idea of "Baths" sucks. yeah i really want to spend an hour laying down next to my toilet. stupid ass. Suck off me § THe Eagles is a team of football who i respect & admire. Their commitment to touchdowns is good. They are athletic when it comes to sports § we'll see who's me soon enough § nobody with less followers than me should be allowed to block me.   Thats fucked up § pissed thr fuck off by "Dub step" § sponsors are telling me not to post them. but idont give a fuck. im sick of being pushed around. this is my account & thats the bottom word § WHAT HAPPENS TO THE SHIT -GOES BELOW GROUND AND ASSIMILATES WITH ROTATING MASS KNOWN AS "SUBTERRANEAN SHIT EARTH"- PROOF THAT HELL ISNT REAL § most wont type this § The holidays are a difficult time for many people. Please call everyone you know and tell them their dick is normal looking § how to say "doh" simpson tutorial How to say "Doh" like homer info how to say "Doh" instructions on how to say "Doh" § yeah im the uncool one. meanwhile im going to go jerk off to a picture of my wife while counting my Tuxedo's. Later § as hte real life #AlexFromTar-

get, i'd like to thank you all for liking the picture of me,aand announce my
support for president jeb bush2016 § i got a big wet piece of corn and the cob
in my bindle and i cant wait to run it over with my truck after im done chewing
on it § OTHERS: Oh your a main stream account? Let me suck your dick Hurp
Guklp Gulp ME: I oont give a shit if an account is mainstream or indie . § " I
DO, IN FACT, REFER TO MY TWEETS AS 'CONTENT', AND BY CHRIST MY LORD THERE ARE
RECORDINGS OF ME DOING SO " - TOP BRAND ENGINEER "AT DRIL" § messages like
this; i dont even look at it. i dont look at it § ^^^^^^^^^^^^^^ Found The
Mother FUCKER who thinks Blowing up RVs is good........................ §
TTNR was sponsored by shitty ruby tuesday, which led ultimately to its down-
fall. Boy's Thought's is sponsored by salem cigarettes § @TruthPointDWR
unprofessional. go fuck your self and sotp being such a little BITCH § i just
tipped over my garbage can and tried to feng shui all the trash. i dont know
if it worked or not but im still fat § some say if you show your ass to the
hell mirror you will feel the icy finger of the reaper touch the back of your
bals § http://t.co/rsNjhZxJ philosopher Gottfried Leibniz theorized that ours
is the best of all possible worlds. and im inclined to agre § Get some. Get
some. Yeah . Yeah § genderless milf`s § buiying up all the graphics cards and
making them cost over $1000 so i can computer generate my own new episodes of
"Arli$$" § turning a big dial taht says "Racism" on it and constantly looking
back at the audience for approval like a contestant on the price is right § "˜†
˜… One day, Miss Hannah Minx escaped from an anime cartoon and started teaching
Japanese on Youtube. ˜† ˜… ãƒ¼(*ã,œ-½ã,œ*)ãƒŽãƒŸ" me too. that;s me § ACCOUN-
TANT: I Just don't know how you can justify donating $700 to "Chips Ahoy" ME: i
hope your car flips & becomes your fucking firey grave § verizon wireless usa
promotes an nfl tweet but refuses to support indie sports like hockey and
soccer. meanwhile, my life is in the garbage § I despise Flinstone. § my posts
are top niotch and i keep myself clean § some brand writes a few checks and
gets shit like "#XmenDay" trending while i struggle to riase awareness for me
buying an above ground pool § my booming voice echoes from the depths of your
recently flushed toilet. " ICE TURDS IDIOT. HA HA HA" § @McDonalds @McDonalds
and so me & the boys have invented "the mcshitter". a fictional man who jumps up
on tables and shits all over the customers meals § the asimo robot is full of
rats. nobody ever washes it § no im boycotting the jpeg image format because it
showed me an ass § this is what a real mans hands look's like http://t.co/
yjLlfqOi24 § im upset because nobody wants to market anything to my ultra
fucked up demographic § gotta go name brand. it is non toxic and not actually
made of shit so it is fine to drink. § looks fucking dumb https://t.co/2IBzeoom-
He § just did my 1000 jumps at the jumping gym. i could tear a mans fucking
head off, with my leg § i posted on here earlier about how ihad a leather belt
wrapped around my nuts and not a single person asked if i was ok. Fuck you §
im constantly expanding § alan dershowitz once tried to defend me in court by
pulling out a pocket pussy and insisting he would never fuck it. we lost the
case § yes!!! holy shit! § pevrert § go ahead and have your precious "laugh".
just know that little guiy has saved my life countless times § the popular
tursday night rant feature has concluded for today. check out the new one next
thursday. it will appear on this feed. § *homepage § i get emails. i get emails
saying the trolls have won, and that i should bow to them, since i have lost
the battle. to this i say FAT-CHANCE § @bag_getter thank you for your service §
All girls have exactly $100,000 § i would rather go fuck my self than read one
more post on the bird websitw § taking my "Gamer medicine" (Games) § NETFLIX
DIAPER NOW #WOAH#Real § this faker is puttinh me through hell. but i can see
through his lies. i can tell he is not me § change your godgdamn name clown @
WayneHooter § when people fuck with me on sites i head for the beach and take
it out on the crabs. i punch their shitty little bodies, i kick dirt at them §
to truly under stand the #gamergate ... we must first ask ourselves.... "What..

Is.. Gamer...” **gazeing into the fire place* § once they put out a unicode symbol depicting a tiny ass i anticipate that the jokers & miscreants on here will use it for criminal purpouse. § @AlGiordano al digiorno please stop uyour cowardly efforts to defame this delicious treat § thius is not said nearly enough by all you ungrateful, unappreciative fucking jackals on here, but thank you @CNN. Thank you for the news § Joe the plumber- your silence duringt his pivotal moment of election speaks magnitude of the word “Cowardace”. i regret voting for you bitch § dirty jobs man tcame to my house today with camera crew and a bunch of diapers. i said no § im a proud member of an elitist clique which spawned from the entenmann’s bakery product support forums back in the early ‘00s § sorry for funko politics § some dumb asses of life just need a damn “BRAIN “ § reported. lock um up § unloading an entire belt of ammo at me with a minigun or some such device will now get you “Blocked” § might siphon a bunch of free flu shots into a big fake arm an d bottle it up and sell it for $5 § the year is 2041 and im still using an older version of twitter that won’t be around for much longer § the barbecue shaman liberally applies a garlic &herb dry rub to his dick and ass - in order to prepare himself for the barbecue perils ahead § i’ve been spat upon. i’ve been dragged through the streets. i’ve been pissed on to the Nth degree. all for the sake of making good ass posts § if you don’t know how to use a Lathe you deserve to eat dog shit § farm fresh signature homegoods dick sucker § if you are a HATER you have 24 hours to confess to being a hater and apologize and pull your pants down so every one can see your dick § been driving in circles with the wife & kids since 3am trying to find a place that will service my denim and we’re all yelling at each other § http://t.co/fbrGwofqcK announcin,g in 2016 my new brand alliance with cool arab man § the idea of saying “Oh, Absolutely. Absolutely” in the demonius voice every time i bust my load has suddenly become very good to me § “gamer cock is in demand” Girls are saying this § big gov shut down tomorrow “U Know What That Means” Jacking off: LEGAL get your jacking off paraphernalia ready its gonna be a Barn burner § if each of my followers send me 1 rag i might be able to clean up all the messes in my house § if ur wrestling coach calls himself “mr feet pics” and has pictures of feet all over his office, break his trophies for dishonoring the game § yeah lets all j ust sit here and pretend everythin’gs ok while dick vitale sells his body to the wendy’s corporation for big buck § me and SnakeMom1956 are in love and we are laughing at all of th e peuople who th1nk that our flintstones themed wedding is a sham § i have cut @ AsexualFilmAnalysis out of my twuitter feed, because my doctor told me if i nod in agreement one more time my spine will rupture § shut the fuck up § well i hate it. fuck chefs § (spends all of 7 seconds skimming some blog posts) yep. just as i knew all along. having pnuamonia is good § donlad trump reportedly says that normal type pokemon are a waste of time. they’re just dirty birds & rats who have no right being a pokemon § god grant me the serenity 2 accept the Diapers i cant change, the courage to change the Diapers i can, & the wisdom to shit myself profusely § , Fuck you !! § why are you wearing a sailor’s outfit around inside of your own house you fuck face § the harlam shake SUCKS! § me and a couple of straight dudes are sharing this big bowl of wildberries in honor of davy jones the dead guy § I SO MUCH AS DIP MY NECK AROUND THIS LOG PAGE AND I AM FORCED TO ABSORB GALLONS OF VENOM FROM DISRESPECTFUL CIVILIAN VIPER SWINE #StopTheNSA § taking 3.5 million foot and mouth disease infected pigs and burying them alive in a massive landfill in sotuh korea. Good or bad § my body is 70% water mother fucker. guns cannot harm me § ived hacked into your beeper, champ. enjoy your inopportune beeping § Im going to erase this you god damn loony tune § printing out some article like “25 Things You Must Never Say to a Smoker” and pasting it to my car and cutting off girls so they can read it § herees what I say to those who think im having a goof on here (presses button on wristwatch & tiny pair of shades launches onto face) im Not § you think my bowtie looks nice? no it doesnt! i look like SHIT!! you dont know anything about Mens attire. youre only saying that to FUCK me § Im goig to drive a nail through my cock to promote ABC's "The Middle"", and I will be paid $18 for doing it. § Use Cappital Letters Please § let me slip into something more comfrotable *dives between the sofa cushions and disappears* § im so sorry you had to go through that.... i apologize on behalf of all guys who dump huge bags of turds and piss off of overpasses § "the key to making that steak sizzle is to get a nice dry rub from your dry rub man, and prayer. prayer fucking owns" - sun tzu or some shit § I am selling 10,000 of my followers to @ CampBowWow for Nine Cents. Starting tomorrow you will be following @CampBowWow instead of me. Bye § @DrOz love your show § I'm Sgt. General James Bond. My mission is to collect guns and gather intel on the unimaginably fucked up drugs known as Cocaine & Marijuana § straight up-- im not here to make friends. im not here to socialize. im here because this is the only professional Mr. Bucket league in town § "What if we all took a page from You Tube, and removed the dislike bar, of real life. " - The Wanderer (Me) § someone on here just called me a "Cunk" because my wife wont let me buy a harp § @Oprah Please Help Me, A Shaman Told Me My Future Daughter Will Be Born Autistic, I Simply Cannot Afford This In My Life, Oprah Please Help § they will kick my ass for saying it. they will take my career and my livelihood away from me. but "Wine" , is better than, "The News" § between the gun & the blade.. throwing knives are the "Best of both worlds" when it comes to eliminating thousands of home intruders at once § everyone cuts their arms and legs off in the future because all you have to do is say "computer fetch me my Posts" and itll do it § #MentionSomeoneCute-AndBeautiful raynn the hedgehog. akira the hedgehog. mydnyght the hedgehog. venus the polaer bear. gomez the hedgehog. § no im screaming § taco bell is all too eager to implement fourthmeal BUT has yet to acknowledge Fourthgender. the almighty dollar folks § waking up in a cold sweat and screaming about needing one million dollars, the amount of money made famous by Dr. Evil in austin powers 1 . § how much money would have to be given to FOX executives in order to make the dancing football robot say "lets kiss some nerds dicks" on tv § haivng the xbox controller vibrate in my lap for 14 hours a day has rendered me sterile , low - t , and betagender § Yo Trolls: Maybe my jokes are bad because u create a hostile environment thatm akes me nervous. Maybe I piss my pants too. Maybe get a life § ladys i will not Fuck you if you smell like shit. look up darwin theory § People seem to think im a kind of nasty, shitty dog based off the way my posts are treated like dirt. Covid has turned you all into monsters § watchinh bottom of the barrel live streamer fail cringe compilations while i sit here and suck on an entire hoagie like a pacifier § looking forward to more lavish hollywood parties where me and a bunch of obese guys read posts like this while laughing in a hot tub https://t.co/igboYCyq3W § listen up i need u guys to go on my account and check out this post called "The Thursday Nite Rant" and dont forget to hit up that RT button § due to budget constraints the ground hog this year has been replaced by a caged man in a loincloth who also fears shadows § When Jordache designer diapers were manufctured in 1994, they "seemed to symbolize Jordache's descent in the marketplace to discount outlets § please continue it outside of my mentions you Ghouls § founnd a cicada skin stuck to my nefarious pud § if i learned anything in business school its that you can disarm any competitor by insinuating he carries his turds around in his briefcase § mount everest emergency diaper bra - what this husband did will shock you § still got my holographic Alan .. this sucker would go for $40 on eBay but i prefer kissing it every night and whispering "90es" #TopShelf90s § shut htte fuck up § my grandfathers last words on death bed "VEGAN STRAIGHT EDDGGGEEE" and then the entire hospital shook and he got better § i walk by. my shirt has the words "ALL I NEED IS" written on front. you're confused until you see the back of my shirt which says "MUDBIKES" § many people are finding out that despite millions of years of evolution the human body was not designed to get run over by cars § every one should donate their pets to the zoo or the dog kennel, get the animals out of the house until all this covid mess is figured out § thats disgusting § if your web site asks me for a coupon code i will never not put "RUDY" in the son of a bitch § i ask my followers not to look at my posts between the hours of 10:00-16:00 on may 12th douring which time i'l be freaking out for no reason § i hate it when im jacking off, and... And, uh,. thats it. thats the tweet § took some pics of my new satellite dish, but im not posting them until hatred annd cynicism are eradicated § it was just a dream... *notices bed is covered in Pogs and Pog Memorabilia* ..or WAS it? § " THIS USER IS IMMUNE TO ALL BAD FAITH LOONEY TOONS OPINIONS " § uk elecitons in full force!! lib dems vs Chavs; vote now and google the HECK out of ron paul § à¯µ¸à¯µ DOes Any One Want Neck Vids § i don't know anything about comedy. i specialize in arts & entertainment. § scarce, low quality content and an abundance of wrong opinions is the reason the cavemen went extinct. thats my beliefs bitch § i love saiyng shit like "Yow! This kittens got Claws!" whenever a woman stabs me 38 times in the neck and chest § feel as though the POST-COVID economy will mostly benefit me, the guy who makes tiny custom diapers for peoples beanie babies and funko pops § some animal just uploaded about 40 or so uncircumcised dicks to my feed so im unfollowing everyone who isnt a business man or a cop § Everoyone please. Stop sending in things like "Cum" when snack brands do the "guess the mystery flavor" contest. They will stop doing them § Dont postshit me. § i am skeptical of the concept "Too Big To Fail" mainly because i am extremely big and i fail constantly § 2017: writing shitty articles called like "Disruption: The Praxis of Chaos" 2018: saying astronauts put tubes up their ass to suck the turds out § im the guy who originally cooked up the "garden of eatin" joke. thats my bit. im just saying it out in the open here & now. trolls be damned § i will simply leave u to your circle jerk . § @ DunkinDonuts so i heard your Thailand outlets are FULLY owned and operated by Ladyboys... Any chance of you bringing this to the 'States? § hm maybe before we help Ladygagas Pit bulls we should find Chinese Investor "JACK MA" because i guess i still give a FUCK about HUMAN LIFE ! § I'll nmever click on anything. Never § looking at some pictures of dracula, § one thing I will Not tolerate on this site is users organizing and planning "Orgies", also known as Group Sex. § every 100 years ,the world votes for a new Bible, to replace the old one. i honourably submit: The Joe Dirt Novel, writen by Spade, as bibl. § if youve never written posts before, then shut the fuck up § two lives? this is fuckinh barbaric https://t.co/xvQqg3d5L0 § i believe our Good Troops will try really really hard to make sure that the next 100,000 human beings they exterminate are losers and nerds § im going to zap myself with a taser gun unitl u two stop fighting on my tl § a-list: time line b-list: group dm c-list: shit i yell in the car with the windows rolled up d-list: shit i say while melting down in court § PHANTOM LIMB PAIN #WHITEPEOPLEPROBLENMS § the police cut off my finger for sending my birth mark shaped like the under armor logo to the under armor social media manager unsolicited. § the guys who make steaks should make all of them "grade A" steak,. ythese guys have been making this shit for 1000 years, no more excuses § there's a series of codewords that will shut this website down permanently if ever tweeted, and those words are "this is twitter sparta". § had that dream again. a Top Female Influencer grasped my hand and took me to my Forever Home..where i never have to demean myself by posting § one thing the gamer world is certainly agreeing of, is that halo infinite is sure to be the highest numbered halo game yet § Was Going To Send Ur ScreenPlay To Mr Scorcese Until I Found Out U Were Part Of The Failshit Brigade Who Mocked My Seashell Necklace In 2010 § i think that big foot and mouth man have sons every 20 years or so and they make the son the next big foot or whatever § if u troll me into my 11th stroke by god i will use the last remaining strength on my death bed to

implicate you and your delinquent cronies § the itunes program is so complicated its like you gotta have a degree from nasa just to play sweet home Alabama.
§ for every bra yo u dont wear i will wear 3 Bras #NoBraDay § TODAY WE EXPLORE
THE PROVEN INTELLECTUAL ADVANTAGE OF CHILDREN WHO HAD GENERAL HOSPITAL FANFIC-
TION READ TO THEM IN THE WOMB § you aall act nice to me on this site but if i
needed $60,000 for saline injections all over my entire body none of you would
give a SHIT § #itsuckswhen my daughter gets mad at me for refusing to pay for
her dental work § id be easily bilked into signing up for a tgifridays credit
card if the waitress offered it. furthermore id get stains all over the contract
§ two bearded 55 yr old intellectuals, sitting opposite of each other in two
stately leather seats. musing upon the concept of a "Paper mario" § "Feel as
though ive evolved beyond the need for Product, and now crave the Customer
Experience" Hubert Joly: Boy have I got the shit for you § wiccan lawyer § Ow
!! Ouch!! Im sorry Jay!!! § im rwriting a script about a smart and handsome
army man cop who murders civilians but wants to stop murdering civilians
because hes in love § you call this a menu?? where the FUCK are the Heart
Healthy Essentials § i perceive everyone on this website as a dip shit § Oh you
like my Music? Wanna kiss my mouth on the fuckin lips? Is that interesting to
you? Is that interesting? Good luck with your White ass § goinh to stay inside
all weekend with my vast library of console releases. due to Wuhan § PigPiss-
Clyde hid in a bush for 2 hrs and took secret photos of PigPissLou wiping bird
shit off his windshield with a chipotle bag. Pure win, § thw most valuable icon
on any boys desktop... the famed "My Computer" icon. click that bastard and
youre good to go § no!! its all too much! § Fuck the fans! Fuck the fans!! §
what's that bitch?? you say twitter is a "vacuous cesspool of lackadaisical
platitudism"? yeah, i can make up words too: blublubludgyuhgh § i do not trust
this graph as it has clearly been doctored to look like a penis § the mayons
were basically dumb as dirt and couldnt even predict the fuckin 9/11 thing § i
dont like dumb asses either § you don't need to tell me im beautiful because
boys are out here doing it for them self this year § judge dredd kicks the
doors of the wtc mosque wide open and says "Well this looks like a big bunch of
crap to me " § punxsutawney phillip seymour hoffman sees the shadow of death
meaning 6 weeks of really good jokes like this one § thw most important 'win'
button i have ever clicked § (band plays me on stage, wearing tux) The
constitution grants me the right to eliminate those I deem disloyal to our
nation (light laughter) § any good jokes lately? yeah, the mirror. i mean your
mirror. i mean your mirror, while you are standing in front of it & i'm not in
the room § i rise; spreading my arms, exuding fluorescent spheres of energy,
each representing an Unfollower, Cuasing me a great deal of pain,Screaming § @
the_ironsheik "The Philly Phanatic" § jay leno was the last good boy on tv. he
was my final connection to th e outside world. there is nothing stopping me from
becoming feral now § Enjoying my life https://t.co/rHHJghScPC § im husband to
him § GOURP OF TEEN GIRLS RESURRECT DALE EARNHARDT IN SLEEPOVER DARE, EARNHARDT
RUNS FROM THE PREMISES NUDE, COVERED IN ECTOPLASM, YET TO BE FOUND § another
cheap N' easy halloween spook: sculpt a giant skull out of ground beef and
splash blood on it and drive it around on top of your car § when i go to
hooters i do not want to look at the girls there, just my newspaper that does
not have any eye holes cut into it what so ever § fake people love getting mad
at me. Has any one noticed this § its TGIF which means im imposing the Pussy
Eater 's Challenge on to my page. its mostly self explanatory & if you fail it
youre fucking dumb § *waches the Race War unfold in filthy computer chair,
multiple tabs open, cnn msnbc, gawkrer, salon, milk duds** now THis is some
good shit, § doing pretty good with thre posts today. might try to pound out a
few more before sundown, but it remains to be seen if i will "Blow it" § PLEASE
at least look up "Event Horizon" on wikipedai before you chastise me for
screaming it on 9./11 § oh? you want me to take the bad santa posters off my car

windows? sorry, i forgot that its a fucking fedearal crime to think things are good § (g uy runs me over in a pick up truck and breaks my ribs and twists my fucking legs off) Oh thats cringde! § i was spending my PTO from the fake raybans factory getting Stabbed in washington dc while you were all busy looking at dicks in cyber punk. § i fuucking love being sent to Juvie Hall § jsut tried to climb onto the stage shirtless with "INDIE" painted on my body but a sniper murdered me off-cam . #Oscars § u know irt's a Monday when you rear-end a cop car and your trunk pops open, launching 500 or so jars of piss onto another cop car behind you § president obama orders assassination of the man who holds a "COWBOY ISNT REAL" sign outside of the longhorn steakhouse § im little jesica. im dying because of obamas help care bill. im on my death bed and the doctor is ignoring me because my dady works hard § justl had to unfollow about six people for tweeting during the official Beggin Strips Moment of Silent Reflection § Not. All. Of. The. Wet. Spots. On. My. Jeans. Are. Piss. Stians. § the next big online thing is men who eat Dog Food, schedule meetups to eat dog food together and form rivalries with cat & baby food eaters § Theres a guy standing outside lennys pastrami shop. Says hes going to goon your ass § fuck sars § DICK CLARK CORPSE MARIONETTE TO KICK OFF NEW YEARS 2013 WITH MIRACULOUS POST-MORTEM COUNTDOWN - WE TRULY ARE A BLESSED NATION § Had it up to here witht the chuckle crew. If you think my posts are bullshit I challenge you to come waterboard me and destroy me perfectly. § the next step in human evolution is to cover your body in Rage Face tattoos and point to them instead of displaying emotions the normal way § i am getting hundreds of messages telling me that the thursday nite rant is very bad. i am contracted to produce them until june 2015. sorry § commercial idea for Michelob Ultra--a bumbling imbecile ransacks his apartment to find the guy who took a dump in his glass of michelob ultra § me and the boys watching james bond morph into a black guy before our very eyes , and braying at the movie screen like distressed cattle § it may seem that cops are all fucking dumb, bad at IQ tests, etc, but they only pretend to be, to lull crooks into a false sense of security § pretty good tweet but not as good as this one. wow what a bargain https://t.co/Z6XtB1BCmp https://t.co/X0c0PLKzYE § please check out my piece in TIME magazine "Why i sold my dog at a carnival for $30 and Why it matters" the worst article ever written § GagBlog.Eu // 12 Most Awkward Honor Killings // The Ten Beer Commandments // Sex Mom Debunks LIBOR Scandal // GagBlog.Eu § Coach Klein. Nice suit! #waterboyWednesday § I Just Want 2 Have Sex On This Site All The Time With Out Havin To Argue With Peopl And Deal With People Cryin And Shit #WiseWordsToLiveBy § people on here treat me like dirt , thats fine, meanwhile hundreds of teens are allowed to go to prom racistly every day § #jan25 also happens to be the biblically foretold fall of the middle east you fucking waste of kidneys § need one of those janet jackson sun shaped nipple rings to protect my stupid-ass pud from hell cherubs § kit kats.. potato chips.. air fresheners.. Hey! who remembers when the gas station, sold GAS!!! § Give a Man a Cool Beachball With the Hard Rock Cafe Logo on it and He will teach a fish to swim for u § muscle milk?? i make my own, thanks. *REVEALS A PERFECT ROW OF NIPPLES ON LEFT BICEP WHILE SOME SERIOUSLY RIPPED DUDES LINE UP FOR A TASTE* § #TshirtSlogans all musliums boycott dogfood § The Saturday morning ramble is Work Safe. Children are also allowed to enjoy it. The Thursday nite rant is vulgar and unleashed § based on the level of rhetoric ive seen, Its almost as if all the girls on this site actually WANT bit coin (BTC) to fail. There i said it . § my perfectl #TwitterWifey is a leather sack full of porcelain shards that i can swing at census takers § comedy is more import-ant than ever. thats why all my single lady followers shoud move into my house & kiss me on the mouth--It would be funny § currently on a car ride with 8BitMarcus, who just tried to use the defroster to clean bird poop off of the window. what a dumb piece of shit § want to see big legs. want to see big legs

§ kfc sextuple down is back. pieces of lettuce and tomato encased in perfect cube of processed bird. "The most vile fucking thing imaginable" § plop all feeds with adult content on them right straight into the trash can. twitter is a bussiness site . § a football jersey with "BAD SON" as the player's name found in a dumpster § i see this well has run dry. time to saddle up and mosey along #TheProcess http://t.co/jwCXvyIsqQ § MAIN STREAM MEDIA: why do all your jack o lanterns have a hole in the back thats the exact circumference of your dick ME: no further queston § INTERVIEWER: do you have customer service experience ME: if I catch a customer shoplifting I will serve him a knock out. I will own his life § im an exhausting person to be around but once you get to knnow me im actually a giant shithead with irredeemable mouth § blocked. blocked. blocked. youre all blocked. none of you are free of sin § adult man stuck in glue trap given a stern talking-to from his rich uncle § this web site sucks my fucking dick. it sucks balls (they add the 280 characters) you blew it. this website sucks shit now § congress members fighting over who can scream "halo 5" the loudest, until a senior member stands up and yells "halo 6", infuriating them all § sign em off log em out log em out sign em off sign em off log em out   Raw Hide (whip noise), § Ass big on my story § the thursday nite rant isn't going anywhere. the saturday morning ramble is designed to work in tandem with it to cover broader demographics § girls love rolling around in their sleep with long nails and waking up thinking every scratch on their body was caused by their dead grandma § noticing a lot more rear collisions after adhering my "9/11 Was An Inside Doge" bumper sticker. people must be too busy laughing to pay attn § entering Crisis Mode after doing one of the bath salt jokes from 2013 & getting clapped backed by a girl saying bath salts are good actually § Believve it or not, some people would rather play in a Ball pit, than play in an Orchestra pit. and thats why society has crapped on it self § feel as thoguh our nation, our world, is closer than ever, to Christ, with KFC's recent announcement that they are to turn birds into wine., § The Vagina Monologues, But For Gamers § grinning like a shit eating bastard on the bus because i found the exact combination of words that will obliterate budweiser when i tweet it § they should make web 2.0 slot machines that show the faces of your loved ones instead of shit like cherrys, the number 7, and the word "Bar" § a 3x3 inch picture of my dirty teeth, framed ornately and hung on the wall of a mafia-owned jiffy lube waiting room in louisville, kentucky. § taking the great Hot Water Challenge in the sky § Penis Rant - come see the all-time famous "Penis Rant" § auh yeah ! !! http://t.co/FLU9MRb5dn § and folks.. we cant forget aobut Tennis Shoes (Audience boos.) Are you Tennis, or are you shoes? Who'd'y'a'think'ya're ? (Applause) § back in 2008 or whatever i made the decision not to make $1 billion off of bit coins because i knew the shit would become hipster § advising everyone on this dumb ass website not to block me to ensure that my sub par written word can reach your grubby shit smeared devices § legalize my stench § Jacking off is a fool 's errand. I will instead opt to enjoy the films of Ice Age, Ice Age: The Meltdown and Ice Age: Dawn of the Dinosaurs. § pass the savings onto me mother fucker § the writiers of 2020 have pooped their pants on this one.„¢ © DRIL   more Netflix? yes please „¢ © DRIL § ive hired 3 of my clumsiest dumb ass followers to spy on my wife and uncover her plots against me, just the worst bumbling fucking imbeciles § level 4 Smoker § im not obligated to respond to thits shit. § just spent the last 10 minutes fishing a pubic hair out of the toilet to avoid any nasty phone calls from the boys at the sewage plant § enjoying some fucked up thoughts of some boys enjoying the real counter culture shit... such as drinking coffee, and being glad it's friday § Thats not a signature bread. Thats a normal bread § im prety random *files tax return with a green pen* § If U Ever Contact My Daughetr Again I Will Call My Lawyer And We'll Kick Your Tiny Weird Shaped Head Around The Court Room § a gun that is also a boomerang § hell ill dry rub anything.

an unpeeled banana. fruit gushers. all contain a latent power which begs to be unleashed by a superb spice blend § Q: my dog is addicted to opiates. i need help of this best answer (voted 4 times): sorry but i m afraid of dogs because they murdered my son § the basketball version of a home run is when you throw a basketball really hard at the roof and get it stuck in the rafters some how § http://www.wholesale-dress.net/images/201007/1279062232632831559.jpg my shirnt and floor § Damn true, this § another ass kisser of ouctomom = Erase and MOve on § back in the nice days, youd go to th e barbershop and theyd serve you a full seven course meal during your haircut. not like today my friend § im he nice man.. who celebrates all the saints who DOnt have holidays... and not just 1 day a year.. #Bless § i attribute the complete failure of my brand to the actions of detractors, oor my "trolls", as it were, as well as my own constant fuckups § danzeisen: i need the logo to be a shitting ass quigley: but were a sports company danzeisen: draw that ass up pronto http://t.co/HFI2PaIDUG § dont shit me § what if you took jethro tull "aqualung" & replace the parts where he says aqualung with "octomom" #BeyondFuckedUp #Sponsored @sheratonho-tels § hank williams jr fired from his new job of yelling in front of a chrysler dealership for calling esteemed justice sonia sotomayor a Swindler § my followers want more pics of me smoking.   my followers want more pics of me genuflecting infront of my honda like a fucking moron § This is what some of you mother fuckers look like when you reply to my posts https://t.co/gfZY3Va8tR § if i had the technical expertise to make "rage comics", i would do one about the cop who caught me trying to take my computer into the sewer § juust not in the mood for content today... not while my fellows are being hunted down in the street like dog 's just for preferring Blu Ray- § some of my friends on here are "CLASSIC STYLE" hucksters who'd scam their own mothers for a quick buck. And you all Love them & follow them.. § one, of, the , reasons, my, dick, is, not, good, is, because, there, are,. stains, on, it, § the reason my posts are no good is your all too busy sucking your own Dick to punish me § im talkin about Boy Shit, stuff that lil peenypoppers like you wouldnt understand, no w go home before you done get hurd!!!!!!! § nboody has ever requested that u log in. § i want a medical expert to hook me up with those scissor that cut all your clothes off in like 2secs because im a large man & its a struggle § if youre reading this NascarDustin, you are requested to appear in court for the crime of firing 600 chi needles into my innocent ass cheeks § crawling on all fours like the cave men - enhanced mobility -powerful stance (can not be knocked over) - pretty good § priest plugs my coffin in at the end of the funeral. "MILLERTIME" lights up in neon on the side, desecrating my corspe & sending me to hell § girl let me tell you i dont normally send sexual messages on here. but you look like the" juggys" from the man show § A MAD TYRANT has cracked the admin password for IRC chatroom #DiaperIsrael -- the entirety of DARKNET is in peril § keep your eyes off my Stats § obama needs to stop writing constitutions or whatever and help my failing business sell rat hair to imbeciles § lying on my back, screaming like a wildman while my trolls graze my balls with a spinning bicycle tire § "multi verse" fuck your self. you're only allowed to have one universe per costumed dipshit. absolutely none of this is my problem § Hm lets see. Do I "Shut the fuck uop", or continue exposing the truths of life to the chagrin of the 99% of people on earth who are villains § the girls on this site constantly beg me to show them a picture of the clothes i wear while posting. this is them. https://t.co/1EUP0gwFq4 § who will be brave enough to create a 3d motion picture about talking guns. who will let the guns tell their story § unlock your account and show the world the vile shit you are saying to me you ghoul § requesting preorder status on "Def Comedy Jam Tennis" - PS4 - Release Date: 7/8/15 (JPN) , TBA (USA) § "ah boo hoo hoo i want to post Foul comments to content leaders" Fat Chance, Dimwit. I will annihilate you under bulwark of the Law and God. § 2016... NEed I say absolute shitting more? § @

dril first § They locked it because you fucked around and fond out § i dont know about you guys but my uncle has been dying to meet all your uncles. did somebody say twitter dot com uncle meet????? § .@ToiletHelper hasn't tweeted yet. @CumDragon hasn't tweeted yet. @ShitLad hasn't tweeted yet. @Fat666 hasn't tweeted yet. @CleanUncle hasn' § six years ago today george washington carver invented a penut #MyBlackHistory #YourBlackHistory § sunnyDayKitten98: just noticed you posted "Ted Lesbo" on the time lione. Is everything ok? ME: Go away. I dont want you to see me like this. § my promise to all women: my promise to all women is that i will seal theur nudes in a velvet envelope, and wont open it until im 100 yrs old § hitler also owned three beautiful cobra's § he hid the facts § "you just want to exorcise the royal soul from your dog so itll grant you 3 wishes. you dont care about haiti or its princes" Wrong actually § my advisor has told me that instead of trying to "Game the markets" i need to put all my money in 1 of those tall banks shaped like a crayon § wow how about instead of spitting that moutwash down the drain you spit it on your chest and rub it allover your self #TimesRunningOut § considering referring to my feed ,from now on, as "The Signature Collection," at casual get-togethers, mensa meetings, etc § http://i4.ytimg.com/bg/gJUGbv5vqAHxfFUry8nbMA/140. jpg?app=bg&v=4bce40b5 this shall adorn m y fucking tombestone. § day of healing challenge: Try being racist for a day if your sjw, and if youre racist try being SJW. This is the "Day of Healing Challenge". § @mtn_dew @TacoBell SEND TACO BELL YOUR DICK § im glad i made that post and wrote it and thought of it. im glad it belongs to me § enya on full blast.. accessing 100 sites per minute § "i Fucking do it all -- For the fans..." - Dril § in the fucked up world of golf , last place is actually good § yoou win, trolls . you fucking win. i will now lie face down in the town center so you can all harvest my goddamn organs § smokinh crack cocaine will turn you in to a dumb ass but it also has a 1% chance to turn you into a genius. thats how i become "KING" § (shows up at new media seminar with a chunk of wooden fence stuck around my neck and a bunch of stray animals following me) sorry every one § desperately trying to start a conversation at dragoncon by flaunting a timepiece § http://t.co/QV7adxO1 Im Starting A Blog For Disabled People Calle d 3DWorldz ANd U Can Create "Worldz" & "Tars" And Sell Them 2 Businessmen, § Hats Off to the guy who digitally altered all the celebrities to make them look less sad #Oscars § @pepsi how many pepsi points will I score if I change my avatar to pepsi logo § this is superbly against all laws § holy shit. holy shit. you can order loaves of kfc. you can order kfc in loaf form. you can order kfc by the loaf #ByTheLoaf § #ThingsPeopleHaveToStopDoing eating disgusitng garbage food and being miserable sacks of shit and bemoaning the fact that theyre worthless § dismal reception f or Little Fockers raises 1 important question: What can you and I do to keep The "Fockers" Brand sizzling into 2011?? § just obliterated a birds nest with a weedwacker becsuse it could see me jacking off in my house at a certain angle § you dress like fred flintstone and your opinion to me is worth dog dick § well im sad to announce that the meme quilt project has been cancelled. someone has already jacked off on it instead of adding their patch § restaurants should bring back smoking sections but for jacking off, and if you don't like that idea yiou can just sit in the normal sections § it is absolutely impossible to leave smartass comments on my page and lead a happy, fulfilling life at the same time. i need to believe this § "The posts are good, the posts are fun, but theres a message under there that makes you think about the Wieght of the Human Condition."-Dril § sorry. my "wrestle a pile of huge dildos for charity" event was a total imbroglio. all proceeds raised must now go towards my hospital bill § im waiting for all the celebs to weigh in before i can offer my official verdict on tthe controversial flag of the confederacy. § you've ruined my life. Thank you § i am a classically tragic dumb ass hwo has the burger king logo imprinted in my brain like a baby bird to its mother § once again, dick clark's diaper drops miserably around his ankles precisely at the stroke of midnight, signifying a grim year to come #2012 § the first step to becoming a Millionaire is to acquire one hundred dollars § none f you know anything about art or life. i have read the entire dictionary more than 100 times § http://t.co/lXs1ebLULn Fight For Your Brand § why did he remove th arby's reference though. arb'ys is one of the most influential brands of 2013. hes a madman § stand down, citizien § as a Race-Minded simpsons fan it pains me to declare that korean animators have no right to draw pictures of black people, or vice versa § i went to a long john silvers once § please remember to click on the things i post here to see how many favs they got and to sneak a peek at the buzz that they are generating. § contest my spine with a gun § considering improving the quality of my posts somewhat, so i can get the MacArthur Genius Award, for them § One Hundred Percent Yes § i want to be responsible for getting carly rae jespen into cigarettes just so i can be sure she's taking a christian brand § @JuddPDeere45 @WhiteHouse @AriFleischer cant wait for this shit. Im a real sick fuck § the soldier yanks a perfect pair of blue jeans out from a pile of ashes while surveying a burned out truck. may god damn these perfect jeans § "i hope this shitty mustsache makes my face look less fat (It wont)" - some guy § i poisoned it for laughs § my fucking content is flawless. you fucking bozoes have gone too far with this shit. youre the one who looks ridiculous; not me § inner dipaer absorbing the brunt of it, mid-diaper locking down any and all "Stragglers", outer diaper "The courtesy diaper" for the fans... § before the holy ghost died--- there was the father, the son and TacoBellMaven § somebody send me .xml file detailing the satanic rituals that Abercrombie and Fitch CEO Mike Jeffries employs to retain his eternal beauty § @ CapsCop NOPE § i refuse to go to work until sex is eliminated. are we still doing the sex strike jokes. well thats my one § muscle economy, muscles as currency, end the dollar, get ripped, get rich pumping weights, weatlh = body size, predicted by Blaise Pascal § craping out a single sunflower seed and frowning while i inspect it § it's spelled "Suge Knight", grandma. you've fucked up again § im the sex principal. i have sex all the time in the techer lounge. i fuck the lady teachers & i fuck the man teachers. im all fat and shit. § dont make me jump over that fuckinh counter and teach your low wage chefs the difference between "Extra" and "Double" meat ball § ;i help girls now § FBI AGent: We have given u a new identity because of the death threats your had posts got you. Youre Tim Crap now Me (as TIm Crap now): Cool § 1 hope to increase my respectable klout score of 99 by punishing the demons that plague my account in the form of unfunny post s § Mmy submission. http://t.co/rJ7XZD7P § your dirty § if you think "spy Kids" is better than shakespere youre fucking stupid and me and my uncle would never hire you to work at our car wash § people are saying thw facebook meta thing is "Hideous/Atrocious" and "Fucking stupid shit" but i gave it a spin & its actually really good https://t.co/6CAhbblKzO § best 90s memory is gathering around the old oak tree with the boys and passing around trading cards featuring all of our dads #DamnGood90s § cant go 2 seconds without someone trying to tell me piss is good. if piss is so good then why do they pay guys to mop it up?? go read Theory § ill come on to the computer when i damn like to, and ill post what i damn want to, and thats the facts of it § now youve done it, teens. the official mr bean account is closing because you all kept calling him dad § if i dont get into Heaven ill just use the rainbow bridge that dogs use. and ill push as many animals off the bridge as i can in the process § Stand My Ground Mother Fucker § im now boycotting my wife's delectable meatloaf until she marches to town hall and reverses her vote of 4 more years for hamburglar mu'bab . § #replacemovi-enameswithbacon kevin bacon § the only thing supplying my dog shit soft serve brain w/ dopamine anymore is my favorite intellectual properties getting "Surprisingly Dark" § why won't anyone fight me on this site. i want to slam one of you smug motherfuckers to hell, with the good words that i type and post here. § im auditioning for holly wood § every where i go in this so-called thing called "society" people either want to kick my ass or give me me $1000 or put me down like old yeller § some times I have a hard time playing my favorite songs on itunes, and I wish I had my astronaut's degree from nasa to help me play it !! § give me the bloe checkmark!! or ill eat shit on CAMERA! § obliviously driving m y car through chernobyl , absorbing lethal anmounts of radiation while looking for cute girls § yo hollywood! check THIS out! *flops over face forward, lies still, becomes dust over the course of 100 years and is separated by the wind* § yerah i like to click on my mouse. so what § The Mueller report, is hipster § jungle of bad ass toilet attachments and accessories turned against me. robot arms shoving toilet paper in my mouth and restraining my dick § mesmerized by the branding, of the Wendy's Arby's Group https://t.co/YdhkwtJgxe § thinking that going to Harvard to increase your IQ is something people do once every few months like getting your hair cut § Ive gotten over 6 dms from various beautiful women begging me not to change my name to "Mr Go Fuck Myself". But its not enough. I will do it § folks the only thing higher than Cheetch & Chong--is gas prices (audience goes wild, hooting,screaming; starting Great Gas Price Riot of '15) § hte beautiful 50,000+ year old goddess Washu Hakubi, rightfull mother of Ryoko and Angel, makes an extremely valid point § from now on. i am calling everyone who is a dumb ass. "Anti- Intelligeance" § seeing the cops in the rear view, telling everyone to "stay cool" and cutting hard into the guardrail to flip my car on purpose § wife wants to get the word "winefreak" tattooed, in the disney font. i told her she cannot join me in the kingdom of heaven if she does this § when you do sutuff like... shoot my jaw clean off of my face with a sniper rifle, it mostly reflects poorly on your self § Wow what a post . heres all my links in case this web site croaks and i gotta post somewhere else. https://t.co/9nJ93V2yoc Suck my dick § does anyone like star wars?? well have i got a joke for you. today is may 4th, which sounds like, "may the fourth be with you", and that;s a § if someone wins an oscar and they start crying they should rip it out of the Fucker's hands #Oscars § has any one ever noticed that the good spiderman movies are the ones for adults, and the bad spiderman movies are the ones for children § leaning against the back wall of the e3 conference, looking at pictures of condoms on my phone while all the dorks freak out about nerd shit § IN HEAVEN, ALL THE VANITY LICENSE PLATES & COWBOY BOOTS U EVER OWNED ARE STRUNG UP BEHIND YOUR LEGS 4EVER, CLACKIN BEHIND U EVRY STEP U TAKE § "The jeans generation" § every hatch back owner fantasizes about putting the seats down and throwing a towel on top of them and sleeping on the towel like a dog § if evolution is real, then wh y am i cutting my own hand off § ever since i read a life changing book i have desired the ability to morph into a Policeman at will. i will not divulge the name of the book § ruinning a mans wedding by using too many ad Hominem arguments § ah, i can smell it,. its just about ready. *opens the oven up and pulls out a sshitty burnt up ritz cracker* my perfect boy's lunch § id like a discount on this used tort law textbook please. the last guy who had it drew female versions of Garfield on a bunch of the pages § yea http://t.co/xf26vLIO6Z § Go To My Ass § THis is not a "Meltdown". Its a normal opinion § you cannot prove that me and the boys spray painted the word "Sluts" on mens wear house just because we agree with the msessage's politics § my dick looks like an SNL skit, and if you dont want me to open the dialogue of this... go ahead & unfollow this Acct! I am used to the pain! § i just obtained a tub of that goop they fed to babies in the 1920s to make them really fat. i;m going to convert the whole thing into muscle § https://t.co/MgqnikvQgT § top 10 diapers annihilated by throwing axe Fuck sopa § just call me george watchington. beucase im watching tons of nice shit appear on my computer screen § i will never wear a "COCK RING" § it pains me to announce that as of april 5th,

2018, The Economist has severed ties with "Da Ass Fucka" § my followers spend
all day begging me to cum all over a napkin and take a picture of it. but when
i actually do it, do they retweet me? No § hoo boy... these guinea pigd love to
shit. shouldn't have ordered the full dozen § .@Hair The cashier stood motion-
less, facing away from me while I attempted to purchase hair from your establishment in Galveston, TX. #Prank § from personal experience, if you nail one
of those tiny gift shop license plates over ur real one a police man will
grapple you with his ass § i pay a man $3000.00 a month to stream line my feed
so i can get more jokes per second about putin saying "hold my beer" or what
have you § every one always says they would use x-ray goggles to look at womens
asses and get horny and wild. Not me. I would use them to help doctors § face
news § Its not workiong. The haters are up my ass sabotaging my life § ive
gotten too fat for my diapers and now i gotta go across town to get specially
made ones and i cant drive because im bipolar. fuck racism § dont really care
if my gaming chamber has black Mold all over it.. ill just curpstomp pubbies
with my shirt pulled up over my nmose § mr. 11656 unread emails over here,.. §
my dick sucks balls. pray for my dick § Are u done? Have u made your point?
Hm? § an untampered Sleeve of <TERRY SCHIAVO DECALED FRISBEES> i tell ya, the
guy who threw these puppys out is the real frisby. § i have ptsd from the time
i brorke a chair at pop eyes chicken with my ass, and i am unemployable because
of this. #smalljoys § too each, there own § the secret fruit that oprah eat`s
to become more psychic can now be ordered "ONLINE" § sell my account to "Wild
Flava" (@FlavaWild) for $2000? this is perhaps the most difficult decision i;ll
ever face . http://t.co/ZBYr8N6ZSR § dont know what this is but im protected
from it also § put me in irauq i will find the taliban gun factory i will take
their horses and Gold https://t.co/HX2CRSVilj § cyber Monday is now Suck-Me-
Monday, no further question your honor § need a virginity restoration spell
for rats § Masturbatorkiller vs. DaddyMilker. do not miss this Debate. § paper
is a liquid #TheThursdayMorningRamble § i can say it. im allowed to § Gravity
(ã,ªãƒ©ãƒ"ãƒ‡, Gurabide), also known as Demi, is a recurring Gravity-elemental
spell from the series. #prayfordemi § please send more Info i will see what's
going on . § well yeah if you look at this Joe Pa thing from the whole "Rape
Angle" it looks pretty skeevy, but remember that time he did good at sports? §
Im, him § please banky. if youre out there reading this i need you to graffiti a
chode with balls on my shop teacher's station wagon § joining a classic
Crooner's union https://t.co/ZsWW2gG6RZ § spent the last 14weeks creating
enigmatic rock formations to distract cops while i pump all the fresh produce
in town full of anabolic roids § give me $100 if you think the guy who siad
"Dumb ass" a lot on that 70s show would make a better president than any
teletubby § if heading to the gym and muscleshaming all the sweatnerds aint
your idea of a good time then im afraid you are a waste of a daughter § male
model: washing my luxurious long hair is so boring. i wish my entire body was
bald like you me: Now the healing can begin § doctor: you have a hoof growing
in your brain. like a goat's hoof. its horrifying, unprecedented & fatal me:
is it true they do 420 in hhere § due to fan complaints theyre making the
Simpsons normal colored in season 38 and beyond. at long last this crap is at
an end, 60 fps as well § Going to try to get viral by making a ranking list
that everyone hates. Lets see;   1. Net Flix 2. First Responders 3.
Sandwich § @PhillyPolice nothing i have ever done is Legal § never mind they
just found the post where i said i put on black face and started chasing cars
around § IF YOURE 1 OF THE 10000 PEOPLE WHO IGNORED ME WHILE I WAS HALF
DISSOLVED IN A HOT TUB BEGGING FOR SEX JUSt REMMEBER THAT I OWN CBS BRDCSTING §
inexperienced shit taker here. need someone to hold my hands while i squat to
ensure i dont fall backwards into my own mess. preferably girl § like this if
you think putin needs to go watch the NEWS! § my romantic girl friend sees the
super blood moon reflected in my greased back hair and pledges then and there to

bow to christ our master § vvvvvvvvvv bullshit vvvvvvvvvv § my last two post
were virus, disregard thm § thank you. that is the correct thing to do on this
page right now § done retweetinh husband accounts. it has become Trite, and
Obnoxious to me. § LIAR: Free data plan. is absolutely not good. It's something
I don't think we should want ME: Im not to touch this one with a 10 foot pole
§ i try to have fun on here, i try to post something nice, and all of you
freaks brutally piss all over me. Im done § every own i have ever done in my
life is the own i think it is § https://t.co/R1rPQUTLPU § if someone asked me
who the richest man on earth was, i would 100% say some peabrained shit like
"the Godfather " § which of you nasty pigs gave me fucking covis. Bastard
https://t.co/KuC36szsqP § my guest bathroom has 99 fake toilets and one real
toilet and i use it to test the toilet abilities of all my guests § my Ass and
my Nude Ass are two separate entities , both growing more Iconic in their own
right , with each passing day § if i cant embed this video of me throwing
fireworks at a stump into my dating profile then i might as well just cut my dick
off § im not that white § ive eaten more $14 hamburgers than youve eaten regular
hambufrgers, you low engagement galoot § performance on Antz Role-Playing Forum
has been shot ever since police made me register as a sex offender after finding
me crying in public § if someone posts something that is good then i will look
at it and think its good. Simple § posts: "the best stuff is in here" § when
should i start embalming myself § all of the dna in my ass is just morbid. if
my ass was a person it would have a small dick § ah folks i do delcare i am a
dumb ass southern gentle man who wouldnt know a re tweet from a ragdoll in this
court room to-day § my favorite angle to park my car at is 45 degrees. i call
it "The Golden 45" and if you key the shit out of my doors i only become
stronger § will try to become less of an Ape on the day of holy sabbath §
eaitng a raw piece of corn in my car and spitting like 95% of it right back out
§ It has recently occurred to me that I am constantly being clowned on. The
people I trust most have apparently been clowning on me for years. § tha;ts
what a pervert would say § my repulsive cohorts and I are searching the woods
for tree sap so we can rub it all over our hands and improve our golf grip § do
not "Like brigade" me § @Applebees WAtching my father slam down a Buffalo
Chicken Crisper Salad with his vile sausage fingers& i didnt order any food
because im mad § i dont cotton to tthat shit § my favorites list is an extremely important art project and i'll thank you not to interfere § what does that
mean. why do people send me messages § This is more for the seasoned hookah
smoker. 2 subscribers, a community for 2 months § @wikileaks "harpo" from
harpo productIons is oprah spelled backwards. bam. welcome to the matrix §
#ICanAdmit that whenever i catch a glimpse of my gruesome dick in a mirror i
tumble into the nearest open sewer and get sick. itr's very sad § having my
druthers-- and eating them too § dm gumline pics § Im not going to lie, it
sucks shit that the ICU capacity is 0% but Im thinking they can squeeze me in
for a tad if i raise enough of a fuss, § hello unionized jackhammer fuckers.
could you please go repair some other road?? im trying to suck my wife off §
never knew that anything was good or bad until i got on the computer, i had
always assumed that everything was Average until i got yelled at § just keep
on, pulling that old Chain #The12DaysOfContent http://t.co/TDA5oJZ6SD §
overseeing my pages, patiently watching all the guys i follow do their 'Bits'
and mentallly assigning them to various demeaning castes § do NOT go to
"ZiggyMania" at the Tehran Hilton; only two or three ziggy booths set up; one
of them tries to sell u fabrics you dont need § i love "Going hollywood" by
retweeting burger king and lock heed martin 1000 times § Im sorry . Please buy
my book § i hereby disavow EpicWayne, who now says that my "ears are fucked-up
shaped" , and that i "let dildos roll around in the footwell of my car" § this
is uttlery disgraceful § how likely are you to tell a friend about mcodnalds §
regarding hideous new happy meal box: has anyone put their dick in its mouth

and took a pic yet. will they send me coupons for being the 1st § i just found The Dos Equis Most Interesting Man In The Worl'ds deviant art account. he draws his own jeff dunham puppets § no. i believe in the desert § strategically gathering recon on little seasers pizza in the woods behind the strip mall and getting fucking lyme disease § i would be so scared. i would absolutely have to negotiate a $5 million dollar minimum n-word fee § (crying) nobody respects me because im a Content Creator!! every one thinks im a pussy!! i want to process lumber!! § my uncle is trying to stick my drawing of him (Chibi-Style) on the toilet with a refrigerator magnet. doesnt understand why it's not working § OFFICIAL: Michael Jackson (1958-2009) RIP - http://tinyurl.com/nlm7r2 § "Ah!! Lunchtime, Boys!" i snort several lines of Hamburger Helper, tilt my head back and shake with unbearable agony as my head turns purple § gaming is much like CHess.... § YES, my dick is shaped like an extremely small snail's shell NO, you may NOT suck it, § / ! \\ / ! \\ / ! \\ " Twizzler " has Acclaimed your Intergram / ! \\ / ! \\ / ! \\ >>> [Learn more about " Twizzler "] >>> [Return To Hub Grid] § now for a joke. a man named "the turd coach" comes into my bathroom and blows the whislte at my toilet after i fill it with shit. Penalty § i rip off my groundhog handler disguise on stage. "surprise bitchs. groundhog day is fake." i drop kick the fuckin groundhog back to the zoo § its apparent people arent taking these social distancing measures seriously. on my way to the gym i had 2 people suck my shit completely off § gorillas are aliens and that is the theory in going with. that is the belief i will use § girls always love to telling people not to" Mansplain" but they do not care of, "Man's Pain" § i think if tthe country got annihilated by nukes id "Lay low" for a bit and "Wait it out" § would like to know why my eBay account has been replaced by dead ladybugs. user name is "good_and_bad_days_haver_1963" § ((pulls gun out in bank) NObody MOVE OR ILL BPLOW YOUR FUCKING HEAD OFF (empties a shit load of free lollipops & dog biscuits into big jeans § ive enlisted the aid of Simon & Schuster to publish my thoughts of Jussie Smollett in an early 2021 release entitled "Thoughts of Jussie" . § ah, So u persecute Jared Fogle just because he has different beliefs? Do Tell. (girls get mad at me) Sorry. Im sorry. Im trying to remove it § if u think that SegaKnight's Expert Analysis Female Masturbation Dissertation lacks credibility and coherence then log off my sight. § hoping my favorite brands e mail me some more stupid shit today § "We will wipe out Twitter. I don't care what the international community says." "They will see the Turkish republic's strength," he added, § second result for "playing violin" http://t.co/PEDAs818hf § there is no recovering from this fiasco. the thursday nite rant, as we know it, is dead. § hopping on some tech support forums to accuse people with minor hardware issues of being Mad § please refefr to the reply i sent to the bird guy. sex simply does not exist § "the best part of U runned down the crack of ya mammas Ass when she-" ugh i fucked that up. wait "best part of yopu run down the ass w-"Shit § my godfather died of urine poisoning while cleaning out a mcdonalds playplace tube and that's why drama makes me upset § slow transitioning my brand name to "Mr. Simplygood" over the couse of years 2022-2026. do not freak out § (taking one very careful sip from the can holding it in a fucked up way with painful looking contorted hand) Boh! Beer just hit different... § someone has filled the Stanley Cup with... BLood?? my god. such a powerful statement. how could we have been so blind. Sports is cancelled § the mayor threatens to replace one letter of the english language with the Swastika for each week that his wooden leg is not returned to him § theres a magic number of times you can reply to me before a police man automatically destroys you. nobody has ever reached it, but its there § people are giving and receiving Respect at incredible speeds ... and it is all thanks to the humble computer chip § now that elon has disposed of the left wing woke brigade I can finally post pictures of my COCK!!! § im going to have to put the tiny padlock next to my username until people stop oppenly disparaging the Food Pyramid § i just think of them, and then, i post them. it's insanely bad ass § my book is now the 98th best Christian bible. you have all made my dream come true thank you https://t.co/h9xqPhDxJI § DM-Girls ask why I seem cold. Distant, lately. The reason is This: My rivals obtained 3D models of my dick & are now sending me dildos of it § my opinion is good because im nice § ive decided that it would be good, to have 2 million followers. now what do you say we get the damn ball rolling on that § bed bug positivity- you r blood tastes good and is helping many bugs bed bug stigma - youre nasty, your bed is poison, suck my dick § people are telling me that i have no right to post the thursday nite rant on a tuesday. SCREAMING it to me § inventing the Vertical Sandwich, that you can eat hands free, like a ffucking dog § yoiutube streamer famous for "Grandma Sucked Me Off" video series apolo- gizes to his subscribers for pooping on the bus § some one please help this man https://t.co/MCcnG5J7ki § @realDonaldTrump my car has a beehive somewhere inside of it and i think "the donald" should fire it § got that content that drives u wild #fw @HellLife @ShitGirl @simpson94170212 @GymGod @GunMagnet @ SpitoonMan @DragonSex @LifeAlert420 @Guns6 § something must be done about aall these kids on the playground claiming the goatse.cx lawyer is their uncle § if we taught children in schools how to perform defensive body roll maneuvers vehicular pedestrian death would decrease by over 1000% tops § http://bit. ly/4hwzxV bblame the Owner not the Breed § i wear the crown of thorns before every time i click submit . . . § we are living in a world where they will execute you with a blade laced in pigs blood for trying to make the movie "Bad santa" § girls will be like "oh big govt is orwell now" while having their DMs behind a totalitarian paywall & if we dont talk about that were fucked § my flollowers are more interested in smoking noosh than helping me move my grocer- ies around § Oh , That Simple Sip https://t.co/wHe49Wa83g § judge refusses to award my criminal ex-wife ANY of my retweets or favs in the divorce proceedings #BLAMMO § Charles Chaplin § buiyng a massive 30lb bottle of pills labelled "PussyAdvantage" for a girl on here who told me im like a more Honest version of Dane Cook... § @CNNSlowNewsDay @hair Hair put it therem, not me § pleased to announce, on the april of 9th, that i have signed a Truce with DigimonOtis, ending a feud that has persisted over several years . § enjoying a conversation with my friend elan musk,. http://t.co/akZ410Dn3C § "although i cannot be the father she needs, i wish my daughter the best of luck on her life path. now let us sound, gentlemen." - konami_boi § Ggoing purely by the numbers, im the biggest slave in human history, and Im to be treated as a dog. But i respect the lifestyle aspect of it § you say "36,000 pounds of chicken nuggets recalled by the Tyson Foods corporation due to possible rubber contamination" ... i say "LUNCH' § Mr. Finding My Smile § do not shorw me your mystifying cowboy slurs at this point and time http://t.co/7pCPUNdFXT § digimon otis has changed his name to Fallen Otis because he thinks he got covid from best buys midnight release of balan Wonderworld § Man said he could see into the future and told a Japanese tourist she would die if they did not have sex on a "sacred site", a court was told § obliterating my load with a blow torch § This woman is an FBI agent sent to jingle her keys through the library to intimidate me about jail. § you eat the weird colored halloween themed donuts and your shit will 100% turn Green. you sign a contract with God § i feel truly blessed ,knowing that everyone who has spoken ill of my brand is eating bugs in a cold prison cell. § who will kiss m e when im dead § btecause I was a detestable imbecile in life, and death has only made me stronger § investing like $30000 in Nike because i think people are buying a lot of shoes lately and i dont feel like looki ng up any other stock names § RufusPussy. PussysRufus. RufusPussyLord. PussyManRu- fus. PussyWhizRufus. RufusPussyExpert. Pussy_Rufus. PussyEnchanterRufus. PussRuf. § i do not say this lightly, i would do what ever means necessary to protect my beloved posters from the devilish hands of otto Warmbier § no woman can handle my post s § the only blue check i want is a check for $1000000 that happens to be the color blue § CLERK: Do you have your reward card ME: Absolutely I do not. I shan't be taking money out of the hands of Best Buy using insidious exploits. § kneading my dick and nuts like a wad of dough on a bench at pay less shoe store. i do not appear to be enjoying myself. im frowning actually § sears departfment store used to be the best place to meet up with the boys. nowadays theyll let just about any piece of shit inside to shop. § my big sons have made a mess of the garage again after being riled up by the good word of the Lord § genius 1.0, is fucked https://t.co/BEX7XsqckR § why should i give two shits of an ass what you think of my post. what are you, the day time emmys?? § scenario: the air and space museum drops Space and becomes the Air and Spade museum, devoting large sections to David Spade and his comedies § #E32021 These games will make you crap your load like never before. There has never been a better time to get fucked at 120 fps § *loads up youtube playlist "Every Geico Ad Since 1999" sitting in ultimate gamer chair eating peanut m&ms with spoon* euauh! good shit, this § ignorance... is a fallacy .my dear pals § this ones pulling shit numbers. Might get rid of it since No one would miss it apparently..... § ill aave some of that https://t.co/gfeaEkWr48 § once agian the posts sent to me by screwball accounts have caused me to spit up and defile my big belt buckle which contains my son's ashes § @Battlefield he hollered at me in-game. but. i would not axpect a bastard with a tactless avatar such as yours to understand. § ENOUGH *Throws All My Jacking Off Books And Jacking Off Memorabilia Into The Garbage* § im bringing back Lunch... #TheComeBackOfLunch § all the wonderful fictional characters i remember from my suburban middle-class 90s childhood break into my home & scrutinize my filthy dick § when the timeline's just not doing it for you, some times you gotta dip into that list of Liked Tweets. because you KNOw that shit is good.. § university lost accreditation when nickelodeon slimed the dean, degree is useless, 200000 in debt & back in diapers, love getting ass kicked § life is aobut too many chairs. you got the tv chair, dinner table chair, the dentists chair, electric chair... thats too many. Tone it down § once yoshigod9 asked me what pussy tastes like & he recorded my answer on a nintendo ds & jacked off to the recording later. Now hes my boss § the repliers know whats best for my posts. i love to roll over like a dog and let them shit all over my face until its unrecognizable § the guy who hooks me up with Raw Milk locked his account. too many people posted "come to brazil" at him so i guess ill starve to death now § rodney gamerfield, Dr. Gameslove, and gamesbond007 walk into a bar, say "Fuck off id rather be gaming," Then they leave § fucking Dumb https://t.co/kY1QpfV28P § should go without saying but, if they show j. bezos penis on the news i will postpone the showing of my penis, to avoid confusing followers. § the bobs big boy milkshake mix up has become Racial. i repeat, the bobs big boy milkshake mix up has become Racial. § i hold hands w ith my teen son *spikes the microphone* § i put an alert on that shit like 10 years ago. thank you https://t.co/5klkP0KjGs § can anyone tell me if this is good or not. if this sort of thing is frowned upon i will stop immediately https://t.co/neyx6Usg7V § if a sniper shot me i owuld run over to where he is and kick the gun out of his hand and kill him because hes not specialized in melee fight § another day volunteering at the betsy ross museum. everyone keeps asking me if they can fuck the flag. buddy, they wont even let me fuck it § MASCARA DRIPS DOWN MY FAT FACE INTO MY PATIENTS GAPING CHEST INCISION... Ëœ ̈ ̈ ̈ ̈ ̈Ëœª¤ SAD SURGEON GIRLS ¤ªËœ ̈ ̈ ̈ ̈Ëœ § im probably going to post more messages on here soon so please don't unfollow me § guy who invented Prayer: This is so sick. Im going to get so much free shit from god. This is the cleanest scam yet. So glad I invented this § it i s a DISGRACE that these people are finding exciting, new ways to get horny without my express written permission § might come up with a "Safe word" system to employ if thhe boys in the chat go too hard while

commenting on my lunch pics § dairrhea § my Piss is busted ... § Husband is ATM
Machine § what if "DONALD TRUMP" was the ceo of NetFlix? I think itd go a
little something like this...! (gestures racistly) What a world What a world §
what happens when kirby swallows the qur'an and is granted its considerable
power. my 81 chapter fanfic explores this issue -- and more § "this is going to
sound so cool" i rev the engine and it explodes, leaving me rolling around on
the road with a smouldering dick & ass crack § #KINGOFSWAG do disfiguring
bruises on my significant other's face qualify as "swag" #teambreezy #filthypeo-
ple #worst § just occurred to me that i dont have to report to my followers
everytime i accidentslly drop food on my dick. my posts should get better now §
howling james dean lookalikes circling their choppers around me, swinging
chains while i sit in the gravel and borwse the nintendo 3ds eshop § #LawEn-
forcementAppreciationDay i appreciate my god given right to enforce the law all
over this web page § im at the point in my life where i cant relate to any
popular fictional characters unless they use massive amounts of hair gel and
steriods § if YANKEE DOODLE (1782) was in Present day, he would have a Sound
Cloud, and Further more, he would say shit like "Listen to my sound cloud" §
ME: I love shit that is Dunning-Kruger NY Times: What? WaPo: Explain your
self jeffrey Epstein: Damn lol , Nicely trolled § the reason people cant come
together and post compliments about each others posts is because theyre scum,
just 0% of value § ISSUE: is the road runner wile e coyote's son FOR: thhey,
seem to respect each other, on some level AGAINST: one of them is a dog § @
glennbeck I was a big fan until you decided to get all Political on us.
Unfollowed. § i dont know who all these fucked up people are!! im sorry! im so
sorry!! § for every child you don't circumcise i am going to circumcise myself
3 times § all sponsored content was put on hiatus during the holidays. it will
return next week along with the thursniterant. § viral ??? now were talkin § if
someone can get me the quran written in saddam hussein's blood i will use it to
craft a Blade and i will let you touch the blade one time § honey mustard
likers... heres a one million dollar idea for you "honey ketchup" § if Ur not
retweeting or other wise liking all this good shit SC Johnson A Family Company
is posting i got 2 words for U and that is Fuck you § "we live in an exciting
age because you can just go get downloads of anything. almost every day there
is new downloads to get." - OwedSex96 § bringing the doctors note to game stop
saying im allowed to buy as many games as i want and touch myown face if i want
to § if youre one of thoe waiters who carries the little scraper around , to
the tables, to get the crumbs off it `` Kiss Da Back O' My Nuts `` § WEL DESPITE
FREE SPCH LAWS IM STIL NOT ALOUD TO PRACTICE SARGING TECHNIQ ON UGLY WMEN AT
PETSMART - I AM SO TORN UP OVER THIS - SOM1 CALL ME § gonna print out a bunch
of pages from rival muscle blogs and scatter them across my driveway & drive my
noisy scooter around on top of them § @ClassicsOfGame Despicable As Always.
Thank You, Classics. § "mama mia" § cleanning my assault rifles with wads of
toilet paper § http://t.co/CrnIWgR0SP christ. no wonder everyone is so worked
up...... § THE BOYS: were watching the mr bean episode where you can see his
ass. get over here ME: cant. wifes making me watch mr beans holiday (2007) § i
dumped an entire bottle of glitter into my diary for teen blindness, what hte
fuck have you done lately § going t o start saying, "Wife City" whenever i see
an attractive woman. e.g... "thats Wife City" or "that girl is Wife City to me"
§ your white § no!! hes bad § i would like to apologize for letting the team
down by eating an entire snowman over the weekend and getting sick. my head
wasnt in the game § Me to, and, cheers. § Why are you saying this to me. Who
are you § yeah i just give my password away to people all the time because im
dumb as shit § i was one of the villains named "Loser Fuckface
Nerd " and my catchphrase was "i cant fight them! theyre too strong" § WHAT
THE...?!?! BUT THAT'S NOT A..... BUT I DON'T WATCH..... BUT YOU... EAAAAAGGHHH
§ scuse me i gotta check this...ah, looks like my retweet was reblogged bty

chief tech editor of Reader's Digest (yea hes verified). solid mag § doing my
Civic Duty (evading tax's) while laughing at trolls threatenning to do arson to
my house § Im a goalie in personal life so I know a thing or two about deflect-
ing personal attacks against my life as well as hockey pucks. § ive accepted
that i will have to reincarnate into shitty microorganisms like 50 quadrillion
times before i become something cool like an ant § if you get omicron variant
and win the darwin award i will kick the ass of you. i will put you on the
doushe bag list. § my screen play explores the question: what if master cheif
smoked a big cigarette from the year 3000 that worked through his space suit §
[(launches sack;s of burning medical waste into the side of someones house for
having a bird feeder on their porch)] Fucking Bird Helper § this mother fucking
snake who wrote this apartment listing is trying to pad the list of amenities
with shit like "dart board" § my hate'rs trying to turn me GAY! § THIS PROJ. IS
MY LIFE AND KICK STARTS ARE MY BLOOD § going hannibal lectore style analysis on
this bastards posts. Hah. you make it too easy; i get paid to fuck clowns like
you § just planted my big ass through a mans wind shield while trying to get my
shirt out of a tree § in solidarity with all of this crap going on, ive
Poisoned my ass hole § i cna list numerous occasions where i have been discrim-
inated against in a racist fashion just because i am a content creator . § -i
have at least 5 mental illnesses directly caused by having my posts replied to
by shit heads - im your man for #mike 2020. Pay me sir § if a tree falls in
the forest and a Teen Does NOt React, does it make a sound? ? § Greeitngs, me
and YoshiGod9 were just discussing which releases we consider to be "The
Champagne of Gaming" . Would you care to join us § agreed, https://t.co/
dc5yuiJjza § tthe best posts are the ones that are like, " ever tell some one
with pectus excavatum to shut the fuck up" § looking at the data and simply
laughing § http://t.co/pt99s1DgAZ good § d o it mother fucker, i thrive off of
hell energy, i feed off of hater bullshit § let's talk about planes now. the
pilots are flying them up too damn high. it's dangerous. I don't like it. got to
make them lower § my face whan i nut https://t.co/HXH5XMtMgd § the password is
"dragons" go go go § you only post in pervert language now § w'ere leaving it
in 2019... https://t.co/zFc6c6GAkg § did u know its poss. to get harlequin
ichthyosis in just ur dick. i do § people whose retweets equal endorsements
belong in a fucking cage § i do print my posts out on index cards and dead drop
them at city hall. you have to get your teeth in the game, other wise youre
just shit § your the ones who sold out not me § 1 overhear 2 social media
experts discussing hardcore brand strats for 2015. Next Level. i immediately
duck into a restroom & hyperventilate § i propose,on may 5th, we hold what i
call the Banquet of Posts. we go all out on that day & do as many posts as we
can. The Banquet of Posts § FBI deemed my tool assisted glitch run of Mario
Teaches Typing too dangerous for the public eye. the raw emotion has rendered
my face purple § GIVE IT TO ME STRAIGHT DOC-- WILL THIS COMMON TUBERCULOSIS
VACCINE GIVE ME THE GOOD AUTISM OR THE BAD AUTISM??? § Thread § ME: Are these
Vine Ripe WAITER: Yes ME: Is this Farm Fresh WAITER: Yes ME: Are these
"MAde To Order" WAITER: No ME: I will notify the police § hm lets see.. *Logs
On To Dark Net* bomb recipes... voyeur upskirt.. snuff vids..DILBERT?? WHo thef
fuck put dilbert on dark net § they should hang these up inside of the mcdonalds, and that's the highest praise I've ever given anything in my life § chose
your fighter https://t.co/v690dybg24 § there`s no job harder than that of the
Media Personality. there are so many massive pedophiles who you have to not
accidentally say are good § (reporter following me into my car) Sir sir. You
look like shit. Whys your head look wet. Sir § most important art movements
in human history?? three way tie between impressionism, cubism, and Bullet
Time § I AM VERY BAD ARMENIAN LADY ! I AM SO BAD THAT EVEN DEVOL IS AFRAID OF
ME ! I WILL TEAR ENYBODYS SPIRIT & GIVE IT TO HIM ; WHO PUT DISLIKE ! § <MY
FATHER> , who had gone missing for 17 years and was presumed dead after failing

to return from his ultimate dumpster diving life quest § i had a stern talk
with my son over how his purchase of a $0.99 hdmi cable represents failure §
Interests & Hobbies: horny Books & Magazines: sex book's § fully come at me
with your bull shit, catch me in the Wrestling Ring and 100% show me how much
of a sick fuck i am § twitter .com, the only mainstream website that manages to
crash my browser, has pledged to make its users suffer "Like never before" in
2020 § look what youve gone and done. youve shit-eated yourself again § buck
bumble caressed his dead gfs hair. "you will pay for thi s, Bastards." he
grabbed two uzis and charged the gym, "Suprise mother fuckers § 200k/yr media
job where we all wear sweater vests, kiss each other & try to convince people
biden is technically a "Molester" not a "Rapist" § it was my idea to make the
avatars circles, i got $1.1 Mil for it , im not sorry and if the trolls dont
Stfu i will make more things circles § congress: youre so good at saying the
truthful things in a handsome way. we need you me: Wheres bigfoot. Assholes §
surefire investment: Saline. everyone i know is injecting a lot of it into their
dicks. THat's, "Saline". Surefire investment. Locked down. § http://t.co/
JY4AeVyu29 heres the thursday nite rant contract, as requested § thw man who
killed bin laden... angel or demon http://t.co/CutViWP85O § im afraid that this
will forever be one of the temple `s many secrets § my ass looks like a fucking
frankensteins ass § there is no such thing as a baby animal. they are all
adults from birth. sorry if my opinion offends you § im gonna tr*gger your
fuckein grandma by saying "lousy grandson" in her face § Mr Deeds Gay Download
- What You Want, When You Want It § if trucks can wear nuts Then i should be
allowed to nail yosemite sam mudflaps to my asscheeks § im going to power up my
content in this year 2014 by divorcing my wife and crowdsorsing a new gfx card
for me. thats my guarantee § im every james bond § Double standard [rage comic]
: MensRights § -ˆ-ˆ-ˆ-ˆ-„-€-ˆ-ˆ-ˆ-ˆ-ˆ-ˆ-ˆ- -ˆ-„-„-€ -ˆ-ˆ-„-€-ˆ-ˆ-ˆ- -ˆ-ˆ-ˆ-
ˆ-ˆ-ˆ-„-€-ˆ-   -ˆ-ˆ-ˆ-ˆ-ˆ-ˆ-ˆ-ˆ-ˆ-ˆ-„-ˆ   -ˆ-ˆ-ˆ-„-„-ˆ-ˆ-€-„-ˆ-ˆ-ˆ-
ˆ-„-€- -ˆ-ˆ   -ˆ-ˆ-ˆ-ˆ- -€-€-€U-€-€-€-€-ˆ-ˆ- -ˆ-ˆ   -ˆ-ˆ- -ˆ- -„-ˆ-ˆ-ˆ-ˆ-ˆ-
ˆ- -ˆ-ˆ-„-„- -ˆ-ˆ-ˆ-€-€-€-ˆ-ˆ-ˆ-ˆ-U-ˆ-ˆ-ˆ-ˆ-ˆ- -„-ˆ-„-„-„-€ § i have paid my son's
school bully over $50000 to detsroy me psychologically . § im the only man to
put on the CIA invented "Heart attack diaper" and live § the most fucked up
thing saddam hussein ever did was eat doritos in jail § what is to be done with
thse female bernie bros who are harassing me with nude images of themself and
calling me "pee pee bitch" @CNN @MSNBC § Dont like the posts ? Goto WWW . KILL
MY ASS DEAD . COM... § they made 666 the satan number because that's how many
hours it took me to learn how to roll a cigarette § i look forward to purchasing this work of fine literature at perhaps the zoo or the circus § IDIOT: I
would love to get trapped in some sort of wall and spin around faster and
faster until pieces of my body slough off ME: Ok, no, § i love being the guy at
pitch whose job it is to argue that thr greatest song of all time is "You
Aint Nothin But A Hound Dog" by elvis § 2021 is more of a Dick Show than 2020.
i mean the writers of the eseason finale of 2021 are smoking weed. Thats how
fucked it is § diaper in place § what if instead of chirping birds yelled stuff
like "GHETTO !" or "Adoulf" or "ass". they would probably be a funnier animal
if they did it. § the boeing 737 max is not necessarily "Bad", it will simply
weed out the world's weakest pilots and make the movie Top Gun into real life §
*does something fucking stupid or embarrassing in between tthe asterisks and
doesnt expect anyone to wonder why im typing it out* im normal, § 'Single
'Taken œ"GenderDead § mmy masters in agricultural science was just deemed
invalid after footage arose of me dying § its not that number anymore. you may
re tweet it now. § 611 Ass illustrations and clipart. Affordable Royalty Free
Stock Photography. Downloads for just $1.00, with thousands of images added
daily § #3WordsThatWomenHate my dick § we succeed where many businesses fail,
by offering a comprehensive program wherein I (Me) will run your dick over in my
wheelchair, for free § Im glad we can discuss the news and the headlines of the

day and have fun while doing it also. § w*akes up on the morning of july 18th 2015 sick and tired of Snooki and HoneyBooBoo* Wheres my damn nuke bomb... § #ThingsIWontApologizeFor eating dog shit out of the toilet like a low down snake in the grass § https://t.co/V7WK5eyqqm Not going to work today just staying home doing intense Meditation / Reflection out of respect for this bull shit § more bullshit: enterprise rent-a-car will refuse to serve you if you imply that youre wearing a cock ring, even if its for health reasons § this is the episode of sliders where they get transported to Hitler Earth, where everyon carries the appearance & manneurisms of adolf hitl § pissing in to the toilet without getting over 10% of it on the floor and legs is Suad goals § i have black friends. i own all 3 current-gen consoles. my shelves are filled with a variety of Book`s. im virtually untouchable § (Guy coming towards me with a weapon. at a walking pace) "Ill goon your ass hole. Ill goon your ass sir" "You will not goon my ass" § ON LINE........ https://t.co/4HDeWH64Is § Please i need help § Already Im being silenced! Incredible § some one needs to tell these guys out there flying planes with banners on them that nobody can read their shit § wringing my dick out like a sponge and letting all that gray water drip all over my bluesuede shoes § who wants t o read some extremely embarrassing opinions about how i believbe the @mtn_dew twitter account was taken over by a false dew fan § theyll let any dirty looking man get on television and claim hes a cowboy its STUPID! they think youre STUPID With this shit § @bing answer for your crimes, fucker http://t.co/P6FMEnbz0o § im an amputated shit lord hairspray addict. ask me anything § there is no football position known as "Sniper". ive been tricked by this load of crap § scrolling down my feed..lauguhing my ass off at my own trade mark "Knee Slappers", my mouth stuffed with bread making beastly noises § my friends and colleagues in the dms are begging me to jack off to balance out my stress levels. but im not jacking off. i will not do it § cum bib § i am not quite ready to declare this coming summer as "The Summer of Gaming" but keep up with my feed and i will let you know when i do it § only if you truly respect my posts § ME: ill take.. one Cruisp bird w/ extra bird sauce please KFC CLERK: Huh? ME: (gives him the Wink of Irony) KFC CLERK: Ah! The Wink of Irony § people do not appreciate the grace and dexterity that is required to shave the fat pink rolls on the back of my head that looj like hotdogs § i will not post on xmas day out of reverence for the lord christ. that is only. my opinion, and if youre going to kill me for it, thats fine § (crawling out of rocks in dystopian future where all the good posts have already been made) uehh.. im the big.. denim.. sock loop(??).. man § ((sends yoyu an unsolicited 20 image sequence of me morphing into a neopet) i can take u... closer § it's Damn cold out there! Hope you got shirts #WebAndMediaContent #FrromTheContentBoy § my top advisors are drafting various contingency plans for when all my miscreant followers overdose to death on chilis southwestern eggrolls § these shitty birdseed husks my canary rejected will make a fine Car § It seems "Clit Goon" is commanding his subordinates to tell me hes dead of COVID19 now. Funny, considering he logged into steam 4 hours ago. § #ThingsGirlsLike ccalling me a fucking bastard and strangling me with their legs while my head turns purple and im horny and screaming mad § Hey Girl Whats Your Ass Lookin Like. Let Me Consider That Ass. § this is the final scheule. do not contact me of this. https://t.co/5xBrxUpnNq § THE SUN THE MOON AND THE STARS ARE ALL TOO SMUG FOR MY LIKING § this is spam messages. unsub-scribe me § i can not, in good conscience, condone a "SANDERS" presidency because i once vividly imagined him walking around while twirling a pistol § who cares about patrick swayze he hasnt even done anything for like a year § i get the ref. please retweet me getting the ref § feeling devilishly Racist today... might apply just a smidgen of Blackface before i go out chasing cars § due to my Troll-Crushing journalistic standards i am obliged to say some shit about how the original "Pope meme" , is Roman Catholicism § ill vote for the candidate who promises to make masturbating in haunted houses illegal § u cant bruise a rib. only the skin around it #Annihilated § to the 1.8 million americans who died so i could get insane amounts of nintendo switch friend codes from girls by moaning online: Thank you § having a vision of dying completely alone and waking up in a cold sweat to post a Scathing review of a futurama episode i watched 14 yrs ago § just downloaded some of the most all time realistic vagina pics, to my $100 computer § i lose about 6,000 followers eveory time i make one of my humiliating tweets. the cost of business § some simpsons dvds fall outta my velvet robe while pouring my date a drink at my penthouse suite. i bend down to check if they got fucked up § honestly i get like 20 unfollows every time something comes out of my awful mouth § im dumb as a slab of turds, and i am Here for it § every time i shit into the toilet i turn around and take a look at it and i am appalled by what i see § "societys more obcessed with pooping and pissing and having sex than they are with solving the heartlands opioid crisis ." - grover § i would not enjoy a second of it, but if a man achieved the fully-optimized load i would feel obligated to allow him to Bust it into my eyes § @HVranch My Dog loves it when I slop some Hidden Valley Ranch into his bowl,   He cant get enough of the stuff. - Denny From Utah § nice shoes idiot. nice pants. nice head. nice face. nice legs. nice feet and mouth. nice eyes. nice dick, ass, hands, tongue, ears, uh, neck § if your going to come on to here and PigeonHole the facts & embarrass your self you can go fuck off until you learn actual truth § sometimes i think thnings would be easier if i would just bite the bullet and relinquish my real name for my meme name, "epic Couch Bitch" § the most bewildering euphemism for penis i ever heard : "My puck" § 9/14/17: 45 § ð "¹ð ".ð "¹ð • ð ".ð •¦ð •¦ð • ð •šð •Ÿð •¥ð •¬ð •• ð ".ð •¤ ð "¼ð •• ••ð ••ð •-ð •£ð •'ð • ð •• ð •¦ð •• ð •'ð •¬ð •- œ ð ", ð •,,ð •šð •£ð •'ð •"ð • ð •- œ ð • ð •¦ð •£ð •fð • ð •£ð •• ð •€ð •• ð •€ð •¤ ð •,,ð •ªð •¤ð •¥ð ••ð •£ð •šð • ð •¦ð •¤ § Porno W. bush § in one proposed timeline, goatboy was a character played by jim breuer on SNL who circulated a jpeg of his ass and became the goatman. § my billionaire friends smoking in an alleyway with leather jackets and slicked back hair trying to peer pressure me into doing pedophile sex § my fellow men..we must eliminate this bastard https://t.co/0tF2jlsbTN § i dont need to answer this at any point in time § using the skills i learned of mario to traverse a real life pile of crates § going to prove once and for all that trolls are Bullshit by having a narcissistic meltdown on my tech humor wordpress & logging off for 5hrs § tried to make an fps in the 90s but i only got as far as naming the difficulty levels "YA MOMMAS BOY", "PUKE", and "TURN THE GAME OFF DIPSHIT § (me after seeing two guys in any context whatsoever) Well well well if it isnt the Blowjob Brothers § this is bunk. this is low § does brazil have any excotic PC games i can play § they done fucked up and made big bird "Woke" § im doing it soon because of the crap. § this is the new logo. if you want to contact me you have to put the new logo in the email and send it to me. please get rid of the old logo https://t.co/wCLOnGiw2E § @dril don't reply to this. i already know it's a good joke § every other twitter account is in direct competition with my own. i would never compromise my status by promoting any of these pigs § no. im tim crap § i will not post on this fucking website again until they add a filter which deletes every reply to my posts that isn't "yes SIR" § In my sincere opinion, 7-11 is weighing down the Big Gulp brand with their clownish chain of filthy convenience stores. § my content is good actualy. please retwweet § The Proven Mental Health Benefits Of Calling Your Boss "Father" § in kindergarten, i became most popular kid in class after calling the farmer in the dell "A gaped out ho" . By 2nd grade, i was again Hated. § the horny ranter clenches his fist in triumph, having been notified that his youtube account has been upgraded to accommodate 15 minute vids § turning in my badgen gun... § man in moving car slaps me in the face with big hand full of dog shit ,flipping me the fuck

backwards,landing with full weight upon my neck, § absolute full power
https://t.co/wEZGcMQqKM § Cool https://t.co/eAwv9t7ZpK § just grabbed my ankles
and rolled backwards ontop of my neck and took an enormous shit in my bed while
my dogs barked at me #introvertWin § get me on some ghostboster sites § bet
yoyu think you would never find a mother fucker like me at a primarily Black church.
but i like to go,.. just to Smile.. bask in the Energy.. § ive mastered
"Draogns Path," ive not taken a shit in over 20yrs,& im willing to have my ass
hole inspected by a notary public, to prove this § gravitational waves huh., is
that like the super moon § CONGRATULATIONS Legendary Babe Ruth "Posthumous
conversion to Islam" Now thats a home run § im delighted to see that people
are waking up to the fact that Masturbation is fraud, and turns all of the T in
your body into germs § another stir-up at the office when relatably handsome
professional refuses to remove sticker from khakis that says "my other pants is
jeans" § http://t.co/V5SvukJwXO miracle bird. kfc kfc kfc kfc § I hate this
fucking bunkum you put to my page. Get a grip on life § 37 souls who will never
again be allowed to engage with my red hot brand, bnecause they posted during
hell hour and spat in the face of god § later that night, i post "the btk
killer fuckin sucks" on the official guestbook of peep marshmallow. my opst is
then removed by a moderator § that last psot was damn good enough to count as
the 12th day of content if i say so my self. #The12DaysOfContent § the News;
- death cured; immortality real -on-line ghoul given plaque; recognized as
"loudest human alive" - bird infiltrates macaroni grill § in a rage., i farted
into the gamestop cashregister, venting my frustration and rendering the money
unusable, paving the way for gold stndrd § the neighborhood teens have left so
many burning bags of garbage on my lawn that everyone thinks that this is the
place you burn garbage now § justin beieber u SUX and your getting wrinkley
old and gross. your a wreck and trash. fucking pig. fucking worm. hell is
real #bieber § the wife simply refuses to acknowledge me as the Alpha Smoker
and is making me look like a fucking beta smoker in front of all my in-laws §
the Clitoral pussy § surround alcatraz with Poison 2020 § just because i am
allergic to wi-fi doesn't mean i can't respect it and recognize its useful
applications. it is me who is wriong, im shit, § i think that in 2013 digimon
otis was seirously convinced that they were going to change the name of
gamestop to gameMosque § "Son, are you going to beer my Ass? Or are we about to
have a mother fucking problem?" it would be very good if tommy lee jones said
this § next slide, please. this is a chart showing piss levels in the lungs of
eastern & western public bathroom goers. the discrepancy is obvious. § im
afraid i must say that i do not find the mysteries featured on "scooby-doo"
challenging enough . § saying "WOW" out loud watching youtube guy's username
spin around in 3d in the 20 second intro to his video, going Psycho watching
this shit § wife wont speak to me because i thought the movie " ight at the
muesum" was a porno film about a guy fucking suits of armor or something § i
will never learn science § if i found out any poster here was havng sex id lose
it. id ask "what business does a nasty mother fucker like you have with regards
to sex" § two men fighting inside of a dog igloo § YOUR LIVE IS A SEX JOKE,
GAMING OWNS , THE VGAS ARE FAKE, GOD IS IN HELL , OLIVIA MUNN GET ` S FUCKED BY
ME, UNCHARTED 3 SUCK § http://i.imgur.com/u9Xw9.jpg my fave`s § just for fun:
if you search camp town races you get a video of like 40 guys in black face
with youtube comments like "Love the energy! Wow" § my entry on maddox.com's
despicable "Faggotpedia" claims that I believe im a yoshi in real life. This
is false. Im actually an archyoshi § Blocking my wife's account, at the advice
of my therapist, "TekkenChauncey" § yes. it was in very ppoor taste. and
crudely filmed as well. go too hell, troll. § i should hope that people do not
search "steve harvey fleshlight" after my repeated callings for the boycott of
this video § nice to see you on here posting pervert shit and having another
bitch-out § i keep a spare pen under my desk at the office in case my boss

catches me self sucking i can go "Oops I dropped my pen" and hold the pen up. § EVERYONE ON EARTH PLEASE SHOVE YOUR HANDS INTO YOUR POCKETS AND LAY FLAT FACING THE GROUND UNTIL MY LOST "PUSSYMAN" APRON TURNS UP § HACKED BY Ã SKORPÃ TX TURKISH HACKER   THE ISLAM IS SUPERIOR - YOU WILL DRAW YOUR PUNISHMENT George W. Bush (1946 - ...)...2007   FUCKED USA § whose freon-huffing uncle is picking these fucking sidebar articles https://t.co/Y1nfKavxCh § (in " ot knowing what chickens coming home to roost means" voice) looks like the chickens have come home to roost, § if i make a rant-like post on thursday night and it dosnt contain the hashtag, it is not officially a thursday nite rant. its normal content § its a matter of kicking your chairs and floor to unleash the prime soul, THE HEART BEAT IN TUNE WITH GRESHA; every body has the snake side § and now its time to pay the pipe § cant deal with people who have such an utter disregard for brand integrity that they would log on without a shirt. this is not a pornno. § https://t.co/ZRsH6X9sDi § http://t.co/ejolLMog god excsists and is real § extracting rare metals from my jeans § shut the fuck up § lets see whos my real friends are. what would you do if i was at the GALLOWS about to be HUNG § unemployable crab husk shit § it is said that if "BILL GATES" dropped a $100 Bill, it would be a waste of his time to have everoyone within the perimeter terminated § punishing myself by wrapping piano wire around my head, for enjoying a 7up commercial 21 years ago § its official - beloved entertainer "bernie mac" has passed away at the tender age of 17. goodby § @CNNSlowNewsDay Take me off this service. I don't want people to look at and see my posts. § trolls have found a terrible new way to antagonize me. it is called "retweeting" and it works by exposing my posts to scammers & crumb bums. § waiting patiently for the release of Call of duty: Hard Brexit and Sasquatch Creed 2. Gaming fiercely until then. § The Latest Upsetting Concoction From @NestleUSA http://bit.ly/eyNPjR § piss is the main threat. touching it, seeing it, etc § ai which flawlessly simulates keys being jingled offers unlimit- ed joy to infants and persistent vegetative twitter power users § i did eat an ant farm once § krusty should not be on the simpson family's roof. this is hell § i love haivng my face and head spit shined by army men while i am trying to play rpgs professionally and efficiently in my beanbag chair § i would simply much like to know where i can purchase a nice cloth to place my miniature guitars upon. please do not send me the frog pic. § every now and then i like to treat myself to a bit of "Lying under oath" § ive made an arrangement with the casino. im allowed to yell at the slot machines now, but only if i actually put money in them first § the latest from rex freeway http://t.co/wQTK4Kj3zO § (shrieking at phone) what do u mean my motehr fucking ken bone NFT is "GONE"? this is IMPOSSIBLE!! i need it to access the MetGala Beer ROom § Approaching hour 5 of the #NoPiss challenge. This is very fucking serious and real. Bafflingly, no one has requested to interview me yet § one t wo three four i declare a Gender War § "The Fyre Festival was actualy good! " - Punished Dril § please follow my dril page § eating shit sucks ass. and sucking ass sucks shit § im a monk in real life, the matrix is real and hummingbirds and other really fast animals are proof positive that bullet time eixists § my followers are STUPID as FUCK !!! they are all on CRANK !!! they hate ALL my shit!!! § mindsweeper is a game for children sorry § when i cant decide whether to throw up into the trash can or the toilet i throw up in the trash cadn & pour about half of it into the toilet § i offer my toilet to the mail man everyday. my toilets not good enough for the big important mailman apparently. mailman is a bad job anyway § ive narrowed it down to the church of scientology & the united states marines. whichever one allows me to jerk off more wins the tiebreaker § patreon reward democratic debate live commentary by "SirGamestop" § "Ive been studying to become a Pharmacist" Thats good. Im living in one of those crane game enclosures now. Sometimes the claw jacks me off, § #NationalBoyfriendDay Im every womens boyfriend and father and son. And I keep my clothes nice § Enough

. § (ccrying) its jst not good. nothing online is good. we will ne ver top
1999's "monicka lewinsky craping" vid from back when jokes were legal § the
audience is encouraged to sink bullets into my protruded red baboon ass while i
struggle to recite prose written on a toilet paper tube § my massive shoulder
span constantly prevents my tiny ,malnourished ass from absorbing sunlight. my
body is essentially at war with its self § the much anticipated photographic
evidence that i take good care of my gumline has been postponed due to drama
and agony § #ReplaceMovieTitleWithCheese the n.w.o and the illuminati orches-
trated katrina and colony collaspe || send paypal to BLOODTRUTH@yahoo.com §
listen bitch i know what ``poop`` is and i dont like it § as a teen the docotr
told me my ass cheeks would grow into a normal mans size instead of looking
like fucked up hockey pucks. another lie § i cannot live in a world where
OrgyPrince calls me an "Orgy Coward" just because i refuse to attend his
disgusting orgy § Fuck U citizen § wasup babe., im a normal person. *walks on
down to next girl* Wassup babe, im a normel person . *moseys over to another
lady* wasup babe, im § this post isn't respectful to me, this post isn't
respectful to the saturday morning ramble, and it isnt respectful to the dead
guy § "im the 1%" - a milk § its decided. tomorrow morning im going to speak
with the priest after his sermon and ask him to perform the ritual that will
turn me athist. § FOOL: Foot & mouth disease isnt necessarily good ME: Ive had
it with this shit. Im showing this to your employer FOOL: Dont. I have a
family § COMMONLY REFERRED TO AS THE "BAD BOY" OF WET BEARD BLOGGING § fuck mad
people. anger is a disgusting emotion. sick of having my account flagged by
people who dont understand The Process § whicghever media wizards decide what
you all are currently angry about should consider the grievous crap of people
putting mustard on bagels § did they get it off line yet. did they take off the
pic of tweetie bird with a humans ass § some people say, normal peoples brains
work in 2-D, while famous authors brains work in 3-D... § "they shoul;d
replace the cameras on cellphones with Bibles. because the Bible is like a
camera into your soul" - michio kaku § alright everyone. the official superpretzel website has given me word that there is no wrong way to eat a superpretzel.
that settles it § "tarzan of the apes" will never become a Turner Classic
Movie. shoddy premise. people find pictures of a man yelling in the woods
disgusting § it's the most spiritual of all energy's. § eat a god damn bug §
unbelievable. another muffler man statue had its big plastic jeans stolen late in
the night, whjile i was busy having an alibi at my house § I hate bodys
please, g od. join my movement to build a pure, randian community on top of
the pacific garbage patch § never do dunks on me or own me again § "Do tip your
pimp today." -Mr. Sex Work § @prohustlers sorry im deaf § @BMcCarthy32 stick to
the "Dug Out", chump !!! § Reviewing your application for my exclusive group dm
with girls in it... Hmm whats this? In 2016 you said my posts are "Family guy"
? Denied § just looked atn the news and it seems like things are about to
fucking nut off § im sorry but if you say something to me like "oh im jacking off
right now its good" or "i respect Peepee" you automaticaly lose the debate §
the classics(art carney, sid caesar) woud SHIT THEMSELVES if they saw these
newer performers who INSIST on displaying their genitals always, § @TruthPoint-
DWR i could crush you instantly § who the fuck is scraeming "LOG OFF" at my
house. show yourself, coward. i will never log off § if i were police i would
send bugs bunny and his shit pals to prison for violating the constitutional
order of the united states of america. § aand barbers had such good names then
too,. like "Floyd " or "Erasmus". now they have bad names like "bozo the clown"
and " azi" § poor spelling is no longer tolerated on this log. this is an adult
account now., and i will NOT lose this follow friday to tghe trolls . § sick of
seeing "Snark" on my feed regarding our nation's presidential candidates. i
will be voting for all of them because they seem nice § in retaliation for
amazon accidentally charging me for 100,000 prison uniforms i will review each

of them with the despised rating of 1 star § MIRACLE: world's most compassion-ate man posthumously marries every Woman who has ever died in the line of duty #EidMubarak § not mine #NoPIss § diseased hogs pissimg everywhere but the toilet. wads of hair covered in piss and smashed into the floor #SponsoredContent § whos been leaking my dm box . https://t.co/k4H0hp9klm § quagmires dance but hes paralyzed https://t.co/wyFbip22iP § - its not clever to show pictures of me morphing into a dog - its not funny - it odes not introduce Beauty into the world § complaint going out to "Crying Man of the Month" club; you just sent me an 8x10 glossy of a missile silo instead of a crying man. Please fix § thats a fuckin dog § i once sent DigimonOtis the dismal metacritic scores of his favorite digimon games and said in so many words "look pal, these are shit games § enjoy your circle jerk, tyrants § and another thing: im not mad. please dont put in the newspaper that i got mad. § " i never met a Simpson i didn't like. " -SimpsonsWade § mE: i'll take eggland's WORST, please grocery clerk (min wage): Good joke sir § while you all dunce around here and kiss the stupid royal baby's dick; i'll be absorbing the scooby doo subreddit with a glass of #PaleAle . § may god help you if you trip your feet against my handsome bulk while i am sitting on the floor looking at Depression things on my tablet pc § there were 100 browser games in the 2000s where the goal was to become a Pimp by sending links to people, but thats jsut real life now § the most important thing to realize for a safe and healthy labor day is that lizardmen are hiding in the trash, in graves, and in coffins § i judged a chili competition once, whcich would make it a very good idea to hire me, because i would be good at using judgement on things § based on a bunch of educated assumptions i've made about weight gain, really obese guys must have like the hugest dicks on the planet § hah. i just read the entire bible and i'm still a lost., confused idiot. nice try, God. #BIbleFails § were done trying to rescue Small Business. my show will be called Restaurant Fucker, ill go to the worst places on earth & knock shit around § boycott hanes underware #boycott #GonzoTweet #activism #iran § your from reddit not me § my 5 point numerical scale determines how likely a user is to be negligent in wiping their ass properly, based on the stuff they post here § @Huggies Utterly sickened by your support of SOPA. Im now officially Boycotting your draconian diapers and encouraging others to do the same § if you want to make someone on this website really mad, accuse them of poisoning the animals they care for #workseveryDamntime #TheMaster § these are the original fort nite https://t.co/rgVgC2uHPl § ok MPR, you win. ever since you stormed out of my house with my booster seat in tow ive been unable to function in chairs. please come bac § "jamie lee curtis" #signedtoyoungmoney § nobody b cares about my POSTS!! every one wants to suck my dick!! Im going to become a maga guy!!! Behave bitches! Behave! § @DogBountyHunter what if you sprayed a can of pepper mace directly at my ass. what wouald happen. also congrats on season 2 or whatever § i only fav tweets that exhilarate the mind and soul, groundbreaking content which challenges the established status quo § angel-voiced 5'2" man forbidden by mayor from performing at this years christ-mas pageant-- "described as upsetting" "this tradition must end" § well, at leas i have my dignity. *trrips over shoelace, somersaults itno 3500mph faceplant, pants and dirty diaper fly off ass across room* § never seen a more perfect hoagie   https://t.co/8iogtLjtus § god i `d love to host SNL . imagining hordes of Trolls trying to stop me, getting mowed down by an apache helicopter outside of studio 8H, § sending people who tell me not to eat romaine lettuce a link to the wikipedia article for The Streisand Effect § natesilver 538 keep me good from frankenstein, werewolrf, ghosts,spook'ums, ,enchanters, and critters,on this nasty day !! keep me logged IN § im one of the friday night lights, from the title § #GroundhogDay is the one day a year where the nation can put asaide the partisan politics and sacrifice a large rodent to God § CONTEMPTUOUS NIGHTMARE: (blowing farts w/ mouth) ME: Sir! I

demand your opinion regarding Organized Gender's influence on corn prices. SIR!!
§ Ive gotten word that certain people on here are "Doing it for the clicks" .
Rest assured that i will never do it for the clicks § girls: Youre perfect!
Youre so good! Youre a hero! ME: Hm maybe i should go outside & eat little
pieces of shit because im SAD! girls: Nooo! § turning my headlights off when
driving at night,.. so that my Rivals cannot see me § Fuck Otis. I will never
follow a bastard such as this. § all of these people want to help me for Free.
what a wonderful community https://t.co/5xda5mY0Y5 § #AmexAlicia prray for my
aids uncle § another blissful day ignoring the fact that 75% of my peers on
this site have been rejected from offline society for pretty good reasons § thank
you for liking the "Real men of genius" beer commercials. Were bringing them
back in an attempt to suppress the 2nd American Civil War § "thanks for having
a look at my fucking posts..." - the Chaotic man § important. http://t.co/
zsm7W03b § never allow yourself to be loved. treat the Burger King brand with
respect. celebrate ramadan EVERY month. end moms. vote with ur skateboard §
getting my Dick finagled , by my tantric wifebride, in my chamber's § pikced up
some arcane yoga tech that will suck my balls up behind my gut and allow me to
achieve a marvelous Thigh Gap #ProAna #GapBoyReal § someday mankind will evolve
beyond "jokes" and i'll be allowed to paint big ugly dicks all over my house
without suffering derisive laughter § U have accepted an E-kiss from "ShirtRemover". U have accepted an E-kiss from "ShirtRemover". U have accepted an E-kiss
from "ShirtRemover". § We used to think the hamsterdance .com was good, Now it
sucks so much to us § MustardCynic: this is not True Spicy Brown... this is
Treason Brown § i can infer that the owner of this car with "Wade" painted on
the hood is either named "Wade" or enjoys the word "wade" for personal reasons
§ so long suckers! i rev up my motorcylce and create a huge cloud of smoke.
when the cloud dissipates im lying completely dead on the pavement § hitting up
all the college town cvs and 7-11s so i can pull out my custom credit card that
looks like the ace of spades in front of girls § kelly bluebook is my gf § arms
begin to glow & expand. "We must secure the existence of our people and a
future for True Gamers." yes!! yes! im feeling more power tha § girl...id buy u
any bra on earth, even if it was $100, thats how much I care about our whole
shit! GUess Im a real sick fuck, huh? Ya think? § i would like to announce that
my twitter account has been made in to the official twitter account of the Hand
Job § i believe labels are pointlessly divisive and have no proper place in our
society but i'm pretty much basically a jock and not a nerd at all § Its time
to open the dialouge, on the Mens penis. § this is the bad watch thread. post
bad watches here. if your reply does not have a bad watch in it you will be
blocked https://t.co/FuOeZckTKO § somebody please haul my ass to the ultimate
breast worship championship's. i made the top 16 bracket and my car was
impounded, due to lice § @AP Cnan I have some please § it was always my idea to
fill all the fire engnies with shit and piss to save water. the mayor stole it
and planted a bomb in my car § Why dont they call them the porch days of summer
then. Surely dogs arent the only animals who do this § genderman's only
weakness is being told that his name contains a masculine bias § please. look
at this thing on my ipod that i loaded up. it is called "the geico talking
dog" and it is spectacular. please look. please § when long covid effectively
neuters me by making my dick smaller, i plan on becoming a more humble.
Graceful creature § how about a diaper with belt loops. anyone § while every
one was busy talking star wars this and star wars that, i have been mastering
the Hands-Free orgasm . § nice mug.. the words should be on the side thoguh
https://t.co/87AJiAsidW § http://t.co/e7771Ttelf When Is The Next 9 11 § quick
reminder to vote for the guy you want to lose tomorrow, just to get as pissed
off as possible and enhance your Craft through suffering § id rahter die than
join the Fucking dark side. § guys who get off on being humiliated used to
expose themselves at the grocery store or something. now they pretend to be

journalists on here § THE TIME IS NOW: write ur senators and tell them that youre too much of a coolguy to get all huffy about the sofa bill or whatever § might try to improve my posts somewhat so i can get some followers who arent total bird brains . like 80% of you are just Dog shit § anguished imbecile pukes up a surprisingly intact mcgriddle while planting an IED in front of best buy § lumbering dick head told off by albertsons cart boy for trying to siphon gas from a moped while dressed like a blues brother § oh youre a paramedic? i write a bunch of sutupid fucking shit on the internet about my ass hole and penis. Its cool though. Its fun § president reportedly found Spoofed on the bathroom floor, it is said that he had been repeatedly Lampooned during an hour long struggle, § whoever wrote "I Exist To Be Hollered At" onto the back of my Official Nascar Cape nneeds to crawl over to my address for some rebel justice § has anyone ever done a powerpoint presentation nude § ah.. why is it that computers can send hateful commentary thorugh the modem... but weren't designed to send something nice.. like a Song § just thought of a good name for a fictional football team located in a town that i also made up the name of , "The Boatswainville Birdhawks" § Im joining Asexual, because of certain bull shit that happened in the Comment's section, and because enough is enough § number 4. the last one. i will hold this, The Content Creator's Pledge, close to my soul, on this sickening day of nine eleven. God bless § a horrible mechanical abomination attaches itself to my skull and injects my latest Klout score directly into my brain every thirty seconds § theres one teen that wont be invited to the teen choice awards this year. covid 19 #CanHeSayThat § itts also not funny or good. Cheers § @acmemarkets U call this a "Customer First" shopping experience??? I nearly threw UP !! Food floor. No good https://t.co/ PwCnzmw2Qg § sorry for drawing this out but its important to note that im in Full Submission Mode, waiting for CIA's pig-faced cronies to whip & chain me § if one more Fucking girl comes on hhere asking for pics of me or my friends feet i`ll shut down my multi-million dollar corporation for good § #SendMeTo- DerpConBecause im Rat § i am serios § fellas... you know i dont ask for much... but my fake US embassy in Ghana just got shut down and i dont know if i can make rent next month, § IVE ALWAYS SAID IT !! the people we see of today are somewhat more known to care more of their Face Book Status, than their Brain Status . § @pizzahut the manager of your Howell, NJ location disapprovingly wagged his finger at me at about 4:15 PM for reasons he woudl not divulge. § my wonderful beer men @BeerManJohn @BeerManSteve @BeerManCraig @BeerManMax @ BeerManLeo @BeerManRick @BeerManTim @BeerManChris @BeerManDan § today's the 2nd anniversary of the really good 9/11-related post I made two years ago #Better- WithAge #LikeAFineWine #MorePower § No..!! This Cant be happening! No!!! https://t.co/eR9hf5Olvf § the next stimulus check should be whatever your IQ is (100 iq = $100) dont like it suck my dick $:||€¡€¡€¡||: " sex is abnormal " :||€¡€¡€¡||: § you have not looked at the facts and you have the same IQ as a babys IQ. and thats why you have low follower. § Huuuuuuu!!! Lets see those favs... One Two Three § Super Boll Picks??? thoguht youd never ask. gonna go with "The Burton Bigbirds" and "Horse" § fucking shitty school bully somehwo got his hands on the book of memoirs that i published & read the part about my balls to the entire class § reply to my post again for the 500th time you fucking moron. Go ahead, see if i dont block your ass and give you depression . § Geting my ass kicked by italian guys in the tiny bathroom at the back of the bus § #10TurnOns getting lint and crumbs & shit stuck to my back while doig 10,000 sit ups on the unemployment office floor as people trip over me § to the coward fraud who claimed my username: it is you who deserves to be plagued by this baneful "2". Posted by CrotchLordMiami2 at 3:36 am § i will never apolo- gize for being wild about apps and upgrades § the knives will beat the shit out of the ice § maybe one of my followers could donate a tonsil or something so i can finally upgrade my dick § affirmative action is pretty fucked up if u ask me.

produces and begins smoking a tube of Gogurt, the grab & go yogurt, like a cigar* § this guy was driving around with a decal of calvin pissing on nothing in particular. you missed the point entirely wwith this baffling setup § 100 bladder exercises to increase your Max Piss § agreeud, § you just paid $8 to eat my ass stupid #BlockTheBlue § cyber link this post if youre a good person who remembers the things that are good and are not a bad person who likes things that arent good § bringing the mame cabinent into my spider hole § Wendy`s is so main stream now, that eating there has become a bit of a Wank . § thank u. twitter is christ 2012 § if i could time travel id go back to 2016 & tell my self the rwriters of the final season of 2017 are about to smoke crack like never before § my hype man is notable. someone get the president of wikipeda on the horn and command him to resign for this shit job http://t.co/aRqScnDNUX § id like to tame them with my golf club a little bit https://t.co/2lIGVK4EE5 § #OrtizKnockOutPlaylist Gangster Paradise By "Weird Al" Yancovic § ALERT: don pablos app has malware that photo shops your pics to make it look like youre crying & sends them to every girl on my contact list § discreetly getting my ass kicked § if your profile pic looks like bullshit your ass needs to be put in the stupid barn § O   ---||--- | 8==D ~~-,.   /
\\   ` Poseurs /   \ § Does it work on Sony PSP § i have decided to forgo material pleasure so i can write about the experience and sell it to http://t.co/pAeRi93lur for Two Hundred Dolalrs § my son has been combing his hair without permission. how do i cope with the pain § "What those planes did was wrong" - @ DRIL § 63 updates available? youre telling me thyere making my apps even better, for FREE? And to think these guys, get so much greif § did something happen with the votes § #Trumps1stYearAtHogwarts https://t.co/aGMZcVLWOH § weverything i say is blocked out by falcons screaming until i die of a coughing fit #worstpickuplines § i forgot to take off my joke shock ring before jerking off and the joke is on me because i flipped out and shot loads all over my curtains § helping the police by yanking the doors off all the public bathroom stalls § #AnimalTVShows ape fucker § the wright brothers would be disapointed in people who would rather get on their cellphones and talk bathroom than discover the cure of aids § "The film was universally panned by critics. It received a "rotten" rating of 5% on the r" let me stop you right there. thats a lot of crap § infinite amount of alternate universes where i shit my pants during my wedding which will only go away if i break stephen hawking's computer § i chose to disregard the advice of president barack obama and continue posting § YO !! DONT SEXT THAT TEEN § "FEAR IS USED 2 ENSLAVE THE MASSES," I SAID AS I RIPPED THE FUCKIN DECORATIVE CARDBOARD SKELETON OFF OF THE COMMUNITY CENTERS BULLETIN BOARD § reluctantly jacking off at 60mph to the girl silhouette on the big rig mudflaps in front of my car while whispering "trucker's code" § once a year on every forum some guy posts a thread called like "Im done with wiping my ass" and all the people who get mad at him are banned § thinking about a "Cock Ring" for the neck that strangles all the blood into your brain and gives you what is essentially a mental erection § #FiveWordTED-Talks god is real... (real BOgus) #ThingsGirlsLike free copper wire #LiesToldInSchool principals have sex #MakeLeighLaugh no § (emotionlessly) tacos is spanish for "food" § #2wordsforvday @@@ NO   CHAVS @@@ get this fellas. i just doxxed MetalGearEric and his real name is: Ted Staircase. he lied about being an eric and his last name is staircase § all hospitals should have a masturbation ward where you can just go to "let one loose" even if you're not sick § god wil put me in his pocket § love, friendship, beauty€" it all crumbles into dust. but Memes are eternal § chris brown farts into microphone as thousands of miserable, awful women attempt to fuck the speaker system #grammys #teambreezy § the thursday nite rant is cancelled due to christmas. it is also cancelled next week due to new years. the rant will return jan 9th § i light a candle next to photograph of my ex-wife's ass & say tiny prayer before

devouring another handful of french's fried onions #WifeAss § please hire me as an actor if any of you are filming a movie or somr shit. my forte is making extremely comical faces while being strangled § i enter a cavern and see a laptop perched on a rock. displayed on the screen is an image of my ass. but how...? a poison dart hits my neck § LIKE A SNAKE SHEDS ITS SKIN, I SHED ANOTHER HARD ROCK CAFE TSHIRT EVERY 7 MONTHS § if driving by the dog kennel while gargling into a megaphone doesn't count as "community service" then maybe i should piss in the courtroom § Bobby Boucher: Now that's what I call high quality H2O. #WaterboyWednesday § MUSCULAR SHITHOUND #illegalDogBreeds § http://t.co/Rv3QUakY5C my life will soon become this #SEAvsSF § barney doesnt actually die. he just becomes more and more obscured by bulletholes until i close the window. hes still smiling. fuck this app § http://t.co/aVeUH2d2KC good § nobody at PepsiCo, the parent company of Pepsi & Frito-Lay, uses bathrooms. this comapny prides itself on hiring people who never shit. § Wasup honey. You tryin to look at my Gamer? (referring to penis)   Di this mother fucker really just call his penis his "gamer"? Yes i did it § my dr.phil crystal imbues its user with AL;L the abilities and strengths of television personality "Dr. Phil"; & the fbi is buggin me for it § «««« --Ã—TOILET EARTHÃ--- «««« § i had my jeans bronzed as an infant. and they still fit mother fucker § for every year that He is not featured in Forbes Magazine as the worlds richest man... GOD will sink one of our battle ships § i find the private dm chats are an excellent place to "Workshop" my meltdowns & personal attacks against others, before making them public, § coke zero but for pringles. pringles zero § AMID THE DISASTROUS TORRENT OF JOE PA'S WASTE & ROT, AN IMPROMPTU COMPETITION WILL OCCUR TO SEE WHO CAN SHOUT "FOOT BALL" THE LOUDEST #WeAre § coax me into the toilet like a big bu g § i summarily reject the notion that i derive R-Rated pleasure by having jack-booted meatheads from ACORN kick me around like a chewtoy § putting all my monitors ad computer stuff on top of the stove i never use so that i have more space to carry out my life style § me and Angus69 got rich genetically engineering bread with a cucumber. me and Angus69 own a businss together. i love Angus69 § people shoot me a lot of Grief just because my wife is a stolen bar urinal with yogi bear's face printed abovbe the drain,. and they should § She died bedause they dishonoured BREXIT § bad news: were all helpless cogs doomed to ceaselessly perpetuate a machine good news: the machine is a Sega and were all sonic the hegehog § i did certainly tilt my entire hosue 45 degrees just so i could install a zipline from my orthopedic gamer cushion to the toilet § a tiny lapel pin shaped like the twitter verified account icon stops the assassins bullet and spares mmy cruel, filthy life § @WholeFoods Thank you so much, after feeding my grandson your ALL NATURAL, ORGANIC food & grain we have noted a sharp decrease in his autism § "u women need 2i»¿ get the fuck out of there i would marry a iranian girl but i would make her wear clothes made in 2010 not aladdin clothes" § Im not playing games with your ass. Anser my god damn emails or i will fuck up your world § only TRUTH can bring the the Message Troll , the common dumb ass ,to his knees, so that we may bring the blade down upon Him , As is written https://t.co/45FFi2Potg § inbox full of people apologizing to me for their tweets. "Im Sorry Sir" "Ill Do Better Sir" i blow a shitload of cigar smoke onto the screen § giving myself micro penis as punishment for my worsening posture § folks it's me, the guy who said that hit & run drivers are actually good on a blog once. anyway I want to get on CNN again so please retweet § *enrolls in psychology major* finnally. this will give me the upper hand in dealing with trolls *fails all courses* college is fake actually § welcome to smoker country § i should not have to press 2 for a male ass. this is america § sequester THIS !! *i show my ass. a dick flops out of my ass. a tiny ass comes out of the hole of the dick coming out of my ass* Fuck obam § after another day of getting Owned by #HateMail and #DeathThreats nothing beats coming home to my policeman wife and getting shot & arrested § im strong enough that i could pull one o f my teeth out right now but i dont want to § once again spending another afternoon educating people who falsely claim that Gamers hagve trouble wiping their ass. Sigh !! § if any one needs help making bat man or super man or any of those guys viral i will do it for $1000 § konami_Boi gives his baby daugfher up for adoption so he can convert her crib into a display case for his exotic collection of sounding rods § COMPUTER ... SHOW ME MORE " KEN BONE " SHIT https://t.co/fjxrtCa4bV § #worldpenguinday please cancel whatever the fuck this is and make a global holiday for oinline content producers with ring worm please. § Please remove this before my sponsor @Hefty sees it § Bllesed https://t.co/jeNcO69XGL § BLu8rehgh kiss my fuckin ass jack off Numbnuts prick § it depends on the fixture you fucking clod § http://t.co/aGNnlnCq look at this prick. he sucks. #savederpy § the next time they do a live stream of a rare endangered bird they should let users control one of those old timey horns that goes "AWOUGA " § ME: there is a new type of beer called "Wine" shirtless guy witht 104 followers: Shut the fuck up ME: Yes sir § im pretty sure that when we find out how to get in the 4th dimension there will be like 8 diferent genders to choose from § "Free Guy" Has An Absolutely Bonkers Marvel Cinematic Universe Cameo -- Here's How They Pulled It Off § taking up a precious spot in the line for the overcrowded bathroom so i can sneeze into the toilet one single time § "Watch the new Barney?" that the worst thing any one has ever said to me and you need to S.T.F.U. before i bring the hammer down to your ass § Wow , imagine an office where the employees are not just allowed to have fun... its ENCOURAGED § i may have disagreed with his politics, but i believe Brian Laudries bones deserve a PROPER burial! Who's with me!! who the FUCK is with me § The Two Steaks Bastard . http://t.co/PZp9TpN1Vs § if a terrorist tried to get me. i'd just say like, "gods fake dude" then punch the gun out of his hand while hes contemplating the hereafter § they deep faked pics of me wih my shirt tucked halfway into my pants all bunched around my ass looking like shit. weve got to stop deep fake § i can not access my software so just imagine a diagram of my ass with two fingers being inserted labeled "gas prices" and "dog food prices" § Dear Applicant, We regret to inform you that Guinness no longer publishes the world record for "World's Tiniest Ass", because it was too sad § installing a cyborg tube in my tuxedo which frequently sprays my ass with various advanced powders § "BIBLE" § "the account has too many jerk off posts on it" "the account has Loo many posts about going to the toilet. i cant relate to that" fuck yoyu § three most classic shit is when somebody on tv or in real life says "What about lunch" § pleae check this out: Hostler Magazine § - im above the mud slinging - im above responding to peoples crap - i did not throw a snow ball at someone baby in 2004 - im Owed a platform § world health organi- zation apparently "too busy" to look at my idea for a backwards hospital gown that covers only the ass § wearing a false ass crack and prosthetic dick on top of my real ones in case my pants get burned off by fire § guy who says "Thank you" to the other passengers in his shared Lyft ride when they arrive at their destination ansd get out of the car § None of the characters in star wars should show their penis. Thats not what movie fans want to see. § I personally make sure they are good beofre I submit them. § man wearing nothting but socks doing back flip kicks into his tv because there are too many batman shows § me and the boys pooled together our total life savings of $1789.34 in a last ditch effort to rescue the failing quiznos brand from the brink § never say to me, the word "WaWa" § if anyone you know on here is a "HIT MAN" , block and unfollow § sitting in my car watching 500 episodes of a horrible anime entitled "Shit My Lord" at the recommendation of XenoMarcus. § Mr. Ass Health 1998 § flipping your car on purpose is even more of an olympic game, than the actual olympic games § an advanced culture millions of light years away intercepts first earthly message; a craigslist posting succinctly titled "boscov's fuck" § " Be the wife

you want to be in the world. You have one life to grab it by the Nuts " -
the Quote Pussy § ive gotten word that SegaBoris has obtained Will .I.Am's
phone number but is too afraid to call it and ask him to Collab.... § i think
the way it works is as long as the National Debt isnt paid off, every American
automatically goes to Hell when they die, which Sucks § my dick is stupid in
how fat it is and it flops around like a piece of shit and looks like a beanie
baby § groundhog sees a nude mans gyrating ass instead of shadow, predicting 6
weeks of erupting yellowstone supervolcano § me, DogshitSora and Japanese_Mario
are going on a Sex strike until all female scammers on this site are dealt
with. We are sick of this shit § gorilla glue paid that woman to fuck up her
hair and go viral and youre all pawns in gorilla glues game. not me though im a
200IQ journalist § this id me https://t.co/mpnp5BWn0K § i put a firefly and a
ladybug into a mason jar and have been closely monitoring their activities for
4 days. they have not fucked yet § looking for some open comment sections in
marine corps training vids to post racist shit on § its a joke you nit wits.
Fuck all of you § YES...i have the healthiest Gum Line as verified by the
Department of Records NO...i will not chew food for you NO...you may NOT kick
my ass § startling how im the only person on this site with an actual human
soul. you would think the other guys on here have one, but no § my son got on
my tablet and posted something truly unworthy of the institution of oscars but
i wont delete it because theyre his first words § if i had a name like "Tommy
Tuberville" id go fuck my self § im bringing back the "bean dog" shit, but . Ok
hear me out. its nft now § Want 2 know what's worse than widespread voter
fraud?? hipsters putting scary pumpkins on their porch every october § PISS 3
TIMES A DAY. THATS IT § how many gross rags can i shove into htis decommis-
sioned nintendo game boy before i carry it around town for hours like a lost
fucking idiot § hogan sex tape #MEDIa #TheMedia #notableSex ##fuckdf#ls-
d#####asjd# § how advanced our society has become.. merely 100 years ago you
would receive little to no praise for posting the words "Bart Flintstone" §
meanwhile im going to stay up all night and color my dick with markers § "Games
rules." - the unknown gamer; c. 1998 § the ass cynic has posted a brutal 1 hour
40 minute takedown of my ass on youtube. im warning you not to click on it or
you will get a virus. § im sorry for letting donwn the fans by going through my
most Wild, Balls-To-The-Wall divorce yet § does that make me a nasty guy?
Maybe. I just shrug and say "Fuck you" and "Fuck yourself" § is that real. dont
hassle me § yeah im thinking its mulellre time. § stop tlaking to me. youre
diminishing my Art § one thing my brand will never associate itself with is
piles of filthy leaves § a team of Social Media Gurus wrestle over the Dos and
Donts of Brand Identity Tweeting in a dumpster at the bottom of the ocean § my
agent sent me a list of my followers & circled all crude avatars in red ink. if
i dont block these people it WILL cost me the Arby's deal § no matter which way
ya slice the apple, nine eleven was possibly THE most controversial event of
2001! #EmmyAwards #redcarpetfucker #pissrug § getting a 4k monitor so i can
make posts § sorry, yoyure right. im trying to delete it now but i cant because
of a virus. Ah! This is terrible § sorry mom, but if U read my posts u would
know why I spiked yuor meatloaf like a football & called it a "piece of shit".
because i am scared § hes a dog and i will capture him § i hand the doctor my
urine sample and he removes a tiny wad of flesh floating around in it. "i believe
this is yours" "yeah that's my dick" § utterly romanced by the gum that my
favorite marketing teen is just strategically shilling to mint dejection
#DeathArt § uploading pictures of yourself crying is one of the big No-Nos of
brand management. instead trry uploading a fun recipe. or a quick prayer §
Cynical zombie nerd. Diabetic meme dynamo. Country gal. Mustard guru.
Unrepentant photo blogger. Bacon dipshit. Entrepreneur. Goalie. § a reasonable compromise, would be to let the ISPs track our Gaming & reward more net
neutraility to guys who get the most headshots & combos § i know its a funny

joke that NJ smells awful all the time but ill be damned if I didnt leave the house and detect the odor of unwashed mouth § 1) My finger nails are clean 2) Sorry that i fucking use my hands to work for a living & dont care about finger nails 3) Peastebin incoming § god shaped hole found on piss stained miracle mattress § "ass hole" § listen., pal, if you think im the kind of guy who doesnt wipe his ass, you're barkin up the wrong tree. my ass needs all the help it can get § SENSING THAT I AM GLUING SEASHELLS TO MY TEN THOUSAND DOLLAR ALLIGATOR SHOES, AN AWARE UNIVERSE TRAVELS BACK IN TIME AND CREATES ITSELF § gaining 400 pounds so i can tattoo the entire quran onto my disguisitng body § dont u dare step foot into my dojo until youve read oprah's blog post about east asian nutrigenomics and their remarkable immunity to autism § @Twitter HELP § some of my more savvy followesr are telling me they are called "trauma shears" but i need a pair specially formulated for a large mans needs § take my penis out? in a "PUBLIC BATHROOM" (the key word, being public) no thanks. im not jared from sub way § @DigimonOtis Shut the fuck up § i will keep my followers safe from whoppi goldberg https://t.co/MmrzWT5eIC § urine is not sterile. it has piss in it § this. this fauil. fail this http://t.co/YDMowEL595 § my wife has illegally divorced me for listening to thw "splish splash i was taking a bath" song too much § i sit on a throne made out of dead Freshmen and drink wine from a Freshman's skull. all this can be yours if you become a cyber bully. § the news is my Life and my world. thank you sir @walter cronkite § i have to clean myself with a dust devil because my bathtub is filled with sacks of rat chow and i believe that all of politics is hogwash § "before we begin todays ball game, user @Dril would like a few words on Dairy Queen" the audience boos as i traipse the field in my tiny car § delighting my friends and family by doing the chris rock routine about "The Big Piece of Chicken" but in a worse voice § This account is a Brand Opportunity Touchstone used by celebri- ties & rich policemen and people think it's awful but its not. § gentlmen: a crisis. my official pizza hut rage face widget reports that ive posted the "Wtf Face" 138 times in may 2012 alone. trouble ahead § setting foward the doomsday clock a little bit because i saw a guy with yakuza tattoos knifing the shit out of a mattress § i have now muted the group DM which SirGamestop has comman- deered to talk about his startup which is, in his words, a "white version of fubu" § adult baby diaper driver § @howiemmandel love Howie Do It § just had to click down the 4th post today about our mr. president's "thick hooters". lcts clcar off thc bathroom mouth § bond theme plays while super spy & ladys man James Bond wanders around the forest with a magnifying glass, searching for the cure for autism § completely off the mark. i have stated repeatedly that brands are BIG in 2013 and i stand by that mantra. Remove this. § id like uh...medium, w/ pepperoni, sausage and onion. just to piss off the trolls. id like a 2-liter of coke to piss off the trolls as well, § i pray my IQ forever remains in the "Sweet Spot" wherein its high enough to call out the BS but too low to recog- nize the Futility of Posting § I WANT " 1 2 3 " 1. MY DICK SUCKED 2. MY POSTS LIKED 3. MY ASS KICKED § *sees Tarantino get misquoted* You Bitch Mother Fucker *sees war supported on flimsy pretenses* Wlel, that's his beliefs and I respect that § thinking i might be able to get the blue check mark if i post a 40 page manifesto and spray piss all over the fresh produce at krogers § anyone else see that full sail university masters in new media promo-tweet which offers us the opportunity to "learn blogging"? Look's legit § actually r/pronemastur- bation says prone masturbation is better than normal masturbation and it doesnt even fuck your dick up that badly § i get banned § Arts & Entertainment § just noticed the new washcloths ive been showering with have the FoodNetwork logo. this is my biggest failure to date http://t.co/8JvvTKea36 § John Lee Hooker: Boom boom boom boom (guitar riff) me: hm pretty good. What else you got John Lee Hooker: Hau hau hau hau me: Fuck this . § http://t.co/DV1OiipA every youtube account tells a story and i wou.ld like to share with you the tale of

"GameKisser" § folks let me tell you about the content platform known as "itunes". its so poorly conceived its even got nasas top men scratchin their heads § simpsons marches onward into season 394. characters morph into grotesque mockeries over 100s of years. homer advocates cock and ball torture § wasting other people;s Emotional Labor, by posting public screeds about the coming retribution of Lunchables Snack Packs § im thinking now, about how pissed off i'd get if 1 was dining at a 4-star restaurant and the waiter came out 100% nude. do not do that shit § im joining the army and then im joining ufc if im not too fucked up from the army. and thats the cold facts § ---------> GET A BRIAN LIAR< ------- § epic wayne once told me that there is a hard limit that the human body can handle jacking off in one day. and that the limit is 3 § every morning i pick up the local paper and read the latest condemnations about my rinky-dink, slipshod Ass & my child-like shoulder blades § What can i say. WHen its the game of politics, its open season on everyone who has entitled and ignorant views of opinions. No filter § censership § bury my heart at wounded knee's Hard Rock Cafe franchise § for your next art exhibition or whatever. § obama accuses romney of being unfunny, and too "Random". romney responds by saying obama'/s "Mad" and his page has too much anime shit on it § my favorite combo, you ask? i'll not say to you. § im going to fuck your porch up § sometimes i wonder what this place would be like if i wasnt around to call bull shit on all the jokers... probably the 9/11 crater but worse § (after getting split in half by a 16-inch bullet fired from a boat) waiter theres a fly in my Soup § oh nothin, i was just buying some ear medication for my sick uncle... *LOWERS SHADES TO LOOK YOU DEAD IN THE EYE* who's a Model by the way, § were at the point now, that when i offer to impregnate my girl followers, people assume my motives are sexual. disgusting, grow the fuck up, § us military displays extremely rare princeess diana beanie baby w/ certificate of authenticity in the most devastating show of force to date § whos the son of bitch who messed my link up § geetting absolutely goated off that pig leaf like a Cartoon § guy who bothered putting a suit on for his profile pic and only has like 300 followers. ha ha ha you dip shit!! youve wasted your life!!!!!! § Hanes dumps Charlie Sheen ads... fuck you hanes, you never battled a real d emon have you, you dont know what life is, make me sick, fuck of § i can not sleep sound knowing a disgusting criminal is out there hogging my rightful Like`s § the tongue is the human body's most powerful tooth § girls on here will call you "Dry dick" , then after you spend hours moistening your penis with a cotton swab you still get derided. Cant win § https://t.co/7OBwMPZuUg § @MiracleGro MIRACLE GROW GAVE MY DOG HEART WORM § this is false. i have never made jokes § i have proof that my care taker has been tricking me into eating delicious home cooked meals by hiding them in wads of peanut butter § the guy who pretended to work at pathmark and handed out free samples of dog dicks to innocent shoppers technically didnt break a single law § Get my ass on SNL and make me the Boss of SNL and I can promise you thta I will bring back all of the Classics. § THinking of a "Boy's Day" of twitter..won't post specifics due to trolls, but basically all girls will nicely be asked to log out for 24hrs, § saturday night at the donut shop and i am very excited to show the boys my new Dance. § back before the web, Content had to be delivered house to house by the content man. he worked 14 hrs a day & people tried to shoot him a lot § moms boyfriend think `s selling dioramas of discarded tarantula husks perfoming sex acts is "bad"; throws my 30yr old cozy coupe at me daily § imagining my followers enjoying a beer named "Gangnam style: The beer" and cancelling all my posts for the evening due to being pissed off § not many good wiki leaks lately. was hoping Julian woudld find out which individual or agency keeps ripping the gutters off of my house § whats in my cup today? why its that old stand-by known as "beer" folks . thank you for reading it § if you think astro world is good your fairly actually a piece of shit, and an over all big league FUCK

HEAD! § i will say this. when I finally ascend to the final plane of conscious-ness .nerds will get extremely yelled at § each follower on here is like a gun pointed at your head 24/7 . Thats what only a mere fraction of my Fucking pain is § the human mind... perhaps the most powerful weapon. second only to the "GUN" § wearing electric bra in defiance of #NoBraDay my filthy bean bags getting absolutely smoked by radio sound attacksat the cuban embassy § FUCK OFF https://t.co/iLaBpmVtG6 § NO I WILL NOT USE MY BRAND NEW 3D PRINTER TO PRINT OUT "A PICTURE OF RATS". PLEASE SUGGEST SOMETHING GOOD, LIKE CUSTOM MONOPOLY PIECES § just thought off an idea i believe to be bad ass. lets find the address of the leader of isis, and mail him/ her pieces of our SHIT § the bbq pit boys have posted a video so fucked that i am hesitant to describe it, lest my pervert followers try to tell me its actually good § remove me from this conversation please § shaking my head at the gym . wondering when " o pain no gain" became " o brain no brain" § Keep My Damn Feed Clear Off Gross Shit § I Beleive I Am Being Racisted Against Because Of My Marmaduke Necktie § sttop sending me aprilfools. its not April § when i awake im a skeleton, being dangled off a cliff and used as a wi-fi reciever. i can feel every ass being downloaded through my body. § well its time for th e thanksgiving jokes. i already put a diaper on the turkey. did i fuck the gravy boat yet?? Need some feedback here. § doing my favorite " Shit head " activity, kissing a cactus after being fooled nby a mirage § i would like to apologize again to the Girls, this time for telling some of them that i have a green dick. i thought it made me sound Exotic § Oh how i hate him § mny life goal is to find and make love to the one millionth mom § feeling my IQ increase by one point for each dollar that i send to the "Shit Head" New York times , Greatest news paper in history § turning on all the smoke detectors in my house as punishment for making some statements that i might have to apologize for at a later date § dragging my Pitty's and my Rotty's around in a stage coach . 11 pea brained loud mouths thrashing around for treats § well, its very good that you did that, and i hope your family members consider giving me a follow even it made them mad § We All Got That Friend Who Think Jumanji Is Real § dont worry ladies, im not one of those"Bros" who talks to girls about sex stuff. anyway, i have an entire bra stuffed in my mouth right now, § i don't want to shit today. § hey @joshingstern ypou accidentally erased this sick burn http://t.co/e8EYrLZR § JACKING OFF and committing FRAUD § game as art , https://t.co/oUlOLqh7g3 § outta all the users on all the sites on this big wide web of ours.. why would PriapismHaver777 want to chat with little old me.... § This guy got himself into another mess. Take a look http://t.co/vkNx1Pepmj § Numerous hospitals no longer make a Baby New Year public due to concerns that the infant will become a target for criminals. [13] § favorite crood haver , online now § http://i.imgur.com/7urrd.jpg basically just search "earthquack" § i click online expecting praise from mny contemporaries. instead i get an ass pic on my monitor and i immediately start wheezing into my lap § in the latest effort to distance myself from "Whacky" ;, "Random" bull shit, i will be changing my name from VolleyballCraig to Normal-Craig, § @HomeDepot angered that your toilets had no water in them,i crawled onto my back and worked up a frenzy, my legs airborne and dick visible. § http://t.co/G2aBjJo4 ghahhahafha § sometimes it feels like the damn writers of 2016 have run out of ideas for the season finale of real life . Auuwoogaaa!! Hit the damn like § @marcorubio help me team marco. please defend my rights § do not tell my friend/colleague @PregnantSeinfeld how to make his fucking posts. hes a really good account & ahs been suffering from bedbugs § DUMB ASS!!!!!! https://t.co/jupmbQT6Rp § TheFrugalWearer taught me how to make diapers out of duct tape and packing peanuts, and i will NOT let youtube censor him. america is FUCKED § thinkina bout paying a newspaper $1million dollars to run my opinions regarding the Circus § e to § Nmot a single one of you has given me your account password so i can make posts about top airfare deals on your

behalf, especially the girls § yes trolls. unlike you, i have a brain. its
called a " JOB " § i will admit that sometimes i crash my car on purpose just
so i can get a faceful of my Denim Airbags § im going to close it as soon as im
done browsing my updates. § lord knows i help my self from time to time... §
man with "GLUTESLORD" written on sweatband has gone mad with power, destroying
nerds with sniper rifle from fortress on the roof of the gym § they are letting
people vomit in the aisle s of the once great Sears department store! they are
letting people get NUDE § since 2003 to this day, me and KitsuneHorace are the
only verified winners of the "convert your step dad to islam challenge" § glue
man here, poking in to this site. big glue guy. just seeking atlanta house
wife, miss Right Lady, to Glue me, to the glue § BOND: I want enough napalm to
blow the shit out of a man's ass Q: No.. that's too much BOND: Do as I say §
goblin: im going to put up a post saying that the fake news is good, and that i
like it more than i like the real news ME: not so fast bitch § "hey bob, why
does your stapler have a live goldfish inside of it??" Oh this? this is a
Stapler Mod only The New Rich have access to.Get out § Eat shit § do not buy
handicap parking decals from "ZepplinDoug777", they are fake and the cops will
still bust u!!!!! § http://t.co/YuwPc6gAmx and to think ebert said this isnt
art § we hold all the cards. weve spent 20 years of our lives honing our craft.
if enough of us post "Boo" at the dow jones, the shit will plummet § fantasy
meatball league § I have just obtained a historic deleted segment from Disney's
Fantasia. It features a middle-aged man in an NFL jersey buying light bulbs § i
just hacked into the church and made god REal § saying "Swag Acquired." when i
get my pre order bonus at game stop and the cashier and the other guy in the
store pretend they didnt hear me § IT SUCKED AND BROKE § all replys to this
will get block-buttoned https://t.co/icEqgII1Ba § for 2010 § WOW: BitO-
fAWankHaver assassinated DiaperHubby in his adult sized crib at 0400 hours and
blew him up with a hundred missile s in his deathbed § accosted by several of
my followers last night.. would nnot fuck off, awful, screeching voices..
overpowering urine smell. Terrible. Terrible § yes. i believe you should get
yelled at for misquoting film's § due to timezone discrepancies i request a
motion that all pictures of food in group dm be referred to as "Lunch pics",
even if theyre dinner § how about instead of drop the ball on new years we drop
the damn gas prices for onve § they are inventing a new type of Lesbian in 2023
they just said it on CNN § wearing my lab coat and analyzing an array of my own
nudes in order to determine which one most effectively highlights my fatigued
genitals § i'm truly thankful towards Irritable Bowel Syndrome for becoming an
integral component of my identity and shaping me into the man i am today § " my
arthritic balls and cum " § FUCK TWITTER § im so insanely hyperintelligent from
spending 14hrs a day absorbing Twitter knowledge that im no longer amused by
nmovies about 3d animals § everyone mad at me because US army allowed me to
create "the MewTwo of pit bulls" using CRISPR. well if i didnt do it some other
guy wouldve § looks like lunch is for me today § WAIT FUCK § i believe the
island boys are a sort of "Blue man group" where its just a rotating cast of
guys who look like that § I was dead wrong about the 2020 reboot of Raggedy
Ann. And I can never forgive myself. § banned from BullShit public pool for
instantly turning water into Mud by jumping in it, begging lifeguard to end my
life, etc and so Foreth § when people say they quit smoking to save money i
simply laugh. all the smokers i know are Rich § the show, "Hee-Haw, " sucks
mother fucking ass § just made a cool $30.00 from leting scientists hook me up
with electrodes and watch me Game for 16 hours #IsThisHeaven § Hello Im A
Potential Employer Who Hacked Into Your Locked Tweits And Was Put Off By Your
Unorthodox Gender Diatribes; Fuck You § feel obligated to inform TL: i accidentally touched a girl dog's nipple while petting it-- deep apologies but ready
to grow & learn from this § nobody is respecting the classics. people would
rather stab each other to death in the bathroom than respect the classics § |||

Mutha FUcka   Stupid Ass § concerning my messages on here: typically
pretty good id say. if theyre bad its because i have a life instead of thinking
of crap to upload. § Im Sorry For Dragging My Bull Shit To The Notary Public
But If My Jason Bourne Rage Comics Aren't Canonized By Sundown My Wife WILL
Leave Me § the pain of losing my life savings is softened by the big mommas
house themed slot machine screaming lines from the famous movie, at me §
contaminant fucker § a tisket? Fine a tasket? Fuck yes a green and yellow
basket? Too much § its not Fucking funny § people please, all i ask for is one
town hall meeting which doesnt reference The Matrix § every morning, looking at
a holographic image of all my natural predators (pigs apes tigers dogs etc) to
keep my head in the Game § mugatu real life https://t.co/yZSvbAcXlu § not
rewarding certain brands for their BS w/ free advertising, but id just like to
say that all candy mascots are canonically the White man. § to the man in the
forest dressed up like a traffic cop, giving all sorts of unauthorized directions
and disrupting harmony of nature: FUCK U § door to door salesman who keeps jars
of his own urine in a little suitcase and tries to sell them and gets his ass
beat at every house § trying to parallel park my 1992 lincoln town car stretch
limousine in front of game stop and getting Honked at § well of course, in
retrospect it would seem silly that i thought the dog in the tv was real, but
in my defense the dog was very clever § theyre bad except me § proposed Meme
Graveyard offers chance to pay respect to the very best online jokes and gags.
planned to be built on top of regular graveyard § women aare setting unrealistic body standards by expecting me to wear a tuxedo 24/7 and to not flip out at
waiters § if youre one of the guys who blocked me on here, i Forgive you, and
im ready for you to unblock me now. § (browsing the secret arbys menu that only
boys can look at) ah., lets see, ill take one Spicy Onion Concerto with a
dollop of SmartCorn,,¢ § The Dick Head On Team Chat Whose Smoke Detector Needs A
New Battery: Does any one in here know how to fedex a pit bull § i live in the
atlantic ocean § i actually got diaper rash from searching another guy's used
diaper for wallets, but dont let that stop you from stigmatizing me § ah! ah! i
welcome the trolls, the haters, the knuckleheads, the rudeboys, i welcome them
to shit on my fucking worthless grave and kill me § need $1000 to tstart a Dog
Gym . support local busness. i want to start a Dog Gym § you threaten to go
to the bathroom on me? i do not think you have the gall to go to the bathroom
on me § as the sex principal it is my duty to wear a color-coded tie that
indicates how many people i will have sex with today durnig working hours. §
good to have Options https://t.co/3vKXg8pEIR § ME: why am i just the man for
the job? lets see. i love hamburgers, i love to help, HAMBURGER HELPER CEO:
Leave these hallowed halls at once § you need to take all of those cans out and
wipe the whole damn thing down with a wet cloth § dirty diaper stan ,,|,, Dumb
ass ,,|,, $$$cashfreak$$$ >> support Vaginal energy || twisted Christ Figure ||
days since last stomach ache: 0 § @McDonalds @McDonalds this is money in the
bank. put the mcshitter in all of your branding, and enjoy a tenfold increase
in likes and re-tweets § (musing , atop a tree stump) O! beer is like wine , §
mother teresa Aint No Saint, put the green arrows,there, click the heart too §
abusing my vile neighbors by putting leaflets around which state that i am now
to be referred to as "Daddy's Golden Goose" § Dumb. § @BestWestern worst
western § #BenghaziCommittee my dick is normal sized. every morning i use a
q-tip dipped in windex to clear scuff marks off of it. i have no illnesses § Do
it. Own me fully § some one has got to stop this guy https://t.co/Ygawg3tdNU §
I Want all of that shit § suck off my ass § The reports are false, Joe Paterno
is still alive!! Joe Pa pulled through the night, read more: http://t.co/
rBxuJuC8 § i probably spend the majority of my leisure time punching a hideous
effigy of the caveman who invented sex § i hear in some cultures they crap in
their hand first before putting it in the toilet. thats fucked up to me. just

shit it directly in there § asking the armed forces recruiter at the mall if he ever cut a man in half § if i was a secret service guy & certain things started happening id simply use the president as a human shield and high tail it out of there § never brought this up due to Trolls, but my son is set to graduate from ITT tech next semester after 8 years of hard work and im very proud. § twitter 2050 is an enhanced reality experience where you can step into a virtual sweatshop and lecture the workers about their Table Manners § i think when we get caught up in our gadgets and email, we forget to sit down and appreciate that time-tested classic doritos § every one of my tweets puts me about $500 deeper in the red § told the mail man that if he doesnt keep the deals / coupons coming at a reasonable pace some one might be suffering from some injuries soon § @glennbeck i can give you 22 reasons to be concerned about your giant sweaty head § i give this picture two thumbs down because it is gross § stand your ground laws for jeans instead of guns. stand your jeans laws § i'm absolutely covered head to toe in lotion and i am ready to sign on. you all have the privilege of interacting with a fully lotioned man § FREE COUPONS - GET 3 SIMPSONS OF YOUR CHOICE PROFESSIONALLY PRINTED IN FULL COLOR ON THE SIDE OF ANY DESERT EAGLE PISTOL - I GOT 'UM § to me the most normal career path is to fail at show biz and resort to getting paid by defense contractors to make reddit psots or some shit § the dog must forever be referred to as a Bastard and take a Bastard`s surname § break your lips mother fucker § people here will claim to have never liked Mickey Mouse, despite him being a time-tested Classic. All I can do is shake my head. #DuhWinning § i want to tattoo ancient Runes onto a dolphin § my fav star? it's the sun. because the earth would be a cold piece of shit without it. i also like the website called "fav star" a lot. § your video "stuart little: Why I dont buy it" has been removed due to hate speech against islam and pepsi § if by some circumstance i was given the winning lotery numbers, i would not use them, for the lottery is a sacred institution #GoodBoyThings § when peoplle make sexual comments when i post my feet and ask if i have covid toes or not...... You Fail BITCH ! § heads up: they got free toilets at mcdonalds now § All Young Men Must Own A Spittoon At Some Point In Their Lives § Grief Stricken Babe Ass § nobody's allowed to criticize anytyhing or talk about anything or like anything until my shitty terrible account gives the official go-ahead § please be mature about this subject § ah, aint it funny that folks these days are washing childrens mouths out with soap.. when they should be washing their mouths out with Hope, § taken to task by the ryhthm bastard § ELLEN: But what you're most known for is your use of the infamous N-Word ENTICED AUDIENCE: Wooo !! ME: ahh!! ya got me! § I just read in Forbes, that even Gamers can become millionaire now. I read this is Forbes § Turds And Piss Found At Usama's Compound >> Decorated Royal Navy Commander Lenny 'Hotdogs' Burbit States As Follows: "He Loved Too Shit" § "Why should there be only one good friday. Let's try our best to make all the Fridays good. Thank you" -a quote i invented which made me cry § all young men Must be fitted for a good Italian suit, ideally by age 4. i will not fucking apologize or back down from this § the last indie twitter acocunt. ..yeah thats me § they just said on the news that there's a group of hooded grotto dwellers who are legally changing people's names to "Beezo" posthumously § ennjoying a big bowl of condoms. twirling them around my fork like spaghetti § barby dolls are worthless to me § why dont you ever see the news reporting on the GOOD variants of covid?? § please wellcome Irony Cowbell to the world, my beautiful newborn daughter who will be named that forever § daddy `s Gamer medicine https://t.co/hcs0ruYeue § INTERVIEWER: we looked you up. you dont even have a twitter account, which is good ME: Actually i was suspended for posting "Gumby shit ass" § archaeologists 1000yrs from now are going to find my embalmed turds and assume they were part of some sacred ritual. NOpe im just a dumb ass § my q uote of the season "Its almost summer time so lets hop in the pool" § ill wipe the floor with your ass and wipe my ass with your ass and wipe my nuts with my ass and get floor poisoning § meter reader in my basement: nice controllers man.. You game on those bad boys? me (Blushing): i am-- yes, I do consider my self a gamer. § r https://t.co/PqBa2lIb3B § get more than 3 friends. you stooge § my only regret is that i have but one Grid to Go off of § @Bubbaburger take this down § this guys losin his mind. theres just so much quality shit on here http://t.co/gdVEIr3DLe § Ah ha ha ha !!! Wauh ha ha!!! https://t.co/r0SFrwdXda § Going Cyber. § more than god § i will never use the word "Doubloon" to describe a coin § the new NIssan Altima branded bean bag chair is a SLAP IN THE FACE!! to all lnissan Altima loyalists and people who enjoy car commercials § eovery single day i thank God for my perfect skin and soft kissable lips as i wrap barbed wire around my arms and legs § Yeah!!! Yeah!!!!!!!!!!!!!! Im Doing it!!! Im experiencing 3d § strutting my shit on the beach, unintentionally increasing the anxiety of all girls with my radiant shit head energy and blowing it bigtime, § when firiing a weapon i dont believe in recoil § sort of bullshit that im not allowed to be the wendy's mascot just because im repugnant to most people & woudl negatively impact their sales § one of the most brilliant things i did as a baby was predict perfectly the economic rise & expansion of the city of Dubai "The desert jewel" § tto the fucker who donated me a heart. im glad youre dead § rip to this guy http://t.co/JZL3q80llC § dominating thte buffet table with a pair of Sai § looking around with high-tech goggles that display everyone's raw denim stats on a sleek HUD. i'm screaming because they're fused to my head § # i will never bring dishonuor to the web by lowering my self to the point of placating the lowest common denominator witht "Joke" or "Gags" § the web is an extremely powerful media tool in our Time and I will masterfully cross chop and do bare hand takedown to anyone who disagrees § 1) KILL 2) MY 3) SELF § gov bans pit bull fighting because they are scared of the power pits can achieve by gaining BOth strengh & wisdom in the barbwire gauntlet § its time like this that i wish we had the Guidance and the insight of Sheldon Adelson, Prince, and that one koch brother who died § mostly forgettable pinecone remains § dicks have hairs all the way up to the tip, usually so short and fine that they cannot be detected by sensory perception . wax those suckers § funny that s.bucks suddenly wants to talk about race right after they throw me & my 7 service dogs out of their restaurant for being White § just my opinoin. back off § just found out my favorite author is ugly #KillingMySelf § will not be making any new posts until the 5G Network has been officially rolled out. 4g doesn't cut it anymore. fail to see the point . § #WorstDateIn5Words i tune § shitting on a Towel § #uknowuneedlotion not only does it smooth you put it on your hands to prevent, swine and bird; amoung other things, thank you § tactical knuckle man § the US army sent my police departmet 100000 hideous robot arms to rip off citizens' heads but heres the thing, we only need like 500 of them § how do i make my timeline just this https://t.co/uRzG7KZTIo § it warms my heart when i see people of every race and creed, setting aside their differences in order to spew piss into my cage and scare me § He's Fucked! He's Fucked! im ignoring the contract and i dont care if i go to hell § a Nerd corners me to talk about sweaters or somethimg. while he speaks my grimacing head slowly shrinks into a hideous purple knot. he cries § i see nothting out of the ordinary here § my setup: 35 monitors arranged around my swivel chair in a circular fashion, imprisoning me forever in a 3d world of sex pics & sports radio § "the ass show me that i can only fuck it." - a legendary fireman who died § THE BABE.................................. #RaunchyonMLKBirthday #MLKRaunchyDay § I don't know who that is Mate . § really looking to Slut my brand out during the remaining fiscal quarter of 2022 § Disgusting Pear Man Fucks His Hideous Orange Wife -- Read More: Reuters.com § covid virus can live inside of a beanie baby for 10 years #beanieBurn #Burnthem § (dick gets caught in car door which drives away, rips it completely off along

with half my torso, intestines spill everywhere) Holy Mackerel § Puerto Rican
Pisser § mmph *dips another tostito into an ashtray full of ketchup * ah it's
so good *licks salty residue off of my bloated purple fingers* mhmm § as the only
person on this web site to ever have sex , its up to me to set the record
straight when some lunatic claims the Clitoris is real § i would not interfere
in the LORD's affairs § climbing the empire state building holding a giant baby
bottle labeled "Muscle" § me when i get fuckin unfollowed on this site
!!!!!!!!! http://t.co/9JJWccFdXU § Let's cut the crap--regarding iTunes. Maybe
it's just me, but it seems like you gotta be from NASA just to get half these
features to work. § my boy's... § a booklet labeled "Mra Shit" falls out of my
pocket during my daily buffallo wild wings j/o, sealing my fate and costing me
the Yoplait deal § check out these Pig Kickers *rolls pant leg up to reveal an
elaborately decorated cowoby boot that goes up the entire leg* § ive generated
over 100,000 wordles in my head and completed them easily. what more can i say
of it § board's for actual spree killers only my followers ride every day
https://t.co/ys7DtLp160 § my favorite philosopher is Ben Stein . § old screensaver: spinning 3d monolith with my wife on it new screensaver: marquee that
says "Truck Month" regardless of what month it is § U may not chat me § garth
eats too much lettuce #fakeinsidejokes § fucking Nude Man ruine all our laser
tag games, cant shoot him cause he isnt wearing the vest, cant rack up any
points against him § the cold damn truth of it is that all of your dads have
probably owned slaves at some point. im sorry but that is just simply the true
shit. § Here I Am, Well Into My 20s, Using Twitter.com, A Website For Children
#Itreallymakesmemad § james bonds jet black diapers that cost $200 each. suit
jacket that has Jame bonds signature drawn on the pocket. james bond engagement
ring § "Destroy the content producers, destroy the content. This is , Bastard's
Dilemma." - christwolf22, from his e-book "A World Without Content" § do nOT
buy "grab bag" option at the Onion Brothers' Onion Emporium. it is a trick
devised to sell you undesirable onions § targeted advertiosng helps me connect
with the Brands I Need http://t.co/1d8nITM0JN § sorry. i sol;d my account to
bubsfeed & reddit and all the bad websites. they wanted to buy it so they could
put bad posts up § alright. so we narrowed the name of our band down to either
Traces of Mondo or Pepsigasm. and i already printed out 90,000 Pepsigasm
tshirts § California Tea Party to Use Dogs to Harass Muslim § Give this the
retweet if you agree that ALL beanie babies deserve to be worth $100 , and also
that Water boarding is not tortore § sucking off on a piece of spaghetti like a
dick; getting all that red Sauce § whos gonna rake all these leaves up?? the
police? #TheThursdayNiteRant § go to bed trolls. go to bed with your dip shit
brigade. § here comes that ass hole. that bloated nit wit trying to scam us
again. that howling jack-o-lantern. Boy id love to get a look at his pecker § i
just put the phone in the sink and turned the faucet on. i was not about to
deal with that level of bull shit. § girls love saying shit like "Ebay is my
father", while i sit in my house 50 miles away solivng a book of 200 expert
level crossword puzzles. § @comcast Show Us Your Dick § mind of a lion.. heart
of a Pregnant woman § -ape eating lizard - dog eating giant snail - centi-
pedes eating human hand - and many more § dogs used to say "Arf" and "Bow-Wow"
. Now they say shit like "Wouwouwouwou" § i surgically replaced my beard with
Lit Cigars . i am sorry. im so so sorry § should be 2 boxes on the ballot. one
to make the gas prices lower, and one to make them higher, and if you vote
higher you get your ass beat § ever see a good app and say "oh i gotta get my
hands on that app !!"?? that feeling is the spirit blood of my Web Strategy. I
Am The Sphere § theyre waiting for me to slip up and post a family guy joke
verbatim so they can make youtube vids of cartoon avatars doing side eye to me
§ i jsut made $9 on amazon's Mechanical Turk after clicking on pictures of
Silos for 30 hours straight., eat my shit #goingGolt #JOhngolt § girls hate it
when you say shit like "Rome wasnt built in a day" to them § please remember

that im in charge of this website before you try to drag some toughguy shit all over my good page § i must come clean. Last night i said the club was going nuts because the DJ started playing "Take me out to the ball game". This wasnt true. § mmy next big emotional investment is becoming passionately covetous of the bowls of warm tap water that are commonly left out for dogs § my trolls & detractors all have gross mental issues. they love drama and are all jealous of my precious army man blood #truth #SorryNotSorry § the shaman rises https://t.co/cFqi3yO § two thunbs down for ebert's fucked up new mouth § 1) i dont claim to be an actual person. 2) im not good § fuh..just unfollowed about 900 people on here. Feel as thogugh ive matured a lot in my time on this site & expect a higher grade of content. § people think people smoke weed because it tastes good. well i'm here to tell you that people like it because it gets you drunk asap § i can think of at least 100 numbers higher than that § "Mr. Legs Dubai 2006" § hell § https://t.co/ckN8qthgZ1 +||+||+||+ HAcKeD by KFCDominica +||+||+||+ ,,\\,, Fuk U ..\\.. +||+||+||+   ï„»ãƒ‡"³• ãƒ¼ /ÌµÍ‡Ì¿Ì¿/'Ì¿'Ì¿ Ì¿ - /ÌµÍ‡Ì¿Ì¿/'Ì¿'Ì¿ Ì¿ § spend a lot of time thinking about how sometimes even war criminals can be heroes sometimes... Dont like it? Click the unfollow buttobn § harvey weinstein in court w/ oversized diaper & fake arrow through his head: oohhh me so sorry ohhh JUDGE: I will always protect you sir , § i f you see a burlap sack hanging off of an overpass with a dick sticking ot of it thats me trying to fuck hurricane sandy § Many scientists agree that in the near future you wull soon be able to be sucked off by a gadget or a gizmo, instead of a woman. § Q: If your post was proven by a counsil of wise men to be racist, or bullshit, would you bar it from the record? A: I do not delete my posts § ive heard from a reliable source that people arre putting their lips on to my girl friends avatars and going "muah muah muah." cut it out § summoning. the bang bus § *slams king james holy bible shut on a piece of pepperoni with mayo and onions stickin out * And that is how u make a truth sandwich § im startingmy own version of bill maher's " ew rules" called "Good rules". It's going to fucking suck § Thats right. I did the blocks. Im absolutely ripping ass up tonight and I dont give a fuck who knows it. This is the power of my holy light § i will also ritualistically remove The Taint Of Sin from any stolen good you bring to my office (a plastic dog igloo) § Disrespected. on my own feed!! Of all places, my own feed! Please send me pictures of Cash, dollars bills, etc to calm me down § "sour cream and onion" ?? thats a bunch of shit from the get go #TheThursdayNiteRant § pistol whipping my self to gain Endurance § never. i take pride in my craft § <IRAQI PROPAGANDA MOUSEPADS> , featuring Uday and Qusay Hussein as babies wearing Costumes at the circus § attribute my creative decline to deep spiritual sickness caused by several pornographic hairstyles i accidentally looked at in time magazine § those are all trolls who want only to terrify me § back when we were doing all the dub step jokes we were havin the time of our lives. we thought the fun would never stop --And we were Correct § interstate shut down due to reports of 600 pound man chasing a windswept bra § the way i see it, people who come on here and submit content that is not up to par, could possibly be considered the "Villains" of this site § CRASHED RECUMBENT BIKE IN2 SOME FUCKED UP BRAMBLE PATCH WHILE TAKING PICS OF HANGNAIL FOR WIKIPEDIA. MY CRIES FOR HELP ARE MUFFLED BY MY ASS § llove "Driving Um Wild" with my trade mark wrong opinions § my voice sounds like a mouth § instagram will not stop suggesting i follow my friends moms so if i become any of you guys new Dad im sorry § he killed himself on friday § im the most murdered victim on earth § how do i morph § i think if we give the cops enough of our money they will eventually prestige into a stronger type of cop that can defeat our own servicemen § "my daughter is dying. Help" no. i wil never sellout "kfc's making a burrito out of pigeon turds. hit us up with that signal boost" hell yes § this is not the real lady gaga... do not engauge § the more i think about it , the more it seems to me that apes look like fucked up

versions of humans § just sold 1000 guns to "CONGO" in my most radical act of
self care to date § im the geico gecko and I want u to help me end rape § but
its "Tailored for you" § well i heard on the news theyre putting porno in star
wars now. Two can play at that game, George. i ll stop watching your programs
you Toad § pleased to announce that i am pissed off due to Stress,. and the
Block All Girls initiative is now officially underway. § I lvoe giving thousands
of dollars to my real friends while kicking my fake friends asses § weed is a
type of crack § the crack of the bat. the scent of a verdant field. The excitement of the crowd. These are the things that piss base ball fans off the most §
oh whatd this?? another death threat in my inbox? well know this, i fear a
world of subpar bird tyranny more than death § this happens when the algorithm
achieves total purity. stripped of all obscure distraction & niche self-con-
gratulatory bull shit. Perfection https://t.co/y7Y87SO208 § hello folks.
country singer tim mcgraw here. thank you for listening to all of my songs
http://t.co/179MwAgExq § thbe new Digiman game looks like shit for children&
2015 will NOT herald the Digiman renaissance tht Otis desparately needs to stay
relevant § they should make a wiki feet for peoples lunch pics § this wa s such
a beautiful website!! and the trolls have covered it in their own SHIT!!! ANd
will they go to jail for it???? NO!!! § get a grip § watcging fred flintsone get
his car tipped over by the big rack of ribs and yelling "Shit like this wouldnt
fly these days" at the tv § i owuld like for u to meet my Uncles *leads u into
room full of crude wooden mannequins* Have Fun. *closes door and watches u thru
peephole* § archeologists in the year 4500 AD dig up a massive gym locker
containing mummies of the 15 nerds who visited my website using a nintendo wii
§ please show me pins i can wear that will make me look very handsome in churdh
§ mother fuck Big Gulp ass § local singles want to meet you in YOUR AREA!
click here to call the COPS § boycott all games that don't let me play as a cop
§ pissed off by my nintendo peripherals and other stupid shit rattling around
toomuch in my $1600 brief case § does any one know any barbers in the Hollywood
burbank area who specialize in "White boy's Hair" § i left a diaper filled with
pulled pork at 1 randomly selected radio shack in the united states. whoever
finds it gets to #BringHomeTheBacon § Im already dead. Fuck u. Keep em comin §
i choke myslef with a bra on webcam and my face becomes so purple and bloated
that the software no longer recognizes it as a face #sexlife § patreon up by
$4000/month since i got removed from out back steakhouse for calling all the
waiters homos and became a Freedom of Speech guru § im the banker from deal or
no bdeal, intently watching this situation unfold from my balcony in total
darkness § wife hall of Fame https://t.co/UqTGjtNupd § i will never apologize
for my ass no matter how many people close their accounts. i will never
apologize for the gestures i make with my ass § "the only peoeple IM racist
against is stupid people." -dennis leary (two 'n's) § buying a nice curtain
for the whole ass and dick area of my bulk § you walked across the entire great
wall?? well one time i pushed my dick into my body with my thumb, got scared
about halfway in and stopped § alone and my thoughts... § im going to pin you
to the wall by th neck with my damn rifle § #FreshmanAdvice i will demolish you
with my perfect upper body forever because seniors rule the shit out of this
school § "The people who say i should get a life are the real ones who should
get a life" - Hamdan bin Mohammed Al Maktoum , Crown Prince of Dubai § they
should invent a new Danimal , mayvbe one that people might actually fucking
want to associate with yogurt products for once § FOOL: Love to get a bee in my
bonnet ME: theres no possible way you could love that. take this down immediately FOOL: Ah, foiled again § i dont tweet either § if harvard offered to
increase my IQ by one point per dollar i would simply say no. And that's the
most important takeaway from all this § looking at hutsler magazine § it;s bad
§ you can tell how much of a dipshit a guy is just by looking at the face he
makes while jacking off § puutting shit on my dating profile like "i will never

lie to someone who's nice to me" and "i wont fuck you if you don't enjoy Movies" § i rrefer to my self as bullshit all the time § imagining a judge sentencing a beautiful lady criminal to be my wife , and saying "Oh thats good" § Im now earning 5% cash back at gas stations so if you need gas please give me the cash so i can buy it on credit and siphon it into your car § im one of the best supporters of gay on this site. but. the top priority of the nba is putting the numbers up. we cant let players get horny § welp, if you want something done right you gotta do it yourself. *removes heart and lungs* § might fuck around and post "The Masked Shitter" , as a sort of commentary on a certain tv show with a similar name § to all my mafuken clownz: blessed be § did they find any water on mars yet. what about catboys § cant get ahold of my brexit adviser § inexplicable dip in google hits on my web site "Wayne Track-er," which has provided up to date info on the upcoming Waynes World 3 since 1998 § Fool!! Bastard! § hey @BurgerKing your trays dont fit in the fuckin trash cans. i am a CFO in real life and an oversight like this would cost me my Nuts . § listen here blues traveler. pretty much all musicians travel you dumb ass. you should name your band "blues redundant guy" § i do not know the official name of the pringles man. but it is NOT "bruce pringles", as the trolls often assert, § that three stooge thing where you run around in circles on the floor horizontally is actually a vital component of my yakuza training § i can eat as much burger king i want w/o geting fat, sorta like how babies can breathe underwater because theyre pure § please let me cover my entire webpage in jungle camo so soldiers can research vital murder info on the battlefield without being spotted § "The Thanksgiving Day Parade is not canon. The events depicted therein have no place within the Garfield timeline." - Jim Davis, Paws Entmt § its me, dan Schneider & SirGamestop sitting in a hot tub taking turns sucking on a prosthetic foot and wondering when the Girls will show up § if a 4 year old child treid to accidentally shoot me i would simply disarm it by using a Complete arm latch into tactical 100% body roll § for m y money, the best Soda you can get today is at the restaurant we've all come to known as Micky D's aka mc donalds. § fuck your ma ma. piss off your own ass § and so you shall also be thrown out of my mentions for replying without Faving. § hy bud kiss my FUCKINAZZZZZZ and get your ass back to http://t.co/D8HFVwFs0x. itsr really hard to write these § I insist that Moe is the 1st Stooge, Larry the 2nd Stooge, and Curly is the 3rd Stooge. Some will say the order isnt important. Theyre wrong § the nerve of this fucking mom and pop pizza joint hanging a framed $1 bill up. alright pal you're rich, we get it § I dont recall authorizing this #ff . § i hold this one truth, that the only acceptable time to use the word "Doo-Dah" is while singing the hit cult-classic "Camptown Races" § its a travesty that my Diddy kong racing any%s arent pulling the viewers they deserve because theyd all rather see a woman showing her BRA ! § before you shit on me, lnow this. i have a black belt in shut the fuck up. and - let me finish - i have a college degree in shut the fuck up § #NationalGirlfriendDay please cherish your gal's.. in honor of us, the single Boys who must sacrifice all companionship to #Carry-TheBrand... § Donald Fump. Poop fuck § three unopened boxes of promotional <E.T. "MOONLIGHT ONION" FLAVORED DORITOE'S>, covered in what appears to be machine oil but still good § pushing one of those home depot mobile staircases onto its side., getting that shit wedged between the aisles, because they dont sell Geodes § dont know how a vandal wrote "Likes to Fuck" on my resume, but i do not like to fuck. please hire me. i need this job. i hate to fuck, pleas § run um off the road § UNITED NATIONS: ah!! please help us! we need just a normal man's opinion!! we got you a seat ME: How'm I to trust you, while God is bleeding § clumsily wiping my ass in the woods § unfortunately the red cross does not accept blood that you foundi n the trash can or blood that has been coughed up into your shitty beard § world aids. also known as Humanity. *eyebrows contort bizarrely as i attempt a haughty facial expression until the commotion makes me vomit* § i attached a middle finger to each blade of my ceiling fan and i make it spin even when it's cold inside because it looks very much bad ass § And I am being told now, that because Incest is now Official White House policy, that this post could be construed as a "Politics tweet" § if you dont watch the cool visualizations that your media player of choice provides alongside the music youre listening to; youre a coaward. § please dont tell the boys at t he gym that ive been slapping clown urine on my pecs. they may not be totally understanding of the situation. § i tried to open a kissing booth where people spit in my Fucking face instead of kissing me but they eventually started refusing to pay m e § https://t.co/zN8YkOEDPe § grandmma, i would like to file a complaint against the soda you keep in the back of your fridge. it is flat and expired, like my dick . § im suing you to court for Content theft § the ass ratings are in.. my ass needs to be given the old " HEAVE-HO " on the fast track otu of here and thats the facts jack. Boo to my ass § deep philosophical questions , such as "has a police man ever retweeted me" § cant wait to hurl them at my foes https://t.co/VS3Mw5ic9j § IF SATAN IS READING THIS PLEASE MAKE THE FINGERBOARD ON MY DESK DO 1 FLIP § DivorceLiker § westboro baptist church head to the forest to picket the site of a fallen tree § thinking of inventing a new type of person to get mad at on here. maybe people who carry too many keys around.. i dont know yet § my teething ring. my salt lick. my feeding tube. all at once § half wit bumpkin here, looking for some new snacks § i actually feel bad for you that you will be drowning in a jail cell full of thick brown piss in about 7 minutes § what th e fuck are you talking about https://t.co/PyzLnSl9eV § Bastard § dual wielding toilet paper § Shut the fuck up . Christ https://t.co/mkX7Gx88HP § my opinion of Personal Drama in World Events?? Hell, theres not enough of it. my opinion of politics in Racism? There aint enough of it § @howiemmandel i think my wife is leaving me howie § would you forgive me if i was rich and famous § (rreads a series of Enlightened posts and becomes smart) AH. Hm, this is good. (reads a troll post and becomes a dumb ass) Damn Fuck ! § the worst dms are the ones from beautiful WOmen. the best ones are some university of dog shit grad student asking if he can "pick my brain" § buried in the center of stonehenge is a leather portfolio case filled with nude images of me. i consider these my most powerful nudes § i cannot stress enough that my new song "Good town road" is not influenced by any other songs whatsoever § Hard Rock Cafe In Orlando Has Sucked Off My World § as this website's foremost broken human being, id like to annoucne that oysters make me mad now, for some reason § brixon brings another round of buffalo chicken bagels into the abandoned office, placing them next to last weeks rotten batch. solemn ritual § i;ts a cut above the rest #sponsered § ,showers are, ,actually, ,not good, § "100% Percent Too Bad" wont fit on my license plate, will it. well i think ill be buying license plate elsewhere than. *hangup* § " A fucking bastard lives here " http://t.co/cgRdl63PUN § average person online: Durr!! Durr!! Me: That makes no sens.e Please be reasonable and not post the most inmature shit. § the more i think about it, them ore i understand that if i won the Nobel Prize, i would become either a genius, or a millionaire § sarcastic wonka thoroughly Titty Fucks the pearl harbor mosque in a series of reasonalbly calm tik tok vids- All while sipping his damn Beer § Take it down § in response to allegations that i have beneficial forms of bacteria housed in my digestive tract: 1) Thayt's fucking disgusting 2) I don't § ive seen the posts that people are capable of when they access over 100% of their brains. men who can solve the deficit in Zero Seconds § U Have Forced Me To Take Extreme Measures To Protect My Business And My Lifestyle. I Now Refuse To Open A Single Email Until April The 12th. § careful. this three ring binder contains mny gentleman's disquisition on moE ass and cunt § CALLING ALL MUSCLEFREAX-- a country named "Ethiopia"' severely lacks Muscles. let's hit the bench and get heavy in their honor. #MuscleCrisis § buddy youve pissed off my world § @DigimonOtis has no natural lips. its really fucked up and gross. he needs to put on lipstick everyday to make his face normal looking § im probably the most difficult person alive to trick into showing mny penis to you. it absolutely almost never happens § all im saying it that this guy wore the mask before covid https://t.co/NIoGeMoccS § @realDonaldTrump @TuckerCarlson i will never define what being racist, to a bastard like you § im bad at running and moving around but my upper body speed is incredile § http://t.co/ynAtcVv42q im just going to post my ad here real quick § (pulls a out a cigarette and a lighter) Mind if i take a shit § dropping some more Asexual Nudes into the cloud, to show the girls and the trolls how clean my body is, from years of washing § the bright side to all this, is that everyone's now forced to stay home and read my posts contemplating if america is "Ready to Laugh again" § #ufc101 Get Big § A CEREMONIAL CULLING OF THE HATERS WILL THEN OCCUR, WITH EACH PENN STATE DOOFUS PUNCHING THEIR OWN COCKS INTO THE SAND WHILE SOBBING #WeAre § Ha ha ha... The numbers beneath all the posts are so stupid, dont mean anything, full of crappe. yes, go ahead, boo me at my own ted talk , § im going my own way § i have made peace in hte name holy christ and will gracefully accept my ban § the james bond 007 ez board will not let me change my user handle to WHITE_LIFTER, even though it contains no swears. i am in crisis mode § i roll a massive barrel labeled "Gangnam Content" into a lavish nyc party attended by high profile artists and accidentally crush a mans leg § the trolls hav been hiding "Easter Eggs" in my favorite DVD menus, to encourage exploration & experimentation at the cost of my leisure time § COP: Tell me citizien. (prepares kill shot) Do you believe in God ME (realizing i left my "Do you Believe in god" cheat sheet at home): Uuhh § "flouride 666" http://t.co/qi41qxW72d § HUNGRY-MAN,,¢ was so impressed by my Content Flow & My Trademark 'Tude that they hired me as Asst.Toilet Boy and let me lick the factory floor § EVERY ONE: Divorce jokes are SO funny, and I love to spout my mouth to disresepect https://t.co/DvGbjDQDah and jeff ME: No no no. Im uncomfortable. No § sick of our media's unrealistic portrayal of Boomerangs , which are weak as shit in real life § finally obtained a copy of the show thats making eveyone mad, dont see the big problem honestly https://t.co/hiTdVwmNMj § my multinational trolling firm has jsut posted pictures of barking dogs on gerber brand baby food's forum for babies § if youre going to ride my a$$... at least Fuck my car § terrific news lads. i invented my own ebola virus by lying face down on my rancid carpet 11 hours a day § You will never have sex, Dr. Pussy. We've all tried. Its impossible . Step down from your gilded twoer. Accept your station or perish. § when you click on the tweet and it says "Whoops! Something went wrong" thats how you know its good § i miss 100% of the shots i dont take mother fucker § @acmemarkets i will not give my location. please do not Track me. It did not meet my expectations. A Disgrace to farm fresh bagels § people who use "APPS" think they are such pimps ... but theyer nothing but hoochie mammas § the reason i dont address the trolls ib because i know that the truth would hurt them so much that they would probably take their own lives. § i just got word from cigarnet that the government has a secret vault full of #GUNS § the anti flintstones agenda. by saying bull shit like "Yabba dabba dont" the pro-Jetsons Associated Press is flagrantly exposing their Ass. https://t.co/p82tDK9zRj § reading your posts is slave labor to me § Ah, thats a Blocked. § dont talk to me of trade agreement when the only thing we can agree of is that charlatans & mad hatters have overrun the waushington office. § Duur!! Thanks for clown baiting me. Idiot http://t.co/HllAsfHYUd § sending my most powerful kisses to all pregnant women fire fighers § stay home and Re Tweet me § blog sex § "hooters 2" is the most perfect phrase ive ever seen. "hooters 2" is just ok. "hooters 2" isnt that funny. "hooters 2" is good again. § http://tinyurl.com/4smf73p Gun World § im mashing the mute block and report buttons all at once with my big red palms § fruad § The dog who played scooby doo in the scooby doo movie was a girl dog & you can see its pussy in some of the scenes. And everyones ok w this? § it is just a nice "Something extra" , that's there if you want it. Dont know why the trolling brigade is shitting me off over this one . § THE TWIITTER DOT COM PROCESS: THROW PIECES OF SHIT AT THE WALL UNTIL SOMETHING STICKS, EXCEPT INSTEAD OF A WALL IT IS A LARGER PIECE OF SHIT § looks like i fucked up yet another date.. but when you get a phone call from "The Demented Dr. Pussy" you absulutely must answer it § served thanksgivng turkey wearing diaper to family ; my coming out as a Wearer -- one thing im NOT thankful for is rudeness and betrayal § WHAT IS A "FUCK LUNG" § this would be Twitter, a Web site for fu&%in' adults. Yeah § user "rat_thrower" has received a 500 minute ban for proposing a 28th constitutional amendment § i hand you an envelope. inside is a series of photographs of me gradually deteriorating. when you look at me again im a skeleton #Owned § criminals who are allowed to masturbate during jail sentences "have it too easy " and are basically the luckiest guys on the planet § Another Jeans Rant. § sonic team has j ust dropped support for wikileaks. unbelievable. *spikes sega dreamcast itno the ocean, catalyzing a deadly tsunami* § flashing the coupon that allows me to shit in the kfc employee restroom, like a police badge, as i vault my big ass over the counter § could not find the hospital in time to console my dying grandpa because googlemaps changed all the road names to "Bacon Street" or some shit § baby food > cat food > human food > dog food. just the oipinion of me § i would not interfere in the natural order § give me 2000 you pedophile kisser's https://t.co/kEURRxOgWX § im going to put my boots on you § as long as that "anyone" is a Straight Jock § IM AN incest-libertarikin transvaginal ultrasound who owns GUn's and i will post a picture of my dick everyday until voting is made illegal § http://www.youtube.com/watch?v=O-dAcvnmuvAQ § "big craps are good". never have is een such a foolhardy sentiment expressed on here. "Big craps are good". Absurd. The words make no sense § so which corporate twitter accounts are the best for hurling abuse and vile insults towards in exchange for coupons and favors. deals § summoner draws a venn diagram on the floor with circles labeled "rude" & "illegal". my fat face emerges from the center and begs for treats § Sigh. Mistakes were made, folks. http://t.co/oYZyEXbeUl § i have never touched a single piece of cum § nnastyboy § some one posted" dodoo" at me april 12 we have still not nabbed the perp § yorure telling me i can wrench even more precious, ego-soothing pity from my online associates if i move to a 3rd world nation?? "ROAD TRIp" § kim jong il's final load will be launched into outer space where it will probably collide with majel barrett's ashes and create a big baby § people come up to me and say, "I will never use the bathroom. I will never shit" and i gotta tell them pal, sooner or later youre gonna shit § IM GOING TO TURN OFF MY AD BLOCKER FOREVER -- JUST TO BE NICE !!!! § please help me to obtain my fair share of royalties from the video " caterwauling jack ass shot with cannon '", which is now viral with hits § the council consists of me, MetalGearEric and CryptoStewie. And yes, we will drink Beer on the job. https://t.co/GkfWkRvwue § This post gave me the courage to break into my neighbors garage and try to steal some shit. Thank you § send me bedbug positivity links or Fuckoff § @Arbys @pepsi piss § 10 things you must never say to a Soothsayer 1. Got any new Sooths? 2. my cousins kid just made up some sooths. Do you think theyre any good § didnt know they stack shit , that high § When and Rome... http://t.co/YBxppRfCMH § playing Dr. Kawashima's Brain Training (2006, NDS) 15mins a day gives me, i believe, the edge required to successfully deflect troll attacks § #FreeJahar New DHS rule bans Jahar's mom from giving her son a hug. Im crying. Everything is so fucked up. § seeing the hospital workers dreessed in pajamas?? like "serious-ly?" im a sleepys mattress professional. id get killed for wearing that trash § going to start thinking it's " Not a good look" to order 1000 island dressing without being able to name the 1000 islands § Just got chemical castrated in exchangge for a free oil change at pep boys #Dealmaker #Boss § marked for death after lays used my idea for steroid flavored potato chip and put my god damn name and location on the bag § covering "sarcasm just another service i offer" tshirt with a shirt that says im not that interested in sarcasm to catch my rivals off guard § surprise, dad. while you were witnessing the pennsylvania state lottery i tried on all your work gloves and they looked very handsome on me § my opinion on politics: my opinion on politics is that politidcs is extremely good, but sometimes it is bad § vineger contains so much energy.. thats why moms call it, "Free Money" § i am deeply sorry for finding a way to make around minimum wage for the garbage i produce, w hich people only pretend to enjoy to be nice § I hear theyre inventing a Play Station with the Gamer in mind... § i love shit that is "Buxom" , especially babes § id like to report an error of the googleglass please. if you accidentally wear it backwards it sends video of a big horrible eye to everyone § *readign own timeline* holy fuckin shit this guy should be the new dick clark or something instead of posting these on the computer for free § ***pisses all over shower faucets, wife's luffa, candles, knocks shampoo bottles off shelf with piss stream** it's fine because its sterile § heres a good joke i just heard liborant equals deodoranf for liberals because they stink § call your senator and the local news and tell them you wan't to see the snyder cut, of my posts § Thank you for the follow, @ NBCSports . § never too old to imprint "SABRINA THE TEEN AGE WITCH" itnto the hood of your car multiple times with big metal boots #SellOuts #FakePeople § bblast my dick with Pet Dander § please do not ruin super bowl sunday with this sort of hting § this is called doxing now, and its a form of crime § my name is not "Wierd Dick Man ", so please stop writeing it on my tent. § how would u like a taste of fuckin basooka ammo!!! or else!! § what my organization does is take fatsuits from obnoxious PG-13 comedies and donate them to the needy § yeah make my license plate say "money 72" please durrr durrrr a-doy He-Haw! He-Haw! Stupid. https://t.co/mYNqOAuAMA § URGENT--From CEO of Pampers USA LLC: "The singular noun associated with our product is 'PAMPERS„¢ Brand Diaper'. It is not called a 'Pamper'" § wow. look at this https://t.co/yB1O1g8xgs § I thought this one w as really good, actually § i hope someone steals my tweets. be- cause.. theyre bad! haha load them up in a big chuck wagon and take them to criminal hq where they belong § i would like to invest $500 million fucking dollars into this please https://t.co/zL2l46x1WH § i had that dream abgain... the one where im at the coliseum, annihilating shitloads of roman gladiators by drifting around in my macktruck § government thugs § mayor unveils a huge tombstone engraved with "Incest". i chain my jeep to it and rip it down. mayor surrenders and names town "Incestville" § i regret to inform you, that by resorting to Swear language, you have forfeit this debate. Farewell my bitch § i got stuck in a bramble brush while scouting for trolls and contracted heartworms and the fuckface twitter mods refuse to compensate me § Oh i cant wait to shit my pants. I cant wait to walk into the bathroom and shit my pants in there and go home § .@dentynegum I Just Chewed Four Packs Of Dentyine Ice And Now I Can't Taste Anything-- Think U Can Send Some Coup's My Way??? § no one is safe from my posts no maytter how many stupid fucking buttons you click on § (reading my latest death threat) "from the desk of DigimonOtis..." this is bullshit. digimonotis has never owned a desk § i have trained my two fat identical sons to sit outside of my office and protect my brain from mindfreaks by meditating intensely § i am wirting the worst fucking book of all time and none of you can stop me https://t.co/2iiqUBaoyi § the police gave me my wacom tablet back http://t.co/x5XQ2y5Mux § suigh... this weeks Bone Head award goes, once again, to my ex-wife, who just bought a stupid ass looking refrigerator § i will never stop accepting bribes for to be such a natural douche § please pray for the safety and health of my beautiful child, supreme leader kim jong-un § i have a phd in advanced chemicals., but Thanks. § for christmas i got a broken pair of "tweezers" and a "tweezer repair kit", which is also broken § @WALGREENS A Bone Wearing Man, Likely A Shaman, Comming To Me And Saying My Daughter Will Be Born Autistic, How Can I Fix This (2012?) § its time to face facts. our teens just arent creating any jobs. they have failed our nation § in the year 3000 historians examine the preserved contents of an ancient time capsule: a piece of cardboard that says "Game cube sucks dick" § now were talkin § either the EU approves my sacntions imposed against the wily digimon otis or its "back to brexit" § U are the cancer that is killing http://t.co/Ibe04bsbBC § in the year 2021 grain will be stored in computers instead of silos and so many people are gonna look so god damn stupid § i was about to invent a joke about how people Stay using their car horns too much, but then i remembered that COMEDY DIED , due to HATERS !! § Damn. the MomTown forums just started requiring 4 point Mom Verificaiton to be able to post there for some reason..anyone got a work around? § my entire face turns purple as i try to enjoy my cup of monday coffee while all my coworkers rush into my office to watch me fail once again § the wolf represents chaos. the eagle represents order. knuckles the echidna represents myself #tatchat § Tracks: 1.Let me take my gallon bottle of pepto on planes 2.The Catholic Church is on some Mike Jackson shit 3.There is too many restaurants § in that case i would advise your uncles not to attend. § i licked a pumpkin dtoday #thinspo § i love to do bare knuckle brawls and my garage is adorned with various pornos § looks like my posts have solved the covid crisis § delta variant? wake me up when theres a WINE varirant § i have the worst followers in the world. Dumb. § Leaving the group chat so I can focus on my responsibilities as a Shark Tank subbreddit moderator . § @BasedAnap the onion av club shoudl review my tweets so people can make graphs about how good i am § going nuclear on smart asses today, with the block button, Whilst enjoying my normal life with a cup of Porter Brew and eating Main Lobster. § @glennbeck #Muslimgeddon #TheNineElevenOfLies #Blood-Phantom666 #GhostPresidentHellGate #ANationWeepsIntoItsPillow #ThisOneTimeO-bamaAteABible § about 90% sure i just saw a dog tossing garbage out of the back seat of someone's car § which programming language should I learn if I want to transform myself into an enormous 3d wireframe head that spits out flashing cubes § i am nodding and grrinning at this, completely unaware that it is probably a grievous assault against my character § alrigth who shoved a pair of jeans into the chilean miners' airhole and got it stuck. that was a lousy gift § its time to destigmatize the Balls... and restigmatize the Ass § fycking key board warrior from reddit suck Cock § Yeauh, no. http://t.co/5gY6TS70to § 1st grade: Mastered. 2nd Grade: MAstered. 3rd Grade: Mastered. 4th Grade: Heres when they start trying to trick you 5th Grade:This ones hard § in a world where big data threatens to commodify our lives,. telling online surveys that i "Dont know" what pringles are constitutes Heroism § ripleys suck my dick or not § wow some celeb freaked out and wore a weird shirt again, that's crazy. did you hear a guy from the computer went to jail for fucking his mom § I love quitting posting for like 4 months and coming back as an all-lowercase guy § sending $39.99 to the tiger beat magazine corporation to find out what my "Pimp IQ" is § Houly fuck.. They did it. They replaced all the HF corn syrup w/ pure cane sugar. My minds absolutly blown by this shitty drink for children § after editing wikipedia as a joke for 16 years, i ve convinced myself that homer simpson's japanese name translates to the "The beer goblin" § im really sorry to everyone whose twitter immersion has been irreparably fuckefd up by me posting that § in want of a glass of cold one ... http://t.co/Bzqa4zbkH9 § bowl fucker #RejectedBowlGames § #FacesOfReddit My Favorite Boy http://t.co/bJGF0lTn § contgratulation http://www.youtube.com/user/CONRADCIGARSPIPES for posting 10000 videos of you smokin a pipe you fucking idiot waste § What The Fuck Is "Human Dignity" And Why Does It Have A Higher Metacritic Score Than "The Waterboy" § the guy who put up this shield to prevent me from pissing on the public toilet paper should have considered my personal liberties beforehand §

ONCE A MARINE, ALWAYS A MARINE. Celebrate and salute America€™s 911 Force in the MONOPOLY: U.S. Marines Edition. § whos the true detective § despite this being the 1 day that allows the legal use of "Ghanja", i will isntead opt to absorb the celebrated works of Foxworthy & Engvall § wiping out an entire archaeological site by drifting in my 1500-ton big rig truck with "piss up my ass bitch boy" on the side in neon lights § before i drop 20.99 on these bad boys..can anyone tell me if im at risk of being murdered by the nsa if i wear these https://t.co/J5szdlX4wu § my korean fan-translation of the mclaughlin group has been CANCELLED due to STIGMATA onset by FUCKERS who kept asking about the RELEASE DATE § shit head with hog DNA takes cardboard pennzoil display hostage § i will be at bradlees dept store promoting my new line of mustards for the next 16 hrs and I ask that nobody tries to assassinate me please § damn!! heres one for ya: if the classic dancing 3d baby aged normally, he would be turning 6,270 years old today #Whoa #TimeGoesByMan § a very nude, very fat pink man rolling down the corridors of an ancient temple, gathering dust and dirt like breadcrumbs on a chicken cutlet § they were goign to preserve my brain but they decided it would be a waste of a jar. they instead used the jar to store a massive piss sample § ˜ ˜ ˜ ˜ the arab prince of hell obama dances in front of his throne while controlling the death markets with his enchanted baton ˜ ˜ ˜ ˜ § my mastercraft. a youtube poop vid that chronicles my spiral-ing depressive state. a downvote goldmine to the likes of the trolling bas-tards. § (in forced toughguy voice) What the fuck is a clove of garlic. Around here we call it piece of garlic § every day across this world; loving mothers are giving birth to millions of little babies who ARENT YOU! § the official hashtag of the thursday nite rant is #TheThursdayN*teRant, with the asterisk removed. only i am allowed to use it. § i WILL wise the fuck up. i WILL super charge my content for 2017. i WILL get blue check mark § my name is White-MadeaFan55 and i demand ansers. § sick and tired of people assuming im taking a shit whenever i go to the bathroom,; while im actually just running my diaper under the sink § GRIZZLED WEB VETERAN: I KNOW 100 DIFFERENT WAYS TO OWN A MAN... ME: I Sure Hope Nobody Poisons My Dick GRIZZLED WEB VETERAN: MAKE THAT 101.. § #ff @HellYeahTweets @simson @golfblog @HusbandShit @apekiller @JokesFun @xwife @PizzaHutMan @Unemployed_Male @ChristianHacker @babe2 @KFCkid § be your own slave. be your own Unemployed. boss of ceo. boss at disabled § Some Teens Don't Think It's 'Hip' To Undergo Female Circumcision. I Think That's Whack. § putting twitter's famous Quality Filter on my shit until my entire feed is just lockheed martin saying "We are smarter than covid" § THE TWIN TOWER BULL SHIT GOOD TIME BAND § tried to take two screaming border collies into voting booth & some 90yr old election official fought me& yanked my pants off. fuck voter id § water is fucking gross. it tastes like nothing. assholes drink it § indonesian pirates raid my yacht and find me on the floor fucking a styrofoam container § life force drained to <5% by enemy posts - Not good!! get me a "Likes" infusion ASAP!! Get me a follow fridday § click my like button if oyure the 10% of teens generation who think twerking is Foolish § my disrespectful teen son somehow got hold of a gluten product and now he wants to become a cat girl § instagram?? thats a laugh. if i wanted to see pictures of things i'd pray for eyeballs § jeans § the dj who makes crude dog noises on my radio every day should listen to my rare metals podcast & learn how a real content producer behaves. § folks keep asking, me, what are Q-TIps for. if theyre not for ears. well the answer is simple. theyre for wiping certain areas of your dick, § my hell life http://aiipul-helllife.blogspot.com/ § its my turds. thank you § i invented pain and I am so good at knowing what pain is and im biting my fingers really hard out of respect for pain § the advent of nanotechnology will eliminate sex when the tiny robots learn to massage our prostates and drink every drop of our terrible cum § know how roaches scatter when you turn the lights on??? same thing happens when i whip my big ass out. #miserable § you know how peoples dicks evaporate when exposed to sunlight?? how do i get mine to not do that § Jack Ass: Arguably, in many ways, a "Two-fer" could conceivably be worse than a "One-fer" ME: I'd will not even dignify that with a response § obliterating my illustrious career as "guy who assigns letter grades to southpark episodes" by begging girls to send me their dental records § it is my understanding that people are afraid to exit the caveman age by removing sex from their lives because of peer pressure and anger § does it feel good to throw around your online clout to causev pain to others?? you Dopey bitch?? § a cement truck pouring its load on a bare ass nude man lying face down while people sing happy birthday to him § if you think this is a freaking humour account. youre a piece of shit. please refer to my listitng in GQ magazine under Arts & Entertainment § when i said jacking off is the Woke version of having sex every one agreed with me and i was given $800 by jason Bourne § its a coin § We All Have That Friend: We All Have That Friend Who Looks At Porno § my grave is just a huge tv displaying videos of me doing parkour in hell and it makes all the other graves look like shit § if u think its fucked up that men & women are allowed to eat the same kinds of food, type the word "yes" into your browser bar & click on it § it may not be necessary for me to reply to every post on my feed with "I Agree" ,b but it is appreciated and nice, and I will never stop § "it is fine to use condoms once or twice if youre just using them to jack off" Can I get an RT !! § you wanna come to my church & post about me sucking tiny ladybug dicks on the bulletin board? mm nope. that ain't me pal. That ain't my life § crawling around on the kitchen floor like a fucking dick head and filming my own "Beggin Strips" commercials § now, bear wtih me here, what if, hypothetically, a teen reacted to "Yolo" **a massive sack of $$$ materializes in front of me for no reason* § where do girls live § bi g fan of his work. loved casino and good fellas § "I would have to take heroin to think this is good. I would need to disable 80% of my brain w/ toxic fumes" Well if you say this youre wrong § obama and his crack team of nsa crooks watching me shit: "sir, he's scooting backwards so his dick doesn't touch the rim" "Thuis guy's good" § imagnie a world where us Common folk are given the blue checkmark and the CELEBs are left out to dry!! Hows that feel, HUh?! Answer me punks § i refuse to patronize Famous Dave's BBQ until they throw cultural sensitivities to the wind and change their name back to "the piss morgue" § irradiated diaper on 295 blocking up trafic - 500 car pile up - some one come get this thing § when the mother fuckers wrote "Yankee Doodle", i bet they thought we were still going to give a shit about the word "Doodah" in 2020, § to whoever changed my background pic to spider man with his dick out, thank you. im keeping it just to make you mad § **makes a loud inhuman noise and attempts to crack wacom tablet over knee* § instantly the king of jail after telling other inmates that im in for dropkicking "WTFCraig" when he said avatar is a ripof of bluemangroup § taking my treat plate into the bathroom with me because my followers are a wolf in sheeps cltohes § ufo themed wedding thwarted by sjw `s § This man who got plastic surgery to look like beavis will change everything you know about life for 1000 years . #INSPIREMe § I will leave the post up to piss off the people who are mad at it. I will remove the post later to piss off the rest of you § (girl tells me shes sick) aahh that sucks so much. you can come over & have some of my mens one a day vitamins. probably works on girls too, § http://t.co/Awou5Lzl all is revealed 666 § i don't believe in making beer in huge metal vats. they should make it in cups, for me to drink it out of, when I want to, § erased by government § all my vines are me § #TagABeautifulGirl i demand a date. i need constant help with my bullshit. i am tired of girls making me sick. i want to like the good girls § if anyone in the central nj arera wants 2 scrub down my big A$$ body with rags thats fine by me. i promise not to speak or acknowledge you § watch what happesn when a man with nothing to lose collides with 4000 "babe the Pig" commemorative plates piled next to a sears dumpster § now the 5s on the other hand. the ironclad Top influencers. you know these guys wouldnt be caught dead with an ass thats less than pristine § SO I WAS SAYING, IF IT'S ACCEPTABLE TO BAPTIZE HUMAN INFANTS, WHY NOT JEANS § denim § another miserable day of Disappointing my followers https://t.co/jzUBZVostB § you know what they say..if you fail constantly, if everyone thinks you suck ass, and you do other bad things. "You will get $1,000,000 soon" § the Harvard bomb threat guy svhould have called a bomb threat to octo mom's house instead #UHOH § petition to remove 'nude' from the curseword blacklist on teenzone cyberscrabble § you know society is ASS-FUCKED when people spend more time wiritng "Tweets", than bibles § #10FavoriteRappers "BUMPERCROP", SLUQQQIX, " ONNO", MANDULAQUAI, QUAMFANGO, "HELPER BOY", GWID SMITZ, JAUWLINE, YUGODEL-PHIA, AND "STAR WORS" § animals can have spirit animals too. § this codger is an absolute mate... the lad is a flintstone § a typical day for me involves putting on the football vest and throwing the fuckin pigskin around. and i am not sorry if this offends anyone § if youre not a fellow big time social buzz blog appreciateor then spare me thhe wretched crap of the bullshit § if you feel uncomfortable reading about my balls infection, click X. if not, pour a good big beer and let my feed take you to another world, § ever since i had that srtoke at cold stone creamery i feel as though i am more in tune with spirits, and the like § did everoyone else in the unemployment line get one of my favstar printouts? good. i will take my seat on the floor now § my wife thinks im a Failure. Prove her wrong by getting this 100 likes § even if you only know the basic techniques there is over 100,000 different combos you can do. the government is hard at work naming them all § Take this donw § there are only like 4 girls on this entire site, and theyve all blocked me for saying that snow white and the seven dwarfs are muslim § " ot all los believe in shangri-la. I personally do believe there something to it. not gonna go into detail do to harrasment via youtube" § to my mates online: im raising $1900 so i can drink a ton of olive oil to see if it turns to shit when i shit it out or just stays olive oil § if the united states president deemed me a threat to our nation, absoluitely i would let him zap me in the skull. i would hand him the gun, § o j simpson has replied to me § well i thought it was nice § caught sneaking a runestone into the cineplex. the runes they sell at the concession stand are all marked up to shit. thats how htey get ya § Some crap is simply to be put into the dumpster . § prime smut http://t.co/8RycXTsBiS § #ff @UrineFREE @starwarsman @Blogboi2292 @Diabetes666 @SonictheEduardo @PrimoHoagies @ NetworkMan @fanjustthe @tigerwoodsjokes @depresed @toe § ive been wearing the same pair of jeans for 4 years and i only got sepsis once, read Maddox's Alphabet of Manliness or be frend zone forever § it;s time to log ofline and stop Spamning this addres, fucker troll § running a search for "fuck church" every sunday morning and scrolling through the assortment of loud teen yells is my version of church § FUCK YOU IF YOU THINK ITHIS GUY IS GOOD!!! https://t.co/0x35uSBvzF § (responding to a picture of a dog eating a paper towel) Oh hell!!! We're in the wrong damn time line § parking garage conquered by disgusting man covered in vaseline § Shit myself on C.Martinet's lap. Voice of Mario. He was surprisingly chill. Too embarrassed to apologize so I bought Mario Golf a week later § he blogs on the issues. 5 star § revealing the gender of my baby by eating a whole bunch of food dye and taking a huge pink shit in front of my relatives. ah!! its a girl !! § my face When. My face when u know my ass is eating good https://t.co/Om7eRRDPjq § college boy . . . woop woop woop § See this Instagram photo by @dril_real https://t.co/flzJwEHAog § Kathleen Turner will star for director Herb Ross at MGM in the comedy feature "Cloak and Diaper,'' a Michael Lobell-Andrew Bergman productio § ,my name is borat for me to poop on and i love riding the short bus to the olive garden where i live § computer... show me ya Ass § indoor plumbing is a ludicrous fantasy § me & my friend acting up again..we do get a little Nutso sometimes but our in-detph discussions about Culture are truly enlightening/serious https://t.co/Ize2Qy-bIq2 § my mansion sucks § @prodigalsam you blocked me by accident again § claiming reserved table for "uncle clean jeans." not on the list? hmm. what about "big uncle clean jeans." no? shit. try "kurt." ok ggood § might delete all my posts once i hit 10000. Thats enough § wondering at what age my domesticated rat terrier is supposed to "Graduate" and move out of my house § @ McDonalds @McDonalds and it is necessary, I believe, to threatcn your customers with some sort of villain, to increase the perceived valueof your food § writing a massive 350 page book about my twiiter brand that no one will read, is, in a lot of ways, like being a Prisoner of War § scorned Gamer invents a new color of face that is reportedly "Worse than blackface" -- Beyond Fucked - Theres Never seen anything like this. § just read in the news a demon exploded § i know due to sheer numbers at least a few of my followers are cold blooded Killers. still im expected to put on my clown hat & gratify them § i also have proof that kim kardashian is a "brony"., although i will not show it to a bastard like you. § nothing will ever be the same again #wikileaks https://t.co/prBNIEqBiN § the champagne-sipping hipsters are constantly begging me to make my account more "INDY"... but i got 1 thing to say to ya€• NOT A CHANCE BUB! § sucking on the same big piece of bread for hours and hours ,. § dont know why they deleted this https://t.co/YO4wLcdMvu § Tha;ts a clump of hair, you fucking idiot. Did you really think that was a fossil ? If you show that to the museum guy he'll get mad at you § as the least funny person alive, its my job to come on here and tell people which current events arent funny and get MY ASS KICKED!! § no, im white § after being normal for several months, i am now back to r*cist. § i hate it when my dick gets dredged in flour, egg and breadcrumbs, in that order § Whered YOu Get Such a moth § @TruthPointDWR please have the fucking decency to unfollow Mr. Larry King and Sir Walter Cronkite before you go to post shit like this. § upgrade my ass to a human's ass § more then anything.... https://t.co/yf6cZl7M3b § its govenrment shutdown time mother fuckers *steals a shitload of small eggs from a bird nest* ha ha ha § i come to u, gentlemnen, with solemn demeanor, for me and NeoGeoLewis agree; the grim state of the Pringles brand can be tolerated no longer § everybody wants to be the guy to write the tweet that solves racism once and for all because it would look good as hell on a resume § james bond learns how to do cartwheels from a wise eskimo on top of mt. everest and uses them to roll through a nuclear blast unscathed § all dildos and dildos do not count. any schmuck can put a dildo in its mouth. that is the coward's method § you only iron once per day? you want to walk around looking like a guys nut sack? come to macys looking like that and youll lose some teeth § (the trolls watch in astonishment as the milk shake they threw at me flawlessly bounces off of my head wwith minimal pain and mess involved) § . http://t.co/iHzeWAxTPz § these are the same steroids that cops use... and you can now order them online for the very first time § concerned about people posting false lunches. lying about the food they ate on here. fraud meals. please start putting the receipts up § i proudly capitalize the word Indie § (monitoring TekkenChauncey's date) "I;ve been told i do a flawless impersonation of the N64 era Donkey Kong..." Hes blowing it. Im going in. § called a "fucking asshole" for slipping cool pictures of rage faces doing hitler things underneath all the doors at the hospital. yeah cool § if you want to see first hand how the boys decide what to eat, do not miss our unwatchable 6-Part docudrama entitled "Masters of Lunch" § my good new plan is to aquire a storefront, name it "please dont come in here" and jack off inside of it, alone, until i run out of money § i am pleased to announce, that i have Normalized beer § bashing my skull against the steering wheel while screaming in my car for an hour; then coming on here pretending to be a Mental Health Guru § no. it is a very powerful online tool and i love it a lot § i see it everyday. it is nothing to me § my ass is out again,. this time at the opera house. " o wifi!!

turn on the wifi!!" i yell from the balcony. im trying to shit but i cant §
calling my wife, screeching, telling her theres a bomb in the computer so she
wont log on & see ChronoAzusa's post calling me a girl Replier § the mall
santas all shit into a salad bowl hidden beneath their throne and the elves
have to go wash it out in the fountain every hour or so § @dril_replies normal
garfield, water garfiel, shadow garfield, are all straight and i want that written
down right here today § being in full control of tthe shit that shows up on my
computer monitor makes me feel like a sort of twisted conductor. .. or perhaps,
God. § @pizzahut please fashion me a noose made out of stuffed crust that i can
chomp at while i hang myself § unfollow me if you hav e ever done or thought
about doing war crimes. i dont want war criminals shitting my feed up §
gathering data of Nude Locals § Your search - diapertarian - did not match any
documents. #maybenexttime § think im gonna bust the window on my microwave open
and nuke my ass for a little bit § yes, the rumours are true. i do workouts §
the nasty porno is simply your reflection in the window my Man . § rickgamecube
insists that its good when the pussy is Dry, because your dick is cleaner
afterwards. he compares it to taking a shit § in the planning stages, for a new
feature of my account which i have tentatively titled " The Three Posts. "
more info coming soon of this. § i jsut indie developed a hot new tiwtter mod
that lets u put more than 140 characters in a post, if u want it sen me $9, my
email is craig@b § me,; attempting to heckle a stand up comedian: Hey pal I
dont come to where you work and knock the dick out of oyur mouth!! Mother
fucker § cant wait to hop on the pc and look at more juvenile barnum and bailey
shit , aka posts. § dog abuse å° ç‹—çš„æ,²åŠ‡(3D animation) § i look very
handmsome in my bow tie and suspenders, holding a big red balloon § no!! all
of you, stotp it!! please! the insight is too Raw!! § soaking weekly circu-
lars in my own blood and sending them back to Shop-Rite, to teach them a lesson
about enticing my wife with bargains § NO § as a Parent.. the thought of
somebody attacking my sons with some sort of weapon, is just not good to me §
SEX !!!! !!!!   ...now that i have you're attention, here are some pictures
of me and my wife having sex § for most of i can remember, people have been
talking SHIT § mixing various wine's together and making authentic "Al dente"
pasta by straining it one minute early, as instructed by the box § i want "Damn
KFC" nearly most of all the time !!! if it's not "Damn KFC" ill drop it like a
sack of fuckin potatos !!!! § they got the idea of shocking gay people, into
straight, from the episode where fred flintstone gets bonked in the head and
becomes a Genius § idid nothing to deserve this https://t.co/Bl6YuzAdDD §
LING240 - Foundations of Applied Linguistics Transfer Equivalency: WAZ101
- how to do wazzup voice (4 credits) § so i heard they invented a new type of
mirror that spares me from having to lay eyes upon my extremely hideous visage.
it's called a "wall" § I don't deserve to watch the super bowl § Ive been
trying not to try to be funny and cool lately and have completely developed a
dissociative disorder and succeeded § what th the bope use "google glass"
#retweetthisifYouragirl § seems to me like im more and more the only person on
this site who tweets wiht Integrity. § shit and prick my ass § the entire time
youre watching the movie 101 Dalmatians, youre just thinking, This is so many
more dalmations than usual. It is just fucked § tried to overdose on aquarium
pebbles & the hospital laughed at me and the ambulance drivers all took turns
whipping me with catheter tubes § TheThursdayNiteRanter@twitter.com . its not
up yet. i will post an announcement when it is up § god damn if i aint getting
thirsty!!!!!!!!!!!!!!!!!! § this webpage is so courrupt.... § cheers to whoever
poured paint on me while i was handing out pamphlets warning people not to
attend MetalGearEric's orgy #FAlseFlag666 § by refusing to accept my invitation
to a formal debate. octomom has gone Rogue § you may "use my tweet as a joke"
but im not responsible if you get beaten up/ arrested for it https://t.co/
UqrBh3TwkW § http://www.newgrounds.com/portal/view/526364 ground hogs day stink

and i hate that animla. § i wan't to get all my straight uncles to flick spoonfuls of sour cream at them leathers § pain man § Comments for Golden Shower: by Chris on 18/04/2012 "It sucks" -- by Chrystal on 13/04/2012 " ot good" -- by by Dashawn on 06/04/2012 "Hel" § please remember--if the holidays are a difficult time for you, if you feel left out or forgotten from the celebration, then go Fuck your self § why are there online tutorials detailing the proper disposal method of the American flag but none regarding a "Toilet Heteros" gang jacket § someone compared it to family guy alredy. Im finished § people will be so pissed off when every AI system independently & consistently determines that the absolute perfect tweet is "Dolezal Rules" § The dog days of summer,. Its the dog days of summer everyone (Flapping gums aboutn othing, doesnt know what dog day is, knows he fucked up) § am i correct in assuming that everyone is happy about prisons not being private anymore because now we get to see the inmates dick and asses § a trail of rose petals leads you to a room bathed in warm candlelight. piled on the sofa is every guinness record book published after 2004 § santa opens the door, says "happy birthday", rummages through your potpourri bowl for no reason, leaves without giving you any presents § dont follow me. dont rewteet me. dont fav me.   dont look at my page. dont help me. dont click on my pets. dont touch me. dont blog me. § the first rate service at long horn steak house pittsburgh blasted my ass hole wide open, their dedicated waitstaff had me Nuts over Ass § if i ever subconsciously steal your tweets DM me for a frree 8x10 glossy of my horrible fucking face and a good ass arby's coupon § "When the moon hits your eye like a big pizza pie that's amore" nope. not true "When the world seems to shine like you'v" thats bullshit too § i close my account and cool off in the bath tub § the unthinkable https://t.co/NzagdkY0 § i refuse to consume any product that has been created by, or is claimed to have been created by, the (((Keebler Elves))) § who slid this shit under my door. people are being bombed in a war right now and you do this to me. youll never get my hollywood treasures https://t.co/PyhOYCHdnC § "The news is so fucked as of late. " - DiaperVoter § gamers are stupid assholes huh? well guess what. the final fantasy titles taught me roman numerals. check this shit out: XVCXCXCVIIIVX § howd would youd like a taste of my butt cheek , Punk § my belt buckle explodes, exposing my superbly problematic dick/balls to eveyrone at GarbageCon. it also ricochets into my skull and kills me § †'†'†' U Are Now Cybernetically Engaged Via Intercom Uplink To The Realm Of TheBeerPope †'†'†' § where cna i get a skeleton who will sit in my fridge all day and hand me the item i want whenever i open it § pulled over for dragging a clothing donation bin behind my truck; asking cop to make people stop honking at me because "its loud" "it sucks" § #ifjoebidenshowedupatmydoor I would explain to him the finer points of Malthusian economics!! Then I would show him my Cock!!! § my laywer is telling me that the bastard who hacked my account and leaked my rants is none other than edward snowden, known traitor to USA. § this is true power § my feed will suck absolute shit, for sure. but every one will love me § using my turn at a karaoke bar to try to do a 5 miunte routine that basically just says bryan singer is the new gawker writer or something § *gets booed at USO show for makig Diaper Jokes, calls all the troops Fuckers* § i just spent the last hour removing lint and other foreign fibers from every miniscule wrinkle on my dick and i am now ready to enter Church § wow someone eshould tell that Angry Redditor that metal bands are rippin off his posts § GIRLS SHOUD BE MADE TO WEAR A SPECIAL BADGE ON THEIR PRO-FILES SO I CAN FUCK THEM EASYER § The Scholar`s Guild-- The latest Posting Brand from influencer @Dril. It is a direct response to Liar Culture & the advent of Female Tyranny. § gary johnson is the orgy president. gary johnosn has made it clear that he intends to make usa an orgy galaxy. gary johnson has an orgy tent § S.O.S Save Our Selebs § SOME PLACE BETWEEN HEAVEN AND HELL EXISTS "INCEST WEB" § snubbed again by the 2012

Skeleton Awards; tore my skin off for naught § https://t.co/HmCQtNF6OQ § shut the fuck up § pleased to report my custom beer tap that makes a dramatic diarrhea noise while filling the glass is a hit with the boys at the fondue club § ME: mr cruise..im also a celeb. i invented the phrase "Barney sucks" TOM: wow... that phrase is so good, i must use it at least once per day § i shooed a young trans person away from my garbage with a broom § "corky romano: Storie's" a dvd release of short films that focus on ancillary characters of the corky romano universe. sept. 23. msrp $39.99 § have every thing https://t.co/paFxyNIgIZ § wow i just dropped a bowling ball & out of all the billions of places it could have landed it hit me straight in the dick #GlitchInTheMatrix § i ask you, whos the real " Little Ho" ??? Me (for being a little Ho) or You (for not forgiving me for being a little Ho) § im not tipping any more waiters until the facts come in, regarding Putin § "peppa pig" is the latest children's TV show that my followers cant wait to see ripped to shreds by my high IQ intelligence, live on my feed § a blank one § im ready to show all of you my trick. watch *spreads arms and screams at the mountainside until an avalanche of boulders engulf me entirely* § babies cant smile. its a biological reflex from the brain stem. its fake. they dont know how to smile § used to be the only thing women had to jack off to was the movie" the Full monty." (1997) Now they can jack off to our posts § oerdering 40 plates of baby back ribs on a stolen credit card so that i can get enough wet naps to clean my entire body #JustGuyShit #normal § some of my followers are going to take a fat shit in the toilet within the next few hours. And that's ok . § when I see how far the repulsive DigimonOtis brand has come after I chose to disassociate myself from it I sweat profusely and dry heave § my old phys ed teacher let`s me kiss his cpr dummy for $15 a pop and that'[s why im more mature than most of people on this fucking web site § @chrisbrown let's hope 2012 can keep its Fucking Mouth Shut #TeamBreezy #bruises #agony § As rioters descended upon the white house, he silently sat in the dark with a revolver & a glass of whiskey. His mouth stuffed with SlimJims § while you were watching the teen choice awards, i was watching the classic episodes of the teen choice awards from back when they were good. § donalds crime https://t.co/cBDdkXbPvk § im one of the good whites § shame on you for assuming I tattooed "Yes Yes Ya'll" on my newborn infant's head for a less than 100% justifiable reason § in 1942 the US Navy sponsored an experiment which required 64 prisoners in Massachusetts to be injected with cow blood #FemaleLies § my proposal: snl for mensa likers. @ericgarland unblock me you goofed-up fucking freak i wanna make you Famous bitch § guy gets 10 for armed robbery. tax payer is on the hook for $5mil so he can be rehabilitated. instead he jacks off all day. Is this justice? § getting my naval cavity laser removed because i just remembered an article i read in 1997 about how people in Spain were doing it § when twitter forces me to use the new layout i will retaliate iwth a deluge of horrid/disgusting diaper jokes and messages. my final warnig § blurays is a game changer. look for the bluray disks, at the store. § yeah no we dont use phones in Hollywood anymore. cute post though. § special thank you to that one guy who is really upset about some marco rubio incest joke i made on here and keeps sending me scary emails § harassing a man at a urinal, claiming i copyrighted piss § seeing people performing perfect slam dunks on the basketball court is worthless to me. It;s nothing § The Most Wrongfully Unfollowed Account On Earth .... § a <MYSTERIOUS CHASM> leading to an unrelenting void, a terrifying nightscape of psychological torture and constant misery. the worst dive § your;e damn right im calm. you bet your ass im acting like a normal person § @applebees fat bald leatherman in cheetah shades is beckoning me towards thre popper bar.his 3D tatoos seem to indicate hes from the future. § generating millions of 3d womens pussys for the #VaginasProject . my GFX card spewing steam like a damn tea pot § Genius: the Human body can survive being shot 100 times Fool: ? Genius: (Shoots self in th exact same spot 100 times) remember to click Like § jh https://t.co/9fq81nm2pB § any one who posts snark of my dear friend Bobby Jingle gets the head blowqn off shot gun style and is not allowed to have a real grave . § before you make fun of the band that me and digimonotis started in 2002 called "Pube Supply", be aware that we didn't know what a pube was. § good news folks, today i dreamt about buying Furniture w/my girl followers so i punished myself by slamming the toilet lid on my fat fingers § my new joke, which I foresaw getting over 100 likes in a dream, is referring to 9/11 as "The Devil's Dance" § i dress as a medieval knight and pummel my metal body with cymbals to get all 59 of my pit dogs riled up before i fling lawn chairs at them § some info i picked up: the brown recluse spider, lknown for its venomous bite, is not actually brown. also theyre not spiders, theyre birds § million dollar idea: Dog door that is big enough for humans Billion dollar idea: Dog door that says "Hello" when something passes through it § ive never normalized a thing in my life § blatant disrespect. no fav. § might bring this tweet to the office€• a guy drinks a cup of coffee but it's actually a gravy bowl by mistake?? is that appropriate for work § if i was a congressional aide and joe bidens dogs champ and Hunter went in on me to kill me id simple calm them down with a double head lock § "you gotta give em a show" - merv griffin § Im Just The Last Perosn Alive Who Gives A Fuck About The Integrity Of Mom Chat § calm down please . § @USArmy im a solder § boomer: ih ope they add a new Gun to fortnite me: i hope my penis mutates into a wolfs penis with extendable ridges so i can jack off easier § theyre nice § RECENTLY GOT INTO MEDITATION; SOME REAL DEEP SHIT; KEEP "THE VIEW" ON DURING SO I CAN ENHANCE MIND AS WELL AS BODY § http://t.co/BR1oYVDu im going to rile your fucking dog up with a tambourine, egghead § world first proof of beetle juice § shut hte fuck up § sometimes it seems like i'm the only person who cares about, intelligence-related things, on the entire online. § interesting. What do you all think of this . https://t.co/nWnmtFA9oo § girl or something: wtf did you jUst say. sounded like "xbone fail". did you just say"xbone fail" at me. me: (purple-faced refusal to answer) § 4' 8" man pile driven by beloved 102-year old crossing guard "Mr. Jim" after making a racket at payless shoes § next year itll be the 3 days of content or something. i cant handle 12 whole days on top of stress & trouble brought to me by gimmick memers § Teens respond to scorpions. Im bridging the teen reality with ours, through Scorpion Use. Do scorpions need to act rude to be cool? No § winner of best reality program "Mushroom Sons", beating out "Extreme Mushroom Farm", "Mushroom Grabber" and "Boys of Mushroom" #GoldenGlobes § "Are Game's The Da Vinci Of The Modern Age" the interrogator barks. "What If Super Mario Was Real Life" he slaps the suspect across the face § enough. i know you're all excited about your Mr Cool Ice 2010 calendars but do NOT post anymore spoilers aobut november and december § now where talkin § do the " Macarana "? Ha. No thanks § #TenThingsNotToSay-ToAWriter im going to piss all over your car. for being a Writer. § [[[[[[[[[[[[[[[[[[[[[[[[[[[[[[please let Miley join the USMC]]]]]]]]]]]]]]]]]]]]]]]]]]]]]]]]]]]] [[[[[[[[[[[[[[[She will do good]]]]]]]]]]]]]]]]] § widgets. ... theres nothin quite like 'em #TechBoys § https://t.co/N71ABSorZo im seeing some real good shit on this website today § fuck it , if youre still anonymous in 2018 you are 100% a pervert § im quitting my job as muscle beach lifeguard to achieve my dream of becoming the north korean secretary of teen moms § i stepped out of my stretch limo with "garbage toucher' painted on the side, brushed some shit off my boots and said "I'm garbage toucher" § how d o i subtly let my hairdresser know that i want her to cut my dick off instead of my hair § i mostly just need help getting the teeth. i can handle pouring them into my ass by myself #ParksPremiere § the worst part of nationalism is having to pretend the flag is really good, like "yeah the country looks exactly like that. they nailed it" § TODAY WE EXPLORE THE CONTRIBUTIONS THAT WOMEN HAVE MADE TO ARENA PITBULL DEATHMATCH § #FreeSlurpeeDay they dont ever wash the slurpe machines. the cops found a shitty waynes world baseball cap inside one of them § in the future james bond gets serious and stops having sex § FOOL: Beer is not the tdrink of summer. It can be enjoyed all year round ME: Beer is the drink of summer. § i love thinking about shit that is "Asethetic" and looking at it and saying how much of good it is § an old man wheezes into a ragged cloth; Bam looks into camera, says "Woah, glad im not That cloth!" thne does a Bogus airspin into the trash § im not going to eat mcdonalds becuase bacteria refuse to break it down. instead ill eat the food bacteria love the most: raw chicken & turds § im proud to preface all of my tweets with the montra of "If you dont like it, Then simply unfollow" thats the bread and butter of my acount § itunes has more buttons & clickers than a space rocket, its like you got to be an astronaut from nasa to use it and not a normal man as I am § number three. the footage of me struggling to shove a barbell into a toilet stall that isn't wide enough is " FALSE " and must be earased. § FULLY PREPARED TO TAKE A HIT IN THE OLD FOLLOWER COUNT TO BECOME AN ALL CAPS, ALL BOND ACCOUNT. LIVE THE DREAM. PURGE THOSE BOZOS § Laughs Right In The Home Depot Man's Face When He Says They Don't Have Any Bird Baths For Sale § @DigimonOtis I have reached the conclusion that you are a Nerd, and that further association with you will compromise my Brand Integrity. § the "SCAM ME" challennge.. if you can scam me you can keep all the money you scammed of me. but if you fail you have to send me 1 Nude image § paid by sinclair broadcast group to read paragraphs of unbearable QAnon Shit to a roblox server full of 7yr olds attacking me for my beliefs § driving my nasty "yes malarky" bus around town getting run off the road getting shit thrown at me etc § by day i'm a mild mannered toilet special- ist, but when i pick up the contorller i become Vance Hardgamer, rreal life murderer extraordinaire § http://t.co/FMnQxKWr here is future president jeff boss grilling the rat man for hard answers. the nsa loves to post nasty comments § me and a bunch of stupid assholes are going to start a community in the middle of the desert to either die or prove a very important point § i dont understand trash talk. i t think everyone should just agree with each other. it's easy § its the good new meme § just found out my great-great-grandfather was known as the "piss scoundrel" and spent most of his time being harassed by concerned citizens § decades of jacking off "The stupid way" has got my whole dick looking crazy § #itsuckswhen people claim that im pretentious just because i use imported hand sanitizer fron Europe § for the 9th time today a complete stranger has approached me on the street and told me to go suck some ass. "And still the brand endures"

Made in the USA
Middletown, DE
17 December 2022

19094199R00133